Tsunami

Also by L. Timmel Duchamp

Alanya to Alanya

Renegade

The Grand Conversation

Love's Body, Dancing in Time

The Red Rose Rages (Bleeding)

Tsunami

Book Three of the Marq'ssan Cycle

by L. Timmel Duchamp

$7
Duchamp

Aqueduct Press, PO Box 95787
Seattle, WA 98145-2787
www.aqueductpress.com

ISBN: 1-933500-09-3
        978-1-933500-09-6

Library of Congress Control Number: 2006909162

First Edition, First Printing, January 2007

COVER ACKNOWLEDGEMENTS
Cover Design by Lynne Jensen Lampe
Cover photos Ocotillo, Sunset, Prisoner: © Royalty-Free/CORBIS
Cover photo of Emma Goldman speaking in Union Square,
© Bettmann/CORBIS collection
Cover photo of Red Square, Courtesy University of Washington
Libraries Special Collections, UWC0121
Book Design by Kathryn Wilham

Fingers Touching by Lori Hillard

Printed in the USA
15 14 13 12 11 10 09 08 07   1 2 3 4 5

This book was set in a digital version of Monotype Walbaum, available through AGFA Monotype. The original typeface was designed by Justus Erich Walbaum.

For Thomas Duchamp and Kathryn Wilham

Two thoughts: There is no liberation that only knows how to say "I." There is no collective movement that speaks for each of us all the way through.

—Adrienne Rich

Chapter One

The core of Security Services had huddled deep below the surface of the earth for so many years that when it finally emerged into daylight, many of its executives said they felt like inmates on parole from prison. *Free at last! Free at last!* Elizabeth Weatherall repeated the words like a mantra as she transferred eyes-only materials from her private vault to the mobile safe in which such materials had to be shipped. The move felt like liberation from a confinement she'd long given up hope of escaping. Not that the Rock had been cramped: having originally been designed to hold the most significant portion of the executive population for the duration of a nuclear-attack or biological-warfare crisis, the mountain base provided an embarrassment of space they had never come close to filling. But her consciousness of one hundred thousand people working inside a single structure had, over the years, grown oppressive. And security concerns at the Rock differed from those typical of quartering in DC. One worried less about breeches from without than about violations of compartmentalization within—less about the opposition's efforts and more about the internecine infighting endemic in Security. The Rock had proven to be a hotter rumor factory than an HQ scattered widely over DC and its suburbs.

Elizabeth's headset chimed.

"He wants you at your quote 'earliest convenience,'" Jacquelyn said.

No doubt Sedgewick wanted her to pack his private safe for him. He, of course, had nothing in it he'd want to conceal from her; whereas she couldn't entrust her safe to anyone, least of all Jacquelyn. The pecking order did not replicate downwards with any substantial degree of equivalence.

Elizabeth locked both safes and crossed the hall. Entering his office, she saw at once that Sedgewick had his private vault open and the mobile parked nearby. *And* he held a cup of coffee in his hand, a good sign at four in the afternoon. Perhaps the end of the war did not mean the collapse of his interest in Security.

He glanced up from the sheaf of flimsies balanced on his knee. "Pack my safe for me, will you Weatherall?"

Elizabeth went to the far wall and started shifting files into the mobile safe.

"I had lunch with Goodwin today," he said.

She had reminded him of the appointment and arranged the chopper to Denver herself. "Anything interesting?" She squatted to reach the bottom shelves.

Sedgewick laid the flimsies on the sofa beside him. "You remember the tentative studies we had done, extrapolating postwar conditions?"

"Mmm...Bennett coordinated that project, didn't she?"

"It's more than time now to get moving on putting the taskforce's recommendations into effect. The propaganda effort will be as critical as the economic recovery program. Between us, Goodwin and I have arranged for Bennett to act as Security's liaison for the project, along with Com & Tran's Welkin. They've worked well together in the past."

Quite a plum for Allison. It was a position functionally close to the sub-deputy director level, even if it lacked the title—as it probably wouldn't were the position going to a male. "Bennett's an excellent choice for the job." Elizabeth dumped an armload of files into the mobile safe. "She's demonstrated considerable ability over the last seven years." She paused to look at Sedgewick.

"I thought you'd be pleased," he said dryly. "She's your protégée, after all."

Elizabeth turned back to the safe and pulled out a long cardboard box weighing perhaps twenty-five pounds.

"But Ambrose...that's another matter," he said. "I doubt he'd even want the honor of being your boy."

Elizabeth snorted. Chase Ambrose, the little ass, was a fool, but a well-connected and wily one. Somehow he'd managed to work himself up the ladder—starting out as Stevens's chief assistant and leapfrog-

ging over Stevens to the position of supervising all domestic security
branches, forming one of a triad—with Allison and Elizabeth—running the domestic side of things during the war, allowing Sedgewick
to ignore everything but foreign operations. They could have done
without Ambrose, but Elizabeth hadn't wanted to deal with the kind
of imbroglio Ambrose had the connections to stir up against her. She'd
figured she'd let one of the directors or deputies take him out. Only
none of them had... And scuttlebutt had it that Stevens now feared
Ambrose would be moving someone of his own into Stevens's directorship of ODS.

"Is Ambrose anyone's boy?" Elizabeth said. She glanced over her
shoulder with an arch look to accompany her flippant query.

To her surprise, Sedgewick smiled. And Elizabeth prepared herself for something nasty.

"Perhaps he might be my boy." Sedgewick drawled the words, as
though savoring the taste of them on his tongue.

Elizabeth shifted her body around and locked eyes with him. "You
have something particular in mind?"

His eyes glittered. "I thought I'd try him out as Deputy Chief. See
how he comes along."

Heat rose into her neck and face as a wave of rage surged through
her body. Sedgewick had let the position of Deputy Chief lie vacant
since his accession to Chief.

"Thought it might be a good idea to groom a successor. You better
than anyone else can appreciate why." Those damned glinting eyes,
watching her, fairly invited her to lose control.

Elizabeth swallowed. She tried to think before speaking. She
could appreciate why, yes. He had some gall so casually referring to
his breakdown, his drinking, his dereliction of responsibility at a time
of acute crisis. After everything she'd done for him and Security, he
would pass her over for that pig? It was incredible. With calculation,
she challenged his proposal on the grounds most removed from her
personal interest in the matter: "You might cram this down the throats
of the domestic branches—you never much cared for their opinions,
anyway—but you must expect flak from Company people."

"I'm only talking about trying it out, Weatherall. Part of that
includes seeing how he makes out with Company people. Naturally

the position demands someone suited for dealing with the Company." Never had there been a Chief who hadn't been a Company man. And Ambrose had started out in ODS, the absolute bottom of the barrel within Security's complex of branches and agencies.

Elizabeth said: "I'm the person best suited for that job. As *you*, Sedgewick, can appreciate better than anybody else."

He nodded. "Oh, I agree. There's no question of *that*. You've demonstrated more than adequately your capacity for handling the job of Chief. Barring the problem of dealing with the Cabinet, of course."

"That problem would be solved by official recognition of the position," Elizabeth said evenly. "And you could make that acceptable to them, if you...ah...*groomed* me for the job."

"Yes, I could see that happening. It would be difficult, but not beyond my powers."

Her throat tightened. Damn him! Sitting there, admitting barefaced that she was best suited for the job and that her holding it was not outside the realm of the possible. After several tense seconds she said, "Then why? Why Ambrose? Why not me if you're suddenly so hot for a Deputy Chief?"

His face defaulted into its usual mask of apathetic stillness, and his eyes grew so cold and dull they might be taken for a corpse's but for their occasional blinking. "That long cardboard box, Weatherall. Take it out of the mobile safe and open it."

Was this a dismissal of the subject? Or did the box have something to do with this outrage? She bent, slid it off the shelf, and set it on the end of the long conference table a yard away. When she lifted the flap and pulled up the lid, her breath caught in her throat. She turned and stared at him. How had he gotten it? *How?*

There was only one possibility. It had to have been Allison. Damn her, had she no sense of loyalty? "How?" she asked him. "When?"

"Surely you must have known I'd pursue it, Weatherall. I knew you'd have kept records. Though I never dreamed you'd make verbatim transcripts." A shiver snaked up her spine. "I've been thinking for years of how best to avenge Zeldin and punish you for disobeying my orders. What is it you want most in the world, I asked myself again and again. You're so ambitious, Weatherall. So damned ambitious. It was staring me in the face all those years, and I didn't see it. It never occurred to me you'd not be satisfied with behind-the-scenes power. But of course, watching you as I have, I did eventually see it. And you do so despise Ambrose." He smiled, letting his teeth show.

"To avenge Zeldin," Elizabeth said numbly. "I don't understand. What I did...was for you."

He hurled his coffee cup, and it smashed into the table only inches from the cardboard box. Shocked, Elizabeth stared at him. He hadn't had such a violent episode in years.

"I came to see you just after Zeldin's capture. You remember, Weatherall?"

That was the last time he'd indulged in uncontrolled violence. She said, "Yes, of course. We discussed what I intended to do with Zeldin."

"I specifically told you that I didn't want her lobotomized. You disregarded that order. You claim to have done that for *me*? Leaving her so anguished she couldn't bear to go on living? I made myself clear to you, Weatherall, and you disregarded my wishes for your own purposes. How amazingly cool of you to discuss those purposes with Zeldin herself. It's all in the transcripts."

Zeldin, yet again Zeldin, this time reaching out from the grave. Still that woman had her hooks in him. "She was perfectly fine when she left the Rock," Elizabeth said. "Note that she didn't kill herself the first chance she got. No, it was after a week of you that she—"

"Shut up!"

Elizabeth recoiled from the fury blazing in his face. "Don't think you can get out of this one, my bitch! Perhaps I should give you Wedgewood's job! Because by god, Weatherall, you have the mind and soul of a torturer. You could teach him a thing or two, couldn't you. With your instincts and talents you'd soon leave him far behind!"

Elizabeth's stomach heaved. With shaking hands she jammed the box into the mobile safe and resumed transferring materials from one safe to the other at speed. Given his history with Zeldin, he had an incredible nerve. Just what was it that had happened between him and her that last week, anyway? Enough to drive Zeldin over the edge. She'd promised Zeldin he wouldn't... Elizabeth whirled and stared into his furious face. "You couldn't leave her alone, could you," she said. "I told her, because it never occurred to me it could be any other way, that you'd keep your hands off—"

"Get the fuck out of here!" His voice rose in pitch, and he fairly screamed at her. "Get out, now! Send someone else to finish packing! I want you out of my sight, bitch!"

"With pleasure." Elizabeth spoke softly and wrenched her mouth into a teeth-baring smile. "With the greatest pleasure imaginable." She strode to the door, aware he was barely restraining himself from physically attacking her. Her tight, grim smile widened as she thought of how the knowledge that she could take him physically if he started anything must be leashing his most violent impulses.

Small satisfaction, though, considering what he had just done to her. Chase Ambrose. Christ. The bastard was right: he'd gotten at her in the worst way possible. And all because of Zeldin. Always with him it was Zeldin. And probably would be until he himself bit the dust.

Which, considering Ambrose's promotion, had better not be any time soon.

[ii]

Celia was finishing ordering the month's rations just as Elena arrived home. Judging by the droop of her mother's shoulders, it must have been a bad day at the hospital.

Her mother detoured to the desk to drop a kiss on Celia's cheek. "Any luck?" she asked, gesturing at the form on the screen.

"Sorry, Mama. Another month of only tubefood. Going through channels, there's no way we can get anything fresh."

Elena squeezed Celia's shoulders and began kneading them— probably, Celia thought, because she'd noticed they were rock-hard with tension. Elena sighed. "Even though I know better, I'd been hoping that with the war over..."

Celia pressed her thumb on the signature plate and logged out. No one in their house—not Celia, not Elena, not Luis Salgado—could risk a black-market transaction. ODS would use the slightest pretext to jail them, and they all agreed that the rare occasions on which they managed the elaborate efforts necessary for eluding their watchdogs could not be wasted on a small thing like food that was not needed for survival.

Elena moved to the window and looked out. "There's a new one out there, Cee. For you, it must be. A Latina this time."

Celia got up from the terminal. "Really? I've had white females, and males of every shade, but never a Latina. What, are they getting desperate, recruiting Latinas?"

Elena left the window and sank onto the sofa-bed. "Maybe they recruited her just for you, Cee." Her smile was sour. "After you lost them that day in the market."

Celia laughed with pleasure at the memory of outsmarting that particular watchdog. "Never did see *him* again," Celia said. "Think they transferred him to another case, or fired him?"

"Probably transferred him to guard duty in one of those desert prisons." Elena sighed—the second time in only a few minutes, Celia noticed. Which wasn't like her. "Would you get your old mother a bottle of water, Cee? I'm parched."

Celia pushed through the beaded curtain into the kitchen-alcove and grabbed one of the half-liter bottles lined up on the shelf above the microwave. "Poor mamacita," she said, stepping back into the living room. "What you need is a day off. And now that the war's over..." She handed her mother the bottle.

Elena broke the seal on the bottle. "Now that the war's over we'll have hundreds of the physically wounded and emotionally damaged overflowing every medical facility in the country. I'm not expecting big changes for the next year at least, Cee." She lifted the bottle to her mouth and drank down several large swallows at once.

"They've officially lifted martial law," Celia said. "That changes the situation—legally, anyway. I'm going to be spending every working second of the next few weeks procuring and serving writs of habeas corpus. Those jerks will have to do it by the book—at least superficially—now. Or we'll have them in court so fast their heads will spin."

Elena shook her head. "Oh Cee. Haven't you learned anything yet? You forget, don't you. Ten years ago—"

"Ten years ago we were free to come and go as we pleased without trailing watchdogs," Celia said. "Ten years ago there were no economic refugee- or prison-camps. Ten years ago ODS had to have evidence to keep people in jail. Ten years ago—"

"Ten years ago," Elena in turn interrupted, "judges let ODS do as it damned well pleased."

Celia stared at her mother. "There's a big difference between then and the last few years, Mama. And you know it."

Elena shrugged. "We'll see whether things change that much." She lifted the bottle to her lips. "We'll see." It really *had* been a bad day, Celia thought. Her mother prided herself on being an "optimistic realist."

Celia slipped on her coat and picked up her attaché case. "Well I'm off," she said.

Elena, as usual, did not ask her destination. The less she knew about Celia's doings, the safer they would all be should anything "happen." Besides, *they* might be monitoring their conversation. "Will you be late, Cee?"

"Maybe ten or eleven. I'm hoping to be given dinner." Celia grinned. "And I don't mean tubefood. Most service-techs eat better than we do, Mama, did you know that?"

Elena leaned forward and set the empty bottle on the coffee table. "I'll probably be asleep by the time you get in. Try not to wake me."

Celia bent and kissed her mother's forehead. "Nighty-night, Mama. Sleep well."

Celia opened the front door. Yes, there she was, leaning against the adobe wall surrounding the executive property across the street. Celia sauntered down to the street. "*Buenos dias*," she called.

The woman stepped forward, out of shadow into sunlight, and Celia saw that the watchdog was even younger than she'd thought.

"I hope you're up to a brisk walk downtown?" Celia said facetiously. "Public transportation's not too frequent between Banker's Hill and downtown. They tell you I do a lot of walking?"

The girl's lips tightened.

Celia shrugged. "Just thought I'd warn you. Well, I'm off!" She turned on her heel and took off down the road at a good clip. Down down down the hill they'd wind, she and her watchdog. She herself free, her watchdog bound to follow where she led. Thinking this was an interesting way of looking at their relationship, Celia fantasized initiating a discussion with the woman about it. It might even be amusing.

[iii]

"Sit down, Allison." Elizabeth spoke in a superior-to-subordinate tone she had used to Allison at most three times in Allison's life. Allison's gaze darted to Elizabeth's face; cautiously, she advanced to the desk and took the chair Elizabeth indicated.

Elizabeth resisted the urge to rise. She knew that if she left the confines of her chair she might lose control. She wanted to shake Allison. (Or worse.) She gripped the leather arms of her chair and drew a deep breath. "You must have expected this to happen long before now," she said. "Were you surprised when nothing immediately came of your treachery?"

Allison paled. "What are you talking about, Elizabeth? I'm as loyal as you are. Whatever it is that I've done, it wasn't intentionally treacherous!"

"You know damned well that's not what I'm talking about. But then perhaps you place such a low premium on loyalty to *me* that you don't consider such treachery betrayal at all?"

Allison's eyes flared. "I've always been loyal to you. For that at least you can't fault me. I may not measure up to your standards and expectations in other ways, but when it comes to loyalty—" She visibly swallowed before going on. "Tell me what you're talking about, Elizabeth. Please."

What kind of fool did Allison take her for? "Today I learned in the most unpleasant way conceivable that you gave Sedgewick the Zeldin transcripts," Elizabeth said flatly. "After everything we went through when you first blackmailed me with them—"

"I didn't give Sedgewick the transcripts! And it's not fair for you to say I blackmailed you. Somebody had to protect Anne—"

"*Protect* her? But don't think that by dragging in past history you'll evade the issue now. Sedgewick has those transcripts, Allison. It's that simple. I saw them, and he made me see that he does."

Allison leaned forward. "He didn't get them from me! I give you my word, Elizabeth. I shredded the copy I had long ago. And I haven't touched those data files since!"

After everything she had done for Allison... Elizabeth pushed away the old memories, of holding Allison as a baby, of teaching six-year-old Allison to ski, of talking to teenaged Allison about her education, of bringing grown-up Allison into the Company... No. She wouldn't let herself be swayed by sentiment this time. Always she excused Allison everything, telling herself that she must simply accept Allison's ambivalence toward her. "Your *word*, Allison?" she said, disgusted that Allison thought she could play her.

Allison's eyes filled with tears. "Did Sedgewick explicitly say I'd given him the transcripts?"

Elizabeth shoved her chair back from the desk. "He didn't have to. There's no other way he could have gotten them."

"Thank you for your trust." Allison's mouth scrunched up in defensive, resentful childishness. "You're willing to believe the worst of me by drawing conclusions from one piece of information. You didn't even bother to ask Sedgewick how he got the transcripts. You just assumed I'd given them to him. Is that right?"

Elizabeth stared at her. The silence pounded in the air between them. Elizabeth lifted her hand to her ear and tapped five on her headset.

Sedgewick's voice snapped in her ear.

"How did you get the transcripts, Sedgewick?"

There was a pause. He said, curtly, "You think I don't know your system for hiding electronic files, Weatherall? After all these years?"

"You found them yourself?"

"I suspected their existence, so I looked for them. And naturally found them." After another pause, he said, "Was there anything else you wanted, Weatherall?"

"No, Sedgewick. Nothing else." She tapped the disconnect button and looked across the desk at Allison. "I'm sorry for that, Allison. It was unforgivable of me to accuse you without grounds."

"Unforgivable to think the worst of me right off." Allison's eyes shimmered. "Much less accuse me. And now I find my word means nothing to you, either. I don't know what I've done to deserve this, Elizabeth."

Damn. Allison was going to cry. And *she* was forced to stay on this side of the desk helplessly watching her do it, too. She hated the ease with which Allison was hurt; she hated Allison's vulnerability... And of course any move she made to comfort her would only give Allison another pretext for rejecting her. Elizabeth looked away from

Allison's tears. "I know you won't forgive me," she said, pressing her fingers into the arms of her chair. "So I won't belabor my apology. But let me instead give you some good news."

Allison sat up straighter in her chair. "Of course I forgive you," she said stiffly.

Elizabeth let that pass. "It's been decided that you're to coordinate a major public education project for postwar adjustment. You'll be working as our liaison with Com & Tran. With Welkin. It's a wonderful position, Allison, and will give you substantial power. Naturally there'll be a significant salary increase with it."

Allison looked crestfallen.

"What is it?" Elizabeth said. "What's the matter?" Anyone else in her situation would be crowing with triumph. Could it be that Allison had been entertaining wild expectations of something better?

Allison stared down at her hands in her lap. "I'd hoped that after the war I'd be transferred back to Europe," she said in a very low voice.

"Back to Europe?" *What the fuck?* "Doing *what?*" Did Allison think she could jump into the upper echelons of the Western Europe desk the way the men sometimes did?

Allison shrugged. "I don't know. I suppose maybe I thought I could have my old job back, or something like it."

Elizabeth was incredulous. "You'd settle for your old job now? Wouldn't you be bored out of your mind—besides being wasted? My god, Allison, you've been operating at the highest levels of Security, and you talk about going back to being a drudgery operations officer?"

Allison bit her lip. "I suppose that sounds stupid to you."

Elizabeth thought. Then, "What about Anne? You couldn't take her to Europe, you know. Not on the kind of salary you'd draw doing that work again."

Allison looked startled. Ah, yes, that had gotten her. Where her precious service-tech was concerned she could always be reached. "I hadn't thought of that. Anyway, I expect you're right about my being bored and wasted. Considering the mess everything's in, I really should be doing the things I'm specially skilled to do." She half-smiled. "This project will be a challenge. You think I can handle it?"

Elizabeth said, "It wouldn't have been offered to you if I didn't think you could." And that was true. She could have vetoed Allison's being given the position. Likely one of the reasons Sedgewick was giving this job to Allison was in order to keep steady what he had deliberately shaken up with his attack via Ambrose. Give with one hand, take away with the other. Telling her she's still on the team while he's breaking her bones: classic Sedgewick.

"I suppose you're nearly packed?" Elizabeth asked.

"Yes. I'm a bit worried, though, about finding a decent place to live in DC. Anne will probably be returning to the place she lived before—if it's still around. You at least have some certainty about your place being intact."

All those repairs that had had to be made after the Civil War—Military having deliberately wasted the place, precisely because it was hers—had been completed long ago. "You needn't worry, Allison. On your salary you'll find something. At any rate, you are welcome to stay with me, as you like." Not that Allison would ever do *that*. Not voluntarily.

"Thank you. Was there anything else, Elizabeth?"

Elizabeth sighed. "No, Allison. Nothing else."

Allison rose to her feet. "Then I'll get back to my packing."

Elizabeth watched her go out the door. As always after such encounters, she felt the sinking weight of failure press against her heart. Her relations with Allison would always be a burden, ever tormenting her.

Elizabeth glanced at her watch, got up, and went back to the packing of the mobile safe. Only the two bottom shelves of her private vault remained to be transferred to the mobile. She opened both and crouching, swiftly moved the files on the next-to-the-bottom shelf of the vault to the mobile. Then she started on the bottom shelf. Pulling out the files at the front of the shelf, she transferred them without even looking at them. When her hands reached for the rest of the stuff on the shelf, they encountered objects obviously not files. Frowning, she pulled some of the objects forward. She stared at the leather book, the satchel, and the box of miscellaneous objects—and remembered: she had stowed everything to do with Zeldin on this bottom shelf. She hadn't wanted to think about what to do with it after Zeldin's death and yet had not been able to dispose of it once and for all.

Elizabeth sat back on her heels. Damn Sedgewick for dredging it all up again. One part of him lived permanently, obsessively in the past, in a ghost world she could not begin to imagine much less inhabit. She should simply throw all this stuff out now. There was no point in hanging onto it.

She lifted the lid of the cardboard box and stared at the rich red silk within. She had retrieved this gown of jouissance silk from the island for obscure reasons she hadn't understood then and certainly couldn't grasp now. Though she fingered the silk, she averted her eyes from the leather book lying inches from her foot. *You have the mind and soul of a torturer.* He was wrong, completely wrong. He believed what he wanted to believe. In that leather book... The story Zeldin told in that book incriminated him. Not that he'd see it that way. As for her own relations with Zeldin...the silk told its own story, too. No, she would keep it all. If he forced her to she would use these things against him. She must retain the power to vindicate herself.

Her throat tight, Elizabeth packed the remnants of Zeldin into the mobile safe. Zeldin had been her worst failure of all. In the end, Zeldin had won—against her, and against Sedgewick. And Zeldin was still raining destruction on them, seven years later, the bitch.

Elizabeth closed the mobile safe. Jacquelyn's girl could pack the rest of the office under Jacquelyn's supervision. Thank god they were leaving the Rock. She had so often felt as though she would suffocate from the lack of fresh air and sunlight. It would be the most blessed relief.

[iv]

Celia put her finger to her lips and took from her attaché case the pad she carried for such occasions. She wrote in block letters:

IF YOU HAVE ANYTHING TO SAY NOT FOR PUBLIC CONSUMPTION, WRITE IT. I'M PROBABLY HOT.

She watched Emily Madden's face as the latter read the warning, and when Madden nodded, was satisfied the executive understood.

Madden reached into her shoulder bag and held out her hand. In her palm lay a small brass instrument dotted with a glowing green light. A jammer, Celia decided—of a fancier than average design. Madden said, "We'll be all right in here."

Celia glanced into the mirror at the reflection of the door. "Not for long. My watchdog will be in anytime now."

"Then let's make this brief. The story is we've hit it off chatting upstairs by the bank of display terminals where we met. I invite you to dinner at my club—that's what we're doing now. You accept. Our cover is that I think you're a legal scholar whose work might interest me. And so on."

Celia said, "I'm not the one who needs to worry. It's you who will be tainted by contact with me."

Madden slipped the jammer back into her bag. "Unimportant. My club is on Twenty-Eighth Street—on the east side of the park. Shall we meet there, or do you need transportation?"

Celia thought. "No, I can get myself there." It would give her an excuse to make a stop along the way to see—or fail to see—a client who hadn't checked in when he should have. "What time?"

Madden took the pad from Celia and scribbled an address on it. "Any time around eight would be fine. I'll tell them to expect you. If you get there before I do, have a drink. You'll find it an easy, relaxing atmosphere."

Celia doubted that: an executive club was one of the last places she'd expect to be comfortable or relaxed.

The door opened. The watchdog came in, walked past them, and shut herself into a stall.

"So I'll see you then," Celia said. She listened to the watchdog begin to pee.

"It's been a pleasure talking to you," Madden said, going out the door ahead of Celia. Celia looked ironically over her shoulder as she left the restroom. Dare she try to get away while the watchdog was taking a piss? But surely they had relief for her stashed nearby. And if they had some kind of tracer planted on her... Celia hurried up the stairs to street level. They could have done anything to her two of the times she'd been jailed and they'd drugged her. She thought again of her mother's plan for CT-scanning her entire body. Every time they'd discussed it, they had discarded the idea; people on the run needing medical attention, people just out of the hands of the butchers and suffering untreated fractures and other injuries, had first call on such cheating. Always, always it was a matter of priorities. They lived their lives in a permanent state of triage.

She'd have to set off for Golden Hills now or she'd never make it to that executive club in time. Accessing the only surviving child of the most powerful man in the county? Incredible. And to find her carrying a jammer (but then someone in her position might do that as a matter of course), to find her "simpatico" as the Movement labeled the "interested" professionals and executives... She had hoped to be given dinner. But at an executive club? And her clothing all worn and patched. She was embarrassed to wear such clothes to court; going into a place full of executive women would be even worse.

Celia glanced over her shoulder as she crossed the street. Yes, there she was, poor lost soul, trudging dutifully behind, talking into her sleeve, giving them everything she could glean from that meeting in the library. It was a dog's life for ODS flunkies. But did *they* know that? Celia turned and waved. The smile died on her lips as she noticed the long gray van pass. A chill ran over her; angrily she accelerated her pace. Let the flunky suffer the agony of blisters and leg cramps. Celia had no pity for those who sold out. A woman like her should know better than to work for butchers.

Celia pressed on. Doubtless, the man she was going looking for would be gone without a trace; he would have gotten word to her otherwise. That was, after all, the point of checking in. So. Though the war was over, there would be one last disappeared client to seek out. The thought of all the forms and legwork and investigative tasks weighed on her, especially when she knew the hardest part would come later, when she found him in a hospital—or was shown his remains.

Celia shifted the attaché case to her other hand. Maybe this executive would be useful. Maybe things would change, now that the war was over. It couldn't go on like this forever, could it? Up, up the hill Celia Espin, she urged herself as she began the ascent. One foot in front of the other, just keep on moving. That's all you can do.

But Celia was tired. She had been trudging uphill for six years now and was seemingly getting nowhere. Was hers the task of Sisyphus? No! *That's the wrong story!* She squared her shoulders and marched forward. Martial law had been rescinded; everything would change. And then the world would be sane again, as it had been before the aliens had wreaked their terrible havoc.

Chapter Two

Martha added her name and com address to the list and passed it on. Making a quick scan of the room, she counted sixty-three students present. Damn. Unless a couple dozen people dropped, the class would be confined to the lecture style. Straight lectures might work for the first term of the course, but surely not for the second, when they'd be "exploring"—as the syllabus promised—emerging economic systems in the post-Blanket world.

When everyone had signed the class list, the students passed it to the professor, who continued outlining the first term of the course. As he was speaking, his roving gaze lighted on Martha—and stuck. He picked up the list; Martha watched his gaze scroll down the sheet, then stop. He looked back at her. "It *is* Ms. Greenglass?" he said.

Heads turned. Martha's cheeks heated up. "Yes, I'm Martha Greenglass." Her voice was less than steady. The first day of her first college-level course, and this had to happen?

The professor's eyebrows lifted. "Could you spare me a minute or two after class, Ms. Greenglass?"

"Sure," Martha said, anxious to be relieved of the pressure of his digression.

He resumed laying out the course content.

For the rest of the hour Martha worried about why he had singled her out and what he could possibly want with her. Did he think it inappropriate for someone with so little education to be taking his course? But that was absurd. Most of the other students were service-techs who probably'd had less preparation than she, and Sam Pace had a reputation for teaching service-techs with tact and skill. Everyone spoke well of him. And David Hughes certified him as not only a sound but also an innovative and creative economist. Maybe he had a bone to pick with her, something to do with her work for the Co-op? Yeah, she supposed that was it. He probably wanted to tell her about aspects of her coordinations he didn't like.

After class a crowd of students swarmed around him. Martha bit her lip and stared at the open battered and scuffed attaché case lying open on the desk, and at its contents, which included an urgently blinking handset, a NoteMaster, and two pens; she tried not to fret about making it on time to her lunch appointment, tried not to speculate about what he wanted to talk to her about. When the other students had all finally melted away, the professor confronted Martha. "What the hell are you doing here?"

This blatant a challenge? "I thought anyone was allowed into this course." Martha lifted her chin. "I realize I'm not as well-prepared as most college kids, but—"

"Cut the crap, Greenglass."

Martha stared at him. "I don't understand."

He folded his arms over his chest. "Do I really have to spell it out? You have as much business taking this course as Shakespeare would have taking sixth-grade English. So what are you doing, checking up on me?"

Martha's eyes widened. "*Checking up* on you?"

His gaze hardened. "It's common knowledge that certain Co-op people are making a new attempt to push through a purge. What kind of fool do you take me for?"

"You're way off the mark, Professor," Martha said. "In the first place, I don't believe in purges. And in the second place, I'm taking this course because I believe that it's about time I learned some of the theory that bears on my work. I'm shamefully ignorant, and more and more I've been feeling at a disadvantage because of it, especially now that the Free Zone is beginning to be recognized by governments. I thought that if I—"

"You don't expect me to buy such bullshit, do you?" Pace's light brown eyes narrowed, and Martha found herself thinking that his eyebrows looked a lot like soft, furry, gold and brown caterpillars. "Are you aware that the second part of this course is to be devoted primarily to studying structures you yourself helped create?"

Martha looked uncertainly at him. "What do my coordinations have to do with economic theory? I don't know anything about economics."

He snorted. "Keep your ingenuousness for your negotiations, Martha Greenglass," Pace said ironically. "It ill suits you."

Martha ran her fingers through her hair. "Does this mean I'm not welcome in your class?"

"Anyone's welcome in my class." Pace's lips thinned. "That's the policy here."

Martha swallowed. "Right. I see." She picked up her briefcase and headed out the door. So much for the excitement of school. Well, she would see tomorrow whether she had the same kind of experience in the political structures course. If so, she'd have to rethink her plan for acquiring an education.

Martha emerged from the building into the soft February drizzle. Academics gave her a pain. Even—maybe *especially*—those who chose to live in the Free Zone.

[ii]

"This may seem a bit far to commute," Emily Madden said as she took the Leucadia exit, "but I can't bring myself to be in constant residence in my father's monstrosity of a house. Not only do I hate that house—one of the most ghastly examples of twentieth century architecture it would be possible to dig up—but I find that even in a house that size I get claustrophobic living with Daddy. Because it seems always to be swarming with Daddy's Military associates, I suppose. So I live up here—knowing Daddy can understand my having a beach hideaway for taking my lovers to and so on, when he wouldn't understand my keeping a separate house in town."

"I see." Celia worried that her response sounded fatuous—or if not fatuous, judgmental. But what else could she say? She knew nothing about the kind of problems—if that's what they could be called—people like Emily Madden had.

They headed west and were soon driving parallel to the shore. From time to time the view opened up, and Celia snatched glimpses of the water, today a soft, light shade of turquoise. She seldom got this close to the ocean, for she had never taken much pleasure in sharing the city's few public beaches with the hordes. And besides, she had little time for recreation; life was too short for dallying on the beach. She peered sidelong at Emily Madden and wondered again about this executive's motives in getting involved in the Movement.

The thick dark brows pulled together, and the almost-black brown eyes shot a quick look at Celia. "You've got questions, haven't you. I'll try to answer all of them. Trust between us is essential, don't you agree?"

"Naturally," Celia said dryly. How old was Emily Madden? Facts about executives were not a matter of public record, so one never could tell. But she looked barely twenty.

Emily pulled off the road and stopped before a wall at least fifteen feet high. Celia hadn't noticed when the wall had appeared. But then someone like Barclay Madden could wall off the entire beach from the border to Pendleton if he chose. There'd be a struggle, but if he wanted it badly enough he'd eventually get his way. A gate Celia hadn't distinguished from the wall swung open—presumably keyed to a signal from Emily's car—and Emily drove in. The gate swung shut behind them. Most of the land enclosed by the wall had been allowed to remain desert scrub and beach; only one building, a relatively small house, stood in all that space.

Emily parked the car near the front door. "And now we're entirely protected from all surveillance. I have it seen to by someone who answers only to me. There's no chance we can be spied or eavesdropped on. Not even the Chief of Security or the Secretary of Defense could access this place."

"The unsinkable *Titanic*, eh?"

Emily said, "I suppose paranoia is an occupational hazard for human rights lawyers." She opened her door and got out of the car. Celia grabbed her attaché case and followed.

They entered through the front door and passed directly through to a heavy glass door at the back of the house, which faced the ocean. "I spend a lot of time out here," Emily said, unlocking and pulling open the door onto a slate terrace overlooking the beach. She waved at the lounges and chairs upholstered in pleasant earth tones. "Please, make yourself comfortable while I get us something to drink."

Celia sank into one of the chairs facing the water. A tall, spiky thicket of bird of paradise flanked one side of the terrace, bougainvillea covering ornate Spanish grillwork that served as a trellis the other. She laid her head back and closed her eyes. Somewhere nearby the fronds of a palm tree or two flapped in the breeze. The sun soaked through her eyelids, and she thought idly that she should probably be wearing sunscreen...Now *this* was her idea of luxury.

Emily returned with tomato juice for herself and coffee for Celia. She seated herself in the chair next to Celia's and offered Celia a friendly, easy smile. "Please," she said. "Feel free to ask me anything you like."

Celia sat up straight and sipped the hot, strong coffee; she watched several waves roll in before speaking. And then she returned blunt-ness for bluntness: "I don't understand your interest in or motives for getting involved with us."

Emily fingered the stem of her glass. "Someone in my position should be on the other side, I'm sure you feel that. I'm an executive, and I'm wealthy. But you see, I don't think the way my father does. It's quite clear to me that the executive system has gone awry, has perhaps outlived its usefulness. It brought prosperity to everyone in its first decades. No one went hungry, no one lacked work, human life was protected and respected. Never had there been such domes-tic tranquility and prosperity, even in less-advantaged countries than ours. But when the aliens came, all that changed." Emily pulled her gaze from the ocean and turned her head to look directly into Celia's eyes. "I was fifteen at the time, Celia. It was the biggest event in my life. I hardly remember what it was like before the Blanket. And then came the Civil War. My brother was dining in a Del Mar restaurant at the time it was bombed. Ironically, it was a place patronized mostly by Security executives and was hit by Military—with whom my father has long enjoyed very close ties."

Emily's gaze returned to the ocean. "I couldn't believe that my father continued siding with Military after that. It made no sense to me. But then the Civil War was an insanity I never understood. I learned from it, though. I learned how corrupt the executive system had become. I learned that people were starving, were being locked up, were disappearing, were being killed... I was nineteen when I had the blowup of blowups with my father. He, you see, regards me as his successor now that he no longer has a son. As a consequence, tensions became exacerbated between us. I began concealing my opinions from him. At some point I saw that I could use the power he increasingly gave me for doing what I could to return the executive system to fulfilling its responsibilities."

Emily turned her head to look at Celia; her eyes gleamed. "I think he has some idea of what I think and is willing to live with it. You see, he wants his illusions. He *needs* them. And I'm willing to play along." She grinned, was it with self-derision? "Not very pretty, Celia, is it. But there you have it."

Celia wondered: was she to assume that Emily wanted to overturn the executive system, or reform it? That Emily dreamed of a golden age of responsible executives? Talk about illusions!

"Anything else, Celia?"

Celia set her empty cup on the table between them. "No, I don't think so. I'd like to get started going over some of the files I've brought with me. I have one of disappeared people we've traced far enough to make writs of habeas corpus a possibility—if you can steer us to a reliable judge. I have another of people who need help getting out of the country—"

"Where are they running to, Celia?"

The wind was sharp, the sun weak. Celia pulled her jacket more tightly around herself. "The North American Free Zone. There's no other place for them."

Emily's breath hissed in. "You're sending them *there*? But the aliens—"

"They have no choice, Emily." Celia lifted her attaché case onto her thighs. "Of course they wouldn't seek asylum there if they had any other choice. But it's that or risk their lives or the lives of their families and friends. Unless you think they'd be better off in a prison camp out in the desert?"

"No, I don't think that," Emily said quietly. "But do you ever hear from people who've fled to the Free Zone?"

"These are the first we're sending there," Celia said. "Previously they ran to Mexico. But then we heard what happened to some of the people who fled there."

Emily's gaze met hers. "What happened to them?"

Celia snapped open the latches and lifted the top of her case. "Either sent back or killed or put in labor camps. They might as well have stayed here." Celia pulled several files from her case. "And, oh yes, there is a file—our fastest growing file—documenting atrocities in the desert camps. We'll need to do something about it. I'm hoping you can suggest courses of action to take and contacts to help us carry out whatever we decide to do." Celia stared at Emily. "Unless you are of the school of thought that prefers to bury and forget such things?"

Emily's eyes did not flinch. "I want to help you, Celia. With all of it."

Celia nodded. "Good. Then let's get down to work. There's enough here to keep us busy all day and night."

[iii]

Elizabeth stood up to stretch. *At last.* She felt confident that her new system for concealing files was Sedgewick-proof. For weeks she had been working on it, mostly at weekends and late at night. When Sedgewick had shown up that morning, she'd sworn to herself that she wouldn't leave the office until she could be certain her private cache was safe from his prying eyes. She had been taking a chance, working on it with Sedgewick in residence across the hall, but she had no intention of working late *this* evening.

As Elizabeth cleared her desk for the night—securing sensitive materials and inputting last-minute memos to her personal calendar file—her thoughts flashed forward to her plans for the evening. Though she barely recalled the girl's face, she had no problem recollecting the lush body beneath the service-tech garb the girl had been wearing when Elizabeth had encountered her at the silk-work shop. This would be her first evening of play since returning to DC, her first tryst in more than a month. It had been so long that her body was aching with anticipation.

She had already removed her headset and was slipping into her sable when the office phone buzzed—Sedgewick's line, damn it. She stared at the handset for a second, then went to the desk and picked it up. "Yes?" she said, not patiently.

"When you've decided to call it a day, I want to see you, Weatherall."

Elizabeth bit her tongue. After half a second she managed to say, "Yes, Sedgewick," without expression. God *damn* that man. But perhaps he wanted to tell her he was returning to Maine, that his only reason for coming to DC had been to publicly announce Ambrose's promotion?

Elizabeth shut down her office and set the locks on the door. The remodeling had worked out well, considering she hadn't wanted to be in the Chief's suite at all and she'd had to supervise the entire project herself. She now had an office almost the equal of Sedgewick's, its only drawback being its proximity to his, located physically closer to him now than when she had been merely his PA. She tried to regard the proximity as an advantage, as a concomitant of her power and a sign to everyone else of that power, yet the truth was she felt more surely at his beck and call now than she ever had. She consoled herself with the thought that he was bound to retreat to his island, and soon. Ambrose, as his deputy, could front for him with the Big Boys. Something *she* had never been able to do herself.

The first thing Elizabeth noticed as she entered his office was that Sedgewick had already gotten about two-thirds of the way through the bottle sitting open on the table beside his chair. And it wasn't yet six. "What is it, Sedgewick?" She stood in the doorway that had been cut into the wall of his office for faster access to her own.

"You might as well take off your coat, Weatherall, and sit down."

"I haven't much time," Elizabeth said evenly.

"Plans for the evening?" The malice in his voice flicked at her nerves. Did he resent her ability to enjoy herself—when he could never enjoy himself?

"Yes, I've plans."

"Well you'll have to cancel them. I'm in a garrulous mood and thus require your attendance for the evening."

The surge of anger that coursed through Elizabeth almost knocked her off her feet. She leaned against the doorframe and—staring down at the gleaming mahogany planks in the floor—steadied her breath. He could still do this to her, whenever he liked. It was as though nothing had changed, as though he were still in control... Well, in *some* ways he *was* still in control. Though the perfect retort came to her—*Won't Chase Ambrose do?*—she did not voice it, for she realized at once that if Chase Ambrose would do, the very base of her power would be substantially undercut.

Without looking at Sedgewick, Elizabeth pulled out her personal handset and called the Diana. The woman who answered named herself as Kate. Elizabeth recalled that she was the professional who managed the club. "Kate, this is Elizabeth Weatherall. I've arranged to meet a guest at the Diana tonight. Her name's Hazel Bell." Although it had eluded her before, an image of the girl's face swam into her mind, as though the girl's name had the power of summoning it... such strikingly colored eyes—a sun-struck amber. "Unfortunately I won't be able to get away from work in time to meet her. Will you offer her my apologies and assure her I'll be in touch?"

When Elizabeth hung up she crossed to where Sedgewick was sitting. He laughed as she threw her fur onto a sofa and took the chair opposite his. "I'm glad to know my call on your time isn't interfering with anything important," he said.

Elizabeth smiled. "Just my pleasure, Sedgewick. Which is such a small thing, after all." When nothing gave him pleasure, nothing at all, unless one could call pleasure the gratification he was feeling now at vexing her.

"Oh, but don't you find my company pleasurable?" He tossed off the last of the wine in his glass.

"Just a constant delight," Elizabeth cooed.

"Said in the best sycophantic style. We're perfect for one another, Weatherall, positively absolutely perfect." He poured more wine into his glass. "By the way," he said in a serious tone that teased her with the possibility that he might actually talk shop, "you handled yourself very well this afternoon. You always do, of course, but I was still impressed. There's no doubt in my mind that not a soul in Security will ever for a moment entertain the idea that you had expectations. Well done, Weatherall."

Another kind of taunt: that no one in Security would ever take her ambitions seriously or ever imagine she could have anything but behind-the-scenes power.

Behind-the-throne-manipulator: that's what she was. Staring at the almost empty bottle of wine, it occurred to her that Sedgewick might be afraid to give her up-front power. But why? What did any of it matter to him? Could the only thing motivating him be his twisted version of the Zeldin affair? It was possible; where Zeldin was concerned he was entirely off-the-wall. But was there some part of him that clung to the possibility of exercising power again if he should so choose—if he should somehow pull himself together or regain the desire for his previous degree of control? Was he thinking of making a comeback (if it could be called that, since formally at least everything was as it had always been)?

"The car's ordered for eight, Weatherall. Watch the time for me, would you? We'll be dining at my house."

The entire damned evening with him. Elizabeth got up and went to the refrigerator for juice. It was a pity his tolerance for alcohol was so high; it usually took several hours of steady drinking before he managed to pass out. She wished she had the nerve to drop something in his wine. But she wasn't prepared to face the consequences if he caught her doing it. And her rule was never to do something the consequences of which following exposure she was not prepared to deal with. When it came to Sedgewick, that meant—generally—playing every hand straight. For Sedgewick was about as safe to handle as gelignite. And about as predictable.

[iv]

Martha's run-in with Sam Pace rankled. That evening, en route to the party at the Austrian Consulate, Martha grumbled about it to David Hughes. "He has a point, Martha," David said after she had described the encounter. "You're one of the key players in the Zone's economy. It's easy to see why he'd find it fishy. Didn't you just say that some of the material to be covered in the second half of the sequence will involve structures you've invented or otherwise helped bring into existence?"

"What does that have to do with it? As you yourself are always pointing out, I'm abysmally ignorant about economic theory."

"Yes, but you've engaged in significant economic practice." David said this with a dry rather than flattering tone of voice that made Martha's lips tighten. "That makes you something of an expert on economic practice, if not theory. I have no doubt that after all these years, you understand, as well as anyone can, the basic theoretical concepts Pace will cover in the first half of the sequence." He snorted. "In fact, Martha, your attendance at parties like this shindy tonight is proof enough that Pace's estimation of your abilities and comprehension is correct. You don't think you're invited to these parties because they think you're such a charming and lovely woman?" He flashed her a grin. "Not that you're not charming and lovely. I merely mean that those particular attributes are beside the point with the diplomatic community."

At the navigational processor's suggestion, Martha switched lanes. *The diplomatic community*—yes, the Free Zone now had such a thing, their damned war had seen to that. It unsettled her; it reeked too much of government. She suspected those people mistook her for a representative of a government claiming not to be one, for they still did not really believe the Free Zone was governmentless. She knew David, in twitting her, was in his kindly way trying to soothe her discomfort at these suspicions—which she had many times discussed with him—by suggesting they invited her because they saw her as "a key player" for securing their business deals. Martha did not believe it was that simple, though certainly she knew herself to be a valuable contact for outsiders wanting to do business inside the Zone.

Martha turned onto Harvard. This old section of Capitol Hill, where most of the old houses and their grounds had remained intact for more than a century, was beautiful; it was hardly surprising that executives occupied so much of it. "Actually," Martha said as she parked, "as far as I can tell my main attraction for the diplomats is their idea that they'll be able to work deals with the Marq'ssan through me." She looked at David—and found him frowning.

"Which diplomats, exactly?"

Martha studied his face. "The idea upsets you?"

His face smoothed out. "Let's discuss this later." He opened his door.

Martha had no intention of discussing it with him at all, not while the Inner Circle remained divided on the matter, and not while they were waiting to hear what their contacts in the other Free Zones had to say about it. She rebuked herself for having volunteered that much to him.

As they walked the two blocks to the Consulate, Martha braced herself. She loathed these affairs—loathed dressing in a style so alien to her, loathed accepting service from people in the employ of executives giving the parties. She refused to go through the valet-parking nonsense. One of the uniformed men stationed at the door (and that was another disturbing thing, the number of obvious guards these places flourished) scrutinized Martha's invitation before admitting her. Just inside the door, a woman dressed entirely in white took their outer garments and passed the two of them along to another woman in white who conducted them up the staircase. At the entrance of the ballroom, Martha gave her name to the white-clad man at the door, who announced them. An executive woman Martha knew approached. She said, "How nice to see you again, Ms. Greenglass."

"This is Dr. David Hughes," Martha said after she shook the executive's hand. "David, this is Margot Ganshoff. She's the Austrian Consul's chief administrative assistant."

Saying "Pleased to meet you, Dr. Hughes," the executive slid a frankly speculative look at Martha. "I think you'll find some interesting people here tonight," she said to Martha, apparently dismissing David from her notice. "There are several in particular who specifically asked me if you would be present."

It was too soon, Martha thought. Nothing had been decided. But perhaps empty preliminary talk was part of the way these things were done.

Ganshoff took her arm. "If you're agreeable, I'd like to introduce you to one or two of them."

Ganshoff was making it clear she did not want David tagging along. Maybe she shouldn't have brought him with her, after all? It had been a selfish idea, wanting moral support for enduring the ordeal. He would be bored to death.

David said, "Don't give me a thought, Martha. I'm a resourceful kind of guy."

Martha laughed, not least at the expression on Ganshoff's face. She said, "Lead on, Ms. Ganshoff."

Ganshoff squeezed her arm. "Please, call me Margot."

"Of course, if you'll call me Martha."

"You see that woman there?" Margot indicated an executive wearing a multilayered silver tunic over severely cut, silver pencil-striped black trousers. "Until recently she was Austria's ambassador to the UN."

In other words, Martha thought, she must be a good rhetorician and probably experienced in espionage. "And she wants to talk to *me?*" she said aloud.

"But everyone wants to talk to you, Martha," Margot said, fairly purring, and again squeezed her arm. Martha was getting strong vibes from this woman. Surely she must be wrong in her reading.

When the former ambassador to the UN saw them approach, she broke off her conversation with the classically beautiful blond man at her side. "I've captured Ms. Greenglass for you, Eva," Margot said. The blond moved away. "Martha, meet Eva Auerbach. Eva, this is Martha Greenglass."

Eva Auerbach had lines in her face. A personal idiosyncrasy? Or an inability to tolerate longevity treatments? Her face creased into even more wrinkles when she smiled. "I've been hearing of you for some time, Ms. Greenglass," she said in a low, gravelly voice. "That you are a woman of initiative and ingenuity. I can see why the Free Zone didn't send you to the UN to represent them."

Margot's laugh rang out.

Martha sketched a smile. The Free Zone sent no one to the UN, since the UN existed to serve governments. Why did these people persist in pretending the Co-op was a government?

Margot lifted a finger, and a white-clad woman carrying a tray of drinks appeared. All the glasses seemed to be filled with fruit juice. Margot and Eva Auerbach each took a glass from the tray. "Unless you'd prefer something alcoholic?" Margot asked.

Martha shook her head. "No, I prefer juice." She took a glass and lifted it to her lips. It was delicious: a mixture of orange and mango, she guessed.

"Very wise. Women, preferring to keep their heads clear, have an obvious advantage at these affairs. Don't you agree, Eva?"

Eva shrugged. "That depends on how serious they are about getting things done. If we were really serious we'd slip away to your suite."

Margot reclaimed Martha's arm. "Why not? Unless you are too amused by the rest?"

What did this pair of executives have cooked up between them? They were looking at her, waiting for her answer. "Sure," Martha said. "I don't see why we can't sit and chat for a bit."

Margot's smile grew broad, and Martha caught a brief exchange of looks between the two executives. She took another sip of the juice. What was she even *doing* at this kind of function? Martha wished that some of the professionals active in the Co-op would agree to handle these situations. Whenever she attended such functions she found herself feeling a mere service-tech again, plunged into an executive world.

Margot drew her forward, and they moved to a side door. "You can hear, it's already getting noisy," she said.

Martha glanced over her shoulder as she went out the door and glimpsed David in conversation with a silver-haired male executive smoking a cigar. Had the man discovered David was an economist and jumped at the chance to pick his brains? The two looked intent on their conversation. More interesting was how obvious it now seemed to Martha that David was a professional—even wearing formal evening clothes—while the other man was just as obviously an executive. Their very postures and gestures seemed to mark the distinction.

"This way, Martha." Margot steered her to the stairs. "My suite is up on the third floor. Wait until you see the view from my sitting room window. It's quite, quite spectacular, even on an overcast February night."

"It's true," Eva Auerbach said, "that after going so long without seeing city lights at night one is deeply moved by the sight of them. First the Blanket, and then the war... Ah. What a terrible decade. What a terrible, terrible decade."

They started up the stairs, the three of them abreast. Margot said. "But now we begin a new decade. And this one will be different, *ne c'est pas?*"

Eva Auerbach clasped Martha's other arm. "But that's up to Martha, yes?"

Margot laughed softly. "We shall see," she said.

A shiver rippled over Martha, and she felt an urge to cut and run. But she steeled herself to go on. She was too curious not to.

Chapter Three

Elizabeth woke well before dawn. As she liked to do when there was time, she lingered in bed, savoring her sense of the day's energy coiled ready to spring. But recollections of the night before flooded her thoughts, and she grew languorous, stretching her limbs to the bed's very edges, smiling as she reviewed her evening with the voluptuous Hazel. Had the girl been so extraordinary, or had it simply been that her own responses had been heightened by prolonged abstinence? It was hardly unusual for her to have been so excited by her partner's response. But merely rolling the girl's nipple between her thumb and finger, feeling through her fingertips and palms precisely what she *knew* the flesh she touched was at that moment experiencing, had made her crazy with urgency. She had lost all control of herself—and thus of the fuck—and pre-empted Hazel's pleasure, unable to stop herself from turning everything upside down, even to demanding that Hazel attend to her first—and then…oh the come, spreading everywhere, not only to her buttocks, but rippling so far out, so far down, into her thighs and knees, in shimmering waves and spasms, all the way to her toes…

But Hazel: what had *she* thought? Probably the girl simply assumed her ordinarily that selfish, knowing, after all, little about her and nothing of her usual sexual self…

The mere memory of it made her thighs slick. She must, must, *must* see her again, if only to discover whether it had been the girl that had made the difference—and to show her a better time… Had the girl resented her greediness? Or did she understand what had happened? The expression in those feline eyes…so opaque, so fathomless; watching, waiting…

Elizabeth scoffed at herself: reading romances into the girl. Just an ordinary service-tech met by chance in a shop, a girl working for a woman in the Justice Department, out running errands for her boss, promiscuous, an easy pickup…

Elizabeth bounded naked out to the kitchen to make coffee. "Lights on," she flat-commanded, then blinked and added, "dim lights to medium-low." San Diego this afternoon, she reminded herself, sipping orange juice as she waited for the water to boil. This would be the first time in years that she would be visiting that city. She dreaded seeing the devastation she knew she would find. The city had sustained a lot of damage in the Civil War, and then been shelled almost constantly during the last years of the Global War.

Worse, she loathed going into a place so heavily Military in orientation. Seven years after the end of the Civil War she still felt a powerful distrust, even an aesthetic distaste, not to mention downright anxiety at the sense of Military's power—whether when visiting Military's territory or when recognizing the sub rosa struggles occasionally waged between Security and Military personnel. Surely she wasn't the only one who felt this way. Sedgewick's sending her there—obviously with reason, for the Executive had explicitly requested an investigation and possible action on the persistence of a black market and local scrip that the Executive had made the mistake of tolerating during the war, and if Sedgewick wouldn't do it himself, someone with his proxy powers must… Might he have a hidden purpose for sending her? Might he be sending her out of Central for his own reasons? Why exactly *did* he continue hanging around DC, anyway?

Elizabeth slid the plunger to the bottom of the pot and poured the coffee into a bowl-like porcelain cup. What was going on in that psychopathic head of his? Why had he given her that hunk of TNC stock—a "bonus" he called it—and the diamond-encrusted sapphire pendant after that hellish night spent listening to him rant and rave about Zeldin? Why the fuck didn't the man just retire gracefully to his island?

She carried the coffee into the bedroom. "Morning, Liz," Maxine called out from the next room.

Elizabeth went into the dressing room. "Good morning, Maxie. And happy birthday."

Maxine looked up from the tunic she was repairing. "I don't know how you remember a thing like that," she said, flushing.

Elizabeth set her cup down on the dressing table. "Thirty-nine, isn't it?" she said. She knew because she kept it on her personal calendar.

Maxine made a face. "I don't even like to think about how old."

Elizabeth smiled down at her. "Your present is something different this year." Elizabeth paused, to anticipate the other's pleasure. "I've arranged for you to have a longevity treatment."

Maxine dropped the tunic. "Longevity treatment?" she whispered. "For me?"

Elizabeth felt uncomfortable at the start of tears in Maxine's eyes: the treatment was as much for her own comfort as for Maxine's benefit. She had no intention of watching Maxine begin to age before her eyes, each year more obviously and painfully; she had no intention of losing her.

"Oh, Liz, I don't know what to say!"

Elizabeth squatted down and took Maxine's hands. "Just say you're happy, Maxie."

Maxine nodded, speechless. Elizabeth leaned forward and kissed her forehead. "Everything's arranged. All you have to do is call them to specify when. It will be best, I think, if you do it while I'm away. I'm leaving for the West Coast this noon and will be gone a few days. I'm not sure yet how many. So without me around, you'll have plenty of spare time on your hands."

Maxine swallowed and nodded again. "Then I'd better do some packing for you," she said. "What part of the West Coast? What kind of climate do you need to be prepared for?"

Elizabeth straightened up. "San Diego. Nothing heavy. Temperatures in the sixties and seventies during the day. And it'll probably get down into the forties at night." She carried her cup into the bathroom and started the shower running. Who looking at the two of them would guess that she was almost twenty-four years older than Maxine—Maxine who had lines at the corners of her eyes and mouth and scattered threads of gray in her hair, Maxine whose knees sometimes ached and whose back gave her intermittent trouble?

Elizabeth stepped under the shower, dialed the massage, and closed her eyes to enjoy the sharp hot pressure of the water pulsing against her skin. It occurred to her that she should take a commercial flight into Lindbergh Field, unannounced. She needed to make a stealth attack. She would avoid notifying Lisa she was coming. There was no telling who might be involved in this situation and which side they might be on. God. Lisa would *freak.*

Damn Sedgewick for sending her. He should be sending his deputy. But he had little faith in Chase Ambrose's abilities, he made no secret of *that*; no question, he would have sent that little asshole instead of herself if he'd been confident the jerk could handle it.

Elizabeth stepped out of the shower, primed to kick ass and wishing it could be Chase Ambrose's.

[ii]

Martha said, "So how's your book coming, Venn?" She and Venn had just finished talking business.

Venn made a face. "I've run into a wall. A very peculiar wall. I guess I shouldn't be surprised."

She sounded discouraged, Martha thought. "What kind of wall?"

Venn got up from her desk and shoved her hands into her tunic pockets. The long, dangling pendants on her earrings, set in motion, jingled and tinkled with a soft, melodic sound that reminded Martha of wind chimes stirring in the distance. "Well, you know that the book makes a general survey of the kinds of innovative journalism that have evolved in the Free Zone since its inception, right? Well, I was intending to devote one section of it to making an exposé of the use of newspapers to disseminate disinformation and make ideological stands against the Co-op. Naturally the *Evening Examiner* has been one of the publications I'm most interested in for its ideological pugnaciousness and continual dissemination of disinformation."

"Most Co-op people think the *Evening Examiner* is funded and managed by an arm of ODS," Martha said.

"That's my suspicion, too. But did you know that there's no known address for the *Examiner*'s editorial offices? The circulation and advertising departments operate entirely online. The street boxes that print out the flimsy edition download it from a file-transfer site that's got a different net address every day, as do online subscribers."

"Have you tried tracing any of the net addresses?"

Venn laughed shortly. "Come on, Martha. The *Examiner* is owned by TNC. You might as well try to hack into the transcripts of the Executive's meetings as trace an address hosted by TNC."

Martha's gaze met Venn's in a long exchange. There were so many things they didn't look into very closely these days. *Too* many. "What about the people who have bylines in the *Examiner?*" Martha said. "Have you talked to any of them?"

"I've been investigating and interviewing…a few of them. Most, though, I haven't been able to locate. There's something creepy about this setup, Martha. And it's starting to dog me." Venn ran her fingers through her short, dark hair, and in the process set her earrings in motion again.

"I suppose you could stick to an analysis of the content of the *Examiner*'s so-called journalism," Martha said. "Though it wouldn't be as interesting or useful as a full-blown exposé."

"I'll have to decide what to do soon. I don't want this project to drag on forever." Venn looked speculatively at Martha. "Would you keep your ears open for me? And if you hear anything about the *Examiner* let me know?"

"Sure, though I doubt I will. It's not the kind of thing I'm likely to hear about."

Venn grinned. "If anyone is likely to hear about anything going on in the Zone, you are, Martha."

Martha zipped her briefcase and stood to go. She bit down hard on her lip to muzzle her urge to retort. Why did people always assume she knew about everything going on in the Zone? "You might try talking to Louise Simon of the Women's Patrol," Martha said, making an effort to keep her irritation out of her voice. "As you know, she's been rabidly interested in ODS's activities in the Zone for years."

"Good idea." Martha went to the door. "Are the rumors true?" Venn asked before Martha could get the door open.

Martha looked over her shoulder. "Which ones?" Was there some new rumor about the Women's Patrol making the rounds?

"The ones about refugees pouring into the Zone from all over the US."

Martha needed to be gone; she couldn't afford, these days, hanging out just to chat. Without taking her hand off the doorknob, she turned just enough so that she could see Venn's face. "Yes," she said. "Those rumors are true. And the things the refugees have been saying..." She sighed. "A group of them from Southern California made contact with us through Jess, who still maintains links with some of her old friends in LA. It sounds as though some pretty horrendous things went on during the war. We've been placing some of these people in the clinics the Marq'ssan helped us set up for the Cuban torture victims. We don't have a clear picture yet of what's been going on...but what's so far emerging is...disturbing."

"You mean...Americans have been torturing Americans?" Venn asked, sounding shocked.

Why was she shocked? Martha wondered. The torture wasn't what was new in the situation, but the range of targets and the extent of it. Martha's hand tightened on the doorknob. "We'll be discussing this issue at the meeting this weekend. I hope you're planning on coming?" Professing herself to be "not into politics," Venn didn't often attend Inner Circle meetings: by implication labeling the rest of them politicians. Some people held that against Venn and called her elitist. When Venn did not immediately assure Martha she was attending, Martha said sharply, "You know you might pick up better information and contacts leading to information for your book if you regularly attended meetings."

Venn smiled. "I know. But I find it hard to bring myself to get that involved in..." She hesitated, then said only half-ironically, "politics."

Martha snorted.

"I don't know what else to call it, Martha." Venn raised her eyebrows. "You know what I mean."

Martha turned the doorknob and pushed open the door. She said, "Good luck with the *Examiner*, and be careful."

Martha dashed out to her two-seater. If she stopped for lunch she'd be late for her next meeting. Maybe she could grab a yogurt or a tube of something before class. There didn't seem to be enough hours in the day to waste on luxuries like eating and sleeping. Not, at least, if she also wanted to get an education and keep doing coordinations besides.

[iii]

Elizabeth's neck and scalp crawled as she disembarked from the plane with fifty other passengers at her back. She wondered whether she had made a mistake taking a commercial flight. Wouldn't she be better protected—and here she squirmed at her resort to this phrase, for why should any executive anywhere in the US need "protection"?—if her visit were out in the open and undertaken with the usual formalities lending her the support of the local branches of Security? Still, she did not turn her head to check that a portion of her escort followed, but moved swiftly through the terminal and out to the curb.

Her escort had orders to attend to her luggage, requisition a car without using her name, and drive her to the club. If Lisa and Leland were trustworthy—and there was no reason to suspect that they were not—neither Military nor the Military-connected interests thwarting the Executive's plans would have any idea of her presence. She must assume that Whitney would have discussed the Executive's perturbation with his top men here...who would then naturally put two and two together once they became aware of her presence. The longer it took for that to happen, the better.

Sedgewick had not been forthcoming about either Whitney's stance or the extent to which the Executive was bringing pressure to bear on Whitney to crack down on his people. He had in fact offered little assessment of the current balance of power in the Executive. Reading between the lines, however, Elizabeth surmised that in general Military was not behaving very well in the Executive's scheme of things—due perhaps to a hangover of resentment at the imbalance within the Executive itself following the division of its loyalties during the Civil War, or perhaps to the arrogance that clung to Military after years of conducting the Global War largely independent of Executive control. A serious power struggle might well be in the offing. Elizabeth's hackles rose at the thought; thanks largely to Sedgewick's debilitation and his refusal to provide adequate substitutes for functions that only he himself had over the years attended to, Security would probably not fare well in a power struggle. And yet she gathered from Sedgewick that the majority of the Executive was counting on Security to rein in Military. She had discussed possible projects for subtly revealing Military's gross misconduct of the war with Allison. Military hoped to project the impression of victory, and the Executive had seen to it that all public discourse presumed victory, but given the reality of the Madrid Accords, anyone paying attention would realize that one could at best characterize the disposition of the war as a draw. But then the Executive itself was pretty much in denial about the significance of not only NATO's having been routed from Eastern Europe, but also the Russian-dominated trade agreements that had severely cut into some of the US's strongest markets. Individual members of the Executive might not care about the heavy loss of life sustained because Whitney had refused to accept the evidence Sedgewick had furnished him with as "conclusive enough" to warrant deep suspicion of their supposed mole operating at the highest levels of the Kremlin; but when they began to see that the end of the war would not mean the return of their quarterly dividends to pre-war levels, they might well be willing to let Security connect the dots. So far, course, Military had enjoyed the short-term advantage of being able to boast about taking back Cuba, and Cuba, after all, was closer to home than Eastern Europe, Africa, and Asia...

Kirkby pulled up in an armored four-seater, and Elizabeth climbed into the backseat. "Do you have a postwar map?" Elizabeth asked him, suspecting that the car's programming might be out of date.

"Yes, madam. It should be easy enough to get over to Twenty-eighth Street."

"And what did you tell the requisitions officer?" Elizabeth wanted to be sure they hadn't screwed up. You could never assume with service-tech males that they'd followed orders to the letter.

"That we're here on a classified operation and need the car. We showed him the authorization from M & S. He advised us to check in at station headquarters."

Elizabeth repeated her instructions covering the times she would be in the club (which never under any circumstances admitted males), what they were to watch for outside the club, about keeping their com link with her open, about their cover story should they happen to have contact with any Security, Military, or civil police forces. As she talked she gazed out on a landscape of devastation far bleaker than DC's, though DC had taken considerable pounding in both wars. She knew San Diego's residential sections had been at least as heavily shelled as the harbor, the university, naval installations, and the business district—destroying quite a lot of executives' residences. Out of malice, she was certain. Why else bother with areas of no strategic significance? It had only been chance that had preserved the lovely old buildings housing station headquarters. Balboa Park and the zoo, Elizabeth wondered as she grew aware of their circuit around the park: had they been spared? She couldn't recall mention of them in Leland's reports.

Kirkby parked in front of the club, and Bradley carried her luggage to the door, where it was taken in by a pair of women service-techs. Elizabeth followed, nodding at the uniformed male holding the door open for her. At the desk she registered in her own name and went in to lunch.

After surveying the sparsely populated dining room from its threshold, she requested a table by the windows overlooking the east side of the park. The professional in charge smiled and led the way to a corner table offering views on both sides. A girl followed with a half-liter bottle of water and a menu, but Elizabeth waved away the menu and ordered at will. She was starving.

How pleasant, looking out on the park: for an hour or two she would have peace of a sort. And how blissful to be away from Sedgewick! That man could single-handedly generate more stress in an hour than an all-night aerial bombardment of an entire city could.

Elizabeth pulled out her handset and input station headquarters' most confidential number, connecting straight into Lisa's office. Lisa's girl answered by repeating the number.

"Mott, please." Elizabeth said.

"Ms. Mott is away from the office. Is there a message?"

"Is she anywhere on the premises?"

"No, madam."

Very properly, the girl wasn't going to divulge Lisa's whereabouts. "When do you expect her return?"

"Later this afternoon, madam."

"I'll call again." Elizabeth put her handset away. A slight setback, but nothing serious. She broke the seal on the half-liter bottle and poured water into her glass. She always felt so much thirstier when in San Diego. Awareness of the desert stretching for miles and miles to the east might, she speculated, induce unconscious anxiety about having enough water. Did permanent residents suffer this same affliction? She would ask Lisa sometime. It would make a good subject for innocuous dinner conversation.

"What the *fuck* are you doing here?"

Elizabeth jerked her head around to face Lisa. "How convenient," she said—and fairly beamed at her. "I was just trying to reach you at your office."

Lisa glared at her. "Since when does Elizabeth Weatherall ride into someone else's territory without exercising the courtesy of announcing herself?" Lisa's lips pressed tightly together, and her brows drew down in a scowl.

"Sit down," Elizabeth said. "Have you lunched?"

"I'm meeting someone here." Lisa crossed her arms over her chest. "Damn you, Elizabeth, answer my question."

Elizabeth sighed. "Sit down, if only for a minute. I need to talk to you. And I refuse to brawl with you towering over me. I'm getting a crick in my neck."

Grimly Lisa took the chair opposite. "When someone of your status visits a territory," she said, "it's customary for—"

"I know what's customary," Elizabeth said. "But my visit is in no way customary. So spare me the lecture."

Lisa's eyes grew wary. "What's going on?" Lisa lowered her voice. "Are you investigating the station?"

"No, I'm not investigating the station. Don't jump to conclusions, Lisa."

"But it's something clandestine."

"Partly. Simply because we're not sure what we're dealing with. I don't want everyone in the territory knowing Central has sent people out here to do what we've come to do."

"Are we to be told what that is?"

"Don't get huffy, dear," Elizabeth said.

Lisa bit her lip. "I think you can understand why I'm not exactly thrilled at your deportment in this situation."

The girl served Elizabeth a tall glass of grapefruit juice. "What may I get for you, madam?" she asked Lisa.

"Nothing. I'm meeting someone else."

The girl withdrew.

"I'm here because the Executive isn't happy with the opposition it's encountering in San Diego County," Elizabeth said.

"We're doing the best we can, Elizabeth. But not only is there the physical devastation of the war to cope with, but also a turf battle with Military. I don't think you have any idea—"

"Lisa," Elizabeth said, her tone again one of warning. Lisa clamped her lips together and waited. "I want as complete and full a report as you can muster in the next twenty-four hours on who and what is blocking the Executive's Regeneration Plan. Clear?"

Lisa's eyes widened. "Is *that* what this is all about?" She sounded incredulous. "Opposition to the Executive's economic strategies?"

Elizabeth sipped her juice. "What was it *you* thought I was talking about?"

Lisa said, "Haven't you been reading *any* of the reports that go out from this station? What the fuck are you people doing at Central anyway? Do you have any idea how isolated we've been feeling out here when we've got a population close to out of control—"

Again Elizabeth stopped her: "Don't get belligerent with me. Of course we read your reports. What do you take us for? I'm perfectly aware you've got a hotbed of revolution breeding down here. We're patient, though, and have confidence in your ability to deal with it. What I'm talking about is far more serious. The Executive—"

"The Executive can fuck itself!"

Elizabeth let the silence drag on for almost ten seconds, long enough to give Lisa leisure to regret her loss of control. "If it's that stressed and insurmountable a situation," Elizabeth said softly, "perhaps Sedgewick himself should come in?"

Lisa went white to the lips. Yes, that had shaken her. She would probably rather have the aliens on her doorstep than Sedgewick. After about half a minute, Lisa said in a near whisper, "We're getting no support *whatsoever* from Central. And fucking Admiral Melvin Precious

Aldridge has the gall to assign responsibility for the assassination of one of his commanders to *us*, just more ammunition for the turf fight, as though we're responsible for the safety of his officers. The bastard had the gall to rant and rave at Leland for close on a goddam hour." Lisa glared at Elizabeth. "We never had a chance to regain our footing down here—not with the war going on and Military for all practical purposes dictating every damned issue south of Pendleton. If we'd kept headquarters in LA, at least we'd have something to work with instead of—"

"Lisa," Elizabeth said.

Lisa put her palms to her face and rubbed her eyes. Elizabeth watched her without speaking. After about half a minute, Lisa returned her hands to her lap, and Elizabeth continued. "I want that report. And if you want something from Central, ask for it." Elizabeth smiled. Lisa would never allow Leland even to hint at desperation in reports to Central. She'd be too worried Sedgewick would take it as an excuse to dump Leland. Or to come put things in order himself.

"Very well," Lisa said woodenly. "But I can tell you right now you're going to be up against Barclay Madden. Which means you'll necessarily be embroiled in our turf fight. Because Madden controls local Military."

"We're up against one individual?"

Lisa's smile was derisive. "Don't sound so incredulous. Basically one individual. He controls the area. I'm sure we operate here at all by his gracious indulgence. I suppose he finds our presence halfway useful." Lisa steepled her fingers under her chin and raised her eyebrows. "If that usefulness should cease..." She shrugged.

"Are you saying local Security is compromised?"

Lisa's brows pulled down, and her eyes narrowed. "Not compromised, but...under pressure."

Elizabeth said, "I don't want anyone but you to know I'm in town for business. You can mention I'm here...for pleasure. I'll put up a good show to lend that cover credence. But not even Leland is to know why I'm here. Clear?"

Lisa stared down at the tablecloth. "Understood."

"As for the report…I'm sure you can think of justifications for ordering its component parts…which I expect you to assemble for me yourself."

"Will there be anything else you'll need?"

Elizabeth took a long swallow of juice before answering. "That will depend on what the report turns up. I suspect a great deal will be required if I'm to bring down the kind of shakeup I surmise from your remarks will be necessary."

"I must go, Elizabeth. My appointment…"

Elizabeth said, "I'll be in touch. Perhaps we could go out together in the evening? You still own that place in Mission Bay?"

Lisa half-smiled. "Yeah, it's still in business." She stood. "Have a pleasant lunch, Elizabeth."

The girl arrived with Elizabeth's prepared-to-order curried shrimp. Ravenous, she dug in and thought about how she'd be able to spend the rest of the afternoon in the park since she'd so neatly taken care of the afternoon's business with Lisa. As far as the world was concerned, she was on vacation. There was time enough to think about Madden and the local Military—later.

[iv]

Martha emptied two liter-and-a-half bottles of water over the beans and fastened the top on the pressure cooker, turned on the gas, and checked the time. Then she started peeling onions. Often these household tasks took the edge off, though sometimes at the end of one of her rougher days the last thing she was in the mood for was household labor. But this day hadn't been bad, and she had the evening earmarked for studying.

Ruth burst into the kitchen. Her eager young face brimmed with excitement. "Martha, I've tons of messages for you!"

"Have my calls been bugging you today?" Martha smiled apologetically. "Sorry about that. I don't know why people won't just leave their messages at the office instead of bothering people here. They know I'm never here in the daytime."

"It doesn't bother *me*." Ruth grinned back. "It's sort of exciting living around a celebrity like you."

Martha said, "Wait till you've lived here a couple more months. By then you'll wish you could kick me out of the house."

Ruth giggled, and her pale freckled cheeks grew pink. "I can't believe anyone in the house feels that way about *you*."

Martha wiped her hands on her apron and took the list from her. Margot Ganshoff, she saw, had called three times. Probably because she had had her personal phone set to voice mail for most of the day. She dreaded having to deal with her. The woman had a way of making her feel out of her depth.

"Thanks, Ruth," Martha said as Ruth turned to go. She put the list aside and resumed chopping. She needed to think of a course to substitute for the econ sequence. David was right, she could pick all that stuff up for herself by reading textbooks and could always ask him to explain things she didn't understand. It wasn't important enough to risk the kind of bad feeling her continuing over Pace's objections might generate; the Co-op didn't need more unfavorable PR. Though David seemed to think she should stick to the course anyway; he said he found Pace's fears "interesting." His theory was that Pace intended to criticize Free Zone economic structures and that Martha's presence would saddle him with unwanted opposition. Though Martha wondered about this, she still did not think it a good idea to set herself up as an opposition force in Pace's class. Word of such a thing would spread fast, and people would begin saying the Co-op was "controlling" the New University.

Social psychology? Or perhaps a language course? Or maybe history? There were so many courses she needed to take she hardly knew where to start. Contemplating the possibilities, Martha's thoughts raced. Education was like magic: stimulating, empowering, transforming. With education, the slings and arrows deployed by people like Margot Ganshoff would deflect off her, as though her skin had been rubber-coated. With education, she would magically understand and be able to figure out what the hell they should be doing now in the Free Zone. And with education, she would finally see everything clearly, sharply, wisely...

Martha put down the knife and wiped her tearing eyes. Onions always did get to her.

Chapter Four

Elizabeth looked away from the terminal: staring fixedly at it wouldn't start the amber light strobing. She checked the time. Five minutes more and she would start tracking him down by phone. Where the hell was he? She'd told him she was going to be getting back to him once she'd digested both the stuff Central had sent her on Madden and Lisa's report. Why couldn't he manage even half-assed cooperation? The fact was, when she wasn't physically there beside him he degenerated into total uselessness. God how sick she was of nursemaiding him.

Hearing the whir of the flimsy rolling out of the printer, Elizabeth whipped around. Finally. The whir stopped after half a second. Elizabeth retrieved the flimsy.

Handle as you see fit. Usual arrangement re authorization. S. Translation: don't bother me with this, I'll rubber-stamp anything within the scope of my authority.

Damn the man. She might have expected it, except that since the Executive itself was so hot on this situation she'd thought he'd take at least a *slight* interest in it. No, she was to fix everything up, do whatever it would take to get Madden and possibly Military under control, and then he would report back to the Executive that everything had been taken care of. Period. Not that it would matter to the Executive who exactly accomplished their will. That Sedgewick had someone around to take care of things only redounded to his so clever credit. Sedgewick's vaunted art of tool-choosing, indeed.

Elizabeth stepped out onto the balcony and stared down at the main terrace where women lounged in the sun sipping tea and juice and chatting. Mostly maternal-line, of course. Why, why was she so upset about Sedgewick's use of her? It had never troubled her before;

she'd always been aware of this aspect of her power. She ground her teeth: clearly the worm of Chase Ambrose had burrowed its way into her gut—just as Sedgewick had intended. Had he been imagining her reaction at the moment he had spoken his message into com? Or had he been stewed in indifference? As though not able to remember what time of day it was, Elizabeth again checked the time. Four-forty. Which meant seven-forty in DC. Stewed in *alcohol*, no doubt. She had forgotten to take that into consideration.

Four-forty: which meant that Lisa should be arriving in twenty minutes. She would try the carrot first—namely restoration of Scripps, Salk, and all the other research institutes previously associated with UCSD. That Security had managed to evacuate them at the outset of the Civil War had been—for years—a thorn in Military's flesh. If Madden was interested in more than local power, he'd have an appetite for this particular carrot. As for the stick, that was easy: threatened with total isolation, he'd soon find himself in difficulties. What individual executives like Booth could do to someone so locally concentrated as Madden would be damage enough; but the combined clout the Executive—minus Defense—could command would be stunning…unless, of course, Defense was prepared to draw this thing into a larger arena. That was the incalculable variable, the x-factor…

Elizabeth went back inside and dressed. One thing she had to discover from Lisa—deviously, of course—was whether she (and therefore, probably, Leland) would be relieved at Central's getting involved, or worried. In other words, she needed to get a feel for how deeply Madden's people had infiltrated the station. Given the dominance of the black market in the county, it would be unlikely that the station was entirely free of his influence, at least in the lower echelons. Lisa would have if not certain knowledge, intuitions… The important thing was not to raise her anxiety level on that particular subject. And the best way to deflect Lisa's attention from Central's possible suspicions would be to create anxieties in other areas.

Elizabeth buttoned her tunic cuffs. Given Lisa's weaknesses, that would be child's play.

[ii]

Celia snapped her attaché case shut and strode briskly out of the courtroom, aware as she passed them of the chatter of the client's friends and family—aware, too, of the photographer snatching pictures of herself and said friends and family. Since the media did not cover such events, she could imagine only one possible reason for their being photographed.

The judge had ordered the Military Police to produce her client within forty-eight hours or face contempt charges. (Who? Just *who* would face contempt charges? And would that ultimately mean anything?) And an investigation by the internal affairs division of the state's attorney general was to follow, too, the judge had ruled. Celia smiled as she emerged from the San Diego County Superior Court Building into the brilliant March sunlight. She'd been right to trust Emily Madden. Without her tip about the judge and her help in fixing the docket, the petition would have been thrown out of court as had happened so many times before. This was the first time she'd ever managed to effect a writ of habeas corpus, the first time in the nine years she had been practicing law. And no, it wasn't because the war was over, either. She wasn't *that* naive.

The state's attorney hadn't looked happy at the outcome. No, Jerry Carrizo had looked first startled, and then uneasy. He hadn't bargained for such an outcome. The situation would be ticklish for him. No doubt he had his orders and knew as little as he could manage about these cases. An occasional show trial, to keep up appearances, another blow against traitorous subversives, all under the fair and impartial eye of the Law…

The Law. That's what ODS liked to call itself: *the Law*.

Celia averted her eyes from the ruins of Horton Plaza. Each time she glimpsed the mess she could not help recalling her mother's description of the human wreckage that had washed up in the hospital in the wake of that hit. The lesson that one big hit took anything around the main target down with it had provided an insight Celia had lately become obsessed with.

She glanced over her shoulder. Yes, there she was. She really must find out the woman's name, invite her in for water, and pull her sad

sad story out of her. Of course once she did that they'd assign someone else, and who knew what would happen to this one. Celia sighed.
Celia Sisyphus Espin she should sign herself. Not *Speranza*. What had
ever gotten into Mama for tagging her with that? Must have been the
giddiness of the triumph of a safe delivery. Nothing else could account
for such mis-naming. Celia S. Espin? Did some report-reader in ODS
laugh at the elaboration of that S? *Speranza/Sisyphus.*

Schizoid, Celia, schizoid.

Because she hadn't been paying attention to the street, Celia didn't
notice the car that had pulled in at the curb a few yards ahead until
the door opened and the black-clad professional got out of the back.
She knew at once, even before the man staring at her said, "Afternoon,
Espin."

Celia nodded coolly. "Good afternoon Mr.—I didn't catch your
name?"

He gestured to the car, and the front passenger door opened, dis-
gorging a second man.

Celia weighed her chances if she ran.

The first man said, "Get in, Celia."

Celia knew better than to waste energy she would soon be in desperate need of. She got into the car.

[iii]

"You're correct about one thing," Elizabeth said to Lisa when
they had seated themselves in the far corner of the back lounge.

"Just one?" Lisa rolled her eyes. "I guess I should be grateful
for that."

Elizabeth gave Lisa a sharp look—and saw how haggard she looked,
how stretched and jumpy. Too many stimulants? Or stress? "It's clear
to me," Elizabeth said, ignoring Lisa's sarcasm, "that Barclay Madden
is the key to the problem. The only question is the size of the body of
water we're dealing with. If it turns out to be a lake then the ripples
he can make could well turn into waves. But if we're dealing with a
nice reasonable-sized pond, handling him will be simple."

Lisa's eyes narrowed.

Ah, yes, Lisa knew precisely what she was talking about. But Elizabeth had never taken her for a fool. She was at times foolish, yes, but never a fool.

"I'm not sure it's possible to find that out in advance," Lisa said, glancing around the mostly empty room.

"Here's the girl now," Elizabeth said in warning, her gaze fixed on the service-tech's breasts swinging and bouncing as she swiftly zigzagged around the sofas, armchairs, and footstools scattered about the room. Elizabeth ordered coffee, Lisa juice. The girl returned Elizabeth's smile. Elizabeth detected flirtatiousness in the way she pivoted and strutted away, swinging her hips with unusual flair.

"Forget her," Lisa said. "She's frigid."

Elizabeth took her gaze off the girl, now fetching their drinks from the other end of the room. "I've heard that one before," she said with a smirk.

"It's a well-known fact. She has a great come-on, but bedding her is like wrapping yourself in a body-sized ice-pack. The locals avoid her like the plague. Which is why she puts herself out to woo out-of-towners like you."

Elizabeth ignored that. "What I need is an intermediary. Someone I can talk to who Madden trusts to deal for him. I suspect that my dealing with him straight-on would put me at a strategic disadvantage."

Elizabeth knew that Lisa understood exactly what she meant— and that she must be wondering why the Executive had sent Elizabeth in the first place…and why Sedgewick, if it mattered so much, was not taking care of it personally.

The girl returned with their drinks. "Can you think of anyone who would meet my requirements?" Elizabeth said as the girl set her coffee on the side table. When Elizabeth paid her no attention, she flounced off with studied defiance.

Lisa, frowning, sipped her juice. "Let me think…" Her eyes widened. "But of course, it's obvious! Emily Madden would be the perfect intermediary!"

Elizabeth picked up the cup and saucer. "That's the daughter?" she asked as she lifted the cup to her lips.

Lisa nodded.

Elizabeth sipped the coffee and identified it as having been dripped from a strong dark roast. "I don't know, Lisa. Someone more in the way of serious access to him would be——"

"But she does have serious access to him," Lisa said. "She handles a good bit of his business for him."

Elizabeth's eyebrows rose. "Not standard maternal-line breeding fodder?"

Lisa stared at her. "Christ, your mouth is vicious, Elizabeth."

Nice going, Lizzie. You're starting to sound like Sedgewick. No doubt Leland had a different style from Sedgewick's: his sentimentalities had entirely other objects than Sedgewick's. "Sorry," she said. "Too much time spent with Sedgewick." Hiding behind the cup, she took a long swallow of coffee.

Lisa's cheeks reddened. "About Madden's daughter," she said carefully.

Elizabeth set the cup back into the saucer and nodded.

"Emily is like no other executive I've ever met or heard of. She comes and goes as she pleases. She's a scholar. When Stanford shut down during the war, Barclay Madden simply imported dozens of tutors for completing the job. And when his son was killed in the Del Mar bombing, he switched all his attention to Emily and let everyone know she would be what the son was to have been. It's said he's emotionally attached to her." Lisa shrugged. "But that part of it's just rumor." She smiled sourly. "People are always looking for reasons explaining the seemingly incomprehensible."

"Whenever I think I've got male execs tapped, I run across fresh anomalies," Elizabeth said. "I think we have to face the fact that getting fixed makes them unstable. As for the ones coming up now, the ones fixed before maturity..." Elizabeth shrugged. "Who knows what *they'll* be like."

"True. There's one working out of the LA base who freaks the shit out of me every time I see him. I think he freaks even Leland."

Elizabeth drank down the rest of her coffee and reflected that she'd recovered her fumble nicely. "At any rate, I'm certainly willing to try it out with Madden's daughter," she said as she set the cup and saucer down on the table. "I'd always deal with women if I had my druthers."

"You want me to arrange a meeting?"

"Yes." Elizabeth stretched her legs before her and gave Lisa a thoughtful look. "I wish there were some way I could get her off by herself for a good bit of time. If I had a house up Ramona way...or if you had such a house...we could have a long weekend billed as a house party..." Elizabeth sighed. "Sedgewick's nearest house is just south of San Francisco."

"It has to be remote?"

"That would be best. Of course if I have to, I'll settle for the usual meeting over dinner or the like."

"I have an idea..."

"Go on," Elizabeth said.

"I propose we get up a party to go camping in the desert. Just Emily, you, me, and my girl. We'll go in by four-wheel drive—or chopper, if you prefer, though in my opinion that would rather spoil the ambience—and have an extended, elegant picnic." Lisa's face and voice grew enthusiastic. "It's a perfect time of year, Elizabeth. The desert will be blooming. Nobody around for miles—we can make sure of that by arranging to have all permits other than our own canceled." She grinned. "I do that all the time when I go into the desert."

An extended elegant picnic? In the *desert*? It sounded positively grueling. "I don't know," Elizabeth said. "It hardly seems...and besides, how would you ever get Emily Madden to agree to it?"

Lisa laughed. "That's the best part of the plan, dear: Emily and I have been camping in the desert two or three times—not alone, but with larger parties. She won't suspect a thing!"

Lisa had been camping with Emily Madden? "I had no idea you knew her personally," Elizabeth said, her stare hard on Lisa's face.

Lisa shrugged. "You didn't ask. Of course I know her. Do you think there are many women executives living in San Diego County I'm not likely to know? Just how many of us do you think are here, anyway?"

"How well do you know her?"

"Superficially," Lisa said. "She keeps everyone at arm's length. I'd say, though, she has some pretty unorthodox interests, judging by..."

"Judging by?"

Lisa hesitated. "Judging by some of her non-executive connections."

"You'd better clarify that," Elizabeth said.

"Her name pops up—occasionally—in routine surveillance reports on known subversives. When we first heard about this we ordered ODS to make special notation for bringing such occurrences to our attention. When it's a matter of someone like Emily Madden…"

"You think she's a renegade?" Elizabeth asked with growing disquiet.

"No," Lisa said. "I don't think she's a renegade. Or near to going renegade, either. My guess is she's a simpatico."

Elizabeth made a face. "What in god's name is a simpatico?" The horrid names people called themselves! This one was positively tacky.

"A simpatico is an executive or professional who sympathizes with the plight of subversives whose civil rights have been disregarded," Lisa sing-songed.

"Textbook definition?" Elizabeth said. "Then there must be a lot of them around locally."

"They're called that by the subversives, and they call themselves that," Lisa said. "Renegade is too strong a word to apply to a mild simpatico; though some of the more zealous types…" She sipped her juice.

"And Emily Madden is of the mild variety?"

"So we surmise," Lisa said. "After all, she is working for her father. Who, as you know, is tight with Military. If she were a renegade he'd do something about it, damned fast."

"Look, Lisa. If I'm going to be dealing with her, you'd better put her under surveillance and run a thorough background check on her. I want to know everything you can find out about her. The nature of her, ah, sympathies will inevitably emerge in that sort of workup. Clear?"

"Understood. Then I'm to go ahead with setting up this outing?"

"If it can be soon. This weekend, say." The sight of the girl—now at the other end of the room—swinging a tray loaded with glasses onto her shoulder caught Elizabeth's eye. Enjoying the sexy grace of her movements, Elizabeth continued watching as the girl turned from the bar toward the passage leading to the adjoining lounge; she apparently did not see the woman barreling down the passage, presumably because of the tray on her shoulder. Fascinated with the inevitability of the collision, Elizabeth held her breath as the girl swung forward into the passage and seconds later let it explode out of her as the woman shot over the threshold straight into the girl and her tray, sending glasses and ice cubes flying. Even from where she sat, Elizabeth could see the beverages the glasses had held spattering both the girl and the woman (though mostly the latter) and making a mess on the patterned turquoise, beige, and peach rug.

At the sound of the crash, Lisa turned around to look. The woman screeched furious invective at the girl. Apologetic, the girl leaned forward and dabbed with a napkin at the woman's tunic. But this— what the furious maternal-line executive named an "uninvited violation"—appeared to whip her into uncontrollable rage, for she shoved the girl from her and shrieked for the manager, who was at that second sprinting into the room, braced for catastrophe.

While the manager apologized and the woman spewed shrill invective, the girl dropped on all fours to retrieve the dishes and glasses scattered over the rug. "My god," Elizabeth breathed, excited by the sight of the girl crawling around on the floor—and grew aware of Lisa staring at her. "Don't underestimate the amount of heat *I* can generate," she murmured. "My heat could turn a body pack of ice into not just water, but steam."

Lisa made a sound of disgust. Or was it derision? "You'd be a fool to have anything to do with her. In any case, I'm sure she'll be out on her ear after this. The maternal-line she had the collision with has never quite gotten over that one having duped *her*. It's a matter of pride, you see," Lisa said, presumably ironically.

After the girl had slunk from the room and the atmosphere had returned to its previous tranquility, Elizabeth looked at Lisa and grinned. "I don't give a birthing fuck for pride. What matters is that my pants are delightfully wet."

Lisa's mouth twisted. "You've got to be the crudest woman I've ever known," she said. "If you have to talk that way, you could at least save it for your pickups."

Elizabeth's grin broadened. "Oh, that's very nice, love. A little hypocrisy makes everything so pretty. Of course you whisper nothing at all in their ears? And of course you yourself don't have a cunt between your legs, or if you do, not one that creams? None of us do, I suppose, except me?"

Lisa spoke through tight lips and clenched teeth: "Some of us don't have to have every girl that appears on the scene, either."

"Oh blissful monogamy! Virtuous Lisa Mott! You know, I'd be tempted to call you a prude except you can't really be one, can you, given your habitual procurement of girls for Leland."

Lisa's face lost all color, signaling a direct hit.

Good. Elizabeth was sick to death of this bitch's primness.

"You know about that?" Lisa whispered.

Elizabeth raised her eyebrows. "Surely you knew that we did? We have to know all there is to know about our territory heads. We have to ferret out any possible vulnerability to blackmail. For godsake, Lisa! Leland himself knows that Sedgewick knows—Sedgewick made a point of letting him know so that he'd realize any blackmail attempt would be best brought to Sedgewick to deal with."

"God you people are sordid," Lisa said, staring down at the floor, her hand at her throat.

"And you're not? What is it he does with the girls, anyway?"

Lisa's head jerked up. "What about Sedgewick? He's not exactly the driven snow when it comes to perversion. His thing with Zeldin— don't forget, I saw him with her. I saw it all. And you had nothing to do with any of that, I suppose?"

Elizabeth leaned forward and patted Lisa's hand. "Sordid, love, that's us, the pair of us sordid accomplices of nasty old perverts."

Lisa said, "I can see you'll be a real hit with Emily Madden. Five minutes of this kind of talk and she'll be radioing for a chopper to make her escape."

Elizabeth's eyebrows raised. "She's squeamish? With a father like Barclay Madden?" She snorted. "I bet it's like living with Sedgewick. How many years has she been handling business for him?"

Lisa glanced at her watch. "If you want me to get the workup on her started, I'd better be getting back to station headquarters." Her unfriendly eyes waited for Elizabeth to release her.

Elizabeth nodded. "Yes, I'm sure you're right."

As soon as Lisa had gone Elizabeth left the club to walk in Balboa Park. The meeting with Lisa had been less than satisfying. She hadn't managed to learn what she needed to know about Leland and his people's possible involvement with any of Madden's projects (the black market, for instance). Well, that could wait for another time. But the hostility she'd stirred up in Lisa...that was a luxury the price of which she'd probably have to pay later, and would likely regret. Elizabeth, staring up at a eucalyptus tree, sighed. She was sick of executive women trying to pretend they were as detached from their sexual pleasures as fixed males, who had no possibility of sexual pleasure. (Though what *was* it Leland wanted with the girls? What was it that had compelled Sedgewick to whatever it was he had done to Kay Zeldin?)

Elizabeth stooped to pick up one of the long narrow leaves scattered over the ice-plant ground cover. Her thoughts turned to Emily Madden. Curious, curious, this new generation. She must try to understand them, for they would inevitably make their impact on the world and for that she needed to be prepared... Their difference presented yet one more thing to anticipate having to deal with in the future. But such marked the difference between her and Lisa Mott, and even between her and Sedgewick: she could look ahead the way the best chess players could conceptualize a dozen alternate games for each move that was made. They, like most people, saw the future as an inevitable continuation of the present. But Elizabeth had long since realized that the future belonged to those who know that the present tense is an illusion.

[iv]

Trembling and aching with fatigue, Celia shifted from one foot to the other and leaned her head against the filthy lime green wall that she'd resisted touching for as long as she could. It was the same old story, employing the same old anxiety-generating techniques. The game never changed and in spite of her understanding of how it worked never failed to psych her out. Like clockwork, it made her stomach churn with acid, her neck and shoulders rigid with tension. And yet it never cowed her, never deterred her from doing everything she could to secure due process for her clients, either. Each time they detained her she balanced on the edge of the precipice, wondering if on this particular occasion the game would go further, to the point of pushing her over the edge, they having genuinely "lost patience" (as they liked to put it).

This time the stakes were higher than they'd been in the past. Today's procedural victory had broken fresh ground, had taken them by surprise. She imagined the chain of three or four phone calls: one from the courtroom, possibly another to a superior, and then a call from the decision-maker to one of the men who'd picked her up (or their superior). Which people this time? Not ODS. Celia closed her eyes. Did it *matter* which ones? There were so many…and they all used the same techniques, all used the same approach, all had the same stone faces, the same hovering subordinates longing for action. (How tedious of her to require intrinsically boring attentions.) And this building…she had never been here before and had no idea of its location. Once they had transferred her to the van she had seen nothing of where they had taken her. She'd been in a lot of different jails, for herself, for her clients—but never in this one. In fact, she didn't even know that this place was actually a jail. Briefly she wondered— but no: it *smelled* like a jail.

As she waited in the hall and the hours passed, the bodily irritations standard to arrest grew oppressive—thirst, hunger, the pressure of a full bladder, the cramp of being too-long cuffed… Eventually a tall skinny Anglo—the first person Celia had seen since having been dumped here—came into the hall. Acutely conscious of his approach, she held her breath and fastened her gaze on the floor. He passed her, though, without stopping, and pushed open the steel-plated exit door at the opposite end of the hall.

His brief appearance had probably been for her benefit.

The memory of the first time she had been left in a hall flooded over her…three years ago, it was…she had thought they had forgotten her, and she had attempted flight, giving them the excuse they had wanted for beating her and keeping her a week in isolation. She shuddered. They must know she would never try that again. *They?* But all her previous arrests must be known to all of them even if some of them operated within different jurisdictions… How much more disturbing to linger in the hall than to wait alone in a room—even in a room with one-way glass, even in the most disgusting of cells. The transience of hallways always grew upsetting after a time, for hallways were spaces not meant for lingering…

After a long while—Celia had no notion of time since she could not manage to glimpse her watch while cuffed—a door several yards down the hall opened and a head twisted around the doorframe. "In here, Espin."

Celia drew a deep breath, straightened her spine, and shakily approached the now empty doorway. She paused on the threshold, then went in.

"Close the door," he ordered from behind the desk.

Celia obeyed awkwardly, using her shoulder, elbow, and back to swing the door to, aware that if she used her foot he would likely abuse her for kicking his door, and waited for an order before advancing into the room.

He looked up from the file opened on the desk before him. "What's the matter with you?" His breath puffed out in disgust. "You trying to put on a retarded act or something? Get over here. We've got some talking to do, you and me."

This was the first time she'd ever been interrogated in an office—bar Judge Barnes's chambers, of course. But this man, she recognized this man. He'd been the controller the last time, he'd been the one to take her to Barnes's chambers. She remembered that she'd formed the distinct impression that he had once been a noncommissioned military officer, something to do with the way he handled himself.

Celia stood before the desk. She had scant hope he'd tell her to sit down in the chair just inches from her hip.

He leaned back in his chair and glared at her. "You've crossed the line, Espin. You remember what Judge Barnes told you last time?"

She nodded.

"Say it."

Celia swallowed to generate saliva in her painfully dry throat. "Judge Barnes warned me I'd be at the very least named if I were ever brought before him again."

"And here you are in trouble again. But you know, Espin, it's sure as hell going to be more than naming. There's not the slightest doubt in my mind it'll be banning, unless..." He smirked, and his smirk made him look distinctly simian. "I'm sure you know what I want from you. You're a smart girl. Even if you do pretend to be retarded."

Banned. Celia's head swam. She braced herself against the chair, hoping he wouldn't notice. Named, she could still give counsel, even if she were not allowed to speak in court, even if she were disbarred. But banned she'd automatically be endangering any clients she might have, for the banned were prohibited from so much as speaking to anyone up on any subversion charges. Celia drew a deep breath. "Martial law has been lifted. None of that applies now. Judge Barnes no longer has the authority to name *or* ban," Celia said.

He gestured her to move away from the chair. Celia did so, wondering why he hadn't used it as a pretext for violence or verbal abuse. "For a lawyer you sure are dumb, Espin. Don't tell me you haven't heard of the Subversion Control Ordinance?"

Oh christ, the state must have gotten something new on the books, fast, when martial law had been lifted. And legally there was nothing that could be done about that. The Reformed Bill of Rights applied only to federal laws. So why had the demand for a writ of habeas corpus worked? Oh, of course: because the judge had used his discretionary powers to allow it. "But aside from that," Celia said, "there is nothing I have done that is illegal. Every defendant has the right to legal counsel and representation." But had they perhaps caught one of her clients on the run and discovered she'd passed on information and money to refugees? Could it be that, and not the writ of habeas corpus?

He was shaking his head. "Nobody's questioning any defendant's right to counsel and representation, Espin. Nobody." His thin, sandy eyebrows sailed high in his short, mole-splotched forehead. "But suborning a judge and tampering with the judicial process?" He pushed his pale, dry lower lip out as far as it could seemingly go. "Now that's serious, Espin. In fact, you'll probably do time for it. But at the very least you can be damned sure you'll never practice law again."

Suborning a judge? It was too soon for that judge to be caving under pressure. They had nothing on her, nothing but their desire to break her.

"Judge Barnes is going to be annoyed at your having wasted his time and patience." The controller rubbed his thumb over his chin. "Considering all the advice he took the trouble to give you the last time. No, I imagine he'll throw the book at you. Besides which, he takes a pretty dim view of officers of the Court disgracing the Law."

Celia reeled under the blow. This was a twist she hadn't anticipated. "I haven't suborned a judge," she said into the silence. ":That
Judge Sands authorized a writ of habeas corpus is no reason for such
an accusation." In her surprise at this tactical move, Celia spoke rashly. "Isn't that rather serious, charging a judge with being bought?"

He sprang to his feet and leaned forward with his palms flat on
the desk. "You watch your mouth, bitch." A fleck of spit flew out of
his own mouth. Celia stared down at the floor and braced herself.

He moved around the desk, and though she was braced, she was
still taken by a surge of alarm that fairly stopped the breath in her
throat. "You're so mixed up in the head, Espin, that I think you need
some time to think about your situation and the wisdom of cooperating with us for a change. Before I take you to see Judge Barnes."
He stood so close to her she could feel his breath on her face. "Judge
Barnes would be very interested in learning about how you tampered
with the Law and who helped you and so on. He might even be willing to go for naming rather than banning—if, that is, you show tangible signs of rehabilitation." Grabbing her arm, he squeezed it so
tightly she gasped at the pain, and he hauled her toward a side door
she hadn't noticed.

This time *was* different, Celia realized as she stumbled along at
the controller's rapid pace. Very different.

Chapter Five

Over the years, Martha had become a champion brooder. And on Saturday morning, Martha brooded as she drove from Ravenna to the Co-op's offices downtown. She told herself that she should not let her ingrained social defensiveness cloud her thinking. But what David Hughes had told her about women executives had jacked up her distrust of Ganshoff.

Sometimes David amazed her. He knew so much about so many things; his level of sophistication rose far above the norm, even for professionals. "Basically," he told her when she'd seen him a few days after the reception at the embassy, "there are two things I always bear in mind about executive women. The first is to never ever, even by accident, touch one, no matter how innocuously. I think I must have been about twenty—I was an undergraduate at the time—when I saw something that made a profound impression on me. I was waiting for an elevator in the library. A male professor and a young woman executive—she was a student, I think—were discussing something literary…Dante, I think it was. When the elevator arrived, the professor unthinkingly put his hand on her back to usher her into the elevator with him. It's the kind of gesture most men use with women, one quite natural between male professor and female student. Only this student was an executive. Before I understood what was happening, this female executive—and my god, she was several inches shorter than the professor, it was incredible—this female executive gave him a shove that sent him crashing back into the corridor wall. And then she decked him with a smashing kick in the knee cap. It was shocking. I mean, there we were, in the *library*. And this is a *student*—a woman, yet—violently assaulting a *professor*. So there he was, lying on the floor, moaning. And he looked up at her and asked her what the fuck she'd done that for. There wasn't any kind of expression on her face as she stared down at him. All she said was, 'If you ever touch me again, I'll put you in the hospital.' And then coolly stepped into the elevator as though nothing had happened."

David's anecdote had made Martha rethink Margot Ganshoff and Eva Auerbach. But David's second observation was far more disturbing, especially considering Margot's...pursuit of her. According to David, executive women—unlike executive men—were sexually active, with a preference for women. But service-tech women, only. They never slept with one another. When Martha had uneasily asked David why that was, his answer had deepened her disquietude: "There's no way to be sure, of course, but I suspect it has something to do with power-relations." He'd grinned at her reaction. "Why, did any of those witches come on to you, Martha?"

In short, Martha thought, the executive women were as bad as the men, maybe worse. Having to fend off the sexual approaches of the person you were doing business with was vexing and disgusting but not surprising when one was dealing with a man. But a woman? The sexualization of the business relation was degrading enough. After what David had hinted at, though, Margot's attitude and behavior disturbed Martha more than such behavior would under more ordinary circumstances.

"Executive women are said to be master handlers. I wouldn't take anything any executive—male *or* female—says to a sub-exec: that's what they call professionals and service-techs, you know—I wouldn't take anything they say to the likes of us at face value," David had said. "They have one set of ethics for dealing among themselves and another for dealing with us."

Martha parked in the Co-op's garage, grabbed her briefcase, and took the elevator up to the fifteenth floor to the windowless conference room the Women's Patrol took special pains to keep bug-free. "Good morning, Martha," Jan sang out as Martha entered the room. Five minutes early, she was the first one there. "There's coffee and rolls and cheese and fruit," Jan said. "A little bird told me this is going to be a super-heavy meeting, so I thought I'd really lay on the grub."

Martha dumped her briefcase on the table. "Which little bird was that?"

Jan laid her arms in an x-formation over her chest. "Sorry. I'm sworn to cross-my-heart-and-hope-to-die secrecy."

Martha shed her rain gear and hung it on one of the coat racks. "I suppose the Women's Patrol have already been in here?" she said.

"An hour ago."

Martha poured a cup of coffee and seated herself.

"Since you're here and I've got everything set up, I'll be getting back to my desk," Jan said.

Martha opened her briefcase and arranged her papers, yellow pad, pen, and NoteMaster. She always seemed to be the first to arrive at these breakfast meetings.

A few minutes later Laura, Louise, and Grace came in together, cackling and chortling at a joke Louise had just finishing telling. Martha recalled having heard that Louise was in love. Louise, seeing Martha, grinned. "Oh hey. Will you look at that!" she said. "There's old Martha, already here, working away like a dog." She dumped her attaché case on the table just across from where Martha sat. "I don't know about you, Martha. Do you *never* stop working? Do you even bother sleeping anymore?" The gleam in Louise's eye was not entirely innocent.

"I sleep, I eat, I'm human," Martha said good-humoredly.

Louise nodded. "Right." She turned to the others, who were also settling themselves at the table. "Did you hear that? Martha's human!"

Martha flushed. So Louise was in one of *those* moods.

Lenore burst into the room and threw a newspaper down on the table. "Take a look at our favorite rag, girrrls."

Louise grabbed the newspaper and read out, "'When the Big Girls Get Together on Saturday Mornings.'" She looked at Lenore. "That's us?"

"Apparently," Lenore said shortly.

Louise laughed. "The Big Girls. That's good. They've got some truly talented and inventive writers on their staff, don't you think? So I'm one of the Big Girls? Coming up in life, I am."

"Oh but there's more," Lenore said. "Much, much more. For instance, the existence of our group—thank god they don't know how we ironically refer to ourselves—"

Louise interrupted: "Ironically, Lenore? Are you sure?"

Lenore glared at Louise. "If they knew, they'd say it confirms all their longstanding accusations. As it is they say we're the secret government of the Free Zone. And," she said through her teeth, "we are promised that every Friday afternoon for the next thirteen weeks each of us in turn will be 'profiled' in detail for *Examiner* readers!"

"Damn the jerks," Martha said angrily. "There must be *some* way of stopping them."

Louise's face lit up. "You want the Women's Patrol to try a physical intercept? I'd love to undertake such an operation, only thing is it'd be violent—which we all already know Ms. Greenglass here wouldn't approve. Besides which, the Co-op would be accused of censorship after the fact."

"Shut up, Louise," Martha said.

"They're starting with you, Martha," Lenore said.

"Oh, that's super."

"Well you know why they're doing it, don't you?" Louise said. "They can't get any of their bugs past the Women's Patrol. I'm sure they think this smear campaign is the next best thing."

"They say they're starting with Martha because she's the most powerful in the group," Lenore said.

Everyone looked at Martha. In the mushrooming silence, she felt as though she'd taken a blow to the solar plexus.

"It's true enough," Louise said casually. "Martha *is* the most powerful. Let's face it, if she doesn't like something around here, it doesn't fly. Who should know that better than I?"

Martha glared at her. "What you want to do is generally opposed by almost everyone else in the group, Louise. And we all know why that is."

Damn those bastards, Martha thought. Whoever planted that little barb in the paper must have had a shrewd idea about the kind of trouble it would stir up. Once declare someone in a non-hierarchical group to be the most powerful member, and dissension was sure to follow.

But the issue was forgotten as Maureen entered with three Whidbey women. "I've brought Gina, Beatrice, and Susan because they have an important contribution to make to this meeting," Maureen said.

Maureen glanced around the room. "Does anyone know if Venn will be making it today?"

Martha said, "Not clear. I asked her, and she said she'd try but couldn't promise."

Louise snorted.

"What about Cora?" Maureen asked as the four of them took chairs around the table.

"Cora attends regularly," Laura said. Martha caught a whiff of irony in spite of Laura's politely keeping her voice free of sarcasm.

"Neither Bert nor Aster will be coming this week," Laura said. She glanced at her watch. "But where *are* Tanya, Beth, Cora, and Kate? It's already ten after."

"We're right here," Kate said, coming into the room with the others. "Sorry to be late, but we got tied up in a snarl on the mass-auto. It must be some kind of problem with routing." Kate threw Lenore an arch look. "Has there been much of that lately?"

"What fine moods everyone is in," Martha said. Kate and Lenore had never gotten along and needled one another whenever they got the chance. Louise and Martha almost always disagreed on everything. And Cora and Laura found Venn's difference from the rest of them—exacerbated by her making no effort to disguise her general attitude towards "politics"—nearly intolerable. Usually these personality clashes had little effect on meetings. But this morning the level of irritability seemed unusually high.

"Before we get into ordinary business," Maureen said as the latecomers helped themselves to coffee and rolls, "I'd appreciate your listening to what Susan, Beatrice, and Gina have to say. I think we will want to act on this as quickly as possible." When everyone had expressed agreement to her request to bypass the usual order of business, Maureen said, "Beatrice, why don't you start."

Beatrice opened the file she had brought in with her and stared down at her densely handwritten notes. "It's hard to know where to begin." Frowning, she pressed her palm over her mouth. After a few seconds she dropped her hand to her lap and sighed. "All of you are aware, I think, that like activist health-care workers in the other Free Zones, Susan and Gina have set up a clinic retreat for refugees who have been tortured. You may recall the Marq'ssan bringing a load of them from Cuba." She glanced around the table. "And you may recall that there are a few other clinic retreats in this Free Zone, one on the Oregon coast, another in the Cascades northeast of Seattle. We started out on Whidbey with twenty-four refugees. Since peace, quiet, and isolation from the outside world are highly desirable during the first phase of recovery, we were reluctant to ever have more than twenty-four at one time." Beatrice took a swallow of water, and Martha wondered where this review of the obvious was leading. "I think Susan and Gina—who are the most involved of any of us in the clinic—will agree that in some cases there has been a slow healing process. In fact, a few people left the clinic, thinking they were ready for the outside world, though it turned out that was premature, and they each ended up returning, shaken and demoralized. So we decided to set up a second-phase place, for those who've gotten beyond the first stage of healing. That's worked out pretty good, I think—they're set up near Sweetwater and mix with Sweetwater people. They've all found work and are beginning to do more than simply hang on."

Beatrice brushed back the strand of hair that had fallen onto her forehead. "I can see you're wondering why I'm going through what most of you already know." She stared down at her notes and nudged them into precise alignment with the brown folder beneath them. "The thing is, we've started getting a lot more refugees—far more than we can reasonably accommodate." She ran her swollen, wrinkled index finger up and down the edge of the folder. "Some of you already know about them and know that they're coming from the US. But you probably don't know that we've been hearing from them about a widespread, apparently systematic practice of torture in US detention centers." Beatrice looked up. "What I'm saying is, that piecing together the stories we're hearing, it's become clear that something must be done to stop the torture—which apparently didn't cease when the war ended. There is also the matter of setting up more of these clinic retreats, but that goes almost without saying. As for what action we should take..." Beatrice's sad gray gaze, traveling around the table as she talked, paused when it met Martha's. "We need to discuss the matter of what the Co-op will do in its own name, as well as the matter of what action we should request of the Marq'ssan."

Cora rapped her knuckles on the table. "Well one thing doesn't need debating." Her tone was as brisk as Beatrice's had been sad and deliberate. "And that's the necessity of exposing this to the world at once." Cora would think that way. Martha wondered if she had visions of the Marq'ssan making a global vid monopoly available to them for the purpose.

Susan cleared her throat. She so seldom spoke when among non-Sweetwater people that Martha knew this must be important to her. "It won't be easy to do that," she said in her soft, hesitant voice. "It's not as though we can simply hold a press conference where the survivors tell all." She looked at Martha—as to a friendly reference point, Martha thought. "Very few of the people pouring into the clinic—and you understand we are now far above our capacity because of this sudden influx—very few of these refugees would be able to face the ordeal of a press conference. Some haven't even been able to talk to *anyone* yet about what was done to them, and still others are afraid that if they speak out publicly there will be retaliation against friends and relatives who in almost every case were left behind." Martha broke out in gooseflesh. She thought of how long it had taken Susan herself to return to even a semblance of a life after her own ordeal. And Susan had had all of Sweetwater to support her.

"Are you saying we won't be able to expose the US Government through the media?" Cora said, looking and sounding mightily pissed-off.

Gina spoke. "The point, Cora, is that it will have to be handled extremely carefully. *We* can speak at a press conference—Beatrice and I, at the very least, and others as well. But as for the survivors, it is inadvisable that *they* do so... Well, it may be possible to videotape some of them in private one-on-one interview sessions. But that would have to be handled very very carefully. There are, of course, other measures than press conferences. What is most important now—though later we will definitely want to give voice to these victims and to denounce and single out those responsible—what is most important now, though, is stopping it. It's not clear that instant exposure will do that. We must think very very carefully before we go ahead. Yet we can't afford to wait long. Every day there are more and more victims."

"You can speak as a physician, Gina, to verify the physical evidence?" Louise said.

"Certainly. There's no question about that kind of evidence."

"What I am wondering," Maureen said, "is whether it would be useful for the Marq'ssan to bring certain pressures to bear on the Executive for stopping it. If perhaps that wouldn't be the best place to start."

Martha picked up her pen and quickly jotted down some of the ideas flooding her mind. "It's too bad Venn isn't here," she said.

"That's why I asked," Cora said. "We need to get some projects going with the Rainbow Press as soon as possible."

"We also need to get word to the activists we're in touch with around the country," Louise said. "Like the Boston Collective. The Atlanta League for Social Justice. The El Paso Mothers. They can start doing some local investigating and tie in what they've heard with the stuff we're getting here. And we need to coordinate closely with the other Free Zones."

And so the discussion began.

They would need to have a plan ready for when they would be meeting Sorben on Sunday. That gave them roughly twenty-four hours in which to work out their strategy—in a situation in which every hour counted heavily in human lives and suffering.

Which is how it happened that the *Examiner* article passed under their collective radar, forgotten in the meeting's moment.

[ii]

Strange country, this. The clouds stretched in thin strata across an otherwise blue sky, casting long shadows on the lush green hills rising out of boulder-tossed chaparral. When they passed one of the few small adobe houses squatting along the roadside, Elizabeth wondered how the obviously indigent inhabitants managed to live in such a place—from whence they got potable water, and how they managed to live off such inhospitable land; some, she thought, likely tended the sheep and horses raised on the area's occasional large ranch. The distant ridges fascinated her: their strikingly different coloring, suggesting layers and layers of light—the first ridge a deep midnight blue, sharp-etched, almost as distinct in outline as shadow in moonlight, then behind it a rising fuzzy gray-white smoke, hardly discernible as a ridge but for its contrast with the first and the one behind it, which, almost black, met the azure, cloud-strafed skyline.

The variety of color in the vegetation surprised Elizabeth even more than the distinctiveness of the ridges. Many shrubs had flowers—purple, red, orange, lavender, pink, white, yellow—of diverse shapes and sizes. The vehicle moved too quickly, though, for Elizabeth to distinguish them clearly. Squinting, she sought to seize impressions before they blurred. When they stopped once for Lisa to check the map, she saw in another direction a ridge she had not previously made out: gray, it could hardly be perceived against a slate horizon. The sky had changed so quickly she had not even noticed the thick massing of clouds in that particular quarter.

They passed a battered, rusted sign that bore the name "Anza" and an arrow. Elizabeth's breath hissed in. She stared at Lisa. "Is that *Anza* as in *Anza-Borrego Desert?*"

Lisa glanced at Elizabeth. "Of course. Where else did you think we were going?"

Trembling, Elizabeth sank back in her seat. The Anza-Borrego desert had been the site of the aliens' first landing to take humans to their starship. Kay Zeldin had come in and gone out there. The realization mainlined a dose of uneasiness hard into the pit of Elizabeth's stomach.

After several minutes, she said, "It's very dry. My nose, my skin… I suppose people go into filter-failure quite easily out here?"

"Stop worrying." Lisa kept her eyes on the road. "We've plenty of water and other fluids. And we have a radio. We have only to give the word and a chopper will fly in and get us. We're not going to the ends of the earth, you know."

It almost looked as though they were, Elizabeth thought. They had seen no people for miles and miles, only the harsh albeit brilliantly colored landscape, only the glaring blue sky, the constantly changing ridges, only birds and flowers and insects…and rocks and sand.

They jolted along a dirt road. A sign announced "Terwilliger"—a designation so humorous Elizabeth wondered if the naming had been a hoax, since nothing, after all, existed in such a place to be named.

A while later, Lisa stopped at a turning she apparently knew, for no sign marked it. Elizabeth gazed out at the purple flowers low to the ground—clover? —and at the bright orange loose weed that seemed to blow free and erratically lodge in the scrub. "Now we start the rough stuff," Lisa said. "We'll be going down the other side of these mountains. Lots and lots of rock fall. It's strenuous, challenging driving."

"There *is* an easier way," Emily said from the back-seat. She didn't sound as though she were giving advice, Elizabeth thought, but as though she were amused at Lisa's preferring "challenging" driving.

Lisa smiled over her shoulder at Emily. "Yes, I know. But I come that way nearly every time." Lisa looked at Elizabeth. "We'll take that way when we go out. It's picturesque, in a softer way, than the terrain we'll be covering going in. But I want to give you a look at the more rugged aspects of the desert." She put the vehicle into gear and turned onto a road heading straight into the hills.

After the first couple of miles their progress became excruciatingly slow. Elizabeth had to grip the looped strap hanging from the ceiling to hold herself steady against the terrific bouncing.

"This is lovely on horseback," Emily said as they started the switchbacks winding down the hills? mountains? they'd just ascended.

Emily Madden came out here on horseback? Sure, it was pretty with all the flowers and the shading of the distant ridges. But for any length of time…Lisa said she sometimes backpacked out here but that it was a pain since one had to carry so much more water than in other terrains. Elizabeth enjoyed backpacking in the mountains; she had done it whenever she could get away in Colorado. But there the solitude was not quite so bleakly godforsaken as it seemed here. The hostility of the terrain… She tried to imagine it in summer when presumably none of these plants would be in bloom, when none of the hills would be green, when the scrub would be dustier and the air unbearably hot and sterile.

The aliens had chosen this place.

They rattled and jolted along, often crawling or even coming to a complete stop in order to get the vehicle over especially treacherous piles of boulders, until at last Lisa said as they drove onto a patch of loose white sand, "All right, it gets better from now on." Twice they drove in the creek-bed where the willows brushed both sides of the vehicle, and the smell, sound, and humidity of the water delighted Elizabeth. The willows—their branches flowing and green with long narrow leaves—not only offered aesthetic relief after miles of bleakness but also tantalized with their trumpet-shaped flowers of a delicate shade somewhere between mauve and lavender. Lowering the window and sticking her head out, Elizabeth gazed down at the surprisingly tall, thorn-spined shrubs thrusting out of the banks of the creek—wet, stratified, caked formations that she could only think of as walls. The refreshment from simply being there in the water made her smile with pleasure. She looked at Lisa. "It's quite beautiful."

Lisa, swinging the wheel and pumping the accelerator to lift them up out of the creek onto more dry, loose sand, chuckled. "It's creeping over you, Elizabeth. I knew it would. By the time we've had several days out here you'll be sorry to be returning to the real world."

Elizabeth doubted that, but she allowed Lisa her satisfaction. There was enough satisfaction today to go around for all of them.

"And now," Lisa said as they picked up speed along the wash, "we're entering Collins Valley. Which is where the aliens came in and out. When we come to it I'll show you where the army had a big pavilion set up for us that first day we all came out here."

Elizabeth wondered that Lisa ever wanted to remember anything to do with those occasions when Zeldin had been present. Why hadn't she buried all that stuff?

"Ten years ago," Lisa said.

"Ten years is a big chunk of my life," Emily said.

Elizabeth turned in her seat to look at her. "This has been a long ten years for all of us," she said. "But how old were you at the time of the Blanket—if you don't mind my asking," she added politely, knowing perfectly well what the answer was.

"Of course I don't mind," Emily said. No, of course not: Emily could have no idea yet of how the context of longevity treatments would change her consciousness of age. "I was fifteen at the time. So you see, more than a third of my life has taken place since then."

"Just think of it. There's a whole new generation of people who came to adulthood after the Blanket," Elizabeth said. "People with no notion of what normal is." How extraordinary those fiery bushes were—long graceful arching branches springing up almost from the ground, something like the light sculpture in the foyer of Sedgewick's Colorado house. "What are those orange-flowered bushes called?" she asked.

"Ocotillos," Lisa and Emily said together.

After a few minutes Lisa said, "Okay, Elizabeth. It was right around here that they had the pavilion… And how well I remember that day…"

Elizabeth drew a deep breath. "It looks untouched. Are you sure?"

Lisa laughed scornfully. "The desert is resilient, dear. Far more so than humans. It's the water and the wind that call the shots out here."

They drove in silence over the flat desert floor until they turned into one of the many canyons branching out from Collins Valley. "We'll be parking fairly soon," Lisa said. "See that stand of palm trees close on the north canyon wall? We'll be camping near there. There are all sorts of trees over there—palms, alders, sycamore."

Elizabeth looked and found said palm trees—a strange sight in the desert, considering… "And those yellow flowers on such bizarrely long stalks sticking up from huge, spiky leaves?"

"Agaves, also known as century plants," Emily said.

Lisa halted the vehicle in a flat clearing that included what looked like an iron hitching post for horses. "Okay, this is it, women. We'll have something to drink and then start hauling our things over to the campsite."

Elizabeth turned her head to give Lisa an incredulous stare. "We?"

Lisa shot her a look of warning. "There's too much and it's too far to saddle Ginger with carrying everything. And we're big strong healthy women: it won't kill us to carry at least one load apiece. And then Ginger will come back for the rest later."

Getting out of the truck, Elizabeth sighed. Why have the girl along at all if they were going to do all this work themselves? She was nothing to look at, that was for sure. How ridiculous of Lisa to bother extracting a promise from her to leave the girl alone—as if she'd want that pale scrawniness… Ginger took plastic bottles of fruit juice from the cooler and handed one to each of them. Elizabeth, hot even in her loose cotton clothing, rolled up her sleeves and welcomed the breeze on her sweat-beaded arms. The grapefruit juice slid down her throat, cold, wet, but not quite refreshing. "I think it's water I want," she said, staring out at the section of Collins Valley still visible, taking in the variously colored ridges rising up in the east. The sun was almost directly overhead, and the enormous moonscape-like rocks glinted and shimmered with heat.

"Can't it wait until we get there?" Lisa asked. "It will be so pleasant over there. And it's almost lunch time."

Elizabeth glanced at Emily, who seemed to be staring at the world around her in something of a trance, her face curiously intense yet serene, her body giving the appearance of drinking in the air, light, and scents surrounding them.

So the four of them loaded themselves down—Elizabeth carrying more than any of the others since she was so much bigger and stronger—and trudged through the sand to the site Lisa had chosen. Elizabeth had to admit that this weekend might be a unique experience for her—which was nothing to be sneered at. Not given the kind of life she led.

[iii]

After dinner the three of them—bundling up in layers as the heat left the rocks—lay on their chaise lounges and sipped steaming hot tea and talked. Elizabeth still had not let Emily know the point of the trip. She had decided to broach it when they were out on the day-hike Lisa had planned for the morrow. It seemed sensible to have this easy introductory period to lay groundwork for communication before plunging into confrontation. Certainly Emily should be easier to manage if Elizabeth had a notion of how she thought and reacted in non-stressful situations. And once Elizabeth brought the conflict into the open, Emily would be on her guard.

Elizabeth listened to Emily's pleasant voice and tried to make out her face in the dark, but the lantern's light did not reach far enough to be of much help. For someone so young, Elizabeth found her extremely interesting. She did not lead the kind of life most young executive women led. When maternal-line, by age twenty-five they tended to be thoroughly wrapped up in the life-style, for at such an age they found it still somewhat new and free-seeming after the restrictive years of executive girlhood. If career-line, they generally held dull jobs and were simply struggling to cope, to adjust, to find a way of living (which was not easy, given the lowness of their status and income while facing the ordinary demands of executive life). Allison had been most tiresome in those years and had had trouble adjusting upwards when her salary and status had begun rising. But Emily…Emily seemed to take the world on her own terms, and not narrowly, either: she had a big sophisticated picture of things, unlike that of any other executive woman at twenty-five past or present whom Elizabeth could think of.

"My mother lives permanently in Mexico," Emily said in response to Elizabeth's ritual questions about her maternal connections. "She and her family were based in the Yucatan—until the aliens made it into a Free Zone. I've seen little of her in the last fifteen years. She detests North Americans." Lisa had told Elizabeth a little about Silvia Alvarez, the daughter of a large executive family in Mexico. Many of the Latin American executives lived very differently from American and European executives; they had larger families and often maintained heterosexual arrangements, including marriage, and many of the men declined getting fixed. Elizabeth grew curious about how Silvia Alvarez and Barclay Madden had ever managed to make an arrangement—and *why*. That sort of mixing was not at all usual. "Also, she is, ah, religious." Emily's voice paused, and Elizabeth wondered if Emily, in saying this, could after so many years be as genuinely perplexed as she sounded. Emily sipped her tea. "She argued most strenuously that I should live with her after the Blanket, because San Diego was such a dangerous place then. But Daddy would not hear of it. And I, I must admit, was thinking mostly of my education then. Besides, the very idea of staying for more than a few weeks with Mama's family…" Emily made a choking sound Elizabeth assumed was a laugh. "I can't begin to describe what a stifling household my grandparents maintain. Religious rituals, rules about staying in and going out, constant social mixing with the males of the family…"

"It sounds like quite another world," Elizabeth said. "One always tends to think of the executive life-style as being universal."

Emily made that choking sound again. "*They* live in another century. Ah…the way Mama fusses at me… And she is scandalized by my having an active sexual life."

"You're not saying she's heterosexual?" Elizabeth said incredulously.

"No, no, I'm not saying that," Emily said. "More accurately, she disapproves of all sex that is not for procreation. I don't think she has a sexual nerve in her body."

"Incredible," Elizabeth breathed. And this was somehow accomplished without surgery? "Does she feel equal to fixed males then?" Elizabeth asked half out of curiosity, half ironically.

"Certainly not! As I said, she's of another century…women are for breeding and praying, and apparently little else. She is a good daughter, my mama is. That may be how one can best sum up her life."

Another great gust of wind soughed through the canyon, and Elizabeth thought she could hear its progress from the upper end down to the mouth, whipping through the palm branches along its path, rustling over the miles and miles of scrub, whirling sand and pollen and fallen flowers through the air. And then, just as suddenly as the wind had risen, it died.

"That's a cold wind," Lisa said, speaking for the first time in perhaps twenty minutes.

"Is there more hot water for tea?" Emily asked.

"You'll be getting up half the night," Lisa said. "I'll check and see, though. I don't think Ginger's made it back yet." Ginger had set off some time ago with a flashlight to wash the dishes, pots, and pans in the creek. Lisa got up from her chaise lounge, and Elizabeth watched her barely discernible figure stumble towards the cooking area.

"You're not worried about her?" Elizabeth asked. "She's been gone a long time."

"No need to worry," Emily said. "Ginger slows down considerably when she's out here. She's probably staring up at the stars between pots. Of course it would have been more sensible of her to wait until the morning, but she has a marked preference for the romantic."

"You've done this with Lisa often, then?"

"Oh yes. Sometimes it's been essential to get away. Sometimes the shelling would start to get to us. And all the rest, of course. I think I like horseback trips out here best. There's a different flavor then… But this is relaxing, too."

Lisa returned with the teakettle and poured hot water into the pot. "Ginger put the second kettle on before she went down to the creek," she said. "So we won't expect her back for a while." She set the kettle down on the ground near the table.

"It's a curious thing," Elizabeth said, interested in picking up one of the threads of the conversation. "My mother's generation was—and still is—terribly confused about sex. Apart from the change in the aging process, and the males getting fixed younger and younger, and Birth Limitation making the absurdity of heterosexuality apparent, I find that my mother and other women her age seem to struggle under loads of guilt and fear. They have in their minds of course the usual negative attitudes about the effects of active sexuality on the personality. But they also have a strange paranoia about the men perceiving conspiracy, disloyalty, and so on at their getting it on with women—as opposed to men. I don't really follow this, though I do understand their anxiety that the men will suspect them of being influenced or even subverted by sub-exec lovers... My mother once told me that when she was younger there was a faint tinge of an idea in peoples' minds connecting preference for women with feminism..." Elizabeth held out her cup to Lisa, who was pouring out the new tea. "And then there's also the bizarre fact that my parents *married*, and when my father was not yet fixed. *That's* hard for me to take in. Can you imagine it? And my mother was socialized for that, too."

"I'm young enough that my mother was less in the vanguard of such things," Lisa said, setting the teapot down on the table. She returned to her chaise lounge. "But she said she always worries that the men will exclude us. Thinking we're too much like sub-execs since they're our lovers. Tarred with the same brush, so to speak."

Elizabeth laughed harshly. "That will be the day. The bastards can't survive without us."

A silence fell. Elizabeth, sipping her tea, scalded her throat.

"That's true, Elizabeth," Lisa said belatedly, "but I don't think it's a good idea to be saying it out loud, even among ourselves. They *are* paranoid—sometimes, you know. One must be very careful."

"Lisa dear we're miles and miles from nowhere. None of us are carrying bugs—I hope—and we're all discreet creatures. Where *is*

your girl, anyway?" Elizabeth interrupted herself, remembering that actually they weren't alone out here.

"Ginger is as discreet as they come," Lisa said.

"Yes, I'm sure." But how discreet did they come, sub-execs?

Emily stirred. "I think I'm going to be turning in now." She got up from her chaise lounge. "I usually read a bit before sleeping. But if you decide to come to bed before I'm finished, don't hesitate, Elizabeth. I won't mind putting the light out."

"Oh, I think I'll stay up for a while yet to chat with Lisa," Elizabeth said.

Emily moved off toward the sleeping area; a few seconds later Elizabeth heard the sound of the tent's zipper.

"We had to get the longest tent possible for you, Elizabeth," Lisa said.

"And the longest bag, too. Yes, I'm more than familiar with such problems. I'm rather a nonstandard fit."

Lisa chuckled. "In more ways than one."

"I'll take that as a compliment." Elizabeth stared up at the sky. "Why don't we douse this lantern. We've no real need of it. The starlight would do just as well."

Lisa leaned forward and switched off the light. "I think you like it out here."

Elizabeth put her head back and lifted her eyes to the sky. The Milky Way was astonishingly vivid, fairly pulsing with energy. "Yes, I do. I wonder which one belongs to the aliens."

Lisa gasped. "I've never thought of that."

Elizabeth laughed shortly. "Well I have. I think it's about time we started thinking about such things, now that the war is over."

"It's somehow hard to believe..." Lisa began, then stopped.

"That there really are aliens and that they really do come from out there somewhere?" Elizabeth asked ironically. "I share your sense of disbelief. Perhaps if they showed themselves or their ships...but it's only a sort of hearsay evidence we get about them. And then there are so many more important things to think about."

Lisa sighed. "Funny your talking about your mother's generation being confused. I feel just as confused—only about different things."

"Yes," Elizabeth said. "The world is again in upheaval." She stated this matter-of-factly, then thought about how she would have some control over the upheaval, about how she was a major player in the game, unlike her mother and the women of her mother's generation, who merely reacted to social strains and cataclysms—and unlike Lisa, who floundered and cared only to survive.

Staring up at the sky, Elizabeth thought, as if making a fresh discovery: I am unique. Absolutely unique. In interesting times unique persons thrive. And these are most interesting times.

Through the dark came a rustle and a metallic clanking. "Your girl's back," she said.

"Yes," Lisa said, "I hear her. A good thing. Even I was starting to get worried."

Elizabeth got to her feet and groped her way around rocks and bushes in search of a place to piss. Leaning back against a rock taller than herself, she listened to the wind and sniffed the desert's scents. Perhaps some time she would come out here by herself when she needed to do some thinking. Really, it was that kind of place, and she knew of too few such places.

Pulling her pants down, she squatted and peed into the sand, the urine hot and acrid as it streamed out. Emily would be easy. Which meant it all depended on how well Emily could manipulate Barclay Madden.

And if the men knew how they worked most of their business? Sedgewick must suspect... Would it matter to them? Allison had been afraid it would. But that was something that always remained unclear, even, Elizabeth judged, to the men. She doubted they ever thought about it, only used vague formulations and stock stereotypical characterizations of them, so that they had little idea of the reality of these things.

Which was fine with her. The less they questioned, the less they understood. And the less they understood, the better. And so all executive women knew, too.

Chapter Six

The filthy steel door groaned and creaked as it slid open. Celia clutched the soiled blanket and pulled it up to her neck. Her stomach clenched like a fist, and her heart pounded as she watched the young Latina creep into the cell. But—this was the woman who had been tracking her since that day she'd first met Emily...

The door wheezed shut, locking them alone in the cell together.

The girl glanced over her shoulder at the door, then stared down at the floor before her. "I have your clothes for you, Espin." Her voice quavered. "And food and water." As though forcing herself to it, she darted a furtive glance at Celia.

She's terrified, Celia thought. But of what? Though Celia tried to make herself think, the misery pressed so densely against her that she could hardly grasp that one thought. "What are you doing here, girl?" Celia whispered. "What are you doing in this place? Does your mother know you are here?"

The woman's eyes flew wide with alarm. "Don't talk to me!" She flung the clothes down on the platform.

Clothes. Did that mean...Celia's eyes filled. "One thing about being made to take them off is that at least they weren't destroyed," Celia heard herself saying. "I need them so badly, you see. They are the last clothes that I can possibly wear to court."

Wear to court? Celia wondered, confused by her own words.

The watchdog stared at her. Gingerly she set the bottle of water and tube of food beside the clothes. "Why do you—" But she could not go on. Hastily she backed away.

Celia forced herself to sit up, and winced at the pain. "Do you know what they did to me?" she whispered.

The girl's head jerked, and she swallowed. "They tell me those things," she whispered back. "They make me listen to them telling those things. You shouldn't have spoken to him that way, it wouldn't have been so bad. He said so."

Vermin? But if I am such vermin then how can you bring yourself to...

"A girl like you shouldn't be here," Celia said, clinging to the thought.

The watchdog ran to the door and pounded on it.

How can she be so afraid of me? Celia wondered.

The door creaked open, and the watchdog rushed out.

Celia closed her eyes and sank down down down, back into inarticulate, thought-stopping misery.

[ii]

Elizabeth woke lathered in sweat. She groped for the zipper and tugged it down to the foot of the bag and stripped off her wool socks and long thermal underwear. She had been cold when she'd gone to sleep yet now her skin burned with heat. The air in the tent seemed warm.

Why start dreaming about Zeldin tonight? It had been years since she'd dreamed about her.

Elizabeth raised herself onto her elbow to peer through the dark at Emily sleeping, then crawled to the foot of the tent, located her sandals, and unzipped the door as softly as she could. She paused a moment, but Emily's breathing held steady. Then she crawled outside, zipped the door shut, and got to her feet. To Elizabeth's astonishment and delight, the desert was awash with light from the silver disk of moon—almost full—hanging above the ridge to the southeast. She looked at her watch. Two-fifteen, it read.

She slipped on her sandals and moved easily over the rock-strewn terrain—one could see fairly well in the moonlight—to a place well away from the campsite. The calcite and pyrite permeating the rocks and sand glinted in eerie beauty. Occasional wisps of breeze—the wind seemed to have died—played over Elizabeth's hot, naked body, carrying the scent of creosote. Leaning against a cold rock she savored the sensation of the stone leeching the heat from the flame-licked flesh touching it.

Why Zeldin tonight?

And she knew: somewhere in her mind she associated Zeldin most with this desert. Not with the Rock, not with Sedgewick's island, not even with Seattle, but with this place.

The instant I saw their craft I realized I might lose her, just when I'd finally recontacted her... The possibility that they might kill her became thinkable, but it was too late then to do anything about...

Out there on that big flat plane shaped like the floor of an enormous bowl—Collins Valley, Lisa called it—the aliens had landed their bizarre craft while the pavilion full of executives watched, waited, submitted themselves to the insanity.

She knew my blood pressure, she knew I'd taken a tranquilizer only seconds before. She gave me the impression that she could close her eyes and see into my body. But of course she must have used a piece of technology too small for me to perceive, too sophisticated for my recognition or comprehension.

The craziness: it still seemed insane—no, impossible. Like a nightmare. And who had ever seen—in the flesh—aliens, but those Free Zone women and their counterparts around the world? She and Sedgewick had—briefly—but they'd been drugged and in a state of shock. While Grausch and Fenton and their sort were useless hysterics: one could never take their witness as meaningful or credible. If it weren't for the aliens' ability to atomize enormous physical structures, one would never have come to believe in their existence. From where up there did they come? Why had no one undertaken to answer—or even ask—the important questions about the aliens? The scientists... No, the scientists were too busy with defense projects... But surely they were agog with curiosity?

Elizabeth planted her feet far apart and squatted to pee. She could have questioned Zeldin about the aliens—and she hadn't. She hadn't wanted to interfere with more important objectives, and the Zeldin affair had been so damned delicate... Where were the aliens now? What were they doing? What was their purpose? What sort of creatures—biologically—were they? Were they doing things that humans could not perceive, thus imperceptibly handling them, directing them toward something, the way humans managed lower creatures?

As she moved away from the sharp smell of her piss Elizabeth observed how long and thin her shadow in the moonlight stretched before her. Higher creatures, lower creatures...why assume the aliens were "higher creatures" than humans? Because of the superiority of their technology? But really, how superior could it be if all they had accomplished had been the establishment of that paltry place in the Pacific Northwest, a sort of mass-commune that did little but toss pots and weave baskets, and a few other, third-world Free Zones... Elizabeth headed back to the tent. One new thing—after how much time?—occurred to her: without Zeldin, the Free Zone probably threatened them less than it might have had Zeldin remained there to run things. Perhaps the aliens needed Zeldin-types to handle humans precisely because they weren't themselves human and thus found humans incomprehensible... Elizabeth slipped back into the tent. Lying naked on top of her bag, she listened for a few seconds to Emily's breathing...and dropped swiftly back into sleep.

[iii]

Martha, Maureen, and Cora made it to Sweetwater before eight, in time to join Beatrice and a few others at breakfast. Most of the women in residence were usually up and out of the house before six-thirty. Martha sipped coffee but ate nothing, for her stomach hadn't been tolerating food for most of the last twenty-four hours. She hadn't slept much, either—having been haunted most of the night by recollections of her own brush with ODS. She had put it behind her soon after her rescue, yet the memory, once it had surfaced—having remained peacefully submerged for almost ten years—affected her powerfully. She wished for a few minutes alone with Beatrice. Not that there was anything they could really say about it. But Beatrice had helped her so much that time; Beatrice *knew*. Martha just wanted to share the fact of the memory with her. Not to discuss it, just to acknowledge it. To know that Beatrice remembered... Martha stared at the tablecloth. The wish seemed childishly egocentric. She looked across the table at Beatrice—nodding at something Maureen was saying—and thought: but of course, it would be Susan she would be thinking about. By comparison, what happened to me...was nothing.

Martha swallowed more coffee and felt instantly nauseated. Best to stick with water today. The problem with planning strategy for this new situation was that they still had not come to grips with certain fundamental questions about what their relationship to the governments should be. She had discussed this with Sorben about five years ago, and the Marq'ssan had said then that the people of each Free Zone would have to decide that for themselves. The Co-op had been trying to decide whether or not to strike a deal with the Executive that would extend the area of the Free Zone down into northern California, straight across the 40th parallel, in exchange for giving safe haven from the war to various people—mostly executive children—sent by the Executive. Some people had thought the Free Zone shouldn't be dealing with the Executive—or with any government—at all, that the initial experience on *s'sbeyl* had shown the futility of such dealings; others thought it wrong to extend the Free Zone without the consent of the inhabitants of the area involved; while still others insisted that as long as the Free Zone continued to absorb immigrants, the Executive should be forced to extend the Free Zone into Idaho and possibly Montana. But these issues seemed almost minor compared to the recently presented possibilities for dealing with other governments than the US's.

The Free Zones' immunity to the more direct vicissitudes of the war (excepting the difficulty it had created of communications among themselves) must, Martha thought, be primarily responsible for the governments' blossoming interest in dealing indirectly with the aliens through the Free Zones. If the Co-op had had better communication with their counterparts in the other Free Zones and had already worked out a definitive position on relations with the governments, it would have been in a better position to work out a strategy for dealing with this other atrocious situation. As it was, their method suffered from being piecemeal. Martha's misgivings exacerbated her anxiety. If only Sorben would propose a plan for them! But Sorben would not. None of the Marq'ssan would ever give them that kind of advice. They might offer criticism or insight, but they would never propose an actual strategy or blueprint.

"Martha?" Martha started. "Are you there, Martha?"

"Yes, I'm here," Martha said wearily.

"I expected you to argue with Susan's position. Back me up: don't you think that that particular attitude is dangerous, that it might in some way offer a subtle, insidious sort of legitimacy to those monsters' behavior?"

Martha, flushing, sent an apologetic look down the table to Susan. "I'm sorry, but I'm afraid I haven't been paying attention."

Maureen turned her head to look back at Susan. "Should I recapitulate, Sue, or would you like to do it?"

"I'll do it." Susan toyed with the spoon in her bowl of yogurt, glanced briefly at Martha, then stared down at the yogurt. "The thing is, Martha, that I don't believe it would be a good idea for me—or for someone like me—to be interviewed as exemplary of a person whose human rights have been violated by the Executive. The first thing people would say on hearing me speak is 'Oh, she was a spy, she was a bad girl, anyone who spies knows what they're risking, and worse, she's a renegade and a traitor. She deserves what she got.' I know how people think." Susan leaned forward and leveled an earnest stare at Martha. "The same goes for people who have been actively dissident or revolutionist. I think it'd be best if we concentrate on those whom ordinary people can immediately identify with and will immediately perceive as innocent bystanders monstrously dragged in." Susan's gaze dropped, and Martha realized she had finished speaking.

"That kind of omission," Maureen said, turning her head to look at Martha, "is bound to make itself felt. Don't you agree, Martha?"

Martha kept her eyes focused on Susan's face. "What I think is that if instead of feeling outraged and angry Susan feels she is to blame for what happened to her, then she certainly should not speak publicly. Most people haven't the faintest idea about these kinds of mind-fucks and they'd completely misunderstand."

As Martha spoke, Susan's gaze—first shocked, then angry and hurt—bored into Martha's. From the first time she'd met Susan, Martha had always taken pains to speak gently and carefully to her, as though an ordinary tone of voice might break her. Martha realized that Susan might well perceive this abrupt break with her custom as an attack. "That's what you think I'm saying, Martha?" Susan said in a high, trembly voice. "That I'm not angry, that after all these years I'm suffering from the Stockholm Syndrome?"

"Yes," Martha said quietly. "That's what I think. Please don't misunderstand: I don't blame you for it. But I don't think you can see straight because of it."

"*I* don't have the Stockholm Syndrome," Cora said, "and *I* agree with Susan." Cora's eyes flashed in her broad, dark face. "We have to think about public perceptions in the way we handle media exposure."

"First, last, and always a media-person, eh, Cora?" Martha said— and at once regretted her tone of voice.

"Will you Co-op people do the rest of us the favor of getting a grip on yourselves?" Beatrice said. "We're not interested in your infighting. What matters to *us* is people's lives!"

Beatrice's tone of voice shook Martha. When had she ever seen Beatrice *furious? You Co-op people:* it had never occurred to Martha that Beatrice thought of her—or even of the others—in that way. "I'm sorry," Martha said with constraint. "I've expressed myself badly. People's lives matter to me, too. And that's the point of what I was saying. I'm not just trying to be politically expedient. I think many people's lives could depend upon this very point which you, Beatrice, seem to think we're quibbling over." Martha drew a deep breath and rushed on as Cora also drew breath to speak. "I don't want to see certain people written off because they are not as quote innocent unquote as other people... *Nothing* justifies killing and torturing; *nothing*, and it's a mistake not to make that clear from the outset. Say we exert enough pressure to get the Executive to stop the killing and torture— stop it for the so-called *innocent*, that is...maybe they won't feel they have to stop it for others who they might think they can justify persecuting—namely anyone in political opposition to them."

"What you say may be correct," Beatrice, still angry, replied, "but you're not correct in talking to Susan that way. Who are you to interpret what she has to say like some goddam shrink? I've never liked the way when you get into a tight spot in a discussion you shift the argument to a place in which your chief opponent is emotionally vulnerable. You lack certain scruples, Martha. And right now you owe Susan an apology."

In the long silence that fell, Martha and Beatrice locked gazes. The others, their gazes lowered, kept very still. The hush hummed loudly in Martha's ears.

"You don't have to fight my battles for me, Bee," Susan said softly. Martha's gaze shifted to Susan's face. "It isn't the Stockholm Syndrome, Martha," Susan said.

Martha swallowed. "Beatrice is right. I shouldn't have said that. This whole thing should have been discussed in the context Maureen first proposed. I apologize." But though she felt ashamed for having attacked Susan, Martha still believed she was right about Susan's reasons for taking the position she had taken. She pushed her chair back. "I think I'll go for a walk before the others get here," she said, rising. She could feel them watching her as she left the kitchen.

People seemed to do nothing but argue these days. *You Co-op people.* Well we Co-op people are a contentious lot. What's happened to us? Martha wondered as she slipped into her raincoat and strode out onto the gravel drive. Whatever it was, they had to get themselves straightened out before they could handle this new crisis. Was it a question of personalities? Or a structural problem? Was she, Martha, lacking in something? Wasn't that what Beatrice had implied when she'd accused Martha of a lack of scruples?

Lack of scruples... The very phrase stung. Was that what she had come to, because of all these years of doing, acting, taking responsibility? A lack of scruples? Had she become too goal-oriented?

Martha halted under a big, bare-branched maple tree and stared out at the mist covering the mountains nearby. Would it always be like this? Would things never be right no matter how long they worked at it? Not even between individuals who respected and listened to one another?

A lack of scruples...

Martha's vision blurred. And to think she had hoped for comfort from Beatrice. How terribly alone she was.

How terribly alone they all were.

[iv]

"Look at that woman, Emily," Lisa called out. "She takes these boulders like a goat. Imagine having legs that long!"

Elizabeth pivoted and stared down at Lisa clambering up a rock—effortfully, in spite of Emily's giving her a hand to grip. "This is great fun," Elizabeth said, grinning. "These rocks are neither wet nor mossy nor ice-covered—what could be easier? The ascent is gradual enough, too. And the scenery! It's incredible, I never imagined such an infinite variety of flowers in a place like *this*!" All around them strange wild things sprang up from cracks and crevices, seemingly through rock: flora of strange forms and brilliant colors, most especially the purples.

"If you're going to strip out here, Elizabeth, you'd better get the sun block from my pack and cover the parts you haven't already blocked," Lisa said, apparently just noticing that Elizabeth had taken off her shirt. "That skin of yours will fry in no time." Pointedly she offered her back to Elizabeth.

"I'm deceptively fair," Elizabeth said. "I don't burn easily. But you're probably right. UV radiation is not to be taken lightly. And my face and neck are already a bit leathery from the wind and sun yesterday afternoon."

Emily dug the tube of block from Lisa's pack and tossed it to Elizabeth. Elizabeth grinned at her. "Do my back for me?"

Emily took back the tube and squirted cream into her palm and stepped behind Elizabeth. Soon Emily's palm was spreading the slick, delicious coolness over her shoulder blades and down the length of her spine. "I'll let you do the rest yourself," she said dryly, handing the tube to Elizabeth.

Elizabeth smeared the cream over her arms, neck, breasts, and stomach. From the look on Lisa's averted face, Elizabeth knew her shirtlessness displeased her. No doubt Lisa was one of those who fastidiously observed the convention of never revealing more than her hands, arms, and feet to anyone but one's lover, except when engaging in a sport where one dressed in the usual uniform. Absurd! Emily obviously didn't mind. In fact, if she weren't too well-mannered to risk offending Lisa, she'd probably be shirtless herself.

They resumed their climb up the canyon. That moment in the tent when Elizabeth had inadvertently glimpsed Emily's thighs flashed into her mind. No, no, and no. If ever anyone had been off-limits to Elizabeth it was Emily: executive, daughter of an enemy—and almost forty years younger. It was obscene of her to think of the woman sexually, even for a moment... One of the worst aspects of that old relationship with Allison had been the change in the way she had looked at certain other executive women. She could reap only trouble from such attractions.

No, she should be thinking about what she would say to Emily once they reached the waterfall and pool.

Up, up, up, one long, stretching stride after another. More suited to a more compact build than hers, but Elizabeth was in good shape. She turned to stare back down the canyon. Little of Collins Valley showed now, and the stand of trees that marked their campsite was no longer visible. The sun—almost directly overhead—lit up the rocks on either side of the canyon. The heat and light would not last long, Elizabeth thought, for the canyon walls cast long shadows over a large area of the canyon for most of the day.

She felt the vibration and heard an ear-splitting rip fairly tear open the sky a nanosecond before the thunder broke through and boomed the length of the canyon. Startled, Elizabeth looked up. Blinded by the glare of the sun, she cupped her hands around her eyes and scanned until she spotted the monster. The plane circled and dipped a wing, then passed over the top of the ridge. "Goddam those bastards are loud," Elizabeth said through her teeth when the quiet had returned. She looked at Lisa. "What are they? Navy?"

"Yes. F-104s. They always buzz us when we're out here. I suppose it gets boring making the same damned runs over and over again."

"More like checking up on us." Elizabeth glanced sidelong at Emily. Barclay Madden's daughter, however, showed no reaction.

Lisa said, "They know who we are, but it doesn't matter. They do it to everyone who comes out here—have been doing it for over a hundred years."

God how she hated Military. Anything Military. She would never trust them again. *Never.*

Elizabeth's spurt of temper dissipated when she came upon the waterfall. Palm trees and alders grew along the creek here, their trunks often shaped by the massive boulders—some of them fifty or more feet high—they grew in relation to. Tall graceful grasses offered a startlingly lush contrast to the stark chaparral only a few yards above and away from the creek. "An oasis," Elizabeth, delighted, breathed to Lisa. She stared down into the rushing water; suddenly she noticed the dozens of frogs scattered over the partially submerged rocks. Pleased with herself and the world, she stepped onto a boulder and moving from rock to rock picked her way up the creek until she came to the pool at the foot of the waterfall.

Lisa chose a flat-topped boulder, half in sun, half in shade, on which to spread their lunch. She broke the seal of the two-liter bottle of water, drank from it, and passed it to Emily. "Don't forget, Elizabeth, you need extra water out here. In addition to the other fluids you drink."

Elizabeth smiled. "You've become such a mother-hen, Lisa. I hardly recognize you."

"Well you don't know shit about the desert," Lisa said. "Did you read the book I gave you the night before we came out?"

Elizabeth's smile broadened into a grin. "Actually, no. I was too busy with that girl you claimed was frigid." Seeing Lisa's mouth tighten, Elizabeth could not resist adding, "She's not, you know."

Emily handed Elizabeth the water bottle. "So you like challenges in the sexual field?"

Elizabeth's eyebrows rose. Arch little thing, Emily Madden. "Sometimes," Elizabeth drawled. "But it's not a prerequisite."

"No," Lisa said, "almost anything with the correct physiological configuration will do."

"Lisa the hyperbolic," Elizabeth said lightly, passing her the bottle. Her gaze swept the creek until it lighted on a likely rock on which to perch. Once on the rock, she removed her boots and socks and rolled up the cuffs of her trousers and—thinking she would sit with her legs dangling in the creek—plunged her feet into the water. But when after a few seconds the tingle from the icy cold of the creek became pain, she drew her legs out of the water and stretched out full length, satisfied to feel the cold rock pressing into her back and the breeze ruffling her sweat-lathered body.

Her hat slipped off; lazily she left it, for the moment careless of the damage the sun could do her hair, *pace* Maxine. Out of the corner of her eye she caught movement and turned her head slightly to look. Emily, it seemed, was undressing. Interesting. What did Lisa think of such brashness? But Emily, once undressed, slipped off her rock and down into the water. Astonished, Elizabeth waited for her recoil. But though Emily shivered and exclaimed, "It must have been snow,

just melted minutes ago," she continued wading toward the pool and
waterfall. Incredible: Emily obviously intended to immerse herself!
But when Emily made it to the pool—where the water crept up to
her waist—she went one step further and stood under the waterfall.
Squealing and giggling, she cried, "Come try this, it's wonderful!"

"What is she, part polar bear?" Elizabeth called to Lisa.

Lisa grinned. "She always does this. I tried it once, and that was
enough for me."

She had a beautiful body, especially that long, long neck and the
strong bone structure of the face. Elizabeth couldn't take her eyes off
her. After a minute or two Emily clambered back up on her rock and
stretched out to let the sun dry her. "And now I'm chilly," she said.
"From sweat to goosebumps in five seconds flat. How invigorating!
Not to mention exhilarating!" She folded her arms behind her neck.

In spite of herself Elizabeth could feel the ache spreading outward
from her vulva. She tore her gaze away and stared instead at the baby
fan palm growing on the bank a few feet away from her rock.

"There's something out here that makes everything different,"
Emily said in a dreamy voice. "One wants to do certain sorts of
things—like plunging into pools under waterfalls—that ordinarily
would seem absurdly uncomfortable. One doesn't mind trudging with
a heavy pack on one's back for miles and miles through loose sand
when there are wild flowers everywhere one's eye lights. And then
there are the dreams... Every night I'm in the desert I have strange
and wonderful dreams. And when I'm out here I feel those dreams
have a special significance I'd ordinarily not attribute to them."

Elizabeth sighed. "I had terrible dreams last night. Twice I
dreamed that I had lost something, and that one person knew what it
was; but contact with that person was so horrible that I knew I would
never find out what it was..." To dream that dream about Zeldin
twice in one night...Elizabeth shuddered. If coming out to this place
meant dreaming about Zeldin, then she would not do it again, not for
any reason.

"I have crazy story dreams out here," Lisa said. "Long, long sagas
filled with people I don't know."

"Mine are relatively simple dreams," Emily said, her voice still
lazy and far away. "I dream about the desert. About seeing lizards.

About birds. And about meeting old Indian women at various places—like this place, for instance."

A romantic, Emily Madden? But one who was tough enough to take painfully cold water for the sake of that romanticism—which was something to be borne in mind.

"Shall we eat?" Lisa said, her voice suddenly brisk.

"Yes," Elizabeth said. "I'm famished. And thirsty for water, too." She sat up and untied her shirt from around her waist. Maybe if she put her shirt on for lunch Emily would dress. It would be difficult concentrating on business if Emily persisted in running around naked.

To Elizabeth's relief, Emily did put her clothes back on, with a remark about how quickly the sun and air had dried her.

As they ate Elizabeth recalled Lisa's telling her about how Emily had been invited to join the most exclusive women's club in San Diego—a club Lisa knew would always remain closed to herself—and had declined, to the shock and consternation of the membership. A woman after my own heart, Elizabeth thought, remembering how Felice Raines had offered to get her into that club in Aspen and how she had refused on the grounds that such clubs were boring and a needless expense. But she had known Felice would have had to go to some trouble to get her in, thus placing her in her debt (and Elizabeth had suspected that Felice had begun to feel that she was so heavily in Elizabeth's debt that she feared that some day Elizabeth would reel her in for something truly costly in personal terms), for by that time she had already been living in the area for two years and knew there wasn't an executive for miles who wasn't aware of her existence and power. If they'd wanted her, they would have asked her long before. No, she could live without their nonsense—in the real world of real power. Let them play their paltry games... Which must have been how Emily had looked at it. Emily was someone who exercised real power. That gave them a great deal in common.

After lunch Elizabeth signaled to Lisa to make herself invisible. She did not care if Lisa managed to eavesdrop. The important one to exclude was the girl, who had been left behind at the campsite, presumably to attend to various housekeeping chores.

As Emily pulled a book out of her pack Elizabeth said, "And now we can talk."

Emily looked at Elizabeth. "That has a very businesslike ring to it."

"I asked Lisa to arrange this weekend precisely so that you and I could talk without interruption or the possibility of being overheard."

Emily set the book down beside her and clasping her hands over them drew her knees to her chest. "I don't do business out here," she said. "These trips are meant for relaxation and pleasure. If you want to talk business with me, make an appointment with my office when we get back to town."

That was said coolly enough. "This is not ordinary business," Elizabeth said. "You may take it that I'm on the Executive's business."

Emily's eyebrows raised. "What on earth would the Executive want with me? I'd have said they didn't know of my existence."

"They know of your father's existence," Elizabeth said dryly.

Emily smiled faintly. "Ah, yes. My father. Then your business must be with him. In that case don't make an appointment with my office when we get back. Make an appointment with my father's office."

"I want to keep this as friendly as possible," Elizabeth said, and her voice hardened. "Which is why I'd like to talk with you. You then can talk with your father."

"I'm to be a message carrier?" Emily's tone was flippant, but her eyes had grown cold and wary.

"Something more than a message-carrier," Elizabeth said. "I should think it would interest you that your father is getting in the Executive's way. And that if he isn't careful he'll find himself up against all of them."

Emily's eyebrows lifted. "*All* of them?" she said delicately.

Ah. This child was already thinking of Whitney's possible stance in any fight to come. "If not all of them, enough of them to bring him down," Elizabeth said.

"I'm sure he'd be most concerned to hear this. I think you'd better talk to him about it. I've no doubt he'd give Elizabeth Weatherall an appointment."

"You sound as though you aren't interested in whether your father's empire crashes or not," Elizabeth said, hoping to goad her.

Emily, grinning, shook her head back and forth, back and forth. "Oh, Elizabeth, I hope you don't expect me to make you confidences about my feelings and interests and concerns? Do you think that because I'm so young I haven't heard about you?"

Elizabeth stared at her in consternation. "I'll wring her neck!"

Emily's grin faded. "Whose?"

"Lisa's."

Emily gave her another of those long, cool looks. Assessing her? "And you're vindictive, too. But Lisa told me nothing about you, except that you were an old, ah, *friend.*" Elizabeth's ire rose at Emily's facetious tone. "You surely don't think you haven't been talked about in local Military circles? Especially after all your visits here toward the end of the Civil War?"

Child? Elizabeth taunted herself. She had probably sprung full-grown from Barclay Madden's brow. "Hail Pallas Athena," Elizabeth murmured.

Emily's forehead puckered. "I've missed something?"

"No, dear," Elizabeth said. "I must be sun-touched. I assume your father would be interested in the return of all the big research institutions Security evacuated ten years ago?"

"It's no good talking to me, Elizabeth."

"You mean you're not going to tell your father we even had this conversation?"

"If you want me to act as go-between, arrange it with him first. That's all I'm saying." Emily picked up her book and rose to her feet in one fluid, graceful movement. "I'm sure you won't be offended if I find a quieter place to read." And so saying, Emily Madden climbed out of the creek and further up the canyon.

Insufferable, Elizabeth thought. Absolutely positively insufferable. Only twenty-five years old and she'd won the round hands down.

Pallas Athena, indeed.

Chapter Seven

[i]

Waking, Elizabeth found the tent flooded with heat and light.
She unzipped the bag and exposed her naked body to the air. As the
sweat dried, cooling her fevered flesh, she checked her watch and saw
that it was not yet six. Lazy but no longer sleepy, she lay with her
eyes closed and listened to the elusive, sometimes mysterious sounds
outside—the wind brushing over the tent and, further off, whipping
through the canyon's scattered palm trees, soughing like ocean surf;
the chatter and twitter of birds she did not recognize; the heavy drone
of bees; the discrete noises she imagined to be made by small animals
scurrying; the occasional scraping and rustling of branches—wind?
birds? squirrels? lizards? That deep thrumming vibration she knew,
for throughout the previous day she had remarked that hummingbirds found the desert a paradise of sweet suckling.

Vividly she imaged a hummingbird hovering over the willow tree
only inches from the tent, its wings whirring in place as it dipped its
long beak into the lavender bell of a flower and sucked out its sweet
liquor. So pleasurable did Elizabeth find the sight of this drinking
that for much of the previous afternoon she had gazed fascinated each
time a hummingbird arrived to suckle, watching it plunge its beak
like a lapping tongue into a bell until, having depleted the liquor, it
moved on to the next, always picking and choosing before sipping,
until sated it darted away, only to return a while later for more...
Before her very eyes the flowers on the tree were drying and shrivel-
ing as the hummingbird made its progress...or would those flowers
have died and shriveled anyway? Had the drinking of the liquor anything to do with the withering of the flowers holding it? Elizabeth's
sigh verged on a sensual groan. So beautiful to see, so lust-arousing to
think of. What could be more sensual than that moment of suckling

with the bird's beak plunged into the flower's trumpet-like bell? The butterflies though colorful were nothing to it, nor the bees, though their drone could seduce one into a near hypnotic trance.

Elizabeth drifted back to sleep. Later, she woke to the sound of voices outside the tent, voices she identified as Lisa's, Emily's, the girl's. She imagined Emily basking in the sun, still in her nightshirt, sipping coffee, watching the light on the ridges. Lisa would be paging through her book of hikes and the girl pottering about the campsite preparing breakfast, keeping the coffee coming, or simply sitting beside Lisa, chattering. Really she did talk too much. It would be enough to drive one out of one's home to have that talkative a service-tech constantly around. But it was Lisa's fault; she encouraged her.

Elizabeth checked her watch and was astonished to find it eight-thirty. She had thought it close to seven, perhaps a little before. Lazy, lazy woman, she chided herself. What was she doing out here in the desert now, anyway? She had no justification for spending another day here, delightful though it was... She would not fool herself that progress could be made with Emily by staying longer. No, she must radio for a chopper to pick her up. She should by all rights have done that yesterday afternoon when they'd returned to the campsite. Her time was too valuable to fritter away like this. Elizabeth sighed. She must get up immediately and have that girl pack for her while she arranged transport. She'd have to tackle Barclay Madden directly, that was clear—after seeing whatever intelligence the station had been able to scrounge up since Friday...

But before Elizabeth even got herself out of the tent, Lisa came to the door and said, "Elizabeth, are you awake?"

"Just getting up," Elizabeth said.

"They want you to return at once. There's a mother of a cable no one has the code for at the station come from Sedgewick, and he's wanting you back in DC stat. A chopper's already on its way to pick you up. I said we'd meet it at the mouth of this canyon in Collins Valley in half an hour."

Sedgewick sending for her... Could it be a crisis? Or was it simply some bizarre vagary of his? That was the worst of Sedgewick: one could never know what would strike him as "urgent." What could be more important to him at the moment than this particular mission?

Unless some new super-crisis had whipped up—to do with the aliens, or maybe the Eastern Alliance. Elizabeth grabbed her clothes and stepped outside the tent to dress. Speculation was useless in these situations. Supposedly the cable waiting for her at the station would give her some idea of what it was all about.

The girl handed her a cup of coffee and without being asked began packing Elizabeth's things. Elizabeth sank down on a chaise lounge and looked around her for the last time. *No more hummingbirds, Lizzie.*

Just Sedgewick, damn him.

[ii]

Celia woke to the hissing of her name: "Espin!" Warily she opened her eyes. The watchdog was bent over her, her mouth inches from Celia's ear. "I've brought you these," she whispered, indicating the towel-wipe packets lying on the platform beside a new bottle of water and tube of food. "Don't give me away. Please," she begged, her eyes wide with fear. "Flush them down the toilet when you've used them."

Celia nodded. "Your name? What is your name?" She could not go on thinking of her as her watchdog.

The young woman's face contracted as though she were debating the wisdom of giving Celia that much. She whispered, "Angela. Call me Angela."

"Thank you, Angela. Thank you so much. You don't know how…" Celia's eyes filled with tears. There was no way this woman could know how filthy she felt and how degraded the filth made her feel. But she was obviously capable of imagining it, or she wouldn't have taken the risk.

Angela scurried to the door and banged on it. Celia quickly covered the towel-wipes with the blanket in case the guard happened to look in. The door creaked opened. And then Angela was gone. Celia ripped open one of the packets, removed her trousers, and began scrubbing her skin. It was the only part of her where she could get at the filth. Angela. A watchdog with sympathy. What a terrible terrible thing this young woman had gotten herself into. Did she know it? Celia wished she could do something to get her out of it. But right now she couldn't help herself, much less a stray in the clutches of wolves.

Celia scrubbed and scrubbed and scrubbed, thinking sadly of all the delusions she shared with every other human. Even delusions about hygiene. It proved a bond between her and Angela. But it also gave the others a powerful means of hurting her. If she were truly strong she'd be able to put it out of her mind. As though it were nothing, like a disagreeable brush with cockroaches... *But I'm only human.* Just a weak pathetic human trapped in the ideas of her own culture, trapped in the constructions of her own mind... It was for that that things were hopeless. That's where the problem lay. And knowing it didn't seem to help, not even in this situation. Of what use was it to understand if understanding failed to alleviate the misery?

Celia scrubbed and scrubbed and scrubbed.

[iii]

During the flight back to DC Elizabeth read Sedgewick's lengthy cable, which her personal terminal had decrypted without a hitch. Going by its text she could not be certain that the crisis was bona fide acute, as Sedgewick claimed. Whether or not it was, she had no choice but to return—being always and ever at his damned beck and call. Did he intend for her to drop the Madden situation? Or did he have some crazy idea that she could handle it from a distance while taking on this new thing?

The cable did not make clear precisely what this new thing was. It involved the Free Zone, the aliens, and other governments—some of them US friends. The reports coming from the Edmonds station had alarmed Sedgewick enough to insist on her return. Did he conceive some sort of international cabal with the aliens? Or did he fear that executive countries might start giving significant ground to dissidents? Or was it simply a perception that if friends weren't prevented from dealing with the Free Zone, the situation would rapidly get beyond them?

Wasn't it beyond them already?

No, Elizabeth decided. Nothing much had happened—yet. Certainly Lauder's people were correct in wanting more definitive action taken with regard to the international situation and in warning about where the things they had been observing in the Free Zone might conceivably lead. Yet Sedgewick's sense of urgency... Unless he simply wanted to jerk her back to DC for reasons of his own. Sedgewick's deviousness... She had never taken issue with his deviousness before now. Only recently had it occurred to her that he could deploy that deviousness against her, his right hand. (Left hand against right?) Since the day he'd told her he was promoting Ambrose to Deputy Chief, she had come to suspect every move he made. Well, that made sense: since he had declared his intentions toward her, she would be a fool to take anything between them at face value.

Elizabeth rubbed more moisturizer into her face and hands. The desert had weathered her skin to rough dry leather, albeit golden. Maxine would be fussing at her about it for weeks (and about her hair, which she hadn't yet inspected for damage). Still, it had been amusing—though Emily Madden surely had gotten the better of her.

No, no time to think about that.

Elizabeth made a list of possible measures to be taken regarding the Free Zone situation. She'd review the list after wading through the pile of reports the Edmonds station had flooded them with over the last few days and then decide—unless, of course, Sedgewick chose to take a hand in it. But no. He wouldn't—otherwise he wouldn't have dragged her back to DC. Elizabeth fumed with exasperation. Really, she might as well be Chief herself for all the use that Sedgewick was.

Or Deputy Chief.

Elizabeth worked furiously until the jet's wheels touched the runway, then packed up and transferred to the chopper waiting to zip her over to Central. Sedgewick certainly was in a hurry if he had gone to the trouble of having her met by chopper rather than the usual car. Curiouser and curiouser... Sleet whirled against the windows. Elizabeth, shivering at the cold seeping into the cabin, wished for her fur. It annoyed her that Jacquelyn hadn't sent it along with the chopper.

They landed on the roof. "Your badge, Ms. Weatherall," the sentry holding open the door for her said, and Elizabeth pulled her badge from her tunic pouch as she flew down the stairs.

In Jacquelyn's office Elizabeth paused to ask whether he had anyone with him, then went straight in.

"Glad you could tear yourself away, Weatherall," Sedgewick said when he saw her. "Even if it did take you all day."

Ever faithful bitch still comes when called, Elizabeth thought. That was her, Elizabeth Weatherall, man's best friend. "All day?" Elizabeth said, glancing at her watch. "It's only one. I call that pretty damned fast."

"Four, Weatherall. It's four." He got up and went to the conference table. Amazing, he had files strewn all over its surface: which meant he had been working—something he hadn't done much of since the end of the war.

"You do understand you've interrupted the other assignment," Elizabeth said.

Frowning, he put on his reading glasses. Elizabeth took her usual seat at the table. "This is of equal if not greater priority. Surely you've taped out enough of that situation by now that you can plan and deploy a strategy for dealing with it?"

"Possibly," Elizabeth said, digging a yellow pad out of her bag.

"This Free Zone situation," Sedgewick said—and sighed. He looked bored, Elizabeth thought. "You'll want to debrief Ambrose and Baldridge yourself. As soon as possible."

"Ambrose? If he's already in on it, why doesn't he handle it?"

Sedgewick's gaze met hers. "Ambrose came to me with something that needed approval. His brilliant strategy for dealing with the situation was to excise the thirteen women running the Free Zone."

Elizabeth's mouth dropped open. "Excise them?" she said blankly. "But that's madness! And Baldridge consented to this plan?"

"Ambrose pulled rank on him."

Incompetent fools, these males: Baldridge unable to manage Ambrose without getting into that nonsense? Baldridge had been in Operations for years and years, and Ambrose knew shit about Operations! Elizabeth thought—but did not say—that Sedgewick should for godsake send the asshole back to ODS. "I always knew Ambrose was stupid. But *that* stupid?"

Sedgewick said, "The idea in and of itself isn't necessarily stupid. What is stupid is the context—and Ambrose's failure to conceptualize with a reasonable degree of imagination. He apparently sees excision as a final solution for bringing down the Free Zone. He seems to have missed the sorts of consequences it would rain down on our heads. If he had, for instance, decided these assassinations would serve the purpose of bringing the aliens into the open, that would be quite another matter. His vision, at the moment, is really quite limited."

His tone was so damned matter-of-fact; that was what galled her most. *Yes, I know, Ambrose is inadequate, but that has nothing to do with why I made him my deputy.* That was essentially what Sedgewick was saying to her, wasn't it? "Why not let Baldridge handle it?" Elizabeth said.

Sedgewick took off his glasses and shot her a critical look. "Several reasons. First of all, this is not simply a matter of Operations: we'll necessarily be working closely in liaison with State, and possibly Commerce as well. Second, if I pull Ambrose and give Baldridge his head, everyone will know it, and that would severely undercut any future legitimacy Ambrose might have in the Company, especially considering Baldridge's years in Operations. And third, I trust neither of them either to comprehend the full picture with all its foreign policy aspects or to handle it properly. No, it must be run from this office."

Elizabeth gave him a straight-on look. "You mean you'll handle it yourself?" Of course he didn't mean that, or he wouldn't have dragged her back here—but she would make him say it, explicitly. It was the least she could get out of it, damn him.

"I mean it will be run from this office—you will be controller and will brief me daily. You know as well as I that neither Baldridge nor Ambrose can coordinate this kind of thing with State."

Ambrose couldn't coordinate anything, and Baldridge had some not-so-friendly competition over at State. While she, Elizabeth, had all sorts of contacts and assets over there. Apparently Sedgewick wasn't interested in opening his files to Ambrose to give him a bit more leverage and advantage.

"And if Ambrose pulls rank on *me*?" Elizabeth said archly.

Sedgewick's eyebrows soared almost to his hairline. "Surely you're joking? How's he going to pull rank on this office?"

This office: Sedgewick's neat euphemism for designating her position. Carrying the scepter in her back pocket, sure... One thing positive: Baldridge had been her man since she'd taken out the Director of Operations and put Baldridge in his place. Yet because of Ambrose's position as Deputy Chief, they'd have to try to keep everything tactfully unspoken. Elizabeth picked up her pen. "You know, Sedgewick, the Ambrose Problem isn't going to go away." She tapped the pen on the table. "Baldridge is going to find it fishy. And then the speculations on why exactly you put Ambrose into that slot only to turn it into a do-nothing .piece of gloss are going to flourish. Which will mean that the already extravagant level of speculation about you will escalate dramatically."

"I don't give a fuck about speculation, Weatherall. If necessary, we'll simply give Ambrose enough rope to properly hang himself, and then we'll get rid of him."

We? "That's pretty cool of you," Elizabeth said. "And there are fools who think he's your new favorite." She laughed. Sedgewick hadn't had a favorite since Zeldin. He was too far gone to take that much interest in another human being. Elizabeth pulled her handset from her pocket. "I'd better have Lennox start setting up appointments for me."

Jacquelyn answered immediately. "Yes, Elizabeth?"

"See if you can't arrange a meeting for six o'clock with Baldridge and Ambrose." Elizabeth debated whether or not to ask Jacquelyn—with Sedgewick likely listening—to make an appointment for her with Rosamund Washburn. "And find out for me if Roz Washburn can dine with me tonight. If so, make reservations at the Diana for eight-thirty." That should give her enough time for the initial debrief with Baldridge and Ambrose. Elizabeth put down the handset, prepared to tell Sedgewick should he ask about the dinner engagement that she was laying the groundwork for coordination with Commerce. But what she needed, she thought, was for him to be more forthcoming about the whys and wherefores of the Barclay Madden affair: if he were, she wouldn't be having to go to Roz for answers.

"What galls particularly about this Free Zone mess," Sedgewick said, "is the way Military gets credit for recovering Cuba after a century of socialism and we get blamed for losing the Pacific Northwest to a bunch of amateur female anarchists. Now that the war's over we're going to have to seriously consider how to regain control of that territory. This will simply force our hand a little sooner than we would like."

Elizabeth frowned. Was *that* what he thought would come of this? "You have some plan already in mind?" she asked, half-incredulous. Though with Sedgewick you could never tell.

"What I'm saying is that we must bear that ultimate objective in mind in everything we do concerning the anarchists and aliens." He started stacking file folders. "I imagine you'll want to go through these right away. Before your meeting with Baldridge."

"You don't care to be in on that meeting?"

"Oh," Sedgewick said absently and held up one of the folders. "I'll include this one, too. I want you to use Daniel in the Free Zone project."

"Daniel?" Elizabeth said, unable to place the name.

Sedgewick looked up. "My son Daniel," he said dryly.

Elizabeth stared at him. His son? She was supposed to use that Wilton-produced horror in her operations? "I don't think that's a good idea," she said.

Sedgewick removed his glasses. "When you've read what's in his personnel file... Well, you'll see why I want you to take him on. He'll need a very tight rein."

Elizabeth's stomach dropped. "Then you are the best one to handle him," she said.

He shook his head. "Not at all. I'm too emotionally involved. Not to mention that the little ass goes into challenge stance every time he sees me. There'd be murder if I tried handling him."

So she was supposed to play surrogate and earn the little monster's hatred? "He's a graduate of Wilton," Elizabeth said. "He won't react at all well to a woman controlling him."

Sedgewick shoved the pile of files at her. "There's no one else I can assign to do this for me, Weatherall. There's no one else in Security who can take a tough enough line with him. He's been trading on his name all damned year." Elizabeth tried to remember what Daniel had been doing since graduating the spring before from Brown. Some kind of Company assignment in South America, wasn't it? "As for outside Security..." He shrugged. "Frankly I'd like to bring him along in Security. Once he matures a bit, he might work out. And to tell the truth, I don't care to have him raising hell in someone else's bailiwick. It was bad enough taking flak when he was a kid in the page program."

Elizabeth stood up, slung her bag over her shoulder, and piled the files into her arms. "I still don't think it's a good idea, Sedgewick."

"I'll make it worth your while, Weatherall."

Ah, there it was: the bribe. His way of dealing with the world. "What, you'll make me deputy chief?" she said facetiously, staring into his dead, dead eyes.

"That's not precluded."

Elizabeth's mouth quirked. "Such generosity. How can I resist?" *The ever faithful bitch comes through again. Let's go for a pat on the head, Lizzie.* What would he do if she walked out on him now? she thought, crossing the hall to her office. Suppose she went to another Cabinet officer and offered her services. She snorted. Apart from getting excised by whichever faithful bitch she might displace, she'd have to be a yessir rightawaysir perfect PA again…Elizabeth dumped the files down on her desk. She could never go back to that, never. Even if it meant having to play surrogate-chief for the rest of her life.

She sank down behind her desk and picked up the handset. God how she hated men. Every damned last one of the bastards.

[iv]

Martha spent a solid two hours at the Austrian Consulate reviewing the terms of the Co-op's agreement with the Austrian, Dutch, and Greek governments. They sat at a long polished mahogany table as they went through the draft agreements point by point. Martha took special pains to be certain that everyone was clear that the paperwork was to name the Co-op as the party she represented—not the Pacific Northwest Free Zone nor the Marq'ssan. The Austrians, Dutch, and Greeks were dealing with her because they believed the Co-op could "deliver" the Marq'ssan goodies they were so anxious to procure. But could the Co-op trust the Austrian government?

Could they trust *any* government?

According to Sorben, the Korean Free Zone was currently negotiating with the governments of Hungary (which had taken a real beating during the Global War) and Poland. Because of that, Martha wondered why the governments of Austria, Greece, and the Netherlands hadn't just gone to the Korean Free Zone, too. Did they think the Pacific Northwest Free Zone would be more naïve and easier to manipulate? Or was it a racist preference? Laura and Lenore had set up a meeting with the Koreans. No question, the Co-op needed to be comparing notes with them.

"We're going to have to try it," Martha had put the case to her peers. And they had all agreed—reluctantly—that they must take the gamble. What made Martha most uneasy, though, was that the gamble involved dealing with Margot Ganshoff.

Every time she saw that woman a slimy feeling crawled over her, pushing her to great lengths to avoid physical proximity—much less contact. Margot's protuberant, globular eyes (so pale, so uncanny) watched her like prey, as though preparing to move in for the kill. Martha felt those eyes on her while she was poring over the numerous contract-like documents the foreign consuls insisted were necessary for sealing the deal; once, glancing up, she looked right into those pale globes and shivered. Don't be an idiot, Martha told herself. The only reason she was feeling and thinking such things was because of what David had said to her. Quickly she returned her attention to the documents. Each one must be read carefully; she knew the ways of the executive world. And yet she couldn't help thinking that David, if he had known about this gamble, would have advised her not to take the chance, would have told her flat out that neither Margot nor the others could be trusted.

Apart from whether or not the Austrians or the other governments in on the deal would betray them, there was always the possibility that someone in their consulates might pass the information on to the Executive. Despite the rift caused by the Global War, the intelligence organizations of executive-based governments tended to cooperate with one another, whether officially or not, when it came to sharing information about "terrorists"...

After the meeting, Margot kept Martha a few minutes longer, trying to persuade her to join her for lunch. By the time she got away, Martha felt itchy and irritable, as though tissue deep inside her body needed sharp and vigorous scratching. She hurried out to the car, put it into gear, and headed back to the office; she needed to tell the others how the conference had gone. Though she had talked every aspect of the thing through with Sorben, she kept wondering if she were making a mistake. Human rights were important, but they needed to keep themselves from getting too involved with governments. The Marq'ssan seemed to think that getting governments to negotiate at all was a necessary "first step." But it seemed to Martha that the very act of treating with governments risked affirming the governments' legitimacy. She supposed that was why, though the deal she was negotiating was a sort of breakthrough, she had a sour, anxious feeling.

At the corner of Stewart and Seventh Martha spotted the woman who usually sat on her right in her social psychology class. She pulled up to the curb and opened the window. "Need a lift?" she called, remembering years and years of trudging through the rain at the end of a long, hard day.

The woman turned, recognized her, and walked up to the car. "Hey. Going anywhere near the Market?"

"Yeah, get in," Martha said, releasing the door lock. "By the way, I'm Martha Greenglass."

"I know. And I'm Verdell Whitefeather."

"That's a Native American name, right? What tribe are you from?" Martha asked, punching in the new destination.

"Whitefeather was my grandmother's name, not a name I earned. When I left Montana, I decided to use it instead of my father's name, which is Anglo. Out of respect, you know? She died two years ago, my grandmother, not long after she'd moved up to Butte to live with my parents. And I'm her only surviving grandchild. Hey, I didn't mean to take you out of your way," Verdell said, gesturing at Martha's tapping a new input into the processor.

Martha had guessed North Dakota or Minnesota from the accent. "Only a few blocks. I'm going to the Co-op Building. So it's no trouble at all."

"I go down to the Market almost every night after work." She laughed. "I'm getting to know some of the vendors pretty well. One of them's even offered me a part-time job, which I'm seriously considering taking. I love having all that going on all in one place. There's nothing like it in Montana. There they've got mostly strip malls, you know? And nothing much to do at night but hang out in bars."

"That's where you're from? How long since you got here?"

"It's been about six months. To tell the truth, I thought I was about to be drafted. I didn't think anything would come of those peace talks. Got to say, I heard some pretty dire things about Seattle, but I also heard that it was a good place to be... Kept thinking about it for a long time, until it seemed to me that it couldn't be that much worse than the way things are in Montana. Dreary, stagnant, no decent employment to be had. The feds really didn't have to draft that many people. Oh, and everyone totally paranoid about everything—although I didn't really realize just how paranoid until I came here."

Martha turned left onto First Avenue. "Did you have trouble getting out?"

Verdell shrugged. "Some. But I made it, that's the thing. Idaho was pretty hairy, they have all those army patrols on the border, you know, not to mention those creepy cults that live out in the sticks, just waiting for the feds to vacate, like they did with Washington State ten years ago." Martha stopped at the corner of First and Pike. "Well thanks for the ride. Guess I'll see you in class."

Martha watched Verdell march off into the Market until the vehicle behind her sounded its horn. That woman probably has a great story to tell, Martha mused. But then so did almost anyone newly arrived in the Zone.

[v]

"Answer the question, Celia." She could see by the way he was looking at her that he was thinking about coming around to her side of the table.

Celia strove to control her ragged breath. "She's a scholar. She'd read an article I wrote as a student, published in the *Quarterly of Californian Legal History*. We talk about scholarly things. Mostly historical." This was the same answer she'd given him the last time. And last time...Celia's mouth dried as she watched his eyes narrow. The only difference this time was Angela's presence in the room. For some reason he had Angela in here, watching.

"So you talked about 'scholarly things,'" he said, sneering. "Was that while you were doing things to each other's cunts, Celia?"

This was a new tack. Did she go along with the story of their being lovers, which Emily had thought a good "cover"? Or did she deny it and stick to what she had already said? Surely if he pressed her into something more he'd be able to use it as a wedge to go further? And at the very least as another source of filth to sling at her. "There's nothing like that between us," Celia said. "We just share some intellectual interests."

"What is it I wonder that a high-powered bitch like her would see in a piece of shit like you?" he said. "I know executive bitches have pretty bizarre sexual tastes, but it baffles me, Celia. A simple guy has to wonder." He paused in that way he had, and Celia tensed for the blow. His gaze shifted; Celia knew he was looking at the guards standing behind her. "Since we're talking about this kind of thing, it's a cinch she'd talk better about it with her clothes off." His eyes stared again at Celia's face. "Give the boys your clothes, Celia." Unless she wanted them ruined. It would be the same as last time, only this time with this new twist. How could she bear it? Celia unbuttoned her tunic with shaking fingers. She must not implicate Emily. She must not. Not for Emily's sake, for they'd never dare to do anything to Barclay Madden's daughter, but because speaking would endanger the entire simpatico movement. She must not must not must not speak. It was all she knew, even as he was telling them to take her clothes away, to go fetch the stool, even as the tears came before any of them had even touched her... She must not must not must not speak...

Chapter Eight

God, these meetings were a bore. Elizabeth glanced at her watch without caring whether anyone noticed. Allison's plane should be landing just about now, and that gave her as good excuse as any for winding up the session. Really, she could take only so much of Ambrose in one sitting. His ridiculous habit of prefacing at least one third of his remarks with *Speaking as Deputy Director, I'd be inclined to say...* made her want to smash the little fucker's teeth down his throat. When Ambrose looked at the wall behind her, at the portraits of the Chiefs of Security past and present, did he fantasize his own, hanging there beside Sedgewick's? Of course he did. The sap had no idea what was happening or how Sedgewick was using him.

"All in all," Elizabeth said when Baldridge had finished outlining the trajectory of Operation Galactica, "it's fortunate for us that though an analyst, Hughes turned out to be such a good operations officer. Especially considering that particular CAT."

Baldridge's gaze flitted off somewhere to the side of Elizabeth's head. The shiftiness of his eyes bugged the shit out of her: he never could look her straight in the eye for more than a second or two, and she always had the impression that that second or two was a matter of accidental collision. And then there was the way he spoke out of the corner of his mouth, as if he were speaking off the record. "He does all right," Baldridge said. His tone was grudging. Of course. She had forgotten how deep the prejudice against analysts ran among operations people. How it must gall Baldridge that Lauder—the erstwhile super-cowboy—had sunk into ineffectualness while Hughes—consummate academic professional—had waxed so dynamic. "The masterstroke is Goodwin's, though. When the Galaxy crew bombs that TNC site, the newspapers in question will suddenly be in great demand and the

Women's Patrol will be blamed for sabotage, attempted censorship, and unprovoked violence."

Elizabeth said, "Yes, and the next Steering Committee meeting will accordingly be preoccupied with this fresh source of outrage. Which however excellent an effect, gets us no closer to the international angle. Do you think Hughes could work Greenglass more tightly than he's been doing? I realize he's probably been optimizing his rapport, but the time's come to reel in the catch, so to speak." Elizabeth sighed. "It's a damned shame that after all these years he hasn't found a way of running her. That would be enough to about give us the Zone on a silver platter."

"If she's that important, why not simply arrange an accident—if not outright assassination?" Ambrose said. "I don't understand your squeamishness at getting rid of the key person in the setup."

Elizabeth exchanged a brief look of exasperation with Baldridge, then stared Ambrose down. Lord the man looked like a pudgy blond cherub dressed in executive clothing. Absolutely ridiculous. Did he have any idea of how absurd his appearance was? It would be easy enough for him to change it. "It's not a question of squeamishness," Elizabeth said. "The Chief and I have discussed this in extensive detail." How ridiculous to say "the Chief": but with Ambrose, such tags carried psychological clout. "Assassination would, apart from being an admission of desperation, merely create a martyr. The Zone is at a stage where it's ripe for the dynamics of martyrdom. Further, the aliens would retaliate. Greenglass, as everyone knows, is in close personal contact with one of the aliens. Third, Greenglass is our main conduit for information about the inner workings of the Co-op. Without Greenglass, Hughes would have no in whatsoever, and they've gotten sophisticated enough that electronic surveillance is difficult."

Ambrose's watery blue eyes blinked. "An accident wouldn't create a martyrdom."

Elizabeth smiled. "You may as well drop the idea since the Chief isn't buying it. As far as I'm concerned, the subject is closed."

He stared down at his yellow pad. Good, his control was in place: he didn't want to lose face before Baldridge. "What I'd like you to take care of, Ambrose—" Elizabeth said, but at the look on his face interrupted herself. "I mean, what the Chief would like you to see to, is a thorough background workup of all the foreign nationals involved in negotiations with the Zone and Greenglass." Elizabeth surmised he would be pleased to have a reason for engaging with Company people for a change. Only Company people would be able to handle in-depth background checks of foreign diplomats. "As well as arranging 24/7 surveillance for Auerbach and Ganshoff. I see no reason why the surveillance detail should be inflicted on the already burdened Edmonds station." Was that an ironic glint in Baldridge's eye? But surely Ambrose did not see it.

Elizabeth opened her attaché case and dumped her NoteMaster, files, yellow legal pad, and pens into it. "I've an appointment imminent," she said. She shoved her chair back and rose to her feet. "Let Lennox know if any questions, problems, or startling developments arise." The nebulous structure of the Chief's office provided certain advantages in its baffling appearance to outsiders. No one knew whether Elizabeth was Sedgewick's PA, or Jacquelyn, or whether Jacquelyn was Elizabeth's PA (though the notion of a PA having a PA must seem unlikely). The single most important fact was that most people could not get access to either Sedgewick or Elizabeth except through Jacquelyn. Ambrose did not know yet that Sedgewick had given Jacquelyn orders denying Ambrose access to him except through Elizabeth's specific intercession. Sedgewick, of course, had no intention of getting embroiled in the situation he himself had constructed. Neither the frustration and rancor that would build up in Ambrose nor the inconvenience this would create for Elizabeth mattered in the least to him.

As she walked back to the Chief's suite she wondered whether Sedgewick had some notion of *her* finding a way of taking Ambrose out. Might he possibly have some kind of grudge against Ambrose? An absurd notion. He'd seen so little of the man. No, as far as Sedgewick was concerned, Ambrose was a non-Company nit who'd been at the right place at the right time for Sedgewick to make use of. If he thought about it at all he would probably be amused at the sorts of speculations Ambrose's meteoric rise in Security had provoked—since, after all, Sedgewick seemed not to care much any more about Security's functioning. If he still cared, Elizabeth thought, Ambrose would be a minor functionary in ODS. But then if he cared he would be handling the Zone situation himself. Not to mention Barclay Madden.

The girl at the front desk, babbling into her headset, visibly jumped and flushed when she saw Elizabeth walk into the reception area. She would have to go, Elizabeth thought. She had been unable to catch on and could barely handle even the ordinary pressures of the Chief's office. There was every reason to think she would be useless in a crisis situation. They should have brought the previous girl out from Denver with them, as Alice Warner had brought Allison's girl, as Hazel's boss had brought Hazel. Jacquelyn had been wrong. But then Jacquelyn had had some peeve about the previous girl.

"Has Allison come in yet?" Elizabeth asked Jacquelyn.

"Not yet. But Cindy says the car was there waiting when the plane landed about five minutes ago."

"Good. I'll want to see her first thing." She went on to her office.

After skimming the log of calls that had come in while she had been in conference, Elizabeth settled with her terminal in her favorite armchair and requested Hazel's personnel file from the general Justice Department directory. As she waited for clearance from the site's security protocol, she spared a thought for Sedgewick. Ought she to go in and see whether he had read the flimsy she'd left on his desk for him? Surely he'd have devoured it by now with the memo square screaming "Something New on Zeldin" to flag his attention... He would know, of course, that she had left it for him to give the knife another twist. She smiled. What a find the new Greenglass-Zeldin connection had been. It almost made having to put up with Ambrose and handle the Zone situation worthwhile, for she would not have run across that little gem if he hadn't forced the Zone situation on her...

BELL, HAZEL DOREEN, *born Denver, CO, 10/14/2055...* 115 wpm keyboard input, very good indeed and useful, given that the aliens could strike them with an EMP at any time... All the usual neural hardware augmentations and software and communications interface and multi-tasking adaptations (none of it fried by an EMP), PA's clerk and reception skills... And of course as Elizabeth already knew, so beautifully poised that she might even be able to manage limited contact with Sedgewick... Only two questions remained: whether to mix this kind of pleasure with business, and whether it would be much trouble getting her away from Justice. Obviously valuable as techs went, they'd be piqued at having brought her here from Denver only to lose her to Security.

The tap on the door drew Elizabeth out of her reverie. Smiling, she admitted Allison. "Welcome back to the land of the grim and dreary. It must have killed you to come back to this."

"Elizabeth, you're tanned!"

"I wasn't so very far from where you were. However, you're *not* tanned. What a shame, dear!" Elizabeth returned to her armchair and gestured Allison to the sofa, but Allison sat on the rug. "Can I get you something to drink?"

Allison shook her head. "No. I'll wait until I get home." Her eyes searched Elizabeth's face. "Imagine my surprise when I found the car waiting for me at the airport. Needless to say I knew at once I was wanted for business."

Elizabeth suppressed a sigh. Why did she have to say these things out loud? Allison had an excess of spite and cynicism where she, Elizabeth, was concerned. She could be generous with other people, but never ever with Elizabeth. "There is a matter I want to take up with you, but that doesn't mean we can't socialize as well," Elizabeth said evenly. "There's the *fino* you like in the refrigerator. As I've told you before, I keep it just for you. Or there's wine. Or juice or tea or coffee."

Allison folded her knees close to her chest and leaned her chin on them. "Thanks, but I had coffee on the plane. And I have a report to finish writing before I can go home tonight."

"I wanted to ask you if while you were in Vienna you knew or knew of Eva Auerbach or Margot Ganshoff."

Allison's eyes narrowed. "Ganshoff…I don't think so, no. But Eva Auerbach, yes, I knew of her. She moved in the highest circles. Someone once pointed her out to me at an embassy party. If I remember correctly she had an important position in a combined shipping-investment-brokerage firm of the sort the Austrians and Dutch specialize in."

"I see," Elizabeth said.

"May I ask why you want to know about these women?"

Elizabeth smiled at Allison: it had been a long, long time since Allison had invited anything resembling a confidence. "It's a tangled mess, Allison. But my hunch is that there will be further upheaval—beyond that directly effected by the war—in the international balance of power unless we can find a way to stop whatever it is that is happening between the Twilight Zone—which means the aliens—and certain corporations and governments. Including Austria, and whatever interests Auerbach represents. Some new alignment seems to be shaping up." Elizabeth frowned. "It's becoming obvious that the settlement of the war is going to change the European picture considerably. There's real danger of the US losing its pre-eminence in western Europe, too. Naturally we've been doing a good deal of informed speculation along those lines, but we never imagined the aliens moving into the picture."

"Ganshoff and Auerbach are in the Free Zone?"

"Yes. Ganshoff is with the Austrian—" Her headset chimed, and Elizabeth broke off. "Yes Jacq?"

"I think you'd better look in on Sedgewick." Jacq's voice wavered. "I went in to see if there was anything he wanted before I left. I thought at first he was just very drunk, but…I don't know, Elizabeth. I think there may be something wrong."

Elizabeth's heart pounded. Had she gone too far? "All right, Jacq, I'll take care of it. You can go home if you like." She turned to Allison. "Do you mind waiting for me? I have to go in to see Sedgewick for a minute or two."

Fear, fear, fear, pumped her up with adrenalin as she hurried across the hall. What would she find on the other side of his door? Elizabeth fumbled her keys in the latches; pushing the door open she recoiled from the blast of music rattling every piece of glass and metal exposed to the vibrating air of the room. *Oh hell not the Brahms.* Hopefully this was only a momentary backslide and not an all out plunge into the abyss… "Sedgewick," she said sharply. She wrested the remote from his clutch and pressed the off button, creating sudden, deafening silence. She knelt beside the sofa. "Sedgewick." How much scotch had been in the bottle when he'd started?

She steeled herself to touch him and took his chin in her fingers and forced his head back. He opened his eyes. Bad, bad, it was very bad this time. *Though at least he's not lying on the floor curled into fetal*

position... "Ever faithful, ever faithless." His words dribbled out in a barely audible mumble.

"Ever faithful, Sedgewick. Believe me, ever faithful," she said, relieved that he was conscious and speaking. He wasn't as bad as he sometimes got.

"Just the opposite of her. Though generally disloyal, she was without rancor. You, though generally loyal, are vindictive, without an ounce of compassion, utterly merciless. If I had her guts I'd've killed myself too, long ago." Slurring, but coherent: he couldn't be *that* drunk.

"All nonsense, Sedgewick," she said briskly. "A: I've compassion—even for you; I'd no idea this revelation would do more than vex you." Jaw clenched, she deliberately put her hand on his forehead and stroked his clammy brow, and he closed his eyes. "B: she had plenty of rancor, you just never saw it." He flinched, and she rushed on, "C: it's not a matter of guts, but a lack of forward vision. She couldn't see past the immediate present or she wouldn't have chosen that way out; while you, Sedgewick, know in your heart that there's something there you're expecting to move toward." She stared at his absent visage. "Though if you'd been like this a hundred years ago no one would have had any doubt of your intention to kill yourself. Only thing is, a man can no longer drink himself to death. Not unless he has his filter removed."

He opened his eyes. "Damn shame. No guts. But you're wrong, there's nothing *to* move toward. She was the last of it. It's like being an unburied corpse. After they half-killed me and she left, only the potentiality of her very existence kept me breathing... Said she'd been eviscerated—like me: said she'd become as dead as I am. That's what she said that night, Weatherall. That's what she said. Eviscerated. Like me."

His words made her flesh creep. She spoke sharply: "Stop feeling sorry for yourself. I thought the idea was to bypass all desire for the maternal other."

His eyes stared past her. "That's all there is. That's what we didn't know."

"And these boys? What about them?" Elizabeth asked, thinking of all the Wilton horrors being successively unleashed on the world: his son, for one.

He looked confused. "What boys?"

She snorted. "Come on, Sedgewick. I'm taking you home." Sleep, then depressed hangover, then forced sobriety under her personal supervision with Higgins's customary assistance. She slipped her hand behind his neck and pulled him into a sagging but upright position. "Do I have to get Bennett to help me?" she said sternly when he clutched at her shoulders.

"I thought it was the beginning that day when I took her out there to supervise the investigation of Greenglass's escape. I thought I was setting her up to live in our world. And all the time she was setting me up—for a fall, Weatherall. Duped me into thinking Torricelli was behind it all. What else, Weatherall? What else did she do that we still don't know about?"

Oh god now he was getting sloppy—worse: teary-eyed. He pressed his face into her shoulder. She'd have to bring in Allison just to shame him into getting some control over himself. Sighing, she put one arm around him and patted his back. "It's all long past, Sedgewick," she said. "You've just had too damned much scotch." Words for herself more than for him. She didn't want him catatonic or bingeing.

After what seemed an interminable five minutes she managed to extricate herself from his clutching hands and prop him up against the back of the sofa. First she'd call downstairs for the car, then get Allison. And she'd have to have that corridor from his elevator to the side door cleared so that she could get him out of the building without being seen by those who would talk. Cavalier though he himself might be about his reputation, she knew her own power depended on it.

[ii]

"From this day forward, Celia Speranza Espin, you shall be 'named,' which is to say that it shall in every case be forbidden that your speech or writing be by any manner reproduced, that you be more than merely named in public, that you be heard to speak or your words in any way transmitted at any public gathering, that as a public person you exist as anything other than the mere name Celia Speranza Espin. All penalties for any violations of this sentence shall be paid not only by yourself but by anyone a party to violating the ruling of this Court. Your name will henceforth be placed on the list of individuals named, which it is the responsibility of any public person or gathering to be advised of." Judge Barnes slammed his gavel. Saying "Dismissed," he reached for a fresh bottle of water.

The interrogator and his minions harried her all the way to the door at the back of the courtroom. "You're walking, Celia," he hissed in her ear, pinching her arm where it was already sore. "I just hope for your sake you're going to be a good girl now." One of them opened the left-hand door and gave her a shove, and she stumbled into a vaguely familiar corridor. After several long seconds of panicked disorientation, she grasped that she was in the courthouse and that they were walking away from her, leaving her there by herself.

"Celia!"

She turned her head; a woman was running up the corridor toward her. Celia stood frozen, not understanding. And then she recognized Emily Madden standing before her. "Come, Celia," she said gently. "I'm taking you home with me. Just for tonight. Your mother is there, waiting." She took Celia's elbow. "I didn't think she should go through the ordeal of waiting here with me." Celia shivered. "Come, Celia. The car's outside." They moved down the corridor toward the side door. "I was out of town," Emily said. "Your mother's message reached me only when I got back. I've been raising every sort of hell I could think of..."

Outside it was night. Emily led her to a large, expensive car, chauffeur-driven, and helped her in. "My mother?" Celia whispered, speaking for the first time in hours. "My mother is safe? They said..." They said she'd been arrested, they said they were "shipping her back to Cuba"—though that threat made no sense, since her mother hadn't come from Cuba, had never in her life even been to Cuba.

"Your mother is safe, at my house," Emily said.

Celia huddled in on herself, unable to think of anything to say, wishing Emily would not touch her.

"Here, Celia," Emily said, putting a half-liter bottle of water in her hand.

"Thank you," Celia said. She had a terrible taste in her mouth, and her mouth was so dry she had constantly to stifle the desire to cough. She had no idea how long it had been since they'd last given her water. She broke open the seal and drank until the bottle was empty, then held tightly to the empty plastic. A nice safe feeling, empty water bottles gave one's fingers. Cool clean impersonal plastic, flexible, smooth. Celia had never noticed that before. Such a simple fact of life, empty water bottles. Yet she hadn't noticed—like so many things she had just begun to see.

[iii]

"You understand," Martha said, glancing up and down the long, gleaming table at everyone present, "that if premature word of this leaks out all arrangements are off. And future negotiations would be placed in jeopardy."

"Certainly," the Austrian Consul said. Frowning, he caressed his rabbity chin with his forefinger and thumb. "It is we, after all, who are taking the Free Zone on trust. We are risking isolation for materials and systems to be delivered at a future date, and we have only your word for it that certain of these materials and systems actually exist and function successfully."

Martha said, "But the more substantial risk belongs to the victims of human rights abuses. If you are isolated, your assistance to these victims will not be directly cited as the reason."

"Pretexts are easy enough to invent."

"And everyone would know the true reason," Laura said. "Which would win you a certain amount of sympathy."

"Perhaps," said the Dutch Consul, "but those who determine international economic policy probably would not be impressed. Bad enough that we were a member of the Eastern Alliance for most of the war."

"Times are changing," said the Greek consul. He had intoned this several times already. "The US Executive is not as powerful as it was a decade ago. New political and economic configurations have been evolving over the last decade, and now that the war is over the new alignments are taking increasingly firmer shape. Greece will benefit greatly by these technologies. The fact that scientists and technologists in the Free Zone have not only had the expertise of the aliens to aid them but also been able to put their considerable combined energies into areas not related to the war will prove fortunate for anyone with initiative enough to change course."

He sounds, Martha decided, as though he's making a speech justifying the decision.

Though these meetings were not quite like the negotiations on *s'sbeyl*, Martha found them reminiscent of those days. And she knew they were a harbinger of things to come, not only for the Pacific Northwest Free Zone, but for the other zones as well. As always when she did business with governments, she had mixed feelings: she hated behaving as though any government had legitimacy, and she particularly detested having to deal with executives. But the prospect of creating this network for information and a mechanism for granting asylum to anyone who physically reached the official consulates and embassies these governments had established in US cities elated her, and that elation was buttressed by the recent revelation that similar arrangements were in the making in the Korean Free Zone. Through these governments, contact with victims and victims' friends and relatives would be greatly facilitated. Marq'ssan would be able to arrange pickups through these governments' agents. And each of these governments had promised to set up clinics—to be supervised by persons specifically designated by the Co-op—in their own countries, for American as well as European victims. Martha's only qualms pertained to the degree of secrecy that could be maintained until they had broadcast Cora's vid program.

After the principals of all four parties had reiterated the basic provisions of their agreements, Margot and the other female executives present circulated the thick sheaves of paper until the four of them had signed every copy of the four-way agreement. A video camera recorded this portion of the formalities.

When they had all finished signing, the six male executives attending shook first Martha's hand and then Laura's, and then they exited—leaving their female executive assistants behind to look after the documents they had signed. Martha and Laura packed up their papers. "You'll join Anna, Thea, and me for dinner, won't you, Martha?" said Margot, indicating the women executives from the Greek and

Dutch Consulates. Martha exchanged glances with Laura. "And you too, of course, Laura. To celebrate."

"Celebration is a bit premature," Martha said. What were they to celebrate? Signing a sheaf of contracts?

"But this marks the beginning of friendly cooperation between your government and ours," Margot said.

Martha picked up her attaché case and turned around. "I don't have a government," she said as she had several times before to this executive.

Margot sighed. "I beg your pardon. But you know what I mean."

Martha glanced around the room at the other women—all executives, except for her and Laura—and tried to imagine their sitting down to a meal at Sweetwater. "I'm sure you won't be offended," Martha said, matching Margot's smile, "if I admit to you that we find it awkward mixing socially with executives. We appreciate the gesture." Suddenly anxious to get out of there, she maneuvered around Laura's chair to avoid brushing against Margot. "But we must decline." She moved toward the door.

"Martha's probably right," Laura said from somewhere behind Martha. "Everyone in such situations is inevitably uncomfortable."

Martha waited in the hall for Laura—determinedly flanked by Margot—to catch her up. "You've put me in my place, haven't you," Margot said, no longer smiling. "I suppose if any of the men had asked, you would have graciously accepted. Instead of telling them how socially inept you presume them to be."

Martha flushed: *she* had been inept, thinking she could get away with responding honestly. "You're wrong," she said. "I wouldn't have accepted an invitation from any of them, either."

Margot's mouth twisted. "You'll do business but not eat with us, is that it?"

Worse and worse. "I beg your pardon," Martha said stiffly. "I had no intention of offending you."

"But I am offended. I'm offended that it is so inconceivable to you to dine with me."

Laura put her hand on Martha's shoulder and squeezed it. "If you'll accept our apology we'd be honored to accept your invitation," she said. "Agreed, Martha?"

Martha swallowed her distaste. What else could she do, unless she wanted an enemy where she least needed one?

Margot said stiffly, "*D'accord.*" She held out her hand to Martha. Reluctantly Martha shook it. She should have pleaded the urgency of their need to get back to the Co-op. But it was too late for that now.

Another lesson in executive manipulation...learned the hard way.

[iv]

After they got Sedgewick safely tucked up, Allison agreed—for a wonder—to dine with Elizabeth at the Diana. Elizabeth suspected that the sight of Sedgewick in such a state had disturbed Allison to the point of discombobulation. Certainly it was a subject she would not under any circumstances discuss with her girl—or so Elizabeth hoped.

"It's so weird," Allison said when they'd finished the soup. "One day he seems perfectly competent, rational, on top of things, the next he's like...*that.*" Her mouth scrunched up. "Infantile." She dabbed her napkin to her lips. "He won't remember I was there, will he?"

"He hasn't any of the other times," Elizabeth said. "Don't worry about it. I doubt if he'd mind that much. He's not easily embarrassed."

Allison sipped her wine. "Was it like this, all that time before, ah, the war broke out?"

Elizabeth leaned her head back against her chair. "What you mean is before he took Zeldin back to the island with him." Allison's face tensed. "Much of the time, yes, though not always. He had lucid spells then, too. The really bad time was the first few months after Zeldin stranded us on the island. He was...incoherent, I suppose is the word." Elizabeth shuddered at a sudden, vivid recollection of those days. If Allison thought him infantile tonight...

"There was something I wanted to discuss with you, Elizabeth," Allison said, running her finger along the rim of her water glass.

Ah. So there'd been a different reason Allison hadn't resisted dinner? Perhaps she was actually going to ask for a favor? Elizabeth smiled. "I'm all ears."

"I've been thinking about something Jacquelyn said to me last week." Allison looked down into her wine glass; Elizabeth observed as she had so many times before how thick and long Allison's eyelashes were against her pale cheekbones. Allison looked up and caught her staring. "She said she was concerned that all of us had gotten into such a habit of using the women's network you built up during the Civil War. That we use it too much for ordinary business. That eventually the men will realize it, or else one of the women will give it away, and then all career-line women will lose everything."

"I've heard this from her before," Elizabeth said. "The fact is that the men couldn't survive without us. They'll close their eyes to the way we get things done for as long as we do get things done. Look at Sedgewick! He couldn't care less whether I go through Georgeanne Childress when I want to get something done at Com & Tran." Elizabeth gave Allison a sharp, loaded look. "As for Jacq—I've warned you that you have to be careful with her. She's not entirely to be trusted."

"Then why did you bring her into the office? I've wondered about that since the first time you warned me about her. Why include her if she's such a risk?"

The girl served their entrées and poured the wine Allison had chosen for this course. When she had gone, Elizabeth said, "At the time I was anxious to firm up my connections with Booth and Booth contacts. Jacq's mother is Booth's first cousin. As it happened, I made good use of Jacq's connections." With a few deft, economical movements of her fingers, Elizabeth removed the spine from her grilled rainbow trout and draped it over her bread plate. "Of course I don't need her for that these days, but I don't see how to move her out without putting up her back. I don't need that kind of strain just now. Besides, she's worked well in the general scheme of things. Her presence in the office adds a nice touch of confusion for anyone outside." Elizabeth popped a bite of trout into her mouth.

"What I don't understand," Allison said, spearing a chicken liver, "is where Chase Ambrose fits into the picture. I mean, he's something of an outsider—isn't he?"

This was almost like old times, Elizabeth thought. Sometimes they could still be like this. It was balm on an aching heart to have Allison slipping back into the role of confidante—even if it lasted for only one evening. "Yes," Elizabeth said, "he is an outsider. I'm not sure what Sedgewick has in mind for him, but I suspect he's simply a spectacular red herring." She sipped water and made herself go on.

"But as for the appointment to deputy chief...Sedgewick did that to hurt me. As far as I can tell, that was his sole reason. Lord knows it's the only one he's given me."

Allison's luminous brown eyes widened. "He would do that—make an appointment that important—for some petty personal reason?"

Elizabeth drank more water. Her appetite seemed to have deserted her. "You remember the day I unfairly accused you of giving him the Zeldin transcripts?" Even as she asked, Elizabeth wondered if the very allusion would make Allison freeze up on her.

Allison, watching her, nodded.

Elizabeth said, "That day he told me he was going to make Ambrose deputy chief because of what he had read in those transcripts."

Allison averted her eyes, and her face closed down. Elizabeth could almost trace her progression of thoughts by the changes in her face. Unable to swallow another bite, she pushed her trout away and poured more water into her glass. Finally Allison looked at her. "He didn't like what you—what we, I mean—did to Zeldin? Is that it?"

"He doesn't blame you, dear," Elizabeth said. "Don't worry about that. Just me. He called me..." Elizabeth could not say it to her. She shook her head. "Never mind, Allison. But you did ask how Ambrose fit in. That's the whole story."

They finished the meal with constraint and returned to the office, Allison to write her report, Elizabeth to dig out the Zeldin relics. She would mine them for ammunition. If Sedgewick thought he'd suffered tonight, he'd soon find that was nothing to the pain she could inflict. She would not let him get away with this Ambrose ploy. She would make him appoint her deputy chief within the next year, or force him to pay the price she had it in her power to exact. She was through letting him use her—as he would soon see.

Chapter Nine

[i]

Hot and sweaty after her workout, Elizabeth showered before returning to the office. The shower did nothing to dampen the energy fizzing through her body, but only heightened the peculiar sense of clarity that sharpened both her perceptions and her thoughts. Quite a different matter, handling a knife, she thought as she dressed. It had made her feel inept and vulnerable; she realized she would have to master a whole new set of perceptions and reflexes before she would feel comfortable using a knife in a personal combat situation.

You surely don't think you haven't been talked about in local Military circles? Especially after all your visits here toward the end of the Civil War? Paranoia? Perhaps. Her usual reaction overflying DC was pure gut-level fear, for though Security personnel now came in and went out at National instead of Andrews, Military owned as much territory per square inch in DC as in San Diego. Granted, with a difference. According to Lisa, Security was merely tolerated in San Diego. Here, Security was…substantial. Still, she'd have felt better if the Executive had chosen to shift out of DC altogether. Damn superstitious fools! As though it mattered *where* they headquartered in peacetime. It might be paranoia, yes: but the image of some hotshot excision specialist taking her out with a hand weapon haunted her.

Elizabeth slotted her electronic keycard to summon Sedgewick's personal elevator. The doors opened at once, and as she stepped in, she thought about how wonderful a tall icy glass of grapefruit juice would feel sliding down her throat. She exuded terrific power and energy after workouts, and that tall glass of juice signaled—far more than the ritual shower—a gearing-down of her physical reflexes. The elevator shot upward. Allison was one of those people who never went anywhere unarmed; she always kept her Beretta close at hand. Total nonsense, Elizabeth often told her. Small arms were useless—maybe even distracting—in any really tight situation. If you were going to pack a weapon, it had better be something powerful. The elevator stopped; Elizabeth ran up the half-flight of stairs to Sedgewick's bathroom. Grapefruit juice and then a call to Higgins, just to be sure he hadn't fucked up and let Sedgewick get started all over again. And a check with Jacq to see if Lisa had gotten the appointment fixed with Madden... Elizabeth unlocked the door into the bathroom and quickly passed through to Sedgewick's silent office—dark with the draperies drawn—coveting as she always did in Sedgewick's absence the Giacometti so carefully preserved by Wedgewood during Security's evacuation from DC, then went out the far door, across the hall, and into her own brilliantly sunlit office. Except for the Giacometti, she didn't envy Sedgewick his.

A shock ran through her, stopping her dead in her tracks, when she saw the back of the head, neck, and shoulders—definitely masculine—of an intruder sitting on one of her sofas. Swiftly she stole to the desk and pressed the blue stud set under the inside edge of the desktop. Silently she crept up on him from behind. The cool audacity of the bastard, sitting with his back unguarded...though perhaps he did not realize there was another entrance than the door off the main hall. She halted a few inches from the sofa, paused, and pounced: and soon had his head pressed back against the top of the sofa, his throat squeezed tight in the crook of her elbow, his fear-widened eyes staring into her face as he futilely struggled against the chokehold.

Sometime after she had pounced—it couldn't have been more than a second or two—the door from the main hall into the office burst open, and first the guards, and then Jacquelyn, shot into the room. Jacquelyn flung her arm out to point at the man as a strangled squawking sound that combined the panic of a shriek with the horror of a gasp emerged from her wide, gaping mouth. It seemed to take her forever to get out the words that had apparently been strangling in her throat. "Sedgewick's son! Must stop, Elizabeth! For godsake that's Sedgewick's son!"

Elizabeth stared at Jacquelyn and took in her white-faced consternation. Belatedly the words penetrated, and she released the intruder. Flicking a glance at the superior of the three guards, she snapped,

"Outside in the hall." She took her time straightening up so as to get a grip on the rage that was boiling up perilously close to the surface. Trembling, she walked around the sofa to get a look at Daniel Sedgewick. His hands probed at his throat; the wary, angry eyes in his empurpled face tracked her every move. Elizabeth turned on Jacquelyn. "Did you let him in here?"

"Yes," Jacquelyn said, now defensive. "Of course I let him in here. How else would he have gotten in?" Her freckles stood out prominently stark in her frightened face.

"Have you totally lost your wits, woman?" Elizabeth's voice roughened into a near-shout. "I could have killed him! Fresh from a workout, still half-psyched up, I find an intruder in my office. You're damned lucky I don't carry firearms or I might have blown his head off before asking questions!"

Two purple spots flared in Jacquelyn's shock-pallid face, clashing violently with the freckles. "If you'd come through the main door—"

"If!" Elizabeth fairly blazed with rage. "If!" She swallowed and took three deep breaths to calm herself. "Get me some juice. And for *him*—" Elizabeth jerked her head toward the sofa— "a half-liter of water." Jacquelyn moved swiftly to obey. "I can't help but wonder what the *fuck* was going on in your brain when you decided to take it upon yourself to break the number-one security rule in this office." Elizabeth darted to the sofa, bent down, and tore the badge from the boy's tunic. As she straightened she saw that her foray had further shaken him. *Good. Let the little fucker tremble in his boots.* When Jacquelyn handed her the juice she flourished the badge in her PA's face: "Look at this, woman. What kind of clearance level do you see on this badge? Anything that would indicate his being allowed in my office unsupervised?"

Jacquelyn looked at her. "No, Elizabeth." Then, very low, she added, "But he's Sedgewick's *son*, Elizabeth. I didn't think—"

"No," Elizabeth said. "You didn't think. You didn't think at all." She looked at the boy. "Give him the water." Jacquelyn did so. "And now," Elizabeth said, "you will sit down at your desk and write up a complete report of what has happened here. I want it within the hour. Clear?"

Jacquelyn's gaze dropped. "Understood."

"I'm glad to hear it." Elizabeth watched Jacquelyn leave the room. She turned her attention to Daniel Sedgewick. "As for you," she said, her voice softening and dropping into a low, husky register. She watched him struggle to swallow the water Jacquelyn had given him. "You're damned lucky you're still alive." She sank into her armchair; sipping the juice, she continued to watch him over the rim of her glass.

After a few seconds he sat up straighter. "You mean *you're* damned lucky you didn't kill me." He achieved a snarl. "What kind of crazy bitch are you to—"

"Shut your mouth, boy," Elizabeth said in the best drill-sergeant manner, and she gave him her hardest look. "With only the slightest provocation I'd be delighted to beat the shit out of you." At the speculative look on his face she added, "And don't think I couldn't. I've forty years' experience, three inches, and maybe ten pounds on you." She smiled nastily. "But try me if you like. It would work off my adrenalin and might even do you some good."

He stared at her, obviously nonplused. What kind of life had he led, anyway, that he entertained delusions of getting away with so much for so little?

She finished her juice, put her glass aside, and leaned back. She could feel her body slowing down, her psyche cooling out. "What are you doing here? Apart from the obvious answer that Lennox let you in?"

"I was ordered to report to you," he said stiffly. "The order came from the Chief's office. I came straight here from the airport. Lennox said I would have to talk to you, that my father wasn't available."

And of course Jacquelyn had somehow been persuaded that Sedgewick's son couldn't be left kicking his heels in the reception area. Stupid bitch. And now she'd have to decide whether to terminate her. Elizabeth picked up the badge, which she had set on the table at her elbow. "Yes, I remember now, I requested your transfer to my control." She slanted a narrow look at him. "Your father thinks it would be good for you to work under me." She snorted. "However that may be, I'm your controller now." She tapped the badge against the glass. "I can't allow this violation of security to pass. You of all people have no excuse for it. Therefore disciplinary action is necessary." From the way he watched her it seemed clear to Elizabeth he expected a slap on the wrist. "First you will write a report detailing your violation of security regulations. Then you will serve seventy-two hours in water-only solitary confinement." His eyes widened. "After which you will re-take the standard course on security regulations all personnel are required to take before their term of employment with Security begins." His eyes fairly smoldered. "And then and then only will I put you to work. Understood?"

"You can't do this to me."

His air of extreme confidence infuriated Elizabeth. She rose from her chair and went to the door, opened it, and gestured the guards in. "You will take this man downstairs to the detention block where he will write a report for you. After which you will see to it that he's held in water-only solitary until further notice. If he hasn't finished writing the report within the next hour you will notify me. Otherwise you will send the report to me personally."

She turned and stared at the boy still sitting on the sofa. "Be easy on yourself by going voluntarily. Otherwise I'll order you cuffed and taken down as a hostile prisoner."

"I demand to see my father," he said, not moving.

Elizabeth turned to the guards. "Take him." She went to her desk and—turning her back on the sight of Daniel Sedgewick being dragged off the sofa—fitted the headset over her ear.

"Yes, Elizabeth?" Jacquelyn said into Elizabeth's ear.

"Have you heard from Lisa Mott yet?"

"She called half an hour ago to say she has set up an appointment for lunch tomorrow."

Daniel was alternately threatening and offering blandishments to the guards. Elizabeth turned around to watch. "Excellent. Then make arrangements for me to go out from here at about ten."

By the time they reached the door, Daniel had begun voluntarily walking. Good. A little shock therapy sometimes did wonders with his type, and of course one thing Wilton boys knew was how to take orders... "You'll regret this, Weatherall," he shouted over his shoulder as they moved him out into the hall.

Yes, she could deal with him easily enough: though at what cost? What would it mean to have made this boy her enemy for life, considering the sort of position he would eventually hold?

Damn Sedgewick for leaving her the dirty work...again.

[ii]

Elizabeth resigned herself to dining with Sedgewick that night. Whenever Sedgewick relapsed, not only her method of handling him but also the balance of power between them shifted. Though only two days earlier Sedgewick had fetched her back to DC with one lift of his finger, the situation had become reversed: it was for her to say now whether to come or go since he manifestly lacked the ability to care for himself even minimally, much less to order others' movements. They both knew this and acknowledged it. However sick to death of his company she was, still she would dine with him tonight and be nice to him as a reward for the good behavior Higgins had reported throughout the day.

In these states of naked vulnerability Sedgewick depended upon her not only because she had nursed him through his worst days after Zeldin's treachery, but also because she was the only person he could talk to freely and with the expectation of being understood. Higgins lacked the security clearance for uninhibited talk about most aspects of Sedgewick's day-to-day existence; more important, he lacked knowledge of the details necessary for making him a comprehending listener to Sedgewick's obsessive monologues. And perhaps most important, Higgins was a professional, which meant he'd have no conception of the pressures Sedgewick lived under, neither those related to his personal life—including being fixed—nor those related to his executive life. Elizabeth, on the other hand, didn't have to be filled in on anything. She usually knew what he was talking about before he'd gotten half a sentence out. For someone as isolated, unstable, and miserable as Sedgewick, Elizabeth's presence during his recoveries represented a life-raft. Elizabeth judged this dependence to continue—though underground—even during his more controlled periods. The difference then, however, was that he could command her presence rather than merely beg for it, and that during his stronger periods she could be as cold and detached and combative toward him as she liked—provided she relented when he needed mothering.

Elizabeth made a face at the very sound of that word echoing in her head. The perversity of her relationship with Sedgewick occasionally made her wish to end it once and for all. Usually she could close her eyes to the more loathsome aspects of it, to the nauseating sorts of manipulations she fell into. But at moments it would come to her that this relationship with Sedgewick as it had developed over the past decade might be imperceptibly contaminating her. Certainly she no longer led any sort of "normal" life.

But did anyone anymore?

And the bouts of pity for him: if anyone was unworthy of her pity it was Sedgewick. He used her and used her and used her—no matter these periods in which she visibly had the upper hand over him. It always came back to his real power over her, his real power in the real world—upon which hers so heavily depended.

Georgetown...*She* could not afford to buy a house—not even a townhouse, much less the palatial edifice Sedgewick lived in—in Georgetown, though her financial situation had improved over the last few years. It galled her sometimes, the difficulties she had constantly to contend with. If, however, she were Deputy Chief and Sedgewick's acknowledged future successor...

She found Higgins waiting for her in the foyer. She handed her coat to the service-tech. "Status report?" she said to Higgins when the service-tech was out of earshot.

"Dead sober, mildly to moderately depressed, but nothing severe," Higgins replied in his quiet, gentle voice. "He hasn't asked for liquor since that one incident early this morning. All the signs are good he'll be semi-operational tomorrow."

"You told him to expect me?"

"Right after your last call." He glanced at his watch. "I've ordered dinner for eight-thirty. Should I put it back, or do you think—"

"No," Elizabeth said, moving into the hall that would take her to the back of the house. "I'm famished." She went directly to the study and was pleased to see that Sedgewick had a fire going in the fireplace. Also, although he wore nightshirt, dressing-gown, and slippers, he was sitting—upright—in one of the tall heavy chairs flanking the fireplace. "I'm ravenous, Sedgewick, so I told Higgins to have them serve immediately."

His gaze drifted onto her face. "I told him we'd dine in here," he said, his voice nearly inaudible.

Elizabeth sat down in the chair that matched his. "I almost killed your son today." She stretched her legs out before her.

"The boy's definitely provocative," Sedgewick said.

"Oh it wasn't that," Elizabeth said, amused. "It was purely accidental—on my part. I came upstairs from a workout, via your elevator, nowhere near cooled out. I entered my office through the door in the rear wall and saw the back of a man sitting on my sofa. First thing that came into my head was that he was an excision specialist sent by Barclay Madden, expecting to shoot me as I walked through the door...someone who hadn't done their homework and so didn't know about that other door. So naturally I set off the Blue Alarm and crept up on him and got him in a chokehold. Lennox and three guards burst into the office—by the main door, none of them bothered to come around the rear, the fools—and then Lennox screamed at me that the intruder was your son. I almost killed him then out of sheer fury."

"I'm sure it was tempting." Sedgewick's voice and eyes remained utterly remote and detached. "Are you going to terminate Lennox for it?"

Elizabeth bit her lip. "I don't know. I'm considering it. I want to weigh the consequences before I take such a step. I have, though, summoned Wedgewood and had *him* on the carpet."

"It's disturbing to find how lax they are." Sedgewick didn't appear to be at all disturbed. "And Daniel? I presume he's still alive?"

Elizabeth grinned. "Oh, he's alive, all right, but smarting. In the first place, I scared the shit out of him. I imagine he thinks I'm a wild woman with a body of steel. In the second place, I've made his discipline seventy-two hours of water-only solitary detention."

Sedgewick's eyes widened, though the rest of his face remained inert. "Isn't that rather harsh, Weatherall?"

"Certainly. But I can't let him get away with breaking security regs. Furthermore, he needs to know I can dispose of him as I please. He was absolutely out of line with me, even after I let him know I was his new controller."

"It has occurred to you he could break under those circumstances?"

"A Company man should be able to take that kind of discipline without breaking. If he can't, he's not cut out for Company work."

Higgins and the service-tech came in with the gate-leg table used for Sedgewick's meals in that room. "I can't argue with that," Sedgewick said as the table was placed before the fireplace. The service-tech carried in table linen, china, and silver. "Still, it seems hard. But then I should have expected that. You have a penchant, after all, for putting people in solitary."

Elizabeth shot him a look around the service-tech standing between them. If he felt he could take that kind of crack at her, he must be on the mend. "You will recall my reluctance to handle Daniel, Sedgewick. If you don't like my way of doing it, then have someone else do it."

He smiled faintly. "I wouldn't dream of it. I'm sure you'll be the making of the boy."

The service-tech carried chairs to the table, then stood before Sedgewick. "Dinner is served, Mr. Sedgewick."

They sat at the table and were immediately served *quenelles de poisson* with Madeira sauce, one of Elizabeth's favorite dishes. She smiled at Sedgewick. "For me?" she asked.

He nodded and took a desultory bite.

Elizabeth dug in with gusto. "Executives of Daniel's generation are not at all like us, Sedgewick," she said, turning the conversation. "Of course there is Wilton, which I'm inclined to hold responsible for all sorts of ills."

"I had to send him to Wilton. Virtually all his peers were being sent there, and I wasn't about to have him handicapped. Not with the background I have. And besides, Raines was mismanaging him."

"That may well be," Elizabeth said, "but the combination of Wilton with the fact of growing up during a time of gross instability…" She shrugged. "Also, it's not clear what sort of effect having the surgery before reaching sexual maturity will have on these young men." She glanced at him out of the corner of her eye. He was the only man with whom she could imagine ever discussing this subject.

"It's bound to be less painful for them than at a later age," Sedgewick said. "They won't know what they're missing."

Elizabeth shuddered. Could he genuinely miss all that ugliness? Take his relationship with Zeldin before he had been fixed. If that had been at all characteristic of his sexual arrangements with other women…Elizabeth drank water. Such details did not bear thinking of. "As for the young women," she said, to shift the subject.

His eyebrows raised. "Surely they are eternally the same? Nothing's changed for them."

"You're wrong there, Sedgewick. This last week I've met someone who doesn't fit either of the molds executive women are cast in. There can be complications other than those brought on by physical alteration, you know."

"That generalization is so broad as to be virtually meaningless."

The service-tech came in, removed their plates and presented the *bouef en daube*. "Then I'll be very specific," Elizabeth said, serving herself from the platter the service-tech offered her. "Barclay Madden's daughter, Emily, is, I think, a law unto herself. Her degree of detachment from the world's expectations takes my breath away." At his look she smiled. "Oh, I admire what I've seen of her immensely. She's not breeding fodder by any means—though one expects she will have to breed since Madden's only other offspring was killed in the Civil War. She's taken on her father's interests. Her mother lives in Mexico; she hardly sees her at all; she's quite independent from the women of her kind in San Diego—declined to join the most exclusive club, and so on."

Sedgewick shrugged. "So she's career-line working for her father."

"Hardly. She's not fettered by the usual constraints placed on career-line women. I'd say she's more like her father's heir—that he's treating her as he might treat a son. It's quite remarkable." Elizabeth took a bite of the tender, juicy meat, and it dissolved like butter in her mouth.

He looked interested. "And it's working? She's handling it well?"

Elizabeth finished chewing and swallowed. "Beautifully from all accounts. And from what I saw, very coolly. She routed my ambush without raising a sweat."

They ate in silence for almost a minute before Sedgewick said, "It's a crime not to drink burgundy with this course."

Elizabeth considered this. She said, "If it's a matter of one or two glasses with the meat, I'll have them bring it."

He shook his head. "It's too late. One can't drink burgundy straight out of the bottle." They ate in silence for about a minute; and then Sedgewick said, "Do you think it's a matter of his having gotten her away from the maternal influence early enough?"

"What? Barclay Madden?"

He nodded.

Elizabeth ate a bite of the sautéed julienned carrots and zucchini; she detected bits of fennel seasoning the vegetables and decided she liked the combination. "Perhaps. I don't know. I couldn't quite make her out. Except to know that she's tough."

"I've been thinking about Alexandra lately."

Elizabeth stared at him. "Indeed," she said dryly.

"I've decided she must be brought out of that unhealthy atmosphere Raines dumped her in."

"Unhealthy?" Elizabeth said. "I'd say Barbados was a rather calm, unperturbed environment conducive to a good quiet upbringing. Especially under Eleanor Dunn's supervision."

"Eleanor Dunn raised Raines, didn't she?" Sedgewick pushed his plate away. "The thought of my daughter turning into another Raines—" He made a sound of disgust.

Fine time for him to be thinking of that now. "How old is she— about fifteen, isn't it?"

"Yes. She'll be sixteen in October."

"So I suppose that means you want to send her to school?"

"That's the obvious thing. To that place in Vermont…what is it called?"

Elizabeth smiled wryly. "My school, you mean?" When he nodded she said, "Crowder's."

"Yes. Much better than her staying down there."

"If she's to go away to school, don't you think Raines is going to want her to go to Layton's?" Crowder's and Layton's were the best schools for girls—and Elizabeth had no doubt Felice would kick and scream against Crowder's. There was nothing like school loyalty in maternal-line women. Even Vivien suffered from this incomprehensible obsession. Sentimentality, it must be.

Sedgewick's face took on its stubborn look. "If it's not too late I intend to do everything in my power to keep Alexandra from turning into another Raines."

Elizabeth sighed. "In the first place, she's been raised an executive girl, and there's nothing you can do about that. Early childhood training tends to stick. In the second place, it's for Raines to decide which school Alexandra should attend."

"I'll be damned if I'll let Raines dictate to me how my own children are to be raised."

Incredible. Suddenly he was coming the paterfamilias—all this nonsense about Daniel, and now taking an interest in Alexandra for the first time since her birth? "It's customary for the mother to make decisions about daughters, Sedgewick," Elizabeth said. "You had your way about Wilton. Certainly it's for Raines to decide about Layton."

"It's within my legal rights," Sedgewick said flatly. "As far as I'm concerned, Raines forfeited any such privileges when she dumped Alexandra on her mother. She hasn't done a damned thing in years to meet her contract obligations. Not only hasn't she given my children the proper attention, she's done none of the other things she's contracted for."

Elizabeth was incredulous: even for Sedgewick, this was a little much. "For godsake, Sedgewick, we both know you couldn't have tolerated having her around to do those things! She doesn't even know your island exists!"

"My point, Weatherall, is that she's had no responsibilities to speak of for years. You don't pay, you don't play. Those are the rules of the game."

And what did he pay? Elizabeth wondered ironically.

"If I hadn't been so damned busy during Alexandra's early years I would have put my foot down. Raines had that girl hogtied, she never had a chance—"

"Oh christ will you listen to yourself!" Elizabeth snorted in exasperation. "Raines was raising her as all executive girls are raised. If you wanted her raised the way professional girls are raised you should have contracted with a professional and not with someone of Raines' caliber!"

He glared at her. "And you, how did *you* turn out so goddam aggressive and ambitious, raised as an executive?"

Elizabeth laughed shortly. "All I can say, Sedgewick, is that you haven't got the faintest idea of what executive women are like. Aggressive and ambitious are adjectives that could be applied to almost every one of us to a woman. It's not *that* that you're bemoaning the lack of." He flushed, and she knew it was because she had made him feel the inferiority of his background. And it was true: executive women were unknown to him—he hardly knew Felice at all, and as for herself, he considered her an egregious exception. All others he ignored.

The service-tech removed their plates and brought out the cheese and fruit. Stuffed Gorgonzola, Elizabeth noted with satisfaction. Judging by the menu, Sedgewick had very much wanted to please her. But before she had a chance to taste the cheese, the handset on Sedgewick's desk buzzed, startling her. Frowning, she rose and went to the desk. It could only be Jacquelyn or the Night Desk at headquarters. Apart from herself, only they had access to Sedgewick's personal number. "Weatherall here," Elizabeth said into the handset.

"It's Bascomb and sorry to disturb you, Ms. Weatherall, but we have a priority one situation. The aliens have taken over the vid and are broadcasting from the Free Zone. You will want to see it. It has to do with the Executive."

"Oh for the birthing fuck," Elizabeth said. "All right, Bascomb. I presume it's being recorded?"

"Yes, madam."

"I'll be here for a while but will probably be returning to headquarters shortly." She turned to Sedgewick. "I need a vid set, stat. The Night Desk reports that the aliens have taken over the vid and are broadcasting something to do with the Executive from the Free Zone."

"Ask Higgins," Sedgewick said. "But don't bring it in here. I don't want to see it."

"This may be important."

"Leave me in peace for at least one more day, Weatherall."

So much for his recovery. She'd apparently misread the nature of his articulation of interest in Alexandra and Daniel.

She went out into the hall. "Higgins!" she shouted.

Higgins bolted out of one of the small rooms along the back hall of the house. "Yes, madam?"

"I need a vid set, stat. Where is the nearest one?"

"In the kitchen, madam."

They hurried to the kitchen, which was now deserted. Everyone, Higgins explained, was in the service dining room.

Elizabeth looked around the kitchen for a likely screen. "And where's the vid set?"

"They must have taken it down to the service dining room," Higgins said.

Elizabeth grimaced. "Lead on."

Higgins held open a door and gestured her down the stairs. Maybe it would have been better to have gone upstairs, Elizabeth thought. This hardly seemed the quickest way to get to a vid set.

Upon their entrance into the room six pairs of eyes moved from the large screen mounted on the wall to Elizabeth. Ignoring them, she leaned against the doorframe and concentrated on the broadcast. She recognized the woman who was speaking as Martha Greenglass. "We have irrefutable evidence that these atrocities are taking place not only on the west coast but in many other areas of the US. Tonight you will hear the personal testimony of just a few of the many victims of this violence and repression. But some of you watching right now will not need to be told about these atrocities, for you have been victims or know of those who have been victims. The Free Zone stands ready to receive such victims and to assist them in escaping. For that reason, an arrangement has been made with the governments of Greece, Austria, and the Netherlands that their embassies and consulates serve as conduits in the United States to the Free Zone. We will provide transport and other sorts of assistance to anyone seeking it from the Free Zone. Any person whose human rights have been violated need only walk into a consulate or embassy of Austria, Greece, or the Netherlands to find help. We strongly encourage the friends and relatives of such victims to report abuses to Free Zone representatives at these consulates and embassies..."

Elizabeth gaped at the screen, hardly believing what she was hearing—yet at the same time deeply believing it. Horrified, she watched an interview between one of the Free Zone women and a male service-tech alleged to have been tortured in a detention camp in New Mexico.

When the program concluded, Elizabeth stumbled upstairs, her stomach churning, her knees shaking. *Some people would call what you're doing to me torture…* Entering the study she found—unbelievably, it seemed—Sedgewick sitting exactly as he had been before she had gone downstairs.

He stared at her, and she stared back at him, uncertain of how to tell him, uncertain even of what it was she had to tell him. He said, "You're pale as flimsy, Weatherall."

She swallowed half a glass of water and cleared her throat. "There's very big trouble," she said hoarsely. "The Free Zone…" She drew a deep breath. "The Free Zone is claiming massive human rights atrocities in the US against US citizens. They have people on vid telling stories about being tortured in detention camps." She gulped another swallow of water. "Worse. They've somehow arranged with Greece, Austria, and the Netherlands to act as conduits for asylum, their consulates and embassies as places where charges can be filed against, quote, violence and repression, unquote."

Higgins came into the room before Sedgewick had a chance to respond. "Mr. Booth is on line three, sir, and wishes to speak with you."

"You take it, Weatherall," Sedgewick said.

Her heart sank. "You know he doesn't like dealing with me," Elizabeth said.

"Tell him… Tell him I think we should have an Executive meeting tomorrow afternoon," Sedgewick said, bargaining. He looked, Elizabeth thought, bored to death at the idea.

Elizabeth bit her lip. "All right. I'll see if I can satisfy him with that." Elizabeth went to the desk. "Line three, Higgins?" she asked, staring at the com-panel.

"Yes, madam."

"You can go, Higgins." She watched him close the door behind him, then picked up the house handset and flat-commanded "Three." In her ordinary voice, she went on: "This is Weatherall, Mr. Booth. Mr. Sedgewick asked me to suggest to you that the Executive meet tomorrow afternoon."

"He's not available now?"

"Ah, he's rather busy just now, sir, because of this breaking crisis. I presume that was your reason in calling?"

"We're going to want a ton of intelligence on every aspect of this, Weatherall. We can't decide how to act until we know just what the fuck is going on. Clear?"

"Understood, sir. We're getting on that immediately."

"Very well, Weatherall. My PA will get back to you tomorrow morning about scheduling the meeting."

"Thank you, sir," Elizabeth said, not quite getting out the "sir" before hearing the click of disconnection.

Elizabeth turned and faced Sedgewick. "It looks like Chase Ambrose's ass has just gone on the line."

His eyebrows lifted. "You think he'll be implicated in this?"

Elizabeth shrugged. "He's the one who had full responsibility for keeping domestic order. The detention centers—all but one of them—were in his jurisdiction."

"You'll have to go back to the office," he said.

"Are you coming in tonight?"

He shoved his chair back from the table. "No, not tonight. I'll leave the preliminaries to you. I'm sure you can manage them perfectly well without me."

Elizabeth headed for the door, then paused to say, "Get an early night, Sedgewick. Use a sedative if you think you'll need it to sleep through the night. You'll have an Executive meeting to deal with in the afternoon."

She had a great deal of work to do before she could call it a night. And what about her lunch appointment with Madden scheduled for tomorrow noon? she wondered as she slipped on her coat and went out the front door. She had made a grave mistake, needling Sedgewick as she had. Her timing could hardly have been worse. She would have to be more careful in the future. She had too damned much to lose, as Booth's call had yet again reminded her. Sedgewick would *have* to make her Deputy Chief, would *have* to make her acceptable to the Executive. They could not go on like this much longer. Sedgewick must be made to understand that, must be made to see her promotion as in his own best interests...though whether he cared about his own best interests these days was debatable.

Damn Greenglass, damn Sedgewick... and most of all damn Zeldin who was responsible not only for Sedgewick's condition but also for Greenglass's very existence. *Some people would call what you're doing to me torture...* Yes, most especially damn Zeldin. Elizabeth climbed into the back of her car and picked up her handset as the door shut, and the car pulled away from the curb.

Chapter Ten

[i]

Yeah, it was morning, all right. Early Saturday morning. Martha pushed her stressed and aching body out of bed just to stop herself from thinking. She crept into the kitchen to make herself coffee and was relieved not to run into any of her housemates. Rather than drinking it at the kitchen table with the *Rainbow Times* as she usually did, she carried her coffee to her room. As she sipped it, propped back against the pillows, she glanced quickly at *The Rainbow Times'* site but instead of reading any of its articles checked out some of the Free Zone's shriller political blogs. She knew it was stupid of her to even look at them, but she couldn't stop herself from scrolling through a few, searching for signs of a groundswell of popular support mounting a defense on her behalf.

A night spent tossing and turning had not lessened the humiliation of reading about herself in *The Examiner's* front-page article, which the bastards had posted prominently on their website the afternoon before. Within hours of the story's release, dozens of people had posted scathing comments about her on several of the Free Zone's political discussion lists, which she had read, sick-hearted, late into the night. Apparently it didn't matter that *The Examiner* was a propaganda rag supervised and paid for by an Executive covert action team: facts, as one of the posters said, are facts, regardless of who is reporting them.

It rocked Martha's faith in herself that so many people were reacting exactly as *The Examiner's* masters had intended and made her so dread facing the rest of the Inner Circle that she actually considered cutting the weekly meeting. She didn't doubt they would all have read the article's ugly recital of selected details of her life, both private and public, as well as its horridly voyeuristic and ideologically hostile "analysis." As she sipped coffee, her stomach churned acid. Last night she had listened to a live, freenet-streamed discussion carried on by a "panel" of four men and a woman who were all elected officials in the Magnolia Neighborhood Association, which had been trying for years to organize a "shadow government" that could pose a credible alternative to the Co-op. Afterwards, she had vowed to avoid all audio posts unless she knew beforehand that someone reasonable had been involved in their production. This morning she scrolled quickly, unwilling to read anything very carefully. Though she found a few posts defending her and attacking *The Examiner* as a scurrilous rag without journalist credibility, so far, these were in the minority.

It didn't help that when everything had broken the afternoon before Martha had voiced her suspicions to Louise that the Women's Patrol was responsible for the firebombing of the TNC site. It struck her now as bitterly appropriate that just as she had doubted Louise, so a good number of people doubted her. But just a little thought had made it obvious to Martha that the *Examiner*'s patrons had perceived a golden opportunity for provocateur sabotage and had seized it. After the firebombing they had not only posted the "exposé" of Martha on their website but also still managed to distribute the download of the afternoon edition to all their subscribers and street boxes. That the firebombing had not inconvenienced TNC in the least would not prevent people from believing the Co-op had perpetrated the firebombing in order to keep the papers from hitting the street. The *Examiner* was claiming that they had mirror sites hosted by different ISPs from which the downloads were distributed and that the Women's Patrol had overlooked all but one of them. Martha could only hope that just as she had had second thoughts about the Women's Patrol's culpability, so most people would, too—and also second thoughts about distrusting her.

A history of ambivalence about her sexual identity: it would enrage Martha if someone were to say such a thing to her face in private. But to print it publicly! They had known about Walt and Louise and David and Sandra. Was her private life such common knowledge? Or was there someone she personally knew feeding them information? Or were they all of them—all of the Inner Circle—under constant surveillance by spies? Martha's sense of violation outraged—and frightened—her. *Greenglass clearly regards the aliens as saviors of the human race, as goddesses descended from the heavens, able—but not yet willing—to sweep the world into an infinity of paradise...* They portrayed her as naive, simple, and confused, and offered theories of personal and emotional inadequacy and immaturity for explaining her determination to drag the people around her—the world, if it were in her power—into chaos, to destroy Western Civilization, to plunge the world into female-dominated barbarism.

About ten minutes after finishing her coffee, Martha logged off. She might want to spend the day hiding, but the longer she waited to face her colleagues, the harder it would get. Just putting on her clothes took an effort. Hoping to invigorate herself, she splashed her face with cold water, dragged a comb through her hair, and brushed her teeth. She glanced at the bed and wished she could sleep through the next couple of months. Presuming that would be long enough for the scandal to blow over...

On arrival at the Co-op Building, Martha parked her two-seater in the garage. Ordinarily she used the stairs, but she felt so flattened by fatigue that she took the elevator. Thinking about the weekly meeting, she reflected that probably the most annoying swipe in the article was the sly allusions to power struggles within the "witches' coven" of "the Big Girls," as the author snidely dubbed the Inner Circle. The public dissection of her made Martha feel as though her self had been maliciously fragmented into a thousand pieces and that sheer force of habit and obligation continued to hold those pieces in a semblance of order that everyone pretended added up to Martha Greenglass... *If the people living in the so-called "Free" Zone were allowed to vote on whether the "Free" Zone should continue to be ruled by this coven of witches, there's no question they would be voted out. Is it any wonder these alien-controlled witches oppose the democratic process with all the force they can marshal? If it weren't for the aliens, these women would be nothing, for the people of the "Free" Zone would refuse to have them. Tyranny must be recognized for what it is. If they are, as they claim, truly interested in the general good of the people, let them show it by holding free and fair elections...*

Martha braced herself as she waited for the elevator doors to open. First she would apologize to Louise. And then...yeah. And then they would get down to business, important business, not nonsense like the *Examiner*'s shitty gossip.

[ii]

The green light on her terminal strobed, and Elizabeth accessed the message on her calendar reminding her that it was time to have the kid brought out of solitary. She called downstairs with instructions to give Daniel Sedgewick a meal, a shower, and fresh clothing, and then send him up to her. She presumed that by the time he'd cleaned up and eaten he'd be well on his way to recovering his composure. She saw no need to extend the lesson: no doubt he'd comprehended the point by now.

Elizabeth continued reviewing State's briefings exploring the new alignment between the Zone on the one hand and Greece, Austria, and the Netherlands on the other. Crannock's meetings with the Greek, Austrian, and Dutch ambassadors had been stormy and polarized, presaging the onset of a cold wave in diplomatic relations. At the Executive's urging Crannock had pressed for meetings with the ambassadors of all other European states in order to clarify their positions and to nip in the bud any tendency toward softening their stance toward the Zone, too. But as Elizabeth read briefing after briefing reporting on each meeting in turn, her sense of unease only amplified. Using the charges of human rights abuses as a pretext, the ambassadors were choosing to hedge. Why? Why couldn't Crannock bring them into line? Elizabeth spoke into her NoteMaster: *Must exert pressure on governments through other than diplomatic channels. Start massive campaign with CEOs and corporate boards. Emphasis should be on carrots over stick. Urge State to avoid negative tactics until essential. And keep Military as far out of the situation as possible.*

It was fortunate, Elizabeth knew, that so many members of the Cabinet now brought an aide or two into the meetings with them, for it had made her presence riding shotgun for Sedgewick much less obtrusive—except for the tiny, insignificant fact that all the other aides were males... Well-briefed and with her sitting there beside him using her NoteMaster's screen to remind him of points that needed to be advanced and/or questions that needed to be raised, Sedgewick had functioned passably. And since he numbered among the few who had been on the Executive for years and years and years—more than half the Cabinet had acceded to the Executive since the Blanket—and because Security carried so much clout, Sedgewick possessed a natural advantage that only the most blatant fuck-up could impair. Elizabeth knew that Booth must suspect the true state of affairs, but since he hadn't been moved to do anything about it thus far, it seemed unlikely he would any time in the near future.

Elizabeth got up from the desk and paced the length of the room. She was having trouble concentrating. Details from Lisa's report on Emily Madden that she'd read that morning kept rattling around in her head, distracting her from thinking about the European situation. What was it Emily had been up to after her return from the desert? Since the surveillance team seemed unable to bug her—everything they tried had been jammed—they had only the bare record of her activities to go on. Elizabeth couldn't help wondering whether Emily's visit to Precious Aldridge at Military headquarters in Coronado had been to brief him on Elizabeth's approach to her. It didn't seem likely, yet why else would Emily go almost straight from the desert to his office? And then that raggedly dressed professional Emily had picked up from the Superior Court Building and taken to her beach home, and the other woman staying there, too…these anomalies were hard to make sense of.

As for the background material…Emily was quite clearly *not* a renegade. She supported a blatantly anti-authoritarian artists' colony and surrounded herself with "simpatico" types, true, but not one definitive contact with subversive organizations could be established—only tenuous brushes with suspected individuals. And though she did not sit on the boards of any of her fathers' armament companies, she did sit on those of companies that supplied clothing and food procurements to Military, which meant she couldn't possibly be anti-system. And her portfolio—what they had been able to discover about it, which hadn't been much, given the kind of security the Maddens provided for themselves—was of the sort one might expect someone of her wealth to possess. As far as one could tell, Emily's "simpatico" predilections were merely the hazy idealism of youth and nothing that one need take seriously.

Surveillance must be maintained, however, given Emily's visit to Aldridge after leaving the desert. It was to be hoped that Lisa's people would be able to discover more about these women staying in Emily's beach house and ascertain that they were simply artistic strays in temporary need of shelter.

Elizabeth's headset chimed. "Yes, Jacquelyn?"

"Daniel Sedgewick is here to see you."

Elizabeth checked the time. "Let him wait at least ten minutes, Jacq." She must make certain that by the time he left her office everything had been made perfectly clear to him. Ten minutes' wait would assist in the clarification.

Elizabeth went back to her desk and sat down. After five minutes she put aside State's reports and took out the hard copy of Daniel's file. At the sight of the two badges tucked inside, she broke into a smile. Daniel was in for a shock, a bigger shock probably than that of spending time in detention. The use of two cryptonyms—one the ordinary working cryptonym, the other known only to those privileged to the information—was not unheard of... But in cases where the officer required no special cover for operational reasons? Elizabeth could not remember ever coming across such a usage of double cryptonyms. But then Daniel Sedgewick was not an ordinary Company officer...yet.

How should she address him? Calling him "Sedgewick" would give him an inordinate psychological advantage. Yet it was his name, she couldn't get around that. And she certainly couldn't call him "Daniel"—only one female would ever call him that, and that was Felice. Well, possibly his sister and grandmother, too. But for Elizabeth to call him "Daniel" would be unspeakably patronizing and precisely the sort of barb that would stick in his memory, festering and infecting... No, to call him "Daniel" would be to provoke resistance to every slightest pressure she would put on him. It would be pointless and foolish. She would simply have to call him "Sedgewick," however much it went against the grain.

When Jacquelyn showed him in, Elizabeth leaned back in her chair and rested her folded hands on the desk. "Sit down, Sedgewick," she said. And while he was still walking somewhat unsteadily across the room towards the desk she continued: "Before you say word one, you'll listen while I lay down the ground rules."

He sat in the chair before the desk. His lips pressed tight, he watched her through narrowed, wary eyes. Good. No outburst, no show of defiance, no sign of challenge. His stylish burgundy tunic— she had never seen such a sash before, she liked the look of it—set off the paleness of his face. He'd obviously cut himself shaving—three times. Apparently he took after his father in preferring not to rid himself permanently of his facial hair. Could it be he didn't know how to shave himself? Imagine a Company officer unable to get along without a valet! The idea was ridiculous, especially considering the easy availability of depilatory creams.

After that one, testing pause, Elizabeth resumed, "First: you will at all times address me politely and formally. As far as you are concerned, I'm your controller and someone you are not on familiar terms with. As a point of advice: it would be well for you to realize that it is in your best interests to get along with me. Any other Company officer would know this, of course. But let us say, charitably, that you are meagerly educated in certain respects... The history of your relations with your controllers as I've read it in your personnel file is, as your father warned me, abysmal." His eyes did not change expression, and he did not try to speak.

Elizabeth picked up the new badge she had had made for him. "Second: for as long as I deem expedient, you will identify yourself by a second cryptonym. By that I don't mean the cryptonym used in reports and cables, but a second cryptonym by which everyone you meet in the Company will know you. More of a pseudonym, actually."

His eyes widened, then narrowed with rage. When he opened his mouth to object, she held up her hand to stop him. "Careful, Sedgewick. You don't want to blurt out something you'll later regret, do you." She nodded at his sullen glare and noted the dull flush suffusing his neck and face that clashed with the burgundy silk. "Your father tells me that your name is making it difficult for you to get proper training. As a personal favor to him I've agreed to undertake your training. Presumably you have prospects in Security, contingent upon your abilities and training. Certainly you won't lack for opportunity."

It was at that moment, staring at the face that so little resembled Sedgewick's, that it abruptly struck Elizabeth what exactly Sedgewick intended her to do with this boy. Her throat choked up; and she struggled against the flare of heat suddenly engulfing her. As Deputy Chief, Ambrose was serving as Daniel's forerunner—a blatantly inappropriate one with so little rapport in the Company, so little experience. In spite of his wild instability, Sedgewick still exercised a capacity for long-range strategizing—when it suited him. So he intended her to groom his son for the job she herself was already suited for? While dragging Ambrose in as a red herring—and psychological preparation—for his real, desired successor? She should have guessed he would try to pull such a stunt, she should have known *immediately* when he dumped Daniel in her lap.

Elizabeth drew a deep breath and strove to control her near-to-tears state of frustration. She must keep her temper. Above all she must keep her head and find a way to control the situation. Damn him, damn him, damn him... The boy watched her with suspicion and hostility, yet still held controlled silence. "I've considered carefully," Elizabeth said, her voice brittle with the strain of control, "and have decided that it would be best for me to keep directly involved in supervising your work. Thus although you will be handled by a variety of sub-controllers, in each case I will receive regular reports on your progress and so on. My idea is to give you a wide exposure to Security with emphasis on the Company since the Company matters above all other agencies and branches of Security. You will not exactly be working your way up from the bottom," she added with a wry twist of her mouth meant to pass as a smile, "since we will skip the usual drudgery jobs like clerking and code work and so on." The jobs career-line women always assumed when they started and often remained in were considered not at all appropriate for a well-connected male like Daniel Sedgewick. "I will require before you leave here today that you give me your word that you will not by any means whatsoever disclose your identity while carrying out assignments. That includes nonverbal cues as well as outright spoken statements." Elizabeth stared down at the badge pressed so tightly between her fingers. Observing the fierceness of her grip, she consciously relaxed her hand. "If I find that you have violated your promise to me, I will wash my hands of you." She looked up at him and smiled. "And if I do that, Sedgewick, I doubt you'll get anywhere in Security. Your father considers me your court of last resort. Clear?"

He stared at her for a long time without responding. Did he intend to challenge her? Elizabeth steepled her fingers together. "Is it possible we have nothing to discuss?" she said in a soft, almost perceptibly hopeful voice.

His eyebrows shot up, and she now perceived a hitherto unseen resemblance to Sedgewick. "Am I to speak now?" he asked, attempting a light mocking tone that failed through the heaviness of his hostility.

Elizabeth gave him a long, cold look. "When a controller asks a subordinate whether something is clear, the rule is that the subordinate responds. This is something the rawest recruit understands. Which makes me wonder whether you're challenging me or are merely stupid."

He flushed. "I doubt if you'll find any judgment of stupidity in that damned file you have on me."

"Ah. Then by default I am to understand you are challenging me," Elizabeth stated. She flashed him a brilliant smile. "Very well. Then I'm rid of you. Dismissed."

He looked uncertainly at her as though questioning the reality of his perceived triumph now that he had achieved it. Would he leave, thinking he could bring Sedgewick around, or would he beg her to take him back? Given her recent insight she hoped for the former, for then Sedgewick would have to deal with the boy himself—and thus face ineluctable disaster for his grooming plan. Sedgewick would never manage to whip his son into shape, not even if he were to stop drinking and become responsible again.

"Tell my father I want to see him." Daniel rapped out the words as though they were an order.

Ah, that must mean he had tried to get access through Jacquelyn, who knew that no one—not even Daniel Sedgewick—could go into Sedgewick's office without Elizabeth's clearance. Jacquelyn would not break an iron rule a second time for this boy, not when it still had not been decided whether she would lose her job for having done so the first time. "You'll have to wait until this evening," she said, "when you can see him at home. He's extremely busy now. While you were in detention a serious crisis transpired. I had intended to brief you on it because the assignment I had in mind for you involved it, but you must understand that I won't be doing that now. The point is, he doesn't have time for personal matters in the middle of a strenuous working day." Elizabeth nodded. "And now, in view of the crisis, I think you've wasted quite enough of my time."

"Have you ever been in solitary, Weatherall?"

A chill seeped into her heart, into her bones. "Must I call the guards to have you removed from this office?"

He stood up. "Quite the high-handed bitch. Well it won't always be that way, I can assure you. Give me my proper badge back."

Elizabeth shook her head. "Sorry. You'll have to get it from your father. As far as I'm concerned you're out—unless, of course, he says otherwise." She touched her hand to her headset. "And that reminds me, be sure to get escort downstairs. It's not a good idea to be wandering the corridors of this building by yourself without a Security badge." Elizabeth flat-spoke into her headset: "Line five."

"All right, I'm going, bitch. Though you'd just get yourself in bigger trouble by having me manhandled again." He strode to the door and yanked it open.

Elizabeth sagged back in her chair as the door slammed shut behind him, then told Jacquelyn she didn't after all need to talk to her. Thank god that was over. What gave him the idea Sedgewick would give him whatever he wanted? Sure, Sedgewick made him a more than generous allowance, tolerated a great deal of nonsense from him, and had several times in the past gotten companionably drunk with him (which wasn't that hard a thing to do). But they hardly got along at all. The boy's arrogance about his ability to manipulate Sedgewick seemed all out of proportion to reality.

Would this put an end to Daniel's career in Security? Well, it would be Sedgewick's move now. She had given it a try and had run into sheer intransigence. Smiling grimly, Elizabeth turned to her terminal and called up Daniel's file in order to write and append the necessary report describing her dealings with him. Quite a dossier the boy had. She could understand why Sedgewick didn't want him working in his colleagues' bailiwicks.

[iii]

Celia lay curled on her side on a blanket on the beach, gazing fixedly at the waves. Emily was out there, swimming, apparently undaunted by the coldness of the water. The waves were coming in at a crooked angle, suggesting that they were being tugged out of line by a serious undertow. What if something happened to Emily out there, what if she were swept away? Celia would be unable to do anything to help and, in fact, would be left in a precarious situation. It was nerve-wracking, waiting for Emily's safe return to shore; it made her realize how thoroughly dependent on Emily she was now. She believed in her bones that without Emily's protection, she surely would be picked up again.

Celia made an effort to stop watching Emily; instead she watched an individual wave form and swell as it approached the shore. Her eyes watered in the fierce, white glare, and she blinked. It was beautiful, and yet... The glitter of the sun on the brilliant green surface hurt not her eyes, but her heart. From the time she'd been released she'd tried not to think about Those Things. She knew it would be better to forget...if only she could. But Those Things were like an indigestible lump of foreign matter inside her, refusing to budge. She hadn't been able to tell any of it to either Emily or her mother, though the latter had deduced much of it through the medical examination she had insisted on. Afterwards, weeping, her mother had held her—while she, Celia, had sat dry-eyed, mute, coiled tightly inside herself.

Like a snail, Celia thought. *I have become a snail...* Snails had shells to protect them. Out of need she had grown a shell, one that she would make stronger and thicker and tougher until it would be able to protect her from even the most determined attacks. She would fuse the shell to her body, making her body and the shell indivisible. Unable to reach the snail fused with such a shell, they would have to crush the shell—and thus kill the snail—before touching her. Being crushed to death would be preferable to having one's shell ruthlessly torn off. Celia dug her fingers into the warm sand and imagined the snail burrowing into the warmth, the invisibility, the protection, of the sand. The image comforted her.

Emily's head bobbed above the waves. She swam naked; and she had walked from the house to the beach without even a towel—strong, confident, easy in her body. Celia could not look at her nakedness, not now. This woman was of another species than herself; they hardly belonged on the same earth, breathing the same air. In her heart, Celia knew that if Emily had been in the same situation she would have reacted differently, would have been stronger, too strong even for those bastards. She could see it in the way Emily moved when naked.

At last Emily emerged from the sea. Water streamed from her hair, and she rubbed her arms with force and vigor. "Brrr," she said. "I need a towel—the air is freezing!" She ran past Celia to the terrace where she had left her toweling-robe draped over the back of a chair. Celia stared out at the water and felt the edge of her tension dull. The sound of the waves racing up the beach was soothing. After a while she closed her eyes, aware only of the rhythm of the sea, the heat of the sun, the brush of the breeze over her skin and hair.

Emily came back down to the beach, fully dressed, and sat about a yard from Celia on the bare sand. "I swim every day," Emily said. "If it's too cold to swim in the ocean then I swim in a heated pool— though I loathe pools. One never knows what so much chemical will do to one."

Celia thought: most people showered daily in a stronger concentration of chemical than that found in the water of a private heated pool filled with fairly high-quality water. Had she any idea of that? Or was she simply not thinking?

Celia turned her gaze back to the ocean and concentrated on its rhythms.

After several minutes, Emily said, "Your mother told me about a doctor she thinks could help you. If I arrange for her to visit you here, would you agree to try talking to her?"

A coldness settled in Celia's belly. Exposing herself to a doctor was the last thing she wanted to do. And besides, such things cost far beyond any means she would ever have of paying. She already owed this woman a burden of debt she would never be free of.

"I realize," Emily said, her voice hesitant, maybe even anxious, "that I don't know very well what to do. To help, I mean. Your mother thinks it would be best for you to talk about what happened to you, but she says you will probably never be able to tell *her* any of it because of not wanting to give her pain." Emily rubbed the spot between her dark, heavy eyebrows and looked out at the water. "Maybe... Well, I thought maybe if you couldn't talk to a doctor, or to your mother, that you might be able to talk to me?"

What, for further humiliation? Emily was the last person she could tell any of it to. Celia sat up and looked at Emily. "All that is pointless." Celia's voice sounded harsh in her own ears. "What's done is past. What we should be doing is finding out about this Cuba thing. Instead of sitting here worrying about poor old Celia's mental state."

Emily looked at her.

"You don't believe me about the Cuba plan, do you," Celia said. "You think I had delusions and made it up."

Emily's eyes were troubled. Celia could see her trying to figure out what to say. "No, I don't think you made it up, Celia. I believe they told you that. They were trying every way they could to hurt you. But that doesn't mean it's true."

Celia said, "Of course you wouldn't want to believe your friends would round up all of my kind and ship us off to Cuba for permanent internment or worse, would you." Celia's voice shook with anger. "They would never do a thing like that, not *your* friends."

Emily's eyes filled with tears. "It will be investigated," she said, blinking.

Celia looked away. She had forgotten how young Emily was—again. With executives age always seemed irrelevant. As if they sprang from the cradle the way all adult executives were. "It will be investigated," Celia said. "I suppose that means you'll go see your friend the admiral again. And whatever he tells you will be the truth of the matter."

"He's not my *friend*." Emily's voice trembled. "If you had any idea of what he put me through before granting me that favor, you wouldn't call him my friend."

Celia watched yet another wave form and swelling push inexorably—and crookedly—toward the shore. Emily had told him they were lovers, had gotten her released as a personal favor to her—it was easy to imagine what he had said. But anyone who could get "favors" from Admiral Aldridge... "You shouldn't have made up all that stuff about our being lovers," Celia said. The words hurt as they burst from her. "You don't understand about those people. They use anything—*anything*—against you that they can. It only made matters worse. Better if you hadn't tried to give that impression to my watchdogs. Better if they'd simply suspected us of conspiracy. They still wouldn't have been able to touch you, and then they'd never have—" Celia stopped, unable to go on.

"What are you saying?" Emily said very low. "What are you telling me?"

"I'm sorry," Celia said, getting to her feet.

Emily stood, too.

"I'm sorry. I shouldn't be angry at you. I should be pulling myself together and trying to do something." Celia wrung her hands and looked at Emily for the first time in several minutes. "I don't know what to do. All I know is that I'm named. And I'm afraid." She tried to swallow the lump in her throat. "I'm a coward, Emily. That's why I'm fussing at you. Because I'm a coward. I'm afraid to leave here. And there's so much work to do, and I don't even know what to do. What I *can* do. Or how to have the courage to do it." She laughed shortly. "All the other times they tried to frighten me into shutting my eyes to it and practicing the correct kind of law. To go back to the old firm I used to work for. They even threatened to pull the license of the firm I'm currently with. But this time..." Celia bent to pick up the blanket. She flapped it to get the sand off it and folded it as she said, "No, I forget, I'm not with that firm now, what am I saying... I can't practice law at all now...at least not in court, nor on paper."

Celia turned and stared up at the house. "I don't know what to do," she said again, and began climbing up to the terrace. She was in one piece, alive, and mentally alert. Yet she was too cowed and full of self-pity to function, too afraid of nightmares to sleep. She, Celia Speranza Espin, did not measure up to her own expectations. That bastard, whatever his name was, had really done her in this time. Amazing how simple it was, how little it took, to break another human being. How odd that she'd never realized that in all the terrible cases she had handled. None of *them* were such weak cowards. Only she. She needed a new name for her middle initial: S for scaredy-cat, soft, subjugated, sundered, submissive, silenced. Yes, silenced. Celia the Silenced Espin. Celia the Shameful Espin—so easily disgraced, so easily cowed, so easily subdued.

[iv]

Snatching a glimpse at her watch, Elizabeth cursed. She needed a Jacuzzi in the worst way, and the time had crept up on her. She was due at the Diana to meet Judith Madison in an hour and fifteen minutes. No time to go home first, nor to use the club's facilities—not without a reservation at this hour of day. So she would have to use Sedgewick's. Why was he still in? she wondered as she crossed the hall to his office. Oh, of course. He'd probably opened a bottle he would finish here or en route.

But Sedgewick was drinking what looked like only his first glass of the evening. "I'd like to use your Jacuzzi," Elizabeth said.

"I've read your update in Daniel's file," he said, stopping her as she was striding past.

She looked at him "As you can see, polite though I was, he was having none of my control."

"Sit down for a minute or so."

"I have an appointment in an hour with someone from the State Department," Elizabeth said.

"I won't keep you long." He was stone sober and serious; she had to do as he ordered. She took the chair nearest his. "I need for you to give Daniel a second chance." She raised an eyebrow at him but said nothing. "If he humbly apologizes, will you take him back?"

"What makes you think he'll apologize?"

"I'm going to give him an ultimatum," Sedgewick said. "A very simple ultimatum. He works for you, or he's out. Which means I'll put his trust fund into effect and wash my hands of him, period."

Elizabeth gave him a skeptical look. "I don't believe you'd do that. He's all you have."

He smiled. "Not quite. You've forgotten Alexandra?"

Elizabeth stared at him, speechless.

Sedgewick's smile widened. "But we'll reserve the subject of Alexandra for a time when you're less pressed. Let me put it this way, Weatherall. If you take Daniel back and work him around Security, I'll give you a house and a reasonable amount of land surrounding it.

One already existing, or one to be built according to your specifications. Wherever you like."

Even Georgetown? But no, she'd have to wait years before any property would be openly put up for sale in Georgetown. "It's a tempting proposition," Elizabeth said. It would be so much better for her in the long term to have Daniel out of the running. Now Alexandra, that could be a different kettle of fish... There would be interesting possibilities if he were seriously considering his daughter for grooming. Elizabeth sat back in her chair. "He expects you to come down hard on me for my heinous treatment of him," she said. "You'll get an earful tonight."

Sedgewick sighed. "Yes, I'm certain I face a boring, tedious evening. But you're evading the issue. Do you accept my proposal?"

What else could she do? As a bribe it was superb. But apart from that, he could still officially assign Daniel to her if he chose. And though Sedgewick couldn't get along without her, neither could she get along without him. He seemed to want this badly. How far would he be willing to shove? "I'd have carte blanche in every respect?"

"With Daniel or your house?"

"Both."

"Yes, of course. I thought that was clear?"

"And if a few years from now I should deliver him up to you fully groomed to succeed you?" His eyebrows soared; now he looked straight at her. "What then? Will you hand Security over to him—leaving me out in the cold?"

"Is that what you think I have in mind?"

"I think it's fairly obvious, Sedgewick." Would she lose an advantage by letting him know she knew what he was up to?

"That's entirely premature, Weatherall."

She snorted, rose from her chair, and started towards the bathroom.

"I want an answer on this now, Weatherall."

She pivoted and jammed her hands into her tunic pockets. "I want something in writing guaranteeing a reasonable position in Security should you retire and Daniel take over."

"Don't you ever consider retiring yourself, Weatherall?"

She gave him a scornful look. "Do I look like I'm thinking of retiring?"

His mouth quirked. "Draft something for me to sign, then, if that will make you feel better."

"I see. You don't really believe such an instrument would be legally binding once you retire."

"What do you want me to do? Extract a promise from the boy? I don't think it's possible, do you?"

"I'm running late," Elizabeth said. "All right, I agree to your proposal, Sedgewick. Remember, no interference whatsoever. Agreed?"

"Agreed." His tone was almost indifferent in its easiness.

Elizabeth turned to go, then stopped and looked over her shoulder. "By the way, Ambrose is driving me crazy with his demands for access to you. It might take the heat off me and Lennox for you to see him. I gather he's most unhappy that you're not bringing him into Cabinet meetings with you."

"I've no intention of seeing him," Sedgewick said. "Part of Lennox's function is to free us from such nuisances."

I knew that'd be your answer: just wanted to remind you that you're playing with fire, boy. Elizabeth aimed a moue at him, turned on her heel, and headed for the bathroom. It was hardly worth dipping into the Jacuzzi at this point, so little time was left. Just as well, perhaps: she wouldn't have time to brood over whether she'd been wise letting Sedgewick know that she knew what he intended for Daniel.

[v]

After meeting with Judith Madison, Elizabeth returned to the office and created a record of the salient points of their conversation. Running through her mind as she spoke into the microphone was Sedgewick's pointed suggestion when she'd told him she had scheduled the meeting that rather than cozying up to the PA of the Assistant Undersecretary of State for Western European Affairs she should be dealing directly with the Assistant Undersecretary himself. "You complain to me about not throwing weight at the Cabinet and sub-Cabinet levels, Weatherall: well I can tell you right now that always insisting on doing your business through women will ensure that that state of affairs continues." When she had countered that she worked through women because the men ignored her, he'd asked her if she had even tried arranging a dinner or lunch engagement with Madison's boss.

She hadn't, of course. She still carried scars from her attempts to deal directly with such people during the Civil War. "If you'd give me some official position making clear my status in Security," she said, "then they might be willing to accept me as their counterpart. Instead they see me as your PA. And thus in their minds though I may wield a great deal of clout within Security, it's all in the family so to speak and nothing to them." His response to that? "I can't afford to give you a deputy directorship, Weatherall. I need you in the Chief's office. You know you can't be spared to a narrower sphere."

Lately she did nothing but go around in circles, it seemed. She used not to care about any of this, it used to be enough to be covertly powerful. But as things returned to normal, the invisibility—and now, added to that, the uncertainty of her future—grew increasingly intolerable.

A few minutes after eleven Elizabeth shut down her terminal and opened the safe. Tonight she would spare herself the transcripts and bring out the leather book. So far she had been unable to pinpoint those conversations with Zeldin that had over the years continued to stick in her mind. A few of them—usually those sessions she had actually enjoyed—were not, of course, included in the transcripts, for they had been in one way or another indiscreet. So far she had only been skimming through Zeldin's initial resistance; and to be honest, the transcripts of the earlier sessions made for uncomfortable reading, though she could not help but admire the woman's strength. Always as she read she had the sense of some underground thing happening with Zeldin, something that lurked on the outermost periphery of her own perceptions, not easily grasped, yet exerting a powerful influence on Zeldin's and her relationship... But it would be the leather book, chiefly, that would give her ammunition to use against Sedgewick, not the transcripts. Sedgewick, after all, claimed to have read all of the transcripts.

Elizabeth lay down on the rug and slid a couple of pillows under her head. Did Sedgewick pore over the transcripts as he pored over all his other Zeldin memorabilia? Or had he hastily skimmed them and put them away, unable to bear so much direct contact with Zeldin's own words? Elizabeth smiled: no doubt Sedgewick had needed to shape and soften his illusions about Zeldin and thus had never given the transcripts more than a cursory look. Careful as Zeldin had been most of the time when talking about him, still one could easily read between the lines much that she had not explicitly said.

Elizabeth opened the leather book. Oh yes, the first entry had been almost verbatim from Zeldin's book... Elizabeth sat up with a jerk. Sedgewick had never even *seen* that book! She'd kept it from him because at the time it was published he'd been in an incoherent babbling phase, and afterwards, when he'd come out of it, because he had seemed too delicate to handle it, and later because she hadn't wanted to negate the possibility of his acceptance of a rehabilitated Zeldin. And then, after Zeldin's death, she had forgotten about the book entirely.

Elizabeth sprang to her feet and went back to the safe to fetch it. Surely there would be material in that book that would be excruciating for Sedgewick. Too excruciating, perhaps? Elizabeth recalled his response to the most recent Zeldin revelation. She returned to her place on the rug, made herself comfortable, and opened the book to the index. She began by looking up the dozens of references to Sedgewick, but as she worked through them she found him mentioned in only non-personal contexts—unless one could call personal those sections discussing the irrationality of Sedgewick's hard-line treatment of rebellion in the cities during the first weeks following the Blanket.

In the process of flipping from the back of the book to the text, however, the header **Executive Sexuality** caught her eye. Breathless with the certainty she had hit pay-dirt, Elizabeth worked her way backwards through the pages so headed until she came to the beginning of that section, titled "Appendix A: Executive Sexuality and Its Possible Implications for Western Civilization." Elizabeth bit her lip. This was a section of the book she herself had only glanced at. It had so aggravated her, she recalled, that she hadn't bothered with reading much past the first few paragraphs. Well, she would read the entire thing tonight. This, whether or not it directly alluded to Sedgewick, would be the ground on which Zeldin would have mounted a personal assault on him. This section of the book had been what had attracted so much notoriety and prurient interest for its revelation of males being fixed.

The first few pages sketched the basic sexual arrangements Zeldin had perceived executives practicing—including getting fixed, child-breeding and -raising contracts, and female executive-service-tech sexual liaisons of the sort favored by women like Felice Raines. Of course Zeldin had had a limited view of these things and had thus extrapolated from those arrangements she had personally observed during the few weeks she had "moved in executive circles." She self-righteously described executive sexual arrangements only from the most sordid perspective, especially where the women's sexual relationships were concerned. Yes, Elizabeth thought, that was why I lacked the patience to read further: so much nonsense as well as heterosexist bias distorted the few valid observations Zeldin had made.

But Zeldin's discussion grew more interesting once Elizabeth got past the attempted sketch of executive life-styles. This must be the "implications" section promised by the appendix's title, Elizabeth thought.

Although the denigration of sexuality—an inevitable concomitant of the mind-body dualism that has characterized most systems of human thought—has been an almost universal phenomenon with the exception of a very few tribal societies, the historical and anthropological literature is absent any instances of sexual arrangements similar to those practiced by executives today. One might speculate that this has chiefly to do with the previous lack of technological capability for accomplishing the surgery that severs executive males from sexual pleasure. Demonstrably, castration would be an acceptable solution neither to the male executives themselves nor to the rest of society should the non-executive population ever happen to gain widespread knowledge of the practice. Castration would in the first instance curtail executive access to the reproductive process, and in the second psychologically handicap executive males with respect both to their own egos as well as to their status vis-à-vis potent non-executive males. For the possession of a penis—and the ability to sustain penile erections—is obviously still of great psychological concern to males the world over.

A male executive would make the point that the difference between himself and a non-executive male is that he, the executive, exercises total control over his sexual functions, while the non-executive male is at the mercy of his lusts, desires, and pleasure. As a matter of record, executive males who have had surgery are occasionally inclined to engage in sexual intercourse of sorts, in two instrumental situations: first, for procreation—since it

seems the idea of "natural" conception without the use of medical technology still holds a certain (albeit devalued) attraction for executives; and
second, for purposes of rape. Robert Sedgewick himself informed me of
at least two occasions on which he had deployed rape as a means of
better controlling executive women. The first instance involved the woman
with whom he had contracted to conceive and raise children; the second
instance (not carried out by Sedgewick personally, though directly ordered
by him to be done by one of his bodyguards) involved the PA of the head
of Security's Southern California station who had sinned doubly: first by
disobeying an order issued by Sedgewick himself, and second, by using
the word "sub-exec" before a non-executive—an offense endangering the
successful manipulation of the non-executive population. [cf. Appendix B,
A Lexicon of Executive Terms and Concepts Not Generally Known to the
Population at Large.]

Elizabeth's breath pulled in. Zeldin must mean that he had raped
Felice! It was incredible. When had he done it? And when had he told
Zeldin about it? Obviously sometime before Zeldin had stranded them
on the island. Felice! And she'd never let on, either. God she must hate
his guts. Yet never once had she lost control before Elizabeth on *that*
subject. Sure, she had ranted and raved about Sedgewick's enrolling
Daniel in Wilton. But Felice had always been careful not to reveal any
personal hostility towards Sedgewick. Her attitude tended to be, "oh
what a tedious disagreeable man Sedgewick is." And Sedgewick, not
mentioning it, when he tended to enjoy letting her know such things
(as though saying, "You'd better be careful, my bitch, or it could happen to you, too")... Why in the hell had he told Zeldin, anyway? It
had hardly been the sort of thing he'd want her to know about him.

So, Zeldin had explicitly named him, and in a highly personal
context. Yes, this might be useful. But there was probably more.
Elizabeth picked up the book to continue reading.

The theory—if by that designation such nonsense can be so dignified—
behind this surgical custom is that ordinary—biologically "natural"—
humans lack control over the material circumstances of their existence
primarily because they are at the mercy of their sexuality, thus still living
with the primitive bodies and psyches *homo sapiens* started out with. The
executives have taken the notion of celibacy propounded by many of the
world's religions (on the grounds that sexual intercourse either leeches

a male's powers or pollutes his spirit and mind) one step further: by ridding themselves of pleasure and the prospect of pleasure, they imagine they can become perfectly "rational" beings. Thus they either destroy their sexuality or transcend it. Most executives being generally unreflective, I have yet to hear an explicit opinion on which of these they think they have accomplished.

Executive females, however, since they are unable—or so the male executives allege—to have physiologically comparable surgery (the nerves stimulating sexual sensation being less centralized in females), are despised by executive males and held to be similar to non-executives, male and female. (This argument is peculiar, given that medically sanctioned clitoridectomies, labial cosmetic surgery, and a wide variety of practices described perjoratively as "female genital mutilation" ranging along a spectrum from limited to radical have been practiced in many societies around the world as well as here in North America. Women robbed of sexual pleasure by these procedures have never been hailed by anyone as being more rational on that account.) Since executive females do still possess sexual desires and the capacity for experiencing sexual pleasure while the men do not, they have created a socially and politically safe and acceptable outlet for their energies in the sexual liaisons they form with service-tech women. [See below.] On the grounds of the instability and irrationality held to accompany active sexual pleasure, female executives are thereby excluded from the upper echelons of executive rule and appear to conduct themselves carefully to avoid accusations of hysteria—which are leveled at executive women whenever they dissent from the instructions, orders, and pronouncements of executive males. Their consciousness of their own inferiority before the superior surgically adapted males is enormous. Yet through the pecking order so cherished by all executives, executive women enjoy a vast sense of superiority over non-executives male and female. Their solution to their sense of inferiority is to submerse themselves in a mysterious decadent life-style barely on the fringes of the executive male world, entirely separate from life as the rest of the population knows it.

Elizabeth snorted. More nonsense! Every time Zeldin got onto the subject of executive women she went off the rails. Well, perhaps it was just as well. It wouldn't do for the real state of affairs to be discussed openly—imagine if the men knew how thoroughly the women despised and manipulated them. There'd be dissension and division on a scale that could well bring about a second executive civil war.

No, it was fortunate Zeldin had been so blind about executive women. Elizabeth continued reading.

> Yet in spite of this theory and its practice, the surgical solution seems fraught with problems. Originally the surgery was performed on mature males only; as time went on, however, because of the psychological difficulties these males had in adjusting to the consequences of the surgery, the age at which the surgery was performed fell lower and lower. At the time of this writing the accepted executive practice is to have the surgery done before the boys even reach puberty. It is widely believed in executive circles that the males who never experience post-pubertal sexual pleasure will find it more natural and less frustrating or poignant than to lose a pleasure they have known. One must wonder what effects this radical practice will have on the individuals, as well as on the psychology and sociology of executive society itself.
>
> Though we must leave it to the biologists, sociologists, and psychologists to evaluate the long-term effects of the male executive's attempt to eradicate his sexuality, one thing can with certainty be concluded from the emphasis placed on sexuality: that executive society—like almost every society past and present—perceives sexuality as all-important to the course of human history. That they are attempting to circumvent it, that they have blamed the general disorder, chaos, and irrationality of human history on sexuality to such an extent indicates an obsession with sex and sexuality of a magnitude previously unknown in human history.
>
> This general obsession takes particular forms in individual cases. Sedgewick, for example, suffers from a peculiar obsessive nostalgia fixed upon his memories of the last woman he was sexually involved with before he underwent surgery; manifestations of this obsession appear to alter materially his effectiveness as Chief of Security. Other such examples—taking a variety of forms—are manifest throughout male executive society.
>
> *Can* the sexual drive be circumvented or transcended through suppression of sexual pleasure? One could support such a thesis only by insisting that the sexual aspects of the psyche are separable from other aspects, by insisting that the human personality is divisible into separate compartments that bear little relation to one another. What in the long run will be the effect of raising a society of males—who, importantly, form the ruling class for much of the world—so altered and divided against themselves and their instincts? Though the historian cannot conjecture about this, at-

tention must be paid to these questions and potential problems. For there lies ahead of us a new generation of rulers who may be warped and who will most certainly be influential in determining the course of human history and development...

Elizabeth laid the book down beside her. If only she had read this while Zeldin was still alive, how much she might have learned picking that woman's brains. Speculation, yes. But clearly Zeldin—though the body of her book only peripherally touched on this subject: thus relegating such discussion to an appendix—had been onto something they all should have recognized long ago. No one would talk about it, of course. Certain conventions governed the ways one could talk about the males' getting fixed, and one did not venture beyond those conventions without risking a great deal of discomfort. It had never occurred to her to discuss this with Zeldin.

Elizabeth returned both books to the safe. She would finish Appendix A another time. She had an early start to make in the morning, and she was sleepy. There was plenty there for her—for ammunition as well as for aiding her own thinking on the subject of fixed males. For now, though, it must be strictly for herself. Sedgewick must not be upset until these crises had passed.

Chapter Eleven

[i]

Elizabeth seated herself across from Daniel Sedgewick and before she'd even fastened her seatbelt established her claim to as much leg space as she needed to be comfortable. His eyes narrowed, but he kept his lip buttoned. She pitched straight in while the plane was still taxiing to the runway. "This briefing is for your benefit, Robertson," she told him. "Hopkins already knows his assignment and is familiar with everything he needs to know about domestic stations in general and this station in particular." She glanced at Hopkins. "Feel free to ignore us," she said to him. After acknowledging her suggestion, he pulled a set of headphones out of his attaché case and mumbled something about brushing up on his Spanish.

Elizabeth couldn't help comparing Daniel with the older executive. The difference wasn't only in the latter's being a seasoned officer, or in his being black, or even in his not having been privileged enough to attend Wilton. It struck her that the difference had less to do with Daniel's having been fixed at such a young age than with a certain injured sense of entitlement the new crop of Wilton alumni fairly radiated. They acted as though the world owed them something it was arbitrarily refusing to give them. Perhaps they thought that the Blanket, followed by first the Civil War and then the Global War, had deprived them of the reality they thought was rightfully theirs... And yet Sedgewick's generation had faced a mess, too—and had taken the mess as an opportunity for radically altering the world to their own purposes. One really had to wonder...

Elizabeth looked at Daniel. "What about your Spanish? I presume after a year in Ecuador—?"

"Not great, but serviceable." His voice was more controlled than she'd yet heard it. His attitude had so far been acceptable, although the previous day he had—briefly—expressed annoyance that he wasn't to be allowed time off before she put him to work.

"We have two objectives for visiting this station today," Elizabeth said. "You'll be in the dark about the second objective until this afternoon. The first will fully occupy your morning. Before going into the specifics of the assignment I'll start with some general information about such visits to stations." The plane arrived at the runway and came to a full stop. The attendant spoke over the intercom, asking them to be sure their seat belts were fasted. And then the plane raced down the tarmac and lifted into the air.

"First, the relationship between Central and a station tends to run a fine line between support—moral, pecuniary, and generally political—and shakedown." Elizabeth looked out the window, then back at Daniel. "What we're doing today falls clearly on the side of shakedown. You see, this station has a special problem. They're feeling embattled because their territory is controlled by Military." The plane oriented itself to the west and leveled off. "It wasn't always under Military's thumb to the extent it is now. But at the onset of the Civil War we pulled all our assets south of Las Pulgas Road, a sort of demarcation line near Pendleton, and moved station headquarters to LA, which was extremely unpleasant in those days, even more so than it is now. Consequently Security lost a lot of its local contacts in San Diego County. And when, after the Civil War, headquarters moved back to La Jolla, the station found itself up against a drastically altered situation. Not only was Military in control, but Barclay Madden, a local strongman with close Military connections, had set up his own little gravy train—most notably a black market, which in addition to other of his activities is obstructing the Executive's Regeneration Plan. What is unclear to us—and this station hasn't been as forthcoming with intel as we think they should be—is the extent to which local ODS personnel and functions have been compromised."

Elizabeth glanced out at the sky again and sighed. "I'm talking mainly about grubs, not upper echelon people." She looked back at Daniel. This briefing—especially the excruciating boredom of such elementary details and analysis—vaguely reminded her of the early days training Allison...although with Allison she had been able to find peripheral amusement as she played the role of teacher.

"Nevertheless, you and Hopkins will be on the prowl for anything, any slightest thing at all. Whatever you hear, however casual, I want written up—if not transcribed *in toto*—in your report at the end of the day. Keep the recorder on your personal NoteMaster running from the moment you enter the station. If you pick up something you think is significant, you'll pass it on to me as soon as possible in case I should need to act on it at once. I suspect, however, that all personnel at the station will be extremely circumspect around you and Hopkins. They're experienced, most of them, and they'll know you're there on a shakedown. Since I never arrive at this station accompanied by 'aides,' that will be fairly obvious from the outset. By the time we've landed, you and Hopkins will have determined the techniques the pair of you judge will be most effective, given your personalities and so on." Elizabeth stared hard at the boy. "You'll give Hopkins final say in everything, since he's very good at this and is in fact your senior. Before we go on to specific things you should be looking for, do you have any questions?"

When Elizabeth had finished briefing him, she told him to spend the rest of the flight discussing techniques with Hopkins and then moved to the back of the cabin to work in peace. Sedgewick had said he would consider her idea of having a national General Election; she needed now to elaborate each point in the preliminary proposal she had given him in case he decided to take it to the Executive. Elizabeth was convinced that an election would not only shift public attention off the accusations of human rights abuse, but would also provide them with a scapegoat on which to blame whatever ugly scandal was brought to light. Wayne Stoddard could easily be made to look Military's patsy and his opposing candidate a spanking new broom ready to sweep clean all the horrors of the war years. Sedgewick provisionally agreed with this analysis but tended to see an election now as a risk—as one more process to keep under the most careful control, since elections provided dissenters with opportunities for stirring up trouble and dissatisfaction. Elizabeth had pointed out that they hadn't bothered with elections since the Blanket and that they'd never achieve the feeling of normalcy now so desperately needed until they had restored them. "Money," Sedgewick further objected. "It will cost pots and pots of money."

"And since when does money prevent us from carrying out an operation we deem necessary?" Elizabeth had retorted. "We need to restore the sense of normalcy," she had repeated. "We've lifted martial law; if we restore the electoral process we'll be all the closer to returning to the forms that give people their sense of the Good Life. With that and our clothing, cosmetics, and entertainment programs we will be well on the way to cutting the ground out from under the subversives."

Elizabeth sighed. Was the kernel of her argument sound? Could they count on an easy restoration? Certainly these things had worked before. But never before had they had to start from such a dislocated mess as they were in now.

Elizabeth stared down at the desert below. The US had come out of the war stabilized domestically while vastly weakened internationally, but the Russians...Obviously the Russians looked better on paper than they had before the war, but they'd lost one hell of a lot of their own infrastructure in the process of expanding their empire. But then centuries of their history had been the expansion and contraction of empire. Expanding for a time, contracting, again grabbing up Eastern Europe, then losing it...

The intercom buzzed, and the pilot told Elizabeth that they would be landing in ten minutes. Elizabeth returned her papers and NoteMaster to her attaché case and went to sit again with the males. "There's another thing I should mention to you, Robertson," Elizabeth said. "It's possible you'll meet the head of station, Leland. He's very old, which means he was fairly well along when he started longevity treatments, and he hasn't had cosmetic surgery because doing so would clash with his notions of masculinity." At Daniel's astonished look, Elizabeth smiled. "He's from an entirely different era. But what I wish to stress is that he is to be treated with great respect. He's had an extremely distinguished career in the Company, and Sedgewick respects and admires him immensely." Elizabeth flicked a glance at Hopkins, then looked back at Daniel. "The only reason he's remained a mere head of station is his dislike of politics. And internal politics are, unfortunately, an inevitable aspect of life at Central."

The plane began its descent. "Oh, and one more thing," Elizabeth said, remembering how people sometimes behaved in new positions of authority. "I would urge you to remember that the people you will be shaking down are your colleagues, not the enemy. Keep your attitude in line with that fact. Not too friendly, but not antagonistic, either." Elizabeth paused and thought of what Daniel would be in for, dipping into the gossip of a domestic station. Undoubtedly they'd be speculating about Sedgewick, and about her, too. And they'd be trying to pump both Daniel and Hopkins for any tidbits they might have to throw into the simmering stew of scuttlebutt. Until now his name had probably kept people around him discreet. Well, *tant pis*. He would just have to get used to it.

To Elizabeth's surprise, she found Lisa waiting on the tarmac with the town car that had been sent to meet her. Pleased, she told Hopkins to requisition a two-seater for himself and Robertson and to get headquarters' location from Lisa's driver. She had no intention of squeezing the two males into the back with her and Lisa, and her escort and the driver would take up all the space in the front.

"*Très très chic*," Lisa said, admiring Elizabeth's new outfit.

Elizabeth grinned. "I happened to be in New York yesterday and had the new styles on my mind." Specifically the style Daniel had been wearing on Thursday.

"I like it," Lisa said. "Its luxuriousness comes as a relief after years of all that grim militaristic shit. I'll have to see if it's hit LA yet."

"Before we get to station headquarters," Elizabeth said as the car stopped at the outermost of the airport's checkpoints, "I want to review my day's plans with you."

Lisa smiled sourly. "Not anything to do with the males you brought with you, I suppose."

The car accessed the freeway. Elizabeth said, "I want you to arrange transport for you, me, Leland, my two males, my escort, and your top ODS man to visit two detention camps—the ones in El Cajon and San Bernardino."

Lisa's eyes almost popped out of her head. "You want to visit *both*? Why on earth would you want to do that?"

Elizabeth cast her a scornful look. "Why do you think? I want to do an unannounced inspection. Which means you'll tell no one—not even Leland—why I want the transport or those people on board with me. Clear?"

Lisa swallowed. "Understood. But must you have Leland? He's out sailing today."

"Get him back here by two," Elizabeth said. "He has to be there. I don't want any doubts should questions arise as to what happened and who was there and represented."

"I don't think I can stand this."

Elizabeth's eyes narrowed; she stared hard at Lisa. "What can't you stand?"

"Inspecting prisons. Christ, Elizabeth! Think what it will be like!"

"You expect to find something unacceptable at either of these places?"

"No, no, that's not what I meant." Lisa said the words so fast they ran into one another.

"If anything suggests to me they've been tipped off, I'll consider you implicated," Elizabeth said.

"For godsakes! I give you my word!"

"Good. I just want to be clear that this is a serious inspection and not window dressing. We need to find out just what the hell is going on."

"And you suspect us in particular?" Lisa's tone was acid.

"We'll be inspecting every detention center," Elizabeth said. "That's partly what I was doing in New York yesterday." She changed the subject. "Did you get anything new on the Maddens for me?"

"We found out a bit more about that woman Emily picked up at the courthouse. Though it was the middle of the night and no courts were in regular session, she had some sort of special hearing before a judge, who sentenced her to naming. It's suspected that military authorities had her in custody previous to her court appearance. My guess is that Emily used her father's influence to have this woman sprung."

"Hmmm. I wish we could learn a bit more about it. Since the woman *is* staying in her house... Don't you have any military contacts you could tap?"

"We're working on it," Lisa said. "These things take time."

"Speaking of that commodity, how am I doing?" Lisa looked confused. "Vis-à-vis my luncheon engagement."

"Oh." She looked at her watch. "You have a good two-and-a-half hours yet. His place isn't that far from headquarters. Just down the beach a ways, on the other side of Scripps. How long are you staying?"

"Only for the day."

"So you won't want reservations or such anywhere. I presume you'll dine with Leland? I'm sure he'll want you to."

Though it would be a bore, it would be good public relations. She had excellent visibility and fairly good rapport with most domestic heads of station. They were used to dealing with her after so many years. She didn't want to lose that rapport. "And the males I have with me? You'll include them?"

Lisa sighed. "Yeah. I suppose we'd better. Leland will want it."

The car left the freeway and headed west. "So now tell me everything you know about Barclay Madden," Elizabeth said.

"Everything?"

"Is he as clever as his daughter?"

"What do you think?" Lisa said dryly.

Elizabeth smiled. "It doesn't matter whether he is or not. I'm going to win this round."

"Hubris," Lisa informed Elizabeth, "hath felled greater mortals than thyself."

"We'll see," Elizabeth promised. "We'll see."

[ii]

Celia still did not feel up to leaving Emily's house.

When on the previous afternoon her mother had proposed the idea of Luis' visiting her, Celia had said without hesitation, "Yes, of course I'd like to see Luis. We have much to talk about, and anyway I'd like him to see for himself that I'm all right." And although she hadn't said it out loud it had occurred to her that such a trip out of town, even if it lasted for only a few hours, would be a welcome relief for him. They could sit on the terrace and stare at the ocean as they ate a non-tubefood lunch. Luis would appreciate a sample of Emily's hospitality. But Celia had tossed and turned through most of the night thinking of how shamed she would be to see him. He knew some of what had been done to her. And she knew what his ideas about sexual purity were; god knew she'd heard enough of them in her adolescence. They were all wrapped up with the history of epidemiology and notions of personal integrity and safety. Never mind that there had been only that one boy from whom she had learned she wasn't interested in men in that way. Luis had changed toward her after she'd announced that she was no longer a virgin. Celia remembered asking her mother about whether Luis had ever (physically) loved anyone. Her mother had looked uncomfortable and refused to say much except that Luis had sworn himself to a life of celibacy before he had finished medical school. Celia felt sure that though this thing that had happened to her hadn't been her fault, he would change toward her now. These things weren't a matter of rationality, not with her, not with Luis. So as she waited, Celia found herself dreading the sound of the gates opening and the car driving into the compound.

Emily had absented herself on the grounds that she had an engagement for lunch. Emily, in general, was almost excruciatingly tactful. She had not tried again to get Celia to talk to her about Those Things. Yet Celia could not help resenting her, guilty though her ingratitude and resentment made her feel. But at least Emily did not pretend to understand—she seemed merely to accept Celia's attitude and aloofness. This Celia grudgingly appreciated; and whenever she happened to recognize this non-condescending acceptance, her resentment would ease—for a time, anyway.

When she heard the gates opening, ever afraid that *they* might penetrate Emily's privacy in her absence, Celia checked the security monitor in the front hall. Only when she had made sure that it was Emily's car did she open the French doors and go out onto the balcony to watch the car approach the house and park. Perhaps something had happened and Luis had not been able to make it... It was possible. In spite of her good intentions, Celia wished she could postpone this first awkward meeting. She knew she wasn't ready.

The back door of the car opened before the driver had time to get out of the car and open it, and Luis stepped out. He glanced up at the house, spotted her, and waved. She waved back and watched the two of them walk along the gardenia-flanked brick path leading to the front door. When they were just below she called out a greeting before going back inside to let them in.

Luis handed her a calla lily and embraced her. Celia stiffened and backed out of his hug and then, embarrassed at her seeming rejection of him, stuttered, "Luis, I'm sorry, I—"

Her mother put her hand on Luis' shoulder. "It's all right, Cee, don't worry about it, Luis understands."

Luis nodded vehemently, "Yes, Elena, of course I understand. Celia's been through so much...it'll take time, I know..." He smiled at Celia, his beautiful dark eyes soft with sympathy. "I'm so sorry, *chiquita*. We'll just take it easy, right?"

Celia said. "Thanks for the lily. It's beautiful." She stepped backwards and gestured. "Let's go sit out on the terrace where we can look at the ocean. The lunch is already on the table out there." Real food in plastic-covered china awaited them, when Luis had had nothing but tubefood for months. She was so glad to be able to share some of Emily's bounty with him that a real smile, which she could feel warming her inside, touched her eyes and lips. And Celia led the way through the house to the terrace, almost as though it were her own house and she a proper hostess.

As they ate Celia reflected on the strangeness of the scene—being here in someone else's house, eating someone else's food, when that person wasn't even present. The three of them were polite to one another in an oddly formal way, as though the stunning fact of the ocean, the house, and the food constrained them to formality, as though the executive who owned all this were sitting there with them, as though under the circumstances they could not be themselves, exactly. Celia buttered the light, flaky roll and spooned dabs of each of the cold salads on her plate. "And there are strawberries with cream for dessert," she said out of a blankness in which only that thought occurred to her.

"Your friend is generous," Luis said. The bougainvillea behind him offered a dramatic backdrop, like something out of a Brazilian soap opera about rich people, its crimson beauty setting off the neatness of his short black hair and the shapeliness of his head to perfection. For the first time, Celia realized her uncle must have been heart-stoppingly handsome in his youth.

"Without her intervention—" Elena said, then stopped.

Celia stared out at the water. Couldn't they ever get away from that subject?

"Elena says you're thinking of going to the Free Zone," Luis said into the silence.

Aghast, Celia looked at her mother: she had only mentioned it as a possibility because she didn't know what to do now that she was too freaked out to be of any use to anyone. Why had her mother told Luis? She must believe Celia intended to go, mustn't she, or she wouldn't have. "I don't know," Celia said. "I don't know what I'm going to do. I only mentioned it as something to think about."

"You're needed here," Luis said sternly. "After what they did to you it's all the more crucial that you stay. People like us can't go running off leaving others to fend for themselves." His lips pressed tightly together. "If all doctors and lawyers and teachers ran at the first sign of trouble..."

Celia stared at him. *The first sign of trouble?* Was that how he thought of it? As though what had been done to her was insignificant, not worth taking into consideration? "I've been named," she said numbly. "I can't represent anyone in court. I can't speak publicly. I can't be quoted in print. I'm not allowed to talk to anyone banned. Half my clients are—were—banned. As a lawyer I'm useless."

"Listen to the girl!" Luis said. "She's telling *me* what it means to be named? I've been living with that for almost three years now, and do you think I let that get in the way?" He glared at Celia. "There's just as much need for named lawyers as there is for named doctors, Celia. It's obvious you're to come to work at the Center now. I can't believe you don't see that!"

Celia turned to her mother for help. "He doesn't understand, Mama," she said, fighting to keep her voice steady. "Why doesn't he understand?"

Elena looked at her brother. "As a physician you admit there are different thresholds of physical pain in each individual, Luis. Why can't you see that that is true for emotional trauma?"

"Pain! If Celia had seen the human wrecks I've tried patching up after those goons have discarded them she'd soon stop feeling sorry for herself. Fractures, burns, contusions! But unlike them *she* had a friend in a high place who for reasons best known to herself chose to step in. Not everyone is as lucky as Celia is."

Celia pushed her chair back from the table. Blinded by tears, she stumbled into furniture as she groped her way into the house. He was right. Everything he said was spot-on. She was lucky to be alive and in one piece, and she had obligations. Except she didn't feel alive—or in one piece. There was something wrong with her; and Luis saw it and despised her for it. That something wrong was weakness and cowardice. Which he thought she should just be able to walk away from. How could she face him again? How could she face *herself*, for that matter? How could she *live* with herself? She might as well be dead for all the good she would be to anyone now.

Celia closed herself in the bedroom and pulled the quilt over her body. All she wanted was sleep, which would, she thought, be a healing draught. If only it weren't so elusive. She listened to the waves. Maybe she could listen to the waves and sleep. Maybe they would lull her into letting go, into dropping into the blankness of oblivion. And then it would almost be like not being there at all.

[iii]

By the end of lunch Elizabeth had conceived a thorough detestation for Barclay Madden. He started out handicapped, of course, by being male; and his Military connections were guaranteed to make him obnoxious. But that he had included a bevy of subordinate males in the lunch party exacerbated that obnoxiousness. The presence of his aide, Shaw—a professional—made sense, since this was a business, not a social occasion. But *four* others? Like Madden himself, they were all dressed with a deplorable West-coast casualness. The two executives wore the same kind of button-up tunic, unbuttoned nearly to the waist, that Madden wore, a dressy version of a sports tunic; and the two service-techs, who were presumably his gorillas, wore skin-tight tee-shirts and loose khaki pants, with holstered guns at their hips. All of the men but Shaw displayed a superbly developed musculature (though Shaw, she thought, might well have one himself, under his ordinary professional business suit). Elizabeth didn't mind the presence of gorillas, of course, but she thought it discourteous to herself for them to be seated at the table.

All of that was bad enough. But when on arrival she had seen just a small portion of Madden's house, so ostentatiously large and pretentiously decorated (Lisa had divulged the interesting fact that when Madden had bought it twenty years past he'd had the inside virtually gutted and redone), she knew he was not going to be easy to handle.

Given the way he flaunted his lack of taste, he would not care much how well he got along with the Executive. Such an attitude, Elizabeth thought, put Emily's refusal of an invitation to join San Diego's most exclusive women's club in quite another light. The Maddens, in short, made it a policy to thumb their noses at the rest of the world.

While she found it distasteful to have to see Barclay Madden's pecs and abs flashing her through lunch, she found it oddly disconcerting to explicitly and visibly connect Emily with him. Though as executive women she and Emily shared that thin, barely perceptible tie between them of being Elizabeth and Emily when out of male earshot but Weatherall and Madden—awkwardly, in this case, since Elizabeth, determined to be excessively polite, as well as to play the role of the Executive's errand girl, called Barclay Madden "Mr. Madden"—when in mixed company, Elizabeth found it difficult to reconcile Emily's presence at lunch with her memory of the naked woman splashing in the desert mountain creek not much more than a week ago.

During the meal Madden lectured at length about his plans for re-establishing a cultural scene in San Diego. Emily contributed details about various sponsoring organizations on whose boards she sat and about the events they had planned for the coming year. Since this was the sort of stuff maternal-line involved themselves in, Elizabeth knew or cared little about any of it. She would go to their functions and contribute money when she had to. But the very thought of active participation in arranging such functions bored her. How did Emily put up with it? Maybe Emily was cut out for a maternal-line existence after all. Most apparent, though, was Barclay Madden's interest in Emily's involvement: he clearly perceived cultural patronage as a means of aggrandizement. The man's insistence on ramming his egotism down her throat made Elizabeth irritable.

"Well," he said as the service-techs cleared away the dessert plates. "I see the haze has burned off. Shall we sit outside? Unless the wind would be too much for you, Weatherall?"

Elizabeth aimed a smiled at the so-smooth-skinned face of her host: "Not at all. I'd be delighted to move outside." So he wanted to play the gender game, did he? As they rose from the table and Madden led the way through the maze to the terrace he had chosen for their talk, Elizabeth worked to assemble an idea of what particular facts and rumors Madden was likely to have been told about her and therefore what sort of picture he had of her. Certainly he didn't imagine her to be a weak female type. Furthermore, it would seem unlikely that the father of a woman like Emily would assume feminine weakness in other women. But who knew what went through the minds of these males? Their view of the world was peculiarly incomplete. They lacked not only perception, but imagination. And what they could not imagine they could not see, not even when it loomed directly before them. Elizabeth doubted that Barclay Madden was exceptional.

Below the terrace lay Black's Beach, where the waves crashed over outcroppings of rock thrust out from the base of the cliff. Madden's male entourage arranged themselves around the terrace, Shaw with a NoteMaster on his knee. Elizabeth accepted a second cup of coffee, which was served in the same gold-trimmed indigo china used for the meal. Barclay Madden took three spoons of sugar in his coffee, she observed as Emily prepared it for him. Shaw drank tea with lemon. The gorillas did not drink anything, and the subordinate executives drank black coffee. Emily drank water. Despite the company, sitting in the fresh sea air filled Elizabeth with pleasure, though she didn't say so.

"My daughter related to me the remarks you made to her last weekend," Madden said, tossing the ball into play.

As she sipped, Elizabeth stared over the rim of her cup out at the water. She looked at Madden only after she had returned her cup to its saucer. "Basically I made four points to her," Elizabeth said. His eyebrows were so perfectly rounded that Elizabeth decided they must have been plucked. "The first point is that the Executive is displeased by your interference with its Regeneration Plan. The second point is that the Executive has in its power the return to San Diego of the various scholarly and research institutions that made your city so prominent and powerful a place before the Civil War. The third point is that if you continue interfering with their Regeneration Plan, the Executive will in all probability take sanctions against you." Elizabeth looked at Emily. "The fourth point is that I would prefer to negotiate with you through an intermediary who would be more accessible than you yourself. Your daughter, for instance."

"Why bring Emily into it?" Madden said. "You've presumably laid everything out on the table; as far as I can see there's no room for negotiation. You offer me a carrot and show me the stick. Either do this, or..." He smiled. "But what I want to know, Weatherall, is what it is you—or should I say the Executive—thinks I'm doing to interfere. I'm just one businessman."

Elizabeth snorted. "Just one businessman. How modest of you, Mr. Madden." Elizabeth tapped her fingernail against the gold rim of her cup. "Your enterprises—and I assume you consider the black market you operate to be a business enterprise?—make any sort of economic normalization impossible in this region. People in this town use almost no plastic credit. Instead they trade in M-dollars printed by you, because M-dollars buy all sorts of things that you middleman. Almost anyone not working for the government—though some of those government workers as well, when the government is an area of Military—is paid in M-dollars. The only difference between what you're doing and what the Free Zone has done is that you're making at least a hundred percent profit on every transaction while the Free Zone makes nothing. Both systems serve to undermine the national economy."

He shook his sleekly shaped head. "The comparison is inapt, Weatherall. There isn't actual hard currency in the Free Zone's system. Just to make sure that good traders can't accumulate capital. They're doing everything they can up there to prevent real entrepreneurial capitalism."

"Which is beside the point. The real point at issue is that you're getting in the Executive's hair."

"San Diego County can't be that important in the general scheme of things," Madden said. "You tell them it will be more trouble trying to destroy me than I'm worth. We're just a tiny corner of the country here."

Elizabeth drank the rest of her coffee and considered how to answer. The truth was there had been pockets of such locally-run places throughout the Civil War and lingering on into the Global War. But most of them had by now returned to the fold. The Executive simply could not afford to have a standout, especially not one this big. And second, the kind of business Madden engaged in—world trading, including his massive military materiel industry—was too big to ignore. Madden's "local" activities effected distant repercussions. The trading arrangements he had established in Latin America alone made him a force to be reckoned with. The main thing working against him was his lack of deference to the Executive and his lack of strongly involved partners. Elizabeth had recommended in her comprehensive report to the Executive that if Madden refused to cooperate, the first step taken should be the squeezing of the few partners who owned significant stock in his corporations.

"You know," Elizabeth said, setting her cup and saucer on the table positioned to the left of her chair, "none of that really matters. What matters is what the Executive wants and what you have to say to what the Executive wants. Am I to assume you are disloyal to the Executive?"

His light blue eyes, which had previously looked amused, chilled. "Are you making an accusation of treason against me, Weatherall?"

Elizabeth let her eyes widen. "Treason? Who said anything about treason, Mr. Madden? I'm sure no one would suspect someone like you of such a thing." Her eyes flicked sideways at Emily and silently continued: *though maybe they might be willing to think it of your daughter, if she keeps taking up bad company.* She looked back at Madden. "What we're talking about is how you stand with the Executive. Let's confine it to that narrow sphere and not confuse the issue with broad generalities."

"I don't know the Executive," Madden said bluntly, "except of course for Mr. Secretary of Defense Whitney. I get along with him just fine. But as for the Executive as a whole—" He shrugged. "I don't have anything against them—yet. Why should I? They're a faceless crowd of strangers. I tell you what, Weatherall. If they want to get acquainted with me and then see how I feel about them, I'll be glad to have them visit." He grinned. "Together, or separately, we can handle that here in this house. We've acres of space for them. And Emily's a great hostess."

Elizabeth couldn't believe he thought he could get away with treating the Executive—verbally, at any rate—like this. She'd never encountered such an attitude, at least not since the end of the Civil

War. She wet her lips. "Aren't you at all interested in preserving the executive system, sir?"

Madden looked at Shaw. "You can call the lady's car. We're almost done here." Shaw pulled a handset out of his pocket and muttered into it. "As you must have noticed, the executive system is alive and well in San Diego," Madden said. "Perhaps it isn't the executive system as the Executive envisions it. Nevertheless, what we have is *an* executive system. One that meshes well with Military's concerns and priorities. Everything is running beautifully in San Diego, Weatherall, and much more prosperously than in, say, the Midwest or the South. Why should the Executive waste its time on us when they've got such a damned mess nearly everywhere else? My advice to them is that they take care of their own business before interfering in mine. Let them do something about Newark or Detroit before they start poking their nose into things out here. Do I make myself clear?"

Elizabeth stood. "I'll deliver your message, sir."

Madden nodded dismissal. "Show Weatherall to the door, Emily."

Shaw rose to his feet. "Your car should be at the door by the time you reach it, madam."

Elizabeth thanked Madden for lunch and followed Emily back into the house. "I have to say I'm more than a little surprised, Emily," Elizabeth said as they negotiated the hallways threading the house. "I think you'd be wise to try to talk some sense into him. Sending that kind of challenge through me, he's begging the Executive to slap him down."

Emily slid her a curious sidelong look. "You think of this as a matter of some local baron out of control?"

"It needn't be put in those terms," Elizabeth said.

"What I wonder about is your stake in this thing. You say you're carrying messages for the Executive. I don't believe that for a minute."

Elizabeth stopped, causing Emily to stop. They faced one another. "Does your father believe it?"

A strange expression flitted over Emily's face and then vanished so swiftly that Elizabeth wondered if she had imagined it. "Yes. Of course he believes it."

Elizabeth smiled. "You tried to persuade him otherwise?"

"Shall we?" Emily said, gesturing. "Your car will be here."

"Anxious to get me out, Emily?" Elizabeth grinned. "Sorry. I shouldn't tease you. It's just that you remind me—" Elizabeth broke off in confusion. It was true, in some way Emily did remind her of Allison, though the two were different in every way. What possible resemblance could she make out between two such different women?

"You know, it's interesting, Elizabeth, the way you simply drop into a town strange to you and expect to be able to make things happen according to your wishes. I don't think my father would be that arrogant."

"Your father would be a fool to think he could drop into DC and set up shop. And since he's not a fool he'd know he couldn't do it. But my delivering messages from the Executive...that's something quite different."

They reached the cavernous red-tiled foyer. "Delivering messages," Emily said, smiling. "Mr. Madden, sir." Her smile broadened. "A stupid move, Elizabeth. He might have responded differently if you'd been straight with him. As it was he hardly noticed you were there. I suppose the next step will be a visit from one of *them*?"

"Why would they want to deal personally with someone so recalcitrant? No, I imagine we'll start putting on the pressure. And then it will be your father's move. Not ours."

Emily said. "It was a pity you couldn't stay longer in the desert. I had the feeling you were enjoying it." She opened the front door.

Elizabeth's car had arrived. "I enjoyed myself immensely. But, you see, I wasn't on vacation at all, and so couldn't have stayed even if I'd wanted to." Elizabeth held out her hand; after an infinitesimal moment of hesitation, Emily shook it. "I hope we meet again...under friendlier circumstances."

"Have a safe trip back to Washington," Emily called as Elizabeth got into the back of the car.

Elizabeth stared out the rear window at the grossly mammoth house and as the car drew further and further away speculated about why anyone would have put so much copper—considering the ugly color it soon turns from corrosion—into their roof. The massive expanse glinted greenly in the sunlight, clashing with the deep blue of the sky. Elizabeth gave up staring at it and relaxed against the seat. She would put her recommendations into action as soon as she got back to the station. If Madden didn't take them seriously now, he would have to be made to see that he must. His attitude astounded her. In some ways it reminded her of Daniel Sedgewick's disbelief that he could be put in solitary or that he would have to take orders from her. But Barclay Madden was a mature male, one with experience. How did he think he could stand against the Executive?

As the car turned onto Torrey Pines Road it came to Elizabeth: Barclay Madden intended to drag Military and all Military-connected associates into the fray. It would be a dirty, nasty fight. Madden could have no other source of such certainty. Would there be a recurrence of civil war, then?

Elizabeth reached for a bottle of water. What should she do? What *could* she do besides going ahead with the first phase of putting on pressure?

For the first time in a long time she wished she could leave it all to Sedgewick. She didn't think she or the executive system could face another civil war. Was it worth pulling Madden in line for? Elizabeth closed her eyes and breathed deeply. She needed a vacation, or at least a brief respite at Vivien's. Vivien would refresh, restore, reassure her. Maybe next week, she told herself—presuming that the powder keg hadn't exploded by then.

She broke the bottle's seal and drank. Whatever happened, she could handle it. She had survived the Civil War, all on her own hook. She must never ever forget that.

Chapter Twelve

[i]

"And in Cell Block D?" Elizabeth said, sweeping her fingers over the area of the floor plan so marked.

"All the prisoners there are subversives," the warden said. "Both male and female, since the hard-core politicals are kept in solitary."

"So in summary," Elizabeth said, "most of your prisoners in for political offenses are in Cell Blocks C and D, excepting the few in Cell Blocks A and B who have been either egregiously uncooperative, evaded the draft, or have incurred minor loyalty charges for activities indirectly adverse to the war-effort. I have that correct?"

"Yes, madam." The warden, though unhappy at having been surprised, was being discreet in expressing his unhappiness. She had caught him aiming a reproachful look at Krebs, his ODS controller, but he had said nothing openly—yet.

"I think then that we will concentrate our attention on Cell Block D." The professional nodded stiffly. "We'll do it this way: Hopkins and Robertson will poke around for themselves, starting first with Cell Block D and then going on to the other blocks. In the meantime, before I make an actual tour, I'd like to sit down at your terminal there—" Elizabeth indicated the terminal on the warden's desk—"and do my own kind of poking around." She smiled at him. "If you don't mind."

He swallowed. "Not at all, madam."

"You will of course supply me with the necessary access codes," Elizabeth said.

"Yes, madam" He pulled a loose-leaf ring binder off one of the shelves of the open safe.

"As for the rest of you," Elizabeth said, glancing at Lisa, Leland, and Krebs, "I'll leave you to your own devices until I'm ready to tour. I'm sure you can find something to inspect for yourselves?"

Leland gave her a dry look she knew to be appreciative of her style. He seemed not at all worried by the surprise she had sprung on him. Lisa, on the other hand, broadcasted nervousness. But then being in this ugly concrete fortress set in the middle of a desolate ghost city—for El Cajon had in water-carefree times been a populous suburb of San Diego—might well be enough to unnerve anyone who had had little contact with detention sites.

For the next hour Elizabeth dipped in and out of prisoners' files. She didn't expect to find anything substantial, for the sorts of things they were looking for wouldn't be spelled out. But she kept an eye out for patterns and possible signs of disappearance-style dispositions of prisoners.

Nothing appeared to Elizabeth's superficial skim. Aware of time passing, she logged out and instructed the warden's PA to notify the warden that she was ready to tour. As far as she was concerned, if there was anything to discover, Hopkins and Daniel Sedgewick would be the ones to discover it. Hopkins was a regular rat-terrier. When earlier that afternoon he had told her that he thought seven of the local ODS should be given loquazene examinations, she had without further consideration approved his recommendation and ordered him and Daniel to stay the extra day to administer the tests. Hopkins had a nose for cover-up, deceit, and, more generally, trouble, so she always let him follow his nose during shakedowns. Even if Daniel failed to acquire the methods and instincts of a crack investigator, he would learn *something* from Hopkins.

When Elizabeth joined the others in the corridor, Lisa took her aside and whispered in her ear. "*Must* I accompany you? The very thought of going in there makes me sick."

Elizabeth patted Lisa's hand. "It'll be good for you, dear. All things considered, your ignorance about certain aspects of your own station's concerns is irresponsible, don't you think?"

Lisa pressed her lips into a taut, thin line and returned to Leland's side.

The tour got underway. An officer assumed point, taking instructions from the warden, beside whom Elizabeth walked, while Lisa and Leland walked behind them, Elizabeth's escort followed next, and Krebs—accompanied by a man of his who had happened to be on-site—brought up the rear.

"Cell Block D has extremely rigorous security," the warden said as they passed through the barriers and checkpoints separating it from the rest of the prison compound. "It has its own physical plant and maintenance facilities so that failure or deliberate sabotage of the main generator cannot threaten its security. And as you can see—" he pointed at the cameras hung at intervals high along the corridor wall—"the entire area is under video surveillance. We even have cameras inside each cell, though naturally we do not keep a constant watch on every prisoner, since that would be a lavish waste of time."

Cameras inside every cell? Not even the Rock had bothered with that degree of surveillance. The thought flitted through Elizabeth's mind that she might have used such a thing for Zeldin. Irritably she pushed it away as she imagined herself spending hours staring at a video monitor, trying to figure out what was going on inside that woman's head.

"Every corridor is the same," the warden said. "Here, midway from one end to the other, is the warder's station." They crowded into the doorless cubicle to look. "Video monitors," he said, waving his hand at the bank of screens, "enabling the warder to scan anywhere in the corridor's territory; a terminal connecting him with the prisoner's files; an internal telephone connecting him with the central office; the usual electronic master controls for the corridor—lights, locks, alarms, tranquilizer gas, and so on; and a drug cabinet. Food and water stocks are kept in the storeroom directly across the corridor. In short, the corridor is a self-contained unit should it need to be."

"And interrogation facilities?" Elizabeth said. "Does each corridor have its own?"

The warden nodded. "Yes, of course. I had intended showing you them next."

"How does one change the scenes on the monitors?" Elizabeth asked the officer sitting at the module.

"Like this, madam," the man said. His fingers danced over the auxiliary keypad, and the scenes on the screens changed.

Elizabeth pointed to the second screen from the right. "Now call up that particular prisoner's file," she said.

The officer glanced at the warden before obeying. When the latter nodded, the officer, from what Elizabeth could deduce of what he was doing, double-clicked on the Query icon, which pulled down a list of the prisoners' names with their cell locations and code numbers, and then single-clicked on the appropriate name. Elizabeth gestured the officer to vacate his seat and sat down at the terminal herself. "Let me see if I have this correct," she said to the officer, who stood at a respectful distance behind her chair. "This prisoner is currently being dosed with heavy tranquilizers, her next dose due to be administered at six; she was arrested six months ago, at which time she was found to be carrying firearms and subversive literature, which she is conjectured to have been intending to pass from one banned person to another? Is that correct?"

"Yes, madam."

Elizabeth looked up at the warden. "Why the drugs?"

The warden cleared his throat. "Standard operating procedure for all Cell Block D prisoners not currently in an interrogation cycle, madam."

"That must be expensive," Elizabeth said. "Considering that they are already in isolation, it can't be to make them easier to handle. What's the rationale?"

"I really couldn't say, madam." The warden kept his face carefully blank. "I'm simply following the procedures laid down for me from above."

Elizabeth frowned. The prison she had toured yesterday had not used drugs, at least not to her observation. "Krebs?" she said, turning to face the ODS man. "What do you know about this?"

He stood correctly at attention. "The policy was begun about four years ago," he said. "As I recall, the orders for it came out of Mr. Stevens' office. I merely passed them on to the detention centers in the territory."

Elizabeth looked back at the warden. "What about prisoners in Cell Blocks A, B, and C, Warden?" Elizabeth said. "Do they receive drugs?"

"We use a selection procedure by which that is determined. The procedure itself was supplied for us."

"By Mr. Stevens' office," Krebs said.

Elizabeth said, "I'd like to see the interrogation facilities." She would interview this particular prisoner afterwards. The monitor's resolution was poor, but she couldn't imagine—aside from a birthmark—what else besides a bruise the marking on the woman's face could be. If she were kept in constant isolation, and drugged, it couldn't have been acquired in a fight.

They trooped down to the end of the corridor, Lisa holding her hand over her nose and mouth in such a way that Elizabeth guessed the heavy odor of chemical mixed with the smell of urine and something acrid (was it vomit?) had begun getting to her. "Is an interrogation in session now?" Elizabeth asked as they stood outside the door the accompanying officer was unlocking.

The warden shrugged. "I really don't know." Elizabeth gave him a sharp look. Of course he knew. He likely knew everything going on in his domain, and at the least he'd have checked out such things while she was fiddling at his terminal. A lot could be done in forty-five minutes. A lot, but not a total clean sweep. Had he realized she had given him the forty-five minutes as rope with which to hang himself?

They entered, first into a room with a table and chairs and a wall of one-way glass (the mirror facing their side), and then into the room on the other side of the glass containing video and other electronic equipment for recording interrogations. She noted a door in the far wall and gestured toward it.

The warden shrugged and opened it, and led them into a room filled with drug cabinets, clinic furniture, a sink, a chemical toilet, and a cabinet of what might be surgical instruments. "For loquazene examinations," he said. "It also doubles as an infirmary."

"You have medical staff on site?" Elizabeth asked. She hadn't completely done her homework, she saw. She should have known in advance precisely what kind of staff they had on site. The facility she had toured the day before had had only med-techs.

"We have one physician and several med-techs to serve the entire facility," the warden said.

Elizabeth led the way back to the outermost room of the three. She nodded at a door on the wall opposite the one-way glass. "And where does that lead?"

The warden's face went still. "Bathing facilities," he said.

Elizabeth stared into his slate-gray eyes. "Let's have a look." Bathing facilities, sure. The warden was visibly uncomfortable. Did he think she would fuss about it, even if the room was used in the usual way during interrogations? Such practices were not what she was on the lookout for. Surely he knew that? Or was there something more?

The accompanying officer unlocked the door and Elizabeth stepped into a room entirely lined with plastic tile—walls and ceiling as well as floors. There were two showers, one of them, the officer said, chemical, the other straight non-potable water, and an enormous tub that resembled a trough. Annulations had been set into the rim of the tub as well as into the walls of the showers.

God, how depressing. Elizabeth sighed and pushed her way past the others, knowing they were standing there simply waiting for her to get it over with. She went back into the corridor and strode at her swiftest pace back to the warder's station. Only Krebs—an inch or so taller than she—was able to keep up with her. In the warder's station the monitors were still configured as they had been. Elizabeth pointed at the prisoner whose file she had read. "I want to see her," she said to the officer.

That clinic-ish room: such a place was all Wedgewood, say, would need to set up shop. Merely checking out facilities would not necessarily uncover anything illicit, unless by accident. Though someone like Hopkins—who would be taking a closer look than the cursory glance she had given these places—would have a better idea of what to look for than she.

"If you will go stand outside her door, madam," the warder said, "I will release the door lock from here. The cell number is 22."

Krebs at her heels, Elizabeth moved back into the corridor and found the door marked 22. The others caught them up just as the door slid open. Elizabeth's breath caught in her throat. The stench of feces hung in the room like an evil miasma. After the spotlessness of the corridor and the interrogation rooms, the cell's filth and disorderliness struck Elizabeth as a glaring revelation: like accidentally opening a closet door in a house one was visiting only to have tons of garbage and filth spill out into the purity of seemingly pristine order. Nauseatingly vile stains and crud crusted the lime-green cement-block walls; one would prefer not to guess what substances had created the stains. The concrete floor looked as if it hadn't been cleaned in years. And in one corner had been heaped trash—dozens of used towel-wipes, empty water bottles, and food-tubes (all of them, Elizabeth noted, a low-end Barclay Madden brand). Perhaps most significantly, a tube of food and half-liter bottle of water lay, untouched, in a niche near the door beneath a slit Elizabeth guessed must be used to distribute food, water, and towel-wipes. As for the smell from the chemical toilet, it made even her want to gag. She could understand why Lisa hung back half into the corridor.

The prisoner lay sprawled on a filthy thin foam-rubber pad on the floor—there were no platforms in this Cell Block—her Day-glo pink plastic tunic hiked up, revealing naked thighs and partially exposing her genitals. She seemed oblivious of their presence.

Elizabeth glanced at the others—and recoiled at the look on the males' faces. She realized, then, that except for Leland (who was peculiar since old as he was, he hadn't been fixed until his late fifties), she was surrounded by unfixed males. It was like being with beasts hungrily eying raw meat. She felt a fierce desire to take control, to put these animals in their place. And she felt, too, the need to cover the girl's genitals from the open obscenity apparent in their gazes. "Get her up, Warden" she said. "I want to talk to her."

The accompanying officer stood over the girl. "Up, pig," he shouted at her. His shout succeeded in getting the girl's attention: she turned her head and stared up at him, her eyes vacant, her mouth hanging slightly open. He nudged her shoulder with his booted foot. "You heard me, I said get up." The girl continued to stare at him, unmoved.

The warden joined his subordinate. Elizabeth's stomach tightened: from his stance she thought he might be going to kick her. It was nightmarish, this scene. She reminded herself that the girl was no innocent victim, she'd been caught carrying firearms and subversive literature, that without places like this the executive system would be overthrown and people like herself murdered or thrown into places like this. Us or them, she told herself. She must not balk simply because she hated the obscenity of this particular situation. She had felt nothing when dealing with a male prisoner the day before.

The warden bent over the girl and grabbed a handful of her hair. "Come, Lisa, stand up like a good girl." Elizabeth glanced involuntarily at executive Lisa, who was hovering near the door with her hand over her mouth. Their gazes met in shocking collision. Elizabeth tore her own away and stared down at the prisoner. The girl's eyes, fixed on the warden's face, had gone wide with terror; she struggled to stand upright. So he had had personal contact with her, Elizabeth thought. Only strong emotional recognition would suffice to pierce the haze in such a heavily drugged mind. Elizabeth noticed, now, the empty water bottles and the tubes of food on the sleeping mat, and saw that where the girl had been lying most of the contents of a tube had spilled out. It looked like some kind of stew, of white beans and peas with small chunks of carrots and potatoes in a thick tomato sauce. The girl hadn't even noticed she'd been lying on the tube. She must have little physical sensation, Elizabeth realized.

"Yes, that's right, Lisa, stand up," the warden said in a smooth, patronizing voice, his pudgy, professional hands gripping the girl's body. He glanced over his shoulder at Elizabeth. "Go ahead, madam. She's receptive now."

Receptive, he called it? The girl's gaze never moved from the warden's face: he had claimed her attention, yes. But the notion of interviewing this girl was absurd. "But she's not exactly in all her wits, is she," Elizabeth said tartly. "I've seen enough." She moved to the door. Outside in the corridor she said, "You've had personal contact with this prisoner, Harrigan?"

The warden looked miffed, probably because she had addressed him by his name rather than his title, and when he spoke, his tone was stiff. "Certainly. I have personal contact with every prisoner in this cell block. The prisoners here are extremely important sources for Mr. Krebs. ODS depends on the intelligence we glean from these politicals."

Elizabeth glanced at her watch. "I'm running late." She glanced at Lisa. "Notify the pilot we'll be leaving immediately," she told her, then looked back at the warden.

He said, "You won't be touring Cell Blocks A, B, or C?"

"Not today," Elizabeth said, moving out into the corridor. "I simply haven't the time." Again her gaze met Lisa's; in this mutual exchange they shared their disgust for these males. Would it be better if the males running these places were fixed? Elizabeth wondered. Perhaps there should be created a separate class of fixed males, not quite executives, but not such obscene beasts as unfixed sub-exec males? No, the executive males would never allow it, Elizabeth decided as they negotiated the heavy security perimeter of Cell Block D. Their being fixed made them superior to everyone else. They would never consent to sub-exec males being fixed for any reason. Well, perhaps it was just as well. Fixing might not improve sub-exec males all that much. At least not for the purpose of running detention facilities located in a sparsely populated wasteland. And anyway, being fixed wouldn't change their basic hatred of women and women's sexuality. Look at the Wilton crop. Would Daniel Sedgewick have been any less sneering and contemptuous at the sight of that girl's cunt than these unfixed males? The only difference would have been in what that contempt might move him to do or fantasize doing.

As they strode up the corridor, Elizabeth glanced out of the corner of her eye at Leland. Was that really the only difference between fixed and unfixed males? No, there had to be more differences—more important differences—than that. To believe otherwise would be heresy. And Elizabeth wasn't about to become a heretic. The next step after heresy was going renegade, the last thing Elizabeth could ever imagine of herself. She would have to think about it later. Who could think clearly around animals like these? They made her skin crawl. They made her long to remind them that they dare not look at or touch her as they would sub-exec women.

They made her itch for a fight.

Elizabeth was glad she had forced Lisa to tour with them, for it would have been intolerable being alone with so many males in the close confines of that cell. As they stepped into the elevator she looked again at Lisa and covertly, lightly, touched her elbow. Lisa's gaze met hers; Elizabeth nodded, almost imperceptibly (she hoped), not wanting the males to see. She glanced around at the others. See? They saw nothing. They were able to see nothing, blindered filthy beasts that they were. And they had no idea of it, either. How bizarre. How utterly and thoroughly bizarre. It seemed, at that moment, as though nothing were real, as though everything were a bizarre, mad nightmare they had all been trapped in together.

[ii]

The helicopter that had ferried them from the detention facility lifted from the driveway as the party entered the main building of the station's compound. "I need a direct satellite uplink," Elizabeth said to Lisa.

The two of them went up the stairs without Leland and Krebs. Lisa pushed open the inches-thick, Spanish-carved door and led the way into the room tucked into the southwest corner of the second story. "Take a break, Pat," Lisa told the young executive at the multimonitor console.

When the woman left the room, Lisa went to one of the windows—both of whose shutters and carved casements stood open—and peered out through the wrought-iron grille at the ocean. "That pig has fucked her," she said, her voice choked and shaking. "I could see it in the way he was standing there, in the way he was touching her, the way he was eyeing her. They're all the same when it comes to *that*, you know. Just like Lamont." Lisa turned around to stare at Elizabeth. Tears streaked her face. "You promised me, Elizabeth. You promised me you'd tell me when Lamont leaves Sedgewick's employ. There isn't a day that goes by that I don't fantasize killing that animal."

"That animal" had been Sedgewick's instrument and had done only what Sedgewick had ordered him to do. But then Lisa wouldn't dare to say out loud what she must fantasize doing to the Chief of Security. Lisa believed Sedgewick hated her, personally and specifically, when the truth was that Sedgewick was barely aware of her existence. That order he'd given siccing Lamont on Lisa had, Elizabeth was sure, been an abstraction unvisualized by him. And at least half his purpose for ordering such punishment had been to make Zeldin react. "I promise you I'll tell you," Elizabeth said. "All the time we were in that cell I felt violent, Lisa. I wanted to take those shits out one by one and smash their ugly faces in. I know how you feel about this."

"No. You *can't* know. Not unless you've experienced it for yourself can you *possibly* know." Her hands clenched into fists; her face crumpled. Her sobs verged on hysteria.

Elizabeth folded her into a close hug. "Sssh, love, ssh, don't think about it; someday you'll avenge yourself and then it will all fade to nothing. Sssh, there, there, love…" Lisa, clinging tightly to her, dug her fingers into Elizabeth's arms. As Elizabeth stroked Lisa's back she tried to remember whether she had any tranqs in her tunic pouch. "You mustn't identify with prisoners, love," she murmured, thinking the admonition applied to herself as well. But for Lisa—it was easy to see why she was so upset. Not only did the experience of rape form a bond of identity, but the girl even had Lisa's name. At the time Sedgewick had ordered Lisa's rape Elizabeth had warned him he was making a mistake, had tried to make him see that if executive women were for any reason vulnerable to sexual abuse, their identification of themselves as executives might falter in the face of being forced to perceive themselves as being like sub-exec females in their vulnerability and victimization. Sedgewick had of course not bothered to listen.

Elizabeth eased Lisa into the desk chair and rummaged in her tunic pouch. "Here, love, take one of these," she said when she found an oblong foil-wrapped tab in her pouch. "It's only a relaxant, nothing strong. Otherwise you'll never make it through dinner."

Lisa fumbled with the foil wrapping and put the tab on her tongue to dissolve. "Oh shit," she said, staring at her hands. "I can see it now: every time I read one of Krebs's reports I'll think of those pigs in that place. And *Krebs*." She shuddered. "To think I'll have to deal with him after having seen him like *that*." Her mouth scrunched up. "It's so disgusting, Elizabeth." She looked up at Elizabeth. "So abominably disgusting."

Elizabeth nodded. "I deal with disgusting characters too, and they're not all sub-execs, either." Like Wedgewood. God how she loathed Wedgewood. But they couldn't do without him. If it weren't Wedgewood it would be somebody else like him.

"That boy, Robertson," Lisa said. Elizabeth raised her eyebrows. "He's from Wilton. It's imprinted on his every gesture and facial expression. They all hold their bodies alike. It stands out a mile."

Elizabeth glanced at her watch. "I hope he and Hopkins make it back before dinner. If they do, I might reasonably be able to get out of dining with Leland—we could leave the three males together and go somewhere by ourselves." Better not to risk Lisa's blurting something at dinner; she could dine with Leland and cement her relations with him another time.

"Oh, dinner," Lisa said, depressed. "I don't even want to think about it. Sometimes Krebs stays on, too."

"Surely not with so many executives present?" Elizabeth said, frowning.

"Oh, Leland doesn't care about such things. He's much more comfortable with Krebs than with people like Hopkins or Robertson. Or you, for that matter." Lisa smiled bitterly. "He finds you, dear, a sore trial indeed."

"More than he would Sedgewick?"

Lisa laughed. "Far more. After all, he and Sedgewick share a background of field experience in Europe. Not to mention later-than-usual fixing. Though Leland is in a category all his own there, still Sedgewick is enough of an anomaly, partly because of that thing he used to have for Zeldin. Leland really sympathized with it, I can tell you."

The tranq had obviously begun taking effect—either that or the calm quiet of the room and its lack of males had soothed Lisa's agitation. "Let me sit down at the desk, love," Elizabeth said, smiling. "I need to get through to Central."

Lisa got up from the chair and moved lethargically to the window seat, and Elizabeth replaced her at the console. Quickly she tapped in her access code and requested a satellite link for scrambled com. Her request elicited an error message. Elizabeth started over, thinking there had been a glitch. When the error message appeared again, she requested specification of the error. It soon became apparent that she was unable to make a satellite link. Either something was wrong with the terminal or the satellite had malfunctioned or there was atmospheric interference—of which only sun-spot activity occurred to her as a possible source. Elizabeth picked up a station handset to call Central: she would have them check out the satellite. But all she could raise was a message saying that all long-distance circuits were temporarily down.

Elizabeth turned to Lisa. "I need something checked out with the local com relay," she said. "There are indications our primary com-satellite is malfunctioning. I can't seem to get through to Central either by com or by telephone. Will you run a check through the local ground station?"

Lisa got up from the window seat. She moved as though she were sleepwalking. "We shouldn't have been talking about that stuff in this room," she said. "It's not shielded. Any number of people could be picking us up."

"Oh christ, Lisa, save such trivialities for later. I've got a potentially serious com problem here, and I want to know what's going on."

"I'll take care of it from my office," Lisa said, tugging open the heavy wooden door. "I'll send Pat back in here. Maybe she can figure something out."

Elizabeth doubted it, though it was worth a try. Something fishy was going on, she could feel it in her bones. She intended finding out what it was, even if it meant staying an extra day. It was just too much of a coincidence that Barclay Madden had declared war on the Executive a few hours earlier. Who knew what sorts of resources Military might make available to him? Elizabeth shook her head. Even if it meant crippling the entire country? Would he go that far? Yes, Elizabeth decided, he would. He was one damned selfish bastard.

When Pat returned Elizabeth let her sit at the console to see what she could do. Elizabeth stared out at the ocean and listened to the tapping of the other woman's fingers on the keys. What a paradise this place was, even if it was surrounded by desert. She could stare out at the ocean forever...

But no, she belonged in DC. That was where the real power lay—as Barclay Madden would learn to his regret.

[iii]

By the time Hopkins and "Robertson" returned, Elizabeth had finished composing, encoding, and printing out in hard copy a long memo to Sedgewick. She had given orders for the chopper returning the pair to the station to be held, for she intended using Daniel as courier—presuming he could make it to the airport. The goddam x-factor again, Elizabeth thought as she sealed the memo in a purple stat envelope. With the satellite link down, there could be no instantaneous communication between here and Central, whether by voice or electronic file. She had had the encoded memo sent by low-frequency cable, but felt uncertain as to its having reached DC. *Had* the satellite malfunctioned? Or had there been deliberate sabotage of some sort? And if the latter, by whom, against whom, and how? It need not necessarily be directed at Security in particular, though Elizabeth tended to believe Security was the intended target. That being so, her real reason for sending Daniel was to get him out of there. If Barclay Madden had—with Military—started something, she wanted Daniel out of reach. Thank god for the double cryptonym she had forced on him. God knew he would make one hell of a hostage.

While the chopper waited, Elizabeth took Daniel into Lisa's office and gave him a sketchy briefing. "In short," she said, "we're getting no response from our primary com-satellite. Aggression may be involved. You'll carry my purple stat to your father and stay in DC until further notice from me. Your father will explain, should he think you need to know any of what is coming down. Clear?"

"Understood," he responded.

"You'll take all precautionary measures for your safety until you've reached Security Central. You will radio ahead for a chopper to be ready to transport you when you reach National."

He met her stare. "You think I need to be careful in DC?" She saw that he found her strictures absurd.

"I don't know what you should expect to find in DC. God knows Military could take DC if it wanted to."

He snorted. "You've got a bee in your bonnet about Military, haven't you."

She raised her eyebrows. "A bee in my bonnet? If you'd been even half-conscious during the Civil War you wouldn't assume such ignorant unconcern."

"The Military-connected people I know are all solid, decent men."

Wilton. *Christ.* "Just follow orders, Sedgewick. Now get out of here."

Watching him move to the door, she thought she could see what Lisa meant about Wilton posture, gesture, and gait. What did they do to so imprint a single identifiable stamp on them? Did they realize what they were doing? But of course they did...Elizabeth frowned. *They?* Whom did she mean?

This was no time to be speculating about such things. She was losing it: how many times that day had she drifted off into such abstractions? Wearily she closed her eyes and listened to the sound of the chopper receding until she could again hear the surf. For a minute or so she let the sound of the surf wash over her until, pulled by duty, she opened her eyes and checked the time. With one hour remaining before dinner, she might as well debrief Hopkins. No point now of that walk on the beach; she would only feel restless to get down to work and impotent at her lack of knowledge.

She picked up the internal phone and summoned Hopkins. Then she stood at the window and stared out at the sea. Though the shore curved in, blocking her view, she knew that perhaps a mile to the north lay Barclay Madden's house. In spite of the armoring of the compound—especially now that she had put the station on Full Alert—she felt vulnerable. With Barclay Madden to the north and perhaps a fifth of the country's navy stretching along most of the coast to the south all the way to the border, it was no wonder Lisa had described the station as embattled. In this seemingly paradisial location, they were, literally, surrounded.

Chapter Thirteen

[i]

"Disobedient dependence is often mistaken for rebellion against authority," Anna Blau said. "However, it would be more accurate to say that disobedient dependence is a rebellion *within* authority. That is, it allows the individual to accept the terms of the authority structure while seeming to flout the will of the authority figure. If the authority figure takes a strong enough line—never allowing the terms to be truly questioned—the individual rebelling not only need not face the uncomfortable fact that his or her weakness is acceding to authority, but also has the comfort of knowing someone else is in charge. The video we will see next depicts a typical situation of disobedient dependence. After we've viewed it we will use it to analyze how disobedient dependence works and will then explore various ways in which it ultimately leads to unsatisfactory, if not—as sometimes may be the case—catastrophic results."

The lights dimmed, and the enormous video screen above and behind the lecturer came alive. But though she found the lecture interesting, Martha had trouble concentrating. On entering the lecture hall she had been painfully self-conscious, fearing that the other students were staring at her and reviewing in their minds all that the *Examiner* had said about her. Most of them likely never read the *Examiner*. Or even paid much attention to any of the Zone's political discussions. Most people in the Zone, after all, just wanted to get on with their lives and only noticed the political scene when some issue touched directly on their daily existence. Martha knew that. Yet her morbid sensitivity on the subject prompted her to imagine that everywhere she went people were staring at her and repeating to themselves the scurrilous trash the *Examiner* had published. And when she recalled some of the things she'd read on some of the Freenet's message boards that she regularly cruised...

She deplored the egotism of her concern. It was the possible damage to the Co-op that mattered, not what people thought of her personally. Her mind should be on the week's activities focusing on the human rights situation—the demonstration on Saturday, for instance, and her trip to Paris, where she would be among a delegation that was to address the UN the next Monday. Though Martha would not be delivering the address, she would be making contact with UN diplomats outside the official session.

Martha paid as little attention to the discussion following the video as she had to the video itself. When Blau called on her with a direct question, she was unable to answer it. Embarrassed, she made an effort to tune in even as she doodled in her notebook. The hour fairly crawled by. She knew she should find the discussion of dependence on authority stimulating for the window it offered into understanding political behavior, but instead she found it merely depressing. It seemed that everyone was doomed to be imprinted from birth with the desire for safe dependency. Except that there was no such thing, not in reality. Worse, according to the social psychologists, people merely deceived themselves into thinking they were rebellious and defiant of authority and thus autonomous by adopting increasingly convoluted subterfuges through which self-respecting individuals attempted to maintain their self-esteem. As far as Martha could make out, the social psychologists contended that human beings were basically infantile, always had been, always would be. It would seem to make the human malaise inescapable.

At last the bell rang. Martha shoved her notebook into her briefcase, got up, and stretched. Yawning, she smiled at Verdell Whitefeather and asked her how she was doing.

Verdell smiled back. "I'm getting along all right. A little tired of the rain, but otherwise fine." She moved out into the aisle, and Martha followed. "I'm having a party tomorrow night," she said somewhat diffidently. "I know you must be awfully busy. But if you have the time and feel like meeting some of the characters I like to hang out with, stop by." Verdell brushed long brown strands of hair out of her eyes. "Anytime after eight."

It might be interesting to see what sort of people Verdell hung out with—she was such a different sort of person from anyone Martha knew. "I don't think I have your address," Martha said.

Verdell scribbled it on a scrap of paper, which she tucked into Martha's breast pocket. "Bring someone if you want," she said. "I gotta run, I have a math class in the Old Geology Building and we're having a test. Bye!" And Verdell did literally run out of Kane Hall, her stocky body moving with surprising speed and lightness. Spirits slightly lifted, Martha trudged through the rain to her two-seater, concentrating on what she would say at the brown-bag lunch at St. Mark's, in the talk she was giving on the subject of what they could do to most effectively address the human rights situation.

[ii]

"Yes, Sedgewick, yes," Elizabeth said into her handset as she rifled through the pile of stuff that had accumulated on her desk in her absence. "I agree, there's a great deal we need to discuss. But I need at least an hour to—"

"Don't argue with me, Weatherall. You were supposed to be back last night."

"As I say, with just an hour I'll be better prepared to tackle—"

"We don't have an hour, Weatherall. I tell you—"

Elizabeth bolted across the hall. The man must be getting senile. If something new had broken, why hadn't he said so at once, instead of blathering on? Elizabeth burst into his office and found him, incredibly, still talking into his handset. "Sedgewick, for godsake what is it? What's happened now?"

He looked at her and—frowning—put down the handset. "What do you mean, what's happened now?"

Elizabeth stared at him. "I thought you just said we didn't have an hour? Which to me implied some new crisis has whipped up?"

Sedgewick rose from his desk and walked around it. "Don't be ridiculous, Weatherall. I would have told you so straight out if that had been the case."

Elizabeth repressed the retort burning her tongue. "In that case," she said quietly, "I'll be back here in an hour." She stalked to the door.

"Get back here, Weatherall. Now." The tone of his voice stopped her cold. Slowly she pivoted and watched him move toward his favorite sofa and seat himself. "Sit down," he said.

Elizabeth sat stiffly in the armchair opposite him. She was damned if she was going to smooth this over. Let him try coming his high-handed crap with her: he'd soon learn what that would gain him.

"I'd hoped to have more time to discuss this with you. If you'd returned last night as planned, it would have worked out. As it is—" he shrugged. He waved his hand expansively. "Alexandra is due within the hour. I've sent my car and told Dixon to call me when they've left the airport. I want you at the main entrance, waiting for her. For a girl as sheltered as she's been, DC—much less this place—will be a shock. All the security downstairs will seem intimidating. She may remember you, I don't know. But what I'd intended to discuss was your mentoring her. The way you mentored Bennett. It seems the best—"

"Wait a minute, Sedgewick," Elizabeth said, shocked first at the animation in his face, and then by what he was saying. *This* was what he was so anxious about? When they had half a dozen major crises on their hands? And when the aliens had knocked out their most important satellite? "I will be happy to mentor Alexandra, if that's what you really want." The thought crossed her mind that if Sedgewick had any idea of where her mentoring of Allison had led, he wouldn't let her speak to Alexandra much less mentor her. "But I really think we can't afford to spend time discussing this now. We very much need to plot our strategy vis-à-vis the Executive for dealing with Barclay Madden. And furthermore, the aliens'—"

"Do you really think," he said, interrupting her, "that you need to be laying down priorities for me?" He steepled his fingers in the air before his chest, as if his elbows were resting on his desk. "Do you think this office cannot function in your absence, Weatherall? Am I to assume you imagine you are indispensable?" The light had gone out of his eyes, the excitement from his voice. He looked and sounded so much like his pre-Civil War self that for a moment she wondered if the old Sedgewick had miraculously reasserted itself.

Elizabeth dug her fingers into the arms of her chair. "Why would I be so deluded as to imagine any such thing, Sedgewick? I'm to assume, then, that you've decided to handle the Madden business and the Free Zone and aliens yourself?" Her voice trembled with rage. "In that case, I think I'll take a vacation. I haven't had one in ten years." Ridiculously close to tears, she rose and moved towards the door.

"I haven't dismissed you, Weatherall," he said as she put her hand on the doorknob.

Elizabeth hesitated, then opened the door and crossed to her office. Her head felt as though it would explode; fragments of her most-of-the-night talk with Lisa about fixed and unfixed males kept popping into her mind, fueling her anger. She began collecting all the personal items she had in the office. She had had enough. He could damned well do without her. He was crazy, that was all there was to it, maundering on like that about Alexandra when so many important things clamored for attention. And how weird, his excitement. She hadn't seen him that excited since he'd brought Zeldin back into the Company.

Her arms raised to remove her Atiyeh acrylic from the wall, Elizabeth froze. *Zeldin.* Had he somehow dreamed up a fantasy about Alexandra that would replace his obsession with Zeldin? But how? Alexandra was only a girl, fifteen, and his daughter to boot. Why in god's name was he so excited about her coming when he had barely acknowledged Daniel's existence the few times he'd seen him in the last three years?

Knuckles rapped on the door set into the back wall of her office. Elizabeth stiffened. It had to be Sedgewick. Jacquelyn never knocked, and Allison always came through the front door. Sedgewick had never once been inside this office—to her knowledge, anyway. Elizabeth debated ignoring him. But if he were determined to barge in he'd just go to Jacquelyn for the key. Or have Jacquelyn open it for him. Which would be mortifying. Gritting her teeth, Elizabeth stalked to the door, flipped open the locks, and flung the door wide—and then turned her back on him to return to the Atiyeh acrylic. Carefully she lifted it off its hanger and laid it on her conference table. She needed boxes and other packing materials, which meant she'd have to call Jacquelyn. And the Atiyeh at least should be properly crated, though she could, she supposed, carry it home in the car as it was, provided she personally saw to it.

"What the hell do you think you're doing, Weatherall?"

She didn't look at him but started taking her collection of vases out of the breakfront. "I'm packing, Sedgewick. I think that's apparent?" Better get packing materials before moving the vases around, she thought, and picked up the nearest handset. "I want enough boxes and packing materials to pack up the personal items in my office," she said to Jacquelyn. "Get them for me as soon as possible." She hung up before Jacquelyn could demand an explanation.

"If you think I'm going to stand for this, Weatherall, you're sorely mistaken." And Sedgewick stepped into her path as she moved toward her desk.

Elizabeth looked at him. One of the facial tics that occasionally afflicted him was twitching his eyelid, and the skin of his face had gone a sick, greasy white. He was flipping, all right. But this time she wasn't going to bail him out. It didn't matter to her now what mess things got into. It was none of her affair. "I'm through, Sedgewick. I've had enough." Exerting great control, she kept her voice steady. "I was willing to put up with your abuse for as long as you let me get things done. But I've had it. I don't care what happens now, to you or Security."

Sedgewick's mouth thinned into a hard, bleached line. "You still don't get it, Weatherall. I thought I'd made my point with you with Ambrose's appointment." His voice dropped to near inaudibility. "But apparently I did not, for you don't seem to realize that when I give you an order it must be obeyed."

I don't know how you can endure him, Elizabeth, day after day after day… Even before he sicced Lamont on me I dreaded his visits and found any contact with him more humiliating than anything else I can think of. He's never acknowledged me as a human being… Leland, at least, has some consideration and sensitivity and doesn't take such exorbitant pleasure in constantly humiliating others… As Elizabeth turned away from him and started toward the bookcases, he grabbed her arm and spun her around. Her reflexes took over, and her body slammed him back into the desk. Panting hard, holding her arms tight to her sides to keep from grabbing him, she said, "Don't you dare touch me again, boy, or I swear to god I'll break every damned rib in your diaphragm!"

He looked furious at her for talking to him that way, but did not push on that particular challenge. Instead he said, his voice actually rising, "Do you think you can just walk out of here without my say-so? All I have to do is pick up a handset. Think about that for a minute, my bitch, you who are so fond of dumping others in solitary. You think I couldn't do that to you?"

This was incredible! He was threatening *her*? The man was insane! "You have no legal ground for doing that," she said. Would the guards take his orders over hers? Everyone knew she ran this office. Would his authority—if it came down to an open challenge—prevail with Security? Would Wedgewood... Oh christ, Wedgewood. Wedgewood hated her guts. He'd be absolutely delighted to detain her. That those sheep would listen to this madman over her was indubitable.

"You don't think I couldn't find something, Weatherall? Besides which, who outside of Security would even notice or care to do something about it? We're all *en famille* here." Sneer of sneers.

Would he go through with his threat? He was desperate, desperate to keep her there. And too enraged to offer conciliation making it possible for her to stay. Elizabeth eased away from the desk and slowly backed toward her armchair, watching him in case he either picked up a handset or tried physically attacking her. (Who could predict what he might do next?)

Keeping her gaze fixed on him, she sank into her armchair. "What is it you think you want of me, Sedgewick? I've played every role you've required of me, without complaint, without prompting, even. But if you think you can continue getting that kind of effort by threatening me, you're wrong." His face did not change. *Shit.* She shouldn't have taken that tack. What she should do is play along with him and then, having properly lulled him, leave DC in the middle of the night. She could afford to charter a private plane. And she could pay the pilot enough to keep him out of DC for a few weeks, long enough to let the trail get cold. But no, she realized, what was she thinking? Sedgewick could freeze her credit at any time just by sitting down at a terminal and entering his access code. And how did she imagine she could live on the run from him with nothing in sight for her? How could she expect to work for someone else with him hounding her?

He advanced toward her until he stood only two feet from the armchair. "We'll discuss all this later, Weatherall. *Ad nauseam*, I imagine." The left side of his mouth tugged up in a half-smile. "I can see it in your face, you've already realized it was a mistake to challenge me." Elizabeth fantasized slamming her foot into his kneecap. He was out of his mind if he thought he could get away with treating her like this. For a moment she toyed with the idea of testing him—seeing if he would go through with putting her in solitary, and if he did, waiting him out. He needed her in the worst way, emotionally as well as for all the work she did in his name. Things would fall apart quickly, and he himself, bingeing, wouldn't be able to do without her... But there was a flaw in her reasoning, she immediately saw. If he knew that she would go if he didn't force her to stay, he'd be in just as much a mess: why then would he release her? Oh christ what should she do? *Play for time.* That's all she could think of—for the moment.

The phone buzzed. "Answer it, Weatherall," Sedgewick said. "And if it's Dixon, you'll go downstairs and wait there for Alexandra and accompany her up to my office."

Elizabeth got up from her chair and moved cautiously around Sedgewick. And what did he think a sheltered fifteen-year-old would make of the heavy vibes that would be oppressing the very air of that office? Nothing, probably. It was a wonder he'd even thought of how she'd react to the open display of security inside and outside the building.

[iii]

Pouring out coffee for herself and Sedgewick, Elizabeth wondered why he hadn't had them serve dinner in one of the smaller rooms, if not in his study. To use the formal dining room when things were already so strained and stilted between him and Alexandra could only deepen the girl's unease. And now to sit here in the formal drawing room, which Sedgewick normally used only for formal dinner parties before or after dinner proper... He usually understood such tactical factors.

Alexandra, sitting still and silent, sipped from a tall glass of mango juice and watched them manufacture conversation. Elizabeth knew what was coming next, though she'd tried to persuade Sedgewick to wait a few days before springing it on the girl. The entire damned day in tatters…not Alexandra's fault, of course, she had no idea Elizabeth didn't usually spend her day shopping and gallery- and museum-gawking. Elizabeth felt sorry for her. The girl had only a few vague memories of DC and almost none of Sedgewick. She was frightened of him. Certainly Sedgewick was a frightening enough presence for most people; but executive girls found most executive males frightening once they had passed the resentment phase, as Elizabeth judged Alexandra to have done. To be peremptorily summoned into such a radically different context must be a shock. Alexandra seemed to be taking it well, though, at least when she wasn't around Sedgewick. She had warmed to Elizabeth, her face growing livelier as the afternoon progressed. All day Elizabeth had been staring and staring at that face; its resemblance to Sedgewick's was uncanny: several times, when it had dropped into stillness, the resemblance had made shivers run down her back. In spite of the sharpness of her features—in Alexandra creating an impression almost of delicacy, especially given her long, thick eyelashes—and the clear replication of bone structure in her face, though anyone who saw her would immediately recognize Alexandra as Sedgewick's offspring (as one would be unlikely to do with Daniel), Elizabeth found her charming. She talked too much and too freely to someone she did not know (and therefore did not know she could trust), but that would pass, especially once Sedgewick had delivered some near-mortal blow of disillusionment (as Elizabeth had no doubt he shortly would).

And what had Felice or Felice's mother told Alexandra about Sedgewick? Probably enough—or so little—that Alexandra would be permanently cautious around him. Though she did seem to be trying, in her own awkward way, to warm Sedgewick to herself.

"Have you kept up with your study of the piano, Alexandra?" Elizabeth asked to draw her into the conversation.

Alexandra turned her head toward Elizabeth; her face came to life again. "Yes, Elizabeth, I have. Grandmother brought a very fine pianist to Barbados last year for me to study with—she said I'd outgrown my old teacher and that I needed someone more sophisticated."

Elizabeth smiled and nodded at Alexandra but glanced out of the corner of her eye at Sedgewick, checking for a reaction to Alexandra's slip. The girl didn't quite understand yet about what she could and could not say before males. Knowing Sedgewick, he'd probably want Alexandra to call her "madam" or "Ms. Weatherall." Just to keep things "clear."

"Which are your favorite composers to play?" Sedgewick asked.

Alexandra turned to her father. "A little Chopin, some Bach, quite a lot of Mozart, but best of all Beethoven." Her golden brown eyes sparkled.

The answer apparently pleased Sedgewick, for he smiled at her. Really, his smiles were ghastly—he'd do better not to smile at all. "Beethoven, eh? Will you do us the honors?"

Oh lord. Damn, damn, damn. Well at least she hadn't mention Brahms...

Alexandra rose from her chair and went to the piano in the corner. She didn't raise the lid...probably there was some rule about that at Grandmother's?

Alexandra began playing the Bagatelles, and Elizabeth leaned back and closed her eyes. She'd expected the girl's playing to be erratic, stormy, and characterized by too much pedal. Why was a fifteen year-old playing with such restraint? No, she wouldn't speculate about that, at least not now... Instead, think about Hazel. The background investigation for Hazel's security clearance had come through while she was away. Which left the loquazene examination, but Elizabeth could have that waived. If she were to stay in the office—and it looked as though for now she would, at least until she'd plotted her escape—it would make life more bearable and would possibly be useful to have Hazel there. There only remained her wooing Hazel into leaving her job in the Justice Department. If, say, she could spend tomorrow night with her—though that wasn't clear, since so much work had piled up and god knew what Sedgewick might take into his head next—if she *could* have Hazel for the night, she could likely persuade her—in one way or another... But all that pressing work she hadn't been able to touch... Suppose she let everything slide and let things get more and more into a mess: what then? No, she couldn't do that. That kind of pressure would never force Sedgewick to straighten up; likely it would only make him crazier.

When Alexandra finished the suite, she closed the keyboard and returned to her chair. "Very nice, Alexandra. You've talent, that's clear." Sedgewick leaned forward and smiled again. "I think we'll have to make sure we keep your teacher on."

Alexandra looked puzzled, but said, "Thank you, Papa," in the demure manner she'd been using with him since her arrival.

"Tell me," Sedgewick said, re-crossing his legs. "When was the last time you saw your mother?"

Alexandra's face tensed into stillness. "Mama stayed a couple of weeks at Christmas," she said very low.

Sedgewick's mouth tightened. "You mean you haven't seen her for four months?"

Elizabeth's fists clenched under the folds of her tunic. Sedgewick hadn't seen his daughter for ten *years*. But he found it convenient to make a show of indignation to justify his breaking executive custom.

Alexandra swallowed. "She phones two or three times a week. Now that the war's over we'll be able to spend a lot more time together. We're going to spend this summer in Europe. Mama wants to show me so many things there. She—"

"I'm sorry, but I doubt that will happen," Sedgewick said, cutting off her rush of enthusiasm.

Alexandra's face went still again. Visibly, she waited. Such good executive training, Elizabeth thought: Eleanor Dunn had once again done the job to perfection.

"We may be able to work something out about Europe," Sedgewick said, as though he thought Alexandra's excitement had purely to do with travel-lust, "but I can't promise. I have something in mind for you for the summer, but everything depends on how you do in what's left of the term."

Oh christ, he was just going to let her puzzle it out for herself? No gentle lead-in, no would you please consider doing this, lovely daughter of mine, no, he wouldn't bother with anything like finesse. Not Sedgewick. Damn him, couldn't he see how this would hurt her?

Alexandra's head tilted slightly to one side: how in the hell had she learned *that* mannerism? Could mannerisms be inherited? Lucky she didn't have his hair, too: at least there were *some* differences. "I'm confused," she said.

This reply pleased Elizabeth for its directness and simplicity. Not a demand to be told what was going on, just a simple statement. Very nice, love.

"I've arranged for you to go to school at Crowder's," Sedgewick said. "It's in Vermont. It's the best school you could attend. It's time we thought of your education. You can't go on living such an unstructured existence at the back of beyond. It's time you were thinking of your future."

What crap. Sedgewick the Patriarch. Sedgewick the Suddenly Concerned Father. Alexandra, of course, didn't have such ironical epithets at hand for protection, guileless lamb to the slaughter that she was. "You want," she said, frowning, "you want to send me away to school? But Mama promised—"

"It's not your mother's place to promise," Sedgewick said, roughly cutting her off. He was annoyed, Elizabeth thought, because Alexandra had not lowered her eyes and murmured the "Yes, Papa" he obviously had thought he would be hearing. "I will decide what's best for you, and what I say will be will be."

All damned day he'd been making his cock in the barnyard dominance show. What had gotten into the man?

Alexandra was shaking her head. Elizabeth's heart sank. The girl was going to try to resist him, which could lead only to humiliation for her and embarrassment between them that Elizabeth had witnessed it. "I'm sorry, Papa, but I don't want to go away to school. My education is highly structured, you can talk to Grandmother about it, she'll explain to you. She says I'm fortunate to be learning so much more than girls learn at school. And there're my piano lessons, too. I would never be able to practice enough if I went away to school. If you would call Grandmother—"

"Enough, Alexandra," Sedgewick said. "I have no intention of discussing your education with your grandmother. As far as I'm concerned, it's none of her damned business. I don't want any argument from you. Weatherall will outfit you for the school and then take you up there and enroll you next Sunday. Clear?"

Alexandra was staring at him in utter frustration. Had no one ever refused to listen to her side of an argument before? Poor girl. "I'm sorry, Papa." She swallowed. "But I won't go."

Sedgewick's face tightened. He was clearly in no mood to have his decisions questioned, not even by a fifteen-year-old.

"Alexandra," Elizabeth said, trying to stave off disaster, "before you make up your mind why don't you and I discuss this together, woman-to-woman? You should at least look at the literature the school puts out for prospective students and their parents and consider it carefully. It's a very complicated sort of decision that shouldn't be rushed into lightly. You haven't seriously thought about it yet, so you're not really prepared to refuse, are you?"

Alexandra's brow furrowed. "But I know that I couldn't bear to leave Grandmother. I don't think you understand—"

"That's enough, Alexandra," Sedgewick said. "You'll go to your room now. I'll expect an apology at breakfast, as well as your word that you will do as I say about this."

Alexandra stood. Her eyes shimmered with tears; her lip trembled. "If you send me there I'll only run away," she said. "You can't make me stay there."

Elizabeth closed her eyes. My god. She had outright challenged him. They'd be lucky if he didn't start throwing things.

"If your grandmother hasn't taught you even the modicum of control, then it's high time you learned," Sedgewick said in his iciest voice. "You can stay in your room until you've met my conditions."

Conditions?

Alexandra walked with admirable poise to the door, opened it, went out, and closed it softly behind her. What more control could one ask for?

"You're a damned fool, Sedgewick, for so botching the job," Elizabeth said. "Consider the fact that she hadn't seen you for ten years—count them, Sedgewick, *ten years*—you're a total unknown quantity to her. Perhaps she's had daydreams all these years about what her father was like and how it would be when he finally did send for her. You had all that going for you, yet all you could think to do was to bash her over the head with the full weight of your parental authority. Nice going."

He rose, went to the bottle of cognac on the coffee tray, and poured himself a goodly amount. "I will not be challenged like that, especially not by a girl of fifteen, even if she is my daughter." He returned to his chair.

"Yes, she's your daughter, Sedgewick. I'd guess, just judging by the look of her, that she'll prove as goddam stubborn as you are. She has your jaw, you know."

He swallowed a large mouthful of cognac. "You'd better go up there and give her the facts of life, Weatherall. You can for openers explain to her that the grandmother routine will get her nowhere."

Elizabeth snorted. "So you can only see this as some contest? That girl hasn't been away from her grandmother in ten fucking years, Sedgewick. Doesn't that mean anything to you? Is it possible the significance of that fact escapes you?"

He glared at her. "That's exactly my point: the girl has to be gotten away from that influence. I don't want her turning out like Raines."

Elizabeth rolled her eyes. "We've been through this once already, Sedgewick. She's an executive girl. And that means—"

"Don't tell me what it means, Weatherall. It doesn't have to be that way."

Elizabeth took a deep breath. "All right. We'll argue in your terms. Let me add this to the pot: if you force Alexandra to attend that school without in some way bringing her to accept your decision, the minute she turns twenty-one you'll lose her. Period. You'll never see her again. Is that what you want?"

His face contorted, then suddenly smoothed out. "She won't turn her back on the money and power that is mine to give her."

Elizabeth smiled. "But you've forgotten one thing, Sedgewick. You've forgotten that Varley Raines—of whom the girl is fond, and who, I deduce from the things she's said to me, is extremely fond of her—Varley Raines has almost as much money to give her as you have. And Eleanor Dunn is not exactly a pauper. She'll go homing straight back to them, and that will be the end of that."

"I've had more than enough of your mouth today, Weatherall."

Elizabeth stared into his eyes. "Does that mean I'm terminated, Sedgewick?"

"We still have things to discuss, you and I, don't we," he said softly. "But first you'll go upstairs and tell the hard facts to my apparently naive daughter."

It was far preferable to have him babbling and sobbing drunk than like this, Elizabeth decided as she mounted the stairs to the second floor. What had brought it on? She couldn't remember seeing him quite like this before.

Elizabeth knocked on Alexandra's door. "Who is it?" Alexandra called through the door. She sounded as though she were crying.

"Elizabeth, dear. Please, may I come in?"

As Elizabeth opened the door, Alexandra turned to stand with her back to Elizabeth. Elizabeth, looking in the mirror, saw that the girl was indeed crying. She went to her and took her by the hand and led her to the bed. Then she sat down and pulled the girl into her lap. "It's hard, I know, dear," Elizabeth whispered, stroking Alexandra's soft chestnut hair—Felice's hair, she thought—"it's very hard being female, but everything will get better, you'll see." Because Sedgewick had been a mere abstraction in this girl's life, she hadn't yet had to learn this particular lesson, a lesson harder to learn at such a late age. Eleanor Dunn couldn't be blamed for that.

"Why does he hate me?" Alexandra choked out.

So strong was Elizabeth's identification with Alexandra that she had trouble keeping herself from tears, too. "He doesn't hate you, love. It's just that he hates being challenged. He's used to having his own way, you see."

"Don't let him send me there, Elizabeth, please can't you do something?"

"I don't think anything will change his mind now, not after you said you'd run away if he sent you there. That was too much for him, dear."

"Grandmother won't let him make me go there," Alexandra said, sitting up and rubbing the tears from her swollen eyes.

Elizabeth shifted Alexandra off her lap and went into the bathroom and wet a face cloth. "Here," she said, returning to the girl and handing her the wet cloth. "Wipe your face; it will make you feel better."

"Only going home will make me feel better," Alexandra said, dabbing the cloth against her blotchy face.

Home. If home meant Barbados, it would be a long time before Alexandra would see it—not if Elizabeth was reading Sedgewick correctly (and at the moment she entertained serious doubts about her ability to read him at all). This was probably one of what Sedgewick called "the hard facts." No, she couldn't tell Alexandra that, not now. Her first night away from home, and forbidden to leave this impersonal guest room...Elizabeth glanced around at the furnishings. He hadn't done anything—beyond ordering (presumably he and not Higgins had thought of it) flowers for the room. "Tell you what," Elizabeth said, rising to her feet. "I think a nice long soak in the tub would do you some good. You must be exhausted, sweetie. I know for a fact there's a Jacuzzi in your mother's suite, which is just down the hall." Elizabeth opened the armoire to look for a dressing gown. "Here," she said, pulling out a bright flowery silk. "Do you have soap and powder?"

"But he said I'm not to leave this room."

Elizabeth sighed. "As I recall he was always doing that to your brother when he was your age. But never mind, I'll tell him myself. I'm sure he won't begrudge you a bath." Elizabeth smiled. "Come on, no argument now," she said crisply. "Get your things together, and I'll take you there myself."

Alexandra jumped up and scurried around the room, visibly cheered. At the bath? Or at in some small way getting around Sedgewick? Elizabeth liked this sign of resilience: Sedgewick would not find it easy to grind this one down—if indeed that was his purpose. But at this point Elizabeth wondered if even Sedgewick knew what his "purpose" was, or if he had merely gone even further off the deep end. Helping Alexandra carry her things down the hall, Elizabeth shivered at the bone-deep chill stealing over her. She intended to look out for Alexandra, but she realized that she might have trouble looking out for herself now.

[iv]

When Elizabeth returned to the drawing room, she found it empty. The bottle of cognac was no longer on the tray: solid confirmation he had moved to the study.

Elizabeth leaned against the doorframe and strove to collect herself. She would have to humor him, have to try to get him out of his mood. The only thing with which to fight him that she could think of was too risky. She smiled bitterly, imagining saying, as though in warning, "I'd keep Zeldin's book out of Alexandra's line of vision, Sedgewick. I don't think it would help matters if she knew you'd raped her mother." But at this point she didn't know how he might react to such a thrust. Given his current state of rage, he might very well turn on her instead of plunging into depression. (What had happened to set him off like this? She would grill Jacquelyn the first chance she got. *Something* must have happened while she was gone; something tangible that would explain this *rage*.) Her impatience of manner and what she had said to him had never before angered him. On the contrary, that method of dealing with his obsession had become customary. She thought wryly of the advice she had once given Zeldin: don't challenge him, but don't let him see you're afraid, either. Well, she *was* afraid: in his current mood she wouldn't put it past him to carry out his threats.

Elizabeth drew a deep breath and headed for the study. She found him there in the near dark, stretched out on the sofa, drinking cognac, listening to Xenakis. When he perceived her presence, he switched it off and sat up.

"I told her to take a bath in Raines' suite," Elizabeth said. "I assured her you wouldn't consider that a violation of her house arrest."

He shot her a poisonous look. For using the facetious term "house arrest"? Or for having told Alexandra she could bathe? "I don't suppose you managed to persuade her to accept my conditions?"

"No," Elizabeth replied, "not yet." She went to the fireplace and rested her elbow on its rose marble mantelshelf. "But I don't think it should be too difficult, unless you persist in taking such a hard line with her." Sedgewick splashed more cognac into his snifter. "I don't think you understand what a shock your attitude is for her. As I said earlier, if you'd allowed for a short period of courtship you would have had her eating out of your hand. But apparently you don't care for establishing a rapport with her. Pawn that you seem to consider her."

"I'm thinking of her future, Weatherall. I've nothing to gain personally by sending her to Crowder's. And it's obvious that I'm the only one who *is* thinking of her future."

Elizabeth said nothing. Arguing with him about this would only make him more intransigent.

"Sit down, Weatherall."

Because of her height he never felt completely in control of her when she was on her feet. Usually she was careful not to stand too close to him, lest the five-inch difference become too palpable. But even when he was sitting and she was standing he sometimes manifested discomfort. It seemed to her now, as she seated herself in one of the massive chairs flanking the fireplace, that he was always ordering her to sit down.

"Clearly it's time we had some clarification, Weatherall," he said. "You seem to think you need answer to no one but yourself." Elizabeth raised an eyebrow, but said nothing. "You took it upon yourself to extend your stay in San Diego, though I explicitly ordered your return in the cable I sent you."

Was that what he was so upset about? But why? What difference could fifteen hours make? "I felt it was necessary that I stay because I assumed Barclay Madden had something to do with our com problems," Elizabeth said. "And by the time I discovered the aliens had caused the problem, it was after midnight—the middle of the night on the East coast, Sedgewick. Naturally I would have gotten your okay for the extension if com had been available—I would have phoned, for godsake. But my inability to do so was precisely the reason I felt I should stay."

"You disobeyed orders, Weatherall." His voice was implacable. "I was prepared to overlook it but your subsequent behavior and attitude when you finally *did* get back made it clear that my orders no longer carry much weight with you."

Elizabeth frowned. Was it a matter of his thinking she was ignoring his dominance? What was it that was going on here? "I only disregard orders when special circumstances persuade me—"

"You're not going to wriggle out of it this time, my bitch." He looked angry, so damned stubbornly angry; she could *feel* the edge of his implacability: there would be no maneuvering him tonight, nor any possibility of reasoning with him. He rose and moved to the fireplace. Staring down at her, he said, "There will be changes. You will report to me daily on the two projects I've assigned you to." God knows she had tried doing that already: but previously he'd wanted nothing of it. "Both orally and in writing. You'll clear every use of the signature stamp with me before you use it. No, better still, you'll return the stamp to me. I don't know if you can be trusted, Weatherall."

Flabbergasted, she craned her neck to stare up at him. He'd entrusted her with the signature stamp a little more than a year after she'd begun working for him. Most PAs routinely used the stamps without any clearance whatsoever from their bosses. What in god's name could be going through the man's head? "You're willing to deal with the most minute details now?" she queried.

"Don't question me, Weatherall. Just do as I say."

No, she wouldn't question him, since ten-to-one he'd take any question as a challenge. "I don't understand what I've done to earn your distrust, Sedgewick," she said, carefully phrasing her question as a statement.

"You've disobeyed my explicit orders just one too many times, Weatherall. And how could I possibly trust someone capable of walking out on me whenever she pleases?" He shook his head. "That's something I won't easily forget, I can assure you."

Her neck was beginning to hurt from staring up at him. "In the interests of further clarification, which you say we are about," Elizabeth said softly, "you will please explain to me exactly what you want of me. I don't have a clear picture of the changes you have in mind. Am I to assume Lennox will become redundant, that you will be taking over running these special projects yourself? At any rate, if I'm to be spending my time taking Alexandra shopping and so on, I don't see how I can possibly manage these projects as well...I'm confused, Sedgewick, as to what it is you expect of me."

He moved close to the arm of her chair, so close his tunic brushed against it. Elizabeth's throat tightened. He knew she couldn't tolerate physical proximity, he knew very well that such proximity was acceptable to her only when he was in his worst depressions, and then only when she initiated it. He stared down at her for several long seconds. Deliberately, he took her braid in his hand, something he had never done before. Elizabeth struggled against the surge of adrenalin that pumped into her blood. At any other time in the past she would have grabbed his wrist and done him physical damage—a thing she knew he had always understood perfectly. Yet now she hesitated, fearing that if she attacked him he'd retaliate by siccing his gorillas on her. One of which was Lamont. She swallowed. Acutely aware of her current powerlessness to control him, she could not help thinking that what he had done to Felice and Lisa he could do to her. "What I expect of you, Weatherall, is the perfect obedience of the perfect tool. You usually know to the nth degree exactly what I want, exactly how I would read a given situation. The next time you disobey my orders—" he gave her braid a yank—"you will surely regret it. Clear?"

Elizabeth dropped her gaze. "Understood," she said, wanting only to get it over with so that she could get away from him.

He relinquished her braid and returned to the sofa to pour himself more cognac. And suddenly she knew he had grabbed her braid to punish her for the shove and for calling him "boy"—and to show her she didn't dare "break every rib in his diaphragm" as she had threatened to do if he touched her.

Elizabeth rose to her feet.

"Where do you think *you're* going?" He spoke in his most grating tone of voice.

Elizabeth paused en route to the desk. "To the phone. To ask them to bring me some juice."

"A good idea. We have a lot of talking to do about Alexandra."

Fuck. So he would make her stay with him until he was ready to pass out. She would not be going back to the office tonight, that much was clear. She'd gotten nothing done today, nothing at all. And he was so crazy that it didn't matter to him that that was the case.

Elizabeth resigned herself to a long, tedious night.

Chapter Fourteen

[i]

The longer she mused on one of the apparently minor points in Gladstone's report on Barclay Madden, the more convinced Elizabeth became of its importance. With her usual intuitive flair, Gladstone had noticed that of Madden's people, two-thirds of the (male) executives at the VP level and above were under the age of thirty. In most corporations, males in their fifties or older predominated at the VP level. Because of the age-skewing brought on by longevity treatments, such positions tended not to be vacated until the individual in question either transferred to another corporation (usually taking a lateral slot) or retired. There was little upward mobility these days except in new, maverick corporations—such as Barclay Madden's.

An image of herself and Emily seated with males flaunting their abs and pecs at the lunch table, among them Madden himself, haunted her.

After lengthy consideration, Elizabeth reached the conclusion that the youthfulness of Madden's high-level execs was no accident. Somehow Madden had seen this demographic problem and figured out a way to exploit it. She had no doubt that under the circumstances, his young male executives tended to develop a fierce personal loyalty to him, as well as resent the lack of immediate access to the highest executive positions in the rest of the executive world. In fact, now that she thought of it, because of this age-skewing problem, many professionals had been ousted from mid-level managerial positions to make jobs for young male executives. Though both wars had exacted a toll on the executive population (especially youths), so had they exacted a toll on the corporations, even taking into account the proliferation of war industries. There had been occasional talk from time to time in the Executive about finding new ways of using executive talent.

Somehow Madden, seeing all this, had used it in his empire-building. Clever man, Barclay Madden.

But she kept coming back to the image of those men wearing casual clothes with their shirts unbuttoned at a business lunch. It struck her as highly significant that he and his minions had chosen to dress and comport themselves outside executive standard. Not to insult her (and by extension, the Executive), for they had shown no self-consciousness about baring their chests. No, she thought, this was their standard style of dress. Madden, it seemed, was inventing his own cultural style and mores. Could there be any clearer indication of the consciousness of Madden's empire-building?

Elizabeth put her handset to her ear. "Jacquelyn, make an appointment for me with Sharon Gladstone, will you? For this afternoon, if possible."

"I was just going to call you. Sedgewick wants you."

"All right, Jacq, thanks." Elizabeth slipped her handset back into her tunic pocket. Jacquelyn had said nothing to her about the canceled order for the packing materials, nor had either of them mentioned the change in atmosphere in the office. But they'd taken to speaking carefully and neutrally to one another—while their eyes questioned and commented.

Elizabeth tucked her NoteMaster into a tunic pocket and crossed the hall to his office. Time for more pretend, she told herself. When she had earlier handed him several reports along with the signature stamp, he had acted as though he had never personally lost control of Security, as though there had never been a time when he had refused to make decisions or assume responsibility.

Elizabeth found him seated at the head of the conference table, a yellow pad under his hand and files strewn all around him. An unusual enough sight, she thought bitterly. "Sit over here, Weatherall," he said, gesturing to the chair on his right. Though Elizabeth always sat on the left with her back to the window, she decided she had better take him literally, in case it mattered to him which seat she occupied and he took her contrary choice of seat as a gesture of defiance. He slid his reading glasses down his nose and peered over their rims at her. "I've been studying your proposal for elections and have decided I'll bring up the subject to Goodwin. If he's interested, *and* if he's willing to include Security in the project, we'll take it to the Executive. I'm not prepared to trust Com & Tran to handle it on their own, however. It's far too risky a proposition for that. Perhaps Bennett could work this into her project."

Elizabeth chose her words carefully. "But everything has changed now, hasn't it, since we don't have vid?" Much less simple things like long-distance phone service and electronic data transmission.

"We'll be launching a replacement for that satellite within the next month, Weatherall. There's no need for concern on that account."

Elizabeth licked her lips. "Does that mean you're going to deal with the aliens? Meet their demands, I mean?" Unless they met the aliens' demands, the aliens would destroy the replacement satellite. They always carried out their threats.

He gave her a sharp look. "That depends on what you mean by 'deal with.'"

"They've warned us that if we continue to harass people going into the Greek, Dutch, and Austrian embassies and consulates they'll start 'destructuring' our industries as they did ten years ago," Elizabeth said.

Sedgewick removed his glasses. "I want you to go to the Free Zone," he said. Elizabeth gaped at him. "We need to convince them that we're investigating their charges. You'll demand to interview the people who say they've been tortured. And if you think the charges can be substantiated, you'll find out where these people were being kept and who is implicated. We need their names and US addresses. You'll see to it that the Free Zone people think that we can't do anything unless we have such leads."

"Why me?" Elizabeth asked. "I have so much to do here. And I'm not a PR expert. It would be better if—" Elizabeth halted: she had been about to say that Allison would make a better choice, but she could not imagine Allison interviewing torture victims. Moreover, Allison's obvious physical revulsion to sub-execs would offend those Free Zone bitches who would be involved in any negotiation undertaken. But surely Baldridge could come up with someone suitable…

"We need someone absolutely trustworthy," Sedgewick said.

Trustworthy? After he'd ranted and raved at her last night about never trusting her again?

"You're so thickheaded," Sedgewick said, "that they wouldn't have a chance at converting you, or whatever it was they did to Zeldin." He smiled at her. "And you have very deep interests here. Like the house I'm giving you."

"Look, if what they say is true and there are verifiable human rights abuses, what do I say to them then?"

Up went his damned eyebrows. "That's easy, Weatherall. I'm surprised you don't see it for yourself. You'll lay responsibility at Military's door. And then we draw the issue into the election project. It's really quite beautifully simple: we'll not only get the aliens off our backs, but we'll get Military so entangled in its own tentacles that it won't be able to move for fear of strangling itself."

Elizabeth frowned. "But what if some of our people are implicated, too?"

His mouth twitched, as though he found something humorous in her question. "You've found the detention centers you've so far had investigated clean. You said in your report you saw nothing suggesting torture went on in the places you personally inspected."

Elizabeth had not reported all her thoughts and impressions about those places: namely about her belief that certain things probably did go on in them—though she had no proof that they did—that might conceivably be interpreted as human rights abuses... She had the nagging sense that she should have dug farther, that she should have insisted on interviewing prisoners more extensively, even if it had required clearing their systems of the drugs. But supposing she had, would they have told her, knowing themselves vulnerable to retaliation afterwards? What was required, of course, were medical examinations... But it hadn't occurred to her to take a physician with her on her tours... It might be argued that she hadn't wanted to find anything at those places... Should she now revise her orders to Hopkins and the other investigators so that physicians would be included on the investigative teams?

The drugs were another thing she hadn't informed Sedgewick of: neither about their routine administration nor the real reason behind the use of the drugs, which she had ferreted out of the pertinent budgets and expense vouchers. She held the proverbial smoking gun in her hand, having found the name of the drug company holding the contract for the drugs and having discovered that Chase Ambrose's father owned thirty-five percent of the company's stock. The connection had become clear and obvious, especially when she'd checked the dates of stock purchase with the dates of Stevens' directive. But she had no intention of handing such information to Sedgewick, for she needed all the clout now that she could muster on her own. Though such setups were often winked at, given the increasing precariousness of Ambrose's situation, he would know he couldn't afford the extra bit of heat such a revelation would generate.

"By the way, Weatherall, what is this thing here that you're asking me to authorize?" He held up a flimsy of a memo to Lauder's team instructing Hughes to go ahead with his exposé of the Co-op bitch who ran the Night Patrol, one of the many pieces of paper requiring the signature stamp that Elizabeth ordinarily would not bother to show Sedgewick. Elizabeth explained the plan, then added, "It will severely damage their credibility, I think, since some of their own people are murdering these men without bothering with a trial. It's terrorism directed at men as a group. Apparently they even kill men when they are alleged to have raped their wives."

"I'm quite familiar with the Night Patrol's activities," Sedgewick said curtly, initialing the flimsy. "When exactly will this scandal hit the streets?"

"If Lauder gets the cable today, it'll hit tomorrow afternoon. Though it might blow Hughes's cover with Greenglass, it's a risk worth taking."

"Well if it hits tomorrow, there's no sense in your going out there yet. We'll wait until next week and see what kind of an effect the exposé has. Besides, we should have more information to go on by early next week, correct?"

"I expect so," Elizabeth said, thinking that by then this fit of his might have passed.

Sedgewick pushed his chair back and rose. "Another thing," he said, moving out of Elizabeth's line of vision. "I want you to put Daniel on Bennett's team to work particularly on the election project."

Allison handling Daniel? He'd have her in hysterics by the end of his first week with her. "Very well," Elizabeth said tonelessly. "What decision have you come to about pressuring Madden?" she asked, to get him off the subject of his damned offspring.

"Decision?" She felt him behind her. Not again. She should not have let pass his touching her. Thinking about it before going to sleep, she had seen that she had been wrong to back down before the risk of his retaliation. By allowing it to pass she'd let him open the door to god knew what. And the cardinal rule among executive women had always been to punish swiftly any incursion on physical privacy. If Felice and Lisa had reacted as they should have, Sedgewick probably would not have touched her last night. Well, she would allow it no more. If she had to put up with being beaten and raped and dumped into solitary, that was too bad. No matter how long it took, he would learn, perhaps painfully, that he could never get her to submit this way... But there stuck in her mind, echoing and re-echoing, the fantasy he had spun aloud to her last night when he'd reached the bottom of the cognac bottle. *We could make it an experiment, Weatherall. To see if you're stronger than Zeldin. I myself would never have thought of your technique, but it's all down on flimsy, all I'd have to do would be to follow your script... How long do you think you'd last chained to Zeldin's platform, Weatherall? Shall we try it and see?* Her only response had been to ask him why he was doing this, why he was so angry at her. But no answer had been forthcoming...just his godawful shrieking laugh and his assertion that he, Sedgewick, did not need a reason for anything he did.

"I wasn't aware that I had a decision to make," Sedgewick said, leaning into her chair.

She could not tell if he was touching her braid. She strove to concentrate on Madden. "Whether you'll bring the sanctions up at an Executive meeting, or whether you'll get them in place minus Whitney," Elizabeth said, holding her voice carefully level.

His hands came down on her shoulders. Now was the time for her to do something. But she was at a disadvantage, trapped by the arms of her chair. She'd have to shove away from the table with enough force to send him reeling backwards.

Elizabeth put her fingers on the top of the table near the edge, pressed her thumbs into the underside of the table, and prepared to shove backwards. *One, two*—Sedgewick's phone buzzed. Sedgewick lifted his hands from her shoulders and returned to his chair. "Answer that, Weatherall," he said, staring out the window.

Sweating, her pulse racing, Elizabeth rose from the table with no real sense of relief. There would be another time, she knew. The inevitable was only postponed. She picked up the handset that had somehow drifted down to the other end of the table. "Yes, Lennox."

"Ambrose is making a nuisance of himself, Elizabeth. I've told him about eight times already this morning that you're in conference. Is there something I can arrange with him, or some message I can give him that would get him off my back?"

Elizabeth glanced over at Sedgewick. "Hold on a minute," she said, and put Jacq on hold. "Since you're controlling the Free Zone project personally now, Sedgewick," Elizabeth said, "perhaps you would take Ambrose's calls?"

"Cut the crap, Weatherall."

Elizabeth got Jacq back on the line. "Tell him I don't want to see him or hear from him for at least forty-eight hours. And then tell the girl—I presume she's screening your calls? —that you won't accept any calls from him at all unless they're priority one in nature." Elizabeth returned to her chair and picked up her pen.

"You'll have to at least talk with him, Weatherall, if not see him," Sedgewick said. "You can't treat him that way."

"Oh no?" she asked coolly. "He's your boy, not mine. You can worry about him if you want to. I'm not concerning myself with such trifles when I also have to worry about your children, Barclay Madden, representing the Executive in the Free Zone, and anything else you feel like dumping on me."

No more would she watch out for Sedgewick's interests: his and her interests had diverged. She would concentrate on getting people of her own into places where she could use them—Hazel would be a start—and concern herself with keeping them loyal and partisan. She would no longer involve herself with matters pertaining to either Sedgewick's or Security's survival. If he gave her an explicit order, she would obey it. But no more volunteerism—as he would soon see. If he didn't give her explicit instructions about Barclay Madden, then the whole thing would slide. She would no longer take the initiative in saving his ass. If he wanted an enemy, he had one. And as for this afternoon's Executive meeting—she would sit silent, she would not prompt him, she would let him flounder in his own incompetence. He would soon see how well he did without her active good will.

"Yes, I realize how greatly you loathe and detest Ambrose," Sedgewick was saying, "but nevertheless when we're done here you'll get him on the phone and see what he wants. There's no point in alienating him. As Deputy Chief one must pay a certain amount of respect to him."

What bullshit!

"Did you hear what I said, Weatherall?"

"Yes, Sedgewick. I'm to call Ambrose. And then what? Oh so sorry but Mr. Sedgewick simply doesn't have time to fit you in. I'm sure that will soothe his troubled spirit quite miraculously."

"Do you have any idea, Weatherall, of how bored I am with your sarcasm?"

"I'm so very sorry you find me boring, Sedgewick."

"More sarcasm, Weatherall?"

Elizabeth lowered her gaze. How had she so lost control of him? Over and over and over she had been asking herself this question, and still she had not even a glimmer of an answer. It couldn't be anything she had done or said. It had to have been something that had happened during her trip to San Diego.

"As for the Madden situation…the obvious thing to do is to have a dinner party. I'm surprised you didn't think of this yourself, Weatherall."

But she *had* thought of it. "Shall I contact Raines?" she queried. Considering how long he'd been in DC and the fact that he apparently intended to remain here—permanently? —it was high time Felice was made to take up *her* responsibilities again.

"Whyever would I want you to contact Raines?"

Elizabeth stretched her fingers over the surface of the table and pressed her palms flat against the smooth, cool mahogany. "To handle your dinner parties—this one and all future ones."

Sedgewick got up from his chair again. He was so fidgety today. "You can handle all that, Weatherall," he said, staring out the window with his back to her. "I don't want Raines here, especially not while Alexandra is in the house."

Hold on to your temper, Lizzie, Elizabeth warned herself. Losing it won't help you get him under control. Don't fall into the trap of believing it will. "At this rate, Sedgewick," Elizabeth said, trying to make her voice light and humorous, "I'll soon find myself breeding. What other little responsibilities of the sort do you have in mind for me?"

He turned to face her, but with the light to his back she could see only his silhouette, not the expression on his face, nor his eyes, only the way he shoved his fists into his tunic pockets and canted his hips forward. So. He thought she was challenging him. Well, she was. So what could he do about it—apart from getting increasingly angry and frustrated at his inability to control her as totally as he apparently wished to do? He couldn't terminate her—though at this point she would be delighted (if later sorry) to have him do so. He couldn't visit violence on her—unless he wanted an escalation the end of which no one could guess. And for such small jabs he wouldn't throw her into detention since he would stand to lose a great deal—and immediately, too—from such an action.

"That might not be a bad idea." Sedgewick drawled the words.

Of all the things he might say, this response she hadn't conceived of. "The point is I don't have time to perform these homely little tasks for you," Elizabeth said, barely able to keep her voice even. "Raines does these things to perfection. You still have a contract with her. The obvious thing to do is to call her back to DC."

"Use Higgins and Lennox for all the drudgery. All I ask of you is your supervision, and of course your directing presence during the dinner parties themselves. Besides," he added casually, "it will be useful for me to have you on the spot when the discussion of pressuring Madden comes up." Hah. He might change his mind about that after this afternoon's Executive meeting.

"You will provide the guest lists?" Elizabeth asked, tapping into her NoteMaster *arrange dinner parties for Sedgewick re Madden*.

"Can't you manage to do that yourself?" Sedgewick asked irritably—as though he always had to do everything himself.

Elizabeth stared at the marks of her hands smudging the high-gloss surface of the table. She shrugged. "It will take me several hours

poking around in our database just to figure out who it would be useful to ask. And even then I won't know the personalities involved."

"Just do it, Weatherall."

"Yessir Mr. Sedgewick."

He stood very still, probably staring at her, though because she
faced the light she could not see enough of his face to know for sure.
This is war, Sedgewick, she thought. You have no idea what you've gotten yourself into. But you will, my boy. And then we'll see, won't we.

[ii]

Checking her watch every five minutes, thinking constantly about
what she herself must do, Celia paced the length of the terrace, from the
bougainvillea to the bird of paradise and back, over and over again.

When at last Emily arrived, Celia, halting, fixed her gaze on
Emily's face—and could not speak. "I'm sorry it took me so long,"
Emily said. "But it turned out that it was ODS that made the busts.
And my connections with them are not quite as cordial. But I did
manage to get a commitment to release your mother." Emily paused.
"About your uncle…"

Celia held her breath. "What is it? Emily, please *tell* me. I need
to know!"

Emily chewed on her lip. "I'm afraid his situation is not so clear.
The woman I talked to said that the entire group of doctors had been
arrested during the demonstration precisely because, being doctors,
their presence was so obtrusive. But it seems they matched your uncle
with a photo taken two days ago of a man coming out of the Austrian
consulate in LA. And…" Emily's voice trailed off.

"Have they sent him to a detention center?" Celia whispered the
words because her throat had closed up.

"That at least I was able to find out," Emily said. "He's at a place
in El Cajon. What we need now is a lawyer who can secure an order
for visitation and try to force ODS to bring charges."

Celia knew she had to get a grip; she swallowed and cleared her
throat. "It's something to work with," she said. She put her hands to
her cheeks, which were cool beneath their sheen of perspiration. "I
have to go home now," she said. "There's too much for me to do to sit
around here feeling sorry for myself. Luis was right—my services are

in demand." Her eyes filled with tears. "Any attorneys willing and able to go into court will be overloaded. I can take some of the prep work off their shoulders."

Emily took two steps toward her, then stopped. "Are you sure you're ready?" she said. "It's important that you not get tangled up in guilt, Celia. I know, because I—"

"None of that's important," Celia said, brushing Emily's words aside.

"If any individual's feelings aren't important, then I'd like to know how it is you think human rights matter," Emily said. "You can't separate these things. If you don't consider your own experiences of account, then how can you take others' experiences seriously?"

"I'm all packed." Celia turned to go into the house. "If you could drive me home now, maybe I could be there when my mother gets out."

"All right," Emily said, sounding resigned. "Go get your things and I'll meet you at the car."

Celia went up to her room one last time and stared out at the calmly rolling ocean, so powerful, so strong, so peaceful. "Goodbye, ocean" she whispered, fighting the tears threatening to spill over. She picked up her suitcase, glanced around the little room, and left without another look backward. *Back to reality, Celia.* The house and the ocean were a fantasy; they never had felt *real.* Mama and Luis busted, *that* felt real. Unreal real.

Celia went down the stairs and out the front door. Emily was already waiting in the car. She remembered then that she hadn't thanked Emily for again helping her. Her debt of gratitude, she thought, just grew and grew and grew.

Goodbye, beach house. Goodbye, ocean. Hello, reality.

Yeah.

[iii]

Elizabeth listened to the silence expand and fairly resonate through the room as everyone present waited for Sedgewick to answer the question. When she failed to scribble him a note or whisper in his ear, Sedgewick said, "Do you have the numbers on that for me, Weatherall?"

But Elizabeth did not, for she hadn't read any of the reports that had poured in following the mass of arrests breaking up demonstrations in twenty-three cities. Sedgewick hadn't instructed her to read the reports, so she hadn't. Instead she'd dumped them into his in-basket. "Sorry, Mr. Sedgewick," she said.

Sedgewick did his damnedest to bluff his way through his colleagues' questions. They all must see that he hadn't been briefed, that he hadn't a clue as to what his own ODS had been doing. Elizabeth concentrated on Hill's gathered tunic cuff. That was a new style, too—big full sleeves that fell in folds from the shoulders, gathered and tightly cuffed with exaggeratedly wide bands of fabric into which had been sewn all sorts of intriguing bits of bric-a-brac. So they were picking up some of the styles from pre-Blanket days and doing new things with them. Other people than herself must be sick to death of military themes...

She'd tried calling Alexandra—worrying over how the girl was taking her forced isolation—but found that Sedgewick had given orders that Alexandra was to be allowed no phone access whatsoever. When she'd suggested to Sedgewick that her keeping contact with Alexandra would work to good effect, he'd merely said she could visit Alexandra if she wanted to communicate with her. When she had asked him if he'd talked with Alexandra at all that day, he'd said it was up to Alexandra to come to him with an apology and submission.

Elizabeth wondered if Sedgewick intended introducing into the meeting his plan to have her go to the Free Zone. It occurred to her that if he waited much longer they might refuse to allow her to represent them on the grounds of her being so ill-informed and of Security being in chaos and out of Sedgewick's control. Already Booth was giving her searching looks—as though he knew something was afoot and did not like it. Elizabeth hardly listened to Sedgewick as he droned on about controlling the damage and how an election would take the masses' minds off the mess the Free Zone was stirring up and how a scandal would shortly be breaking in the Free Zone that would strain the Free Zone's leaders' credibility... Would Booth, once he had figured out she was no longer in control, get rid of Sedgewick? Though they might be tempted to make Ambrose Acting Chief, Elizabeth doubted they would. They didn't know Ambrose from

Adam. And although Ambrose had great connections, they weren't Cabinet-level. No, they'd choose someone from their own little circle. Maybe somebody's son or cousin, the way they had when it had come to filling all the positions in the Executive that had fallen vacant right after the Blanket.

The discussion shifted to Goodwin, whose Com & Tran would along with Security be managing the elections. Elizabeth observed how careful they were not to refer to the Military-Security split or to the possibility that the election could become an occasion for Military-bashing. Naturally Whitney opposed it, saying that it was up to Security and State to scotch the human rights scandal threatening US foreign relations and international hegemony. Hegemony! Only Military would claim American hegemony in the world. American hegemony vanished well before the Executive Transformation. Military people were positive diehard dinosaurs, refusing to face reality and go on from there.

At last the meeting broke up, and Elizabeth was able to return to her office. Sedgewick, however, had to stay to engage in social chit-chat, for Booth clapped his hand on Sedgewick's shoulder and steered him with the rest of his contingent to the suite of rooms reserved solely for the use of the Executive. Finally, finally, she would be able to call Hazel. She would get away from the office early, go home, and start preparations for the dinner she would give her. She would listen to music and forget everything but the food and the girl. Sedgewick would be trapped with Booth for at least the remainder of the afternoon, if not into the evening, since the latter was especially concerned about the com satellite's failure and the damage the economy would suffer as a result, and about the absence of vid, which always created domestic security problems. After a couple of hours with Booth, Sedgewick would be ready for scotch. And this time she wouldn't nursemaid him. Elizabeth gloated. Let him taste the consequences of his making war on her. He thought her without compassion? So be it. He would soon learn what lack of compassion was and regret having thrown away all that she had favored him with.

Back at the office Elizabeth instructed Jacquelyn to tell everyone who called that she was out and informed her that after making one call she'd be going home early. Jacquelyn frowned but made no comment.

Smiling with anticipation, Elizabeth ran a data search for the number of Hazel's work phone. Her call was answered on the first ring, by a voice she recognized as Hazel's. "Hazel, this is Liz," she said, her own voice suddenly husky as her body responded to the sound of Hazel's.

"Liz! How are you?"

"Dying to see you, love."

"Oh—" There was a pause. "I wanted to thank you for the lovely basket of fruit, I couldn't believe it when it came, I've never seen anything like it—it was delicious. But of course I didn't know how to call you."

"Oh, didn't I give you my number?" But of course she hadn't. Hazel didn't even know her last name—yet. "I'm glad you enjoyed it. I had occasion to be out in California, and while I was in the desert..." Elizabeth gurgled laughter. "But let's save the story for later, darling. I was calling to ask if you'd like to dine with me this evening."

"Tonight? Oh I'm sorry, I'm afraid I can't tonight. You see..."

"Yes?" Elizabeth prompted, the warmth leaving her voice. She had to have Hazel tonight. She needed it so very badly. And only Hazel would do.

"I, uh, there's something else I've committed myself to doing tonight," the girl stammered out.

"You're seeing someone else?" Elizabeth said coldly.

"If you mean...the way I would see you, the answer is no, Liz. I'm not seeing anyone right now. In fact, you're the only woman I've seen since I've moved to DC."

Relief swept away an anxiety Elizabeth hadn't realized Hazel's evasiveness had aroused. "Let me confess, Hazel," Elizabeth said, very low, "that I've been thinking about you a great deal. But I've been so busy, in and out of town, that I haven't had a chance even to call you. I've been looking forward so much to seeing you that your refusal is terribly disappointing. This may be our last chance for some time. Things are so hectic for me. Isn't there some way you can postpone whatever it is keeping you from seeing me?"

"I don't know what to say, Liz."

Elizabeth found it incredible that Hazel was resisting her like this. Surely if she didn't have another executive lover she wouldn't want to risk losing her altogether—would she? Or was she simply not interested? "Say you'll come to me tonight," Elizabeth urged. When Hazel didn't immediately answer, Elizabeth relapsed into coldness. "I'm sorry to have bothered you, Hazel. I understand perfectly. You needn't worry about my calling you again." A gamble, for if Hazel didn't immediately protest, she would have to hang up.

"No, wait, Liz, please. I *do* want to see you, very much. But…" Elizabeth let the pause stretch out. "I'll see what I can do, see if I can rearrange things," Hazel said, her voice uncertain. "What time and where shall we meet?"

"Tell me what time you get off work and I'll have someone pick you up at your office," Elizabeth said. "I thought I'd cook for you." She hadn't cooked in weeks. If Hazel knew how few lovers she ever cooked for…

"I get off at five-thirty," Hazel said, her voice subdued. "Let me tell you where I work."

Elizabeth fairly purred. "But I already know. How else would I have found your work number?"

"Oh. I hadn't thought of that."

"Don't worry about it. I'll tell you everything about it tonight," Elizabeth said, sensing the girl's unease at her being able to discover such things about her. "I'll see you around six, then. Bye, love."

"Bye, Liz," Hazel said, and Elizabeth disconnected. Elated, she prepared to leave, knowing her car and driver were still downstairs in the garage where she had left them, waiting for her. She would find oblivion tonight—in total freedom from Sedgewick and everything to do with him. While he drowned himself in scotch she would drown herself in Hazel—and, unlike him, be fresh and energetic in the morning.

To think some women lamented not being fixed!

[iv]

From the moment she entered the apartment—properly escorted by Garcia, in line with Elizabeth's security arrangements—Hazel had been ill-at-ease. Elizabeth had to work hard to draw out the warm, open girl she had been that night at the club. While finishing the final stages of food preparation Elizabeth came to the conclusion that the

car, the driver, the exclusiveness of the apartment, and the expensive-
ness of its furnishings had intimidated Hazel. Elizabeth hadn't expected such a reaction from someone so poised. So just why was Hazel
nonplused? Because she had formed a picture of Elizabeth that bore
no relation to reality? Or was there something else? She spoke with
constraint and sat and ate and walked carefully, as though picking
her way through a crowded antique shop specializing in crystal and
china. And somehow that attitude toward the objects in Elizabeth's
apartment was further directed—as though by association—toward
Elizabeth herself. Lightly touching Hazel's hands, neck, shoulders,
arms, Elizabeth expected the warm, free, easy response of their first
meeting. But Hazel did not touch back, and for a while Elizabeth
wondered if perhaps Hazel really had not wanted to see her again but
had found it too difficult to say so outright.

After dinner they sat shoulder to shoulder on the rug in the living
room—the only illumination that of one dim lamp in the corner—
staring out at the lights of DC. Elizabeth took Hazel's hand into her
own and lightly stroked the palm. "Shall we have coffee and dessert
now, or later?"

"Later, please—I feel as if I've eaten enough for a week."

Elizabeth lightly teased her. "Aren't you glad I gave you something loose to wear? I knew your pants would become excruciatingly
tight if you wore them while dining."

Hazel chuckled, a little nervously, Elizabeth thought. "That food
was Asian you said?"

"Yes. The very spicy-hot dish I didn't give you to eat was Thai,
the whole fish with black bean sauce was Hunan—that is, from an
area of China—and the noodles and the salad-like cold nut and rice
dish that you were so crazy about were Vietnamese."

"And the soup?"

"The soup was Thai. I toned it down for you. If you're not accustomed to spicy-hot food it's impossible to eat without suffering ago-
nies of discomfort."

"Then how do people ever become accustomed to them?"

Elizabeth nibbled Hazel's middle finger. "Just like anything else.
Gradually. Spicy food gets to be addictive you know." Elizabeth ran
her tongue over the finger.

Hazel's fingers moved against Elizabeth's tongue, teeth, and lips. "Then it must be a vice," Hazel murmured. "Anything addictive is a vice." She drew her wet fingers along Elizabeth's jaw and caressed Elizabeth's neck. A pulse in Elizabeth's vulva began throbbing, spreading a sexy, heavy ache into her arms and legs. She pressed Hazel down onto the rug, and suddenly they were tease-kissing, tongues-to-lips, tongues-to-teeth, their lips never quite meeting, immersing Elizabeth, swallowing her whole. Confused by the sensations she felt she knew Hazel was feeling which merged with what she was feeling at Hazel's touch, she lost track of what was happening between them, her tongue over, against, between, Hazel's smooth teeth and inner lip, and again she imagined she experienced both her own and Hazel's sensations, almost unbearably intensifying her pleasure…Hazel's tongue in her mouth might almost be in direct contact with the nerves in her vulva. "Too fast," she gasped, rolling a little apart from Hazel to slow her responses, to separate her self, to draw the sensations out before coming. Threading her confusion was bewilderment at her lack of control. First Hazel's pleasure, she reminded herself, then mine. Don't be greedy, Lizzie.

But Hazel was opening Elizabeth's gown, drawing her palms over Elizabeth's breasts, whispering "You want this now, darling, I know you do," and so Elizabeth closed her eyes and abandoned herself to an almost tidal immersion. Hazel's lips brushed her navel; her fingers on Elizabeth's abdomen trailed electric thrills in their wake. "So soft and golden," the low voice murmured, the fingers now skimming Elizabeth's pubic hair. Elizabeth, floating in darkness, waited, anticipating the fingers slipping inside, moving through the hair, sliding between her labia. *This is what's like for them as I play them out prolonging and prolonging and prolonging until they beg.* Hazel's fingers drew slickly wet up from her vagina along the groove underneath beside inside her lips parting slightly, spasms of sensation surging out out out deep inside her, each wave promising the next, growing, intensifying until cresting as the one great wave washed high high deep into crevices cracks places between the rocks she had forgotten were there, sensation spreading everywhere. Half-sobbing, she pressed Hazel's hand tight against the throbbing pulsing undulation until finally the spasms receded, slowly leaving her, at last, awash with the hot tingle in thighs, buttocks, vulva, the traces lingering and then barely recognizable as her muscles relaxed and smoothed out.

When she had recovered her breath, Elizabeth kissed Hazel's fingers one by one. "You're turning me into a glutton, my sweet," she said between kisses.

A smile curved Hazel's lips. "I wish we could have your hair down, Lizzie. It's soft, isn't it." She touched Elizabeth's hair. "Rapunzel, Rapunzel, let down your fair hair..." Elizabeth stared into the amber eyes. "So soft, the hair on your head, the hair under your arms,"— her fingers brushed Elizabeth's armpit—"the hair on your belly,"— her hand moved to touch Elizabeth's abdomen—"the hair of your cunt,"—her hand moved to Elizabeth's pubic hair—"the hair on your legs"—and her palm smoothed down Elizabeth's thigh past the knee to the ankle. "All of you covered with golden down, of course you must keep your hair long, long, long."

Elizabeth smiled into the shining eyes and caressed the flushed cheeks. "Go ahead, darling, unbraid me," she said. Only with Allison had she so literally let down her hair, but never during sex, never like this.

Smiling, nearly purring, Hazel took Elizabeth's braid in her hands and loosed the long piece of silk winding around and around the end of it. Slowly she freed the braid, unraveling the silk until it lay in a pile on the floor near Elizabeth's head. Elizabeth sat up to let Hazel unbraid the three thick strands of the plait, and soon her hair was cascading over her back and Hazel's hands, curling around both their bodies, tangling them in long golden strands. She laughed at the absurdity of it and at Hazel's sensuously caressing their bodies with it. Slipping her hand through the curtain of hair and between Hazel's thighs, she found it strange to feel her own hair against her naked body, causing another momentary blurring and confusion she eluded by pressing her lips against Hazel's. "I want to tell you about the desert, love," Elizabeth said as she nuzzled Hazel's ear and neck. "Imagine a great rounded bush-like tree dripping with long green leaves, covered with lovely soft smooth sweet-smelling lavender flowers shaped like, like, oh, perhaps the bell of a trumpet, but cup-like, so enticing and sweet and silky...like this spot on your neck, like your breasts," —she slid her fingers over the full, swelling curve of Hazel's breast—"a tree so

delightfully bursting with flowers that all the bees and hummingbirds in the desert come to it to drink their intoxicating liquor…"
Elizabeth kissed Hazel's lips, feeling as if she were a hummingbird
drinking, sipping, tasting Hazel's nectar…

A series of thuds knocked Elizabeth out of her reverie.

Her hair entangled her legs and feet as—moving without thinking—she vaulted to her feet. She paused to listen. Someone was
pounding on her elevator doors. No one was allowed up without her
permission. They should have called from downstairs, which could
only mean—

She ran into the hall and pressed her thumb to the lock of the
safe concealed behind the hall's wood paneling. The pounding continued, filling her mind's eye with images of tool-wielding males
trying to break through into her apartment. The paneling slid aside.
Elizabeth seized the M-27D and rushed into the foyer. She flicked the
closed-circuit video switch, braced herself against the wall, and took
aim at the doors. She did not really expect the video to be working,
for she assumed they had disabled the camera. But the screen flick-
ered on, showing the interior of the elevator, revealing its occupants:
Sedgewick, knocking a bottle against the doors, flanked by two stolid,
expressionless gorillas.

Elizabeth closed her eyes and worked hard to control her breath,
still the pounding of her heart, and ease the cramping tension in
her muscles.

"Liz," came the soft hiss from behind her.

Elizabeth whirled, the M-27D swinging with her. "Hazel!" she
exclaimed—and quickly lowered the weapon. Hazel's wide eyes
moved to the monitor, then back to Elizabeth. "Do you want this?" she
asked in a high, tense voice, holding out Elizabeth's gown. Elizabeth
realized she was naked and giggled hysterically at the girl's concern.
Ignoring Sedgewick's racket, she swept Hazel into the hall. "It's all
right, darling, there's nothing to worry about," she said to reassure the
girl. "But I want you to go into my bedroom, through the bathroom,
into the next room where there's a Jacuzzi, and through that into the
room behind, my dressing room. Close all the doors as you go, darling,
and stay there until I come for you." She stopped with Hazel at the

threshold of her bedroom and put the hand not holding the weapon on the girl's shoulders and looked down into her eyes. "Clear?"

Hazel looked confused; but she nodded and said, "Understood."

Elizabeth bent and kissed her forehead. "Give me that, you're right, I need it," she said, taking the gown, and gave Hazel a little push on the buttocks, into the bedroom.

Elizabeth returned the M-27D to the safe, slipped into the gown, and went back into the foyer. Scowling, she flipped the switch that opened the doors.

Sedgewick staggered out of the elevator. "Why don't you answer your door, Weatherall." His words were so slurred that she had trouble understanding him. Elizabeth flicked a look at the gorillas—one of whom was Lamont—and made the doors close. She was not about to have those animals in her apartment. She couldn't care less how uncomfortable they might find waiting in the elevator. If they had had the sense to deal with Sedgewick instead of merely accompanying him and following his every order, they wouldn't be in this predicament.

Elizabeth stalked back into the living room, leaving Sedgewick to follow. Judging by the bottle's relatively light depletion it seemed reasonable to assume he was on his second fifth. Disgusted, she snatched up the nearest handset, punched in the number of Sedgewick's household phone, and demanded to speak with Higgins. Sedgewick fell into her armchair and leveled a bleary stare at her. "Get your ass over here," she instructed Higgins. "He's verging on the unmanageable." When she hung up she glared at Sedgewick. "You shouldn't be allowed out without a keeper. You're as bad as your son when it comes to breaking security regs. What kind of a dumb-assed stunt did you think you were pulling, coming up here like this?"

His eyes, their pupils dilated and unfocused, peered at her as though he were having trouble seeing her. "Your hair," he said slowly, carefully, "is loose."

She sighed. "Yes, damn it Sedgewick my hair is loose. No, stay over there, just sit down in that chair and behave yourself. I can smell you all the way over here. Sit down, I said," she fairly barked at him as he staggered toward her. The reek of his alcohol-soaked breath was disgusting. Losing patience, she grabbed his arm and shoved him back into the chair. "You'll stay put if you know what's good for you. And if you spill scotch on my chair you'll really be sorry." Deciding not to give him the chance, she snatched the bottle from his tenuous grip and took it out to the kitchen. Remembering Hazel, she hoped the girl had done exactly as she'd directed. The last thing she wanted was for Hazel to overhear the contemptuous language Sedgewick used when talking about the lovers of women executives. It was only a matter of time before he would guess she had someone here.

When she returned to the living room she found his face contorted by a terrible frown. He squinted at her and said, "Betrayed me."

Elizabeth leaned against the plate-glass window and folded her arms over her chest. "You betrayed yourself," she said coldly. "From now on you'll get precisely what you ask for."

Of course he was too far gone to understand what she meant. His face still puckered, he said, "Don't think you can leave me. I'll kill you first."

Elizabeth's blood chilled. "You don't know what you're talking about, Sedgewick."

"You think I don't know what you're up to?" Forgetting to speak carefully, he slurred his words into an almost indistinguishable mush. "She ran away though I loved her," he whined.

"Oh shut up," Elizabeth said, turning to stare out at the city. "Have you any idea how bored to death I am with your fetish? Day after day after day you maunder on and on and *on*, until I'm driven to fantasizing ways of making you shut up. You need a selective lobotomy, Sedgewick. Instead of cutting your genital nerves they should have found the cells in your brain contaminated with that bitch and cut them right out. Christ you're tedious!"

"Why're you so mean to me?" He was just one big whine, Elizabeth thought. Even without turning around, she knew he was proceeding into a crying jag. She glanced at her watch. What time had it been when she'd called Higgins? How much longer would she have to put up with this shit? "Anything you want I'll give you," he blubbered.

She wheeled to face him. "Peace is what I want, pig, and as we both know, it's the last thing you'll give me." She felt so savagely angry that she longed to pull him out of the chair, drag him to the elevator, and pitch him in with his gorillas.

"Anything," he said, tears streaming down his face, "anything as long as you don't leave me."

"Right. Tell me that tomorrow, boy." Again, Elizabeth checked her watch.

Sedgewick subsided into wordless weeping, and again Elizabeth turned her back on him to stare out the window. At last, the house phone buzzed. The guard downstairs announced Higgins, and Elizabeth told him—thinking of how he'd let himself be intimidated by Sedgewick and what she would have to say on that score to him in the morning—to send the man up. She waited in the foyer for him, and when he stepped out of the elevator (the gorillas placed exactly where they had been when Sedgewick had arrived) gestured toward the living room. "He's in there. Just get him the fuck out of here, take him home, and put him to bed. Those idiots there didn't have the sense to do that themselves." She glared at Lamont, then turned and led Higgins through the hall into the living room.

When the elevator doors had closed on the lot of them, Elizabeth switched off the vid screen and leaned wearily against the foyer wall. *Sordid, love, that's us, the pair of us sordid accomplices of nasty old perverts.* The evening was spoiled now, and she felt dirty, soiled and old, terribly terribly old. It was she who should be weeping, not Sedgewick.

When she felt she had her roiling emotions under control Elizabeth moved up the hall, passed through the bedroom into the bathroom and past the Jacuzzi room. She found Hazel in the dressing room, lying on the mauve and gray chaise lounge. Hazel stared at Elizabeth. "It's okay now?" she whispered.

Elizabeth went to her. "I'm sorry for all that, darling." She held out her hand and helped Hazel to her feet. "There was nothing dangerous in the situation, though at first I thought there must be."

Hazel was trembling. "When you took out that, that thing…"

Elizabeth drew her close. "I know, it must have scared the hell out of you. I'm sorry. I'll try to explain everything to you. But first let's go to the kitchen while I make coffee."

Hazel made a sound that Elizabeth identified as a nervous giggle. "I feel as though I won't want caffeine for days."

Elizabeth smiled faintly. "You shall have cognac," she said. "I'll even warm it for you." She kissed Hazel's hairline. "Come along, darling." Gently she detached Hazel from her and, taking her hand, led her out to the kitchen. The worst of it, she thought, was that Hazel might now be extremely reluctant to have anything to do with working in Security. It would be uphill work persuading her. But Elizabeth could see that she needed Hazel more now than ever.

Chapter Fifteen

[i]

As the hours crawled by Celia dozed, nodded awake, and dozed, all the time aware of the watchers outside. She told herself watchdogs were nothing new, but she was frightened.

Two *separate* watchdogs. Emily's words about how this time it was ODS who had her mother, about how Emily's connections with ODS were not as effective as those she had used for obtaining Celia's release, kept turning over in her mind. Did this mean that different branches of the security forces were detaining people? There was always confusion when talking about security forces and detention centers. People tended to name them all "ODS" under the assumption that although there were different people involved in different busts, they all worked under the same umbrella.

What if they had told Emily they would free Mama and had then sent her to Cuba? What if she were already on the way to Cuba? Emily persisted in thinking the interrogator had invented the fantasy to demoralize Celia, but Celia could not dismiss the possibility that they might actually start exiling activist Latinos to Cuba.

Please, Mama, please be all right, please come home to me, I'm here now, waiting for you, I won't leave you again, Mama, please come home now...

Nodding awake from a dream, Celia heard the steps—many of them—coming up the walk. She waited in the dark, her heart pounding, thinking of how often political arrests were made in the middle of the night. But then she heard a key scratching in the lock. Security forces wouldn't bother with picking locks; they'd just break the door down or shoot out the lock. Celia flew off the sofa-bed to the door and threw it open. "Mama!" She flung her arms around her mother and squeezed her eyes tight to feel her mother's presence all the more intensely. When she opened them, she saw Emily and Claire Davies, the latter looking oddly as worn, exhausted, and depressed as Elena did. Celia supported her mother's shoulder and walked her into the room. Anxiously she watched as Elena sank down onto the sofa-bed and leaned her head back. "Are you all right, Mama?" she asked, switching on the lamp.

"Tired, just very very tired." Elena said through chapped, barely parted lips. "My legs are aching and cramped as though I'd been working a thirty-six hour shift. I did a lot of standing this time."

Celia looked around at Emily and Claire. "Claire?" she asked in middle-of-the-night confusion. "You went with Emily?"

Claire sat at the other end of the sofa-bed. "No. They decided to release me with Elena. God knows why. But fortunately they did."

"I didn't know you'd been taken too," Celia said, her throat tight with emotion. Emily had said they had arrested doctors; Claire was an R.N., as activist as Elena. She must have been at the demonstration with Elena and Luis. "Does anyone want anything to eat or drink? We've real food that Emily stocked us up with this afternoon."

"Just water for me, Cee. Lots and lots of water. I'm very dry."

"Claire?"

"The same," she said, apparently too tired to say more than she had to. Celia stepped to the kitchenette and fetched several half-liter bottles for Elena and Claire and juice for Emily, who had settled on the floor.

Elena spoke only after she had finished one of the half-liters. "Emily told me about Luis. She said you'll know what to do, which legal documents to file and so on."

Celia noted how *old* her mother was looking, as though jail had aged her ten years. The lines in her face looked deeper, her hair grayer. She said, "Yes, provided we know for certain where he's being kept," she said.

"We will know for certain," Emily said. "I will see to it."

Celia believed her, for so far Emily had done everything she had said she would do. She was a woman of her word.

Elena closed her eyes. "I can sleep now," she said.

"Come, Mama, I'll tuck you in," Celia said, surprised that her mother's first impulse wasn't to shower.

"And Claire," Elena added as she stumbled to her feet. "Claire can have Luis's bed."

Claire looked with dull, bloodshot eyes at Celia. "I could sleep for a week," she said. "If I weren't so thirsty."

Emily rose to her feet. "I'll be in touch tomorrow, Celia."

Celia locked up, showed Claire to Luis's room, and helped her mother undress. "Good-night, Mama," she whispered as she bent down to kiss her mother's cheek.

Elena had already fallen asleep.

Celia turned off the light and tiptoed out of the room. She hoped she would be able to fall asleep as easily herself now that she knew Elena was safe. She must try not to think of Luis too much except where it might help him. Do not brood, was what Luis had always told her—which, she admonished herself, was sound advice.

If only she could follow it.

[ii]

Elizabeth woke to find Hazel asleep beside her. She kissed the girl's neck and inhaled deeply, to get more of her delicious scent. And then suddenly she came fully awake and remembered everything. She glanced at the time. It was not even six yet. She would have Hazel driven home so the girl could stay until seven. That would give her time to talk to her about the job. It would be a hard sell, she knew, since she had been upset to hear that Elizabeth worked in Sedgewick's office. Her reaction had taken Elizabeth by surprise. She might have expected such a reaction from somebody working in State, Commerce, Health, or Interior and Environment. But Justice worked so closely with Security that it was almost a subdepartment. Jack Hill generally followed whatever recommendations Security made to him, and he always backed Sedgewick in Executive meetings. Why then such a response to her association with Security and Sedgewick?

She hadn't yet told Hazel that it had been Sedgewick in the elevator. If Hazel came to work at the office she'd recognize him, of course... Elizabeth smoothed her fingers over the girl's neck. She was not stunningly pretty, especially when asleep, but the expressiveness of her eyes exercised their own attraction. Hazel stirred. Elizabeth brushed a strand of hair off the so-sleepy face. "Good morning, darling."

"Liz." Hazel put her knuckles to her eyes and rubbed. "Oh!" Frowning, she struggled up onto an elbow. "What time is it? I have to go home before I can go to work!"

Gently, Elizabeth pressed her back onto the bed. "Don't worry, it isn't even six yet. We've plenty of time."

"Oh," Hazel said, putting her hand to her heart. "Thank god."

"You take your job very seriously, don't you."

Hazel gave her a look. "Of course I do. I have serious rent to pay. I really couldn't bear living in one of those horrible dormitories." She grimaced.

"I hope you don't mind my waking you, but I wanted us to talk before you had to rush off. To offer you a job, darling."

Hazel's eyebrows pulled together. "A job?" Her voice was wary. "I don't understand."

"Working in my office," Elizabeth said, interested to note Hazel's frown shading from wariness to puzzlement. "I know your skills, you see, and am convinced you would be perfect for the front desk of the Chief's office. Your security clearance has already come through."

"*Security* clearance? You had me investigated?" She pulled a little away from Elizabeth and sat up against the headboard, clutching the sheet to her breasts. "That's how you knew where I worked," she said slowly.

"Not quite." Elizabeth chose her words with care. "You understand, surely, that most personnel files are easily accessed by the Chief's office."

Hazel swallowed. "I'd heard that, of course. But I never thought—"

Elizabeth understood: Hazel had never thought *her* file would be of interest to someone in Sedgewick's office. She was a good, obedient, law-abiding service-tech. No one could possibly be interested in peeping into her file. "I'm sorry I ordered the backgrounder without talking with you first, darling, but I've been frantic to find someone appropriate for that particular position, and then I thought of you and I didn't have the time to meet with you, so..." Elizabeth shrugged. "I thought I'd go ahead with it and tell you afterwards."

Hazel stared down at her sheet-covered knees. "I'm sorry you went to so much trouble. I can't accept the job."

"Why not, Hazel? You don't even know yet what it involves or what the salary is."

Hazel's fingers kneaded the sheet. "Several reasons come to mind right off," she said slowly, not meeting Elizabeth's gaze.

"Tell me," Elizabeth urged. If she knew the girl's reasons she could talk her out of them.

"Well for one thing, I have the best job security I could ever hope for. They moved me out here from Denver, you know." She bit her lip. "It's terribly expensive here in DC. Oh, they gave me a raise in salary commensurate with the expense, but still I had to use up all my savings for deposits for the place I live in. For utilities and things like that. And also for a few expenses to do with the move that they didn't cover for me. It will be a long time before I can save much. So you see, job security is very important to me."

"But darling, I wouldn't fire you! Why leap to that conclusion? Do I strike you as the sort of person who is unfair to employees?"

Hazel—still not looking at Elizabeth's face—shrugged. "I don't know what kind of employer you are. But the main thing is I know I can do my job well and that I will continue doing it well and to my boss's satisfaction. I don't know that about working for you. It would be taking a risk, and I can't afford that kind of risk."

"I promise you that if it didn't work out I'd help you—both financially, and to find another job." Elizabeth touched Hazel's arm lightly. "I promise," she repeated. When Hazel didn't answer she said, "What are your other reasons?"

Hazel hesitated. "I might as well tell you," she said after a long silence. Her cheeks grew rosy. "I'm sure you won't want me working for you when I tell you that I'm not going to see you again." Her gaze darted to Elizabeth's face and then away.

Elizabeth's stomach fluttered. This was something that had never occurred to her. "Because of what happened in the foyer?" she asked. "I can tell you that that has happened only once before in my entire life. Normally that weapon stays in the safe, untouched except for cleaning and inspection."

Hazel's fingers knotted together. "It's not just that," she said very low.

Elizabeth's throat tightened. "There is someone else?"

Hazel shook her head. "No. I told you the truth about that."

"I could have sworn you enjoyed last night, and our previous meeting too," Elizabeth said. "Am I to be allowed to know why?"

"I did enjoy last night, and the other time, also," Hazel said, finally meeting Elizabeth's gaze. "I'm terribly attracted to you. That's the only reason I agreed to meet you the first time. Your eyes were so warm and engaging that day in the silk shop. You treated me like a human being, and you listened to what I said. I thought the clerk was going to have a stroke when you invited me to sit with you. She's usually very snotty to me."

"I don't understand then, Hazel. You say the only reason. Surely that's the main reason people make love."

"I know what happens to people who get involved with executives," Hazel said, averting her eyes. "I don't want to be hurt like that. I've seen so much of that. Already…" her voice trailed off.

Already what? Elizabeth wondered. "Then yesterday on the phone you lied when you said you had another commitment last night."

"I knew I shouldn't see you again. That it would grow harder each time I saw you. That's how my kind get trapped. But I thought, because you said that this was the last opportunity, that one last time would be okay."

Trapped. What a strange thing for Hazel to think, when usually it worked the other way. Look at Allison—trapped by her girl. And Felice always having to extricate herself from lovers too intense, too entangling. And Lisa with that horrible Ginger. "You can rest assured, Hazel, that I wouldn't trap you," Elizabeth said dryly. "I've never in my life held onto a lover like that."

Hazel wet her lips. "That's not what I mean," she whispered. "I mean emotionally trapped. Falling in love. Only briefly requited, and then there we are, by ourselves again, or passed on to someone else. That's maybe the worst, the way executives pass us around. That's why I stay away from them. Or did until I went out with you."

"You make us sound like monsters."

"You're angry with me," Hazel said. She looked around the room, saw the clock, and got out of bed. "It's time for me to go." And without looking at Elizabeth, she went into the bathroom.

Elizabeth sagged back onto the pillows. So she wasn't to have this girl. She couldn't believe it. She had lain in Hazel's arms half the night with her head on Hazel's breast and had felt so good, so relaxed, so *eased*. Hazel was the first lover since Allison whom she'd wanted so intensely. Hazel's poise and intelligence made her perfect for the job. She was someone she would have been able to trust in an office of sharks.

No. She wouldn't accept defeat. She could change the girl's mind. The one advantage she had was Hazel's strong attraction to her. She had half an hour to make love to her before she'd have to let her go.

Elizabeth followed Hazel into the bathroom. "I'll have you driven home, darling," she said softly, watching Hazel climb into her tight cotton pants. "There's no need for you to rush off. Please, come back to bed for just a little longer. Since this is our last time." Elizabeth went to her and put her hand on Hazel's, stopping her from velcroing closed the waistband.

"You're not angry?" Hazel said, her amber eyes luminous in the sunlight pouring down through the skylight.

"No, darling, just sad." Elizabeth drew her close.

Hazel let Elizabeth move her into the other room and lay her down on the bed. And then Elizabeth pulled out all the stops. Driven by a need she did not begin to comprehend, she would at that moment have done almost anything to keep Hazel.

[iii]

Elizabeth arrived at Sedgewick's house in the highest and best of spirits. A service-tech admitted her and asked if she wanted to talk to Higgins before seeing Sedgewick. Flicking a haughty eyebrow at him, Elizabeth informed the man she was neither seeing Mr. Sedgewick nor interested in talking to Higgins, but was there to see *Ms.* Sedgewick, then left him gaping as she gaily took the stairs two at a time.

She rapped briskly on Alexandra's door. "Come," Alexandra's voice said.

Elizabeth threw open the door. "Spring's come to DC, Alexandra! Up with you! I'm taking you to lunch! What's this? You haven't even dressed?" The girl was lying in the dark, flat on her back in bed; and depression was written all over her face. Elizabeth threw open the shutters to let in some light. "What's this?" she said as Alexandra turned her face away, presumably to hide her tears. She went to the bed, sat on the edge, and drew the thick chestnut hair off the half-hidden face. "I promise you, sweetie, you'll feel better once you get out of this room. But hey, aren't you going to talk to poor old Elizabeth? Are you mad at me, love?"

Alexandra shook her head. Slowly she turned her face toward Elizabeth. "Did *he* say I can come out now?" she asked, fighting a sob in her throat.

"Don't worry about that, love. He didn't begrudge you the Jacuzzi, he won't begrudge you lunch out. Trust me. You know I wouldn't do anything that your father would object to." But how monstrous, Elizabeth thought, treating his own daughter this way. She patted Alexandra's hand, then stood up and went to the armoire. "I bet you haven't bathed yet today, have you."

"I didn't feel like it," Alexandra said.

"Well I insist you do it now. Shower in here or use the Jacuzzi in your mother's suite."

"I'll shower in here," Alexandra said quickly.

"Then hop to it, while I decide how to dress you. I'm taking you to the Diana—where, by the way, you'll become a member on your sixteenth birthday. I can assure you I'll sponsor you myself if your mother isn't here to do it."

"It's a women's club?" Alexandra asked, wide-eyed. "They let people as young as me—?"

"When you're sixteen," Elizabeth said firmly. "Which if I correctly recall is in about six months."

"October thirteenth."

"Old Elizabeth's not senile yet." Elizabeth grinned. "Now go shower, my babe, so we can get out of this mausoleum and into the fresh spring air!"

To Elizabeth's relief Alexandra scrambled out of bed and padded quickly into the bathroom. Soon Elizabeth heard the shower running.

While she waited, Elizabeth chose an outfit for Alexandra—one they had found the afternoon Elizabeth had taken her shopping—and jewelry to match. Curiously she glanced around the room. A book lay on the dressing table, *Jane Eyre*, Elizabeth saw from its spine. Pretty gloomy reading for someone in Alexandra's situation. Only one book. No other sources of amusement? Elizabeth's eye fell on a tray of dirty dishes and food. Looking more closely, she realized they were the remains of breakfast.

Her blood boiling, Elizabeth picked up the tray, stepped out into the hall, and went to the landing. Leaning over the banister she pitched the tray and its contents straight down what must have been twenty-five feet. Then she sped down the stairs so that she was there waiting when a service-tech came running. "Who is assigned to serve Ms. Sedgewick?"

"Barbara is, madam."

Elizabeth kicked a shard of china across the parquet floor and watched with satisfaction as it skittered far into the main hall. "Will you please be so good as to inform Barbara that she's wanted in Ms. Sedgewick's room," she said, making her eyes flash.

The man bobbed his head, and—darting a fast look at the remains of Alexandra's breakfast—scuttled off, clearly uneasy about leaving the mess lying there.

Elizabeth returned to Alexandra's room and found her dressing. "I've sent for your girl, Alexandra. You mustn't let her get away with such slackness. I'm furious she left your breakfast tray here. It's past noon!"

Alexandra flushed. "*He* took my handset away," she said, clearly embarrassed, "and I'm not supposed to leave the room. I just couldn't see myself opening the door and yelling, hoping I would be heard."

Heard and paid attention to. Obviously the staff had decided Alexandra was of little account in this house. Elizabeth arranged the turquoise diagonal sash on Alexandra's flowery silk tunic. "The new styles are very becoming on you," she said, turning Alexandra to face the full-length mirror. "Don't you think?"

A knock sounded on the door. Elizabeth opened it and found a dumpy middle-aged woman staring apprehensively at her. "You're Barbara?" Elizabeth said coldly.

"Yes, madam. Was there something wanted?"

"You're dismissed as of today," Elizabeth said. "I'm sure I don't have to explain to you in exactly what ways you've been unsatisfactory. Slackness of that sort is unacceptable in a house of this quality.

One would think you'd know better than to try to pull this sort of thing on the daughter of the house."

The woman's eyes watered; slowly the color drained from her face. "Please, madam, please give me another chance. Since the Blanket I—"

"That will do," Elizabeth interrupted. "You may go now." Elizabeth turned to Alexandra. "Come, darling, let's get out of here. We've a one o'clock reservation." Sweeping past the service-tech, Elizabeth led Alexandra down the stairs, out of the house, and into her car. "Of course," Elizabeth said, "most of the staff are new here. The house was only reopened—after having been restored—two months ago. Still…"

"I can't believe you fired her, Elizabeth," Alexandra said. "I mean, it was only for leaving the tray, and she's probably desperate for the job—"

"It wasn't only for leaving the tray, Alexandra, and if she were desperate for the job she would have served you properly. She took advantage of a situation she thought she understood. It was a gamble, and she lost." Elizabeth's tone was severe. "Don't feel sorry for her, darling."

"But I do," Alexandra said. "It's as though it was my fault she lost her job."

Elizabeth snorted. "Don't worry about *her*. She'll get a week's severance pay. And she'll soon find something else. Though I certainly won't give her a reference, there are plenty of people in DC who will take her anyway." Time to get Alexandra's mind off that damned house, Elizabeth thought. "Let's see who can spot the most signs of spring today," she said. "Ah, there—look at the fluffy white blossoms on that tree. That only happens in spring," she said.

Alexandra peered out the window. "But I don't know what to look for," she said. "There isn't this kind of spring in Barbados!"

"Oh you poor deprived child," Elizabeth mocked. "Wait until the lilacs are out! You'll love them!"

[iv]

The amber light flashed, and everyone prepared for landing. Martha glanced from Cora to Gina to Louise. What, she wondered of herself, did she think she was she doing, tagging along on this mission? She didn't have any particular skills in demand, and the first-hand experience wouldn't be all that helpful to her in Paris. She could almost do as well visiting the clinic on Whidbey.

Refugees, Martha and Cora agreed, was an ugly word that they must find some way of avoiding. Every alternative they had so far come up with was either awkward or negative. All were now agreed that they must keep trying until they found a designation that worked.

While Cora taped interviews with the asylum seekers and consulate personnel who had contact with walk-ins and Gina made medical judgments and examinations, Louise would sift through the data the consulates had begun collecting from people brave enough to lay charges and report disappearances and known human rights abuses. She, Martha, was to float—which meant she'd probably get stuck dealing with the consulate personnel. The group agreed, however, that her chief function on this mission was beginning the work of figuring out the most efficient but humane way to run things with a view toward designing regular procedures that could be followed at all participating consulates and embassies. Martha was already clear, though, that they should use local activists whenever possible as liaisons between the consulates on the one hand and the clinics and the Co-op on the other. She knew from experience that although bureaucratic procedures tended to generate inflexibility and rote indifference, in many situations set procedures, when administered with determined flexibility and sensitivity, made things run more smoothly—at least for a while. And yet she had also noticed that routine procedures over the long run tended to become cumbersome and irrational impediments to getting the right things done. She told herself that the need for these missions would likely end soon, making worry about bureaucratic deterioration superfluous.

"All set," Sorben said, rising from her flight couch.

"We're going in camouflaged," Magyyt said, "so everyone needs to maintain a chain of physical contact. We don't want to risk even the slightest chance of interference from security forces. We'll let them see us only as we're evacuating people, when it can't be helped, since Sorben and I couldn't possibly manage that extensive a camouflage by ourselves."

"I doubt any security forces will be taking random shots at us as we're leaving," Louise said. "Unless the higher-ups have anticipated such a contingency and have already passed orders down the line. Though I myself doubt they'd want to risk further sanctions."

"Still, once we start loading we will want to be as quick as possible, which means we'll need as many people as possible helping." She glanced at Gina. "I'm assuming there may be people who aren't ambulatory, as in our previous pickups."

"Perhaps," Gina said, "though how such people would have made it to the consulate in the first place..." She frowned. "This won't be like going into an unsurveilled spot."

This being the very first pickup since the vid transmission, they had no idea what they might find.

"I'll need help carrying my equipment if I'm to be a part of the chain," Cora said.

With each of them carrying bits of video equipment (though Cora herself ferried the bulk of it strapped to her back) and holding hands, they disembarked into the warm muggy New Orleans evening. Martha saw that they had landed in the middle of an enormous lawn enclosed by a wrought-iron fence and gates, and for a moment she imagined someone strolling across the lawn and running smack into the virtually invisible pod. As they crossed the bit of lawn between the pod and the floodlit mansion, the air wrapped itself around Martha like a wet, suffocating blanket. By the time they stepped into the light, Martha had begun sweating, and Gina's hand in Martha's went from damp to slippery. "The air smells like it's rotting," Martha whispered to Gina. "Like something old and musty, like rotting vegetation."

Gina didn't answer, for they were approaching the guarded side entrance under the portico through which the driveway curved. What kind of guard? Martha wondered. A guard for the consulate, or a guard for harassing or even arresting people coming for asylum or to lay charges? Sorben gestured to them to stop and wait as Magyyt disarmed the guard, an operation Martha knew to be difficult to pull off without harming the guard. She felt like cheering when the automatic weapon the man carried disintegrated into dust that swirled and drifted to the ground, but confined herself to a silent grin. The guard cried out, and the Marq'ssan withdrew the camouflage. "We are expected by the Consul," Sorben said to the guard. "Let us pass."

He stared at them, speechless as they filed past him into the building. Martha had witnessed enough reactions to the Marq'ssan's use of their powers to surmise that he was probably too disoriented and disbelieving of what had happened to do more than stand there for several minutes frozen in the paralysis of shock.

Inside, the air was dry and cool. The sweat on Martha's skin evaporated, leaving behind an unpleasantly scummy film. As Sorben led them through the hall Martha caught a confused impression of high ceilings, chandeliers dripping crystal, a richly colored rug running down the center of the oak floor, and oil portraits and landscapes lining the beige linen walls. Sorben did not stop at any of the open thresholds or closed doors they passed but led them to the foot of a staircase in a spacious, high-ceilinged foyer. "We're the Free Zone contingent," she said to the guards and service people stationed there.

A guard touched his headset and spoke into its mike. Cora slid the pack off her back and began assembling her vid equipment. The other guards and service-techs in the hall watched the Free Zone contingent—some suspiciously, some curiously, others indifferently. When the guard finished speaking into the headset, he walked over to them and said, very low, to Sorben, "You are expected. Please follow me."

Cora cursed. "Wait a minute, wait a minute. I need to get my gear ready. It'll only take a few seconds. I've nearly got everything set to go."

"We'll wait for her," Sorben said.

The guard frowned and fixed his gaze on Sorben. Martha was sure he was wondering whether she was an alien. After a lot of commotion, Cora set her cam onto her shoulder and started recording. "Lead on!" she said. The guard's frown deepened; wordlessly he started up the stairs.

They were taken to an office on the second floor, a room graced with the same high ceilings and long narrow windows Martha had noticed below. A heavyset blonde executive greeted them and introduced herself as Katje Voets. They in turn introduced themselves. "The Consul would prefer not to be interviewed," Voets said. "He's authorized me to speak for him and has urged me to be as helpful to you as possible." She moved to a long table set against one wall and gestured at an 8"x14"x24" wire basket brimming with flimsy. "This is everything we've got so far in the way of complaints, charges, and requests for help." Her many gold bracelets clanked and jangled with every movement of her arm. "The people seeking asylum—all nine of them—are down on the first floor. I understand the Austrian and Greek consulates also have people requesting asylum?"

"We'll be going to them after we've finished here," Sorben said.

Voets looked at Cora. "We expect you to respect the privacy of this consulate and that you'll confine your, ah, coverage to the refugees and refrain from accosting consular staff."

Cora said, "I would like to interview you, if not the Consul."

"We can do that," Voets said without enthusiasm. "However, I must insist we clarify in advance which subjects may and which subjects may not be addressed before the recorded portion of the interview begins."

"Have there been attempts to harass people coming to the consulate to request help?" Louise asked.

Voets bit her lip and gestured toward Cora. "I have told you I am willing to be interviewed, but under the proper conditions. You will please be so good as to take your camera elsewhere or turn it off now if you wish me to address this question."

Martha looked at Cora and said, "Cora?"

Cora's lower lip pushed out, but she ostentatiously switched the cam off and lowered it to her side.

Voets said, "Thank you." She looked at Louise. "There was an incident two days ago. On the day of the demonstration, that is. Uniformed officers detained several persons."

"Did you demand an explanation from the Executive?"

Voets shook her head. "Our position is difficult."

Louise said, "Don't you think it would be a good idea to pursue the matter?"

"It's something we may want to explore."

Louise snorted. "May I?" she asked Voets, pointing to the basket of flimsy.

"Certainly." Martha imagined Voets must be thrilled to be rid of it. "And now, I'll take you downstairs to see the nine individuals asking for asylum."

Cora lifted the cam back onto her shoulder and started for the door. Martha decided she had better stick with Voets after she had taken all of them downstairs so that she and Voets could discuss procedures.

"Just a minute," Louise said as they prepared to leave the office. Voets turned and raised her eyebrows at Louise's peremptoriness. "Are there any local activist groups in contact with the consulate? NOAFF, for instance?"

Voets's beady blue eyes frosted over. "Certainly not. We would never associate ourselves with people like *that*."

But of course. These people were executives and employed by a *government*. It was going to be more difficult than they had thought, Martha realized. She had forgotten to take such attitudes into account. Martha began to consider what she would have to do to overcome the obstacles such an attitude created. She might not be able to do anything about it by talking with Voets herself, but she was sure there were other ways and other means.

[v]

That evening Elizabeth returned to the office at ten-thirty—not to work, but to continue poring over Zeldin's entries in the leather book. Higgins had persisted in phoning her throughout the day and evening, begging her to see Sedgewick, insisting he could no longer manage him, warning her that though sober, Sedgewick would not be functional the next or even the day after that unless she gave him some attention. "I am dispensable, Higgins," Elizabeth said. "Remind him of that if he asks for me."

"He hasn't asked for you," Higgins said. "He's only asked if you've called."

At this Elizabeth had laughed. "I hope you told him the truth," she said—and hung up. No more mothering, Sedgewick. No more loyally covering your ass. You're going down, and fast. And then I'll be free of you... Though where that would leave her was another matter. She couldn't start over, not at her status, not at her age. She knew she would have to get used to living in a small pond, of being much less powerful. She didn't really see that she had any choice. If he *didn't* go down, at the rate they were going Sedgewick would eventually kill her—or she him.

Elizabeth stretched out on the sofa. She took several leisurely sips of water and found the place in the leather book where she had last stopped reading.

After that second sexual encounter, I hoped never to see him again. But in the middle of December on a bleak, drizzly day he showed up at my scheduled debriefing. At first he was so businesslike, making no reference to our last encounter, that I assumed the sexual aspect of our relationship was over. I asked him if he had permanently replaced my previous controller, and he said that he had. At this point I had no idea Sedgewick was the Chief Controller for Western Europe. I only knew that, as an executive, he must be much more important than my previous (professional) controller.

Toward the end of the debriefing he slipped into what I came to think of as his "charming mode"—his eyes warm and glowing, his voice cajoling and smooth; he flattered me by telling me I was wasted on that operation, that I could be doing "more important things" for the Company. At the end of the session he switched from "Zeldin" to "Kay" and pressed me to have dinner with him. He was so attentive, so complimentary, so warm (now it is impossible to imagine associating that word with Sedgewick, but back then, he exuded magnetic warmth), that my determination to avoid him melted. My sexual attraction to him rekindled, too. I don't know how he was able to get me to forget all my negative feelings, but he did.

He took me to a club, extremely intimate and private, and taught me how to drink Russian vodka. Afterwards we went to his apartment. When one first starts drinking Russian vodka one doesn't notice the alcohol affecting one until one is extremely drunk—sick drunk, for me. I didn't get sick-drunk that first time, and so I had no sense of being affected by it. But I know I must have been very drunk. Certainly later, when I saw my face in the mirror, I found my cheeks flushed a dark purple.

Sedgewick suggested I undress; and then he disappeared into his dressing room. I did undress, completely. When he came back, he was wearing a dressing gown and carrying a silk-covered box. He put the box on the bed and, as we stood at the foot, kissed and stroked me into a state of high sexual excitement. Since he had requested me to be for a time passive, not touching him back, the entire focus of this sexual activity was on what he was doing to me. This request of his didn't strike me as odd, because I'd several times before encountered various unexplained requests from men that I always suspected had to do with a private fantasy they were entertaining as they had sex with me.

I was at the edge of orgasm and was considering what tactics to use to make him fuck me when he started telling me that he wanted to do "something different," that he wanted me to agree to do whatever he told me to do. There was something frightening about this. What do you mean? I asked, what sort of thing…and then he lifted the lid of the box and showed me the enema apparatus, which included a black rubber bag and a long blue hose with a long black nozzle coiled around it. I have a sharp, vivid memory of his sitting me on the edge of the bed and standing in front of me, one hand in my hair, the other stroking my neck—in what I later came to think of as one of his "tableaux." (Always with him certain things had to be done in certain ways.)

He proceeded to talk me into letting him do what he wanted. I know what that is, I said, pointing to the open box, I can't let you use it on me. But he said that things done in a sexual context were experienced differently and observed that I hadn't objected to his sticking his finger up my ass while fucking. And then he changed his argument, saying he knew I was afraid, and that women were always afraid before their first vaginal penetration, that they expected pain, but that because vaginal penetration was a necessary part of fucking no one ever fussed over it, fearful though it was as an unknown…that this was unknown to me and thus fear-producing, but that he knew Kay Zeldin wasn't a coward and that I would try it, that he would lead me to new sorts of sexual sensations I'd never before experienced… It was his implying cowardice on my part that probably made me go through with it. I didn't want to be thought a coward. And I was too drunk to think clearly enough to counter anything he said. All I could think was that yes I'm afraid and that's why I don't want to do this, because something about this scares me terribly. At the time I thought it was the pain I was scared of, but now I know it wasn't that but was something to do with my terror of this particular relational structure… He took from the box a blue rubber sheet that he spread over the bed. And then he took the bag into the bathroom and filled it. At some point he talked to me about water temperatures and additives and the variations on "the experience" one could make along an "incremental spectrum," but I hardly took in what he was saying. He positioned me on my hands and knees—not that easy for a person as drunk

as I was—and gave me my first "sexual-context" enema... It all ended on
the bathroom floor where he finally fucked me. Then we went to bed—to
sleep. He slept, I did not, partly because of the vodka, partly because of
my perturbation. By the end of the night I realized that more than anything
what he had done was humiliate me... By some streak of pride, perhaps the
same that had induced me to go through with it to prove I wasn't a coward, I
determined not to let him see that I felt humiliated. So instead of getting out
of his bed and creeping away in the middle of the night, I lay there sleepless
until morning, going over and over the encounter, then showered, dressed,
and drank coffee with him, terribly aware of having a sort of strange
double vision of him, as he had been the night before and as he had been
debriefing me. He behaved as though nothing odd had happened. And when
we parted, he kissed me lightly on the lips and said goodbye very casually, as
though we would be meeting soon. I was upset all day, kept thinking of how
he had said he was my controller now... Later in the day, I grew angry. And
that's when I resolved to turn the tables on him, to show him he could not
use me that way, to force him to speak more honestly and—perhaps most
importantly—to humiliate him in return. I didn't know if he'd let me, but I
intended to use the same tactics on him he had used on me...

Unable to continue, Elizabeth put the book down on the floor
beside the sofa. What was it she had said to Zeldin, scoffing at the
idea that Zeldin could be anyone's victim much less Sedgewick's? She
recalled extorting from Kay the admission that she had experienced
an orgasm during the encounter she described. What had she been
thinking the first time she had read this entry? She had been full of
triumph, yes, at Kay's capitulation. She had insisted to Kay that she
had had control over her sexual relationship with Sedgewick, that that
relationship had been mutual, reciprocal, and wholly consensual...
No victims, Kay, she had told her, it is Sedgewick who was hurt, not
you... You came out of it psychologically unscathed... But it read
differently now. She could so easily visualize the scene, so easily imagine Sedgewick's executive ease of managing a drunk and inexperienced professional woman afraid of being thought a coward, subtly
mixing in her mind executive Sedgewick as controller with Robert
Sedgewick her lover, fearing his contempt at her cowardice, unable
to think clearly enough to see through his arguments... Elizabeth returned the leather book to the safe. Why read it? Would Sedgewick

care about any of these memories, beyond being avid for a taste of them? If he read this particular entry he would have his own version of it, just as she herself had had a different understanding of it when she had first read it than she had of it now. Suddenly, an insight struck her: Sedgewick often used the same tactic on Company people—on herself, in fact—playing on their fear of being seen as either cowards or soft. As she herself sometimes did. People were so easily managed through their fear of the contempt of a superior.

Tidying the office, Elizabeth wondered how many things she had done out of such fear, done mainly for Sedgewick, too. Did she still have such a fear by which he could yet manage her? Lately, Sedgewick had been finding it necessary to tap other fears—overtly... It was as though every individual were composed of a series of fears through which they would always be vulnerable to those shrewd enough to discern and exploit them. And the best kind of management, of course, was covert. How many times had Sedgewick so managed her? But that was something, she realized, that she would never know.

Elizabeth phoned her driver and asked him which door they should use. He suggested the rear entrance since they had used the garage twice already that day and the side door the last time she had worked late.

She would go home, Elizabeth thought, and forget about Zeldin, her job, and most of all about Sedgewick. She would think, instead, about Hazel and about how she had persuaded the girl to see her again. And then she would sleep.

Chapter Sixteen

[i]

The day after the Co-op made its first pick-ups in New Orleans, Martha woke not much before two in the afternoon to a deserted house. In the kitchen she found a note from Laura reminding her that the Inner Circle would be meeting at seven-thirty that evening. Everyone had agreed to postpone the meeting because the pick-up team had gotten back so late.

After making herself a cup of coffee, Martha flipped open her handset and punched in the number to the Austrian Consulate. The operator immediately put her through to Margot. "There's something we need to discuss," Martha said without preamble.

"I agree," Margot said—a little coolly, Martha thought. "I can see you any time before five-thirty."

Martha calculated how long it would take her to drink her coffee, shower, dress, and drive over to Capitol Hill. "I'll be there in forty-five minutes," she said.

Martha made it in just under a half-hour. A service-tech conducted her up the stairs to Margot's "sitting room." "Coffee?" Margot asked.

"Please," Martha said, still groggy after her heavy daylight sleep.

Margot poured a dark fragrant brew from a thermoflask into a flowery china cup and handed it to Martha. "I realize now that I should have said something to you about it immediately." The Austrian frowned. "But my first thought was that he was running you. Granted, I found it hard to comprehend his coming here with you so openly. But I conjectured you were playing a very deep game—playing *them*." Margot's mouth twitched. "You are such a shrewd one, Martha, that it wasn't inconceivable. Yet I see now that though you are shrewd you aren't necessarily *clever* in the sense of being capable of devious stratagem. It seemed incredible to me that you didn't *know*, and so I decided to be careful, and bide my time. Obviously that was a mistake, since—"

"Wait a minute," Martha said. She might still be feeling a little groggy, but she wasn't so out of it that she had lost her grasp of English. "I haven't understood a word you've been saying. Would you mind telling me what you're talking about?"

Margot gaped at her. "What I am talking about? What I am talking about? What *could* I be talking about but David Hughes, of course?"

"David Hughes!" Martha stared at her. "What about him?"

"You mean you haven't put it together yet, Martha? Is it possible that you didn't immediately deduce when the *Examiner* created the scandal that only he could have been behind it?"

Martha frowned. "No, of course not. I did realize that someone who knew me fairly well had to have been involved to have been able to supply them with the names of all my past lovers. But David? You're saying he works for the *Examiner?*"

Margot snorted. "In the greater interests of accuracy, let's say the *Examiner* works for him, dear. Frankly, I'm relieved to find he isn't running you. That would have been exceedingly inconvenient."

"Running me?" Martha said, unable to make sense of what Margot was saying.

"When SIC officers control and collect intelligence from agents, it's called 'running them,'" Margot said patiently.

"SIC officer! You're saying *David* is SIC?"

Margot shook her head. "You know, even with the aliens helping you, I don't see how you people have managed to stay alive the last ten years. It's written all over the man, Martha! I could smell it on him that day when you walked into the reception with him. And when I took you away from him, he made a beeline for old man Lauder himself, confirming my suspicion."

"You must be mistaken," Martha said. "I've known David for a long time. He's one of the few men I feel I can trust. He's too nice a guy to be an SIC officer."

"How many of them have you known?"

"I've known plenty of ODS types," Martha said. "And none of them were remotely like David Hughes."

Margot rolled her eyes. "The male who escorted you upstairs is as much an employee of the consulate as I am. Yet no one would ever think that knowledge of him in particular would by the same token make me recognizably an employee of this consulate. And that's the kind of comparison you're offering. ODS officers are simply police-men, Martha. While I doubt anyone would ever describe an SIC officer as one."

Martha set her cup down on the side table. "Still, your theory might not be true. Much of what was said in that article about me would be things many people would know, and probably gossip about, too."

"Are you saying that most of the Co-op has been silently complici-tous with this information all along?"

"Complicitous? Isn't that a rather strange word to be using in ref-erence to scurrilous gossip about my sex-life?"

"I'm not talking about your sex-life," Margot snapped. "I'm talk-ing about your associate's Night Patrol activities."

Martha's heart lurched; the blood rushed loudly in her ears. She stared at Margot in horror. "What are you saying?" she whispered.

Margot stared at her. "You mean you haven't seen yesterday's *Examiner* yet?"

Fear twisted and twined Martha's bowels, making her want to run for the toilet. "No. We went to New Orleans yesterday evening and got back very late. I called you as soon as I woke."

Margot rose from her chair and went out of the room. A long half-minute later she returned with a newspaper flimsy. "I suggest you read this now," she said, handing it to Martha.

Martha opened it. **The Co-op's Connection with the Night Patrol**, the headline screamed. Martha's vision blurred as she stared at the photo of Louise in Women's Patrol uniform holding a rifle.

> Louise Simon, though primarily known as the original organizer and perma-nent leader of the Co-op's all-women militia (called "The Women's Patrol"), also engages in other activities of equal if not greater significance. One of her lesser known activities is the training of terrorists in the use of arms and techniques of sabotage as well as propaganda and other arts subver-sive of law and order on this and other continents.

> However, Simon's best kept secret is her membership in the feared terrorist organization that styles itself the "Night Patrol." This gang, under the guise of punishing "known rapists," serves the general function in the Seattle area especially of intimidating men in their intimate relations with women (though the Night Patrol does on occasion venture into other areas of the Free Zone when they deem it judicious to do so). Simon is, of course, a lesbian, a confirmed man-hater. When the Night Patrol decides a man has not been treating his wife or girlfriend as they judge he should be, they murder him, strip his corpse naked, and erect a placard advising other males living in the Free Zone that the Night Patrol is on the job…

Martha looked at Margot. "I don't need to finish reading this to know how they're going to use it against us," she said. Damn Louise. That something like this would eventually happen had been inevitable from the start.

"Read on," Margot said. "You obviously haven't gotten to the part concerning yourself yet."

"Concerning *me?*"

"Read."

Martha continued. Her hands shook so badly she had trouble holding the page steady enough to read. After two more paragraphs lamenting the degree to which males in the Free Zone had been successfully terrorized and emasculated by the Night Patrol's activities, the article shifted to the Inner Circle:

> Of all aspects of the Co-op, perhaps the most revealing is its leaders' connection with the Night Patrol. The most powerful of them, Martha Greenglass [see last week's in-depth profile], was for almost two years Simon's lesbian lover. They broke up abruptly, however, on the day Greenglass, returning unexpectedly early from an out-of-town trip, discovered a garbage sack full of bloody clothing. The naively blind Greenglass thus finally tumbled to the ugly fact of Simon's murderous activities. While Greenglass apparently found this too much for her delicate pacifist sensibilities to bear, she took no steps to stop the Night Patrol from further bloodshed. A reasonable person might wonder why she did not.
>
> In fact, the attitude of Simon's colleagues in the Co-op has always been one of complicity—the unstated opinion being that the Night Patrol serves a "useful function" however "ideologically repugnant" it may be to the principles espoused by the Co-op. (Simon herself, a longtime advocate

of bloody revolution, has never at any time subscribed to the Co-op's alleged principles.)

This silent complicity is characteristic of the contradictions inherent in the Co-op. Moreover, it is utterly indicative of the Co-op's general attitude of contempt—when not one of open hatred—for men. It has been speculated that the reason the Night Patrol's murderous practices have never been stopped is the total anonymity of the members of the group. It will be interesting to see whether the Night Patrol, now that its leader has been unveiled, will be restrained—whether by the Co-op, or by a Men's Protection group.

The rest of the article excoriated Louise's activities "training up violent terrorists" and running the Women's Patrol, for which the author insidiously managed to imply a connection—through Louise—with the Night Patrol.

Martha flung the paper to the floor. "I never told David Hughes any of that," she said. She was sick to her stomach. How could this be happening?

Margot's eyebrows rose. "You don't really believe Hughes has been content with getting out of you only what you volunteer to him?" Her silvery gray eyes glittered with irony. "A man like Hughes can get state-of-the-art drugs and electronic equipment to use as he likes. I'm sure Sedgewick's gang gives him carte blanche. Just think how much the Free Zone is a thorn-in-the-flesh for the Executive. And he's been carrying you around in his hip-pocket for how many years is it?"

Martha flushed. "Something like eight or nine. It was right after I left Louise. I even went to bed with him a few times."

Margot rolled her eyes, and Martha mentally kicked herself for having blurted out what was no one's business but her own. "You're unbelievable, Martha. Considering the shrewdness with which you make business deals, you seem in other respects to be a total..." Margot shrugged. "No, I won't say it. Insulting you won't help." She broke the seal on a bottle of water and poured it into a glass. "You're going to have to dump Simon, and fast, you know."

Martha watched her drink down the glass she'd poured. "You think dissociating ourselves from Louise is the answer."

"Part of the answer." Margot set the glass on the table with considerable force. "Christ, Martha. Think of it. They didn't have to invent anything or even slightly twist or distort a near-truth. All the bastards had to do was report the facts." Margot poured more water into the glass. "I've roughed up a few rapists in my time, and properly so. But *killing* them? Stupid, for one thing. Extremist for another. And third, unnecessary. There are non-lethal methods that work perfectly well with rapists and without calling down the fury and paranoia of the male population. Why must your friend *kill* them? Don't you see that it's going to be damned hard for the Free Zone to sustain its position in this human rights thing?" The question, obviously, was rhetorical. Margot drank more water before continuing. Her eyes, watching Martha over the rim of the glass, flashed with a spurt of temper. "I'll tell you straight out, that if you people can't get your house sufficiently in order for shrugging off the flak you're going to be taking because of this revelation, the Austrian government, for one, will cut its ties with you—honoring the business contracts already signed, of course, but rescinding everything to do with the human rights project. The Consul is very clear on this."

Martha tried to think, but her mind, numbed by shock, seemed unable to do more than feebly register the fact of the newspaper article and David Hughes's role in it.

"You must see," Margot said when Martha failed to speak, "that the Night Patrol comes off as a sort of gender-slanted death squad tolerated or even encouraged by the Co-op's leaders. That being so, you'd better face the fact that the Executive will probably be able to bring world opinion around to its side."

"I've never quite understood the role of 'world opinion' in real events," Martha said slowly, trying to catch at something tangible. "For instance, our business deals…"

Margot smiled slightly. "True. But you yourself have led me to infer that you're more interested in the human rights issue than in all your myriad business dealings."

"We could still connect them," Martha said, trying to think.

Margot gave her a sharp look. "You're very strange, Martha," she said. "If you're saying what I think you're saying…it sounds very confused."

"I came over here to talk to you about ironing out certain details that came up during last night's pickup—our first," Martha said, remembering.

Margot said, "All that's on hold until we see what you and your people can do about that mess." She gestured at the newspaper lying near Martha's feet.

Flattened by confusion, Martha could think of nothing to say. "Well then I guess I'd better be going," she said. "Since there is obviously a great deal of talking and thinking that must be done."

Margot walked her to the head of the stairs. "Keep me posted," she said, putting her hand on Martha's arm.

"Yes." Martha started down the stairs. Thinking ahead to that evening's Inner Circle meeting and what she would have to tell them about David Hughes, she wondered what they *could* do. Had she been wrong not to accuse Louise and Diane publicly? It was like a bad dream, the way all this had come out at the worst possible moment. David Hughes...Martha recalled his efforts to keep her away from Margot and his various other pieces of advice. She thought: gulled—again. Maybe that first article had been "truth," too. Maybe she *was* naive and foolish and confused. Certainly she felt that way now.

[ii]

Celia stared at her reflection in the mirror. Never had she looked so much like an attorney as she did in this beautiful linen suit Emily had had custom-made for her. Though Emily was correct in arguing that she needed to be properly dressed and that it was no fault of her own that her last intact suit had been spoiled in jail, she felt uncomfortable accepting it, perhaps because it was so expensively made. She enjoyed the solid professional feeling the suit gave her, a feeling she had been missing for longer than she cared to remember... Her old cracked flat court shoes looked the worse for comparison, but they were her best and would have to do. At least they had no holes in them.

The new suit made her feel solid, but it didn't go far in cutting her dread of the arts affair she'd agreed to attend with Emily. She had never been good at affairs of "high culture" mixing professionals and executives. And she was still feeling so stressed around strangers that the thought of facing a crowd of them made her stomach ache. She had to get used to seeing people: she knew that. For how would she be of use if she couldn't take meeting strangers?

She stood at the front window and watched for Emily's car. Yes, they still lurked across the street, one in a two-seater, the other standing a few yards up the road. Why didn't they collaborate and pool their efforts?

When Emily's large, chauffeured car pulled up, Celia locked the door behind her and hurried to the street. Emily greeted her with a smile. "Ready for something different?"

When the car began moving, Celia noted that the watchdog without a car was talking into his wrist-phone. She twisted around to stare out the back window and spotted the other car following them. "We're being tailed," Celia said.

"Doesn't matter. They'll have trouble getting past the guard post to the Muirlands, and then we'll be free of them." They accessed the freeway. "Is your mother feeling better?"

"I can't believe her resilience. Believe it or not, she went in to work this afternoon, saying that so many of the hospital staff had been arrested she couldn't afford to goldbrick when all she'd needed was a good solid sleep. You know she slept from the time you left until five yesterday afternoon? I've never known her to sleep that long. Claire, on the other hand, got up at ten and went home, saying something about always waking at ten because she works a shift that begins at noon."

"The woman responsible for getting your mother released is going to be there this afternoon," Emily said.

Celia's stomach fluttered. "She's an ODS officer?"

"Not exactly. She's associated with ODS, but isn't really one of them. Let's say she has influence with them. I intend to press her about Luis Salgado today. But I can't quite decide whether or not I should introduce you to her as related to him—and as the daughter of the woman whose release she obtained."

Celia fingered the crease in her trousers. "Will you point her out to me?"

"Yes. Perhaps I should let you decide."

"You don't think she expects to be *thanked?*" Celia said, outraged at the possibility as it suddenly occurred to her.

"I don't know how these things work. At any rate, she did it as a personal favor to me, and not for you. I've already thanked her." Emily smiled wryly. "And I imagine some day she'll ask me for a favor in return."

Celia watched the oleanders fly by. It was said that the wide strip on which the oleanders and other flowers and shrubs flourished had in the old days held from four to six lanes of traffic and that all the vehicles traveling on it had been gasoline-powered free-wheelers. It was hard to imagine the need for so much roadway—cabled or free.

The car exited the freeway and headed west. Another place by the ocean? she wondered, twisting around to check on the watchdog. Yes, he had gotten off the freeway with them. And was there another car somewhere, following as well? How exactly did they work it? There would probably not have been any other cars matching the description of this one coming down Banker's Hill at the same time as they.

The car halted at a gate and the driver handed a uniformed guard a piece of plastic that was passed through a sensor and then returned to him. The gate opened and they drove through. Celia looked out the back window to watch as the guard held up her tail, but they soon passed out of visual range of the guard post, for the road twisted and climbed.

"Don't *worry*, Cee," Emily said. "Your tail will have to get special authorization to enter. That's the rule. Executives aren't any fonder of being harassed by security services than non-executives. Since they keep such tight security here they're allowed to make outside surveillance types jump through hoops before admitting them. By the time they do get in, this car will be off the street and out of sight. So for all practical purposes it doesn't matter who you see at Mytilene."

"Mytilene?"

"That's the name of the place we're going to. Named after a Greek Island inhabited by women artists and poets several centuries BCE."

Mytilene was certainly not a name in Celia's vocabulary, though she did have a familiarity with some of the classical Greek materials through her Latin and literature classes in college.

The car negotiated a serpentine course through wide, constantly curving streets affording frequent glimpses of both ocean and downtown San Diego. "What wonderful views people have here," Celia said. Barring, of course, the occasional bombed-out ruin.

"Which is why this is an exclusively executive neighborhood," Emily said. "The women of Mytilene are the only non-executives living in the enclave—except for the handful of live-in service-techs some of the executives prefer to dailies."

"If they're non-executives, how can they live here?"

The car stopped; after a few seconds a gate opened in the adobe wall along which many freewheeling vehicles had been parked. "They're artists and musicians and writers supported by an executive," Emily said. "The executive owns the property and lists the residents as live-in service-techs." The car drove in; the gate closed behind them. "Here we are. And now the car is off the street. There's no way they'll find you since they won't be allowed access to the names of property owners here without first getting a court order. Even if everything went their way it would take them at least two hours to manage, but probably more. Though I doubt they'll go to that kind of trouble unless you fail to reappear within a given number of hours." Emily opened the door.

Celia stepped out of the car and gaped at the overwhelmingly green setting. Lush exotic plants, profuse yet orderly in their arrangement, created a jungle-like ambience. She could think only of how much water they must require.

They walked along a flagstone path toward a large twentieth-century house. "The residents designed and built their living quarters themselves," Emily said, pointing at a thicket of exceedingly tall bird of paradise flowers partially screening another building. "If we have time I'll ask them to give you a tour—it's an interesting setup. But this house, here, is where they have their work areas. The rule is that we don't open the doors that are closed. But we are invited into any room whose door is open." They walked around to the front of the house.

About a dozen women occupied the large front room, a space without window-coverings or furniture, except for a long table along one wall. Photographs, etchings, and drawings covered the walls, and most of the women in the room stood in clusters discussing them. Emily led Celia through to a dim room in which the blinds over the windows had been closed. A few women sat in deep, engulfing lounges, each wearing a gray plastic apparatus that covered her eyes and ears and part of her skull. As Celia gazed on this strangeness, a block of light pooled in a corner of the room drew her eye. After looking at it for almost a minute, she realized it was a holograph and that its figures were all the same person arranged in different postures and wearing a variety of facial expressions. She had an urge to circle and examine it, for the idea of studying several manifestations of a single individual from so many different angles and perspectives at once fascinated her. And so when a woman wearing a long pink and purple robe glided up to Emily and put her arm around her, Celia, feeling first in the way and then, when the woman kissed Emily on the mouth, painfully embarrassed, sidled toward the holograph to get a better look at the tableau. Only as she inched around it did the shocking realization dawn on her that it was not a set holograph at all, for the figures' faces and bodies were constantly altering. Celia found something disorienting about the continual slight shifts in the depictions, for though one might be used to seeing stationary as well as moving holographs, one expected those that did not obviously appear to move to stay put as one walked around them and looked one's fill.

"I see you've discovered my mobility piece."

Celia turned to find Emily and the woman in the pink and purple robe standing just behind her. "Celia, meet Jean, the maker of this obsession," Emily said. "Jean, this is Celia."

"Emmie thinks there's something unhealthy in my being so absorbed with a single subject," Jean said, chuckling. "She thinks I must be madly in love with the model."

Emily smiled. "What nonsense, I never said that. But you must admit it's a trifle obsessed."

Celia felt a pressure to say something. "What is it called?"

Jean laughed. "'Portrait of a Woman.' Strikingly original, no? Of course the crucial question is whether it's really one portrait, or even one woman. 'Portraits of a Woman'? 'Portrait of Women'? 'Portraits of Women'? Take your pick. I prefer the double singular, myself. It can be taken as metonymic, or as literal, however one chooses."

"It's fascinating to watch such minute changes," Celia said, "only there's something disconcerting about the way the figures never seem to make contact with one another, don't even seem to be aware of one another's existence."

Jean's already bright eyes brightened still more. "Yes, that's part of the decision I made about this piece. Imagine if I'd made the figures to be looking at one another—the viewer would know it to be faked, of course, something arranged and forced by me—but even weirder would be the almost frightening degree of narcissism—or would it be that? Might it not be recognition? A rare painful self-honesty that such a scene would evoke? It might be like watching someone looking into half a dozen mirrors—only the reflections looking back wouldn't be exact reverse images, would they, since all my figures are in different phases to one another."

Celia's head fairly spun as she tried to think about Jean's suggestions for what the work might have been. "So you decided it would be more...natural, for the figures not to be seeing one another?" she asked, unsure that she understood what the artist had been saying.

Jean shrugged. "It's not natural at all, is it. No, I don't think it was naturalness I was looking for...maybe a commentary on how all one's different selves never quite—or at least only tangentially—connect except through the fact of their physical resemblance."

This reduced Celia to shivering silence.

"Will you be interested in seeing my latest retinal-feedback piece, Em?" Jean asked after a few seconds. "You too, Celia. There are four headsets. I'm sure the people using them now won't monopolize them all afternoon."

"They might," Emily said. "Your last piece was addictive."

Jean smiled. "For you, sweetheart, maybe, but clearly not for everyone. I've hardly sold any."

"Give it time, Jean," Emily said. "You can afford to be patient."

Jean grinned at Celia. "That's my patron speaking now, Celia."

Did that mean that the executive Emily had referred to as maintaining this place had been herself? Why hadn't she just come right out and said so?

"Has Lisa Mott been by yet?" Emily asked, changing the subject.

"I haven't seen her," Jean said.

"Lisa is the woman I mentioned to you," Emily said to Celia. "She lives across the street."

"With a wonderful view," Jean added to Celia. "Which I fiercely envy her." She looked at Emily. "I'm sure she'll be coming by. Ginger brought some pastry over this morning—it's with the refreshments laid out in one of the other rooms." Jean's gaze moved past Emily and Celia. "Anyway, according to Ginger, Lisa intended taking off from work early today so that she could join us." Jean gestured. "You can both have a chance at the piece now, they all seem to be finishing at once." Smiling, she swished past them.

Celia watched the women remove the headsets and set them carefully on the table in the corner. Jean talked for a minute or so with them, then said to Celia and Emily, "I'll be right back to get you set up," and followed the women into the front room.

"Half of everything they make here today will go to an assistance fund," Emily quietly told Celia. "We can use international plastic credits as well as M-dollars, so it hardly matters how they pay. Every member of Mytilene has agreed to this arrangement. One of them, a poet, spent some time in a prison camp three years ago. Her work, for that reason, is a little sensitive. We don't quite know what to do with it. We were thinking perhaps we could arrange for her to read for groups of simpaticos."

So at least someone here was politically inclined, Celia thought. The dreamy isolation of the place had been disturbing her, so far from reality did it seem. "One of my former clients is a cartoonist," Celia said. "Very sharply satirical. He always hoped to make enormous reproductions of his cartoons for wheat-pasting on the sides of buildings, but it never happened. Didn't have the resources or time. So mostly his things are passed hand to hand and occasionally appear in flyers." Celia thought of a recent cartoon of his lampooning Barclay Madden and wondered how Emily would react if she saw it. "Of course, *they* always manage to get hold of flyers and other samizdat. If they ever realize he's responsible for the lampooning cartoons, I shudder to think what they'd do to him."

"Get us in contact with him and we'll give him the resources he needs," Emily said seriously. "We have facilities here, you know. Sandy could probably handle it."

Celia nodded as nonchalantly as she could manage and tried to suppress her spurt of excitement as she imagined Martin's cartoons pasted over the sides of buildings and billboards all over San Diego. For a moment she wondered whether if Emily knew what and whom some of the cartoons satirized she would be so easily offering assistance. How far would she go to help, how far would she go to "keep her word"? "I'll try to get a message to him by a third party," Celia said. "I should tell you he's banned. Which means that it's illegal to in any way reproduce his work." She looked into Emily's eyes. "Are you willing to take that kind of risk?"

Emily nodded, very calmly, Celia thought. "Of course I am," she said.

Of course? The woman must believe she's immune to arrest, Celia thought. Perhaps she had good reason for believing that, but surely there were limits, even for the daughter of Barclay Madden?

Jean bustled back into the room. "A sale, Em!" she crowed. "And she wants *two* of them! I guess she doesn't necessarily consider it a solitary pleasure, as you've been characterizing my pieces."

"Well I don't see how sitting in the same room while another person is doing it will make it any less solitary," Emily said. "Their experiences will still be completely different."

"Ah, but my touch will be on those experiences," Jean said. "For no matter how much the participant's responses determine the unfolding of the piece, all the parameters, structures, and possibilities in it were created by me. So in some sense there *must* be a cohesive Jean Starobinski texture to the experience. You'll see, Emmie, when the scholarly types start analyzing my work."

"Heaven preserve us," Emily said. Jean made a face at her. "Okay, Jean, set us up," Emily said. "If it bores you, you can quit anytime you feel like it," she whispered to Celia as they sat down in the engulfing form-fit lounges.

Celia, having never sat in furniture like it, was surprised at how comfortable and relaxing it was—like being suspended and wrapped in a soft warmth-giving cocoon, like an artificial womb for adults…Jean handed her the apparatus. "Put it on your head and then I'll position the section that closes around the eyes for you," she said. Awkwardly Celia lifted the bulky plastic and glass thing onto her head; it fit like a helmet, only was less inclusive and surprisingly light. The ear pieces fit inside her ears.

"I've only one thing to tell you in advance," Jean said before she moved the largest piece of the apparatus into place. "What you see and hear will be partially determined by your retinal responses. There's a mechanism in the apparatus that will track your eye movements so that you will be engaged in a feedback process. It would be nice if we could do the same thing for hearing, but no one has any idea yet of how to easily track what individuals distinguish when they listen to sounds... So. Enough technical gobbledygook. Are you ready?"

A bit apprehensive at the idea of being so closed in, Celia nodded.

"Okay. Just relax and let it happen." Jean moved the protruding box on its hinges until it clicked into the latch on the other side of the helmet, plunging Celia into darkness.

After a few seconds Celia became aware of fuzzy reddish blurs of color drifting before her eyes. She strained to make out patterns. As she focused on one blob, it sharpened and clarified and exploded into activity. She grew aware of music and realized she had no idea when it had begun. Each time she thought she was managing to focus, the image would elude her, either dissolving or transforming into something else or receding into a larger pattern or exploding into furious activity.

After a while, she felt frustrated. Worse, she became disoriented and grew uncertain whether she was managing to distinguish what she was seeing from what she was hearing and tasting. When the patterns of light and sound began to induce unpleasant visceral sensations, Celia struggled into an upright position, put her hands to the helmet, and clawed at it to get it off her head. "Could somebody help me?" she called out, trying not to give way to her terror of being trapped inside a sensory nightmare.

Someone else's hands did what Celia's seemed unable to do and swung back the visual apparatus and lifted the helmet off Celia's head. "Thank god," Celia gasped, staring up at Jean.

"You're so pale!" Jean's eyes narrowed in concern. "Lie back and let me get you some water. You look as though you might be going to pass out."

Celia closed her eyes, aware only of the buzzing in her ears and the sweat drenching her body.

"Here, Celia," Jean's voice said, and Celia felt a glass pressed into her hand.

She opened her eyes and drank. "So disorienting," she said between sips. "I felt as though I were trapped in a nightmare."

Jean's eyes widened. "You found it upsetting?" She sounded incredulous.

The artist's incredulity made Celia feel foolish. "Yes, sorry. I don't know what's wrong with me, but I found something about it terrifying."

"Do you know exactly what?" Jean asked, looking fascinated. "I've never heard of anyone having that reaction before. I'm very curious, Celia."

"Well the synesthesia, for one thing," Celia said, grasping for something to say that might satisfy the artist's curiosity.

"Synesthesia! Wow! I wish I knew just what it was you experienced," Jean said wistfully. "No one has ever reported synesthesia before. My god, I wonder if I could get you to do some of my other pieces, to see what you make of them?"

Celia shook her head. "Sorry, but I don't think I could stand going through that again," she said apologetically. "It's made me sick to my stomach and given me a headache." The fluttering in her stomach, the vicious pain in her eyes made her feel like vomiting.

"I understand," Jean said, obviously disappointed. At the sound of approaching footsteps behind her, she glanced over her shoulder, then looked back at Celia. "Why don't you lie back for a while until you feel better. Emily will probably be under for a little while longer; it's only been ten minutes since you both started."

Celia emptied the glass as Jean set up the executive woman in the chair on the other side of Emily. What a strange way of putting it, she thought, *being under*. Yet appropriate. Celia shuddered. It had been a truly grotesque experience. But why did other people not find it as horrible as she had? Was there something wrong with her?

She held the empty glass in her lap and ran her finger around its rim. And to think all this was going on at the same time as people were enduring jail and prison camps. How did one fit the world together when people's experiences were so disparate? She stared at the ceiling and tried to think of other projects she might get Emily to support. Publishing the work of named and banned writers, perhaps? Or political analyses of the named and banned? There seemed to be so many possibilities, if Emily truly didn't mind the risk. But she must talk to Emily about that risk, first, to make certain she understood what she would be getting herself into. For if there was one thing *they* wouldn't tolerate, it was the flourishing of a public subversive literature and graphics, which had been all but stamped out since the end of the Civil War. No one was immune to their efforts at suppression, not even Emily Madden. And she had to be made to understand that before she got herself in any deeper.

Chapter Seventeen

[i]

Elizabeth reached across the table and clasped Hazel's hand. "So tell me." She smiled into Hazel's eyes. "Have you ever been in love?"

Hazel look startled. "Of course," she said. "By my age I must have, don't you think?"

Elizabeth toyed with Hazel's fingers, which were freckled and ringless. "So you imagine everyone falls in love when they're young?"

The service-tech interrupted them to set drinks—wine for Hazel, grapefruit juice for Elizabeth—and plates before them, and a basket of bread and a platter of antipasto between them. "I take it *you've* never been in love," Hazel said dryly before taking a first sip of the wine.

"I'm not sure." Elizabeth reached for a plump shrimp that had been broiled in garlic and olive oil in its shell. "I've cared very deeply and have sometimes been extremely, ah, infatuated sexually, I suppose that's the way to put it, but I'm not sure what is meant by 'in love.' Everyone else seems to know what it means, though. Which is why I asked."

Hazel stared into her glass. "When your life turns inside out because of your feelings for another person, I'd say that can be called being in love. I'll confess I can't imagine an executive ever feeling that way about one of us."

Elizabeth wasn't prepared for that. She felt a flash of an unpleasant sensation in her stomach, as though it were performing backflips. Hazel seemed to be as bad as Allison at saying the wrong thing. "Don't talk that way, darling. Please," she said very low. Such remarks implied a deep anger at executives, perhaps even at the executive system, and therefore was something Hazel must be made to keep silent about. Elizabeth knew they couldn't be directed at her personally, for she felt certain Hazel did not resent her. It was possible that Hazel was the wrong person to be bringing into the office… Yet, irrationally, Elizabeth still longed to have her there and felt certain that once their relationship became more settled Hazel would be an intelligent, sympathetic, and above all loyal ally strategically placed to do a great deal of good. "Were you in love with your first lover?" she asked, determined to shift the conversation back onto the right track.

Hazel stared at her a moment before speaking. "Why are you asking me these things, Liz?"

She sounds suspicious of my motives, Elizabeth thought. It's as though outside of direct sexual contact it's impossible to reach her. "Because I'm interested in you," Elizabeth said evenly. "If you think it's none of my business I'll of course back off. Or if you like I'll tell you about my first lover, though for me the subject of my past life is a bore while the subject of yours is completely unexplored." Elizabeth ate another shrimp. "Try these before I gobble them all up," she said, for Hazel hadn't touched any of the food.

"I'm not very hungry." Hazel took another sip of wine.

"Then I'll fill up on this stuff and we'll order dinner much later," Elizabeth said, smiling.

Hazel blushed. "No, don't do that. It's just that I'm, well, a little keyed-up tonight. I doubt I'll get any hungrier."

Oh god. She was upset. It must have to do with all that nonsense in the foyer still. Damn Sedgewick, always spoiling everything. Reaching around the antipasto, Elizabeth took Hazel's hand. "Tell you what," she said. "Why don't we see if we can get hold of a Jacuzzi here in the club. That'll relax you. And then see what we feel like doing after that." Elizabeth grinned. "There are ways of working up a good appetite, you know."

"No, no, don't change your plans on my account," Hazel said quickly. "Let's just have dinner the way we'd planned. It's my problem, not—"

"*My* plans?" Elizabeth said, interrupting. "*My* only plan is to sometime in the course of this evening eat a good dinner and get you into bed." She withdrew her hand from Hazel's and snatched up a skewer of provolone and prosciutto and popped it into her mouth. "There are dozens of ways of doing that, *n'est ce pas?*"

To Elizabeth's relief, Hazel laughed with her. "Too bad we can't reverse the order," she said with a sly look.

"We can," Elizabeth said grandly. "After I finish all these goodies we'll take a room upstairs…and then later we can come down and gobble some more. For a hedonist like me, the prospect is paradisial!"

But no sooner were the words out of her mouth than the handset in Elizabeth's pocket began beeping. Elizabeth's smile faded. "Sorry, darling," she said. She held the handset to her ear. "Weatherall."

"It's Higgins, Madam. Mr. Sedgewick asks that you attend him here at his house at once."

"I'm in the middle of a dinner engagement, Higgins," Elizabeth said sharply. "Tell him I'll see him tomorrow." She did need to see Sedgewick, to work out the details of the arrangements for Alexandra. But she was damned if she'd ruin her evening for him. From now on she would have a personal life that he couldn't touch.

"Um, I'm sorry, Madam, but Mr. Sedgewick asks me to inform you," Higgins said in a palpably uneasy voice, "that he will send you an escort if necessary."

Elizabeth went very still—and then felt the blood fairly exploding into her head. Send her an escort? Higgins' polite euphemism, likely, for the damned flunky wouldn't have the guts to repeat outright the phrasing Sedgewick had probably used. "Very well, Higgins," Elizabeth said coldly. "I'll leave here at once." She put the handset back into her pocket and pressed the call-button set under the edge of the table. Hazel, she saw, was staring fixedly at the rose in its crystal bud vase. "I'm sorry, darling," she said, sighing, "but I'm going to have to interrupt our evening. It's something I can't put off. The hell of it is that I don't even know how long it will take. If I knew it wouldn't take long I'd leave you here and rejoin you as soon as I was able. But I just don't know. I suppose I'll have to have my driver take you home after he drops me off." Elizabeth sketched a smile. "It's so damned disappointing."

All the way to Sedgewick's house as she kissed and fondled Hazel Elizabeth wondered in what state she'd find Sedgewick. He'd never attempted this kind of tactic when drunk. Could he be sober? She had assumed him to be bingeing though she didn't really know since she had refused to let Higgins tell her anything about the man's condition.

When the car stopped Elizabeth unwillingly withdrew, rupturing the rapturous sexual cocoon they had been spinning around themselves. "This is ridiculous," she said as she took her hand out of Hazel's pants. "If only I knew——" She shouldn't have been letting herself get so worked up during the drive; she should have been pulling herself together into cold control.

"Maybe I should wait for you," Hazel whispered. "I wouldn't mind. I'll feel the same I'm feeling now if I go home, only without any prospect of seeing you later."

Elizabeth tried to think. "I don't know, darling, it could be a very, very long time. Tell you what, why don't I have the driver wait until he hears from me. Then, when I've assessed how long it will likely take, I'll get word to him about whether he should drive you home or not. How's that?"

Hazel wound her arms around Elizabeth's neck and pressed her lips to Elizabeth's. Elizabeth pulled away. "You're terrible," she scolded. "I'm going in there with wet pants. I won't be able to think straight." *It has long been recognized that women are victims of their own uncontrolled sexuality. Moreover, due to the extreme diffusion of their sexual sensations, surgery eliminating this source of instability and irrationality cannot be performed with any degree of success.*

Elizabeth opened the door and stepped out into the chilly night. All right, Sedgewick, she thought grimly. This had better be good.

[ii]

Martha managed to track Louise to the Women's Patrol office well in advance of the Inner Circle's scheduled meeting. She stood before Louise's desk. "We have to talk," she said.

Louise leaned back in her swivel chair and leveled a hard stare at her. "Isn't it a little late to be making confessions?" she said ironically.

So Louise seemed to think she, Martha, had a confession to make? "I've just been talking to Ganshoff." Martha said. "All indications are that we've had the ground cut out from under us by this latest *Examiner* article. Ganshoff thinks the Inner Circle should dissociate ourselves from you."

Louise smiled sardonically. "And what does Martha Judas Iscariot Greenglass think?"

Martha gaped at her. "You believe *I* planted that story in the *Examiner*?"

"Who else? How else could anyone know the reason we split unless you told them?"

Martha swallowed. "Remember that bug I found in my collar so many years ago?"

"Yeah," Louise said, "I remember. That was the beginning of our unending campaign against electronic surveillance."

"Well I think I know who planted it. And probably the same person who put it there found out about our reason for splitting, either by bugging us or by using a drug on me. Ganshoff says such drugs exist."

Louise sighed. "I give, Martha. Who do you think bugged you?"

"David Hughes. Ganshoff says she knew the first time she laid eyes on him that he's SIC."

"That economist whose arms you fell into after you left me?"

"I never told him, Louise. I couldn't stand the thought of talking about it...to anyone. Obviously I made a mistake," she added bitterly. "I let personal loyalty override my morality. If I'd done what I should have we wouldn't be in this mess today. I can see now I should've stopped you and Diane. But since I didn't, I'm implicated in all the killings since then myself. Both of us will have to resign from the Co-op."

Louise rolled her eyes. "What bullshit. Since when do the opinions of the executive world matter to you? Or to any of us? The only people whose opinions matter are other Co-op people and the Marq'ssan. I don't know about you, but I refuse to be bound by executive values. And if you cave now, Martha, that's what you'll be doing."

"I know you've never given a shit about killing people. But don't you mind being called a death squad?"

Louise sat bolt upright and slammed her fist onto her desk. "I don't share your pacifist principles, Martha, so don't start trying to load me with a guilt trip!" Louise glared at her. "By my reckoning I'm doing just fine. And while we're at it, let's tell the whole truth here: if you had thought it was *that* terrible you would have stopped me."

"You're wrong." Martha's hands balled into fists. "I just couldn't stand to think about it, at least not enough to drag it out into the light for everyone to see. I was a moral coward, Louise, not wantonly complicitous. There's a difference!"

Louise laughed. "You mean delicacy as opposed to complacency?"

Martha's fists fell open and she leaned back against the door frame. A wave of self-disgust washed over her.

Louise watched her. After a couple of beats, she said, "Lady, your distinctions are far too fine for someone as crude as me." She got up from her chair and went to the water cupboard. "You want some?" she asked as she took a half-liter bottle from the shelf.

"Please," Martha said wearily.

Louise handed Martha a bottle, then returned to her chair and broke the seal of the one she had kept for herself. "I hope to god this meeting tonight isn't going to be a wringing of hands over spilled milk. If I thought it was I wouldn't bother to go. We need to be preparing a strategy of counterattack, not beating our breasts over dead rapists."

Martha drank from the bottle. "I can't imagine what we could possibly do other than purge the Inner Circle of ourselves," she said. The water seemed to make her stomach even more upset, as though strengthening the churning acid tormenting it.

Louise's mouth twitched with disgust. "Oh christ, Martha, since when have you gotten to be so negative? I'm sure there's plenty we can do. You're not going to claim that those bastard governments decided to help us because they felt morally impelled to do so, are you?"

"Look, you're right about that, I'll grant you that much," Martha said. "But it's going to be much harder now——"

"That's no reason to talk as though we've already lost the battle, is it?"

"No, you're right," Martha said. "But I still think we should consider resigning."

"And *I* think we should decide what we're going to do about David SIC Hughes," Louise said. "Don't you?"

Martha's eyes widened. "I hadn't thought of that."

"Well let's think about it now," Louise said. "We have approximately an hour and a half until the meeting's scheduled to begin."

Martha swallowed the last of the water in the bottle. Her throat still felt dry.

"Obviously the first question," Louise said, "is to decide whether we have anything to gain from hiding our knowledge that he's a sickie..."

A sickie, Martha thought. Now that was a perfect tag for the son-of-a-bitch. If it were up to her and it were only her feelings at stake, she'd never willingly lay eyes on the man again. But however personal their relationship had seemed to be, it involved everyone now. And that was something she was just going to have to get used to.

[iii]

Elizabeth stationed herself at the foot of the sofa and stared down at Sedgewick's ghastly pallor and glassy, lusterless eyes. He hadn't looked this bad in years. "Sit down, Weatherall." His expressionless voice was nearly inaudible.

Elizabeth did not move. "Am I to assume this is an all-evening assignment, or should I have my car wait?" she said in her iciest voice.

He blinked. "Please, sit down. There's time enough to decide that."

"Why did you summon me here, Sedgewick? Your threat though discreetly conveyed naturally compelled my obedience."

He closed his eyes. "For godsake, Weatherall, at least sit down before you start in. I don't have the energy to cope with your towering over me while you rail at and revile me."

Pressing her lips tightly together, Elizabeth sat in one of the chairs by the fireplace. "Simply flexing your muscles again, I see," she said. "How much pleasure spoiling my evenings seems to give you. I have so few of them to myself, and then when I do take one you interrupt it. How sad that you have so little pleasure in life that such small outbursts of malice are all that remain to you. Quite a——"

"I apologize, Weatherall," Sedgewick said, opening his eyes and sitting up, "if I've spoiled your evening. That wasn't my intention."

Elizabeth laughed angrily. "Oh then you have some purpose in compelling my presence?"

His face twisted. "Why do you make me ask you to come? You know I need you."

Elizabeth, her eyes prickling, fought for self-control. "The perfect tool does only what it's told to do. The perfect tool does not act spontaneously, Sedgewick. The perfect tool is perfectly obedient. The perfect tool comes only when called. The perfect tool——"

"That's enough!" Sedgewick said hoarsely. "If I'd known your feelings were so tender I'd never have used that expression to you. But——"

"Bullshit," Elizabeth said harshly, drowning out his next words. "You told me what you wanted. We're not talking about tender *feelings*, Sedgewick; we're talking about what you want from me. Remember? You told me what you want from me—no, what you *expect* from me, I believe that was the word you used. And that was well after you informed me I'm not indispensable to you. Let's keep things clear, at least as clear as you made them. Now. If you will tell me in what way you *need* me, the perfect tool will comply with the new orders." She stared at him, knowing full well he understood the nature of her challenge.

"Don't do this to me," he said. "You know I can't take this from you right now."

After about half a minute, Elizabeth hissed at him, "What is it you want, Sedgewick?"

He put his hands to his face and steepled his fingers over his nose. After a long time he dropped them into his lap and looked at her. "Forgive me, Weatherall. I apologize for being so obnoxious and abusive to you. When you didn't return as planned..." He wet his lips. "Can't we forget all this and go back to the way we were?"

"How do you expect to be able to do that? You threaten to lock me up if I don't do what you want, then you threaten to kill me if I leave—surely you don't think I can forget such threats?"

"I *never* threatened to kill you!"

Elizabeth clicked her tongue in disgust. "Of course you blanked out that little scene in my living room. How convenient your drunks are for you, Sedgewick."

He rubbed his face. "If I made such a threat I apologize for it. You know I'd never harm you."

"Sure," Elizabeth scoffed, "the way you'd never harm Zeldin. You do remember what you did to her at Calais?"

"I swear to you I'd never harm you," he said. "Your packing like that upset me. We both know I can't function without you."

Elizabeth let that hang in the air for about a minute before speaking. "Can't function." She rose from her chair and prowled restlessly, unable to stay seated, not feeling in control at a time when she should be, not sure what she should be doing with him at this his most vulnerable moment in years. She came to a halt in back of the sofa and stared down at the crown of his head. "What is it you want of me, Sedgewick? Let's get everything clear once and for all."

He made a choking sound in his throat. "For godsake, Weatherall, you know what I need."

"Let's be clear about it, Sedgewick. Spell it out." She would make him say it; make him pay for all that he had put her through.

His shoulders hunched. "I can't do it alone." He choked the words out, as if having to wrench them out of an unwilling throat. "You can't have any idea how hard it was getting through these last two days alone. I can't manage the office without you; I can't hold even myself together without you. You know I need you to take care of me." He twisted around and stared up at her. "Is that what you want, Weatherall, to hear me say it? Or do you want more? Shall I crawl to you?"

"You need to be punished," Elizabeth said, staring hard into his eyes.

"What more, then?" he asked faintly, accepting her verdict.

Elizabeth swelled with an elation that drowned her anger and misery. Really, there was nothing more she could do to punish him, at least not for the moment. She steeled herself; half smiling, she reached out her hand and lightly stroked his face. He closed his eyes. "No more of your nonsense, Sedgewick," she said softly. After perhaps half a minute she withdrew her hand, then moved around the sofa and settled back down in the chair.

"You'll dine with me?" he asked, his attitude both humble and eager.

Elizabeth knew she would have to. And besides, she could use the occasion to work out all the details about Alexandra. "Alexandra will join us," she said. "I've been discussing the matter of Crowder's with her and have got her to the point of agreeing to go—under certain conditions."

"Conditions?" Sedgewick said, frowning. "I won't make deals with my daughter, Weatherall. She's in no position to exact conditions from me."

She shook her head. "It won't be seen to be exacting conditions, Sedgewick, unless you insist on it. She will simply tell you she's decided to obey you. While you, for your part, will back up whatever arrangements I've made with her."

"Such as?"

Elizabeth stretched her legs out before her. "Such as visits at the school from Raines and her grandparents, and the possibility of negotiating again in autumn if the spring term is unbearable to her. And two or three weeks with her mother in the summer."

"The one thing I'm determined to stop is so much contact with these maternal influences."

"You can't simply cut her off like that, Sedgewick. It would make it very difficult for her to adapt to her new situation. Furthermore, she'd never forgive you. As it is you're something of a monster to her with this iron fist policy you've visited on her. What I suggest is that you make it as easy for her as possible, and wean her. I can help with that since at the moment she sees me as her only accessible friend in a world of cold, hostile enemies. I can mediate between you. But if you don't give her that much she'll just make herself sick holding out against you. She's a stubborn girl, Sedgewick."

"You've made up your mind, I see."

"Yes," Elizabeth said, "I have. I think you've handled it very badly."

He looked down at his hands. "All right, we'll do it your way."

"Good. Then I'll go up and tell her she's to dine with us. And advise her there will be visits and so on. And then when she comes down she'll make her apology to you and so on, just as you demanded." Elizabeth got to her feet.

"Then I suppose we should eat in the small dining room," Sedgewick said.

"Nonsense," Elizabeth said. "We'll eat in here. It will be far less awkward for all of us." She went to the door, then turned and glanced back at him. "And Sedgewick, please try to show her a little less of the cruel father this time. You might be surprised at the difference it could make in her response to you."

Before Elizabeth went upstairs to Alexandra she went out to the car. She opened the rear door first and leaned in to talk to Hazel. "I'm sorry, darling, but our evening's off entirely," she said. She drew Hazel's hand to her lips and kissed it.

"I understand," Hazel said.

"Maybe tomorrow?" Elizabeth said, thinking it would be Sunday and therefore Hazel's day off. "No, wait, I don't think I can make it tomorrow," she corrected, realizing she'd have to work like a madwoman to make up for all the time lost over the last week. "Someday soon, though," she said lamely, wondering how that could be. "I'll find time somehow, darling." She made this a promise as much to herself as to Hazel. She knelt on the edge of the seat and offered Hazel a lingering kiss, then withdrew with the greatest reluctance. She instructed the driver to return after taking Hazel home.

Upstairs, receiving no answer to her knock, Elizabeth opened the door to find Alexandra stretched out on the bed listening to strange, sonorous music on the speakers Elizabeth had bought her the day before. "What is that music?" Elizabeth asked.

Alexandra started and turned her head toward the door. "Elizabeth! I didn't know you were coming to see me tonight!" Her face grew radiant.

"A nice surprise, then. But what *is* this music?"

"It's from the Renaissance. Josquin des Pres. Isn't it beautiful?"

"I've never heard anything like it," Elizabeth said.

"The harmonies and counterpoint are incredibly different from other Western music, and there's something so, so *sublime* about it." Her eyes shone with excitement and pleasure.

How unexpected to hear Alexandra use a word like *sublime*. "I've been talking with your father about you," Elizabeth said.

Alexandra's face dimmed. She got up and turned off the music. The sudden silence in the room seemed loud to Elizabeth's ears. "What did he say, Elizabeth?"

"He's agreed to your conditions," Elizabeth said, smiling. "But you mustn't mention them to him, and you must apologize for your disobedience, and for challenging him. Clear?"

"I understand. But I'll be able to see Mama and Grandmother?"

"Yes. You may have visits and phone calls. What you must do now, though, is get dressed. You're to join us for dinner."

Alexandra bit her lip. "You mean I have to talk to him tonight?"

"Don't you think it would be best to get it over with, love? You'll have your freedom then. Remember, there's a piano downstairs. And plenty for you to do in DC."

"Until I have to leave to go to that place," Alexandra said bitterly.

Elizabeth brushed a few loose strands of hair from Alexandra's eyes. "Don't go negative on me now, love. I'll be there, helping out. You know you're going to have to deal with him by yourself eventually. Better to see him first while I'm here, don't you agree?"

"Yes." The girl was plainly reluctant. "I know you're right. But I wish...I wish it could be just the two of us."

Elizabeth laughed. "The world doesn't work that way, love. And you know it. Now come on, let's get you dressed. Which stunning new outfit will you wear tonight? How can we best dress you up as the sweet demure daughter?"

Alexandra giggled. "Sweet demure daughter? Oh, that's me all right!" She was clearly delighted to be sharing this joke with Elizabeth.

Elizabeth opened the armoire. "Yes, the sweet demure daughter... Hmmm...Yes, this will do, this lovely pink thing, don't you think? Of course, we don't want to overdo it, or he'll suspect we're pulling his leg..." Elizabeth lifted the chosen hangers off the rack and turned to face Alexandra. "But seriously, love. Remember what I told you about handling him. He's got superior firepower for the moment, so you have to let him feel he's winning. Don't, whatever you do, challenge him, or he'll humiliate you for it." Elizabeth sighed. "If your mother were here she'd be telling you the same thing. She knows all about being in that situation with him."

Alexandra slipped out of her gown and took the tunic from Elizabeth. She seemed to be not at all shy of undressing before another executive woman. "How do you stand it, Elizabeth?" she asked.

Elizabeth helped pull the tunic down over Alexandra's head. "Well you must have noticed I get my way a fair bit with him. I suppose that's how I stand it."

Alexandra looked pensive. "I don't know if it would be worth it," she said, taking the trousers from Elizabeth. "Wouldn't it be better not to have anything to do with him?"

Elizabeth laughed. "Oh, love, what an innocent you are. Ten years from now I'll remind you of your having asked me that question."

Alexandra stepped into the trousers. "I guess I don't understand," she said—sadly, Elizabeth thought.

"You will, love, one day you'll understand all too well." Elizabeth sighed. "Take my word for it." There could be no question that Alexandra would understand. Not after all the years of Sedgewick she had lying ahead of her, poor girl.

[iv]

Martha wasn't sure how she had expected her colleagues to react, but certainly not like this. They were almost half an hour into the meeting, and no one had so much as referred—even in the most oblique fashion—to what must be uppermost in everyone's minds, much less opened discussion of it. But all the while they discussed the details of the "Rescue Mission" (as they called it), Martha sensed the group's uneasy restlessness, manifested in their fidgeting, irritable remarks and a tendency to lose track of the subject under discussion. Louise wore her sardonic look: her face hardened; her movements, gestures, and posture studiedly casual, her voice throaty and drawling. Were the others shocked? Horrified? Or merely embarrassed? Had it been a surprise to all of them, or had some of them suspected? And what were they thinking of her, Martha, for having kept such a secret for so long? Or of *not* having kept it—for surely some of them must suspect from the details of the article that the revelation in some way implicated her.

It was Venn who, without warning, parted the thick, careful atmosphere—by creating, as it were, an incision she had sketched out by eye and had through sheer grit determined to open—confronting them all, without hope of evasion, with what they had only pretended to be keeping concealed. "I realize you want all these political education materials written and published and disseminated instantly," Venn said. "But I'm warning you, you'll have to give me priorities. We practically killed ourselves working overtime to get out that last issue of *The Rainbow Times* with an exposé and analysis of the provocateur firebombing of the supposed *Examiner* warehouse. Then there's this personal narrative project you say you're anxious to get out, as well as the extended journalism piece you want based on the collection of data from various sources around the continent. But as I see it, I think we have to wonder whether the Press shouldn't be concentrating on getting the *Examiner*'s propaganda exposé out, first."

Without realizing it, Martha held her breath as she stared down at her yellow pad and listened. She could feel a current of energy rippling through the room and wondered if the others, too, divined where Venn was taking them. Venn continued: "It seems to me that unless we find some way to counter all this muck the *Examiner* is pouring over us, everything else we try to do will be degraded. Our very credibility is on the line, folks. If the first two pieces are anything to judge by, we're in for one hell of a rough ride. For myself, I can easily imagine being labeled the group's propagandist and token intellectual. Considering the style of the one they did on Louise, it seems they're shrewdly directing these pieces toward disrupting the cohesiveness and basic level of trust we've so far enjoyed within this group."

A painful, extended silence set in. Not only did no one speak, but the room was devoid of the usual meeting sounds of coffee cups being moved and papers being shuffled; Martha heard only the occasional rustle of individuals re-crossing their legs or shifting in their chairs. She kept her gaze on her yellow pad for a long time, until, finally, trying to make up her mind to speak, she raised her eyes to look across the table at Louise.

And at that moment Louise broke the silence. "It's true that I'm one of the Night Patrol," she said. "I'm not ashamed of it." Her gaze flicked at Martha, then took aim at Venn. "I've kept it dark because I knew that most of you disapproved of the Night Patrol in spite of all that it's done for this community. But if you can't find a way to reconcile that activity with my position with the Co-op, I'll leave—taking the Women's Patrol with me. I wouldn't blame you if you dissociated yourselves from me and condemned me publicly. I can see the argument that might be made for the political expediency of doing so. And certainly it would delight the Executive's Security forces, who are behind all these assaults on us. But I wouldn't agree that it's the correct course the Co-op should be taking. Not by a long-shot."

"I think your resignation is an excellent idea," Cora said. "We can't afford to have someone known to be a murderer as a leading light of the Co-op." There was a gasp at the word, but Cora ignored it. "Not when we're so loudly accusing the Executive of human rights abuses and offering asylum to its victims." She tapped her pen on the table and glanced around at the others. "And, I might add, right now, while there's still time, if anyone else has any skeletons in their closets, they, too, should consider removing themselves—*before* the damage hits. We can't afford to be castigating the Executive when we're culpable of things equally terrible."

"Wait a minute, Cora," Martha said. "It might be that Louise should withdraw. About that I don't know. I think an argument could be made that it's more important than ever that we stick together and not allow these people to divide us—as they're apparently succeeding in doing. But aside from that, I find the comparisons you're making odious—comparing the Inner Circle to the Executive, as though we were a governing body, and comparing the Night Patrol to the people who have been imprisoning, torturing, and raping innocent people. Killing rapists isn't quite in the same league as that other stuff." Grace started to say something in objection, but Martha drove on, "I don't approve of the Night Patrol. I don't know where the *Examiner* got its information. It's true, though, that Louise and I broke up over it. But that doesn't mean I think we should purge Louise—not to mention the Women's Patrol, though everyone knows how I've objected to much of the Women's Patrol's activities. I just think we need to be careful about how we react." Martha stared at Cora. "Defensive reaction is precisely what they want of us. They're hoping we'll get ourselves into even more of a mess by reacting rashly."

"What gets me, Martha," Bert said in a rush, "is that all the time you let Louise and her gang do this, you used your in with the Marq'ssan to stop the City of Spokane from trying and imprisoning rapists and thieves." Her green-blue eyes glinted with resentment that had obviously been long in building. "You even made us empty our jails with all your damned arguments about not being a government. You gave us no choice at all. And we weren't *killing* them, only preventing them from harming innocent people!"

"So you think I gave the Night Patrol my blessing?" Martha said. "Is that what you're saying?"

"We all know the Marq'ssan wouldn't have sanctioned the Night Patrol," Lenore said. "If they'd had any idea at all that Louise was involved in it they would never have supported the Co-op. I think we should be thinking about how the Marq'ssan are going to react to this. Their opinion is more important than that of the rest of the world put together."

"You're all missing the most important points," Laura said. Her opaque dark brown gaze swept around the table. "The first is that we're all implicated in the Night Patrol's activities, and I don't mean by Louise's participation in the killings or by Martha's knowledge of them. What I mean is that at any given point if we'd considered it important enough we would have done something about it. We could have found out who the Night Patrol was if we really wanted to. But we didn't. It suited our convenience to ignore it. Because let's face it, friends, at the time the Night Patrol started operating, the women in this town were pretty damned freaked out by the rapes going on. And when we finally got rid of the executives, each of us knew damned well—even if we didn't say it—that we had no idea how we were going to deal with violent men. The Night Patrol gave us a sense of safety, it—"

"That's bullshit," Martha shouted, furious. "The cops never did anything to make women feel safe. Why should we feel any less safe without cops? No, the reason I didn't do anything was because I couldn't face the godawful truth about what Louise is!" Heat rose into her face and spread down her neck. "I just couldn't bear to look at the truth. I didn't have what it took. So I pretended…when I could. My solution was to cut Louise out of my life as much as possible. Half the time when she's sitting at this table I don't *really* see her." Martha glanced across the table at Louise. "Oh, I *thought* I was caught by personal loyalty, but that was just something I told myself to explain why I kept it secret. I'd say to myself, 'and to think this person was once my lover!' God, sometimes when I came up against that thought I'd get so crazy I'd do anything to blot it out." Unable to go on, Martha halted. No one, she saw, was looking at her. She reached for a bottle of water, but her hands were shaking too much to get it open. Listlessly she dropped it into her lap.

Louise's voice cut into the silence. "The real point we have to address here is how we're going to keep this thing from destroying either the Co-op or the rescue operation or both. It's obvious to me that we've got to present a uniform front to the world. It's no goddam right of any government to tell the Free Zone how to deal with its rapists. If we let them get a moral victory out of this, we've had it. 'Cause believe me, if we give way on this there will be other things. If we have to have courts of law to deal with rapists, then we'll have to have courts to try civil law suits enabling executives to regain all the property they've lost since we drove them out, and on and on. This isn't a discrete issue."

"If you make that argument, Louise," Venn said, "then they can say they have the right to deal with suspected dissidents as they please. Dissidents threaten the executives' way of life. As rapists—the analogy would go—threaten ours."

Louise snorted. "No one is going to buy that analogy, Venn. For one thing, we've killed exactly eighty-nine rapists since February 2076—and that includes the ones we've done outside Seattle. While they've tortured and sometimes murdered thousands since then. There's no comparison."

Martha put her hands over her face. How could this discussion be taking place? It was *insane.* And what *would* Sorben say? Martha imagined her large gray eyes reproaching her with sorrowful disappointment. *Eighty-nine.* How many of those killings could she, Martha, have prevented? And now what to do? Was Louise's plan the best one? Or would it be better if the two of them resigned and took upon themselves personally as much of the flak as they could? Martha wished she could ask Sorben, but there were certain things on which Sorben would not advise her. She already knew this would be one of them. What a mess, what a godawful mess, and all her own fault for being blind to what David was, for being too weak to confront Louise as she should have.

Martha saw that she must seriously consider resigning from the Co-op on the grounds of being inadequate for meeting her responsibilities. She hoped they would ask it of her, thus sparing her the responsibility of having to decide for herself.

Never had she felt so confused, so lonely. Was this mess what her life had come to, had been all along programmed to come to once she had chosen to shirk her responsibility for stopping Louise? It felt like a bad dream. And yet it was one she somehow could not feel surprise at finding herself trapped in. Somewhere in the depths of her heart she had known that something like this would eventually happen. It now seemed so drearily inevitable that she felt as though the situation had always been a part of her—a part kept hidden from herself as much as from others.

Chapter Eighteen

[i]

Martha met with Sorben in Ravenna Park. As concisely and un-emotionally as she could manage, she laid out the facts of the "situation." By the time she finished her account, her body was trembling with emotion, perhaps because the Marq'ssan's initial reaction put a hard, cold lump of fear into Martha's belly. While Martha talked, Sorben's expression remained one of intent listening. But when she finished, although Sorben's demeanor did not perceptibly change, Martha felt chilled by a reaction she only indirectly sensed. From a corner of her mind came the reminder that Sorben's facial expressions were all voluntarily produced in order to communicate with the humans they were talking to. It was as though in a moment of profound distress Sorben had forgotten about her face and its communicative properties.

"I could never have imagined this happening with you, Martha," Sorben said. "It comes as a blow. You see…you see, you are among the few North Americans I know who not only feel a deep respect for life, but who act again and again without being prompted, out of a genuine personal sense of responsibility for the world you live in. I've come to think of you as being the nearest among most humans I've met to our way of being and acting. Yet you tell me you knew, have known for seven years, about this killing, and not only knew but had the power to stop it—and to struggle with Louise over it—and did nothing. I can't quite take it in, Martha, because it is so devastating to our hopes that humans will wrench themselves out of their death-and-destruction orientation. If someone like you—someone desirous of change, someone who is strong and powerful and committed—avoids acting in such a simple, clear-cut situation, how can we ever hope to do anything here?"

She stared at Martha for a moment without speaking. "What am I doing here, Martha? Why did I stay?" She shook her head. "I'm sorry. This isn't what you need. I think I'm going to have to spend some time alone before I can talk to you about this."

Martha could think of nothing to say. Leaning against the girders holding up the bridge spanning Ravenna's ravine, she watched through tear-blurred eyes as Sorben struck out along the path.

The Marq'ssan vanished from sight, and Martha was left to stare at the concrete foundations of the old steel bridge. Somewhere in the quiet of the ravine an owl hooted. The piercing desolation of the sound seemed to strike Martha's heart, resonating with her fear, echoing her sorrow.

[ii]

Later, they sat side-by-side on the shelf of rock overlooking a small waterfall. Sorben began by asking Martha a question. Martha fingered the plain gray stone she had taken from the ground and stirred the thick carpet of decaying leaves with the tip of her shoe. She tried to think carefully before answering Sorben's question, for the Marq'ssan's gravity made her feel that the answer was important—for both of them. "At first when I thought about this—and I have to admit that I never thought about it until the *Examiner* story came out—I thought it must have been out of some sense of personal loyalty to Louise. But once I put it that way to myself, I realized that couldn't be it. It didn't make sense. Louise might think it would—she'd think *of course Martha puts loyalty to me above loyalty to rapists.* And other people might think that I've been feeling an obligation not to expose Louise to retaliation—for some of those violent male groups might now consider her their number-one target—or to removal from her responsibilities within the Co-op. But all that would be wrong."

Sorben nodded, encouraging her to continue. Martha swallowed to lubricate her throat, and wished she'd brought a second bottle of water with her. "I think the real reason was what I told the others in the meeting last night. Namely, that I couldn't bear to look at the truth, so I tried to hide from it as much as I could. It seemed so horrendous to me—and Louise so, so tainted." Martha's mouth twisted. "The thought of Louise's touching me was truly horrible, so physically

revolted was I. Maybe it was seeing the sack of bloody clothing in the
bathroom, which is how I stumbled into the truth. But apart from this
revulsion, I shut down my mind. I recoiled first from Louise, and then
from even thinking about what I had learned about Louise. *I didn't
want to see.* I'm not sure why this is so, except that it's a weakness
in me."

"Then let me ask you this," Sorben said, her brow furrowing. "If
it had been someone you knew less intimately than Louise, would you
have stopped *them?* Or rather, let me put it this way: whom would
you have stopped, and whom would you simply have recoiled from?
I already know you would have stopped a group of strangers you perceived as the enemy from killing. But among people you perceive as
either neutral or on your side? Who among those groupings would
you have stopped?"

Martha folded her fingers tightly around the stone. "I don't know,"
she whispered. "I suppose most of them." She looked into Sorben's
eyes. "You think it's an us/them-mentality thing? That because the
victims were rapists, and male, I didn't consider them truly human,
and that because I was in love with Louise and because I was used to
thinking of her as part of myself I didn't stop her because I couldn't
fully face up to what she was doing?" Martha swallowed again; one
spot in her throat felt especially dry. "Okay, I think I see what you
mean. You may be right. I don't understand it very well, but I think
it may be more of that damned dualism at work in me." If the people
Louise had been killing had been people Martha could easily care
about or identify with, she would have stopped Louise: of that she
felt certain.

"I'm just trying to understand what happened, Martha," Sorben
said. "How can we overcome these weaknesses unless we find out
what sorts of things lie at the roots of them?"

The question was rhetorical. Martha stared down at the ground
and with the tip of her shoe nudged the layer of dried and decaying
leaves aside to reveal the dead moss beneath.

After a long silence, Sorben asked, "What does the Co-op intend
to do?"

Martha made a face. "We were up half the night arguing it out.
The final plan everyone says she can live with is this: first, to make a

statement saying we do not condone murder and that the revelations about Louise and the Night Patrol will be gone into thoroughly at the next Steering Committee meeting. Which happens to be only two weeks away. For the moment we aren't doing anything about expelling Louise from the Co-op. We've decided that that is not our decision to make, that it's a public matter. And that furthermore it would be politically unwise to allow ourselves to be stampeded by outside governments into forcing Louise out. That this is a matter for people in the Free Zone to decide. Second, we're holding a press conference tonight—but we won't be putting it on global vid: we're treating this as a local problem of local concern. Therefore the press conference will be directed to the people of the Free Zone. Third, in Paris tomorrow I'll pass out a statement to the delegations we're treating with, explaining our position. If the US government attempts to make a big splash with this, we'll take more extensive measures. Going on global vid is our last resort—which would be a sort of defeat, of being forced to react to their attack on us. Fourth, I'm going to be putting pressure on the three governments already assisting us to make sure they don't try to back out of our agreements with them. And since they very badly want the services the Marq'ssan can provide, we still have a good source of leverage." Unless, of course, they decided to open negotiations with one of the other Free Zones. Evening had begun creeping over the ravine. Soon they'd have to climb out and head for the house. Everyone going to Paris would be meeting there in the next hour.

"All that sounds sensible enough," Sorben said. "But I wish you'd think more about what happened to you. I think you have an obligation to understand it and then to communicate what you understand to others. I'm certain there are other people in your situation at this very moment—especially with reference to human rights abuses." Sorben's eyes looked silvery in the dying light. "You see what I'm saying?"

Something opened in Martha, tantalizing her with the promise of relief's being within reach, if only she strove hard toward it. "Yes," Martha said. "I think I do." Painful as this was to face, something positive might still come out of it. But of course, Martha thought. She should have realized that without Sorben's prompting.

It would be painful, so painful.

Sorben rose to her feet. "We'd better be getting back to the house," she said.

Martha rose, too, and shoved her hands into her pockets. Without speaking they walked up the sloping path until they emerged from the ravine into the streetlamp-lighted night. Martha, remembering the stone, took her hand out of her pocket and opened her fingers, and the small gray pebble fell back to the ground.

[iii]

As Maxine pulled the brush rhythmically through Elizabeth's hair, Elizabeth, staring at the new basket of silks for tying her braid that Maxine had given her for her birthday, told herself age no longer mattered. April 17, 2022, seemed a date far removed from the present. She was three years younger than Sedgewick. And she looked years and years younger than Maxine. Still, when she recalled how young Hazel was, thinking of her own age and birth date gave her a strange feeling, for she knew that if Hazel knew how old she was she would probably think or feel something Elizabeth would prefer she not think or feel. (And given Hazel's outspokenness she might even *say* whatever it was she would be thinking.)

"Guess I'm just talking to myself."

Elizabeth looked at Maxine in the mirror. "Sorry, Maxie. I'm afraid I was off in the clouds." She smiled. "Try me again. I promise to listen."

Maxine shrugged; again she drew the brush down the length of Elizabeth's hair. "Nothing important," she said. Elizabeth suppressed a sigh. Maxine had been visibly pleased to be giving her the new braid silks—one among the variety of labor-intensive gifts she produced for the few gift-giving occasions that occurred every year—but her pleasure had obviously been spoiled by Elizabeth's lack of attention. "I suppose you're thinking of that new one." Maxine's tone was offhand.

Elizabeth pressed her lips together to keep from laughing. Maxine could not get over Hazel's having been in Elizabeth's bed that morning last week. It had been years since Elizabeth had had anyone to stay the entire night: so that Hazel's having done so seemed terribly significant to her. "The problem is, I'm too busy these days," Elizabeth said, smiling at Maxine's reflection.

"You mean you think about her a lot because you can't get your fill of her."

"Oh I don't know." Elizabeth drawled the words. "I might still be thinking about her even if I could see her as often as I'd like."

Maxine grunted her disbelief. She clearly thought it impossible for Elizabeth to be absorbed for long by one woman. But Maxine had never known about Allison, since Allison had always left Elizabeth's bed well in advance of Maxine's arrival in the morning.

"It looks as though I'll be leaving for Seattle the day after tomorrow," Elizabeth said to change the subject. "It'll probably be for three or four days. And then I might spend a couple of days in California before returning."

"Seattle! Why would you be going there?" Maxine said, then quickly added, "No, no, I didn't mean that as a nosy question, Liz. It's just a little weird-sounding, that's all. Considering the aliens and the anarchy and all that."

"I'm not looking forward to it, believe me," Elizabeth said. "Still, I'm curious to see what the place looks like after ten years of chaos."

Maxine snorted. "Murder in the streets and muggings and rape is what I'd expect. They don't have jails or prisons in the Free Zone. They don't believe in law over there. Which means that the meanest types will be doing whatever they want. You'd better take care, Liz. Make sure you don't go anywhere without your bodyguard."

Elizabeth grinned. "Oh Maxie, you're so silly. Can you imagine anyone mean enough to succeed in bothering me?"

"Yes, you always *say* you can take care of yourself, Liz, but that's overconfidence. You haven't been in any really dangerous places. That place will be a jungle, take my word for it. You may be tall and muscular, but you're still a woman. And women are disadvantaged when it comes to taking care of themselves."

Elizabeth rolled her eyes. Maxine was incredible. Absolutely incredible. She actually believed all that stuff broadcast over vid. Well, that was to be expected. Otherwise Allison would be wasting her time and the Executive's money with her enormous public education program. Still...one might think Maxine would be a little less naive after so many years working for her. "Are you close to being finished?" she asked, glancing at the clock on the dressing table.

"Just about ready to begin braiding."

"Good," Elizabeth said. "I'm starving and want my breakfast."

As she often did while Maxine plaited the long, long strands, Elizabeth fantasized having her hair cut off. But this time she also thought of Hazel unbraiding it and imaged what Sedgewick had interrupted. *Rapunzel, Rapunzel, let down your fair hair…*

Hazel loved her long, long braid. It would be unthinkable not to keep it.

[iv]

Elizabeth had just finished meeting with Stevens, Ambrose, and Baldridge when Felice called. "I'm at the Georgetown house, Elizabeth," she said. "We have some talking to do, you and I, and the sooner the better."

"How about tomorrow, Felice? I've got a murderous schedule today." Elizabeth called up her calendar. "Unless you want to just say what's on your mind flat out."

"Don't try to brush me off." Felice actually sounded angry. "I'm not having it."

"I have about three hundred pages of reports that I was somehow supposed to have read this morning, another appointment ten minutes from now, and then a lunch engagement. What is it you expect me to do?"

"Cancel your lunch engagement. Unless you're going to tell me it's with half the Executive?"

Elizabeth began to get annoyed. "It's a working lunch, Felice."

"So what? I want a 'working lunch' with you myself. Believe me, it's not pleasure I have in mind."

Elizabeth frowned at the screen. For lunch she was supposed to join Allison, Welkin, and whatever staff the two considered essential for the meeting. She could keep Felice from bugging her by telling Jacq she wouldn't accept her calls, but then she'd have a mess dealing with Felice over the looming dinner party arrangements and who knew what other future projects. "Very well," Elizabeth said. "For you, Felice, I'll go into the meeting late, thereby screwing up my afternoon schedule. It had better be important."

"I'll get us in at Chez Hélène. One o'clock?"

"Make it twelve-thirty," Elizabeth said. "And don't count on my staying much more than forty-five minutes." She hung up, called Allison, and told her to reschedule the meeting for one-thirty in the Chief's conference room, *sans* lunch. Hanging up on Allison's protests, Elizabeth called Jacq and asked her to shift all her appointments accordingly. And then, after checking on Sedgewick to make sure he was getting himself prepared for his meeting with Selby (especially necessary since she couldn't spare the time to sit at his elbow and Farley would be inadequate for doing more than supplying information when asked specific questions), Elizabeth, using Sedgewick's private stairs, went down one floor to be briefed with video footage supplementing the standard dossiers on the women she'd be dealing with in the Free Zone.

[v]

The server stared past her shoulder, haughty in his display of patience. Elizabeth loved to eat. And Chez Hélène boasted one of the top five chefs in town. Yet even with the server waiting for her reply, she couldn't settle on what to order—not through indecisiveness, but because she simply could not wrest her attention from Felice's coiffure. To call it a new style would hardly do justice to the dramatic totality of it. Choosing almost at random, she told the server to bring her the trout pâté, lamb chops, and the house's potato specialty, with cheese and fruit to follow. Felice made a comment about how Elizabeth always ate like a horse, then ordered spinach salad and a slice of Camembert with fruit, period. "I'm still a growing girl," Elizabeth said, smiling. "And I just finished working out. I'm always ravenous after workouts. I wasn't supposed to have it until late afternoon, but you've messed up my schedule."

Felice rolled her eyes. "I don't suppose it ever occurs to you that it's not necessary to work out every damned day."

"In my line of work I can't afford to be that soft, or someday I might have a nasty surprise."

"What, with the gorillas you trail simply standing by twiddling their thumbs?"

"The women in this room can't seem to take their eyes off your hair, Felice," Elizabeth said. "I've never seen anything like it. Are people wearing their hair like that in Como?" Como had been the place to which Elizabeth had ultimately tracked her.

"In Italy and southern France a few women—not men—are playing with this sort of thing." Felice smiled complacently. "I'd gotten madly bored with the same old styles all the time and decided to try this for a while. The only problem is it takes a couple of hours every morning, and one has to have a girl who's been specially trained for maintaining it. Worse, I've no idea where I'll find anyone in DC who'll be able to make substantial modifications for me once I tire of the current configuration. It would certainly be a bore to have to return to Milan just to change it."

"Configuration" was certainly the appropriate word, Elizabeth thought. The hair had been cut scores of different lengths at diverse angles and bizarrely tinted in dozens of colors and was it wired? glued? lacquered? into a grand architectural structure. "It's not sensual enough for me," Elizabeth said.

Felice gave her a critical look. "Don't you get sick of that same old braid day in and day out?"

"Of course. But sometimes…"—Elizabeth smiled, thinking of Hazel—"sometimes wearing my hair long can be delightful." She shook her head. "But the idea of spending a minimum of two hours a day on it? It would drive me nuts. I have so little personal time as it is."

"I brought the Italian girl I found to take care of it along with me. I don't think she's going to like living here. I hope to god Sedgewick doesn't insist I stay long?" Felice's eyebrows inquired of Elizabeth Sedgewick's intentions. When Elizabeth did not immediately answer, she went on, "The mess that household is in—where did you find those people, anyway? And that Higgins character—" Felice curled her lip and sent Elizabeth a look—"seems to have the upper hand. The things Giulietta has been telling me the staff have been saying to her about Sedgewick!" She peered narrowly at Elizabeth. "Am I to take it he's in the throes of severe alcoholism? That's what it sounds like from what Giulietta has gleaned."

The waiter appeared and set the trout pâté, several pots of mustard, a bowl of sweet butter, and a basket of bread before Elizabeth. She leaned forward to inhale whiffs of each of the pots of mustard, then slathered butter, green peppercorn mustard, and pâté onto a thick slice of bread. She said, "You don't really need to hear about Sedgewick," and bit into the bread.

As Felice drank, her gaze met Elizabeth's over the rim of her water glass. Setting the glass down, she said, "What I want to know is what the *hell* you think you're doing with my daughter."

Elizabeth, ready for another bite, paused. "Doing what I can to protect her from Sedgewick," she said before taking the bite.

Felice's eyes widened dramatically and then narrowed, making Elizabeth realize that all the tints in Felice's hair had been carefully matched to the brilliant jade green of her eyes. "You said nothing about Alexandra in the cable, and since there's no using the telephone—" the look on her face suggested she considered the malfunctioning of the com-satellite Elizabeth's personal responsibility—"I had no idea she wasn't still in Barbados. So imagine my surprise not only to find her here, but to discover she's being sent to *Crowder's*. Not Layton's, *Crowder's*. Naturally she shouldn't be going to school at all, I don't think she's cut out for it, and really it hardly matters whether she makes the right friends since quite obviously she will be madly sought after. She's been doing very well with my mother." Felice glared at Elizabeth. "So what in god's name are you and Sedgewick up to?"

Elizabeth prepared the next slice of bread. "Sedgewick has some kind of plan for Alexandra; I'm not quite sure what it is." She would try the grainier mustard this time; it had a delightfully pungent smell. "All I know is that he's determined to take control of her. I did try to argue with him about your customary rights, but he claims they're privileges that would never stand up in a court of law." Elizabeth's gaze met Felice's. "I wouldn't try to fight it legally. It could be damaging for other women if this sort of thing were brought into court—and you can bet given the principals involved it would be a widely celebrated case. Legally he has control. I don't know how the courts would rule on the weight of custom. But I do know that if the court ruled against you it would give a lot of men certain ideas about their rights."

Felice frowned. "I see what you mean. But there must be some way I can stop him. Alexandra's miserable, for one thing. And for another, my parents are going to be very upset by this." She fingered her water glass. "I don't know what my father's going to do once he's fully aware of this situation."

"I've convinced Sedgewick to allow visits to Alexandra," Elizabeth said.

"Allow? Allow? That that pig can talk about *allowing*! And he hadn't even seen her in ten years, Elizabeth. Ten fucking *years!*"

"Keep your voice down," Elizabeth said, sorely tempted to aim a swift kick under the table at Felice's shin. That's all they'd need—a nice juicy family scandal. Bad enough that people in Security gossiped constantly about Sedgewick. But all of executive DC getting interested in his family arrangements?

"And his damned house arrest," Felice said very low, through her teeth. She shot Elizabeth a hard look. "You certainly managed to ingratiate yourself with her. Was that Sedgewick's intention?"

"All Sedgewick wanted was total submission," Elizabeth said coldly. "Don't think I'm in cahoots with him. I've just told you I don't know what he has in mind. Basically I've been doing everything I can to ease the situation for Alexandra. If he'd had his way she'd not only be at Crowder's right now but also out of contact with you or Varley Raines or Eleanor Dunn until she comes of age. I'd be careful if I were you, or that still might happen." Elizabeth took a large bite. She hated talking about this kind of thing while eating. It spoiled her enjoyment of good food.

Felice fingered the many and many natural pearls invisibly strung, wrapped several times around her neck. Were those beads in her hair pearls, too? Elizabeth wondered. "I just can't believe he's doing this." Felice sounded uncharacteristically dispirited. "I didn't fight him on Daniel. Because I assumed that by letting him handle Daniel as he pleased I could raise Alexandra without interference." She stared down at her hands as she moved her heavily ringed fingers over the linen. "I've seen Daniel maybe three times in the last four years. Which is by his choice." Felice looked at Elizabeth. "He's ambivalent about me, you know. In an extreme way. It's so painful for me when I do see him that I suppose it's best that he chooses to see me hardly at all."

Elizabeth had just taken a big mouthful of bread and pâté, so she did not immediately answer. "It's disturbing seeing these Wilton boys," she said into Felice's depressed silence when she had finished chewing and swallowing. "But you know, Felice," she went on, determined to finish talking about Alexandra, "there's not that much difference between Layton's and Crowder's. I gather Sedgewick's only reason for choosing Crowder's is because you attended Layton's. You aren't going to lose Alexandra, you know. She'll be all right." Elizabeth smiled. "She's turned out quite lovely, and has a good head on her shoulders. And stubborn! I suspect she'll be a match for Sedgewick by the time she comes of age. What you have to do is bide your time, patiently, and work as best you can with what you have. I'll help as much as I can. But if I were you I'd save my strength for battles it might be possible to win. I'm quite certain you'll never overturn his decision to send her to Crowder's." Elizabeth took the bite remaining and hoped Felice would be content to drop the subject.

"I'll never as long as I live understand why Daddy insisted on such a piss-poor contract with Sedgewick," Felice said very low. "You'd better believe I'll make sure Alexandra never gets caught in such a thing."

Elizabeth knew very well why Varley Raines had pushed that contract with Sedgewick. But she wasn't about to tell his daughter about it. It wouldn't make Felice feel any better for knowing, that was certain. In fact, Elizabeth had an idea that the only reason Sedgewick had never flung that ugly little piece of history into Felice's face was because Varley Raines had stipulated Felice never be told any of the details. "I'm quite certain Sedgewick has ideas for Alexandra," Elizabeth said. "And I doubt if getting her tied up in that kind of contract is one of them." The waiter whisked away the debris of Elizabeth's first course.

Felice frowned. "I wish I had some notion of what is going through his head. Obviously he's intending to use her for one of his plots." At Elizabeth's raised eyebrows, Felice said, "You don't expect me to believe he gives a damn for her personally. No, she's simply a pawn to him for use in his power games. I know that man too well to believe anything else."

"I really don't know, Felice," Elizabeth said. "But if I were you I wouldn't bring it up with him. You'd do best working on him through me—he gets irrationally obstinate whenever he gets a whiff of you, even indirectly. You'd put his back up in no time if you tried confronting him."

Felice sighed. She had to know Elizabeth was right.

Their entrées arrived.

"So about these dinner parties," Felice said.

Thank god, Felice was going to accept Elizabeth's handling of the Alexandra situation. "They're important," Elizabeth said. "And I've no idea how many."

"Am I to expect having to live here permanently then?" Felice jabbed her fork into her spinach salad.

"I don't know, Felice. Sedgewick's got things on his mind that he hasn't revealed even to me. So I have no idea what you can expect."

"Even to you?" Felice said after swallowing. "And all this drinking…"

"Stay out of Higgins' way as much as possible," Elizabeth said. "His function is more important than you might guess."

Felice shook her head. "I don't understand any of this, Elizabeth."

"I'll tell you whatever you need to know," Elizabeth said. "But in the meantime, why don't you tell me about life in post-war Europe."

Felice happily plunged into a subject that genuinely interested her. "The basic idea is that everyone is bored with the grim status quo and mad for something different. There are tons and tons of parties, and people are spending money the way they used to…"

Elizabeth, attacking her scalloped potatoes and lamb, encouraged Felice to gossip. There'd be no trouble from her. She'd be bored to death here, but she'd let Elizabeth handle Sedgewick and keep cool. Elizabeth would find ways to give Felice time away from DC, and Felice would be satisfied, even grateful. And that would eliminate at least one of Elizabeth's potential problems…

[vi]

Celia left the bus at the freeway exit and quickly walked, senses at stretch, up University toward Fourth. She didn't bother to look behind her to see if her watchdogs trailed her: why check on a sure thing? When at Sixth a shabby runt of a kid swung into step beside her, Celia struggled against panic. Never before had she been frightened by the denizens of Hillcrest, but now the sight of any male stranger set her heart pounding. "Interested in doing some shopping, lady?" The boy spoke with a lisp. His large, round eyes assessed her. Of course. Being a professional, what other reason would she have for coming into this section of town?

Keeping her voice low, Celia warned him off: "I've got two fucking watchdogs, kid. Look behind me and you'll see them. You sell me anything for M-dollars and we'll both end up busted. Get lost before they get interested in you, too."

"You into politics, then," he said, explaining it to himself.

"Better not to talk at all," Celia said.

He got the message. "Good luck, mama," he said softly before dropping behind.

Celia crossed Fifth and plowed through the thick press of milling crowds and open stalls. The last time she'd come here she'd lost her anglo male watchdog by taking off her suit jacket and mixing with a crowd of prostitutes. She passed through and out the other side of the market and turned up Fourth, hoping they were suffering at least some anxiety about losing her.

As she mounted the front steps of the dilapidated building she caught a glimpse of them both only a few yards behind her—one on each side of the street. Huh. They seemed not to be talking to one another. She'd like to know more about why they didn't.

Inside, she chatted with Delia, the person who kept the Center's chaos half-way organized, and learned that she had a client waiting. Celia raised her eyebrows at Delia. "I guess that'll be all right," she said, looking into Delia's eyes. She pulled the jammer Emily had given her out of her pocket and held it out in her open palm. Delia nodded. "Of course I won't use it except when essential." If she used it too much they'd suspect and then shake her down to look for it—if, that is, they had her bugged in the first place. Delia nodded again. "It might come in handy in other contexts," Celia added.

Delia smiled. "That's what I was thinking." Jammers were expensive and hard to come by.

Celia passed through the library where lawyers and paralegals toiled over terminals to the corridor lined with half a dozen conference rooms. Entering the assigned conference room, Celia found an excruciatingly thin woman of perhaps seventeen seated at the table, her hands folded in her lap, her bony shoulders hunched forward. She looked as if she had been waiting for a long time. Celia flipped the jammer's on-switch and deliberately set it on the table where the client could see it. Then she held out her hand. "I'm Celia Espin." And Celia smiled into the thin, anxious face.

The woman hesitantly gave Celia her hand to shake. "I'm Frances Ysador," she said softly. "It's my cousin." Her voice rose in both pitch and volume, as if speaking had released a wave of panic. "I need help for my cousin, 'cause he's in bad trouble. And that's really not fair. He just got out of the service! He's *paid* his dues!"

Celia pulled a chair out from the table and sat facing the client. "What sort of trouble, Frances?"

"Franny," she said, gnawing at her already well-bitten lips.

Celia took a yellow pad from her attaché case. "Tell me about it, Franny."

The client cleared her throat. "They came to our house. Some non-uniformed police, maybe ODS. We were all sleeping, it was something like two or three in the morning. They kicked the door in." Franny cleared her throat again. "It was really scary. Like I woke up to find this man pressing a gun against my head. Like Jesus, I thought he was going to shoot me! And he made me get up, and it was cold and I was shivering, and he wouldn't let me put on my sweater, I was shivering and kept thinking I was going to pee in my pants. And so they made everybody line up against the wall out in the hall, and cuffed us, even my granny, while they ransacked the place. And then, while we were all lined up against the wall, besides Rickie's gun, which he brought with him from the war, they claimed to find a bunch of firebombs. I couldn't believe it! They were like shouting and swearing at us, all the time we were standing like that, with our faces smashed against the wall. And when they finally left they took my cousin and my father. *God!* I had this feeling in my belly, you know, like I'd never see them again. I mean, that was even scarier than that bastard's pressing the gun into my head. My father, they let him go a couple of days later, but not Rickie. Him they charged. With unlawful possession of weapons and some kind of conspiracy charge."

Celia stopped writing in order to look into Franny's eyes, which had glazed over with unshed tears. "Okay, Franny. Let's take it slow here.

Are there are other people being charged with conspiracy? Has your cousin given them names? Or has someone else given them names?"

Franny rubbed her bare arms as though she were cold, and Celia noticed the tattoos of green and black roses, complete with thorns and leaves, covering her upper arms. "I don't know. Like, we haven't been able to see him. We just know there are charges, and he's supposed to be having a trial."

Celia wondered whether the weapons had been the boy's or whether they'd been planted; with ODS, you could never tell. "Have they told you where he's being kept?"

"In El Cajon, they said."

"In the El Cajon Federal Detention Facility?"

"Yeah, I think that's the name of the place."

"Did they give you a trial date?"

Franny pulled a tattered, folded flimsy from her pocket. Celia unfolded it and found it to be a notice declaring that Richard Ysador would be tried in Federal Court on multiple felony counts on May 15, 2086. The charges included two counts of terrorism. Celia jotted the details on her yellow pad. "We'll have to see if we can use his nominal right to counsel to get visiting privileges. Although I won't be able to see him myself, we have someone here who can. But I'll help prepare the defense, Franny."

The girl's eyes fastened on Celia with a degree of hope that Celia could not bring herself to dash. Celia continued. "I'm going to want to talk to all of your family—everyone who was there the night they made the arrest, and to your neighbors." Even if they could get the conspiracy and terrorism charges tossed, the whole thing was a foregone conclusion, and so ODS knew; otherwise, they wouldn't be bothering with a trial. Possession of weapons always meant a stiff sentence. This kid would be in El Cajon or a work-camp (if they decided he wouldn't be likely to stir up other detainees) for the remainder of his youthful years.

Celia got up and went to the shelf, brought two half-liter bottles of water back to the table, and gave one to Franny. "An important thing we need to do, Franny, is find out if they're tying anyone else to this so-called conspiracy, and if so who they are and what their status is. It's likely the prosecutor's office won't give us this information in advance of trial. So we need to do some detective work ourselves. It'd be really helpful if you could tell me—or find out for me, if you don't already know—whether he was involved with others, and if so whether any of them have dropped out of sight recently. Either before or after your cousin's arrest. Okay?"

Franny's face scrunched up. "You mean you believe there was a conspiracy?"

Celia braced herself: the girl looked as though she might be going to cry. "Prosecutors have a habit of calling all sorts of things conspiracies. But I think we need to find out who else might be involved in this thing. I don't know how much information they're going to let us have for trial preparation. Do you see what I'm getting at?"

Franny looked at her for about half a minute, then said, "I'll ask around."

Celia's heart sank. That probably meant the firebombs and gun were the boy's and hadn't been planted by ODS. Which would make everything that much harder, especially if they'd managed to crack one of his co-conspirators.

El Cajon was where Luis was being kept. How ironic to have her first case involve that place, especially when Luis himself had urged her to this work. It must be a sign telling her this was the right thing to be doing—as though it had been meant for her to have been named, so that she would be moved to take up this work in Hillcrest: work *someone* had to do.

[vii]

Elizabeth labored to clear off her desk: she was dying to get away from the office. She could hardly concentrate, so violently did her thoughts jostle and compete for attention. She wanted to implement her brainstorm of bringing Hazel with her on her trip, at once: she *needed* a secretary, somebody she could trust—and would at the same time then have Hazel for an entire week. And besides, such a working trip might prove to be a way of coaxing Hazel into a permanent job... So... *if* she could get away early, *then* she could try to persuade Hazel to spend the night with her (though that, too, was not a sure thing, given Hazel's hesitancy about even seeing her). And *then* she could try to bring her on staff.

When Elizabeth finally finished inputting notes and comments on all the meetings of the day, she braced herself for dealing with Sedgewick. He would be next door still—for undoubtedly he would put off going home for as long as he could; he was as little inclined to face Felice as Felice was to face him. His relations with Alexandra would be complicated now, especially when it came to practical arrangements. Felice could be Machiavellian, and he knew it. He would have to think before reacting, or risk making strategic errors. And Sedgewick hated thinking. He'd gotten lazy, since hardly anyone or anything could require thinking of him.

Elizabeth crossed to his office. Wine this evening, she observed, and he hadn't drunk more than two glasses of it, either. He was being very controlled since the incident in her foyer. "I have something unpleasant to discuss with you, Sedgewick," Elizabeth said, taking the armchair opposite his sofa.

He half-smiled. "Very well, then we'll start with your unpleasantness, and finish with my infinitely more agreeable business," he said, apparently in good humor.

Elizabeth drew a deep breath. "Bennett found Daniel and another young male from Wilton who works for Welkin plugging in." Elizabeth watched for a reaction, but detected none. She wondered how he would react were she to tell him that the two young men were reportedly *sexual partners*. "She of course wanted to terminate him, but I've told her to hold back for now. I wanted to hear what you think about it first."

"Obviously I'll have to have a talk with him," Sedgewick said. "What else can we do? I don't think terminating him is advisable...yet."

"By the book he'd be terminated," Elizabeth said, stating a fact she knew Sedgewick knew. Drug and alcohol abuse could be dealt with. But plugging in?

"Did Bennett confiscate the equipment?"

"Yes, of course," Elizabeth said. "I might add, Sedgewick, that she told me that Welkin claims that plugging in is a common Wilton practice. They do it in groups." Elizabeth smoothed her hand over her trouser leg and looked down at her shoe, which matched the fabric of her trousers perfectly. "Bennett says Daniel claimed to have gotten the equipment from some of the vid performers. Apparently certain of them are supplied with everything necessary for plugging in, since it makes them easier to control. Well, it's obvious that that would be so. Welkin thinks Daniel had the equipment with him all the time, and corrupted his boy." She shrugged. "Who knows where they got the equipment. But I suspect that merely taking it away from him isn't going to prevent his access to it. Daniel's got the wherewithal for purchasing almost anything he wants."

Sedgewick snorted. "You think he could procure it through a simple plastic transaction? Don't be ridiculous. All we'd have to do would be to track his transactions and look for a sizeable personal transfer, and we'd have his supplier. Any intelligent supplier would know that and be appropriately wary."

"You're forgetting, Sedgewick. Southern California has a black market. All he has to do is buy M-dollars or barter something for M-dollars. You'd never be able to track it then."

"You'd better send for him, Weatherall."

Elizabeth sighed. "You don't seriously believe anything I can say will stop him?" Besides, she was leaving town. She couldn't order him to come to her in the Free Zone.

Sedgewick got up from the sofa. "You're right. I'll have to speak to him myself. Just send for him. And then when he gets here I'll deal with him."

"And what should I tell Bennett?"

He moved to the cabinets lining part of one wall. "Tell her he's to be given a second chance, but that you'll want to know at once if she sees any sign whatsoever of his plugging in again." He stooped to unlock one of the cabinets. When he straightened up and turned around she saw he held a large gift-wrapped box in his arms. It must be a birthday present, she realized. He came to her and handed her the box. "I do have the day right?" he asked.

"It's my birthday, if that's what you mean," Elizabeth said, taking the box. Its weight surprised her. She removed the ribbons, lifted first the lid and then the heavy tissue-paper wrapped object from the box. The paper fell away from it, revealing a gleaming, shapely piece of white marble. "Oh," she gasped. She looked at Sedgewick. "How did you ever get this? I can't believe it, it's to be *mine*?" It was *incredible*.

How the *fuck* had he acquired her very most favorite Louise Bourgeois sculpture? It had been in the Hirshhorn the last time she'd seen it.

He grinned. "I hope it's still one of your favorite pieces of art?"

Elizabeth could not take her hands off the cool, white, almost unbearably erotic marble. She had wanted to touch it every time she'd seen it in the Hirshhorn, but it had been kept in a glass case—precisely to thwart such desires. The feel of its smooth round curves under her palm made her vulva cream, no matter that Sedgewick was watching her slightest gesture and facial response. "My god, Sedgewick, I don't know what to say!"

Still grinning, he sipped his wine. "Now all you need is the house that will be the perfect setting for it. I hope you've been giving that some thought?"

Elizabeth—her head whirling with elation—laughed. "I've been too busy." She stared down at the lovely thing in her lap. "I can't quite take it in," she said. How had he done it? And when? It must have cost him a fortune. And simply to please her?

"I imagine you have better things to be doing with your evening than sitting here with me," he said without even a tinge of self-pity. "So get out of here and enjoy yourself."

Elizabeth slipped the sculpture back into the box and rose to her feet. "My cup runneth over," she said, thinking of Hazel. Hazel and Bourgeois. My god. Happy birthday, Lizzie. Happy fabulous birthday to you.

Before leaving his office she went to Sedgewick, bent down, and kissed him on the cheek. The only other time she had done that had been after he'd pulled out of that first terrible episode that had followed Zeldin's stranding them on the island. His eyes glowed with elation; again he urged her to have a pleasurable evening.

The Bourgeois clutched to her breast, Elizabeth flew through the building and down to the garage. All she needed now to make her in every way delirious with joy was Hazel. *Happy birthday, Lizzie. Happy fabulous birthday to you.*

Chapter Nineteen

[i]

In service to the need for discretion, Mark Goodwin met Elizabeth in a small conference-room at SeaTac, rather than out on the tarmac. "I'm astounded by their seeming unconcern over this airport," were Elizabeth's first words to him. "This must be the anarchists' most strategically vulnerable place, yet they allow outsiders to control it."

Goodwin smiled sardonically. "From their point of view it hardly matters *who* uses this airport. As long as they have the aliens protecting them, no one would dare use it for strategic purposes. Say we landed a first-rate direct action force here and retook the Puget Sound area, which we could probably do within hours: it wouldn't matter in the least. The aliens would simply drop in and destroy our hardware. We might get rid of the current leadership by doing such a thing, but basically we'd lose not only hardware but face when we found ourselves evacuating our people a second time."

"I understand all that *theoretically*," Elizabeth said. "Nevertheless, when one *sees* this airport, it's shocking." The airport was held by a private security force employed by the airlines and run by an administration collectively financed by the airlines, and its air traffic was controlled by techs collectively supplied by the airlines. After a decade's experience with the security nightmares of places like LAX and JFK, SeaTac struck Elizabeth as disturbingly wild, open to unknown vulnerabilities—this though she could not claim ever to have felt safe at the most heavily guarded airports.

"I've arranged a car and driver for you," Goodwin said. "Something relatively though not absolutely non-conspicuous. Which is to say that if anyone's interested in keeping an eye on you, they'll have no trouble, but that on the other hand your transport won't attract casual attention."

Elizabeth nodded. "We'll deal through a cut-out after this meeting, Goodwin. I don't want to compromise the Edmonds Station. I also don't see any reason to thrust the relationship between me and the Station's activities in their faces. They'll probably assume it, but they won't know for certain. I'd prefer to keep it that way."

"Understood. And considering their naïveté, there's no telling what we might get away with."

"Have you anything new on Greenglass or any of the other leaders?"

"Greenglass is just back from Paris." Goodwin brushed a speck of lint from his old-style sleeve. Naturally everything executive would be behind the times in such a backwater. "Hughes hasn't had any contact with her since the scandal broke last Friday. We have no idea whether or not she connects Hughes with the exposé. He's planning to contact her tonight."

Elizabeth glanced around the dismally bare room. "Is there nothing to drink in this place? I'm positively parched."

"Sorry," Goodwin said. "Shall I send someone for juice or water?"

Elizabeth shook her head. "Never mind, I can wait. The less time I spend in here with you the better. Now listen, I'll want to know anything new on their leaders as it comes in. Use a florist or maintenance cover or something like that to get reports to me—everything verbal and in person, nothing on paper or electronic. We can't risk documents falling into their hands. Has the climate here heated up any more over the Night Patrol?"

"I'd characterize it is as simmering. The explosion, if there is one, will come at the Steering Committee Meeting, which is two weeks from now. The way they handled it, they've deferred popular wrath until then. I've no doubt every opposition group in the Zone will make the most of the occasion. It could be interesting."

"They've handled it too easily," Elizabeth said. "As it is, it hasn't stopped them from working through the Austrians, Dutch, and Greeks. And they manipulated the UN General Assembly so easily that it makes me wonder why they don't simply ask to have their own delegation seated—which they must know would give them the beginnings of legitimacy. God knows the majority of delegations at the UN would love the opportunity to deal us yet another slap in the face."

"Hughes claims they won't ever take a seat at the UN because of their insistence that they're not a government. Something to do with the principles of anarchy, or some such nonsense."

Elizabeth snorted. "Yeah, well we'll see how well their principles hold up by the time we're through with them." She stood up. "Unless you've got anything else to add, that's it. I have a lot to do today."

Elizabeth went out into the corridor and found Hazel, standing a little aloof from the escort, waiting. She looked uncomfortable. Well, that would pass, Elizabeth thought. Once they got down to work, anyway.

[ii]

"How about here?" Martha indicated the two empty chairs facing the windows.

"Perfect," Verdell said. "We'll even have a view of Lake Washington." Eating in the Hub certainly had its attractions.

They removed their jackets and settled into the armchairs. The women seated at a round table just behind them seemed to be a support group for rape victims. Not intentionally listening, Martha gathered that three of them belonged to the group because they'd had rape experiences, while the other two were counselors. She took a carton of yogurt and a spoon, a bottle of water, and a shiny green apple from her attaché case. "So did I miss much on Tuesday?" she said as she plunged her spoon into the yogurt.

Verdell made a face. "We did some role-playing. It was maximum slow—reminded me of the workshops I used to have to attend at my old job. And she announced that part of the final will be role-playing participation in a scenario we'll be required to analyze in detail. The way we've been doing with the videos."

"What was your old job?" Martha asked curiously.

Verdell opened the seam in the thermal wrap and held the steaming pastry in her fingers. It smelled like curry. "Robo-maintenance. I couldn't even begin to tell you what the robos were making—something defense-oriented is all we were told—but basically we had to keep the robos running."

"Both mechanical and electronic skills, then?" Martha said, watching Verdell bite into the pastry.

Mouth full, Verdell nodded. When she had swallowed, she said, "We had a software specialist on the team, who handled that end of it—though she hardly ever had anything to do, since they'd been using these robos for the same old functions for years. The rest of us were supposed to be able to do both mechanical and electronic repairs, but since we tended to divide the labor up it usually worked out that some of us always did mechanical and others of us always did electronic. I mostly did electronic repairs." She brought the pastry to her mouth to take another bite, then hesitated. "You know, I didn't think about it when I bought this this morning," she said, lowering the pastry. "Does it bother you, my eating this?"

"Bother me?" Martha tilted her head in query. "Why should it?"

"Well, I used my plastic to pay for it. And these things come from outside the Zone."

"It doesn't bother me. Who am I to dictate to other people what they should or shouldn't buy?"

"But you don't buy them, do you." She took another bite.

Martha took a drink of water. "No, I don't, but that's my decision. I also follow the boycotts advocated by the Co-op. But I certainly don't claim the right to tell others they have to do as I do."

"Hmm." Verdell frowned. "I don't really get the sense of your attitude. Which seems of a piece with the way the Co-op allows that scandal sheet to get away with printing such filth about Co-op members. And yet continues to allow it to operate on the FreeNet. No, I really don't get it."

The caustic tone of this comment made Martha feel good. "But it does make sense. I mean, there's definitely a logic to it," she said, "even if we have fucked up over this Night Patrol thing. That was a blind spot of ours. Somehow I didn't see..." She scooped up the last bite of yogurt.

"Well I don't get what's so terrible about killing rapists, either," Verdell said. "Not that I think killing people is a good idea generally—I've always been opposed to capital punishment. But I can see the other side of it, too. It's surprising to me how safe I feel here in Seattle, compared with Butte. All those years thinking that it was the cops that kept men from attacking anyone weaker than themselves on the street—day or night." Her brown eyes narrowed. "But it isn't that at all, is it. I was sort of hoping this social psych course would get into that kind of thing, help explain how it works, but it doesn't look as if it will. Or only very indirectly."

Martha nodded enthusiastically. "You know all those years I was an anarchist—before the Blanket, I mean—I kept telling people that they didn't need cops for personal protection. But hardly anyone could believe it. Yet I *knew* it. After all, as an activist, how could I not know the cops were my worst enemies and would be the last people to come to my assistance if I ever needed it?" Martha crunched into the crisp pippin and savored the first, tart bite before continuing. "Their role was always punishment, not prevention. And punishment obviously never did anything to keep anyone in line."

"But you could think that only because you were going against the system," Verdell said, licking her fingers. "So how did you decide your perception applied to everyone else?"

"Because I knew that in this society authority is deeply internalized, even when we don't want it to be. Most people—the same ones who wouldn't do it in a heavily policed society—would be too afraid to attack one another. Or, conversely, too afraid not to defend one another when seeing someone else attacked by someone perceived as anti-social and without legitimate authority. Except in rare instances, individuals are deeply social creatures. And the people who are going to be assholes will do what they want whether there are cops around or not."

"So it wasn't just idealism—an idea that people are too nice to hurt one another—that gave you the idea cops aren't necessary?"

Martha grinned. "Oh I want to think the best of people. The only thing is, they do terrible things when given the authority to engage in or sanction violence against others. So my theory has been—and still is—that people behave according to the structures they've learned as they are juxtaposed with the structures presently determining their lives."

"Sounds sort of mechanistic," Verdell said, ripping open a towel wipe. "Don't you believe in free will?" Slowly, thoroughly, she wiped her fingers one by one.

Martha laughed. "Of course. But the question is, how free is anyone's will? There naturally are individual variations, but I don't believe any individual ultimately escapes these structures—except for the bone-deep sociopaths, of course. As for the variations, it just seems to be the case that some individuals resist internalized structures of power slightly more than most."

"You're so certain of these things, Martha."

"I've been thinking about them for a long time."

"And acting on your theories, too," Verdell said. "Which is what makes it so interesting. I doubt I'd find it as interesting to talk to someone who sat at a terminal all day writing books on the subject. Who knows, maybe you'll convert the world." She grinned. "Going to the UN and all."

"Hah-hah," Martha said, making herself smile at this teasing. "My days in the Co-op are numbered, I'm afraid. I'll probably be out after the next Steering Committee meeting."

Verdell's smile faded. "You think so? Because of the Night Patrol scandal?"

"Yes. And it's my own damned fault. But maybe we'll all be able to learn from it."

They gazed out the window and inadvertently listened to the depressing discussion going on behind them. After a while, Verdell said, "I'm having another party tonight. Any chance you can make it?"

Verdell's first party had been interesting, but fatiguing: several people there, having discovered who she was, had backed Martha into a corner and harangued her with their opinions on how things should be changed in the Free Zone. One person, who looked like she was only in her mid-thirties and said she had arrived in the Zone two years ago from LA, had been angry that the Co-op wouldn't provide longevity treatments to people until they'd lived for five years in the Zone. When Martha had pointed out that without that stipulation, people would simply drop into the Zone, take the treatment, and return to the US or whatever country they'd come from, her interlocutor had gotten furious at Martha's assumption that services the Co-op funded should go chiefly to Zone residents and not the world at large, and had accused the Co-op of "thinking like a government."

"I don't know, Verdell," Martha said. "I'm not sure I can take that kind of pressure tonight. I think when I'm not studying I should be trying to relax in the evenings, to slow it down, so that I can get my head clear and straight before the Steering Committee meeting."

"I promise I won't let anyone bother you," Verdell said. "It'll only be a few people this time. I can vouch in advance for their good behavior."

Not that an expression of political opinion was bad behavior, but... "Well—" Martha laughed self-consciously—"in that case, maybe I will. Though I can't promise." If she were spared political attacks, it could be a refreshing diversion from the usual. Verdell's crowd was nothing like the parties hosted by the Co-op people she usually socialized with—where every damned encounter seemed to be work-related.

"Good enough."

Martha checked her watch and saw that it was a couple of minutes past one. "Damn! Gotta run." She sprang to her feet and snatched up her attaché case and trash.

"Nine o'clock," Verdell called after her.

Martha looked over her shoulder and nodded to show Verdell she had heard, then barreled hell-for-leather out of the Hub toward the lot where she'd left her two-seater. She had a one o'clock meeting with Margot Ganshoff. Who loathed unpunctuality. Slotting her key-card into the power strip, Martha imagined Margot's reaction to discovering that it had been Martha's conversation with Verdell that had made her late. And she smiled.

[iii]

It didn't take Hazel long to set Elizabeth up with at least one of the appointments she wanted. Getting an appointment with Greenglass, though, was something else. The Co-op person Hazel talked to wouldn't give Elizabeth a hard-and-fast appointment, but would only say that Greenglass would "be around" at three and would likely agree to see her then. The woman claimed Greenglass's appointments could be made only through Greenglass herself.

"What kind of an outfit are those people running?" Elizabeth said to Hazel. "Unless she simply made that up to make access difficult?"

Hazel looked worried. "She said that all the people I mentioned to her handled their own calendars. And when I asked for Greenglass's secretary or personal assistant, she said that no one in the Co-op had secretaries or personal assistants. When I said I found that hard to believe she said, 'Who do you think we are, the Executive?' I don't know, Liz, whether she was telling the truth or not."

Elizabeth seriously doubted it.

Nevertheless, at quarter after three Elizabeth checked her NoteMaster for the map Goodwin had given her to download on it and announced to Hazel she was going out. "Don't leave the hotel without Simmons," Elizabeth told Hazel as she checked her personal computer to make sure it was set to receive and record input from the open transmitter she would be carrying. "I'll leave him behind for you. Under no circumstances go out by yourself. Clear?"

Hazel, who was studying the hotel's instructions for accessing the FreeNet, as the Free Zone called their regional internet, looked up and nodded. Elizabeth knew that the very thought of going out alone on the unpoliced streets of Seattle frightened Hazel. They had talked a little about it on the plane. "What time did you say you'd scheduled Ganshoff for dinner?" Elizabeth asked.

"Eight-thirty."

"Good. I'll be back well before then." She smiled into Hazel's anxious face, then bent and kissed her soft, freckled forehead. "Don't worry so, love. Remember what I told you on the plane."

Hazel, clearly not convinced, sketched a smile.

Elizabeth picked up her attaché case and stepped into the elevator; as soon as the doors closed it plummeted to the first floor.

Briskly walking the three blocks to the Co-op's building, she stared curiously around her, surprised that Seattle's streets resembled those of any ordinary city of comparable size. At each intersection she turned her head to look down the cross street at Elliott Bay, a thrilling blue surface glistening under a deep azure sky, snowy mountains rising on the horizon behind it. What a pity we lost this place to the aliens, Elizabeth thought, for the first time perceiving the territory as concrete rather than abstract. We'll never get it back—not unless the aliens decide, for their own reasons, to withdraw. What was it they *wanted*, anyway? she wondered for the thousandth time. What was their purpose, and why did they want this place in particular, besides the handful of small poor areas in backwaters that they'd also claimed? None of the more imaginative types in the Company had ever been able to suggest a satisfactory hypothesis to explain the mystery. Maybe *she* could discover something while on this mission...

Half a block from it, Elizabeth spotted the sign designating the Kay Zeldin Memorial Building. Pressing back a surge of uneasiness, Elizabeth quickened her pace. This was no time to be thinking about Zeldin, she warned herself. Zeldin was long dead; Zeldin was irrelevant now to the Free Zone. She strode past the sign and through the revolving glass door into a spacious atrium furnished with chairs and sofas occupied by none too respectable-looking people reading, talking, sleeping. After a few seconds' search she spotted a bank of elevators and made a fast beeline for them.

Her air of decision deserted her halfway across the atrium, and she froze in her tracks as she nearly walked straight into...Kay Zeldin. Zeldin's glittering blue eyes seemed to be gazing directly at her. Elizabeth shuddered. No one else had eyes like those, no one. They simply weren't natural. She pressed her hand to her heavily pounding heart. But sanity flooded back over her, and she realized the figure was a holograph, not a human being, and slightly larger than life-size.

Sagging, catching her breath, she averted her eyes from the figure and hurried around it. Still she could feel its implacable gaze watching her, judging her. (Accusing her?) What had they done, turned her into a goddess or something? Elizabeth forced her trembling legs on. She felt Zeldin's presence behind her—as though the woman had been resurrected from the dead—and was aware of Zeldin standing with her hands lifted high above her head in a pose of victory (or was it perhaps a fighting stance?), her presence dominating the large, high-ceilinged space as some charismatic leader's would.

It was creepy. So very, horribly creepy.

A checkpoint controlled by armed women in gray uniforms occupied the area directly before the elevators. These must be the so-called Women's Patrol, Elizabeth thought. As she approached, they told her she'd have to submit to a scanner, and she unhappily allowed it. Her body passed muster, but when they ran the sensor over her attaché case, the instrument shrilled positive.

"I'm not carrying any weapons," she said coldly.

"Electronic equipment?" one of them said, watching Elizabeth as though she thought she might be going to attack.

"I'm carrying an open transmitter," Elizabeth said. "Surely you're not going to tell me I can't take that upstairs with me?" Everyone allowed bugs in these sorts of meetings.

"I'll have to look at it," the woman said. "And then if I find that it is the source of the positive, I'll have to check with the people you're seeing."

Elizabeth laid her attaché case on the table, unlocked it, and removed the transmitter. She wondered what these people did about service-techs with functioning implants—people like Hazel. The woman examined the transmitter and requested that Elizabeth's attaché case be scanned without the transmitter. This time it registered negative, and they told Elizabeth she could put the transmitter back into the attaché case. After Elizabeth had told them whom she intended to see, they let her go. As she waited for the elevator she observed the woman talking into the phone, which meant, she surmised, that Greenglass would have warning she was coming.

Elizabeth left the elevator on the seventh floor. Wandering in search of Greenglass's office, slightly disoriented by the corridor's curves, she realized it had been laid out in an ellipse. The lack of visibly present guards made the place seem almost eerily deserted. Apart from the two she had encountered at the checkpoint, she saw no others. Excision would be a triviality if they ever chose that method of dealing with the leaders.

The door to Greenglass's office stood open. Inside a woman sat at the desk with her back to the door. What a rash act of faith, Elizabeth thought, if that was indeed Greenglass sitting there. Elizabeth rapped her knuckles on the doorframe. "Hello," she caroled, "I'm looking for Martha Greenglass."

The woman at the desk swiveled her chair around to face Elizabeth.

Elizabeth surveyed the dark compact figure dressed in an odd version of the outfit the guards wore. Allison had told her about their clothing, of course—all the pro-Co-op types wore it: loose cotton trousers (like the kind she herself wore for hiking), a tee-shirt with either long sleeves or short sleeves (cotton or wool according to the season), and a long buttoned short-sleeved tunic-coat over the shirt, which they unbuttoned or took off as the temperature changed during the day (as it often did in Seattle). This woman's over-tunic was a dark burgundy denim, her tee-shirt a long-sleeved mauve cotton. It looked comfortable and practical, but Elizabeth knew she would not want *her* service-techs wearing it, for one could hardly make out the lines of the body it clothed.

"I'm Martha Greenglass," the woman said. Her keen dark eyes took in Elizabeth—her height, probably, and her executiveness, Elizabeth thought.

"How do you do." Elizabeth smiled nicely. "I'm Elizabeth Weatherall. Representing the Executive."

Greenglass's eyes widened. "Representing the Executive," she said, as though that were a significant statement. "Then this is official business?"

Her question caught Elizabeth by surprise: she hadn't expected quite this level of play from Greenglass. Elizabeth, still smiling, spoke in a drawl. "Oh, surely you don't imagine for an instant that the Executive will deal with you *officially*. You can't have any illusions about their recognizing the 'Free Zone'—" Elizabeth pronounced these words with a heavy, ironical inflection—"as a legal entity. That, I can assure you, will never happen."

Greenglass said, sounding indifferent, "I won't bother arguing *that* point with you. I just wanted to establish the terms of your representation."

But of course she should have expected that sort of thing from Greenglass, Elizabeth chided herself. Greenglass had been dealing with governments and even a few corporations—the more traitorous ones—for years now. She must long have had the rules of the game well-learned. "I'm empowered to talk with you about possible arrangements to do with the alleged human rights abuses you've charged the Executive with," Elizabeth said.

Greenglass, her face now animated, sprang to her feet. "*That's* your interest?" she said, her voice full of barely suppressed passion.

Naturally Greenglass would regard this visit as a coup for the Free Zone—demonstrating the Executive's seeming willingness to answer the Free Zone's charges—and thus in one sense acknowledging a certain legitimacy in spite of their refusal to recognize the Free Zone as anything other than territory held by rebels out of control.

"Come in and have a seat," Greenglass said, gesturing to the chair on the other side of the desk.

Elizabeth strolled inside. For a moment she stared out at the dazzling view of Elliott Bay and the Olympics behind. From here the harbor looked busy and thriving—full of ships and barges and ferries. Greenglass must like that, she thought, must consider such a sight the fruit of her labors. Elizabeth sat with her back to the window (giving her a certain advantage, especially at this time of day, since the sun would soon be in Greenglass's eyes) and accepted the water Greenglass poured into a glass for her. Greenglass herself—as an affectation, Elizabeth suspected—drank directly from the mouth of a half-liter bottle. "First off," Elizabeth said, opening her attaché case and bringing out the transmitter, "I want a commitment from you that if we investigate, bring to a halt, and take judicial action on these human rights abuses you've alleged, the aliens will leave intact the replacement for the communications satellite they recently disabled."

Greenglass, her eyes on the transmitter, said, "I am to assume everything said here is being recorded?"

"Of course."

Greenglass frowned in concentration; she bent to open a drawer in her desk. Straightening up, she set a small, dedicated recorder on the desk. "As a precautionary measure," she said.

So Greenglass imagined they might alter the recording? The thought amused Elizabeth. "As you wish," she said, smiling.

Greenglass crossed her arms over her breast. "If the Executive fully cooperates with us in uncovering, stopping, and punishing the human rights abuses going on in the US, then yes, the Executive may rest assured that the Marq'ssan will not disable a replacement satellite. Unless, of course," Greenglass added, darting a quick suspicious look at Elizabeth, "the Executive offers other provocation inviting such retaliation."

"That's somewhat vague," Elizabeth said.

Greenglass picked up the half-liter bottle. "I don't think so. The Marq'ssan have always used their destructive powers with discretion. As the Executive knows full well." Greenglass took another swallow from the bottle. "How do you intend to work this?" she said. "Are you inviting outside investigators in? Or do you claim to be able to police yourselves?" Her shaggy brown eyebrows flicked a challenge of open skepticism at Elizabeth.

"We've already begun an investigation," Elizabeth said smoothly. "However, we *might* be willing—under certain circumstances and with certain concessions from the Free Zone—to allow outside investigators to participate in our internal investigations."

Greenglass held up her hand. "Before we go any farther, I'd like to bring a few other people in on this discussion."

It would be considerably more difficult to manage a group than an individual. "It's easier to work things out tête-à-tête," Elizabeth said, "and I know you have the authority here to—"

But Greenglass cut off Elizabeth's flattery before she'd gotten it fully spun. "I think it's appropriate that certain of my colleagues be present during this discussion," she said. She took a handset from its wall cradle and made a series of quick calls to several women whose names Elizabeth recognized from her briefings on the Co-op."

Elizabeth turned in her chair to look out the window. Woman-to-woman, she had planned to put it to Greenglass. So much for her notion of trying to play on this woman's feminism. That kind of approach would be useless if she had to deal with a crowd of them. What was it Hughes had said about Greenglass? Slow but stubbornly sure. That the best one could hope for would be to catch her off guard, to slip something in so that it might fail to be noticed and thus analyzed. Greenglass always and ever analyzed, Hughes said, and then acted stolidly on whatever analysis she arrived at. Elizabeth would have to be careful not to put everything out on the table in this meeting Greenglass was orchestrating. And if she were clever, she might maneuver more cordial—and personal—meetings the next day or the day after that.

[iv]

That evening, as Elizabeth prepared to receive Margot Ganshoff, Hazel revealed that she had no idea of how to serve food and had never in her life done so. Elizabeth barely succeeded in suppressing her annoyance at the inconvenience this posed. Dinner, she realized, would have to be managed without service, for she would not risk using personnel provided by the hotel. Who knew what intelligence services might be represented on the hotel's staff? It was, after all, the best hotel in Seattle. Anyone of importance lacking a private residence would stay there. Keeping agents on the staff would be simple, good sense. Naturally Lauder's team had agents on the staff, but Elizabeth had no idea who they were, so she could not arrange to have one of them assigned to serve dinner. And it was essential that she keep her contact with the station as minimal as possible.

"As soon as the food cart arrives and you've wheeled it to the table," Elizabeth said, "you'll go downstairs to the dining room. You needn't worry, darling, it will be perfectly safe. If you like, I can assign Simmons to stick close to you."

Hazel shook her head with an attitude of alarm Elizabeth could not immediately parse. "No, no, that's not necessary," Hazel said, stuttering. "I don't need Simmons to protect me!"

Elizabeth frowned. "Is there some problem with Simmons?"

Hazel flushed. If Simmons had laid a finger on the girl, Elizabeth thought, she'd *kill* him.

"Not a problem, exactly." Hazel hesitated. "It's just that…he makes me very uncomfortable. He's so…insinuating. Because of our sexual relationship, I think."

Elizabeth sighed. "Do you want me to talk to him?" Really, it would be too tiresome of Hazel if she proved to have a thin skin about public knowledge of their relationship.

Hazel looked away. "No. What would there be to say?"

Elizabeth pressed her lips together. "If it goes beyond insinuating looks, I want to know," she said. "I won't tolerate that sort of thing."

Hazel, still not looking at her, nodded. "And I'm to stay downstairs until Ms. Ganshoff goes?"

Elizabeth thought a moment. "No, I don't believe that's necessary," she said. "In fact, it might be preferable for you to be in your room, on call in case I should want you for some reason I can't think of now. Besides," she added, "I wouldn't like to be interrupted by the phone while Ganshoff is here."

As if on cue, the room phone chirped. Hazel picked it up, murmured something, and put it down. "That was the desk. Ms. Ganshoff is on her way up," she said.

Elizabeth moved to the window to stare out at the lights twinkling in the harbor and on a distant shore. West Seattle? Bainbridge Island? Ganshoff would probably be a challenge, even more of a challenge than the women she had met with that afternoon. If it had been one of the Executive in Elizabeth's place, none of these meetings would have been taking place, not that little hen-session this afternoon, and certainly not a meeting over dinner with either Ganshoff or her superior. Executive males lacked the social ease executive women shared. Though she and Ganshoff were fierce opponents, of different nationalities, and total strangers, they would still find themselves sliding effortlessly into a social relationship that would allow them to talk—albeit guardedly—without either ceremony or support staff. Within the first few minutes they would not only have laid down the ground rules governing their meeting, but would also have established links, connections, and a base of mutual interest and recognition—thus eliminating certain ego problems inevitable for executive males in a comparable situation. Unless Ganshoff were unusual she would not be interested in the challenge-orientation, which inevitably dominated males who were strangers and opponents. Of course that didn't mean Elizabeth wouldn't be on her mettle from the start: she knew from everything Hughes had reported and everything their people in Vienna could scrounge up on Ganshoff that the woman was shrewd, experienced, and—for someone in her situation—relatively powerful. Elizabeth regretted that she could not reread Hughes's reports on Ganshoff's relations with Greenglass—but with the satellite down it was impossible, for she hadn't been about to risk carrying those files into the Free Zone on her personal computer's hard drive...

Elizabeth heard Hazel's voice saying, "This way, please." Elizabeth turned to look at the tiny, well-dressed woman following Hazel into the room. Elizabeth was amused to see the woman's protuberant, globular eyes appreciatively fixed on Hazel (who looked especially voluptuous in the clinging russet velvet suit Elizabeth had given her that morning). A woman after her own heart, Elizabeth thought.

She crossed to meet Ganshoff halfway. Smiling, she held out her hand. "Margot Ganshoff? I'm Elizabeth Weatherall."

Ganshoff, also smiling, shook Elizabeth's hand. "You must be a good foot and a half taller than I," she said, her head thrown back to look up into Elizabeth's face. "You make me feel quite a midget."

"Ah, but *you* make *me* feel a giant," Elizabeth said. "And so the best thing we can do for ourselves is sit." She gestured at the arrangement of sofa, loveseat, and armchairs. "Shall we?"

Hazel served them juice, then left the room to wait by the elevator for the arrival of their dinner. "She's fiercely monogamous," Elizabeth said with a twinkle, "so it would be pointless of you even to try."

Ganshoff laughed. "I'm that obvious?"

"I'm just observant," Elizabeth said, partly joking, warning Ganshoff that it would not be trivial to dupe her. "So tell me," she said, changing the subject, "what's it like living in this godforsaken place? Lonely, I suspect. And how many years have you been stuck here?"

Ganshoff sipped her spiced tomato juice. "I've been here since the middle of the war, for which I was truly grateful, under the circumstances. And yes, as you know, there's no one here to speak of. Boredom is a distinct problem. Apart from mountain and water sports, the only amusement is sex."

"And I don't imagine after growing up in the Alps the skiing is up to your exigent standards."

"It's a very icy pack. So what brings you here, Elizabeth?"

"Oh I imagine you can deduce my reasons." Elizabeth stretched out her legs. "The aliens have this annoying tendency of making life difficult for us when we fail to toe their line. But then you've yet to learn that, haven't you."

Ganshoff's eyebrows raised. "You think we run a risk doing business with them? Have you noticed Elliott Bay, Elizabeth? The leaders of the Free Zone have been in communication with the aliens for a decade now. *They* haven't found the aliens at all difficult. Here in the Free Zone, for instance, it's now actually possible to *fish* in Puget Sound. I wouldn't say they've made life difficult for people in the Free Zone, would you?"

Elizabeth smiled. "But Margot, dear, there isn't much executive life left here, is there. How do you think you're going to get around that little problem?" She sipped her grapefruit juice. "And when they tell you to give a gang of anarchist rebels a chunk of Austria, what will you do then?"

Hazel wheeled the food cart into the room, over to the already laid table, and set out the first course. "We'll be serving ourselves," Elizabeth said, leading Ganshoff to the table when Hazel had gone. "I thought we'd feel a bit freer in our conversation."

Ganshoff slanted an odd look at her. "You don't trust your girl?"

Elizabeth laughed. "She's never served food before. And I don't trust the hotel staff." She picked up her soup spoon. She hoped the hotel's chef was decent. "Tell me," she said after swallowing the first spoonful of the strong clear broth. "What is it that you think the aliens want with this planet? What is it they're really up to?"

"Have you met any of them?"

Elizabeth, remembering her single encounter with the aliens, shivered. "Once," she said. She couldn't tell Ganshoff the circumstances without revealing her connection with Sedgewick. And she wasn't prepared to give Ganshoff that much, at least not yet. "But do, please, answer my question."

Ganshoff touched her napkin to her lips. "Obviously you suspect them of diabolical intent," she said. "I'm not so sure. Greenglass, whom I've talked to quite a lot, seems not to suspect them of ulterior motives—and she is in regular contact with them."

Elizabeth snorted. "The Free Zone leaders are naive fools. I wouldn't take their opinions very seriously if I were you."

Ganshoff gave Elizabeth a superior, knowing smile. "They're not as naive as you might think. At any rate they've managed to hold power for ten years. That's not something to be sneered at."

Elizabeth swallowed more soup. "Only because the aliens choose to use them. They're perfect pawns. Or they were until this recent scandal hit."

Ganshoff's smile broadened. "Oh yes, that so-convenient opposition newspaper story revealing the Night Patrol connection." Ganshoff lifted her water goblet to her lips; Elizabeth watched her throat as she swallowed. "I do believe they'll weather it."

"So you're saying that Austria will continue trafficking with anti-executive terrorists," Elizabeth said flatly. This was something she needed to know for certain.

"If you mean that we'll continue with our trade agreements—"

Elizabeth interrupted her. "I mean this arrangement whereby your consulates and embassies openly aid and abet rebels and dissenters and work in tandem with anti-executive terrorists."

"Terrorists, Elizabeth?"

Elizabeth rose and removed their soup plates, then removed the thermal wrap from the meat platter and spooned generous portions of Pork Carbonnade onto the dinner plates. "You still haven't told me what you think the aliens are up to," she said, setting one of the plates before Ganshoff and the other in the center of her own place setting. "I'm most interested in your theories about that." She sat down and picked up her fork.

"I haven't thought much about their *intentions* one way or another," Ganshoff said. She frowned. "We've been more interested in what they have done for the Free Zone and in what they can do for Austria." She looked at Elizabeth. "Were you aware that they will be helping Free Zone techs to rapidly construct extremely efficient desalinization plants for both the Greeks and the Dutch? The Free Zone already has two such plants and according to the tech literature it's not completely understood how they operate. In other words, incorporated into the design and construction of their plants is alien technology. For us, Elizabeth, it seems eminently reasonable that we make use of the aliens' technology to the extent that we can, rather than scrolling through sinister science-fiction style scenarios." She looked down at her plate, stabbed a chunk of pork, and popped it into her mouth.

"It doesn't bother you that they're out to destroy the executive system?"

Ganshoff finished chewing and swallowed. "It's not clear they're interested in doing that," she said. "The fact that the so-called Free Zones they've established have dismantled their executive systems isn't necessarily an indication of the aliens' intention to do so. I'd say, rather, that they gave power to anti-executives only because the executives in those places were unwilling to deal with them. I'm convinced they destroyed the executive system in the Puget Sound area as an example. They work by example, the aliens. Remember their destructuring of various corporate sites at the beginning of the Blanket? All that was done by way of example."

"Not always," Elizabeth said, recalling the aliens' retaliation following Security's announcement of Zeldin's capture and execution. "But I'd like to point out that their behavior those first few months was completely different from what their behavior has been over the years since. They disbanded their assembly or whatever you want to call it and cut off contact with the governments. And they only punished a few of the governments, not all. I don't quite see——"

Ganshoff, shaking her head, interrupted. "You've remembered incorrectly, Elizabeth. Your government pulled its delegation out of the aliens' assembly and broke off relations with them entirely. It was after that that they cleared you out of this Free Zone. We never took steps to break with them the way you did and consequently we never suffered what you suffered."

Elizabeth took one of the soft yeasty rolls from the napkin-swathed basket and buttered it. "Perhaps," she said. "But I still don't see how that assures us of their ultimate intentions." She laid her butter knife down and stared at Ganshoff. "We know nothing about them. We don't even know what they look like physically, for godsake. We don't know which star they're from. All we know is their gender!"

Ganshoff's eyes looked directly into Elizabeth's. "We don't know their gender," she said quietly.

Elizabeth gaped at her. "What do you mean? Surely they're all females?"

"According to Greenglass, they have assumed human female form for certain political and psychological reasons. But Greenglass herself says they have kept their true gender identities deliberately ambiguous, and that they say for Marq'ssan gender is an irrelevancy."

This revelation stunned Elizabeth and disquieted her. It took her a few moments to recover herself enough to say, "You certainly seem to trust Greenglass."

Ganshoff reached for a roll. "Let's say I understand her, Elizabeth." She smiled—a sphinx's smile, Elizabeth thought. "And now," Ganshoff said, "you can tell me what kind of deal your Executive is going to try to make with the aliens. Which, I assume, is the reason for your even being here."

Elizabeth picked up the roll she had buttered. "I can hardly talk details when everything is up in the air. But as you know, we're concerned about the loss of our com-satellite." The rest of the meal would be spent avoiding saying anything, she thought. The evening's purpose had been accomplished. She could not really turn the screws until some of Selby's people had begun putting pressure on the corporations Austria had dragged into trade with the Free Zone…which would mean a second visit—if, indeed, the Executive chose to send Elizabeth to the Free Zone again.

[v]

Martha was not as convinced as Louise and Lenore were that playing the role of spy would be useful. Miserable with her effort to offer a false front, she faced her dinner partner across the table and wondered how she would be able to eat. "What have you been doing with yourself for the last two weeks?" she asked David after Suzy had taken their order. "It's been ages since I've heard from you."

How could she hide her knowledge of what he was? It had been bad enough lying awake nights thinking about their relationship and the lie it had always been. But sitting across the table from him she found her pain, anger, and humiliation overwhelming. *He* had been deceiving *her* for years, but she was new to the game: she doubted she could play the role she, Lenore, and Louise had cooked up. She longed to fling her knowledge in his face, and—even more than she longed to do that—she longed never to see him again. What would it matter to him how she felt about his treachery? His kind cared nothing for other people's feelings. His calculated use of her… Determinedly she stopped the thought and struggled against the tears suddenly stinging her eyes.

"I knew you were beyond busy, so I decided to keep out of your way." David's tone was casual. Then: "Hey, what's wrong, Martha?" In a lightning-swift shift, his voice oozed warm concern.

The brazenness of his hypocrisy provoked a spurt of rage that surged through Martha's body, making her head pound with nearly blinding fury. Probably he had been wondering if she'd guessed: yet he didn't really seem to expect that she might have figured it out. Well, if it hadn't been for Margot she probably *wouldn't* have. "I guess," Martha said, wishing she were better at thinking on her feet, wishing she were a better liar, "I thought maybe you wouldn't want to see me after that damned article the *Examiner* wrote about me. Since it dragged your name into it." She looked at him with what she hoped was wide-eyed distress and apology. "I'm sorry about that. It certainly is embarrassing." She could feel from the heat in her cheeks that her rage had turned her face red. He would probably, she thought, think she was blushing from shame.

"Hey, Martha." He covered her hand with his. "*Hey*. Don't worry about *me*. I knew straight off that it was a damned rotten tissue of lies. No way you're at fault in any of it."

Martha fought the urge to snatch her hand away. Could she go through with the charade? Would it be as helpful as Louise claimed? "I don't know," she said bitterly, "I suppose I had it coming to me. I've got a lot of enemies, it seems. Just how many will probably become apparent two weeks from now when the Steering Committee meets. I've thought of resigning before then, but everyone says that would be cowardly."

His hand tightened. "No, no, you mustn't resign, Martha." He gave her one of his soulfully earnest looks. "That would be admitting defeat. I'm sure you can handle the Steering Committee meeting. It's not as though you haven't been up against problems there before."

Of course he'd want her to continue with the Co-op for as long as she maintained her link with him, Martha thought. She was probably his best source of information on what was going on in the Co-op.

"What do the others and Sorben say?"

"The others are divided." Martha needed to be careful about what she "fed" him (to use Louise's terminology). "But Sorben definitely wants me to stick with it."

He nodded. "Then you'll stick. If the aliens are set on keeping you, the Steering Committee will accommodate itself."

Martha stared at him. For the first time she realized that he actually believed that the Marq'ssan dictated to the Steering Committee! She debated disputing this opinion, then decided to let it ride. Maybe it would be better for the Executive to think the Marq'ssan ran everything. But how could she know? What was it she should be saying, anyway? Louise hadn't been too clear...

Suzy brought the wine they'd ordered. After she'd uncorked the bottle and poured out two glasses, David proposed a toast. "To your continuing future with the Co-op." His grin was detestably satisfied.

Martha summoned up a wan smile. "I can drink to that," she said, clicking glasses with him. They drank, and Martha felt the wine hit her raw, burning stomach. Oh how he made her sick—the very sight of his face much less the sound of his voice. And how contemptible he must find her...

Suddenly it struck her: he himself had probably written that article describing her as a naive, silly fool, or had at the least suggested those exact words to whoever had written it.

And she was supposed to sit here and drink and eat with him? Louise, this had better be worth it, she thought, remembering that she could have gone instead to Verdell's party.

"So tell me about Paris," David said.

Martha leaned back and took another large gulp of wine. Paris, he wanted? All right. Paris he would get, and precious little else—other than the disinformation Louise had cooked up for him, of course.

Chapter Twenty

[i]

Elizabeth woke at dawn, perhaps because Hazel's bed was too damned short for her. Careful not to wake the girl, Elizabeth crept across the hall to her own room—the room Vivien had furnished with Elizabeth herself in mind. It had been after three when she and Vivien had gotten too sleepy to talk any longer and Elizabeth had gone into Hazel's room and made love to the half-asleep girl. She had intended to return to her own more comfortable bed but had fallen asleep with her head on Hazel's breast. It was getting to be a habit with her, she realized, and an uncharacteristic one at that.

Part of the time while talking with Vivien she had had fantasies of herself and Vivien both making love to Hazel at once, as they had done with another girl, long ago when they had been in their teens and at Crowder's. Elizabeth could not imagine sharing a sexual experience with any executive woman besides Vivien. She had felt nostalgic when telling Vivien about Hazel's special sensuality, poignantly wistful of what they could not share. But aside from whether or not Vivien would accept such an experience with her now that they were mature women, Hazel herself presented the greatest obstacle. The girl had such peculiar sensitivities. And Elizabeth would not risk upsetting her.

After Elizabeth showered and brushed her hair and rebraided it, she wandered through the house to the long glass-walled room that overlooked the ocean. The fog on the other side of the window hung so thickly that she could make out neither ocean nor sky. She decided that after she'd had coffee and croissants she would walk along the beach, alone. One of the things she most valued about her visits here were the periods of solitude they afforded her. Vivien understood her need and simply left her alone unless Elizabeth indicated that she wished otherwise. As on other visits, she would be able to do some thinking. It had been a long time since she'd had the opportunity. And lately she'd felt she'd lost her grip on her life. That much of her existence seemed out of control disturbed her, made her anxious—as she knew from the sort of dreams she'd been having since the trip to the desert.

When the service-tech entered with a tray of coffee and croissants, she said to Elizabeth, "There's a man who's been waiting to see you, Madam."

At that hour? "He's been frisked by my escort?" Elizabeth asked.

The girl nodded.

"Bring me some ID from him," Elizabeth said.

The girl left and returned immediately with a Security badge. Elizabeth returned to her room to run it through the scanner on her personal computer. His name and description checked out, so she went back out to the waiting service tech and said, "I'll see him now."

Half a minute later a man came in alone. Elizabeth checked his face against the badge. "What can I do for you, Feldman?" she said, watching him closely.

"I have a purple for you, Madam." He flourished the 10" x 13" purple envelope he held in his hand.

"You'll wait until I've seen whether there's to be an answer," Elizabeth said, slipping his badge into the pocket of her gown. She had never seen this courier before and was inclined to take precautions; she would give the badge back to him when she'd finished deciphering whatever he carried. She waved dismissal, and he left the room. Inside the purple envelope she found a thick wad of flimsy, a data key, and a handwritten note from the Northern California territory supervisor saying that these were the contents of a cable received from Sedgewick, sent via the San Jose station because Sedgewick had requested them to pass on his instruction that she "look in on" the San Diego station vis-à-vis the current State of Alarm in LA.

This was the first she'd heard of a State of Alarm. The note implied that she should know what that referred to. If only she could pick up the phone or make a com-link through her personal computer… Damn the aliens. Did this note mean she was to go immediately to San Diego, or did Sedgewick simply want her to make a stop

there before returning to DC? "Look in on" could hardly be vaguer.
Maybe the cable would be more forthcoming. Resigned to going to
her room, downloading the encrypted file into her personal computer,
and reading it before going out on her solitary walk, Elizabeth picked
up the tray of coffee and croissants and tucked the envelope under
her arm. Duty first, she thought: for she prided herself on being an
exemplary executive.

[ii]

As Emily made frozen smoothies, Celia ran her observations and
ideas about two different sets of federal forces detaining political prisoners by her. "Well, what you say makes sense to me," Emily said
as she added several handfuls of strawberries to the bananas, kiwi,
and ice already in the food processor. "There's still a great deal of
executive factionalism in this town along the lines taken during the
Civil War." She locked the cover of the food processor into place and
depressed the pulse button. The ice cubes clattered against the glass
sides of the container, making conversation impossible. After a few
seconds Emily lifted her finger and the racket stopped.

"So that means that when people are picked up we have to worry
about which side has them," Celia said. "But does it also mean that
they keep separate records? Or do they pool their information?"

Emily took a pair of balloon glasses out of the freezer and poured
out their drinks. "I don't know the answer to that last question. But I
can probably find out, if you think it's important." She handed Celia
one of the glasses, picked up the other, and led the way to the terrace.

"I'm not sure," Celia said when they had seated themselves on
chaise lounges. It was warm enough in the sun to go without a jacket,
even guzzling drinks made with crushed ice. "But it seems to me that
if they aren't pooling their records there should be some advantage we
might be able to exploit." She sipped her drink, and the flavor of the
fruit fizzed on her tongue. "Or is that wishful thinking?" Celia set her
glass down on the table beside her. The sun wasn't really hot enough
to make icy hands pleasurable.

"The only picture I see is one of confusion," Emily said. "And I
can't figure out how that can help us. In fact, it might make it harder

chasing people down and identifying the police personnel involved in particular cases."

Celia stared at the ocean and struggled to think. "Would you say most executives in the county are divided along Civil War lines?"

"Yes," Emily said slowly. "I think I would say that. Not all, but most. Their ties are too close to allow many people to remain neutral."

Celia felt as though they were onto something important. "That means that judges are on one side or the other, right? Couldn't we play on that in trying to get judges to allow prosecution of the people perpetrating abuses?" The bastard's face flashed into her mind, stifling, oppressing, choking her. What did it matter to her which "side" he was on? They were all the same, those executives' lackeys.

Emily swallowed more of her drink. "I don't know." She sounded dubious. "It's hard to imagine executives not sticking together. Especially now with so much property being destroyed in LA. It's bound to make them more intense in their crack-down here. Through so-called preventative measures."

Celia sighed. "I don't understand all this violence. Was it there all along? Or is it just that I didn't notice it until I started seeing clients in Hillcrest? They're all *children*, Emily."

"Children with firebombs," Emily said dryly. "According to my father, a law has been passed requiring all vendors of glass bottles to be specially licensed. The theory is that firebombs cannot be as effective when they're made from other containers than good old fragile glass."

Whole sections of LA were said to be burning now. That was especially scary since the hillsides always flamed up out of control when it was this dry and windy. "I just hope they don't find a way to tie the firebombings to the rent protest," Celia said.

They sat silent, sipping from their drinks, staring out at the water. Celia recalled fires that had been ignited by bombings and strafings during the war. As had often been the case in those times, her mother hadn't come home the night before. The hospital was crammed with casualties coptered down from overloaded LA hospitals.

After a while Emily stirred. "You know, when it comes to that issue, there may be some division along the lines you were suggesting earlier."

"Which issue?" Celia said, trying to remember exactly what they had just been talking about.

"The rent protest," Emily said. "You know who the rent protests are against, don't you?"

Celia frowned. "Well, no..."

"A number of property owners in Southern California have switched out of the old system of rental contracts by which the rent is automatically deducted from the renter's plastic account on the date the rent is due," Emily said. "The reason property owners have changed from the old practice was so that they could collect M-dollars from their tenants. But of course from the property owner's point of view there's a disadvantage with the new system—namely, that the renter has to physically pay the owner. Also, in exchange for paying in M-dollars, many tenants have gotten reductions in the amount of rent they pay. But everyone else is still locked into the old system. Since money has gotten tighter and the renters have no way of bargaining—say by withholding payment—when their rent is being deducted from their plastic accounts, the other rental system—in M-dollars—seems relatively attractive to renters." Emily paused, as though to make sure Celia was following her.

"I understand all that," Celia said. "But what does that have to do with executive factionalism?"

"It's very simple, Cee: the renters' protests are largely against the property owners who still operate on the old system, because their rents are higher and more inflexible. The M-dollar rents are newer arrangements better reflecting the current economic situation. Further, paying in M-dollars gives renters the sense of being less powerless."

Celia frowned. "And you're suggesting that those executives taking rents in M-dollars are all on one side of a factional split?"

Emily said, "I believe so. It's probably not an absolutely categorical sort of thing, but I suspect that most of the owners preferring to use M-dollars are Military-connected, since that includes just about every local military contractor as well as local retailers, while those preferring the old method are Security-connected." Emily grinned. "You see, Celia, most Security-connected executives will do anything they can to stamp out M-dollars. They're afraid the entire international monetary system could collapse if people had the choice of using a physical currency not directly controlled by the executive system. Also, transactions in M-dollars have the interesting property of being difficult to trace. Which is of course why M-dollars are so useful for interests like yours and mine."

Celia's excitement resurged. "So how do you think we can exploit this difference?"

Emily bit her lip. "I don't know. I don't know that we can. But I think we should at least *think* about it. It would logically make sense that a divided Executive could be useful for the Movement. And this renters' protest is interesting because it's one of the only organized events on this scale we've seen."

"Do you think the firebombings are coming out of the rent protests?"

"I think the publicizing of the holdings of certain property owners may be contributing to it. But violence can only detract from the legitimacy of the rent protests. It may be that most people will withdraw their support of the protest because of the possible tie."

Celia's excitement subsided. So Emily had had nothing concrete in mind when she had made her suggestion. "And the violence here?" she said, thinking of some of the clients she had taken on in Hillcrest.

"It's all small stuff, isn't it. A venting of frustration by children. It gives the political police an excuse to search people's homes and arrest teenagers."

"I wish I knew why they're keeping Luis," Celia said. Her gaze returned to the water. "It doesn't make sense. They don't usually hold doctors for long. Lawyers, yes, because of the nature of the services they provide for their clients. So why Luis? I keep wondering if he had a patient who was in some way sensitive and who might have told him something they don't want known. It's the only thing I can come up with." The sick feeling she'd been carrying around with her for weeks clenched her gut like a fist squeezing a sponge.

"He was photographed going into the consulate," Emily said. "I think, Celia, that we're going to have to find a way to contact those people who say they're willing to help the victims of the security forces. And I think the best means of doing that will be through me."

Celia looked at Emily. "How? By driving up to LA and paying a call on one of the consuls?"

Emily smiled. "By inviting them down here for lunch or dinner at my father's house. All three of them. That way I can sit down with them and see what's what; and then if they seem trustworthy, make arrangements with them. What do you think?"

"I think that's a fantastic idea," Celia said. "Even if ODS suspects what you're up to, there's nothing they'll be able to do about it."

"Exactly. We need to take advantage of my privilege and connections."

Celia's eyes filled with tears. "You amaze me, Emily. You really do." Struggling to regain her composure, she picked up her glass and sipped. "I hope you understand what you're getting into," she said after she'd taken three or four swallows. "It's wonderful that you're so generous with your time and efforts for the Movement. But there *is* danger, you know. Even for you."

"I'm splendidly equipped to take care of myself, Celia. Not only am I an executive, I'm Barclay Madden's daughter. So long as Daddy stands behind me, I can get away with a quite a bit more than almost anybody else around here could."

"You don't think the people fiercely opposing M-dollars won't have another reason for disregarding your special privileges?" In some ways Emily counted too heavily on her position of privilege to protect her from the ruthlessness they were up against. It seemed to Celia that Emily still hadn't taken their enemies' measure.

Emily's gaze met Celia's. "That's something to think about," she said slowly, as though it were an idea totally new to her. Then she shook her head. "No, no, those people especially wouldn't try railroading me. It would rock too many boats, upset too many people, to see assured privilege so easily trampled upon. No, they'd need absolute proof of a serious treason charge to get me."

Long familiar with judicial notions of "proof," Celia sighed. Though she, Celia, lacked much of Emily's sophistication and knowledge, Emily, it seemed, had not a glimmer of something any individual living in Hillcrest was forced to understand from the age of five up.

"I think you should be there when I have the consuls to lunch," Emily said.

"Really?"

"Yes. You can bring all your files."

"If ODS hasn't taken them by then," Celia said, thinking of Delia's warnings about how often their files were searched and seized.

"And that's another thing we'll have to find a way of dealing with," Emily said.

"You think there's a way of stopping their searches?"

"Not stopping their searches, but preventing their seizures. The practical answer is simple: we find a way to dump all the clients' files into another comp system. We'll be devious."

"It will cost money," Celia said.

Emily laughed. "Money is the easiest thing of all for me to provide. What we need now is a systems specialist. Do you know any?"

Celia could think of no one safe. "I'll check around," she said.

"Good," Emily said. "And so will I."

How many projects was Emily willing to take on? Celia felt as though before meeting Emily she herself had barely been involved in the Movement by comparison with all the things she had begun dabbling in because of Emily's push.

Emily rose from her lounge and stretched. Smiling, she said, "Time for my swim, since I missed my usual dip this morning on account of the board meeting I had to attend. Interested in joining me? The water's warming up, you know."

"No, thanks," Celia said as Emily began stripping off her clothes. She was sure it was still too cold for a wimp like herself. "But I think I'll walk a bit." Thinking she would wait until after Emily was actually in the water, she sat back and watched Emily stride naked down to the beach. From board meeting to anti-executive plotting to swimming naked in the sea: what a life Emily led. When Celia thought about it, it hardly seemed real. Emily's blind spot, now, *that* was real. If only she could be made to see it.

[iii]

"What the *hell* is she playing at?" Elizabeth said, closing the file. "It doesn't look good, Lisa."

Lisa swiveled away from her terminal to face Elizabeth. "I haven't passed any of this on to Krebs, you know. I thought I'd better check with you first."

"Good. I think this is something we want to be handling ourselves—with discretion—at least for the moment." Elizabeth paused to think. "You say she brought this subversive to her art party? I just can't figure that into the picture. Do you suppose they really are lovers?"

"I seriously doubt it. You know how most professionals are… though this woman seems not to have sexual interests in men. I suppose it's just barely possible. But she definitely isn't Emily's usual type. She was so very out of place at that party."

Elizabeth made up her mind. "I want to talk to the uncle. Call our vile friend Harrigan and have him sent over at once. I have too much to do to go out there myself."

"And if he's too doped-up to talk?"

"I don't see that as likely. Central sent out an order to cease routine dosing. And I doubt this Salgado is a violent type requiring special measures for control."

"All right," Lisa said with resignation. "They don't like this kind of thing out there. But you're the boss."

Elizabeth couldn't care less what Harrigan liked or didn't like, as long as he followed orders. While Lisa got El Cajon on the phone, Elizabeth walked over to the enormous wall monitor displaying a map of the entire Southern California territory. Desiring greater resolution and detail for the LA area, she entered the appropriate command into the terminal and watched the map reform. Yes, there it was, she could see all the data they currently had, graphically depicted. And before her eyes details in the display were refreshed automatically—the locations of Leland's men, for instance, as well as surveillance subjects' whereabouts and fires in progress.

She knew what Sedgewick would order Leland to do if he were handling this himself. And she knew Sedgewick would expect her to order the same thing in his stead. Could she avoid doing so? Leland tended to prefer a semi-soft approach. Sedgewick, however, simply did not believe Leland's reasons stood up against "experience." It had been clear in the file Central had sent her that Sedgewick considered this current outbreak of disorder to be a direct consequence of Leland's failure to quash the rent protest at its inception. According to Lisa, Leland had reasoned that coming down hard on something so ineffective would add fuel to the other fire: he had seen the rent protest as a sort of safety-valve emission. Staring now at the obviously high degree of property damage in Westwood alone, Elizabeth knew she would have to find some action to recommend to Leland that would satisfy Sedgewick. Not only must she consider Sedgewick himself—for she could, if necessary, handle his dissatisfaction—but the Executive as well. They would be hearing from the people whose property was either under attack or threatened. And in some cases members of the Executive were themselves LA property owners. Elizabeth knew that Booth, for one, had extensive holdings in LA and that the name of his rental corporation had been on the list of owners the rent protesters had named as targets for possible future boycotts.

"Harrigan says Salgado is in an interrogation cycle," Lisa said.

Elizabeth turned from the map. "What does that have to do with anything?" she said irritably.

Lisa bit her lip. "Harrigan is concerned that we not interrupt it."

"I'm not interested in Harrigan's concerns," Elizabeth said. "I'm only here for the day, and I want to see this prisoner. Don't talk to me about what Harrigan wants or doesn't want. Just get Salgado fucking *over* here." She turned back to the map and tried to shut out the sound of Lisa's phone murmur.

Never would Lisa dream of suggesting to Sedgewick, say, that his orders be changed to suit a subordinate's convenience. It simply would not happen. Yet many station people still did this to her after years of working under her. Was it the difference in her personal style? Or because she was a woman? Or her lack of official status? After all, Lisa knew very well that if Elizabeth wanted an order carried out it would be carried out: it had never happened, not once, that Elizabeth's authority had faltered. Sedgewick had never failed to rubberstamp her orders, had never directly countermanded them. No, Elizabeth thought, if he didn't like the way she handled something he'd make her countermand her own orders: carefully preserving her credit while having his own way. So why had Lisa bothered to pass on Harrigan's nonsense?

"They'll have him here in an hour or so," Lisa said.

"Good. That will give me time to talk to Leland first—about this mess." Elizabeth gestured at the map.

"Now?"

"Now."

"All right," Lisa said, picking up the phone. "Let me check to see that he's not in the middle of something."

"If he is, then he'll just have to tear himself away, won't he," Elizabeth said.

When Lisa hung up the phone she looked at Elizabeth. "He said he'll come in here since we're probably going to want reference to the big map. It would be too awkward trying to see everything on desktop monitors."

When the door opened and Leland came in, other differences from the way things would be if it had been Sedgewick here instead of herself struck Elizabeth. For one thing, if it had been Sedgewick, Leland would have been with him the entire time—not only when summoned—and would have probably been passing on Sedgewick's orders to Lisa. Thus if Sedgewick had wanted to question Salgado, he would have told Leland to get the man over here, and Leland would have told Lisa to call El Cajon, and Lisa in turn would merely have relayed the order without referring Harrigan's complaint back to either Leland or Sedgewick. Of course Elizabeth did not want Leland's constant attendance on her: she *preferred* working through Lisa as much as possible, just as she always *preferred* working through the executive women who were the PAs of the men she needed to deal with. Was it this structure that changed the dynamics of the situation? Elizabeth wondered as she greeted Leland.

"I've familiarized myself with your situation in LA," Elizabeth said. "I don't think the steps you've taken are comprehensive and preventative enough for the possibilities inherent in the situation."

"Surely putting an end to the firebombings and rounding up the leaders of the rent protest will be sufficient?" Leland said, his face creasing into exponentially more wrinkles as he frowned.

Elizabeth gestured at the monitor. "Rounding up the leaders of the rent protest would probably have been sufficient a few days ago. It's too late now for counting on that alone. The firebombings have given the protests added publicity, albeit negative. Vid and radio coverage has been cleverly managed, I will grant—the very people likely to be considering getting involved in rent protests will be frightened by the threat of their own apartments being firebombed once it is known that the property subject to rent protests is precisely the property being destroyed." A thought came into Elizabeth's head, and she immediately spoke it: "Do you suppose Madden's people could be behind some of the firebombings? To try to stampede owners into switching their rentals into M-dollars?"

Leland's eyes narrowed. "That hadn't occurred to me," he said, obviously disturbed. "It's hard to imagine, since most of the arsonists seem to be teenagers. Still, it's something we should bear in mind in interrogations of apprehended arsonists." He looked at Lisa. "Make a note of that for Krebs," he said.

Lisa, already scribbling a note on her yellow pad, nodded.

"Naturally," Elizabeth said, "I know your inclinations well enough to assume you would prefer not to use Sedgewick's methods." Her gaze met Leland's. "In this case I imagine Sedgewick would order the Guard to sector the county, impose a dusk to dawn curfew, and use chemical spraying. It's rather important that we make it clear that this sort of disorder will not be tolerated. If we appear to be soft, word will get around to troublemakers in other cities." Elizabeth gazed at the map. "For the moment I will not recommend measures like chemical spraying. However, I do think we need to begin taking steps to effect isolation. Second, I think the news coverage of this could be far more effective. Bennett is in the area, isn't she?"

Leland looked at Lisa.

"Yes," Lisa said. "She's in Santa Monica."

"I'd like to bring her in on this," Elizabeth said. "She's very good with media tactics. Moreover, we can use this situation to press the issue of M-dollars. It's essential that we make people see that using M-dollars will in the long-run undermine their own interests. Bennett will be able to tie in the firebombings with the flow of M-dollars and find a way to focus it on individual types that people will be able to identify with."

Leland looked at Lisa. "See if you can raise her on the phone now," he said.

Elizabeth watched with mixed feelings as Lisa obeyed Leland's order. On the one hand, she was getting instant compliance with her suggestions and wishes. On the other hand, something about the situation made her uncomfortable. Why had he taken it upon himself to explicitly order Lisa to call? There was something absurd about a visible chain of command, when Elizabeth could have told Lisa herself, or Lisa could have suggested making the call.

Elizabeth pushed this extraneous matter from her mind and returned to the subject of which repressive methods they would implement according to each set of contingencies they extrapolated. She hoped they could get the damned satellite replaced, fast, for they needed Allison's vid project to forestall another situation like the current one. All the repressive measures in the world could be employed and they still would not have control. Even Sedgewick knew that such "control" was desperate at best and more expensive than they could now afford.

[iv]

When yet another meeting with the cooperating consuls broke up, Margot took Martha aside and said she had something to discuss with her apart from the others. Elated because she had gotten the consuls to accept all the procedures she had proposed, including using Shoshana—one of Louise's people—as a mediator between consulates and the activist groups local to them, Martha agreed without hesitation and followed the executive to her sitting room.

"So," the executive said when they were sitting in comfortable chairs drinking orange and mango juice. "I hope Elizabeth Weatherall didn't take you in."

Martha's gaze flew to her face. "You knew about her visit?"

Margot snorted. "Oh, really, Martha. She contacted me on her arrival."

Martha thought about this and saw that it made sense. The Executive must be disturbed about other executive governments being involved in arrangements with the PNW Free Zone, especially when those arrangements concerned US human rights violations.

"You know who she is, I assume?"

Martha set her glass down on the table between them. "Someone the Executive sent," she said. The name *had* sounded familiar, but she hadn't been able to place it.

"She's Sedgewick's right hand."

Martha was appalled. "I *knew* her name sounded familiar. But it's been so many years since I heard it. Kay Zeldin mentioned her when she told us her story. And later in her book." Martha bit her lip. "So that means she's a spy."

"Certainly she's with the SIC," Margot said dryly, "and in contact with your friend Hughes, or if not him, his superior."

Martha thought of how she'd had dinner with David the very night of the day she'd first talked with Weatherall, at his invitation. Probably he'd been hoping she would talk about the business Weatherall had proposed, maybe even reveal the Co-op's reactions and plans. What a situation! Louise thought they could use David, but in the meantime David was still trying to use—and surround—her.

"I hope you realize that you're going to have an all-out public relations fight on your hands," Margot said when Martha failed to speak. "For while you seem to have the upper hand over the Executive, they're going to have popular support if—or rather when, for I think it inevitable—they start pounding away again at the evil intentions of the Marq'ssan."

Martha brushed this away: "*That* doesn't worry me. What's important is to force them to change their attitude toward dissent. To stop the human rights abuses." In fact, she would not feel satisfied until they'd overturned the executive system and completely broken the Executive's power. But that was none of Margot's business. She said, "In one sense, Weatherall is the ideal person for us to be dealing through—since it's her people who are perpetrating the violence and repression. It will be a matter of making sure she doesn't gull us."

Margot had started to lift her glass to her lips, but before drinking, she made as if to toast Martha. "Good luck, dear. I'm sure you know you'll have to be looking over your shoulder all the way. I'd make sure she doesn't leave loopholes. And that's going to be damned hard to do. You don't know how these people think."

Oh no? Martha had the impression she knew their thinking very well: goddess knew she'd been fighting it long enough and had personally suffered from it. "I've told her we're going to be insisting on outside monitoring teams—made up of observers of our choice."

"And she agreed?"

"Yes," Martha said. "I made it the condition for allowing them to replace their communications satellite. I think Weatherall understands that the Marq'ssan will destructure it as soon as it's launched if this condition isn't met." Sorben had said that it was up to Martha and the rest of the Inner Circle to use the threat as effectively as possible.

Margot chuckled. "I imagine the loss of that satellite has thoroughly fucked up most US com-systems—including Security's. And of course there's the matter of global vid, their most effective means of control." She fairly oozed *schadenfreude.*

Yes, Martha thought, it *is* their most effective means of control. It's too bad the Co-op needed so badly to bargain. Without the satellite, global vid was difficult—though it was not apparently impossible. According to Sorben, the Executive had begun constructing a system of towers for long distance transmission. In case they permanently lost the satellite? Or to circumvent the effects of future satellite strikes?

"This could be very amusing," Margot said.

Martha raised her eyebrows.

"Your being pitted against Elizabeth Weatherall, I mean. You do realize she assumes she has the advantage, in spite of your having the aliens' powers at your disposal?"

"They're not at my disposal," Martha said. "You always have to be so simplistic when it comes to the Marq'ssan, don't you."

Margot's teeth flashed in the broadest of smiles. "My *point* is that Weatherall thinks you—and the Free Zone—are at the aliens' disposal. I don't pretend to know which is true. But it's clear to me you have some sort of arrangement with them that give you untold advantages over anyone you deal with—provided you understand what's going on."

"And you think that perhaps we don't—or won't—understand," Martha said.

Margot held her hand up in protest. "*I* wouldn't underestimate you, Martha." Martha snorted. "By the way, what *was* it that Hughes told you about me, anyway?"

Martha flushed. "Why do you think we discussed you?"

Margot laughed. "Given the US's need to prevent other govern-ments from consorting with the Free Zone? And given the difference in your attitude after he learned we were doing business together? Don't be absurd, Martha."

Martha swallowed the remainder of the juice in her glass. "Was there anything else you wanted to discuss?"

"Besides Elizabeth Weatherall?" Margot shook her head. "I want-ed to warn you to be careful in your dealings with her."

"Why should it matter to you?"

Margot's eyes narrowed. "Austria has a lot riding on these ar-rangements with the PNW Free Zone," she said evenly. "More than you might suspect. We're feeling a great deal of pressure to get back into line. Austria's emerging relationship with your Free Zone is virtually redrawing the geopolitical map. Not to mention restruc-turing the global economy, and in ways that demonstrate how little influence the United States has remaining to it." Margot picked up her glass and held it to her lips. "Don't you understand the implica-tions?" She drank, then put her glass down. "As one example, I can assure you that the EU will refuse to adopt sanctions against the Free Zone—which is what the Executive is demanding they do. Although the British have proposed it, they are meeting with almost unanimous opposition from the rest of the member states." Margot smiled tartly. "I expect you and the other Free Zones will soon be deluged with of-fers of assistance from other governments than the three represented here today, for they all have projects they'd be delighted to have the aliens' assistance with."

Martha realized that news of Hungary and Poland's dealings with the Korean Free Zone hadn't yet gotten out. It made her smile to think of how furious it would make David when it did.

Martha came away from the consulate bursting with optimism. Once again she'd been given a glimpse of possibilities she could scarcely imagine. She had the sense that if enough people could un-derstand what to do, many of the things they so desperately wanted could happen. But did they have what it would take to understand? If only things had happened differently from the time the Marq'ssan had made their presence felt on earth. If there had been a plan—and if the governments had responded then as they were beginning to respond now—everything might have happened differently. But instead everything had been so chaotic, so little understood.

Not to mention that the Marq'ssan had always declined to engage in what they called management, so wary were they of becoming oppressive colonizers shaping another species' culture.

But now they had another chance, Martha could feel it: human structures, after so much stress, were in upheaval, beginning to crack and break and nearing collapse. And they *would* collapse; Martha felt sure of it. The only question was whether or not the structures replacing those that collapsed would be clones reproducing everything she hated, or wholly new structures allowing change, freedom, and the withering away of the oppressions implicit in the collapsing structures.

Martha decided to track down Verdell. She was dying to talk, dying to share her enthusiasm. And unlike everyone else Martha knew, Verdell was not jaded, which meant that talking with her offered a good chance of giving her a fresh, hopeful, stimulating outlook— which was precisely what she felt she needed most right now.

[v]

They had put the prisoner in a small windowless room in the basement of the station's annex. Elizabeth found him seated at the table, his left wrist cuffed to a steel ring attached to his chair. She said "Good afternoon, Dr. Salgado," introduced herself by name, and set the liter-and-a-half bottle she had brought him on the table, within reach of his free hand. He glanced first at her and then at the bottle, and then stared down at the surface of the table. When she told him she was investigating the possibility that there had been human rights violations and invited him to talk about any that he might know about, he neither looked at her nor spoke. She asked him about his visit to the Austrian consulate. He continued to stare down at the table in silence. Finally, in frustration, she said that she was conducting an investigation of the charges alleged by the Free Zone. Only then did he lift his gaze to her face—letting her see that he believed she was hoping to persuade him to incriminate himself and expose others to pursuit and arrest: this in spite of her treating him with scrupulous politeness.

She should have expected this, Elizabeth told herself, for he was probably too exhausted to distinguish her from those who had been interrogating him at El Cajon. Several tics twitched his drawn face, and his eyes hardly seemed able to focus on her. Elizabeth wished she had the time to spare for restoring him to reasonable physical condition and then going to work on him. She knew she could not entrust the job to Lisa, and for various reasons she did not want anyone else briefed yet on what they knew about Emily Madden.

After half an hour of trying to break through Salgado's silence, she gave up and ordered him returned to the detention facility.

When she opened the door to Lisa's office, Lisa said in an irritatingly bright tone, "Did you learn anything?"

Elizabeth folded her arms over her chest. "Nothing," she said. "When was it Allison said she'd be arriving?"

"At six."

Elizabeth checked her watch; it was only four-thirty. "Hazel's still down on the beach?"

"As far as I know. You'd better warn her about sunburn, Elizabeth. I don't think she understands about the potency of our sun."

"Walk down to the beach with me, just for a minute or two," Elizabeth said.

As soon as they were out of the house and descending the steps to the beach, Elizabeth resumed their earlier discussion of Emily Madden. "So far, Salgado is our only hope for finding out what she's up to. Therefore, his interrogation protocol is to be paused until further notice. I want you to arrange visiting privileges for him. And then I want complete transcripts as well as videotapes of all the visits that are made to him." Elizabeth spotted Hazel sitting on a large black rock about fifty yards from the bottom of the stairs.

"I doubt if that will net anything."

"We have no way of knowing that, do we," Elizabeth said sharply. "The other possibility, of course, is springing him."

"That would do no good at all," Lisa said, very definitely. "Whenever Espin is with Emily we lose transmission. Emily obviously carries a jammer on her person. We'd know just as much as we do now about her relations with Espin. Which is to say, almost nothing. No, I think guile is called for. How about my telling Emily I want to talk with Espin about her uncle? I am, after all, their main hope for getting him released."

They stepped onto the sand. "There's another angle to this, you know." Elizabeth leaned against the rocky embankment, shielded from exposure to the sun, and stared out at the majestically gliding green waves.

"Enlighten me."

"There may be something major coming down because of this human rights mess. And it's likely Salgado is a witness. He's a doctor. I suspect he's seen physical evidence. Such witnesses will need to be handled carefully. If we can cull out cases where Military authorities are especially to blame—" Elizabeth quirked an eyebrow— "or at the very least concentrate on localized cases of twistedness or overzealousness, we might lose the battle without losing the war. It's imperative that Security hang onto its authority, which means its credibility. Putting our own house in order is an important means of doing that."

Their eyes locked in a long, mutually-held gaze. "You mean people like Harrigan and Krebs...would be sacrificed?" Lisa asked softly.

Elizabeth held the gaze. "Perhaps. If they deserved it."

"That wouldn't exactly depress me," Lisa said. "But on the other hand, there's another sort of credibility Security can't afford to lose. Credibility within."

"I think that could be managed."

Lisa smiled. "Are you making a hit list, Elizabeth?"

"I don't know what you have in mind, Lisa, but your flippancy is...unwise." That's all she'd need, having rumors fly the rounds that she, Elizabeth Weatherall, had made up a hit list. She showed Lisa a stone face. "All this is of course in confidence and not for anyone else's consumption. Not even Leland's. Clear?"

"Understood," Lisa responded. "Your girl is walking back this way, did you know?"

Elizabeth moved her head slightly; out of the corner of her eye she noted Hazel's progress towards them. "I think you'd better make sure Salgado is treated...well. You can tell Harrigan and Krebs that Salgado is of interest to Central and that we will be talking with him again at another time."

Lisa bit her lip. "Very well, Elizabeth. It won't be easy, but I'll manage it somehow."

"What do you mean, it won't be easy? Since when do professionals refuse to take orders from their executive superiors?"

"This situation is different," Lisa said. "You've seen what El Cajon is like. They consider that their domain."

Elizabeth pressed her lips together. "In that case I think I'm going to have to arrange for a few more visits by my people. Longer, more thorough investigations."

"You're going to make an example of us then," Lisa said bitterly. "That's all we need. Thanks a lot, Elizabeth."

Elizabeth perceived Hazel approaching. "You're putting the wrong spin on this," Elizabeth said. "The way I see this is that it may help you in your turf fight."

"Not bloody likely," Lisa said. Hazel stood a few feet from them, waiting. "No more than your transferring out five of our people and shipping in five new people from outside. Do you have any idea what morale has been since that went down?"

Elizabeth turned her head and smiled at Hazel. "There you are, darling," she called, stretching her hand toward the girl. Hazel moved closer. "Look at those freckles!" Elizabeth touched a finger to Hazel's nose. "How charming!" Elizabeth looked back at Lisa. "Have someone fetch me when Allison arrives, would you?" she said to dismiss her.

Lisa started back up the stairs.

Elizabeth slid her arm around Hazel. "Have you had enough of the beach, or can you take another walk, this time with me?"

"I'll never have enough of this beach," Hazel said happily.

"Your eyes are like topazes out here," Elizabeth said. They began walking back the way Hazel had come from. "Amber in the east, topaz in the west. You're a jewel according to your setting, Hazel."

Hazel laughed and leaned her head against Elizabeth's arm. "I wish I knew how to talk about your eyes," she said. "They're far more beautiful than mine."

"You're much too modest, love. I'm going to have to feed you a daily ration of compliments so that you'll get a fair impression of yourself."

"Flattery, flattery," Hazel mocked. "Don't think it will get you anywhere."

"No, my Hazel is above that," Elizabeth said, stopping her. She looked down into Hazel's face and, backing Hazel into the embankment, let everything else slip away from her. She knew they could not be seen from above. She slid her hands down Hazel's body; grasping Hazel's buttocks, lifting her off the ground, she kissed her soft, warm mouth. At once her body came alive with sensation that spread through her limbs, tingled in her breasts and groin. In spite of the presence of the station above she would make love to Hazel right here on the spot. Doing so was her prerogative, her defiance against Leland, Sedgewick, and all the other males dictating the nonsense that made her life less than it might be. Whatever their idiosyncratic perversions, those pigs could never again experience the pleasure she now shared with Hazel—if, indeed, they ever had. Who knew what sexual pleasures unfixed males experienced? Whatever it was, it was nothing like her own pleasure, for they knew nothing of female sensuality, nothing at all. One never saw it in their art or literature, only the most barefaced mimicry, it was merely one more thing of which men were oblivious, beasts that they were.

"And this, love," Elizabeth murmured into Hazel's ear upon her discovery of another entry in Hazel's personal lexicon of desire.

"Yes," Hazel gasped, "yes."

Yes, Elizabeth's body echoed, yes.

Chapter Twenty-one

[i]

Together, Elizabeth and Sedgewick studied the enormous and intricate flow-chart Selby's people had made up, devoting special attention to the new configuration Elizabeth had sketched in to reflect the meager results of the previous night's dinner party. "What I don't understand," Elizabeth said, "is why Booth isn't putting himself out more on this. Or the others, for that matter. It seems that only you, Selby, and Wilson are making any effort to handle this. How does the Executive expect us to deal with Madden without their help?"

"You know what's happened, don't you," Sedgewick said, collapsing into Elizabeth's favorite armchair. "They've gotten used to Security's managing everything of importance for them since the Blanket." Sedgewick leaned his head back and closed his eyes, as though to avoid the sight of the chart. "Oh, it's a little more complicated than that, granted—most of the people we've had trouble prodding into action are afraid of losing money on the deal. They're having a hard time seeing the larger picture, the larger risks. They're thinking in very narrow, self-interested terms. As for those on the Executive, they prefer to think that a Security operation—something covert, something not touching them personally—will undermine Madden and bring about his fall." Sedgewick opened his eyes and looked at Elizabeth. "Maybe some of them even hope we'll excise him—and so solve the problem decisively once and for all."

"Excise him!"

Sedgewick looked bored. "It would solve their problem, Weatherall. Madden's a one-man empire. All the people we had to dinner last night are financially entangled in Military-connected undertakings. Which is, of course, why they were there, since these are the people who can put real pressure on Madden. Unfortunately, they're also the ones least likely to do so. So unless we resort to blackmail, I don't see our winning this particular campaign. Which is why I think we'll have to embark on the two other campaigns I see as possibilities remaining to us."

"Cutting off the flow to the outermost circle of trade," Elizabeth said, tracing the outer network of connections encircling the heart of the chart. "That's the only alternative I see."

Sedgewick rubbed his chin. "There's another, of dubious value, that we must consider. To wit, cracking down on the circulation of M-dollars. Doing so wouldn't get us Madden or any of the executives who are dealing in M-dollars, but it would get us their agents and make it uncomfortable for the masses using them. We could make it a Bureau project. Of course Madden and his people would perceive it as harassment and possibly as a sign of weakness—since it would be an admission of desperation. It would net only flunkeys. And it wouldn't, in the final result, stop the circulation of M-dollars."

Elizabeth fingered her light pen as she considered this. "Maybe it wouldn't stop the circulation of M-dollars," she said slowly, "but if done carefully, it might shift the balance of public opinion. As it is now, rental agents who use M-dollars are popular, are perceived as being fair and possibly even reformist. What we need is a media campaign designed to undermine the perception of M-dollars' being economically favorable for the masses." Elizabeth laid down the light pen and took a seat on the sofa facing Sedgewick. "If we linked such a campaign with the crackdown you're suggesting, we might get strong results."

"I thought you'd asked Bennett to start working on that angle already?"

"On a similar angle. This is a bit more complicated—tying in the crackdown, I mean. I'm not quite sure how it would work, but I imagine some of Com & Tran's people should be able to come up with something. They understand such techniques far better than any of us over here."

"Perhaps," Sedgewick said noncommittally. "What about aiming campaigns against specific Madden products? His brands of tubefood, for instance."

Elizabeth wondered at Sedgewick's even suggesting such a thing. "Generating boycotts?" she said. "I don't think that's a good idea,

Sedgewick. Advocating boycotts is illegal, of course. But even if we disguised what we were doing, there's still the risk that it would give new ideas for pressure tactics to undesirable elements. Look what's happened with such things in the Free Zone."

"Speaking of the Free Zone." Sedgewick's voice acquired a sneer as it always did when it hit the words *Free Zone*. "That statement you prepared for me to read is unacceptable. And it indicates a plan you've formulated that is equally unacceptable."

Such a mild reaction. Elizabeth had expected him to be thoroughly unpleasant about it. "It's our only solution," she said, "without sacrificing our com capabilities. With this plan we may come out of it limping, but viable. And Military would probably be deeply damaged, to boot. You know *they* won't sacrifice any of *their* people. They're too rigid to think in the larger picture." Elizabeth deliberately used the expression to draw an explicit connection with Sedgewick's earlier scorn for those executives who clung to their current financial interests without looking at the more complex picture that would affect their future interests.

"It's not an either/or choice, Weatherall. Once this kind of thing starts it can't be stopped."

"I don't see it that way," Elizabeth said. "Morale will be low, true." Though she knew damned well that some people would not be sorry to see scum like Harrigan take punishment. And how many people in Central, for instance, would be pleased to see the last of Wedgewood? Hundreds, probably thousands. Wedgewood, after all, inspired terror within the ranks, and that finely inculcated terror kept both sub-execs as well as all but the highest levels of execs from leaking, insubordination, and doubling. Elizabeth said, almost casually, "But only a small percentage of people in Security would be affected. We can allow the blame to travel upward as far as Ambrose, which would nicely contain the situation and would give the masses the satisfaction of having tasted blood." Elizabeth grinned. As far as the outside was concerned, Ambrose was Sedgewick's next-in-command. She added, "According to our analysis, mostly service-techs would be affected."

"It's an intrusion on our prerogatives," Sedgewick said. "Why should we let those bitches dictate to us how we run our business?"

"If it were only them it wouldn't matter," Elizabeth said, stating the obvious. "But we have to deal with the aliens, Sedgewick. There's no getting around them. No one has come up with a solution for dealing with them except by placating the Free Zone people. We have a hell of a lot more to lose if this com-blackout continues." Determined to make him understand, Elizabeth leaned forward. "Don't you see, even when we've managed to construct long-distance ground-linked fiber-optic networks we'll still have the problem of being set back, of having visibly lost the satellite to the aliens. And *we* will be held responsible, not Military, for we're charged with dealing with sabotage, not Military."

"Christ it goes against the grain."

"I know." Carefully avoiding using any form of the word *defense*, Elizabeth said, "But think of it as advance damage-control."

"Let me ask you this," Sedgewick said, raising his eyebrows. "How are you going to define human rights violations? At what point does a prisoner's treatment get labeled abusive? Have you thought of that?"

Elizabeth relaxed. He had decided to go with her plan. It would now be simply a matter of fine-tuning. "Yes, I have. And I realize we need to define terms very strictly before we start in order to keep the thing from spreading out of control. I think they'll agree to making a strict definition—solely because they'll be overwhelmed by our agreeing to cooperate with them to the fullest extent."

"Those bitches would love pulling down Security."

"They'd love pulling down the Executive and the executive-system, for that matter," Elizabeth said. "And if we don't contain this thing, they'll have a shot at doing it, too. They'll seize any pretext for the aliens' making further strikes against us, and in this case, they'd likely have world opinion on their side."

"They already have that," Sedgewick said. "Look at our defeat in the EU meeting. And that's only the beginning."

My god, he was in a negative mood. What was *with* him today? Elizabeth got up and went to her desk. "Do you agree then to read that statement? And to allow me to contact Greenglass again to hammer out a hard and fast policy agreement?"

Sedgewick twisted in his chair to look at her. "I hope you know what you're doing, Weatherall. I suppose this means you'll be returning to Seattle?"

"Yes. The place will be in an uproar next week, you know, for that's when they're having their Steering Committee meeting. I need to decide whether to work with Greenglass before the meeting or to wait until after. I really can't see an advantage to waiting. It would only hold up our launch date."

"You don't think Greenglass will fall?" Sedgewick asked, getting to his feet.

"No. And if she did I doubt we'd be given an easier time by whoever her successor might be. But I really can't see her falling. She handled the onset of the scandal too deftly. And everyone sees her as the aliens' primary contact. It makes her too valuable to the Free Zone." Elizabeth reached to touch her headset, then paused. "One more thing," she said as Sedgewick reached the door. He turned and looked at her. "May I send out the order to start picking up people whom we know to have been recently held for lengthy periods by Military police? I'd like to be able to hand that to Greenglass as a token of good faith. And of course accomplishing the mid-term effect of spotlighting Military's abuses."

Sedgewick put his hand on the doorknob. "Go ahead. Do as you like. When do you want me to read this statement?"

"I'll arrange it for after lunch."

He nodded, opened the door, and went out into the hall between her office and his. Elizabeth sighed. She appreciated his giving her so little fight, but his docility—not to mention his negativity—portended problems. Perhaps it would be best to get the media people assembled before noon. Judging by the look of him, this would probably be one of those days when he started drinking at lunch.

[ii]

At Emily's urging, Celia and Desmond Seymour accepted the use of Emily's chauffeured car for the drive to El Cajon. Emily was worried that the permission for visitation might be a trap and wanted Celia to take every precaution possible. Celia trembled with nervousness from the moment she got into Emily's car. ODS could pick her up at any time, which made a surprise arrest unlikely. But because she didn't trust them, it meant nothing to Celia that Emily's connection had "given her word" that neither Celia nor Desmond would be in any way harassed or harmed during the course of the visit.

En route to El Cajon, they discussed Luis' situation and their possible courses of action. Desmond argued that the only rational course of action was to try to force ODS to file charges against Luis by bringing his case before the judge through whom Celia had successfully pressed the writ of habeas corpus. "Remember what happened to me after I accomplished that?" Celia said. "Do you want to end up in jail, too?"

"That won't necessarily happen," Desmond said. "First of all, we're dealing with ODS this time. The previous time we were dealing with Military Police. From what you've said, I don't think we need assume they'll behave identically in the same circumstances."

Celia was shivering and sweating at the same time. She said, "I see no difference that matters between ODS and Military Police. And besides, the judge may have since been intimidated. In which case he won't play."

"We won't know unless we try," Desmond said. "And I can't think of a more promising course of action."

"If only Luis were still officially accredited," Celia said wistfully. "Then we'd be able to argue that holding him without charge constitutes public harm, given the current demand for medical services."

"I'd never argue that before a judge," Desmond said, "unless I wanted to see my client ordered to provide medical services inside prison."

I should have thought of that myself. But my brain seems to have turned to mush.

Celia's mouth became as dry as cotton when the car pulled up to the security gate controlling access to the prison complex. Even from the cool, dim interior of the car, the aridity and sterility of the place, glaring bright in the desert sun, depressed her. The officer kept them waiting for several minutes while he verified their identities and permission to visit. When he was satisfied, he told her and Desmond to get out of the car and proceed on foot, and directed the driver to a parking area. Celia shrank from the sight of so many heavily armed men surrounding and watching them. The pair of guards detailed to escort them rapped out orders as though she and Desmond were prisoners. Certainly the way the guards looked at them was the same way her guards had looked at her all the times she had been a prisoner.

After they entered the main building, the guards led them deep into the bowels of the prison. The staleness of the air, the thickness of the walls, the conspicuousness of the electronic shields and surveillance oppressed Celia's spirit. Taken into separate locker areas, they were required to submit to a strip search. The book of poetry and the clothing Celia had brought to give Luis were taken from her—for close examination, she was told. Although they said that if the book and clothing passed muster they would be given to Luis, based on her considerable experience and knowledge of detention, Celia had serious doubts that Luis would ever see either.

After their own clothing had been examined they were allowed to dress, and their guards led them through a labyrinth of corridors. Several times along the way they waited for clearance at steel mesh barriers bearing signs warning that they were electrified. Finally, the two of them were left alone in a place Celia recognized as an interrogation room. She stared at the mirror, certain a video camera lay on the other side of it. She and Desmond and Luis would have to be very careful, she thought. She glanced at Desmond and saw that he had taken in the mirror, too. He looked at her, and it seemed to Celia his eyes signaled acknowledgment of the danger.

More than fifteen minutes passed before the door was unlocked and Luis brought in. Celia flew out of her chair and threw herself at him—remembering only at the last second that he might have become too fragile to sustain a hard, fierce hug. "Luis," she whispered, taking his hand and kissing his beard-stubbled cheek. "Oh, Luis." Irrelevantly she thought of how he must hate having stubble on his face. In normal circumstances he depilated his face twice a day.

He looked dazed. "I had no idea," he said. "I thought when they brought me here that this would be an interrogation."

Celia pulled out a chair and urged him into it. "They've said you may have two visits a month," Celia said. "Do you know where you are?" As a prisoner she had at times grown obsessed with the need to know where she was.

He looked so tired. He said, his voice barely more than a mumble, "El Cajon. In a Federal Detention Facility."

"This is Desmond Seymour," Celia said, gesturing. "An attorney with Karnes, Epson, and Smith."

The two men shook hands across the table. "Would you feel comfortable telling us how you've been treated?" Desmond said, getting quickly to the point. They had been given no idea about how long they would have.

Luis' eyes traveled briefly to the mirror, then settled on Desmond's face. "They've had me in solitary, of course. And at the beginning they interrogated me rigorously, not allowing me sleep or rest of any kind. But a strange thing happened. In the middle of an interrogation they bundled me out to a helicopter and flew me back to San Diego. La Jolla, I think. It was a place right on the beach. There I was taken before a woman who questioned me, first about Celia and her high-powered executive friend—" his gaze moved to Celia's face for a moment— "and then asked if I knew of any human rights violations. She said that it was known I had been to the Austrian consulate in LA and would I tell her what business I had been pursuing there." He shrugged. "It was an episode completely outside my previous experience of detention."

"Who was this woman?" Desmond asked—for confirmation, Celia assumed.

"I've no idea. I'm afraid that when she introduced herself, I was in such a debilitated mental state that I was unable to retain her name, since it meant nothing to me at the time. I will say that she was the tallest woman I've ever seen, blonde, and an executive. She seemed particularly interested in Celia."

"So her interest was primarily in your knowledge of human rights violations and your willingness to act on the knowledge," Desmond said.

Luis, flicking his eyes at the mirror, only shrugged. Celia understood that he didn't want to speak about her and Emily.

"And there's more," Luis said, as though just remembering something. "A couple of days ago they had me talk to someone who claimed to be a doctor. An executive was present. The doctor did most of the talking—wanted me to give him medical details, along with names and dates, of after-effects of torture that I've seen and treated."

Celia looked at Desmond. Desmond shook his head at her. "What did you do?" he asked.

Luis' mouth tightened. "I gave them some case histories, but no names. If they thought they'd find out whom I may have notified the Austrian consulate about, they were mistaken. Don't ask me why I gave them anything." He shrugged. "I suppose I felt angry about those cases and relished the opportunity to confront these people with them."

Celia could understand *that*. "Did they press you to give names, Luis?"

He shook his head. "That's the most inexplicable thing of all. They asked me if I *knew* the names, and then said that if I did that was enough."

"Enough?" Celia said, puzzled. What the hell was *that* about? "And you haven't been interrogated since then?"

"Nothing. Just the craziness of solitary broken up by the delivery of food and the change in the lighting morning and night." He stretched out his hand to Celia, and she clasped it lightly. "Your mother, Celia. She was taken too?"

Celia smiled through the blur of sudden tears. "Mama was released almost at once. Don't worry about her, she's fine, she's working hard. And me, I'm working in Hillcrest now."

His eyes warmed. "I'm proud of you, Celia. I knew you would see what you had to do."

The door opened. "Move it, Salgado," the guard said. Luis and Celia hugged. "Now, Salgado," the guard said in the gratuitously grating tone guards always seemed to use. Luis turned from Celia and went out into the corridor. The door shut with a thud.

Celia looked at Desmond. They would talk only when they were safely inside Emily's car with the vehicle's internal jamming system switched on.

Celia was almost unbearably anxious to see Emily, to tell her about the blonde woman's questions. She hoped Emily wasn't already in deep trouble. It seemed likely she was, though. ODS would never be taking such a line with Luis otherwise.

[iii]

Martha was seated at her desk in her office, toiling over what she had begun dubbing—to herself, only— "the mea culpa speech," when she got a call from the atrium detail of the Women's Patrol. "There's a man down here, Martha, with an ODS look about him, who claims he has papers to deliver to you. We took three weapons off him—a stun-gun, a Colt .45, and a knife strapped to his ankle. Plus a whole *slew* of electronic gear. Should we let him up to see you? And if so, do you want one of us to escort him?"

"Has he said who he is or who he's delivering papers for?" Martha asked. Likely he *was* ODS or SIC, maybe even one of David's creeps. The people she did business with did not send heavily armed couriers to make deliveries of contracts and other papers.

After about fifteen seconds, Ellen came back on the line. "He says he's from Security Central. And that the papers he's carrying come from the Chief's office."

Martha leaned back in her chair and stared at the ceiling for a couple of seconds before replying. "I'll see him," she told Ellen, "but I'd appreciate one of you accompanying him. I don't think such a person should be allowed to wander the building at will. Also, don't let him come armed. Make sure all that stuff stays downstairs." But of course it would. It was a hard-and-fast rule: no weapons of any sort past the atrium, except for those worn by on-duty Women's Patrol.

A few minutes later a burly stranger appeared in the doorway. Ellen stood directly behind him. "Ms. Greenglass?" he asked.

"Yes," Martha said.

"If you'll show me some ID I have a packet of papers from Ms. Weatherall for you."

"We don't have ID in the Free Zone," Martha said.

Uneasily he studied her face. This possibility had clearly not occurred to him. "Well," he said, "I guess I can take it you're she. This is her office, and this person here is one of your officers." He glanced over his shoulder at Ellen. "You can vouch for her?" he said foolishly.

Ellen rolled her eyes. "Of course this is Martha Greenglass. Anyone could tell you that."

"Regulations," he said, extending the large manila envelope clutched in his left hand.

Martha took the envelope. "Anything else?" she asked.

He handed her a KlipBoard. "I need your signature, on the yellow-highlighted strip where the **X** is marked."

Martha took the electronic screen and stylus and duly signed the form. Ellen gave her a droll look over the man's shoulder, then turned and followed him out of the office.

Martha opened the envelope and removed a thick wad of flimsies. On the top of the pile lay a letter printed on thick cream bond paper. The forceful signature—*Elizabeth Weatherall*—at the bottom of the page caught Martha's eye before she even picked up the letter to read it.

Dear Martha:

I'm pleased to report significant progress in setting into motion the human rights project we discussed last week. Enclosed you'll find a copy of the statement Robert Sedgewick, Chief of Security, read to the press this morning, announcing a full-scale investigation of any and all allegations of human rights violations presented to your representatives, as well as a top-to-bottom in-house investigation of all branches and agencies of Security Services. Chief Sedgewick has agreed to allow full participation in any form you wish by you and any agents you designate in this investigation. My suggestion is that you and I work out the exact details ourselves. Naturally I have a few suggestions to offer as to how you can best contribute to the in-house investigation, but would like to emphasize that the final disposition of such details will be your prerogative.

Furthermore, Martha, Chief Sedgewick has this morning sent out an order that all individuals recently released from detention and known to have been held on political grounds be sought out. These individuals will not be treated as prisoners, but will be given the option of emigration to the locations your people have mentioned as places of asylum. I strongly urge that your representatives see these people and interview them for possible testimony they may have concerning human rights violations.

I'll be arriving in Seattle tomorrow morning and will hope to see you shortly thereafter. I'm looking forward to working with you, Martha.

Best regards,

Elizabeth Weatherall

P.S. I've also enclosed for your convenience the following documents: (a)
the prospectus for the in-house investigation; (b) the protocol for Operation
Asylum (described above); (c) a list of all Security Services detention centers and their personnel; and (d) a provisional definition of what a human
rights violation consists (to be worked out between us).

Unprepared for such apparently full compliance with their demands, Martha stared at the letter for some time before leafing
through the enclosed documents. Sedgewick's statement, announcing
Free Zone participation in the investigation, stunned her. She had not
expected so much so soon—and from Sedgewick himself, whose iron
fist policies had been directly responsible for years and years of repression... The immediate question that sprang to mind was in what way
these people were intending to get around them: where lay the decep-
tion in Weatherall's proposals and declarations?

But no, Martha corrected herself, though they may have the intent to get around us, they've offered us the means to thwart them
in their attempt. We have to make use of these means—shrewdly,
vigilantly, aggressively.

Martha picked up her handset to call Maureen. With Weatherall
arriving in the morning, they'd have little time now to prepare their
strategy. It was a pity this opportunity would be cutting into the little
time she had to prepare her statement for the Steering Committee
meeting; but Martha knew her priorities.

[iv]

As Elizabeth finished skimming the daily summary that Stevens'
office wrote for Ambrose (which Elizabeth always received a copy of,
despite Ambrose's being officially responsible for overseeing ODS' operations), she reflected that the uproar over human rights violations
would not be taking place at all if it weren't for the aliens. It was a fact
everyone around her seemed to overlook. Nor would Elizabeth herself be engaged in dealings involving the likes of Martha Greenglass.
What little contact Elizabeth might have with people like Greenglass
ordinarily would be in quite another context, one characteristic of

Greenglass's earlier contacts with ODS. There was something unsavory about Greenglass and her kind, something that made Elizabeth think of the detention centers she had visited, an odor or attitude that clung to Greenglass even in her pleasant little office overlooking Elliott Bay.

Still, for all the grumblings she had already begun to hear around Security, she wondered if it weren't for the best that they would be dealing in a new way with people like Greenglass. Briefly, almost whimsically, she wondered if a change in attitude toward, for instance, the church groups Stevens reported as again on the move, might not be a good thing. The problem with relying on repression was that you could never afford to ease up, with the result that ever more resources had to be devoted to maintaining the status quo. ODS's standing policy was, of course, the one Sedgewick had long ago put in place when the main activity of such groups was agitation against Birth Limitation. And yet, on further thought, Elizabeth doubted not only that she could get Sedgewick to agree to a change ("Bad enough we're dealing with the anarchists, we're sure as hell not going to give an inch to the religious dissenters inside our own borders"—so Elizabeth imagined him responding, unconsciously acknowledging the Free Zone as outside their borders in practice if not in theory), but also the wisdom of opening such a Pandora's Box. Sedgewick would be correct were he to point out that giving them an inch would mean their trying to grab a mile, and that the country was still not in shape to take much stress of that sort. The US was too fragmented, too weak after years of war. And they had not fully recovered from the Blanket, either.

No, Elizabeth thought as she shut down her office, they needed to concentrate their energies on clearing the aliens off the planet. Zeldin had revealed there were only six—though she had also said something about a full crew of aliens eventually returning… What was the time-frame she had given? Elizabeth could not remember. She would have to run a search in the Dahlia files. Why hadn't she taken in the possible significance of that revelation at the time? And why did everyone keep forgetting that the aliens were the root cause of all their problems with domestic order? The fact was, those women in the Free Zone were only pawns in the game. The real opponents were the aliens. All this time they should have been making war on the aliens instead of hatching plans for assassinating Greenglass and her cohorts.

But how? Elizabeth asked herself, crossing to Sedgewick's office. How did one make war on opponents whose very existence remained a shadow difficult to take hold of? She opened the door to Sedgewick's office—and pulled up short. Damn it, the man was sitting in the dark staring at an image from his Zeldin collection. Shit. Damn. Fuck. He'd run and rerun video footage of her last night. And now this. And god knew Sedgewick had long since memorized every fucking one of his thousands of photos.

Elizabeth advanced into the room. "Not a pretty picture, is it," Sedgewick said.

Elizabeth looked to see which image currently held his fascinated attention, and her stomach flopped over. Projected on the screen was an image she had not known existed—of Zeldin, of course—but a post-capture Zeldin—lying on the chaise lounge in the Small Study of Sedgewick's island house. Elizabeth's heartbeat picked up, thudding heavily enough to shake her chest wall. "I had no idea you had pictures of her from that time," she said. How could he have done it? And he'd never told her, never shown her—which meant he had kept them from her.

"Take a good look, Weatherall." His voice grated. "You'd forgotten, hadn't you. And that was your accomplishment, entirely. No one else's."

"No, Sedgewick," she said slowly, emphatically. "It wasn't my doing. It was the fact of her captivity, combined with what I forced her to remember. She couldn't bear remembering her earlier life with you." Elizabeth knew she should stop herself. "That's what kept her from eating. She was in despair over that memory. She couldn't live with it. Or with you."

Sedgewick's tone became abrasively taunting. "You'd like to think that, wouldn't you. But we know better, you and I, we know better. None of it was necessary. If you'd done as I'd ordered she would never have gotten into this state. I didn't require revenge, you know. Never did I require revenge against *her*. As far as I was concerned that was never the point of her capture."

Hadn't they had enough of this? Why must he drag this out into the light again and again and again? In spite of herself, Elizabeth stared at the screen. The eyes disturbed her far more than the painful lack of flesh. This Zeldin looked unlike any of her other images, much less the holograph in the atrium of the building named for her. This Zeldin resembled a medieval allegory of the consequences of damnation. "Why do you sit and stare at it?" Elizabeth said. "Do you enjoy it? Enjoy the sight of her suffering, or enjoy remembering the one brief time you had full possession of her?"

"The people who are making an outcry about torture," Sedgewick said. "Well at least those tortures are on rational grounds of necessity. This," he said, pointing to the screen, "was unnecessary. Gratuitous. Wanton. All for your private purposes, Weatherall. Yet you have the gall to insist that all our people involved in less severe treatment of prisoners should be thrown to the wolves?"

"Turn the damned thing off," Elizabeth said, unable to think while that image was on the screen behind her.

"Yet you were in love with her, too." Sedgewick's tone softened, and became sinister with insinuation. "Do you see, Weatherall, she's wearing the jouissance silk you gave her."

Elizabeth backed toward the door. She would not stay here and be subjected to his obsession. "I'm leaving for the evening, Sedgewick." Her voice trembled. "I'll be in only briefly in the morning before I fly out to Seattle."

He did not reply.

Elizabeth fumbled the door open and stepped out into the hall between their offices. He was insane. But she would not let him draw her into his insanity; she would not enter into his fantasies and reveries. Where Zeldin was concerned, anything he said must be suspect. He never made sense where Zeldin was concerned, never had and never would.

[v]

"A tall blonde executive woman?" Emily said, swallowing the last of the delicious cold avocado soup. The small restaurant in the converted garage two blocks from Celia's house offered only one selection a night, but she and Celia had discovered that it was usually delicious.

"There's someone who immediately springs to mind, especially in connection with Security. I don't like the sound of it, Cee. I think she must be after me, to get at my father. That's what I imagine *her* main interest in your uncle to be. She's someone extremely high up, you know. She's Sedgewick's personal lieutenant."

Celia poured more water into her glass. "You see? You're going to have to be careful," she said, anxious to press the point. "If they're specifically trying to get *you*—for whatever reason—they'll be watching your every move. Even with your privileges of privacy you're vulnerable to them if they really want to get you."

"But aren't you interested in the statement Sedgewick made today?" Emily asked, changing the subject.

"I'm sure it's just empty PR. I don't believe they'll do what he claims they'll do. It would be revolution if they did."

The owner, who was the lone server, removed their soup plates, and Celia asked him to tell his wife that they had loved the soup. On their first visit to the restaurant they had learned that the man and his wife were veterinarians. After their daughter had been killed in action in the Czech Republic during the Global War, they had decided to spend their savings, which had been earmarked for their daughter's college education, on "following their dream."

Thanking Celia for her "kind compliments," the owner set their entrées before them and warned them that the plates were too hot to touch.

"It smells wonderful," Emily said, smiling at the owner. Then, when he had gone, she said as she loaded up a fork with the sticky golden rice, "Do you suppose they've made some kind of deal that entails promoting an appearance of carrying out Free Zone demands?"

"You mean something like promising to leave them alone, or to recognize them officially, in return for their allowing the appearance of an investigation and so on?" Celia asked as she picked up her fork.

Emily chewed and swallowed that first bite of the paella. "Something like that. I just can't see any other possibility—apart from their somehow having successfully duped the Free Zone people into accepting whatever superficial appearance they've cooked up. But I don't see the Free Zone people as being easily duped. We have to assume they're tough for having succeeded in establishing independence from the Executive in the first place and then maintained that independence."

"With the aliens' help," Celia said, spearing a shrimp and peeling off the bit of shell that it had been cooked in.

"Yes, but the aliens can't do everything for them." Emily took another bite of paella.

Celia ate the shrimp, which was juicy and seasoned with red pepper. "You think the Free Zone people are sincere about their concern for human rights?"

"Perhaps. More likely they simply see the issue as giving them a chance of acting as a gadfly, or even as a means of pressuring the Executive into giving them something they want. Which would fit with my first hypothesis about their collaborating in an appearance of justice."

Celia laid down her fork and sighed. "Then you don't see Sedgewick's statement as a hopeful sign of change." Perceiving how letdown she felt, Celia realized she must have taken Sedgewick's statement seriously.

"No," Emily said sadly, "I don't. I wouldn't trust Sedgewick and his outfit to give the correct time of day, much less tell the truth about themselves."

Celia reached for her water glass. She had to agree with Emily. Accepting Security's promises for policing ODS would be like believing foxen could be trusted to guard chickens. The earth would stop dead in its orbit around the sun before either of those things would happen.

[vi]

She wakes early, in the middle of the night really, irritated with the way the braid feels, something wrong with it, she needs to free it, brush it, replait it, it's too vexing to wait on Maxine's arrival, so she goes into the dressing room to take it apart. But turning on the light, sitting down at the dressing table, she sees—in the mirror—Zeldin: Zeldin reclining on the chaise lounge, Zeldin wearing the red and black jouissance silk gown, Zeldin watching her with those horrible terrifying eyes, stabbing at her in the mirror.

She turns and confronts the bitch. "Get out!" she screams at her. "Get out of here out of here out of here!" But Zeldin sits staring, saying

nothing. And then she sees the cuffs, she sees that Zeldin's wrists are cuffed together, lying motionless in the folds of the silk.

Heart pounding, she runs out into the hall, opens the safe, gets out the M-27D. She returns to the dressing room hoping Zeldin will be gone, a mere figment of her imagination, but finds her still there, sitting exactly as before. She backs into the wall of mirrors to brace herself and lifts the weapon. "It's useless, Elizabeth," Zeldin says, speaking for the first time. "Turn around and look in the mirror."

Elizabeth, in her terror almost shrieking, can't keep herself from obeying. She doesn't want to. Her heart in her throat, she inches forward, away from the mirror and then, still holding the weapon, turns. In the glass she sees not her own reflection—the reflection of a tall naked woman holding a powerful weapon—but Zeldin, her eyes the same horrible knowing blue, watching her without wavering, without relenting. There is only one thing to do, she knows. She lifts the weapon and points it at the image in the mirror. It takes an eternity to do; but her finger—weak, feeble, desperate—squeezes the trigger, making the weapon fire straight into the mirror.

"Liz, Liz," Hazel's voice murmured into her ear as her hands held and stroked her. "It was only a dream, love, only a dream."

Clutching Hazel, concentrating on Hazel's physical substantiality, Elizabeth struggled to shake off the dream.

Hazel dabbed with the sheet at the tears on Elizabeth's face. "Shall we turn on the light?" she said. "What do you usually do when this happens?"

"The light, yes," Elizabeth said, feeling foolish, yet still trembling, still carrying Zeldin's image in her mind. Hazel stretched out her arm and the reading light went on. Elizabeth thought for a moment of the dressing room and knew herself afraid to go in there, much as she desired to know for certain that it was empty. Of course it's empty! she scoffed at herself. Dreams are not real, not true. Zeldin is dead, there was no need to shoot her, Zeldin is dead, dead, dead... "Here, Liz," Hazel was saying, pressing a glass of water into her hand. "Sip it slowly, and by the time you're done the dream will be gone."

Elizabeth's gaze sank into Hazel's warm, full, face, her tousled hair, her large round breasts, her fleshy shoulders and arms. "You're beautiful, darling," she said, smoothing her fingers over Hazel's so real skin. "So beautiful. Hold me, please." Hazel lay back and opened her arms. Still trembling, Elizabeth rested her head on Hazel's breast and twined her legs with Hazel's. For a long time she did not close her eyes, but stared to the point of mesmerism at Hazel's lightly freckled arm and listened to Hazel's slow, steady heartbeat. Hazel's solidity gentled and smoothed her fear, and shortly after she noticed that Hazel had fallen back to sleep, she did, too.

Chapter Twenty-two

[i]

Celia had just finished dressing when a fist hit the front door five quick times in succession. It was only eight in the morning. And yet because they'd never come at such a civilized hour before, she answered the door unprepared.

"Celia Espin?" the anglo said, his eyes moving between her face and the photo on what looked like a warrant card in his hand.

Unable to speak, Celia nodded.

"ODS. We have orders to take you into protective custody. You are allowed one small bag."

Protective custody?

Celia wondered at the apparent courtesy. They had never allowed her to take anything with her before. She moved several steps backwards, and they followed her inside. Her thoughts tumbled about in a confused blur. When she went into her room to pack, they of course followed her.

"Why protective custody?" she asked as she pulled an overnight bag from the closet shelf.

"You know as much as we do," the man who was apparently the designated speaker replied. The other one, a Latino, stood in the doorway, scanning the room as though on constant guard against attack or attempted rescue of the prisoner.

Celia crammed things into the bag, careful not to take anything important lest it be lost forever. *Not again, not again, not again...* The words droned through her head in a looped refrain, beating the tattoo of numb, impotent horror. Fear occupied her gut like a lump of icy iron. Her nerve had deserted her. All she could think was that she couldn't go through it again. Not after that last time. She scribbled a note for her mother—*taken by ODS*—and they allowed it, further confusing her. Why? she wondered. *Why?* But she was bereft of answers, and the empty words of fear and despair repeated endlessly in her head. *Not again, not again, not again…*

[ii]

"So we are agreed on the composition of each investigative team," Elizabeth Weatherall said, her deep blue gaze moving watchfully around the table, taking in all the women Martha had managed to assemble on such short notice.

Martha caught Laura's eye and found it hard to suppress the grin she felt tugging at her mouth. The negotiations—albeit mere words on paper—were proceeding with amazing speed and specificity.

"Shall we go on to the next point," Weatherall said, "that of allowing accessibility of your monitors to what you refer to as 'communities'?"

"All we ask is a guarantee that neither our monitors nor the people we interview will be harassed," Martha said.

Weatherall sighed. "Lurking within the apparently simple notion of a 'guarantee,' ladies, is a very complicated, messy situation. What you don't seem to understand about such an unstructured approach is that violence could erupt without notice. In fact, nothing seems more likely, given that we're seeing a good deal of it in LA and Boston at this moment. The appearance of your monitors could provide the catalyst for mass violence and chaos across the United States. I don't believe the Executive could accept such an anarchic approach."

"Then you aren't genuinely interested in making people free to discuss violations," Maureen said in her usual blunt style. "For as long as your people are present, there will be an atmosphere of intimidation at work against our monitors, regardless of whether or not your officers are actually harassing people. Which is why we need a guarantee."

A Women's Patroller entered the room.

"You misunderstand me," Weatherall said smoothly. "Allow me to present an alternative—"

"Excuse me, Ms. Weatherall," the Patroller said. "But one of your people—a courier, he said he was—insisted I ask you to leave the meeting to receive the purple stat, I think he called it, that he's carrying."

The executive's face revealed nothing as she excused herself and left the room with the Patroller.

Martha said, "Shall we take a break? Say half an hour?" At once
the others began pushing their chairs back from the table, getting to
their feet, and stretching.

Martha, Laura, and Maureen went down to Martha's office. "I
can't believe that first point was so easily achieved," Laura said as
soon as the door was closed.

"It was *too* easy," Maureen said. "There's got to be a catch."

"But they haven't felt this kind of pressure before, not since the
Blanket," Martha said, getting out a liter-and-a-half bottle of water.
She uncapped it and handed it to Laura. "For one thing, we've never
gotten any governments to back us before. And for another, they're
worried about their com satellites and know that if we want to press
them they might lose more than just com and global vid. And third,
they're losing ground with their allies." Martha took the bottle from
Maureen. "We have them on the run."

"Maybe so," Maureen said, "but I still don't trust them. They're
probably up to real skullduggery. Like killing any of us who quote
participate. It would be one way to get rid of their most vocal enemies
all at once."

Martha choked on the water she was swallowing. It took her almost a minute of coughing and clearing her throat before she could
speak. "Come on, Maureen! Do you really believe they'd try such a
thing?" Her voice had gone hoarse from choking. She passed the bottle to Laura. "Apart from their knowing they'd have to deal with the
Marq'ssan, surely they'd be worried about world opinion?"

Maureen said, "They killed Kay Zeldin, remember? And lost
Boston for it, too, but I bet they thought it was worth it. Think how
much better it would be to get all of us out of the way!"

"I don't think that's what they're up to," Laura said. "I don't believe Elizabeth Weatherall would sit there so coolly if that's what she
had in mind."

Maureen shook her head as though to say that she couldn't believe
Laura could be so foolish. "Why would they bother telling her? She's
a woman, isn't she? We all know that executives don't let women hold
powerful positions. She's merely their rep, telling us exactly what
they tell her to tell us. The way Kay Zeldin did when she was their
rep on *s'sbeyl*."

"Oh christ," Martha said, sinking down onto the floor. "So what do we do, Maureen? Call off the negotiations? Insist on being surrounded by armed Women's Patrol whenever we venture into their territory?"

"Can we have the light on in here, Martha?" Maureen said. "It's so gloomy today I keep wanting to go back to bed." Clearly, she felt no enthusiasm for Elizabeth Weatherall's apparent forthcomingness. She switched on the desk lamp, then settled down on the floor beside Martha, her back against the door. "My idea is this. Our monitors go into communities without prior notification to Security—the way we've always done, with the Marq'ssan providing our transportation. That way ODS *et al.* won't know where or when to expect us. I think we have to hold out for that, whatever excuse she gives about inciting violence."

Laura squatted low on her haunches, facing them, and passed the bottle to Maureen. "But aren't you worried we won't get anything at all if we hold out for the max?"

"We hold the winning cards in this hand," Maureen said. "It's a matter of not letting them bluff us into doubting that we do. They're desperate to have their technology left alone. We'll make it clear there's no chance of that as long as they don't meet our demands. It's that simple."

Laura said, "I have the distinct impression that some of the others are ready to jump at anything Elizabeth offers because she came across so sweepingly on that first point."

"She's clever, all right," Maureen said. "But we hold the winning cards, whatever she tries to make us believe to the contrary."

"What a metaphor," Martha said. She took the bottle and drank the few drops remaining.

The ensuing silence was broken by a knock. Without rising to her feet, Maureen scooted away from the door, lifted her hand to the doorknob, and pulled open the door. Elizabeth Weatherall stood there, her attaché case in hand. She stared down at them from the height of her six foot-plus. "I'm sorry to report that our negotiations are to be terminated at once," she said. "Whether permanently or not, I can't say. I've received a summons back to Washington, with orders to break off negotiations." She exchanged a long look with Martha. "I'm hoping this is only temporary. I thought we were making substantial progress this morning."

Maureen caught Martha's eye and grimaced. Martha peered back up at Weatherall, then pushed herself to her feet. "I'm sorry, too. Am I to take it that everything we've worked out is null and void?"

Weatherall bit her lip. "For the moment, yes. But I'm hoping…" She shrugged. "We'll see. At any rate, I'm leaving now. I hope to see you again soon." She nodded at each of them, shook Martha's hand, and disappeared down the corridor.

Maureen nudged the door shut. "What did I tell you? I bet she had no intention of letting those arrangements stand, that all that talk was a ploy."

Martha's gaze met Laura's. "That could be," Martha said. "I guess we'd better let the others know."

It wasn't as though they all had plenty of free time to be throwing around with lavish abandon. So back to the *mea culpa* speech. Clearly it would be the Night Patrol issue rather than an announcement of successful negotiations that would be the focus of the Steering Committee meeting.

As Elizabeth Weatherall probably very well knew.

[iii]

As she boarded the plane, the white heat of Elizabeth's rage narrowed and warped her perceptions. Stalking to the rear of the cabin, she encountered the courier who had brought her Sedgewick's purple stat. "Get the *fuck* out my way," she said through her teeth. He scurried backwards. "Didn't you hear what I said, fool?" Elizabeth grabbed him by the arm, whirled him around, and pitched him into the front of the cabin.

"But my papers, Madam!"

Elizabeth snatched up his leather shoulder bag and threw it after him—and saw it just miss hitting Hazel, who was standing stockstill in the middle of the cabin holding their luggage, looking lost. She snapped at the girl in undisguised exasperation. "Damn it, Hazel, stop your dithering and sit down."

Hazel started; she looked around the cabin. "Where did you want me to sit?" she asked, her voice barely rising above the racket of the engines.

"Why the fuck ask *me* that? Sit where you like, girl, just for godsake sit down and stop *dithering*!" Elizabeth turned her back on them all and stamped angrily to the rear of the cabin, slammed her attaché case onto a table, and sank down into a seat. *Sub-execs*, she had to deal with *sub-execs*, and just when she was getting somewhere that moron calls her back, obviously panicked by the Executive—unless he were going into another one of his psychotic cycles. Whatever the case, he had clearly lost the ability to deal with the Executive, the one function she needed him for. If he couldn't do even that, she might as well throw in the towel. Damn the moron. He'd just better get his shit together and pull his colleagues into line, or he could say goodbye to her for good. No more comforting caresses, no more covering his ass for him in meetings, no more holding Security Services together for him.

For the duration of the flight Elizabeth alternated between fuming and plotting. She had had those women in the palm of her hand, she knew she had. Everything had been going so smoothly, so entirely according to plan. Could she salvage the damage—supposing she managed to whip the Executive into line? She snorted at the irony of it: she'd had an easier time running things during the Civil War when the Executive had been in disarray. At the time she'd lamented their impotence. But now she saw that their power was more a matter of thwarting other people's efforts than of taking charge and getting things done. Not one of those dogs had offered a single constructive suggestion for what to do about the loss of their com-sat. And what if the aliens destroyed their other satellites? Or the chemical manufacturing station? If they could kill the com-sat that easily they sure as hell could kill the others. Didn't those fools see *anything*?

When the plane came into radio contact with DC, Elizabeth had the pilot check to see that a chopper had been ordered for her. She could hardly wait to lay into Sedgewick; if she could she'd parachute from the plane to land on the roof of Security Central, so obsessed was she with straightening that moron out. After a few minutes the pilot reported to her over the intercom that a chopper had already been ordered by Central and was there, waiting.

Elizabeth was hardly aware of transferring from plane to chopper, so absorbed was she in trying to decide what her first scathing words to Sedgewick would be. But as soon as the chopper dropped onto the roof she leaped out, ready to charge into Sedgewick's office. Without so much as pausing, she swept past the Guard at the roof entrance and, rushing down the stairs, ignored whatever it was he said to her, and strode into the Chief's suite through its main entrance—ignoring the girl sitting at Hazel's desk—and brushed past Jacquelyn.

Jacquelyn grabbed her from behind. Whirling, Elizabeth moved to strike Jacquelyn's hand away. "For godsake listen to me," Jacquelyn cried. "Booth's in there with him!"

Elizabeth let out her breath in a long, angry hiss. "For how long?" she said, some part of her knowing she shouldn't see Booth in her current state of mind while most of her longed to deliver a blistering tirade at him, too.

"Twenty minutes so far. You don't have your badge on, Elizabeth."

Elizabeth dug into her tunic pouch for her badge, found it, and slapped it on. "Let me know as soon as he's gone," she said, unlocking the corridor door to her office. She dumped her case onto the sofa and poured herself a glass of grapefruit juice.

Eight minutes after entering her office, the handset on her desk buzzed. "Weatherall, get in here *now*," Sedgewick's voice said.

Elizabeth threw the handset onto the desk and stormed across the hall into his office.

"Sedgewick—" she said angrily—then pulled up short when she found that Booth was still with him. She looked from Booth's chilly gray eyes to Sedgewick's muddy, withdrawn ones and her rage frosted. "Good afternoon, Mr. Booth," she said as evenly as she could manage.

"Sit down, Weatherall," Booth said, his tone peremptory in the extreme. Elizabeth took an armchair. "We have been discussing your plans for negotiating with the Pacific Northwest rebels," Booth said.

Elizabeth glanced at Sedgewick, but his face was at its most inexpressively corpselike. "I was making significant progress this morning when I was called back here," Elizabeth said.

"Progress, Weatherall?" Booth's eyes narrowed. "Negotiating with terrorists can never be the Executive's idea of progress." Booth glanced at Sedgewick. "It is quite clear, Weatherall, you have over-stepped the bounds of your authority. You have no authorization to negotiate on the Executive's behalf. And I'm surprised at you for thinking you could assume such a thing."

Elizabeth's throat tensed. Stupid little cock, on the strut, flaunt-ing his comb, imagining he owned the barnyard. And Sedgewick! Obviously Sedgewick had thrown her to Booth to save himself: did he realize what that made *him* look like? A man who couldn't control his bitch? "What I have assumed, Mr. Booth," Elizabeth enunciated clearly and slowly, "is that restoring our com-satellite capability as well as preserving all our other orbital assets from destruction is a top priority. The sacrifice of a few low-level scum within Security cer-tainly seems worth it."

"You're not thinking, Weatherall." Booth's eyes grew, if possible, even colder. "In the first place, the very fact of our negotiating with these sub-exec rebels would create a perception of weakness through-out this country—and the world. The repercussions could be devastat-ing for our global position. Second, Security should be concentrating its energies on taking back that territory: it is particularly egregious that you've let the rebels have it for so long when at the same time Military has recovered Cuba." Booth's fingers tapped out a beat of impatience on the arm of his chair. "Moreover, Security should have by now found a way to make our satellites invulnerable to the aliens' weapons. Instead of playing footsie with anarchist sub-exec rebels."

Elizabeth stared at Sedgewick, willing him to respond to Booth's nonsense. But Sedgewick said nothing and refused to meet her eyes. "There is no material that has proven to be invulnerable to the aliens' weapons," Elizabeth said. "As for recovering lost territory, the aliens' ties with the rebels make that impossible. Our time would be better spent trying to separate the aliens from the rebels. They depend on each other. Separating them would—"

Booth interrupted. "I'm not interested in your theories, Weatherall. I simply wish to make it unequivocally clear that you are to cease dragging the Executive's honor into the muck and mire you seem to delight in playing in."

Elizabeth pressed her lips together and stared down at the rug. "Is that clear, Weatherall?"

The words came hard. "Understood, sir."

Booth heaved himself to his feet. He was getting fat, Elizabeth noticed with disgust. His tunic bulged out ridiculously, as though he were pregnant. He said, "I hope that clears everything up, Robert."

Sedgewick and Elizabeth both rose, and Sedgewick followed Booth to the door. "I'll get that proposal to you by tomorrow morning at eight," Sedgewick said, opening the door for Booth. The two men went out into the hall. Elizabeth ground her teeth in fury. If she'd been an hour earlier—maybe even half an hour, she could have forced Sedgewick to stand up to the pig. Damn the bastards, they were wrecking everything. They were choosing the fool's road to ruin, and all under the guise of honor. Christ! Were they blind to everything in the world around them? They were like small boys scrapping on the playground. Only this wasn't a playground, nor a barnyard: what would the aliens care for Executive honor? What could *anyone*—apart from male executives—care for it?

When Sedgewick returned, Elizabeth sprang to the attack. "Why didn't you just get down on your hands and knees and lick the bottom of his boots, Sedgewick?" she said as he advanced into the room. "How could you be so craven as to allow him to sabotage the only chance we had for dealing with the aliens?" He stopped a couple of yards short of her; still his eyes did not meet hers. "And then to scapegoat me—you must have as much as admitted to him that you're not in control of your own damned people! How the hell do you expect us to function if you can throw away all my hard work in twenty fucking minutes!"

He looked up, and she saw that his eyes were blazing with fury. "Shut up, Weatherall!" Sedgewick was actually *shouting* at her! "If you had even the faintest sense of proportion you would have been fine. But no, you won't be satisfied until you're running the entire damned Executive! Do you *know* what Booth told me, Weatherall?" His body had assumed challenge stance, Elizabeth saw. Did Sedgewick realize he was challenging his own—nominal—-subordinate? "Booth told me, my bitch, that the Executive had been content to allow you your head for as long as you faithfully executed our policies as I had always done." His hands clenched into fists. "Do you understand what

I'm saying, Weatherall?" My god. He was *shrieking*. Surely he must have known that his colleagues were aware of what had been going on in Security for the last ten years? Could he really have imagined they weren't? He *was* a fool! "But this time, Booth informed me today, you've gone too far, you've taken it upon yourself to forge a new policy that is completely out of keeping with Security's past policies, a policy so far out from accepted practice that anyone would know it was not Sedgewick's. Your decision to act *unilaterally*, Booth said, is unacceptable, and far exceeds your authority. Do you hear what I'm saying, bitch?"

"I don't give a birthing fuck what those idiots think!" Elizabeth said through her teeth. "They haven't got the faintest idea of what's going on in the world today. They're dinosaurs and fools, all of them, living in a dream world. Things are not what they were ten years ago; we can't go on using outdated policies for handling entirely different problems and contexts! The aliens exist, Sedgewick, they're real, whether you and the Executive want to admit it or not!"

Sedgewick's eyes, scary in the flatness of their cold, lifeless rage, narrowed almost to slits. His voice sank to a dangerously deep pitch that rasped with an edge that made her want to ram her fist down his manly adam-appled throat. "Who do you think you are, Weatherall," Sedgewick bellowed, "that you imagine you can put yourself above the Executive?"

Elizabeth turned her back on him and started for the door. She refused to deal with him when he was talking to her this way. Let him simmer and stew. In the meantime she had to figure out what to do next, how to salvage the mess without counting on Sedgewick's standing up to his colleagues—presuming such a feat was possible.

"Don't you *dare* walk out on me," Sedgewick said.

Elizabeth kept going.

"Unless you want me to use force to restrain you?"

Elizabeth halted. So he was going to get into that again? Like this, he was completely unmanageable. She would have to get control of him, have to turn him around and make him face up to the situation: he left her no other choice. She drew three deep breaths and pivoted.

Sedgewick stalked to the conference table and pulled out the far left-hand chair. He pointed at it. "Sit down."

She needed to get him past this first burst of rage so that he'd be confronted with consciousness of what had happened, a realization of his isolation vis-à-vis the Executive: she must make him see that he needed to please her far more than he needed to please Booth, that by doing as she said Booth could be handled, but that he would get nothing from her if he gave himself body and soul to Booth's authority. If she capitulated to his threat of violence—for surely that's how he'd see any gesture or word that could be interpreted as obedience—she might lose her authority over him. But if she pushed him and forced him to go through with his threat—for he was probably feeling so pressured by Booth's openly expressed attitude that he would likely not back down for anything—she would lose all opportunity to get control of him.

Warily, Elizabeth sat where he directed, in the same damned place he had made her sit that other time. She thought that it must hold some significance for him of which she was unaware.

Sedgewick perched on the table—allowing him a rare opportunity to look down at her, Elizabeth sardonically observed. "Now that he's incognito," Sedgewick said in his usual tone of voice, "Daniel is constantly hearing Company gossip. Did you know you have a soubriquet by which you are universally known in the Company?"

"I'm not interested in gossip," Elizabeth said. "What is at stake here—"

"I'll tell you anyway," Sedgewick said, overriding her attempt to get the conversation back on course. "You're known as 'SuperBitch,' Weatherall." He grinned. "Appropriate, don't you think?"

Elizabeth folded her arms over her chest. He was afraid, she could see it, he was afraid that they called her SuperBitch because they considered *her* to be controlling *him*. Yet he didn't know for sure if that's what the soubriquet referred to.

"Booth is right about following *my* policies, Weatherall," Sedgewick said. "All along we should have been finding a way to rid ourselves of the aliens. But apart from Lauder's team and the hole-in-the-corner bunch of shrinks and anthropologists supposedly working on analyzing them, there's been nothing. Nothing, Weatherall, nothing to show since the terrorists first struck."

"We had a civil war followed by a global war to worry about," Elizabeth said. "And considering Lauder's experience attempting to capture even one of them, it seemed a waste of time and money to divert valuable resources from more pressing interests."

"That's no excuse." Obviously Booth had harped on this. "Moreover, you haven't pushed hard enough to find a way of making our orbital assets invulnerable. You—"

"Just a minute, Sedgewick," Elizabeth said, interrupting. "You're talking as though I'm responsible for all of Security's activities and policies! But *I'm* not Chief of Security, or even Deputy Chief, *am* I. Why didn't *you* order more to be done if you think we should have?"

Sedgewick did something so inconceivable to her that even as it was happening Elizabeth with her lightning swift reflexes failed to stop it: he slammed the back of his hand into her face. Instantly she grabbed his wrist, squeezing it as tightly as she sought to squeeze her own reflexive burst of rage under iron control. Her eyes smarted from the pain. "That was a mistake, Sedgewick," she said quietly.

His breath came in ragged gasps. He stared at her as though afraid of her response while at the same time daring it; he looked prepared to take it further, as though things had now gone so far that he felt he had nothing to lose by escalation. "I won't tolerate your talking to me like that, Weatherall." He choked out the words, gasping for breath. She could feel him trembling. "Release my wrist. Or face the consequences."

She stared down at his wrist and removed her hand from it. Given the marks her fingers had made, he would most certainly have bruises to show for it—while she herself would likely carry a mark on her face.

"We could work the human rights issue into the elections," Elizabeth said softly, tonelessly, not looking at his face. "When I discussed this with Bennett she said she saw how to use it in the public education project. The risk would be minimal if we did it all very carefully, and—"

"I don't want to hear anymore about it, Weatherall," Sedgewick said. "Is that clear?"

Elizabeth stared at his trousered leg so near to the arm of her chair. "Understood," she responded.

"I'm beginning to worry about you, Weatherall. You seem to have developed a problem with authority."

His hand darted to her face; his fingers stroked her cheek where he had struck it. Elizabeth held herself under tight restraint. She understood, finally, that there was no point in trying to deal with him; things had gone too far. She was beginning to see the pattern.

"Which puzzles me," Sedgewick said. "All your life you've been such a superbly adjusted executive woman, so in control of yourself, so perceptive as to what is fitting and proper. I'm afraid Booth is right; the power we've allowed you has gone to your head. You'd overturn the Executive if you could, wouldn't you." As she stared straight ahead out the window his fingers slid along her neck. Had he been wanting to do this all along? she wondered. To take such a liberty with her? "You must have very long hair, Weatherall," he said.

Her rigidity was giving her a headache; she could feel the constriction of the blood vessels in her neck, spreading tension, forcing her blood pressure higher and higher. Without warning Sedgewick slipped off the table and moved behind her chair. Her braid, she could feel him holding her braid. *Patterns, rituals, habits, everything in our relationship centered on these fixed patterns and rituals that had to be observed. Perhaps they made him feel safe? I don't know why, but there was always this repetition, the differences being mainly in intensity, in extent...*

Why hadn't she seen what was happening? Elizabeth wondered. It was so clear to her now, so many things stood out; it seemed painfully obvious that in some way he was forcing a replication of his relationship with Zeldin on her. For a moment the dream's image—seeing Zeldin instead of herself in the mirror—overwhelmed her. No, she thought, no, I will escape this, I will escape him, I will escape Zeldin. I will make my own life, free of his obsession, free of his warped clutch on me... "But something can be done with what you've started," he was saying, moving away from her, taking the chair to her left at the head of the table. "I see a way we can use what you've been trying to set up with the rebels. We'll lure them into a trap, them and the aliens, and then we'll have them, for without the leaders, and without the aliens, the territory will fall to us. Without the aliens and the anarchists, the other power groups will be so busy fighting among themselves that they won't have a chance to resist."

He was insane. They'd never lure the aliens into a trap: that had been tried again and again. And did he think they could simply kill the monitors being sent without incurring universal condemnation? But he and Booth thought condemnation preferable to being perceived as *weak*.

"We'll have to have some Company people in for the initial strategy sessions," he said. "And then, once we've worked it out, we'll pass the details on to Stevens, for undoubtedly it will occur in the context of their inspection of detention facilities. Rather convenient, the rebels' willingness to walk into our den," Sedgewick said. "Oh, and by the way, I had a meeting this morning with MacPhereson—of the Boston station—and Ambrose. MacPhereson has a plan I think we're going to want to experiment with. We'll be trying it out in his territory as well as in Leland's. An elaboration of the concept of sectoring, as a means for containment, minimizing property damage, and preventing the flow of subversives into other neighborhoods than their own."

Elizabeth let him ramble on, never once attempting to argue with him, never making any suggestions at all, merely saying "understood" when it was required of her. She was through trying to manipulate him; it was no longer worth it. She would give him the illusion of capitulation until she had everything arranged for her escape, and he would believe what he wanted to believe. Knowing she would get away from him made it possible to offer the appearance of submission. It wouldn't be for much longer, and then she would be free of him. Forever and ever free—though forever and ever without his power.

[iv]

Elizabeth got up from her desk, turned, and leaned her forehead against the plate glass window. The world outside looked strangely unreal: already she had begun to separate herself from the known and familiar. She knew she must lay her plans carefully, with excruciating attention to every detail, without hurry. If she rushed she would slip up or betray her plans to Sedgewick. Forty-eight hours? Seventy-two? How long would it take? She must set up a timetable, must sketch for herself exactly what she must do and how long it would take her to do it. If it were a matter of merely getting away and disappearing, then little effort would be required. She could make up the false IDs,

arrange the transfer of funds, wipe all electronic memory of her fin-
ger- and retinal-prints and perhaps even get away that night—if that
was all she wanted. But if she wanted more, if she wanted any kind of
future, she would have to think quite a bit harder, plan a great deal
more creatively.

*Who do you think you are, Weatherall, that you imagine you can
put yourself above the Executive?* None of them would have her now.
She would never be an acceptable PA or aide for any other member
of the Executive. As for the private sector... She knew nothing of
business management; the only thing she knew was politics and government. Anyway, word must have gotten around by now: what male
executive in his right mind would want her as a subordinate when she
was known to control Sedgewick, the man who had himself been a
symbol of control for so many years before the Blanket? No, that kind
of future was no longer a possibility. *Don't you ever think of retiring,
Weatherall?* Hah, retirement. Except that Sedgewick would probably
not allow it to her. No, what he wanted was for her to retire when
he did...

It dawned on Elizabeth: Sedgewick must have some fantasy about
her retiring with him, *physically* with him, once he'd made whatever
arrangements he had in mind for either of his progeny to take over
Security. For it was clear he couldn't conceive of living by himself,
without her.

He had as much as said he'd never let her go.

A knock on the door jerked Elizabeth out of her reverie. Allison,
she thought, turning away from the window. She would have to be
careful not to compromise Allison. She reached for the switch on her
desk that controlled the door. She must be careful to protect Allison
and Vivien and Maxine, and to—

It was not Allison who came into the office. "Hazel!" Seeing her,
Elizabeth realized she needed the girl's arms around her.

Hazel stood a foot or two just inside the doorframe. Elizabeth
made the door close. "Ms. Lennox asked me to give you these," Hazel
said, stiffly holding out several files. "I'm sorry to disturb you."

Why was she standing by the door like that? Elizabeth moved
around her desk. "I'm so glad she sent you instead of coming herself,"
Elizabeth said. "I've been wanting you and didn't even realize it." She

would have to find a way to take Hazel with her, she thought as she approached her. The girl pushed the files at her. "Come in, let's not hover by the door, darling," Elizabeth said, taking the folders with one hand and reaching for Hazel with the other.

Hazel stepped backwards, almost into the door.

Elizabeth got her arm around her and began moving her to the sofa. "Come sit with me a bit," she said, wondering how much she could tell her.

"Ms. Lennox has asked me to prepare a report."

"Don't worry about it," Elizabeth said. "I'm Jacquelyn's boss, re-member?" They stood by the sofa; Elizabeth tossed the folders onto the side table and slid both arms around Hazel. Staring down into her face, Elizabeth realized that Hazel had not once looked at her since entering the room. "What is it, darling?" Elizabeth slipped her hand under the girl's chin to raise it. "Is there some kind of problem with Jacquelyn? If you tell me about it I'm sure we can straighten it out."

Hazel looked at her then. Her eyes had gone dark, almost to brown. "There's no problem with Ms. Lennox," she said, looking away. Elizabeth reached for Hazel's hands, which were hanging unre-sponsive at her sides. "Then tell me, darling, what the problem is. I'm sure I can help you with it, whatever it is."

Hazel stifled a choking sound in her throat: a laugh? A sob? What was wrong with the girl? Gently Elizabeth pushed her down onto the sofa and sat beside her.

"What was it you wanted me for?" Hazel asked, her voice barely steady.

The girl's hands lay limp in Elizabeth's. Could it be Sedgewick? Had Sedgewick said something insulting to her, something crude? "It's not Sedgewick, is it?" Elizabeth asked anxiously, imagining the sorts of things he had it in him to say as a means of petty revenge on her.

Hazel shook her head.

"Then what is it, love? Tell me!"

"There's nothing to say," Hazel said, staring down at the floor.

Elizabeth released Hazel's hands. Obviously the girl's reticence had nothing to do with shyness or embarrassment. "You're upset about something. Something private, perhaps. Obviously what you want to say to me is that it's none of my business. And that as far as you're concerned I'm nothing more to you than a boss." Elizabeth swallowed. Her disappointment was bitter; though she hadn't known it, she had been expecting to be able to count on Hazel, had in the back of her mind been thinking Hazel would be with her, would help her, would stick by her.

Hazel said nothing. Elizabeth watched the girl's hands twisting in her lap as the silence beat on and on. She thought of how she had woken from the dream, hysterical, and Hazel had soothed her. The way she, Elizabeth, might have treated Sedgewick in a similar situation? The thought scalded her with pain. She said, "Did it make you feel powerful, Hazel, soothing away the boss's nightmare?"

Hazel lifted her head and looked directly at Elizabeth. Tears coursed down her face. "I gave up my job for you!" The words seemed wrenched out of her.

"Because you saw a better chance," Elizabeth said. "Working for someone like me, you could see possibilities for manipulation right off, couldn't you. All your prim talk, Hazel: such a very clever girl."

"You think everyone is like you. That all anyone ever cares about is pushing people around."

Elizabeth rose to her feet to pace. Everything was falling down around her ears. Even her relationship with Hazel. That the girl was talking to her this way, was being so hateful, so secretive... She should dismiss her, should forget about her. She came to a halt in front of her. "So that's what you think of me? That all I care about is, quote, pushing people around?" Hazel said nothing. "Go ahead," Elizabeth said angrily, "answer me! And while you're at it tell me how you arrived at this stunning insight, after all the personal time we've spent together. I'd like to know in what way you imagine me to have been pushing you around all the times we've made love."

Still Hazel said nothing.

Elizabeth shouted: "Answer me, damn you!" and reached for Hazel's face, to make the girl look at her.

Hazel flinched from her touch, as though to avoid a blow.

Trembling, Elizabeth turned away. That Hazel should do that somehow hurt the worst. "I don't know what it is you hold against me," she said. "Is this something to do with your grudge against executives?" Elizabeth turned back to face the girl and stared down at her. "Is that it? That you hoped to hurt me all along?"

"I left my job for you!" Hazel's gaze met Elizabeth's. "Don't you understand? You think I'd take that kind of risk for something only a twisted mind would even think of?" She shook her head. "I knew better than that, but I did it anyway. I suppose I deserve everything that follows from such stupidity and weakness."

Elizabeth put her hands to her cheeks. "I don't understand. If you felt you were taking a risk, then presumably that means you felt something positive for me. If that's the case, I don't understand what's happening here. Why are you pushing me away from you? Why are you talking to me like this?" Was this girl trying out some devious manipulation? Could she have been so duped by her?

Hazel swallowed, then wiped her face with a piece of tissue she pulled from her pocket. "I'm sorry," she said.

Elizabeth stared at her with frustration. "You're *sorry*?" she said. "That must be about the most meaningless thing you could have chosen to say." After staring for a time at Hazel's closed face, at her silent tears, Elizabeth sat down on the sofa and, half-afraid the girl would flinch from her again, brushed loose, wet strands of hair off her face. "Please, darling," she said softly, stroking Hazel's hair, "please talk to me about this. It's important to me. I need...I need to understand. I need to be close to you." Elizabeth moved nearer and slipped her arm around the girl. "Your presence in my life has made it possible for me to get through the last couple of weeks, darling, which have otherwise been hellish. I've never felt like this about anyone before. It's more than infatuation, can't you tell? You mustn't just toss all that away, Hazel."

"I don't believe you," Hazel said. "I know I should pretend, that if I did I might even keep from being fired, but it's no use. I can't pretend; I'm just not made that way."

"What don't you believe?" Elizabeth asked, making her voice gentle. Why did this girl harp so about her job? It was some sort of barrier she kept throwing between them each time Elizabeth moved to go around it.

"That my feelings matter to you at all," Hazel said in a breathless rush. "That you care anything about me. For some reason you want me to believe that, and I don't know why, though I'm sure you have your reasons. I guess you think we're all so stupid that you think that just by telling me that I'll forget everything else and believe it. Or maybe you think we're so fatuous and so needing to believe that one of you could feel anything for us that I'll be easily duped."

"For godsakes, Hazel, what are you talking about? Who is this 'we'?"

"Service-techs," Hazel whispered. "Whenever you forget to pretend I see it, though usually I somehow explain it away, or forget about it. Because I don't want to admit it to myself, it's so ugly. Because what does that make me? But then, today..." She shrugged. "How can I forget that? I don't think you even believe we're human."

Elizabeth wracked her brain to understand what the girl could possibly be referring to. "How can you say that!" she exclaimed. "I don't pretend; I've never pretended anything with you!"

Hazel twisted away and held herself stiffly apart. "The only time you weren't pretending," she said, turning her burning yellow eyes onto Elizabeth's face, "was when you were pushing us around. It wasn't so much the way you treated me as the way you treated that poor courier. He was a wreck all the way back here, and so thankful when you ignored him. Through the entire flight I could see his hands were shaking so badly he couldn't even do the crossword puzzles he had been working. And he was so humiliated he couldn't look at me. But the worst was that he wasn't even surprised. Not at all. As though he's used to that kind of abuse. Maybe even from you."

"Hazel," Elizabeth said, troubled by this picture the girl had drawn of her, "you're blowing this way out of proportion. I admit I was in a rage. I was so angry I could hardly see straight! I wasn't polite to him, that's true. I lost control of myself. I should be the one to feel humiliated. But it was only a shove. I don't see why you are so upset by this."

Hazel continued to hold her gaze. "Only a shove. How would you feel if someone shoved you? Not that anyone would, of course, but suppose they did, and you couldn't afford to say anything to help assert your dignity, much less shove back?"

"Oh god." Groaning, Elizabeth put her hand over her eyes. "I do know, Hazel, believe me I do know what it's like." She dropped her hand from her eyes and looked again at Hazel. "Just now, darling. Just before you came in here." She drew a deep breath and nerved herself to go on. "Sedgewick slapped me, Hazel," she said, feeling the heat come into her cheeks. Hazel's eyes widened; she looked shocked. "And I did nothing about it, said nothing. Even though I'm stronger and bigger than he is. Because I'd face unthinkable consequences if I retaliated. I was furious at him for doing that, and humiliated, too. I feel shame just from telling you, Hazel. But I don't think Sedgewick did it because he has contempt for me, or because he doesn't consider me human. I'm the single most important person—living—to him."

"I didn't realize until I met you that there's so much violence in executives," Hazel said. "You even treat one another that way?"

"Please, darling, don't you see I was taking my temper out on whoever was in range? It's nothing to do with the way I feel about service-techs. As a matter of fact I don't have any one comprehensive feeling about service-techs as a group. And I've never felt about any- one the way I feel about you. My feelings for you are unique. As for that courier, I confess it was probably more to do with his gender than with his status. I plain don't like men. I only put up with the ones I have to." She was saying too much, she was telling this girl things she should be telling no one. If this girl *was* manipulating her...

"I'm so confused," Hazel whispered. "I don't understand any of this. I only know it upsets me, *scares* me. In my other job there was nothing like this kind of stress. People were civil to one another. I don't think my boss's boss ever slapped *her*. And then that night you got out that, that *thing* you keep in your safe. That *weapon*. So much violence. Of course, I have no way of knowing. But...I just don't know..." Hazel's voice trailed off uncertainly.

"Darling, I'm not a violent woman, I promise you. Ask Maxine. Or Allison. Or Vivien. Of all people they know me best. Surely they would know if anyone would. I don't think I've ever raised my voice to Maxine, Hazel. Surely if I were as mean and contemptuous as you say I am I would have treated her badly?" It was terrible, this need to defend herself like this. But she had to allay Hazel's anxiety, had to win her back. Thinking of Allison, Vivien, and Maxine, Elizabeth glimpsed the enormity of her coming loss: she would be losing them, losing the people she loved best because to maintain contact with them would be to endanger them. She couldn't bear to lose Hazel, too. Or to have Hazel thinking of her the way she, Elizabeth, thought of Sedgewick. She sank back against the sofa. "I don't mean to pressure you. Please believe me. You mustn't be worried about this job, Hazel. If it doesn't work out between us, I won't take it out on you. I promise you."

Elizabeth let her head rest against the back of the sofa. She was so tired. She needed to be able to think, to plan, she needed to pull herself together. Everything was a nightmare, out of control; she felt as though she were in a car driving along a twisty mountain road and the wheel had just been wrenched away from her by a lunatic who had suddenly materialized beside her. She heard Hazel moving, felt the shifting of her weight from the sofa cushions, and made herself keep silent, prevented herself from saying something to keep Hazel from leaving the room.

"Liz," Hazel said softly, and Elizabeth felt the girl's hand on her cheek. She opened her eyes. Hazel knelt on the sofa beside her, facing her. "I don't want to hurt you," she said, "but I see these things about you that upset me, that make me feel helpless. You are so different from anyone I've ever been involved with, I don't know how to understand. I'm all mixed up."

Elizabeth moved her head to kiss Hazel's fingers. "I could say the same thing about you, darling," she murmured. "You're so critical of me, it makes me anxious. I can't bear for you to think I'm anything like the picture you've painted of me."

Hazel leaned forward and initiated a long kiss. After a while Elizabeth shifted herself and Hazel to the floor so that they could lie full length on the rug, holding one another, cuddling. But a few minutes later, a series of terrible sobs tore out of her chest and throat, as though wrenched from deep, deep inside. How could she bear what she *must* bear? And if Hazel deserted her?

"Everything is unbearably ugly but you, darling. I need you, Hazel. I love you."

Hazel brought out another tissue and handed it to Elizabeth. "What a pair of crybabies we are," she said shakily. "And that's my last tissue too, so I guess we'd better keep ourselves from starting again."

Elizabeth smiled weakly and sat up. "Let's go wash our faces, darling. And hope nobody comes in here. The sight of us would make them wonder, wouldn't it." Elizabeth stood and reached a hand down to help Hazel to her feet. They went into Elizabeth's bathroom and bathed their blotchy red faces. "I feel all hollow and headachy, darling," Elizabeth said, splashing water onto her face. "Do you realize we've missed lunch? Let's order out for some thick, juicy sandwiches, shall we?"

Hazel smiled at her in the mirror. "You're always thinking about food, Liz."

"Can't live without it. But wait until Jacq gets a look at us: she'll know we've been quarreling." Hazel looked surprised. "But that's what we've been doing, darling." Elizabeth grinned. "Quarreling. And you've been taking me to task. You look shocked, my sweet. I wonder why." Elizabeth handed her a towel.

Hazel patted her face dry. "Well, you're an executive, and my boss. It sounds sort of…funny."

"But it's not so simple with us, is it," Elizabeth said, amused—and pleased. "It would be terrible if you didn't feel you could quarrel with me. Don't you agree?"

Hazel gave her a searching look, then put the towel down on the vanity. "I don't understand any of this, Liz."

Elizabeth, looking in the mirror, straightened her crumpled tunic. "Neither do I, darling, but does that matter? Don't you think it's more interesting this way?"

Hazel half-smiled. "I'm starving too, Liz. What kind of sandwiches should we get?"

Elizabeth put her handset to her ear and told Jacq what to order and began thinking again of how much she could tell Hazel and of whether or not Hazel would want to go with her. She had so little time, so very little time left for making decisions.

Chapter Twenty-three

[i]

As the males droned on, continually rephrasing and restating everything they had said in the first half of the meeting, Elizabeth sorted her email. She was beginning to think the goddam fucking meeting would never end. But Sedgewick had insisted she attend, and she had not dared to flout his order. Checking the time, she found it was already eight-thirty. Once she'd repeated to them the initial plan for rounding up people able to finger Military without incriminating ODS for human rights violations and handing them over to the Free Zone's monitors and coordinators, she had had little to contribute. Apart from a certain distaste and anxiety for the possibility of atrocity that the entire plan seemed to breed, she found galling that they would be using her name and reputation as the basis for this elaborate trap for capturing aliens. The Free Zone people might be rebels, but Elizabeth had been negotiating with them in good faith. Sedgewick, of course, dismissed this as immaterial: "People like them aren't part of the civilized community. Ordinary rules of civilization don't apply in our dealings with them. More to the point, nothing could be more important than capturing the aliens—you yourself have said time and again that without the aliens, all our problems would vanish."

Elizabeth didn't believe they would catch even one of the aliens, however many hostages they managed to take. Sedgewick had given orders to Guard commanders in all the western territories to be prepared to enter and take the Free Zone on May 1—which was Tuesday. Security had long since prepared detailed plans for doing so—plans that rested on the contingency of all six of the aliens' absence from the scene. Could Sedgewick seriously think that Security would be able to take out the aliens by May 1?

Elizabeth was tasked with setting things up with Greenglass and her people so that a large contingent of them—preferably including Greenglass herself—would be lured into visiting several regional sites where potential refugees would be quartered. When Elizabeth had suggested that Sedgewick was unwise to set up an operation of such magnitude so hastily, especially considering the harshness of the aliens' past reprisals, he had gotten angry. It was then that he had said she was to be present at every important strategy session.

So here she sat with eight men and two other women, listening to tedious, arrant nonsense. Ambrose was in his element, thrilled at finally being allowed to take action against the Free Zone leaders and letting Elizabeth see by occasional flashes of his watery blue eyes at her that he considered the very fact of the operation a personal triumph. Before the meeting had started he'd slid her—and her bruise—a sly look and said, "Looks like you met your match downstairs, Weatherall. Or can it be you're having a slow day?" Elizabeth had favored him with a nasty smile and offered to take him on any time, any rules.

The officer who would be coordinating the operation, Serkin, was an old Company hand foisted onto this essentially ODS affair by Sedgewick, who did not trust any of Stevens's people to pull it off by themselves. It was a foregone conclusion that all the ODS people would resent having an outsider controlling them. Even Stevens and Ambrose, who were technically overseeing Serkin's performance, showed signs of irritation at his presence.

As they played with the electronic wall maps in their discussion of the sites, one part of Elizabeth's mind continued posing fundamental questions she needed to address before finalizing her plans. Did she want merely to escape, or did she intend in some way to go renegade? The very appearance of that word in her thoughts induced anxiety. Yet the notion of trying to disappear and live quietly—abdicating all power, all responsibility, all activity for the rest of her life—disturbed her almost as much. Whenever she tried to envision a successful disappearance, her resolve to leave Sedgewick faltered. But with the word *renegade*, Kay Zeldin entered her thoughts, and with Kay Zeldin the memory of the rebuke she had administered to Zeldin for having "abdicated her responsibility" to manipulate Sedgewick. It was as

though now, faced with a seeming inability to control Sedgewick—
and through Sedgewick, Booth and the rest of the Executive—she,
Elizabeth, were giving up—running away—through a similar mixture of fear and frustration and sense of impotence. Would she be able
to live with the fact of flight once she had buried herself in safe obscurity? She would have years and years of time on her hands with nothing to do but think about what she had done. Much as she loved to
play, Elizabeth could not imagine spending all her time at it: doing so
would be a sure way to render her favorite activities boring. But if she
chose neither to stay nor to bury herself in obscurity—i.e., if she chose
to go renegade—then the next question was in what way she might
do that. Certainly she would not go over to the Free Zone people, to
the aliens, or to any other anti-executive group she could think of. She
was not cynical enough to contemplate taking over such a group and
transforming it into a vehicle for her own activities and aggrandizement, she was not desperate enough to need their assistance, and she
possessed no inclination for vengeance per se against Sedgewick and
his colleagues.

Her true desire dawned on Elizabeth in a shocking moment of
revelation, even as Ambrose droned on and on about the placement
of ODS's crack tactical teams: she saw that she yearned for a world in
which women like herself, Allison, Lisa Mott, Georgeanne Childress—
and even Emily Madden, for that matter—would be allowed to get
on with their work. All these women possessed a determination and
dedication that the men—those, in other words, who depended on
such women—did not see much less appreciate. Never did the males
acknowledge that career-line women held the executive-system together, especially in times of extended crisis. Never did the males see
that the network that existed served to ease the execution of their interests (and at times subtly circumvented orders and policies that the
males did not realize endangered the executive system itself).

Boldly, Elizabeth made the leap to think the unthinkable: to what
extent—if at all—might she be able to call on that career-line network
in the course of her defection? In general, executive women stuck together up to the point at which their personal loyalties to the males
they worked for intruded. What Elizabeth found difficult to gauge,
however, was whether this loyalty would be considered to cover any

assistance whatsoever to someone defecting. Elizabeth's connection to the network was more extensive than that of any other career-line woman; her use of the network to bring the Civil War to an end had given her contacts with women in almost every part of the country. But could she safely draw on it once she had given up her position in Security?

This question led her in turn to consider whether she could work against Sedgewick while remaining with him. That is, could she somehow mobilize the network in defiance of his direct orders? The idea seemed preposterous. In the end it was usually males who controlled and physically carried out the most critical aspects of the Executive's policies. The women in the network did not *make* policy, nor did they *carry out* policy, they simply *helped* to carry it out. And though their help was critical, it did not allow them much chance for altering policy, except in subtle, largely unseen ways. Elizabeth's past input into real policy decision-making was extraordinary. And the only reason the Executive had tolerated that input had been that Elizabeth's decisions had for the most part conformed with its wishes. And since the end of the Civil War she had initiated far fewer independent policy decisions than during it, when the Executive had barely functioned— and when the Executive had still been in the dark about Sedgewick's incapacitation and his dependence on her to run Security.

At last, the males appeared to have exhausted themselves. As Elizabeth was packing up to go, Serkin asked her for a meeting on Saturday. "I want to work out all the details of your participation in this operation," he said. "Your role is critical."

"I'm extremely busy tomorrow," Elizabeth said. "But I can probably find you some time on Sunday afternoon."

"Sunday afternoon will be rather late, don't you think, if you're to leave on Sunday evening."

"Leave on Sunday evening?" Elizabeth frowned at him. "I can't possibly leave by that time. It will have to be Monday, Serkin. Believe me, it doesn't take long to work things out with those people, if one promises them what they want to hear. It's not like attending a meeting of executives needing to wrangle ad infinitum over trifles." Pointedly, Elizabeth flicked her eyes in Ambrose's direction.

Serkin scowled at her. "I've already set up the timetable, Weatherall." His unpleasantly nasal voice grated on her nerves even more than Ambrose's husky tenor did.

Elizabeth gave him her iciest stare. "Timetables can be changed. I suggest you change yours. I know these people, Serkin. And the less advance notice we give them of our plan, the better. You don't want to give them time to think up precautions and so on, do you?"

He blinked. "Your point is taken, Weatherall. One o'clock Sunday afternoon, then?"

"Make it three," Elizabeth said. "In either my office or Sedgewick's. Just show up in the Chief's suite at three and someone will bring you to me."

Elizabeth left without another word to anyone, and as she stalked back to her office she wondered if all of them in that meeting thought of her as "SuperBitch" as Sedgewick claimed. Let them, she thought. Not a single one of them could challenge her on any ground—she knew it, and they knew it. Since the Chief's suite was a black box to them, they could have not even an inkling of how precarious her position had become.

As Elizabeth entered her office it occurred to her that in whatever she decided to do, putting Sedgewick out of commission would be of immense help. If he fell into a binge-cycle, which he would inevitably do if she weren't there to help him recover from his next big drunk, he would not only be at her mercy, but he'd also be largely unaware of anything going on in Security. While she might not be able to abort the operation, she would be better able to manipulate certain details that would make her own defection easier to carry out.

Bracing herself to face the unpleasant, Elizabeth opened the safe and squatted low to the floor on her haunches. She flashed on the dressing room scene in the dream. What was it that the dream was telling her? That she had become Zeldin? Elizabeth revolted from the very idea of it. She was not going renegade as Zeldin had. Her relationship with Sedgewick was not in any way the same, even if superficially it might seem to be.

Reaching for the leather book, her hand encountered the silk. Unable to stop herself, Elizabeth drew it off the shelf. She held it to her face, breathing in its subtle scent, rubbing its luxuriance against her cheek. The flood of emotion it released almost choked her with poignance. "No," she said aloud, warning herself against the perils of immersion. Anxious, she groped around the back of the shelf until she located the book. And then Elizabeth settled into her armchair, spreading the gown over her lap, letting it drape over her knees to the floor.

She opened the book at random, to a page near the end, a page filled with writing. How could that be? Elizabeth wondered in consternation. There should be nothing in the last half; all the pages should be blank. Zeldin would never have risked the punishment that the defiance of writing for her own purposes would have provoked. Elizabeth stared at Zeldin's writing. Automatically she began to read it.

Elizabeth,

For the first time I name you in this book. I write it, after all, only for you. And I dare finally to write without your instruction to do so, because this is my last night in this cell, my last night under your eye. Although I haven't seen Sedgewick yet, I believe, you see, that you will convince him to take me back with him. How could I now doubt anything you tell me? To doubt one thing would be to doubt everything, which now includes all reality for me. I dare to write because if you ever again open this book it will be after I've been returned here, in which case this sin of unsolicited writing, of unauthorized use of language—the greatest sin among the commandments you've laid down for me—will be a mere peccadillo by comparison with the larger transgression of my return.

I want you to know Elizabeth that I understand what you've done to me. I don't know exactly when it happened. That first time in the closet was the beginning, of course: it was then that I began to doubt the existence of my self, it was then that I saw that self's existence as wholly dependent upon your recognition of it. And I thought you *did* recognize it. The way you sometimes would talk to me, your seeming respect for that self…but that's gone now. It no longer exists, and you do not recognize it. It was the thing you had to kill in order to hollow me out to be merely an object for your use.

I keep asking myself whether you refused recognition of my self (the thing that makes me human, Elizabeth, you do know that?) because you were so contemptuous of me/it, because you so little valued who and what I was that you never felt a moment's qualm in destroying me/it, or whether your contempt came as that self died. My true self is always in the closet now,

Elizabeth, always in restraint, in the void since only you could tell me I exist, and you've denied it. Finally. Irrevocably. When you told me in the car, while I stared at the magnificence around us, I couldn't really take it in. Later I saw, of course, that it was my destruction, my reduction into a creature of the closet, that had been the end you had been striving for all along. How could you do this, Elizabeth? Are human beings so little to you? Or was it something about me in particular that drove you to extinguish me? Of all the things you've said to me perhaps the one I most believe is your statement that you don't hate me. Surprisingly, for hatred would at least explain to me why you have done this…why you have exiled me from my self.

This annihilation of me, Elizabeth, is far worse than my betrayal of Sedgewick. I never deliberately set out to wipe from existence a human soul, not even in my youth. I don't understand these things, Elizabeth. I only understand what you have done to me.

This shattering of any sense of self, this distortion of past into meaningless fragments…you hold up a simulacrum for imitation and identity, as meaningless a representation of a living self as "Good morning, Elizabeth" can signify anything other than submission. All possibility of social exchange for me has been forever negated, just as that use of "morning" never referred to an hour of the day or night. And just as "Good morning Elizabeth" can only be an extortion of submission, can never be anything more, so the "reconstructed" Kay can never be more than a patched together stick-figure manufactured for superficial purposes. There can be nothing behind the stick figure, and the stick figure is all you have allowed to exist.

Ah, I've just picked up the pen again, I can't sleep, Elizabeth, tormented by images of your arms around me. When you treated me gently after bouts in the closet it was to console me for losing my soul—I know that now, I'm certain of it. But did you know that's what you were doing? And then bit by bit, it—my soul, I mean—disappeared as you refused to grant it recognition. When I look into your eyes I see the closet. But then that's what you intended all along.

Again I want to ask you how you could think so little of me? How could you think so little of me that you could destroy me for so slight a purpose? This is what it means to be forsaken. This is what it means to be dead. I truly am the corpse Allison named me. And you are my murderer.

For the second time that day Elizabeth broke down. "God damn you, Kay Zeldin! You wrote this knowing I couldn't answer you, you wrote this knowing you would haunt me." Her eyes streaming, Elizabeth lifted the silk and buried her face in it. It was Zeldin's revenge, she told herself over and over again. But she didn't believe it, not in her heart. She could not escape that face in the mirror, staring at her, accusing her, watching her—and, finally, becoming her.

[ii]

Although Elizabeth had not yet come to a decision about what to do, she took certain precautionary steps in preparation for her flight/defection/exile. For one, she sent Maxine away for an all-expenses-paid vacation, which the latter chose to take as an opportunity for visiting her mother, who lived in New Jersey—which for Elizabeth was not without a certain irony, since Maxine had happened to be visiting her mother at the time of the Blanket, a circumstance that had probably saved her life. But though she had tried to think about it all night as she fought off memories of Kay Zeldin and the guilt and pain reading from the book had evoked, Elizabeth had come no closer to deciding what exactly she should do. She knew she had little time left though, for there were too many details any one course of action would require her to attend to.

As she considered practical details—how to hold on to valued personal articles, for instance, as well as the few pieces of art she owned—she faced the fact that her safety might depend on her leaving them behind. She wanted to think she could send some of her things to Vivien and later (perhaps much much later) retrieve them, but she knew very well she could not take that kind of risk.

Sedgewick would be wild at her disappearance; if he did not go on a prolonged binge, he would pursue her relentlessly. Accounts of his pursuit of Zeldin to Calais (from both Sedgewick's and Zeldin's lips) had recurred to her throughout the night. It would not be exactly the same, of course, but it would be at least as terrible, if not more terrible, for Sedgewick was far more unstable now than he had been thirty years past. She must be excruciatingly careful to leave Allison and Vivien and Maxine out of it. They must know nothing; she must make up her mind to giving up all contact with them, for Sedgewick would be watching. He could be amazingly patient in his waiting games; he'd waited thirteen years before recontacting Zeldin. The only limiting factors in his pursuit of her would be his emotional stability and the possibility of Booth's chucking him out of Security for good. But even if that happened, his successor would be looking for her, too—for other reasons. The Executive's first thought on hearing of her disappearance would be what a national security threat she could—if she desired—pose. She might not have all of Military's secrets in her pocket, but what she did carry would be enough to enable other forces to do great damage in almost every area of national security, both domestically and externally. Most important, she knew everything there was to know about Security Services, which meant she knew almost everything there was to know about anything of strategic significance to the US. Booth would be the first person to realize that.

When Elizabeth finished dictating the report Sedgewick had promised to get to Booth by eight o'clock (it was now nine-thirty, and as yet only existed on a data key), she went out to the front to give it to Hazel. "We need this as soon as possible, darling," Elizabeth told her. "Drop everything and do this now. And then when you're done, bring it in to me yourself, okay? I'm hoping we can have some time today to talk."

Hazel's eyes searched her face. "You look terrible, Liz. As though you didn't sleep last night. I hope it wasn't because of—"

Elizabeth dropped her hand onto Hazel's shoulder. "No, darling, don't worry about it. I've got a lot on my mind, and some of it I want to talk to you about. But this thing here—" she gestured at the key— "takes priority over everything else."

Hazel squeezed her hand, then picked up the key and inserted it into her machine.

Elizabeth returned to her office. She could no longer put off deciding what she was going to do vis-à-vis Sedgewick's plan to trap Greenglass and the aliens. Dictating the report had reinforced her disgust for the operation and made her wonder if she shouldn't disappear before luring Greenglass into the trap. She felt torn, though, for though she did not want to see Sedgewick's plan succeed, she did not want to assist the rebels, either. She was not Zeldin, and she would not follow in Zeldin's steps.

The thought teased her that if the Executive persisted in attempting to take such extreme measures against the Free Zone, they would lose everything, and under such circumstances a significant contingent of the executive community just might be interested in forming an opposition under new leadership. In such a situation she, Elizabeth, would be a likely candidate for taking a strong leadership role. Yet she somehow could not believe that any group outside of either Security or Military circles could survive and succeed. If both Military and Security fell—highly unlikely unless they embarked on a new Civil War, and god knew she would never consciously catalyze such a thing the way Zeldin had—if both of them fell, then someone like Barclay Madden would step into the power vacuum. And Barclay Madden...

What about Emily? Elizabeth suddenly wondered. Would Emily hold onto her things if she sent them to her—without giving her away? Emily felt no loyalty for Sedgewick or Security, Emily could not be intimidated in the way Vivien or Allison could be. But Emily had no reason to befriend her, either. In fact, for all she knew Emily might consider her an enemy.

She could defect to Barclay Madden.

She dismissed this wild, wild idea as soon as it occurred to her. Madden's connection with Military was too strong, went too much against the grain. And besides, he would be an intolerable boss. She knew that. And toward women...even toward a woman like Elizabeth Weatherall... She could not help recalling his bevy of bare-chested males. Worse, he would probably not trust someone who had been a traitor to her own boss. No. Barclay Madden was no possibility.

Should she try to stick it out in Security? Suppose she were able to work up some sort of organized opposition to the Executive's policies within all twelve departments of the Executive? Ridiculous idea. How, for starters, would she know whom it would be safe to sound out? With a soubriquet like SuperBitch, what could she expect? And besides, she could no longer control Sedgewick, and Booth would be openly watching and pressing her from now on. And the very thought of putting her efforts and time and energy at the service of policies she could not believe in and in certain instances felt the greatest repugnance toward, all the while Sedgewick encroached more and more upon her in that disgustingly personal way… She could not. It was that simple. She could not do it. She had to get away.

Her headset chimed; Elizabeth expected to hear Hazel's voice since Jacq took most Saturdays off. But, "Cross the hall, would you, Weatherall?" Sedgewick's voice said into her ear, shaking her.

Elizabeth took a minute to lie on the floor and compose herself before facing Sedgewick.

"You heard me tell Booth that report would be on his desk by eight," Sedgewick said the instant she set foot in his office. "It's now almost eleven and it isn't even printed out. Explain yourself." He was sitting behind his desk for a change, sifting through what looked like station reports. Elizabeth hadn't so much as glanced at them yet that morning.

"The meeting broke up late in the evening," Elizabeth said evenly, taking the chair before his desk. "I didn't finish dictating it until an hour and a half ago. The girl is a crack word processor. It won't take her long to prepare it."

He snorted. "Judging by the condition of your face I suppose you spent the night debauching her."

Elizabeth lowered her eyes to hide her rage. She barely held herself in check, for she could not stand his talking this way about herself and Hazel. Since she could not even fake a smile, she raised her eyebrows. "While she looks fresh as a daisy?" Elizabeth said.

"She's young."

"Not that young." Elizabeth's tone was tart. "She's almost thirty, Sedgewick."

"Does she know your age?"

Elizabeth looked at him. "I was thinking about Zeldin last night, Sedgewick," she said, more calmly than she felt. *And you are my murderer.* "I was wondering about something we've never discussed."

He watched her as though afraid she was about to say something he would not be able to bear. "That's how you spent your night? Thinking about Zeldin?" And yet he was avid with curiosity.

"Pretty much."

"You *are* obsessed with her," he said, as though she had now provided proof for this long-promoted contention of his.

"Why did you kill her?" she asked pointblank.

His face blanched. "What the hell kind of question is that, Weatherall?" he said hoarsely. "You know I did it because she begged me to."

"That's not a good enough answer," Elizabeth said. "Suppose she'd begged you to send her back to the Free Zone? Would you have done that for her because she'd begged you to?"

Sedgewick's tongue ran over his lips. "As I've said before, you had no compassion for that woman, none at all."

"Don't you tell me about compassion." Elizabeth flung the words at him. "Don't you tell me about your compassion for Zeldin. When did you ever feel compassion for her? After you'd beaten her to a pulp, raped, and sodomized her in Calais? Is that when you felt compassion for her, Sedgewick?"

"You'll note she never felt that I destroyed her, Weatherall." Sedgewick's eyes blazed; he looked like a fanatical madman on a mission. "She was in despair, Weatherall. You don't think she wouldn't have found a way to kill me on that island if that's what she had wanted to do? I didn't keep her restrained and hardly had her watched at all, you know. She could have killed me as I slept. But she didn't, did she."

"She wouldn't have killed you even before I captured her," Elizabeth said. "She had her chance, didn't she. She could have killed both of us instead of stranding us on the island. Zeldin didn't believe in murder. Hadn't you noticed that about her?" Elizabeth flashed him a scornful look. "No, of course you didn't. You never noticed much that you didn't want to see, except when she forced it on you."

Sedgewick leaned back in his chair and folded his arms over his chest. "And you, Weatherall, have made up a dream-woman. Something I can't even begin to imagine. Your Zeldin isn't mine."

Elizabeth grinned. "*My* Zeldin, Sedgewick? I'm sorry, but I just don't think of her so possessively."

"Not so. In your hubris you think you know the true Zeldin, that you possess the truth about her. I could see it in the transcripts—you thought it even then. Simply because she was in your power."

Elizabeth's eyes widened as she stumbled onto an insight. "I know what it was, Sedgewick," she said, not bothering to keep the triumph from her voice. "I know why you killed her." She could see the dread coming back into his face. "The reason you killed her is because you were afraid. You were afraid that she would eventually challenge you, or even refuse you. You just couldn't believe it would work." She watched his eyes dim. "That's it, isn't it," she said softly. "You knew you couldn't have handled the old Zeldin. And you didn't believe it would stick. And then when she asked you to kill her—and that's presuming she really did, I have no proof assuring me of that, I have only your version of events—" Sedgewick tried to interrupt, but Elizabeth rode over his weak attempt to derail her— "but if and when she asked you to kill her, something about her made you afraid that the whole thing would go smash. I saw you the day before, if you remember, Sedgewick, and you were riding damned high, you were so confident that you'd finally gotten what you'd wanted for so many years… But a part of you didn't believe it would last. And so you couldn't face that, could you. How much better to have a nice memory of perfection, something to cherish forever, a way of projecting how your life would have been if I hadn't made Zeldin so unhappy."

His eyes, now like dead ashes stirred in mud, accepted the blow and gave no sign of desire or need to fight back. "You know nothing." His voice was almost inaudible. "I couldn't bear her suffering. She was in pain, in terrible pain."

"But you always took pleasure in her pain, Sedgewick. Don't try to tell me you didn't find that pain attractive. The way you found her emaciation irresistible." He looked away from her. "You can't deny it, you told me so yourself. And when you look at pictures of that pain you talk of and the visible emaciation?"

"She said that what had been done to her was like my surgery," he said without looking at her. "That it had killed her ability to be a full person. That she felt hollowed out, empty, without substance. Like me. I understood what she was talking about, Weatherall."

Elizabeth snorted. "If that's what you think, then why don't all executive males suicide, Sedgewick? Yourself, for instance?"

"Because we're not like Zeldin," Sedgewick said, his gaze drifting back onto Elizabeth's face. "We're weak. Instead, we drink. Or plug in. Or engage in more outwardly destructive behavior."

"Zeldin didn't know what she was talking about." Elizabeth leaned forward and braced her hands on the desk, wishing it weren't between them so that she could get right up into his face. "She made up this whole death of self stuff because she felt sorry for herself. She didn't like surrendering. She didn't like losing."

"No," Sedgewick said. "She was suffering. It wasn't a game for her. What you did to her was more than she could bear. Just because she wasn't raving doesn't mean she didn't crack. In some way she did crack, or she would have gone on fighting you. But she didn't crack all the way, for she was still detached enough from her turmoil to know that she wanted to die. Maybe she saw herself disintegrating, Weatherall. Only gradually and not all at once."

The world seemed to have shrunk to a tight, airless membrane surrounding and binding herself and Sedgewick together. *Are human beings so little to you? Or was it something about me that drove you to extinguish me?* "We weren't talking about what Zeldin felt, thought, or said, Sedgewick. The question was why you killed her. And I think I've answered that." Elizabeth stared straight into his eyes. "How she terrified you, when she not only challenged but betrayed you. You realized then that you'd never controlled her. And that you never would. And then when I gave you another chance, when I'd made her safe for you, you couldn't get past that fear. All that I did was wasted on you, wasn't it."

"Get out of here, bitch," he whispered, and Elizabeth saw that he was trembling. "Get out of here, now. The sight of you makes me sick. The sound of your voice talking about *her*, so far above anything you could ever be——" His voice rose—— "Get out, Weatherall, now!" He jerked to his feet and stood in advanced challenge stance, his white-knuckled fists in prominent display.

Elizabeth left his office without saying another word. He would probably start drinking, though she had not intended that when she'd introduced the subject. The answer to that question had been something she had needed to know for herself. She felt positive that if Zeldin had lived—if Sedgewick had refused to kill her—she would have found a way to live on that island. Without the closet, without solitary, without being locked up in an underground cell twenty-four hours a day, Zeldin would have bounced back, she was such a damned resilient woman. Sedgewick must have pressed her too far, must have lost control of himself or given signs of his eventually losing control

of himself, making Zeldin fear the future with him, fear being swallowed up in his paranoid solipsism.

In her office Elizabeth stood at the window and stared out at the
many other tall buildings around, still and silent and deserted. In DC,
only Security and Military offices saw much activity during the weekend. *I want to ask you how you could think so little of me? How could
you think so little of me that you could destroy me for so slight a purpose?* No, Kay, no, there was nothing slight about it. It was a grand,
important, essential purpose. Maybe I was wrong. Maybe I didn't
have enough faith in my own ability to manipulate the Executive
without Sedgewick fronting for me. Maybe it would have been better if they'd been forced to openly acknowledge me. I might not be
at this *point-non-plus* now if I'd had to find a way to manage without
Sedgewick. You knew how much I admired you, I know you did. You
were only writing that night out of fear of the unknown, your old fear
of Sedgewick overwhelming you at your most vulnerable moment. It
was his fault. If he hadn't killed you everything would have turned
out differently.

If, if, if… The knock on the door pulled Elizabeth out of the conversation she was having with Zeldin in her head. Hazel, it was Hazel,
she thought, moving blindly to the door. She opened it and through
the blur of tears let Hazel in. As she closed the door Hazel exclaimed,
"Liz, what is it? You're crying again! Sweetheart, what is going on
with you?" She pulled Elizabeth close, and Elizabeth clung to her.

After maybe a minute Elizabeth drew back and wiped her eyes
and offered Hazel a tremulous smile. "Don't pay attention to it. I think
I'm just tired, darling. Apart from which my life is in cataclysm—but
that is something we'll have to talk about once we have that horrid
report out of the way."

"I have it here," Hazel said, holding out a folder to Elizabeth.

Something in Hazel's tone made Elizabeth examine her face. "Let
me look it over, see if anything needs changing, and then give it to
Sedgewick to sign. After that you can get a page—no, it's Saturday,
there won't be any—we'll round up a courier, then, so it can be hand-
delivered to Booth's office. Have a seat while I skim through it."

Elizabeth took the folder to her desk and read through the report with a red pen handy, in case. But since she cared little about it

she chose to make no changes at all. Sedgewick should still be sober enough to sign his name, she thought sardonically as she went across the hall.

Sedgewick was listening to Beethoven and drinking scotch. Elizabeth put the last page of the report and a pen in front of him. "Sign. It's Booth's report."

He scrawled his initials without speaking to her, and she left without saying anything more. They both knew what was happening. Sedgewick did not care, and Elizabeth considered this drunk a means of keeping him out of her hair and completely unaware of her doings.

Elizabeth sent Hazel to arrange for the report to be hand-delivered and then, pacing, began to consider how to convince the girl to take up a life of uncertainty and danger with her. One qualm troubled her, though: once she told Hazel her intentions, Hazel would be implicated. If Hazel did not want to defect with her, then she would have to go to Sedgewick or internal security—which meant Wedgewood—with what Elizabeth told her, since if she didn't do that and didn't take flight with Elizabeth, she would most certainly be treated as an accessory before the fact and charged with treason. The thought made Elizabeth sick. So Hazel would be caught in having to make the choice between going with Elizabeth, betraying her, or finding herself charged with treason. How could Elizabeth find out whether Hazel would be willing to go with her without forcing that kind of a choice on her? Did she even have the right to force such a choice on another person?

On her return, Hazel said: "So you'll be going back to Seattle tomorrow?"

Elizabeth bit her lip. "I'm hoping you'll come with me too, darling."

"My instructor was pretty p-o'd about my missing class last week," Hazel said.

Elizabeth laughed. "That's too bad, isn't it. Those security people take themselves too seriously. Though of course the precautions they teach are essential in the long run. Still, they can be a bit myopic, not to say paranoid."

"It all seems pretty strange to me," Hazel said. "But then everyone around here is off-the-wall compared to the Justice Department."

"I daresay," Elizabeth said. She seated herself on the sofa and patted the cushion. "Will you sit with me for a while?" Hazel plumped down beside her and let Elizabeth take her hand. "You don't like working in Security, do you," Elizabeth said.

Hazel's mouth twisted, and she sighed. "Not really."

"It's the people?"

"I like you, and Ms. Lennox, and Ms. Bennett," Hazel said. "But everyone else…I don't know, this place makes me feel anxious, maybe sometimes even scared." Hazel's eyes widened. "That man who was here yesterday, MacPhereson was his name, I think. Anyway, there was something about him that gave me the major creeps. Something mean-looking."

"Yes," Elizabeth said, "that's MacPhereson, all right." And what would Hazel say to Wedgewood, if she thought MacPhereson gave off nasty vibes?

"But that's not all." Hazel dropped her gaze. "I probably shouldn't say this." She glanced at Elizabeth, then shook her head. "No. It's better if I don't. Not now."

Elizabeth held Hazel's gaze steady. "You don't have to worry about losing your job, Hazel. I promise you. But I want you to be honest with me. It's important."

Hazel swallowed. "I don't know, Liz. You see, I don't really know exactly what's what in Security. I mean, it's okay to be critical in Departments like Justice, where things are a little less, ah, involved. But here, loyalty seems to be so stressed…"

Elizabeth squeezed Hazel's hand. "Tell me," she said quietly. "I know you aren't a security risk, darling. It's between you and me. A lovers' secret. Okay?"

Hazel studied Elizabeth's eyes before speaking. "Inputting that report made me sick, Liz. I know those women are the enemy, but there's something truly horrible about what you're planning to do."

Elizabeth's heart lifted with wild hope. "I think it's truly horrible, too. And I don't want to be a party to it." Elizabeth's voice dropped to a near-whisper. "I quarreled fiercely with Sedgewick about it—that's when he slapped me, darling—and got nowhere. And I even warned them that if they go through with this plan, the aliens will destroy the US and bring down the Executive. But they wouldn't listen to me." She paused—and resisted the temptation to check again that the jamming system was functioning. She studied Hazel's eyes, trying to read the girl's thoughts. "I don't know whether to continue this discussion or not," she said. "Once we go past a certain point…" Elizabeth thought she saw understanding steal into Hazel's eyes.

"You can trust me, Liz," she whispered.

"It's not that, exactly," Elizabeth said. "It's that once we go past a certain point in our discussion…" She raised her eyebrows. "What I'm saying, darling, is I'd be putting you in the position of having to choose between loyalty to Security—upon which you swore an oath when you took the job—or loyalty to me."

"You make it sound so serious," Hazel said.

"It is serious."

She nodded. "I don't think you'd be wanting to talk to me about it if it weren't important. Go on, Liz. Tell me."

For a moment Elizabeth felt bewildered—never could she have imagined such a scene: not only having this particular discussion, but having it with someone like Hazel. Hazel was as far from her notion of a service-tech as she could be and still remain identifiably such. Her strength, her intelligence, her *confidence* in her own self continually made Elizabeth forget to exercise her usual control. Hazel lent *her* support and confidence, and not the other way around as it had always been with any other lover she had had working under her.

Everything had turned upside-down, topsy-turvy, inside-out. She, Elizabeth, was thinking of defecting, perhaps even of sabotaging a priority-one operation. She was sitting here preparing to launch into a discussion of treason with her service-tech lover-secretary. "I'm thinking seriously of leaving Security," Elizabeth said, her gaze boring into Hazel's. "And to leave Security means going AWOL, for Sedgewick won't willingly let me go. He's variously threatened to kill me or put me into solitary detention if I openly attempt to leave. I tried to quit just before you came to work here, with the result of his threatening me with those things." Elizabeth licked her lips. "I'm also thinking of sabotaging the operation discussed in the report you inputted this morning."

Hazel paled; her eyes grew large and dark. "Do you really think he would do that, Liz? Kill you or lock you up? It sounds—crazy!"

Elizabeth sketched a smile. "But that's the point, darling. Sedgewick *is* crazy. He's been crazy for a long time. And I don't think I can take his craziness any longer. Not when the Executive is in their own way crazy, too." The Executive, Elizabeth realized, had never acknowledged the existence and power of the aliens. They paid lip-service to their belief in the aliens' existence, but for all practical purposes, except for refraining from bombing the Free Zone, they insisted upon acting as though the aliens were not there. If that wasn't crazy, what was?

"Why are you telling me this, Liz?" Hazel asked, her eyes intensely watchful.

Elizabeth's eyes prickled. "Because I'm hoping you'll agree to go with me."

Hazel continued to stare at her. After perhaps half a minute she said, "I'll have to now, won't I."

"You're so quick," Elizabeth said, her eyes filling with tears. "It's either that or turn me in—or risk your life saying nothing and then being found out later when they question you. You know that if you stay they'll interrogate you with loquazene, because of your relationship with me."

Hazel shivered. "I want to go with you, Liz." She looked away. "Because I don't want to lose you. I'm too involved. Not that I wanted that to happen. But yesterday, I realized..." She looked back at Elizabeth. "But what will we do? Where can we go? How can we live? They'll be looking for us, won't they?"

"Yes," Elizabeth said. Her heart grew huge with happiness. Everything was terrible, but that Hazel felt this way made everything wonderful, too. "They'll be looking for us, all right. But we'll have fake IDs, fake plastic accounts, and I have jewels and other assets that will be useful. I'm hoping to be able to liquidate some of my stocks and bonds, though I can't count on that working out. Most of my assets are in that kind of paper. With money and plastic—and, I hope, my being able to wipe our prints from all readily accessible data records—we'll have a good chance. I haven't decided yet where to go. Or even when. But I think it will have to be from the Free Zone, which will give us certain advantages since the Free Zone lacks the density of the Security network that's maintained over the rest of the continent."

"It's incredible," Hazel said. "I can't believe it. It's like being in one of those old movies."

Elizabeth smiled bitterly. "True romance, don't you think, darling? Only it won't be much fun, I'm afraid. But whatever happens, I promise I'll take care of you. If it comes down to it I'll manage a way to fix things up for you, even if I…" She sighed. "What's the point of talking about the negative possibilities? We must simply be careful in everything we do, plan everything with great diligence, thoroughness, and exactitude. We're pretty smart, both of us. If any two people can manage, we can."

Elizabeth could hardly believe Hazel had agreed so easily to a life on the run, uprooted and dangerous. How soon would they get tired of it—if, say, they could not find a place for themselves? But they would, Elizabeth insisted to herself. They would find a place, a niche; they would make a new life. There *were* possibilities. All she had to do was think of them.

Chapter Twenty-four

[i]

Celia woke early, before the light began filtering through the thick plastic panels of the temp-shelter, and listened to the breathing snoring muttering of the twenty-three other women lying all around her. She shivered in the pre-dawn cold, despite the wool socks and sweater she had worn to bed. Her thoughts hovered over the same ground that had preoccupied her since her arrival at the camp.

No one in the camp had openly speculated about what ODS might be intending, at least not loudly enough for her to hear. As one of only two professional women in the entire camp, she found herself isolated. She could see the suspicion in the other prisoners' eyes and in the way they held their bodies when she passed near them. She did not know how to reassure them, how to break through the wall of hostility. They were less suspicious of the other professional—a professor—who had not revealed her comprehension of Spanish. Could they tell that she hadn't learned Spanish at her mother's knee (apart from those few mother-child expressions that Elena's mother had used to Elena and Elena in turn to Celia, expressions not likely to come up in adult conversation) but in school?

Celia pulled her knees more tightly against her chest. When the camp authorities had ordered them to assemble and had spouted all that nonsense about human rights violations and outside monitors and the option of emigration, the detainees had stood stone-faced, and several had hissed. The ODS official had simply shrugged his shoulders and left, implying that he didn't care whether they believed his story or not.

How many of them were there? Close to a thousand, Celia guessed. And of that thousand perhaps ten percent were women. Idle and angry, the men milled around the camp; and already many of the youth had begun forming into gangs. Most of them came from the LA and Bay areas, where excessive violence had been common since the Blanket. Not that there wasn't youth violence in Hillcrest, but Celia's experience of Hillcrest bore little resemblance to what one might experience in certain parts of East LA, for instance...

There had been a number of sociological studies about the secondary effects of the economic crash that had followed the Blanket, causing a lengthy disruption of K-12 education and the temporary loss of service-tech jobs during the Civil War. Such disruptions and instability had unsettled an entire generation of young people—or so the sociologists claimed. Celia doubted that conscription into military service (which she herself had only narrowly escaped) for the duration of the Global War had helped.

Celia took care to stick close to the other women and tried to keep as far away from the males as she could. She needed no one to tell her that the ODS guards were there to make sure no prisoner escaped, not to protect the prisoners from one another.

Ignoring the pressure on her bladder, she rolled over and positioned her body on the spot already warmed. ODS, she was being held by ODS. She clung to the thought as though the knowledge itself could somehow help her. Would Emily be able to help her this time? She already owed the favor of Elena's release to that woman who had influence with ODS. Surely Emily had her hands full simply seeing to her own safety without trying to find Celia and get her released. And this detention was different. As far as she could tell, all of them were political, and in her experience, politicals were usually kept in isolation and not thrown together into a freely mingling mass. It stood to reason that whatever ODS had planned would be terrible.

Every prisoner in the camp knew it, too.

[ii]

"I suppose I shouldn't have let myself hope," Martha said to Sorben as they walked along the waterfront. "I know Maureen never let herself trust Elizabeth Weatherall the way some of us did."

"I've met her, you know."

Martha glanced sidelong at the Marq'ssan. "Who? Elizabeth Weatherall?"

"Yes. That time we went to pick up Kay in DC and she had us transport Sedgewick to an island in the north Atlantic. Weatherall was with Sedgewick, and we took her to the island, too."

"Elizabeth didn't mention that."

Sorben's lips twitched into a near-smile. "No, I don't imagine she would have. So what do you recommend next, Martha?"

Martha sighed. "I think we're going to have to exert more pressure, Sorben. Granted, I'm afraid of what might happen if we make them feel *too* pressured. They might very well begin to consider their victims as hostages." Martha halted, so Sorben did, too. Martha looked directly into the Marq'ssan's face. "That's what frightens me so much about this situation. It's different from all the other times, because we're interfering with what they consider to be their legal prerogatives. And precisely because of our interference they know that the safety of those people matter to us." Martha bit her lip. "Or at least I *think* they know that. Unless they assume we're as cynical as they are and are just trying to make a *cause célèbre* out of it?"

Sorben frowned. "We could go for a target—I'm thinking of TNC, something in the communications industry for a change—or else we could try something new—blanketing one discrete area, as a reminder…" She raised her eyebrows at Martha. "What do you think? Would throwing that kind of scare into them help?"

Martha struggled to conceptualize the immediate practical consequences as well as long-range retaliation each of these tactics might entail. She said, "What about a military target. Since a blanket, however localized, would inevitably mean even more repression than they're already using."

"That's a possibility, though I don't know if it will catch their attention to the same extent," Sorben said thoughtfully. "Our problem is that we have a limited amount of energy for carrying out these destructurings, which means we need to choose carefully. And the problem with military targets is that they seem to have an infinite amount of arms and other hardware, which means they need only shift things around until they produce more. That's not true of their investments and resources at the production level."

"I see what you mean. Maybe you're right. Maybe it would have the effect of reminding them that you could do that to the entire country, which would, from their point of view, be worse than your doing it to the whole world."

Sorben started them moving again. "And now the big question. Are you ready for the Steering Committee meeting?"

Martha watched a ferry nosing into dock. "I think so," she said. "It will be hard-going, but I think I know what I have to say. Whether people listen or not is another thing, but at least I will have said it. Louise will be furious with me, for sure. She still refuses to admit the Night Patrol's killings are wrong. But I can't let what Louise thinks influence me."

"I'm glad to hear you say that," Sorben said. "This has been a problem since the start, but one you and many others refused to see or deal with."

The ferry inched into its berth and was locked into place. They were close enough now that Martha could see the couple dozen brightly clad bicyclists waiting on the deck. "I know that—now," Martha said. "I only hope we can learn from this and not be destroyed by it. Our crises tend to be situations we merely weather, merely survive, with the net effect being negative. Like the reproduction issue: we made a compromise, but we never really came to terms with the problem. Everyone was left sour and bitter, locked into their own interests and opinions. I hope this won't be the same."

"You must make sure that it isn't," Sorben said, somewhat sternly, Martha felt. But then the Marq'ssan turned her head and gave Martha a warm, full smile. "I have confidence in you, Martha."

Martha fairly glowed. "I'll do my best," she promised.

The ferry's horn sounded. Martha's gaze went to the boat, and she saw the barrier rising. And the swarm of bicyclists raced off, the vanguard of the off-load.

[iii]

Elizabeth talked encouragement to Hazel all the way to National. And when Hazel made to peel the plastic from her fingertips, Elizabeth stopped her. "No, darling, you mustn't, not until we've vanished. We don't want them lifting our prints from the plane or our hotel, or any of the cars."

Hazel said, "I forgot. I wasn't even thinking when I started picking at the plastic."

Less able to cope with staying up two nights in a row than Elizabeth, Hazel's face was white with exhaustion. There was so much they'd had to do that at about three that morning Elizabeth had begun to think they wouldn't get it all done in time. But Hazel—in disguise—had even managed to get Elizabeth's parcels to the air-express place near the office—though the timing had been close. Emily would be getting the parcels within twenty-four hours, along with Elizabeth's note asking her to keep them for her. Whether Emily would do so, Elizabeth did not know, but she did know that if she had left them behind she'd have had no chance of ever seeing them again. And Elizabeth found the thought of losing the Bourgeois so shortly after acquiring it unbearable.

"It won't be long, darling, before you can relax a little," Elizabeth said. The girl's pallor made her freckles almost heartbreakingly visible. "When we get to the hotel you can go straight to bed with a pill, and I'll give orders that you're not to be disturbed for anything." Elizabeth stroked the girl's hair and spoke in her most soothing voice. When would it hit her, Elizabeth wondered, *really* hit her? When it did, she might well be angry and feel she had been railroaded. The fact was, even if Elizabeth had said nothing to her, Hazel would have suffered. She would at the very least have been fired...

Planting explosives in her own and Sedgewick's offices, set to go off at four the next morning... Elizabeth had hated doing it; she knew casualties were possible even at that hour. But how else could she assure the destruction of those thousands of flimsies with her prints on them? Though she had wiped everything she could, she knew there remained innumerable other sources. It had taken hours to wipe her apartment, literally *hours*. She had destroyed many of her things precisely because her prints were on them and she lacked the time for wiping them all.

Once the bombs had detonated, the entire Executive would know. But of course they would probably know sometime on Tuesday, anyway.

The car bypassed the terminal and drove straight out to the runway where the jet awaited them. Thank god they didn't check passengers coming off planes, Elizabeth thought, reviewing the plan, which called for her getting her small personal arsenal past SeaTac security.

When the car came to a stop, her gorillas opened both back doors. There on the tarmac she and Hazel were joined by Mastney, Serkin's contact-man, whose assignment was to stick with her. Elizabeth swept past him and boarded the plane, not quite smiling at the thought of how busy she would keep him during the next twenty-four hours. By the time the operation was over, he would look the fool just as much as Serkin and Sedgewick would. As for Sedgewick—she liked to think of him lying at home on the sofa, either drunk or sleeping it off. When Booth dumped him, would he even notice?

[iv]

Returning to her office after her meeting with Sorben, Martha found a message from Shoshana saying that she had "important and urgent" information that Martha needed to have as soon as possible. Martha phoned her at once, and Shoshana asked that Martha come downstairs to her office. Martha agreed, though reluctantly. She had always done her best to avoid the basement. She had been down there maybe three times since the building's construction.

In the basement, Women's Patrollers stopped her several times and asked her where she wanted to go and each time gave her directions. With so much "help," Martha had little trouble negotiating the maze of halls so unlike the rest of the building.

"Close the door and sit down, Martha," Shoshana said when Martha knocked at Shoshana's open door.

To make clear her intention not to stay long, Martha sat on the edge of the chair. Without preamble, she said, "What's going on?"

Shoshana's rich brown eyes gazed steadily at Martha. "Louise asked me to tell you several things and then give you updates as they are appropriate." She leaned back in her squeaky, high-backed swivel-chair. "A few days ago we discovered that David Hughes's gang of thugs were intending to kill Louise." Martha gasped. "You see, once we started concentrating on Hughes, we were able to learn quite a lot about his operations. We know who many of his agents are, for example, and we also know where the local gang of SIC officers hang out."

Martha fairly reeled with shock. *Kill Louise?* "Then David has been behind everything?"

"He certainly seems to be one of the chief organizers," Shoshana said. "But there's more."

"Go on." A bad feeling settled into Martha's gut.

"Louise is at this very moment—" Shoshana checked her watch— "carrying out an operation for capturing Hughes and penetrating the executive enclave where the SIC are based. If she has to, she will kill the SIC people, but she is hoping to take them captive—and to get evidence of SIC's activities in the Free Zone." As she spoke, Shoshana's dark face grew radiant. "She thinks we'll be able to present some of it at the Steering Committee meeting."

Martha felt suddenly weak, as though all the blood were draining out of her body. "Louise is going to *kidnap* these people?" As Martha tried to take in the second shocker, a manic surge of energy overrode her body's initial response. "We've got to stop her!" Martha sprang to her feet and rushed to the door.

"Martha, wait!" Shoshana got to her feet and came around the desk. "You can't do anything now, it's too late. Louise instructed me not to tell you until the whole thing was well under way. She wanted you to be able to prepare for what will happen once the thing is brought off. She thinks this exposé will be far more important than anything else that might be discussed at the Steering Committee meeting."

Martha leaned back against the wall. "Of course," she said bitterly. "I might have known Louise would pull some kind of stunt for diverting public concern over the Night Patrol." She pressed her lips together. "But I can tell you right now that I won't let the subject be swept under the rug." Martha wondered what that gray metal or plastic thing encircling Shoshana's right earlobe was. Jewelry? Or a piece of electronics? She crossed her arms and stared into Shoshana's eyes. "Are you involved with the Night Patrol yourself?" she asked pointblank.

Shoshana did not so much as blink. "Since the Women's Patrol is in solidarity with the Night Patrol," she said, "none of us will answer that question if we are asked." Her eyes narrowed. "Not everyone thinks the way you and your friends think, Martha."

"Yes," Martha said, "I know that." She glared at the intransigence in Shoshana's face and posture. "But everything will come out in the end. You can count on that, whatever disaster Louise causes with this latest paramilitary escapade."

"We'll see," Shoshana said expressionlessly. "We'll see."

[v]

After they'd checked into the hotel and unpacked a few of their things, Elizabeth and Hazel relaxed in the Jacuzzi. The latex gloves they wore to protect their fingertips even more than exhaustion kept it from becoming sexual, as their baths together usually did. Afterwards Elizabeth gave Hazel a sedative and tucked her into bed; Elizabeth then got into bed herself, kissed Hazel lightly on the forehead, and undertook a brief session of self-hypnosis to replenish her own energy. Then she returned to the sitting room.

The meeting at the airport with Goodwin had been short and sharp. She had established that Mastney was to give Goodwin the minimal briefing necessary to ensure that the station would not get in their way yet be prepared to lend support if necessary. So for the moment, at least, Elizabeth felt fairly safe from detection. The trickiest part would be making arrangements for a car without Mastney's or her gorillas' knowledge, and for this reason, she had decided to take Margot Ganshoff into her confidence. The other matter still up in the air was what to do about Greenglass and her people. Elizabeth would have to contact Greenglass, soon, since if she didn't, Serkin would begin wondering why she hadn't already made arrangements for a meeting.

Staring out at Elliott Bay—silvery gray, shimmering almost white under a heavy, lowering sky—Elizabeth told herself she had to make her decision before meeting with Greenglass. Her mind, though, persisted in wandering onto a subject that always seemed to haunt her whenever she was in Seattle. *You and I would have made a great team, Kay Zeldin.* There had been a time when that had been a powerfully seductive thought. But she had to forget that woman, Elizabeth told herself. *This is nothing to do with her, nothing at all. Only to the extent that Sedgewick has acted upon us are our lives and courses similar. I may be a renegade, but I'm not that kind of renegade. Never would I support anarchy. Never.*

Elizabeth turned her back on the view and collected herself—and in a lightning flash of insight realized that she didn't need to think, that she already knew what she had to do. She strode to the house handset, picked it up, and asked the operator for the Co-op's general exchange. When Co-op information came on the line, Elizabeth requested that she be connected with Martha Greenglass. To her surprise, Greenglass answered. "Martha, this is Elizabeth Weatherall," she said. "I'm back in Seattle and hoping we may resume negotiations."

"Oh! You're in Seattle *now?*" After a lengthy pause, Greenglass said, "Your timing is a little off, Elizabeth. The Steering Committee meeting begins tomorrow and will probably continue through the week. I'm afraid we won't be able to resume negotiations until its conclusion."

Elizabeth almost laughed with relief. She was off the hook! Except…Central would expect her to return to DC at once. She would have to stall Serkin by giving him the impression that she might be able to change Greenglass's mind. "Could we—the two of us, Martha, you and me—meet this afternoon, anyway?"

"I don't know, Elizabeth." Greenglass sounded abstracted, as though she were hardly paying attention to the conversation. "Things are more than a little hectic around here. We're all involved in last minute preparations…"

"A drink before dinner, perhaps?"

"Well…tentatively. As long as you understand there's a good chance I'll have to cancel."

"I'll understand if you do," Elizabeth said quickly. "There are a few things I'd like to discuss with you, sort of as preparation. To go in tandem with our efforts."

"I'll do my best. And now I really have to go." Greenglass's voice came from a distance. Elizabeth thought she heard voices in the background.

"Thanks very much," Elizabeth said just as Greenglass disconnected.

She alerted her driver and went into the bedroom to dress.

[vi]

In response to Martha's emergency call, the members of the Inner Circle assembled in the large, bug-swept conference room. When Martha had passed on the little Shoshana had told her, Maureen cursed Louise. "This will shoot our human rights activities out of the water!" she said. "How could Louise be so arrogant as to make such a decision without consulting any of us?"

Cora, of course, countered with the pragmatic view: "I see where she's coming from," she said, nodding thoughtfully, "trying for a diversion—and for revenge against the very people who dragged all this Night Patrol stuff into the open. But the question is whether the public will buy it."

"*Is* that the question?" Laura said. "I would have thought the question was a great deal more complicated than simply worrying about whether the Steering Committee meeting will be successfully diverted from pursuing Louise's involvement in the Night Patrol."

"And we should probably note," Lenore said, "that we don't know yet how serious this situation may become. Whether people will be killed, for instance."

The word *killed* shocked them into silence. After about half a minute, Martha put her handset to her ear. Shoshana answered at once. "Have you heard anything from Louise or any of the others yet?" Martha asked her.

"Just that their van successfully penetrated the enclave. They're in contact with the chopper, which is preparing to close in just as the van makes it to the house."

How, Martha wondered, would they have known where to go? Their leads could only have come from David. And he wouldn't— Martha shut off her speculation; she could not stand thinking about the details. "From now on I want you to keep us informed," Martha said. "We're up in the conference room. All of us but Louise." As soon as Martha put the phone down, it buzzed. Wondering if it could be Shoshana so soon (though knowing it couldn't be), Martha picked it up and said her name.

"Martha, this is Inez Monteforte. I'm calling from the main office; they tell me I'm only a few doors down from where you are now. Can you spare me some time? It's important that we talk, you and I."

Inez Monteforte in Seattle? "Inez, hello," Martha said, trying to make her voice friendly and easy. "I didn't know you were in town." Martha tried to think. She couldn't spare time for trading business just now, not while they were waiting to see what kind of disaster Louise was precipitating. But she didn't want to offend Inez, either.

"Magyyt brought me," Inez said. "Perhaps I should say up front that this is about something more than trade, Martha."

That's just great. "We're in the middle of a crisis," Martha said. In spite of her good intentions, her tone was stiff. "I wonder if we couldn't meet later in the day and—"

"*Please*, Martha. Magyyt is returning for me at five."

Martha bit her lip. "I'll be right there," she said. After all, they were doing nothing here but waiting, speculating, and wrangling. She might as well see what Inez had come for. "I'm going out for a bit to talk to a Guatemalan who Magyyt has brought especially to talk to me," Martha told Venn (who, as usual, was observing rather than participating in the discussion). "If Shoshana calls with more news, please come out and find me. The main office will know where I am."

Venn said, "Lucky you. While the rest of us are stuck here, waiting."

En route to the lounge, Martha wondered why Magyyt had brought Inez for such a short period of time. It had been three or four years since Martha had last seen her: the six collectives Inez represented had maintained the same trade arrangements for years with only minor alterations, which they'd been handling via email correspondence.

Martha found Inez pacing the lounge, around and around the circular room, her gaze bent to the rug, her steps following one of its long spiral arms. At Martha's approach, she looked up. Her bony face burned with excitement; her body held the tension of a coiled spring. "Martha, Martha." Smiling, she held out her hands.

Martha clasped the offered hands. "It's been a long time, Inez."

"Seattle has changed," she exclaimed. "And this building! It's all for the Co-op?"

"Yes. You should see our assembly hall—we finally have something that gets us away from that square-box confrontational setting. More like on the Marq'ssan's starship."

Inez sighed. "Oh, how long *that's* been, Martha. I sometimes get nostalgic, you know?"

"So do I," Martha said. "Everything seemed simpler back then."

"But why? You have your Free Zone, just like our friends in what used to be parts of southern Mexico and Brazil," Inez said. "Which is more than we can say in Guatemala."

"Shall we sit?" Martha asked. "And would you like something to drink? Coffee or water?"

"Water, please."

They settled on the floor with a glass of water each. Martha studied Inez's face. "Your visit is so brief," she said, refraining from asking Inez outright why she had come. Martha had long ago learned to avoid direct approaches with people who weren't North Americans.

Inez sipped, then set her glass down on the rug. "I've come to ask the PNW Free Zone to include us in their campaign for the protection of human rights. And maybe we can help with coordination with the other Zones. I'm sure they will all want to be involved." Her gaze bored into Martha's. "Since the Blanket there have been problems in our country, too. Our model executive system seems to be having difficulty." Inez pronounced the words *model executive system* ironically. An "experiment" undertaken by the corporate consortium that had taken overt control of the country in the thirties, Guatemala's executive system was held to be nearly perfect—supposedly with most of the population living in perfect contentment and prosperity, the economy ideal, the environment protected, and health and education benefits the best in the Western hemisphere. "There's been an upsurge of dissidence," Inez said. "Though there were a few dissidents before the Blanket, they weren't genuine threats to the system and thus though harassed were tolerated. As were dissidents in the US before the Blanket, as I'm sure you recall."

Inez, Martha now remembered, always insisted on giving historical background to everything she intended to say, as though she found it impossible not to review the historical context in which the current situation was embedded whenever she spoke of it.

"With the growth of dissidence and the escalating repression, there has been a spiral." Inez's hands literally described a spiral, a good deal tighter than the ones depicted in the rug they were sitting on. "Naturally the economy has had a great deal to do with this situation." Inez's hands—the fingers spread, the palms down—plunged, then leveled. "The issue people seem most mobilized around, however, is Birth Limitation—on two fronts: on the old religious grounds and of course on the old ethical grounds that the Indian minority is being reduced nearly to extinction." Her right hand lifted, its wrist turning her palm up. "Religious groups, especially, are coming into increasing prominence in focusing discontent."

Martha darted in with a question as Inez paused to draw breath: "How do you mean, include you?"

Inez leaned forward; her hands, now vertical, extended towards Martha. "We wish to join our protests against human rights violations in Guatemala with yours against such violations in the United States. And to expand your offer of asylum to Guatemalan victims. I believe you know Carla Jiminez, of the Mexican Free Zone?" Martha nodded. "I spoke with her about this last week. Although they are happy to provide asylum, the Mexican Free Zone lacks connections with governments that the PNW and the Korean Free Zones have. And so it makes sense, Carla thinks, to join forces with the PNW Free Zone since they've already got such an arrangement in place with the Netherlands, Austria, and Greece. We are hoping, with your help, to get those governments to accept Guatemalan human rights refugees in their embassy in Guatemala City."

Martha bit her lip. She could just imagine what the three consuls she had been dealing with would say to *that.*

Inez's gaze fairly plunged into Martha's. "You must see that you can't stop with the United States. You must see that there must be an international effort, with wide international cooperation. And that all the Free Zones must be consulted and brought into the effort."

Martha could see that, much yes. Presuming the Night Patrol scandal didn't blow up in their faces. "It sounds like a wonderful idea, Inez. But I'm having trouble seeing the whole picture. I mean, this sounds like the sort of thing that could mushroom into something..." She shrugged. "What I mean is, we can be reasonably certain that there are few governments innocent of such violations. Can we handle the issue on that kind of scale, even if all the Zones work together? Our between-zone coordination efforts are still so new. Imagine the sorts of politics that will come into it, in the UN." The very thought of it seemed nightmarish in its proportions—not simply the fact of tens—maybe even hundreds—of thousands of people being acknowledged as victims, but the political complexity of forcing confrontation on such a scale. They were already having trouble with the US Executive alone, even with a segment of the international community supporting their position. But were they to begin really coordinating between zones and focusing attention on the violations of other governments, they would surely lose that support at once. Executives world-wide would consider all the zones working together that way a major threat to their existence.

"The UN?" Inez's tone was scoffing. "It would be a mistake to attempt to do anything through them! They represent the very governments we will be fighting."

"Yes, but we've got to think this thing through," Martha said. "And make contact with others world-wide. We must set up some sort of communication network so that we can act in concert."

"That is, I believe, what I have been saying." Inez produced a faint smile. "We already know that several Brazilian women's groups, both inside and outside the New Brazil Free Zone, are prepared to join us. Magyyt has been—"

Frowning at someone or something behind Martha, Inez halted. Martha turned to see Venn making a beeline across the room towards them. "Sorry to interrupt," Venn said, nodding down at Inez. "But Martha, we've just heard from Shoshana."

Martha touched Inez's wrist. "I'm sorry," she said, "but I'm going to have to go back into the conference. We're in the middle of a serious emergency. I agree that it's very important that we talk. And with others, too." Martha levered herself off the floor. "I don't quite know what to... If I'd known you were coming we could have arranged for you to visit one of our clinics..."

Inez got to her feet, too, and stooped to pick up their empty glasses. She said, "I understand, Martha. Return to your conference. But if there's the slightest chance we can talk before Magyyt returns for me...?"

"Just keep in touch with the office," Martha said. "Certainly the immediacy of this situation will not hold through the entire day."

And yet, Martha thought as she and Venn raced back to the conference room, it could—if it got worse. When they were safely inside with the door closed, Martha—shutting her ears to the discussion going on at the table—said, "Tell me, Venn: what has been happening?"

"Louise and her people have taken over the house the SIC headquarters is in." Venn looked angry but resigned. "They had a stowaway in the van David Hughes was driving and several people concealed near the compound entrance, waiting for him to be passed in through the electronically-controlled barrier. As soon as he was admitted to the compound surrounding the house, the stowaway took him captive and was joined by the others, who'd sneaked in along with the van. They used him as a hostage to get inside the house. According to Shoshana, they are now holding half a dozen more people—everyone who was in the house when they took it—hostage, as well. Three of Louise's people have been wounded—Shoshana has already arranged for medical support to be sent in. Since the people inside the house didn't respond well to the hostage scenario, they—Louise and her people, I mean—used some kind of crowd-control gas to incapacitate them. According to Shoshana, Louise's crew is combing through documents now, looking for incriminating evidence."

"My god," Martha whispered. "I don't believe they managed to do it! I didn't think Louise and her women were capable of it!"

Venn's mouth twisted. "Just what was it you thought they were doing out at Farley's, Martha? Or on the other side of the Cascades in the more rigorous training camps? What *I* wonder is how they got the gas. It's apparently the stuff that ODS uses to quell demonstrations and riots. I didn't realize it was so easily available."

Martha and Venn resumed their places at the table. Cora was urging that they arrange for a global vid monopoly in order to expose whatever heinous evidence was found in the house in Edmonds. Maureen, though, countered with the argument that the less international attention the better, since the major image projected would be one of female warriors successfully pulling off a commando raid against the SIC, which was not a positive or in any way useful image for the Free Zone to be projecting. But Cora insisted: "Knowledge of this thing will be out in no time at all. Our only option is controlling how it's framed. We need to put the emphasis on these SIC agents' attack on the people of the Free Zone and our ability to take care of ourselves just fine, and not get into the position of defending ourselves against the Executive's spin. Since the world will be discussing it anyway, we might as well reap some advantage from it."

"You know damned well that when the Executive dismisses it as terrorist activity the media and government officials around the world will repeat the phrase," Martha said. "And that the Executive will present the SIC's presence in the Free Zone as a part of their on-going attempt to recover the Free Zone from the illegal control of the rebels that the Marq'ssan support. I can already hear their rhetoric, Cora, and considering the propaganda apparatus they have in place it will be rhetoric that will be repeated until this whole thing is allowed to die. And if," Martha plowed on when Cora tried to take the floor back, "we try to talk about the heinousness of the SIC's plans against us—for instance their plan to assassinate Louise—they'll say that the plan would have been carried out by local citizens desirous of ridding their city of a man-killer. And they'll say of all the other plans that only a handful of their people were involved, that there's a strong *resistance* movement afoot that the SIC is only *assisting*." Martha glanced around the table. "What Louise has done will now allow them to talk about 'freedom fighters.' Which is terminology they haven't had much of a chance to push before now, since they never dared move openly against us because of the Marq'ssan's protection of the Free Zone. But since *we* have now brought it out into the open, they'll take advantage of the opportunity." Martha fixed her gaze on Cora's face and folded her arms across her chest. "In short, Cora, their propaganda response will make mincemeat of us. And not vice versa."

Cora launched into a defense of her position and an attack on Martha's negativity. Martha recalled Inez and thought of how they should be bending their collective energies and skills toward the truly revolutionary vision Inez had conjured instead of closeting themselves in discussions of how to manipulate public opinion in defense of Louise's paramilitarism. If they weren't careful, Martha thought, they'd soon be living up to the many misapprehensions that made non-Co-op people think of them as a governing body. All Cora was thinking of was preserving the Co-op's *image*, whatever that was.

After twenty minutes, Martha had had enough. She rose from the table and signaled to Venn, Maureen, and Laura. She would talk with them first, alone, to see what they were thinking, and perhaps to tell them about Inez's proposal. Better to start a private discussion than continuing to argue with Cora. They needed a think session, not a debating field. They needed to think about what they should be doing instead of arguing about which point of view was most "productive."

As she stepped out it into the corridor Martha remembered that it had been Louise who had brought Cora into the group. For the first time, she could see why. They were peas in a pod, those two. But why had it taken her so long to realize it?

[vii]

Ganshoff eyed Elizabeth's face. "You look like hell," she said.

Elizabeth said, "We must talk."

Ganshoff's right eyebrow lifted. "By all means, let's do."

"Somewhere shielded."

Ganshoff smiled. "My dear Elizabeth, this room is fully shielded. This room, the Consul's office, and a room in the basement are all shielded."

Elizabeth frowned. "You're with an intelligence service?" she said bluntly. And would Ganshoff admit it if she were? The background research done on her had turned up no such indications. Still...

"And do only intelligence officers need shielded rooms?" Ganshoff shot Elizabeth an ironic look. "My dear, you surely must know there are important secrets in other areas besides security! We do a great deal of business through this office. And business always has its secrets." The expression on her face became openly derisive. "Or don't you intelligence people realize that?"

So she knew. Of course, that was bound to have happened. Margot Ganshoff was not stupid. She had probably known the morning after having dined with her. "Then you are aware of the position I've held in Security for years and years," Elizabeth said.

"That is so. I suppose you've come here with a proposal for weaning Austria away from its new ties with the Free Zone?"

Elizabeth shook her head. "No. My business is quite a bit more complicated and...delicate than that." She considered how to proceed. Delicate was almost an understatement. She studied the other woman's face, though she knew she would not see in it what she needed to be certain of. There was no way she would ever know for certain in advance. She, Elizabeth Weatherall, was gambling, was playing poker—a thing she had sworn never to do. But her days playing chess seemed to be over. "I need your help," she said at last. "I personally."

Ganshoff looked intensely interested. "Oh? Doing what?"

Elizabeth sensed the other woman biting back a piece of tempting facetiousness; she could see it in her face. "I'm leaving Sedgewick's employ," Elizabeth said bluntly—and shocked herself. "However, it is not with his consent. Nor with the consent of any of the Executive. I fully expect to be on the run from an excision team within twenty-four hours." Elizabeth chose to fabricate the excision team because telling Ganshoff the full truth would be too complicated—and humiliating. For all practical purposes, they might as well assume an excision team. It certainly would sound plausible to someone like Margot Ganshoff.

"You shock me." Ganshoff's eyes glittered with excitement. "And why are you doing such an incomprehensible thing? Are you by any chance going renegade?"

Elizabeth licked her lips. "My situation vis-à-vis Sedgewick and the Executive has become intolerable. I'm willing to trade some information vital to your human rights crusade with the Free Zone, for a small amount of practical help." Again Elizabeth shocked herself. She hadn't realized before she said the words that she had intended to make that kind of offer.

"I'm dying of curiosity," Ganshoff said. "How delicious it would be were Elizabeth Weatherall really going renegade."

"I suppose the main question here," Elizabeth said, the words sticking in her now dry throat, "is whether you will feel an obligation as an executive to turn in someone going renegade. Or whether you'd prefer to be practical and do business with me."

Ganshoff grinned. "That's easily answered, Elizabeth. I've always been, and always will be, a practical woman. I'm loyal to my government, of course, but I don't see how betraying you to your people could possibly be demanded by that loyalty." She leaned forward and dropped her voice. "But of course, you are so clever that you might not be telling me the truth. Perhaps you have some *dis*information you want to feed the Free Zone through me and you find this an amusing way of doing it."

Elizabeth's gaze held Ganshoff's. "But the very nature of my information will allay that suspicion," she said. "Security could have nothing to gain by making up such a thing."

"Okay," Ganshoff said noncommittally. "Go ahead. What is this information?"

"You aren't interested in knowing first what I will require of you in exchange?"

"My dear Elizabeth, your effrontery is magnificent!" Ganshoff laughed. "If your situation is what you say it is, then you're in no position to bargain. You'll have to take my good will on faith, won't you."

Elizabeth's stomach lurched. "Give me your word you won't betray me, even if you don't help me," she said in a voice as rock-hard and firm as she could make it.

Ganshoff waved a graceful hand. "But of course I won't betray you, my dear. I've already as much as said so."

"Your word."

Ganshoff sighed. "How tiresome of you. Very well, I give you my word, Elizabeth, that I won't betray you to your own people."

Elizabeth did not like the qualification implied in the wording of the promise, but felt compelled to accept it without further caviling. She drew a deep breath to do something she had never imagined doing, something it made her quiver even to contemplate doing. "Sedgewick has a plan for capturing the leaders of the Free Zone and the aliens," she said, at one blow violating decades of security-minded reserve, breaking decades of training. Her knees and calves trembled violently; she felt her upper lip twitch. "Through the plan to bring Free Zone monitors into detention centers," she added breathlessly. She gasped for breath. "I was to arrange with Greenglass for the aliens to bring her and other Free Zone leaders to one of those places. Sedgewick intends them to be taken hostage—Greenglass and her people as well as whatever aliens are there on the scene. And then, by using them as hostages, to lead the rest of the aliens into a trap."

Ganshoff burst out laughing. "You surely don't expect me to believe this, do you?"

"What do you mean?" Elizabeth asked in bewilderment.

"That Sedgewick is so stupid as to think he can trap the aliens!"

Elizabeth bit her lip. "He's crazy, Margot, not stupid. He and the Executive still don't take in the aliens. I can't get them to talk sense. They really do believe they can pull off such an operation."

Ganshoff shook her head. "They might be able to capture Greenglass, but the aliens will never be caught. Do you have any idea of how non-human they are? Have you considered at all how little you know about them? They can't be controlled, Elizabeth, not by force."

"*I* know that. But Sedgewick…Sedgewick lives in a dream world."

"You sound frustrated, my dear." Ganshoff's lips pursed into a smug little smile that infuriated Elizabeth.

"They have no intention at all of letting anyone take asylum in the Free Zone or any place else," Elizabeth said. "I suspect they might even try to hold hostage the people Greenglass wants to rescue. They're prepared to go to any lengths at this point. You can't count on rational behavior from them."

"How far developed *is* this plan?"

"Very well developed," Elizabeth said after a moment. "The only thing not in place is Greenglass. I've been sent here to maneuver her into playing her part. The plan designates tomorrow as Day One."

Ganshoff tsked. "Bad planning, my dear. Tomorrow is the opening of the Steering Committee meeting. Greenglass won't miss that for anything."

"But if doing it at once were made a condition of doing it at all?"

Ganshoff shrugged. "Then she'd certainly smell a rat." She looked thoughtfully out at the distant view of Elliott Bay. "But as it is, perhaps she might find it worthwhile missing the opening of the Steering Committee meeting precisely to *seem* to walk into the trap while turning the tables?" Margot's eyes moved back to Elizabeth. "It could be done, you know. With the aliens' help, Greenglass could expose the Executive's plan."

"Why bother taking the risk? Why not simply avoid walking into the trap?"

Ganshoff tilted her head to one side. "Because, my dear, if they don't take up this public proposal of Sedgewick's offer, the Free Zone will be open to censure. This way they can expose the truth of the matter and bring down even greater condemnation on the Executive's head. The whole thing stinks to high heaven, you know." Her eyes narrowed. "Or hadn't you noticed? I suppose your nostrils must be pretty damned calloused by now."

Elizabeth's cheeks flamed. "Thanks very much, Margot. You don't think moral scruples come into this for me?"

"You've been working for Sedgewick for how many years?"

Elizabeth let a beat pass before speaking. "So we can do business together?" She stared hard at Ganshoff, wishing she had a less transparent complexion.

Ganshoff nodded. "Yes, we can do business together. But I want to bring Greenglass in on this at once. You agree to that?"

Elizabeth stared out the window at the view of Lake Union in the middle distance and the Cascades on the horizon and tried to think. If Mastney got onto her meeting secretly with Ganshoff and Greenglass together, she'd be on her way back to DC in no time—in cuffs. "Yes," Elizabeth finally said. "I agree. But we must be extremely careful not to tip our hand to any of my people."

"Doesn't it strike you as absurd, your calling them your people?"

Elizabeth lowered her gaze and tried not to think about what Ganshoff was getting at. "Before we go any further, how about a glass of juice," she said. "I'm positively parched."

"Surely." Ganshoff got up and went to a small refrigerator hidden behind a cabinet door.

So, Elizabeth thought. *Alea jacta est.*

Chapter Twenty-five

[i]

Elizabeth was exhausted. She could not allow herself to go to bed, though, because Mastney's uptightness over the lack of contact with Greenglass had him on the verge of calling for an abort, which meant that the expected call from Greenglass or Ganshoff was vital. So she dozed in the arm chair as she waited. Mastney seemed not to know what to do with himself. When he started pacing, she irritably ordered him to go into his room to call the Edmonds station to see if any cables had been sent them from Central. He gave her a look that plainly said that if Central had cabled, the station would have notified them. But he said only "Yes, Ma'am" and left the room. Elizabeth nodded back to sleep. Let Mastney consume himself with anxiety: she herself was beyond nerves.

When a few minutes later her personal phone buzzed her awake, Elizabeth picked up the handset and muttered her name.

"I'm having trouble arranging a meeting," Ganshoff said. "Greenglass seems to be in the middle of some sort of crisis. And I'm not getting anywhere over the phone. So I think I'll pay her a visit at the Co-op Building. That's not far from where you are. Depending on how it goes, you can expect either to join us or receive a visit from me."

"Here?" Elizabeth said. This suite was the riskiest place they could meet.

"Don't worry, Elizabeth," Ganshoff said, her voice patronizingly soothing. "I can assure you, all will be well."

"Gee thanks," Elizabeth said. "I'm ever so glad to hear it."

Mastney returned shortly after she finished talking to Ganshoff. "Goodwin says nothing's come in." He advanced into the room and stood a couple of yards from her chair. "But there was something strange about our conversation."

Elizabeth scowled. "What do you mean?" Belatedly she remembered to keep her hands out of sight.

"I can't put my finger on it. A girl answered and put me through to him without even asking me to identify myself. Which was strange in itself. And then Goodwin said, 'We have heard nothing from Central all day, nothing at all.'" Mastney frowned. "Why would Goodwin tell me he'd heard nothing at all from Central all day? It's strange."

Elizabeth shrugged. "Maybe you caught him in the middle of something and he wasn't paying much attention to what he was saying."

Mastney shoved his hands into his tunic pockets. "Maybe *we* should cable Central. To let them know we're having problems getting Greenglass set up."

"No." Elizabeth shot him her meanest, coldest stare. "I say we wait until nine this evening before we call an abort. You don't know how fast these people can move. They're not like most governments, you know. They simply do a thing when the idea occurs to them."

"I don't like this uncertainty," Mastney said. "We should have planned for another day. Wednesday or Thursday, maybe."

"Sedgewick's in a hurry," Elizabeth said. "If I were you I'd hold off annoying him with the possibility of an abort." Sedgewick was probably oblivious to the whole operation, either pickled in scotch or lying on the sofa in the Georgetown house suffering the re-imposition of sobriety. But Mastney didn't need to know that: let him think Sedgewick was breathing down Serkin's neck. He'd be far more cautious about the kinds of cables he sent Central if he thought Sedgewick would be likely to be reading them first. "Surely you can find yourself something to do, Mastney," Elizabeth said. "You're obviously pre-operation hyper. I don't like jumpy people threatening to spoil everything on account of nerves."

That hit him like a bucket of cold water, Elizabeth thought, observing his reflexive straightening of his posture and squaring of his shoulders. "I'm an experienced operations officer," he said. "And I've been working with Serkin for twelve years. I know how he likes things done."

"And I've been working for Sedgewick for more than twenty years," Elizabeth said. "Now get out of here. Unlike you, I have an endless amount of work with which to occupy myself while I'm waiting."

He turned on his heel and left without speaking. How it galled male executives to have to defer to her, Elizabeth thought. Well, this would be one of the last times that would ever happen. Once Sedgewick knew she had gone, all such manifestations and consequences of her power would be things of the past.

[ii]

When Jan phoned Martha in the conference room to tell her that Margot Ganshoff was in the lounge next to the main office, Martha immediately thought of the possibility of Inez's still being there and of the potential disaster she could have on her hands if the two women got to talking to one another. "Please ask her to step down to my office," Martha said to Jan. Laura, Maureen, and Venn could continue to work on the others without her.

Martha arrived before Margot did. While she waited, she set out two half-liters of water and a glass on her desk.

"Very interesting, Martha," Margot said as she closed the door behind her.

Martha raised her eyebrows. "What's that?"

"There's a woman upstairs in that lounge where I was waiting for you. She's from Central America—a renegade executive. I don't run into renegade executives very often."

"A renegade executive?" Martha said, puzzled. "You mean Inez Monteforte?"

"A tall, thin, dark woman dressed in khaki?"

Martha nodded.

"Certainly she's a renegade executive."

"How do you know that?" Martha asked, curious. "I've always known her as a member of a Guatemalan collective. She was among the free women at the Marq'ssan assembly on *s'sbeyl*."

"I spotted her as an executive almost straight off," Margot said. "She seemed a little oddly dressed for being an executive, but after a few minutes' conversation it became apparent she was of the renegade variety."

"How do you know someone is an executive if they don't dress like one?" Martha asked.

"How would I know a service-tech is a service-tech when she's dressed like an executive?"

"That's different," Martha said. "One of us would always feel uneasy in that kind of clothing. And there's a whole code of manners and things. And the way executives hold their heads, their postures, their gestures. It would be very difficult imitating all that."

"Precisely," Margot said. "You don't think service-techs have their own set of signals?"

"But we're so simple in our manners, and no, we *don't* have special signals or anything. Anyway, we know that executives sometimes *do* disguise themselves as service-techs, and successfully."

"Not for long they don't," Margot said. "Anyway, this woman, Inez, has executive stamped all over her."

Martha could not help remembering David's warnings about executive women. "I wonder why she went renegade," Martha said.

"Executive women have many reasons for going renegade," Margot said. Neither her mouth nor her eyes were smiling. "Which brings me to the very point of my visit."

"The reasons women executives go renegade?" Martha asked in bewilderment.

"Elizabeth Weatherall is going renegade," Margot said, "and she's just revealed to me the details of a trap you and the Marq'ssan are supposed to fall into."

Martha took one of the bottles of water and gestured at the other bottle and the glass. Her mind remained strangely blank, as though it couldn't process what Margot had just said. "I don't believe this." Everything and everyone had apparently gone crazy. Louise had taken over local SIC headquarters, Inez was ready to start a planet-wide revolution, and now Margot was telling her about a trap and Elizabeth Weatherall going renegade? "Why would she go renegade? It doesn't make sense. Could there be a trap under the trap?"

Margot opened the bottle and poured water into the glass. "There's nothing she'd have to gain from preventing you from walking into a trap, Martha. I've looked at it from every angle I can think of. I don't see her revelation as leading to entrapment. I think she's telling the truth. She says the Executive—including Sedgewick—are crazy and have no intention of ever negotiating with the Free Zone *or* the

Marq'ssan. She seems to think they don't really believe in the aliens, not genuinely."

"Nothing makes any sense." The words came out as a complaint rather than a protest. "How can they not believe in the Marq'ssan? After all these years, and after the Marq'ssan destroyed all their military bases in the Pacific Northwest? *Believe in them*! As though they're claiming that people take the Marq'ssan's existence on faith!"

"Yes," Margot said, "but hardly anyone has ever *seen* an alien. And even then, because they look like us... I find it difficult to believe in them myself, even though I see proofs of their existence everywhere I look."

Martha's handset buzzed. She debated not answering—until she realized someone from upstairs might have new information. She picked it up and held it to her ear. "Martha Greenglass."

"Martha, Venn. Shoshana tells us that Louise has invited a contingent of the press in. Which means that it won't be long before everyone knows—including the Executive. You're going to have to contact Sorben. This situation could blow up in our faces."

Martha groaned. "I can't believe it. I just can't believe she'd do that, too."

"It's crazy, I agree. But I think we've underestimated the extent to which Louise has been taking personally the likelihood of her losing her position in the Co-op."

"You think that's what this is all about?" Martha asked, not really caring. What did it matter *why* Louise had done it?

"So you'll call Sorben?"

It had been only hours since Martha had last seen her. "You think that's necessary? What can she do?"

"Come on, Martha," Venn said sharply. "You're not *thinking*. Once the Executive finds out, they're going to be contemplating taking action against us, especially if any of their SIC people are casualties. What's to stop them from making air strikes against us? Have you considered that?"

No. Martha hadn't been thinking in such terms. "God," she said, deeply afraid for the first time in ten years. If Margot was right about the Executive not believing in the Marq'ssan, then they might very

well do such a thing. "All right, I'll contact Sorben and try to fill her in
on what's happening. Have you brought the hold-outs around yet?"

"There's just Cora, Beth, and Tanya. I think I'm going to start suggesting some of the more horrible consequences that are possible—I
didn't want to get us into that kind of scene, but maybe it's necessary
to straighten them out, to get them out of this glory exposure of spy-
ring stuff."

"All right," Martha said wearily. "I'll get back to you when I
can." Martha disconnected and looked at Margot. "I might as well
tell you now," she said to the executive, "because you'll know soon
enough. Louise Simon has taken over the local SIC headquarters—a
house in Edmonds." Margot stared at her, wide-eyed. "She's taken all
the people there hostage and has started to tell the world about it. She
intends to expose the documents she's found. God knows what's going
to happen then."

Margot, her hand to her throat, breathed, "I don't think I can take
so much excitement in one day. You're serious, Martha?"

Martha nodded miserably.

"That's all you needed to get the Co-op permanently branded as
terrorist," Margot said. "Quite apart from what this will do to the Free
Zone's international reputation, what do you suppose Sedgewick's reprisals will be?"

"That's what we were discussing on the phone just now," Martha
said, toying with her handset. "Apparently Louise designed this as
a diversion from the public scrutiny of the Night Patrol that was to
have taken place at the Steering Committee meeting."

"It's going to be far more than that."

"Yes," Martha said, "I know."

"I think you'd better intervene before they kill someone.
Presuming they haven't already done so?"

Martha shrugged. "They say not, but how can we know for sure?"

"Do you think your aliens can do something?"

"What, get Louise to release her hostages?"

"That would be the best course. And it might save the Free Zone's
reputation in the long run—the aliens' stepping in like that, I mean."

Martha wondered why she hadn't thought of that before. She
unlocked the bottom drawer of her desk, got out the transmitter for

signaling Sorben, and used the frequency marked **absolutely urgent**. "I'll have to be on my way in the next fifteen minutes," Martha said, aware that Margot's gaze was fairly glued to the transmitter.

"You just called them, using that thing?" she said, still staring at the transmitter.

"Yes." Martha dropped the transmitter into a tunic pocket.

"It's incredible. That you can call them so easily."

"She'll know it's an emergency."

Margot's eyes widened. "I think I must contact Elizabeth Weatherall and tell her what is happening," she said. "I don't know how this will affect her situation." She tapped her fingernail against her empty water glass. "Perhaps there's some way we could make use of her? In this crisis, I mean. After all, she'll know everything there is to know about the people being held hostage, and about how Sedgewick is likely to react. Perhaps we could use her as a liaison of sorts?"

"I wish I could *think*," Martha said. "Everything is happening so quickly I can't seem to take in the events themselves much less their significance. I suppose we might consider seeing what she has to say."

"After you talk to Sorben, why don't you and I and Elizabeth meet."

Martha remembered Inez. She looked at her watch. Three-thirty: which meant that in an hour and a half Magyyt would be returning for her. And she *had* to talk to her before then. To at least explain why they couldn't consider her proposal today... Martha said, "How about if we meet in the evening. I'm going to have to come back here to talk to the others after seeing Sorben. If you want to arrange something for, say, seven-thirty or eight, that would be fine." Martha rose to her feet.

"How about the three of us dining together?" Margot said, also rising.

"Sure." Martha opened the door. "Unless things have gotten worse," she added vaguely, not sure what she meant—and not really wanting to know.

[iii]

When Ganshoff called back, Elizabeth explained in as few words and as obliquely as possible that they could not afford to meet openly again because Ganshoff was under surveillance. Elizabeth knew very well that Baldridge had not ordered the surveillance stopped. She had, herself, glanced at reports of that surveillance over the last two weeks. Ganshoff, considering, came up with the idea of meeting at an art gallery owned by an intimate friend. Elizabeth agreed to the plan, then set out on foot for the gallery, which was in the Pioneer Square area, about ten blocks from her hotel.

As she strode south and then west through the drizzle, Elizabeth thought how strange it was that it was in Seattle that her life-long connection with Security would end, in a city inevitably linked in her mind with Kay Zeldin. "Like some crazy kind of fate," Elizabeth thought. She put her hand to her head and felt the wet beading the top layer of her hair. She would have to cut her hair. Knowing she would be less conspicuous as a man, she had—wearing a black wig for the photo—made one of her false IDs that of a male with her own physical statistics. People would assume she had inhibited the growth of facial hair through hormone treatments. Her only question was whether or not to take Ganshoff's suggestion of holing up in the Austrian Consul's cabin in the north central Cascades for a couple of weeks. Her initial plan had been to cross the border, travel north to Edmonton, and fly south to San Diego. But Ganshoff had argued that their first suspicion would be of her crossing into Canada—probably to go somewhere overseas.

Not that Elizabeth had told Ganshoff that she intended to go to San Diego. She trusted Ganshoff, but only so far. If Security began to suspect Ganshoff had assisted her escape, they'd have no scruples whatsoever about abducting her, administering loquazene, and later releasing her with an apology to the Austrian government explaining that they had known she had been involved, as their loquazene examination had proven, and had not been able to afford risking Ganshoff's slipping out of their grasp by going through channels.

Elizabeth found the gallery without trouble. "Elizabeth Weatherall to see Madame Nestor," she said to the professional on floor duty. The woman hurried away, and Elizabeth cased the small front room, taking note of the eye of what she knew to be a closed-circuit camera and of the uniformed guard armed with a stun-gun. She would have to speak to Margot about destroying the video-file documenting her presence in the gallery. It could be taken for granted that Security would manage to acquire and examine all such records existing in the Seattle area. Whoever ran the operation for her recovery would overlook nothing.

The professional led Elizabeth through the gallery's three display rooms to a door marked **PRIVATE**, opened it, and asked Elizabeth to go in. When Elizabeth stepped inside, she closed the door behind her. Elizabeth's gaze swept over the room's interesting clutter until she located a door that she had not at first noticed because it was painted the same color as the walls and lacked a frame. She opened the door and surveyed this second room from the threshold. Comfortable-looking, civilized—all in the hyper-modern style—it seemed to beckon her in. Elizabeth stepped in and looked around. Only then did she see the spiral staircase of translucent gray plastic, winding up into what she suspected might be a loft. Curious, she moved to the bottom of the stairs and peered up. Fragments of music floated down from above. Undoubtedly Madame Nestor was up there. Elizabeth returned to the center of the room and stood in uncharacteristic indecision. Everything had changed. She could no longer afford to take her own security for granted. In less than twenty-four hours they would be hunting her. The fact was difficult to assimilate, especially in a room so comfortable and welcoming.

Hearing footsteps approaching, Elizabeth stepped to one side of the door, out of the line of sight of anyone entering. She should be carrying a weapon, she told herself. She must begin to do so as a matter of course.

Ganshoff walked in. "Elizabeth?" she called, glancing around.

"Here," Elizabeth said, stepping forward.

"Oh!" Ganshoff pressed her hand to her heart. Recovering, she gave Elizabeth a wry smile. "Well you were right. I *am* under surveillance. I must thank you, my dear, for adding that little fillip to my life. I simply don't know what we diplomats would do without the excitement the intelligence services bring to our poor, dull, meager existences."

Elizabeth sighed. It would be poetic justice if orders she had issued resulted in her own capture. But Elizabeth did not appreciate irony in general, much less this very personal particular sort. "I'm sorry about that, Margot," she said. "But I'm afraid there's nothing I can do about it now."

"No matter. I've been under surveillance before. They'll get tired and decide there's nothing to be gained from such an expense, and then that will be the end of it." She raised an eyebrow. "I suppose it was for my association with Greenglass?"

"Just so."

Ganshoff smiled. "I have some news for you, dear. I wonder if you'll think it's good or bad news."

Elizabeth frowned. "Something has happened?"

Ganshoff, laughing, removed her wet cloak and let it fall to the floor. "It's really quite amusing, except that I'm afraid the consequences will be very nasty indeed, and then I won't be laughing. But for the moment I can laugh, for there's something tickling in hearing about an SIC station being taken over."

Elizabeth stared at her. "What are you talking about?"

Ganshoff dropped into an extensor chair. She leaned her head back against the neck rest, flicked the switch on the arm rest, and surrendered herself to the chair's vibrating cocoon. "Louise Simon of Night Patrol infamy has stormed the local SIC station and taken everyone in it hostage."

Elizabeth's heartbeat thundered in her ears. "Christ! The entire *Company* will be swarming into the area!"

Ganshoff peered at her through the narrowed slits of her almost-closed eyes, and Elizabeth saw how those eyes gleamed with pleasure. How widely the Company was hated, she thought. And Austria had been an ally for decades... "Perhaps they'll be too busy to give much thought to you," Ganshoff said.

"Not bloody likely. As it is—" Elizabeth remembered Mastney. "Oh my god, once word of this gets out I'll be ordered to return to DC at once. Especially if they decide to take violent action in response."

"You don't think they'll negotiate for the release of the hostages?"

Elizabeth paced. "Not if the Executive has anything to say about it. Of course Company people might see it as the thing to do, but I doubt it. The current approach is hard line. Negotiation for any reason is perceived as showing softness."

"Just who is it they're holding hostage?" Ganshoff said. "Anybody important?"

Elizabeth swung around to face Ganshoff. "Among others, an old, old veteran of the Company who's turned into a hopeless drunk, and the son of a Cabinet officer. One of the Goodwins."

Ganshoff whistled. "Yes, I can see that they might decide to ditch the old drunk, but a Goodwin? A son of a Cabinet officer? What's *he* doing working out of a station, anyway?"

Elizabeth laughed mirthlessly. "He *likes* that kind of thing, that's what he's doing at this station. He's essentially running the station in the name of the old drunk. He likes the idea of being in rebel territory and running covert action teams. It appeals to a certain strain of romanticism in him. And he probably likes all the old stories the veteran tells when in his cups." The subject irritated the hell out of her. "Christ, *I* don't know why the males do what they do. Don't ask *me*!"

"Why don't you take off your cloak and sit down, dear?" Margot's gaze was shrewd. "Your pacing is making me nervous."

What *was* she going to do about Mastney? Once he found out he would argue with her about returning to DC and at the very least send a courier posthaste with the news, with or without her agreement...But suppose she did get Mastney out of the way: Central still might hear the news before morning and send orders for her immediate return.

Who would be managing the crisis? Baldridge, because he was Director of Operations? Or Ambrose? With Sedgewick out of things—and Elizabeth found it hard to imagine Higgins being able to revive him into taking control—one or the other of them would assume control. Ambrose would prefer not to have her on the scene, for he'd reason that if she were *she* would be in control, not he. If Baldridge, on the other hand, were in control, he would prefer her to be there to deflect and absorb what he'd take for heat. In either case, if they intended a punitive strike, then her presence in Seattle could only be perceived as making her vulnerable to also being taken hostage.

"Do you mind sharing some of your turbulent thoughts with me, Elizabeth?"

Elizabeth came to a halt and stared at Ganshoff. She had forgotten where she was and whom she was with. "Sorry." Realizing she was hot and sweaty, she let her cloak fall to the floor and collapsed onto the sofa. She was tired, so very tired. "I'm not going to change my plans," she said to Ganshoff. "I think we must go through with them as we worked them out this morning."

"So you're not thinking of offering Simon your services in dealing with their windfall at the station?"

"Are you trying to be funny?"

Ganshoff's eyebrows sailed high in her forehead. "No," she said. "I'm serious. You could put yourself at the Free Zone's service and put them in your debt. While furthering your own ends. For instance, you could send certain cables to Washington feeding them misinformation. Doesn't that appeal to you?"

Elizabeth shook her head. "No. Doing such a thing would expose me to further risk. I'm not stupid, Margot."

Ganshoff closed her eyes and sighed. "And here I was, weaving grandiose plans. Greenglass, of course, is thinking of the ultimate consequences. She's very frightened, I think."

"If I had such loose cannons in my government as this Simon appears to be, I'd be frightened, too," Elizabeth said tartly. "I'm no such maniac, Margot, so don't think you can tempt me into trying to use that station against Central."

"All right," Ganshoff said mildly. "I didn't really have anything definite in mind. I suppose it has occurred to you that a lot of intelligence services would dearly love to have your memory and expertise at their disposal."

"I'm not *that* kind of renegade."

"I feel certain that if approached, the Austrian BRN would be delighted to put you on their payroll. Since Austria's no longer a part of the Eastern Alliance, that wouldn't be like working for the Russians or URI, would it."

"I haven't thought of any of that," Elizabeth said. "There will be time enough to assess such possibilities when I've made my escape."

"And then there's the Free Zone," Ganshoff said, as though refusing to hear what Elizabeth had said. "I wonder how many former
executive women are operating here. One almost begins to think the
aliens the patrons of executive women who have gone renegade. Why
just this afternoon I met a woman from Guatemala who is such a one.
She was waiting for a bit of Martha Greenglass's time. It almost made
me begin to wonder about myself. Greenglass asked me why an executive woman would go renegade." Ganshoff fell silent, then opened
her eyes to stare hard at Elizabeth. "As I said, it gives one something
to think about."

Elizabeth said, "My case is an exception."

"I'd dearly love to hear the details."

"No doubt. But that doesn't put me in the mood to confide, Margot."
No one would ever know her story, not even Hazel. Especially not
Hazel. Elizabeth thought of the leather book locked in the tamper-
proof mini-safe. She had not been able to leave it behind to be destroyed, though it was dangerous to her own safety, especially here
in the Free Zone. But if someone tried to break into the mini-safe
the problem would be solved, for the contents of the safe would be
instantly eradicated by a release of acid. Probably, Elizabeth realized,
not even Sedgewick would understand why she had gone: he was beyond understanding, beyond even asking the right questions, though
surely if anyone could ever know her reasons it would be he. Booth
would assume he knew why, but would have only one part of the
answer. Others would conjecture, but all would be wrong. Only she
herself would know why, only she herself could understand why.

[iv]

Martha found Sorben waiting in Old Sand Point Park, their ap-
pointed daylight meeting place for emergencies. Sorben knocked
on the window on the passenger side, and Martha released the door
lock. "We have a mess on our hands," Martha said as Sorben got in.
"Louise has stormed the local SIC headquarters and taken everyone
there hostage." Sorben's sky-gray eyes widened. Martha wondered
irrelevantly if Sorben's hair ever grew: it always seemed the same
length. Did the Marq'ssan have *real* human bodies, or totally illusory
ones that merely seemed to be made of solid flesh, bone, and hair? If

Sorben were cut, would she bleed? "Her spokesperson says that this will divert attention from the Night Patrol issue to the SIC's invasion of the Free Zone. She's apparently hoping to publicize certain documents they expect to find there."

"Have you talked to her since this happened?" Sorben asked.

"No. Shoshana refuses to give us access, on the basis of orders— orders!—Louise issued in advance." Martha fell silent and waited for Sorben to speak.

The silence stretched for a long time. But then Sorben usually took her time digesting information before asking questions or drawing conclusions.

After about a minute and a half Martha spoke again. "Do you think you could go in there and force Louise to free those people?"

Sorben stared at her. "How would I do that?"

"*Couldn't* you do that?"

"I don't see how. Presumably Louise is using violence. What am I to do, threaten her with violence in return? Or do you think I can talk her into giving up her madness?" Sorben looked out at the water. "I don't think Louise can be reasoned with, Martha. And I'm not willing to resort to her methods. I think the best thing you can do is to ignore what she's doing, refuse to acknowledge it. To not allow a diversion of your purpose at the Steering Committee meeting."

Martha swallowed. "That may be difficult, if all the world is talking about it. And if the Executive decides to retaliate."

"The latter is worth your attention," Sorben said. "But I don't think you should allow it to dominate the Steering Committee meeting. You must exert yourself to focus attention where it is due. If you aren't careful, your asylum project will disintegrate."

"Won't it anyway, now that Louise has done this?" Martha asked bitterly. "Not that they were on the level in their negotiations," she said, remembering Margot's revelation. "Apparently they intended to lure us all into a trap. At least that's what Margot Ganshoff tells me—and she says she has that directly from Elizabeth Weatherall, who according to Margot is going renegade."

Sorben gave Martha a solemn look. "If you can manage to keep the Steering Committee on course, Martha, we Marq'ssan will do everything necessary to pressure the governments to force a change on this human rights issue."

"Governments," Martha said. "You know about Inez's visit then."

"Inez? She's one of the activists Magyyt works with?"

"Yes. She came to see me today, to discuss bringing Guatemala and others into our project."

Sorben nodded. "Good. Yes, there will be others, too. And not just the other Free Zones. You do see the potential implied by a globalization of this project?"

"I don't know how we can pull it off, Sorben," Martha said, her anxiety intensifying. "If we can't manage one government that is isolating itself, how can we manage all the governments, who under attack will stick together? Especially if they think the Zones are all working together. It will be chaos! With the result that we won't be able to force *any* of them to change. It will be like our attempts on *s'sbeyl* to force all the governments to negotiate with us."

"And I'm beginning to think we've been wrong to take this piece-meal approach, Martha. We Marq'ssan did so mostly because we were waiting for the war to end. Since it has ended, I think it's time we tried for more than merely preserving the six free zones from being overrun by their previous governments. Don't you?"

Martha's heart fluttered. "My god, Sorben. You're going to try for...*world revolution*?" And she realized that she hadn't really taken Inez's vision of world revolution seriously.

Sorben's gaze held hers. The Marq'ssan said, "We've decided to go ahead with taking the action you and I have discussed. In Washington DC and its surrounding area—including all of Virginia and Maryland because of their military installations—at five tomorrow morning, just before the day begins, we're going to strike with an EMP." Martha gasped. "As a reminder, as a warning, as well as punishment for their negotiating in bad faith. Do you know how complacent they've become, Martha? They've returned their standard military weapons issue to lasers. They don't believe the Blanket could happen to them again. A reminder would be in order. We will start with the US, but will extend the principle to other countries as well, one at a time. We'll have to work this out in close coordination with the other Zones and activist groups worldwide as they come into the project. You see now why it's essential that we not let the Night Patrol issue be derailed? You *must* tell them, *all* of them, your insight, what you learned about your own thinking."

Martha burned with excitement. "Yes, yes, I see," she said, again believing what had for a while faded from her consciousness. But still she was full of dread, dread at what she had to say at the Steering Committee meeting, dread at the enormity of the Marq'ssan's plan.

[v]

Elizabeth shut her bedroom door and unlocked the luggage holding the weapons and ammunition. Looking over her armaments, she considered what would be most useful to have in hand as she neutralized Mastney, Simmons, Bradley, and Kirkby. If she could take them one at a time, she wouldn't need a weapon. But if she got entangled with more than one of them and found herself in a brawl, she would be glad to have something powerful in hand, especially since she must presume that each of them was at all times armed. She did not want to kill anyone. So perhaps a laser weapon would be best, set to the stun setting.

Elizabeth picked up the M-27D and stripped it down into its hand-weapon form. She keyed in the setting, checked to make sure the **READY** button was switched to **OFF** and slipped it into her right tunic pocket. Before relocking the suitcase she removed a pair of cuffs, unlocked them, and slipped those into her tunic pouch. Then she lay down on the floor on her back, calmed her breathing, and made her mental preparation. Finally, she did a few warm-up exercises.

Before returning to the main sitting room, she looked in on Hazel. The girl was lying on her side, one hand nestled at her throat. Elizabeth listened for a minute to her breathing, which was slow and heavy. When she shut the door, she wished she could lock it, to assure Hazel's safety.

Mastney, Elizabeth saw from the doorway of the sitting room, had come in while she had been in the bedroom; he sat in an armchair watching vid. He apparently hadn't realized she had returned, for when he heard her walk into the room he leaped to his feet and reached for his weapon. He froze when he saw her. "You didn't say you were going out, or where," he said, sinking back into his chair.

His tone was accusatory—toward her, his superior. "And then dropping your escort, besides, Weatherall. What's up with *that?*"

Elizabeth moved across the room toward him. "I went out to meet a contact, who is arranging for me to dine with Greenglass."

"Dine with her! How the hell are we going to get this show on the road if—"

"Shut up, Mastney," Elizabeth said sharply. "I'm sick to death of hearing you tell me how to do my business. If you ever expect to work with the Chief's office again you'd better get it through your obviously thick skull that I won't stand for hectoring from subordinates." What an act, Elizabeth thought. But it shut him up, didn't it, even if it pissed him off. She drifted past him to the window, which put her about two yards in back of his chair. Elizabeth stared out at the depressing gray sky for about a minute. Incredible, she thought, an executive watching vid, and Free Zone vid at that. If she weren't going renegade, she would certainly have included that detail in her report on him.

When she judged his attention deeply sunk into the program, careful not to make a sound, she turned from the window, stepped from the polished wood floor onto the rug, and dug her toes into it. Since he wore headphones, she doubted that he was aware of her quiet, stealthy approach. Step by step she crept up on him as the adrenalin pumped into her blood. When she stood two feet from the back of his chair, she used the same dive and chokehold she had used on Daniel Sedgewick when she had found him in her office. Mastney fought far more effectively than Daniel had, but his double disadvantage of being seated and being taken from behind with the chair between most of her body and his grasping hands meant that he could do little against her.

When his struggle grew feeble, Elizabeth thought of getting out her weapon and mentally cursed her stupidity in putting it in her right pocket and thus out of reach of her free hand. She would have to cuff him now and hope she could maneuver him into one of the two rooms the males used. Or should she first render him unconscious, cuff him while he was out, and then move him into the bedroom when he came to? It was difficult to decide. She realized that she should have used a drug on him. One of those idiots might walk in on them at any time. Or even Hazel, for that matter. Though it would be safe if Hazel came in, her merely witnessing the scene would create difficulties because of the girl's sensitivity to violence.

Having made up her mind to press her fingers briefly against his carotid artery, Elizabeth noticed that he had ceased to struggle at all. An act? Or had he gone unconscious? How long had it been? Panicking, Elizabeth released her hold on him and jumped around the chair to face him. He was breathing, she observed with relief, but his face and neck were purple with engorgement. Still, he could come around at any time. Without wasting another second, she heaved him forward in the chair and, pushing his arms behind his back, cuffed his wrists together. Now she would be able to handle him, she thought, getting the weapon out of her pocket. She switched the **READY** button to **ON**. Then she tiptoed into the hallway that serviced all the suite's bedrooms and checked each of the males' rooms to make sure they were empty. She'd have a disaster on her hands if she bundled Mastney into a room already occupied by one of her gorillas.

As Mastney came to he flopped about and groaned. Alarmed at the noise he was making, Elizabeth snatched the silk handkerchief out of his breast pocket and stuffed it into his mouth. At last his eyelids fluttered. "Listen to me carefully, Mastney." She spoke in a cold, clear voice. "Your life depends on it. As you'll soon realize, you're cuffed, and I have an M-27D aimed at you." His eyes opened, and he struggled to focus them. "Yes, Mastney, it's true. So. You'll get to your feet, and we'll go slow and easy into your sleeping room." He looked furious, but also confused. "Get up now, Mastney."

He turned his head to look around the room. Then he looked back at her. He made no effort to rise.

"You'd prefer excision?" Elizabeth said, making a show of taking aim. "I've got the little red bead on your forehead." He could not, of course, see the setting. "If you don't cooperate there will be no point in my sparing you."

Apparently he believed her, for he strained to heave himself out of the chair with his arms pulled behind him. Elizabeth did not help. The drain in energy his effort would entail would be to her advantage. It probably would not take him long to recover from the strangulation.

When he at last he succeeded in getting himself to his feet, Mastney reeled, and Elizabeth took hold of his elbow. "Move right along into the hall," she said, pressing the muzzle of the M-27D into his back. Slowly, slowly, they moved to his room. Elizabeth shoved him backwards onto the bed, then locked the corridor door with the inside deadbolt to prevent any of the gorillas or hotel staff from entering. She went out through the hall door and crossed to her own room to fetch a sedative. Then she returned to Mastney, removed the handkerchief from his mouth, and forced two tabs to the back of his throat. They took a long time to completely dissolve and take effect. But Elizabeth sat on the other bed and watched until he had fallen into drugged, heavy-breathing sleep.

Exhausted, Elizabeth returned to her own room. She wanted to think before tackling the others. Either she would drug them, or she would stun them, or she would take one of them hostage and force the others to cuff one another. They would be harder than Mastney to handle, for they were bigger and trained specifically for personal combat. Simmons was as tall as she and thirty pounds heavier. She had been matched to work out with him, and though she was ultimately faster than he, she knew him to be a challenge in equal circumstances. There was something terribly fatiguing about dragging male bodies around, and something depressing about it, too. It was not at all like the exhilaration of working out with someone. And if she had actually had to fight Mastney, it would have been much worse.

This was a new experience for her, and she had made mistakes. She would have many new experiences to face in the days ahead of her: she only hoped she would be quicker-witted than she had been just now. She couldn't afford many more mistakes like the ones she had made with Mastney.

Chapter Twenty-six

By the time she had finished neutralizing all the males in her escort, Elizabeth had exhausted the surge of adrenalin that had enabled her to do so and was left utterly enervated. Leaning with her head back against the wall, she surveyed her handiwork—the gags and the tangle of limbs and the objects to which they were cuffed—and decided her captives would be safe enough until her return after dinner. Just before leaving for the Cascades she would fasten sedative patches to their arms so that they would not awaken before morning.

It was already seven-thirty. She would have to wake Hazel now. The girl would need a good meal to get her through the night. Elizabeth sighed at the thought of having to get through it herself. Perhaps lack of sleep explained why she was making so many mistakes.

She went into Hazel's room and sat on the bed. The poor girl still looked exhausted. Wondering why she should bother to dine with Ganshoff and Greenglass at all now, Elizabeth hesitated. Hadn't the entire point been to keep Mastney satisfied? She reached for her handset, to cancel, then put it back in her pocket before she'd even flipped it open. Making new arrangements for a meeting would be tricky, and Ganshoff seemed to want it. Elizabeth sighed and fought from closing her eyes and laying her head on the pillow beside Hazel's for just a few minutes.

Elizabeth stroked Hazel's face. "Hazel, darling, sorry to wake you, but you must get up now," she said.

Hazel mumbled incoherently. "So tired," she finally managed to say. Her eyes opened and she squinted at Elizabeth.

"We're in Seattle, darling, remember?" Elizabeth touched the deep circles pouched beneath the sleepy amber eyes.

Hazel yawned. "What time is it?"

"It's a little after seven in the evening, darling." Elizabeth smiled. "Would you like some coffee?"

"Mmmm, yes, maybe that will wake me up." Hazel closed her eyes again.

Elizabeth fetched a cup of the coffee she had made for herself after dragging Simmons into the males' room. She woke Hazel again, helped her to sit up, and put the cup in her hand. "We're going out to dinner, darling. When we get back we'll load the van, which hopefully will be in the hotel garage by then." Hazel's eyes widened. "And then we'll leave Seattle."

"Tonight?"

"Yes, darling. Tonight. We must. They'll begin looking for us in the morning." Four a.m. DC time meant one a.m. Seattle time. It would take Central only a few hours to put two and two together. And then the hunt would begin. Of course, the general state of emergency brought on by that madwoman's attack against the station would complicate matters. Elizabeth thought of how Edwin Goodwin was probably exerting enormous pressure on the Executive, while Booth, of course, must be furiously opposing any kind of negotiation at all. And who would be running Security? An image of Booth storming into Sedgewick's study came into her mind. It was impossible to predict what would happen. Would Booth regret having pushed on her so hard? No. *Au contraire.* He'd blame her for everything, curse her, and swear that never again would a woman be allowed that much power, no matter what the circumstances. Elizabeth watched Hazel sip the coffee. "Are you feeling better, darling?" She took Hazel's free hand in her own.

"A lot better," Hazel said, "though I still feel pretty worn out. As though I'd been sick with a virus."

"Poor sheltered sweetie," Elizabeth teased, "you have no stamina at all."

"Do we have to go *out* to dinner?" Hazel asked. "Couldn't we have it up here?"

"Sorry, darling, but I've promised we'll dine with two other women tonight. Don't worry, it won't be difficult. You might even find it interesting. One of them will be Martha Greenglass." Elizabeth watched Hazel's face as she made the connection.

"Does she know…?"

"About the plan to trap her?" Elizabeth asked. Hazel nodded. "Yes, darling, she knows."

Hazel's gaze held steady. "I'm glad," she said. "I would have hated thinking I'd been in any way a party to that."

Elizabeth got up from the bed and went to the closet to look at the few things Hazel had unpacked. It was a good thing she would no longer be working for Security, Elizabeth thought. There would have been terrible problems; she could see that now. She took out one of the dresses—the new service-tech fashion Allison and the others had begun promoting through their soap operas and other vid shows— she had given to Hazel. Hazel had worn one of the dresses once for Elizabeth—in private. She had said she found the prospect of going out into public with her legs uncovered embarrassing. When Elizabeth had pointed out that people wore shorts and bikinis without embarrassment, Hazel had said that that was different. Elizabeth turned around and held up the dress. "Will you wear this tonight, darling?"

Hazel set her coffee cup on the bedside table. "Oh, Liz, you know how I feel about it! If others were wearing dresses, that would be one thing. But to be the only one? I couldn't do it!"

"But you unpacked it."

"For us, by ourselves," Hazel said. "Because you liked it so much that other night."

Elizabeth put the dress back in the closet, pulled out the pants and shirt Hazel had worn that morning, and laid them out on the bed. "I'm going to shower before dressing. I don't know if you want to?" Hazel shook her head. She had, after all, been in bed all day, not dragging heavy males from room to room. Elizabeth watched Hazel throw the covers back and swing her legs off the bed. "Too bad we don't have more time," she said. Tired as she was, the diversion would do her good, especially since the night was going to be so very long.

Hazel flashed her a grin. Because of that grin Elizabeth lightly tickled Hazel's ribs and hips when the girl slinked past on her way to the bathroom.

As Elizabeth showered and dressed she realized this would be the very last evening she would spend as Elizabeth Weatherall: as herself, using her own name, recognized by others as herself. The thought choked her until she forced herself to remember that scene in Sedgewick's office. Facing herself in the mirror, staring at the bruise marking her cheek, she focused on the revenge she would be wreaking simply through her absence. Sedgewick would immediately fall apart. And as for Booth…he would find his dependence on her far more extensive than he could have guessed. The image of Security going to pieces banished the pain of losing her identity as Elizabeth Weatherall. Whatever happened, she would have the satisfaction of knowing her own power and strength and what the loss of that power and strength would mean to Security and therefore to the Executive.

Elizabeth draped her cloak over her arm and went out into the sitting room. Hazel was already waiting. "We'll drive ourselves, love," Elizabeth said, her eyes drawn to the close neat fit of Hazel's shirt.

Hazel gave her an odd look. "I didn't know you drove," she said.

Elizabeth laughed. "Oh yes, I drive. And a good thing, too, since you don't! How else would we make our getaway?"

Hazel picked up her raincoat. "I don't know how to do very many things besides word processing," she said.

"I'll teach you to drive this week," Elizabeth said. "You'll be learning tons of things, just as I will be doing, too. But you're so clever you'll probably learn faster than I will." They left the suite; as Elizabeth locked the door she hoped Hazel would not ask where any of the males were.

Elizabeth found the four-seater in the parking garage without difficulty. "This place is near Lake Washington," she said as she exited the garage. "In a residential neighborhood, according to Margot." Elizabeth checked the map glowing on the data screen for the best route. Only one executive women's club—a small place in Madison Park—remained in Seattle. But then there were hardly any executive women left in the entire Puget Sound area, and most of them lived in Edmonds.

At the club, a service-tech parked the car for Elizabeth. As they walked the few steps to the door they observed that the rain had stopped. "It smells nice," Hazel said, her voice like soft velvet in the cool, moist air.

"It's all the trees they have here," Elizabeth said. Another service-tech held the door for them to go in. "It makes everything about the air different, don't you think?"

The manager showed them to a small private dining room. Ganshoff and Greenglass were already there, sitting by the wood fire, sipping drinks. "So there you are," Ganshoff said, quirking an eyebrow. "I thought perhaps you'd gotten lost."

"Margot, I think you've already met Hazel," Elizabeth said, nodding at Ganshoff, "but I know you haven't, Martha." She smiled at Greenglass, who looked as wiped as she and Hazel did. "Martha, this is Hazel, Hazel, meet Martha." The two service-techs half-smiled and nodded at one another; Elizabeth exchanged a wry look with Ganshoff.

Ganshoff shrugged slightly, then said, "What can I get you two to drink?"

"Some kind of fruit smoothie for me," Elizabeth said. She looked at Hazel. "Wine, darling?"

Hazel shook her head. "I'd fall right back to sleep. Maybe another cup of coffee?"

Ganshoff urged them to sit and picked up the handset at her elbow and ordered their drinks.

"Any news about the station?" Elizabeth asked Greenglass.

Greenglass's brow furrowed. "I beg your pardon? The station?"

Elizabeth half-smiled. "That which your colleague has taken hostage." Colleague and ex-lover, but it wouldn't do to say so.

"The situation is basically unchanged," Greenglass said. Her gaze moved from Elizabeth's face to Hazel's. "Louise seems rather upset about various papers she's found, which she thinks relate to herself. They don't use her name, but she says they can only be referring to her." Greenglass's gaze returned to Elizabeth's face.

"What is she planning on doing with the fact that one of the people she's holding is the son of a Cabinet officer?"

"I don't know if she knows that yet."

"You mean you haven't told her?" Elizabeth asked incredulously. "It could make the difference between whether they negotiate or not!"

Greenglass shrugged. "That's not something I intend to get involved with. Louise is doing this on her own hook. Presumably she's in contact with your people. I wouldn't know. The Co-op is not going to be a party to this sort of violence."

"You're dreaming if you think you can dissociate yourself from your colleague's madness. If I were you, I'd make the best of a bad situation." Elizabeth smiled. "But then I'm not you."

"My dear Elizabeth." Ganshoff, also smiling, entered the conversation. "I agree with Martha's response completely. I think it would be a mistake for the Co-op to try to extort anything from the Executive. Simon and her group are in an untenable situation. Consider such sorts of tactics undertaken by similar small extremist groups in the last few centuries: they've never worked, they never will. All they do is bring public attention to the group and its grievances, which is sometimes useful, of course, but rarely accomplishes much, at least not until the group has matured and begun eschewing such methods. I could cite you half a dozen examples from history."

Elizabeth rolled her eyes and winked at Hazel. "Lord spare me from history."

"I have a question I've been wanting to ask you, Elizabeth." Greenglass wore a particularly stubborn look on her face.

"Go ahead," Elizabeth said, wondering if Greenglass was going to ask her why she was going renegade.

"Why does ODS do everything it can to stifle dissent? Why has ODS ruined so many people's lives? Why put nonviolent, harmless people in prison?" Greenglass's eyes glinted. "I've always wanted to know, have always wanted an opportunity to ask somebody responsible for the policy. I've never been able to figure it out. Even before the Blanket, ODS hassled people like me. But *after* the Blanket the situation got a hundred times worse. Harassing and jailing people has become routine. Why is that?"

Elizabeth stared at her. "What a perfectly amazing thing to ask! It's so obvious why, Martha! People like you want to overthrow the executive system! And look what happens when they're allowed to do as they wish! Chaos! Look at what your colleague has done! That's what comes of letting people do and say as they please!" Elizabeth shook her head. Seeing that Greenglass was about to retort, she said,

"Now *you* tell *me* something, Martha: why is it that people won't behave peaceably? Why do they insist on stirring up trouble? ODS wouldn't exist if that tiny group of people weren't so intent on over-throwing the executive system. Why won't they respect the rights of the majority to have the system they find works best? The executive system benefits the greatest number of people. Without the executive system, the world would still be suffering hunger and starvation and overcrowding. Until the Blanket disturbed everything, there was a Good Life for everyone!"

Greenglass grimaced. "Right. What a fantasy world you live in, Elizabeth. I suppose you believe that's the truth? That people prefer to be oppressed? That they want the government to make all the most important decisions for them? That argument reminds me of the one that slave owners have throughout history used to claim that slaves are happy under slavery."

"In the executive system there have been relatively few malad-justed people," Elizabeth said, thinking of the service-techs who re-fused vid, refused their own culture. "Why must the entire society suffer for those few?"

"Oh dear," Ganshoff said, "I hadn't realized we were to have a discussion of political philosophy this evening. I don't think I'm quite up to it."

"Let me offer an analogy," Greenglass, sitting forward in her chair, said. "Kay Zeldin told us plenty about Sedgewick, you know."

Elizabeth's nerves tightened. This was the first time she had heard Greenglass make reference to Zeldin. It gave her a creepy feeling, as though Zeldin were suddenly in the room with them, ready to un-mask her.

"Margot told me you work very closely with him," Martha said. "From what Kay said about how he and other executives behave to-ward women, I'd imagine you find his style a bit difficult to take. Of course, you may have a way of rationalizing all that away, the way women in the most abominable circumstances have frequently done. The way a few men invented the theory that women are intrin-sically masochistic, that they enjoy pain, and most women repeated it to themselves for more than a century before rejecting it. Do you find ways to rationalize being thought to be an unreliable, hysterical, irresponsible person, ways to rationalize being treated like shit, Elizabeth?"

Elizabeth—for a moment unable to speak—stared at Greenglass. A fit of trembling attacked her. She saw that it had been a mistake to come here when she was so exhausted. She should instead have gone to bed for a few hours and refreshed herself. "You don't know what you're talking about," she said when she'd gotten her body under control.

Greenglass looked at Ganshoff. "What about you, Margot? Do you find it reasonable the way even executive women—who are so incredibly privileged—are treated? What does it feel like, lowering your eyes and saying 'Yes sir'? You're powerful, sure, but when it comes down to it, how do you fare in their world? It *is* their world, you know."

"Ah, the feminist argument," Ganshoff said.

The door opened and a service-tech came in. She set a thickly frosted glass on the table beside Elizabeth and handed Hazel a cup of coffee. "Thank you," Hazel said.

"There must be order," Elizabeth said. "You are talking about abuses. Hierarchy in and of itself isn't bad."

Greenglass looked at Hazel. "What do *you* say, Hazel? Or does Elizabeth speak for you?"

Hazel flushed, and Elizabeth felt herself getting angry. If Greenglass *dared* upset that girl she'd make her pay. Hazel was completely inexperienced at this sort of thing, and Greenglass, in baiting her like that, obviously knew it, too. "I have my own opinions," Hazel said quietly. "But I'm not very good at explaining things. Also, I have to admit I'm confused. I'm not even sure I know what you're talking about."

Elizabeth smiled at Hazel. "Of course Hazel has her own opinions," she said. "She's intelligent and independent." Elizabeth looked at Greenglass. "I wouldn't begin to presume to speak for her."

"You seem willing enough to speak for everyone else," Greenglass said. "But aside from which, I must say that if a lover of mine talked about me that way while I was sitting in the room with him or her, I'd be saying goodbye forever. Don't you think that by taking it upon yourself to judge Hazel out loud you're being just slightly patronizing towards her? What if she were to do the same to you?"

Though furious at Greenglass for her effrontery, Elizabeth, feeling defensive, grew afraid that Greenglass's poison might work. She looked at Hazel. "I didn't mean to be patronizing you, darling," she said, thinking about taking Hazel and walking out.

Hazel offered her an embarrassed smile. "I know, Liz. I don't consider what you said patronizing."

Greenglass snorted. "And you, Elizabeth, would you consider it patronizing if Hazel were to say to me in front of you, 'Elizabeth's intelligent and independent'? No, you probably wouldn't. You'd probably consider it *impertinent.* But I suppose Sedgewick talks about you that way to his colleagues. How do you feel about it when he does it to you?"

She was too damned tired to be trying to argue with Greenglass. "None of this alters the fact that hierarchy exists and always will exist," Elizabeth said, determined to cut the discussion off. "You don't like it because you aren't typical of your class. You think and behave like an executive, more or less." Greenglass gasped and opened her mouth to protest, but Elizabeth plowed on. "There are a few of you who were made to govern and not be governed. But that shouldn't mislead you into making the mistake of thinking that the rest of the governed are like yourself. As a matter of fact, most people need the comfort and reassurance that someone other than themselves is in control. You can't deny that, Martha Greenglass."

"It's their training!" Martha said. "It's not the way they have to be! It's their training!"

"Yes, but that training is essential for even limited social harmony," Elizabeth said. "You see, whether we like it or not, the men are violent and aggressive. The important thing to them is control." What was it Kay had said in one of their conversations about hierarchy? Something about the original sin being the desire to control, that Adam had spoiled the garden—and therefore eliminated paradise—by insisting on trying to dominate everything in the garden, giving names to everything, bossing Eve around. But even if the desire to control was the problem, Elizabeth had answered Kay, in the end they had to deal with the fact of that desire. "You'll never succeed in suppressing this desire to control. Which is why there must be government, and why in most of society men must be allowed to feel superior to women. Whenever they lose that sense they go out of control and do violent and destructive things." Look at Sedgewick! He was a prime example for the truth of her theory.

But Greenglass was shaking her head. "I'm not an exception," she said. "And the Marq'ssan have confirmed this. The point is that once people can be made to see that they can be much more than they are, that they can enjoy being responsible for themselves, that they can change and thus not have to repeat the same old mistakes over and over and over again, then everything can be different. It's just very difficult to undo what the repressive structures of our society have done. We're all brainwashed, some less than others, but all of us have to fight this bizarre warping these hierarchical structures have forced on us."

The door opened and the service-tech wheeled in a food cart. "Thank god," Ganshoff said. "Saved by the serving of dinner. May I suggest, friends, that we give this subject a rest, at least while we eat?"

"Amen," Elizabeth said, rising. "Oh does that smell good. I hadn't realized how famished I am."

"Me too," Hazel said, coming to stand by Elizabeth, unobtrusively brushing her fingers against Elizabeth's. Relief swelled Elizabeth's heart. So Greenglass's ploy hadn't worked. Hazel would not be corrupted, would not be lured away, not even here in the Free Zone.

They seated themselves at the table and began on the soup course. Ganshoff questioned Greenglass about some dispute to do with logging on the Olympic Peninsula. Elizabeth slid her foot sideways until it rested against Hazel's and guzzled her soup. This was her last meal as Elizabeth Weatherall, she sadly reminded herself. Her last meal as herself.

[ii]

A few miles past the last Everett exit Elizabeth pulled the van over to the side of the road. "Is something wrong?" Hazel said into the loud, rural silence. Since leaving Seattle they had seen perhaps half a dozen other vehicles using I-5.

"I have to make a security check, darling." Elizabeth put her hand on Hazel's shoulder. "Also, I want to prepare you." Elizabeth paused, remembering Hazel's alarm when she'd seen her positioning the fully extended M-27D between her seat and the door. "Under your seat, darling, is a helmet. It's a laser helmet, like the kind worn in combat. It's there in case we get into a bad situation. I want you to know about it and be prepared to put it on when I tell you to if we should get into difficulty. No, no, darling, don't get upset, it isn't likely, but it's *possible*. We must always be prepared to face the possible. That's common sense. Okay?" Hazel hesitated, then nodded. "The helmet is easy to use. You just put it on your head and strap the Velcro strip holding the remote to your wrist. Whatever your eyes—looking through the retinal feedback goggles—focus on, you will be able to shoot with the laser, by pressing the fire button on the remote. It will automatically adjust for distance and so on. Do you understand?"

"I don't know if I could kill someone."

"Listen to me, darling," Elizabeth said, squeezing Hazel's shoulder. "If they catch us, it will be…terrible. You haven't been in Security long enough to know about such things. But the very fact that you work for Security is classified information. You are so classified that any security-related charges against you would never make it into a civilian court. And since you were in the Chief's office—and also because of your being so intimately connected with me—everything would be up to Sedgewick to determine. Ordinarily these things are determined by superiors. Well there *is* no one above Sedgewick. My point is, that under no circumstances do we want to be captured, Hazel. Killing someone would be preferable, I promise you." Talking so explicitly about it made Elizabeth sick to her stomach. "Just promise me you'll put the helmet on if I tell you to?"

Hazel's tongue touched her upper lip before she began gnawing on the lower lip. "I promise, Liz."

Elizabeth gave Hazel's shoulder another squeeze before opening the door. "I'll be only a minute or two, darling." She stepped down onto the pavement. The darkness was solid, broken only by the distant twinkle of a few discrete points of light. Elizabeth got the bug-sweeper out of her tunic pocket. It did not take long to locate the transmitter, which looked to the casual eye like a moth, attached to the left rear mudguard; a tracer, she conjectured. Ganshoff already knew where she was going, but she apparently wanted to be able to count on tracking her in case she went elsewhere. It was enough to know it was there. She could jettison it later, if necessary.

Before climbing back into the van Elizabeth checked her watch. Unless she had made a mistake, the explosives would detonate in thirty minutes. That nagging little fear-spot in her groin spread. If they failed to detonate, she and Hazel would be pathetically easy to track. (She refused to think about the possibility of SIC investigators lifting her prints from places she had been unable to clean up—places like Sedgewick's house. She had to assume he'd be too drunk even to think of it. Or that his staff had been thorough in their routine cleaning.) And if they did detonate... She knew Allison wasn't in DC, yet the fear haunted her: what if Allison should happen to return early, what if she should happen to be at the office at that hour? But Allison *never* worked after midnight or one, and *never* went in before six. And Allison was scheduled to be in California. It was only her fear of something going wrong that made her even think about the possibility.

Elizabeth got back into the van and started the engine. And if Sedgewick were there? Would she regret his death? She pulled onto the road. They had just enough power in the battery to reach the cabin. No detours, no getting lost allowed. Follow the map precisely. Elizabeth stared at the glowing data display. It was simple; very, very simple, even at night.

Soon they came to the Arlington exit, where Elizabeth left the interstate. "Too bad it's dark, darling," Elizabeth said to Hazel. "Margot says this area is pretty, with a lot of mountains visible. Mt. Baker, for instance, which is one of those wild snow-packed volcanic peaks."

Hazel jerked awake, probably because of the sharp change in the vehicle's speed. "Sorry, Liz. I guess I fell asleep."

"Don't worry, my sweet, you needn't stay awake," Elizabeth said, certain she was too hyper to need company.

After Arlington she saw almost no lights at all. Ganshoff had said this road ran through a flat valley filled with farms—one of which hosted one of Louise Simon's amazon training camps. The idea of women trained in such skills appealed to her—how much more pleasant her life in the Company would have been with women as her escort instead of those damned males who as far as she was concerned were the dregs of the Company. She remembered a discussion with

Sedgewick, a long time ago, on the subject. Sedgewick had said that women had for awhile been placed in active Guard and Military roles, but that the Executive had decided to put an end to that since it had become obvious that it would be very difficult to keep service-tech males in the Guard and Military under control if basic gender differentiation in the services were seriously eroded. "There has to be a pecking order," Sedgewick had said. Though they'd had to call up women during the Global War, they'd taken pains to maintain a sense of gender differentiation.

Elizabeth drew a deep breath. Tonight, she told herself, she was free. For the first time since Zeldin's death. And what would Kay say if she could see Elizabeth now? Would she gloat and say *I told you so?* Elizabeth imagined lying down beside her on the bed in that cell and telling her everything that had happened. You were right, Kay, he couldn't be manipulated past a certain point. I tried, god knows I tried. He's so weak. Did you know that, too? If you did, you were afraid to say it to me... Would you forgive me? You know what it is to make mistakes. Big mistakes. And now what can I do? I'm not going to them, you know, the way you did. Did you go to them because you saw nowhere else to go? Because you knew you couldn't live the way Hazel and I will have to live? Because you didn't have the resources I have for even trying to live that way? Why did you join with Greenglass? And you took such a low profile with them, Kay, when you could have been their acknowledged leader. "Our founding mother," Greenglass calls you. They've made you posthumously responsible for their mess. What would you have done when you'd seen your mistake? Where would you have gone then?

Elizabeth's eyes blurred, and she braked. For a few minutes she sat with her hands pressed to her eyes, weeping. She was tired, she told herself, that was why she was so emotional.

"Liz? What is it? Are you okay?" Hazel's voice was tender; she leaned close and rubbed Elizabeth's back.

Elizabeth sniffed and groped for her handkerchief. "I'm fine, darling. I'm just crying because I'm realizing I'm missing someone who's dead. Who's been dead for eight years." She blew her nose and wiped her eyes. "I'm just being silly," she said.

Hazel took Elizabeth's hand and pressed it between both of hers. "It's not silly to miss someone you cared for."

Elizabeth lifted Hazel's hand to her lips and pressed a kiss into the palm. "In this case, my love, it most certainly is," she said. She released the brake and put the van into gear. If she weren't careful she'd soon be as crazy as Sedgewick. "And now, on to Darrington," Elizabeth said. "And then we'll almost be there."

Which would be a Good Thing. If she didn't soon get some sleep she would crack. No wonder she was being so emotional and silly. Everyone needed sleep, eventually. Even Elizabeth Weatherall…who she no longer was, anyway.

[iii]

The population of the camp, swelling with arrivals daily, had broken into distinct divisions and cliques. The most vocal were the religious groups, the most visible the youth gangs; many other, smaller, groupings formed as well. In the busloads that had arrived during the distribution of food, salt-tablets, and water on Monday evening had been a couple dozen discernibly professional people. Inevitably, and with considerable wryness, the professionals in the camp—twenty-eight in all—had drifted together. Celia carried on intense discussions with many of them, and by Wednesday knew the stories of most. After the first sharing of stories the focus of their talk had shifted into two areas—speculation on what ODS might be intending to do to them, and a careful discussion of the emerging camp politics and how they—the professionals—should be interacting with the rest of the camp. Many of the professionals were anglo; only half-a-dozen—who (with the exception of Celia) all came from the Bay area—spoke Spanglish. They estimated that perhaps three quarters of the people in the camp spoke Spanish as their first language.

All except three of the professionals were simpaticos. And except for Celia, all of these had been activists before they'd become simpaticos, sometimes as in the case of two of the academics, because the groups they belonged to had been prohibited. The three professionals who did not consider themselves to be simpaticos were journalists— one a reporter and two editors. Celia had never heard of professional journalists ever doing more than reading what the authorities provided for them in the way of "news." But apparently they had taken it upon themselves to report (and the editor to publish) an on-the-scene account of a dispute between workers and executives at a chemical plant in San Jose involving the cutting of hazard pay for cleaning up a toxic spill. The executives claimed they'd had to cut the hazard pay because the plant was operating in the red and that their only other choice was to close the plant down. Since such high-hazard jobs incurred a strong risk of filter-failure, they had always been well paid. Certain workers counted on such jobs for an integral part of their total income and had thus constituted a sure supply of such labor. Unhappy to be losing the higher pay, they had banded together and refused to do such jobs unless the previous pay-rate was restored. When workers couldn't be found for the next clean-up job that had arisen, Military Police had hauled two dozen of the usual clean-up workers to the site of the spill to force them to work. A riot had ensued; two people had been killed and many arrested. The journalists had dared to interview some of the workers and had reported their side of the story in a Bay area newspaper. The editors responsible for the decision to print and the reporter who had written the story had been fired and later picked up by the Military Police for interrogation. The reporter had been so severely beaten that he now—three months later—needed a cane to walk.

On Wednesday afternoon, almost without noticing it, the lawyers among them hived off into their own small group for further speculation. They established that as far as they knew, everyone had been told at the time of their arrest that they were being taken into "protective custody"; that every night the commanding ODS officer stood before them to give them a speech about reporting violations of human rights; and that all of them had in common a recent arrest followed by a short period of release before they had been picked up again by ODS. Celia suspected that if they polled every person in the camp they would discover Military Police arrests in their backgrounds—presuming, of course, people even knew which of the secret police forces had previously arrested them. She supposed that many people would not have distinguished between them, as she herself had not done until recently.

Celia was delicately airing a few of the things she had discussed with Emily when her voice was drowned out by the noise of an ODS helicopter, landing in the desolate boulder-strewn area outside the barbed-wire fence enclosing the encampment. She paid little attention to it once its racket ceased, but continued explaining the split between Military- and Security-connected executives, though her interlocutors kept staring past her, distracted. Only when the woman beside her put her hand on Celia's arm to warn her did Celia turn to check out what everyone else was staring at. To her amazement, she saw Emily, accompanied by another executive woman and two men—one executive, the other professional—coming toward them.

When Emily's gaze found her, her face lit up. Her mouth moved, and those accompanying her stared at Celia. Celia's heart beat violently. Surely Emily's presence meant she would be released? Unless Emily were in trouble? But she didn't appear to be, for she led them to Celia, freely, easily.

"Celia." Emily held out her hand, and Celia grasped it. Emily's eyes smiled into her own.

"You're being released, Ms. Espin," the other executive woman said. Celia recognized her as the one Emily had pointed out at the art party—the one whom Emily said had "influence" with ODS.

Celia became conscious that the eyes of every inmate in the area were on her. A spurt of guilt spiked her sense of relief. She swallowed. "I may get my things?" she asked the executive woman in a very low voice.

When the woman nodded, Celia pointed at the temp-shelter she had been assigned to. "They're in there," she said.

"Go fetch them, then," the woman said.

Celia stumbled toward the shelter, aware that everyone in the vicinity was watching her. They probably thought she was an informer, she realized. Even the colleagues she had just been talking to might think it. Her knees shook, making it difficult for her to walk. At last she reached the shelter and went inside, hoping no one would follow her in. Blinded by the sudden dimness, she snatched her bag—and saw with shock that two pallets away from hers a pair of women were making love. She ran outside and squinted against the sun's assault. As she walked to Emily she felt the hostility swelling around her. If something went wrong and she were returned here, she would be in serious trouble.

It was a terrible feeling: fear mixed with guilt. And yet a wild hope she hadn't known she had surfaced—the hope of living, the hope of freedom. She was to be saved. She could not regret that, however guilty her reprieve made her feel.

Chapter Twenty-seven

[i]

Celia was safe again. For the second time Emily had rescued her and brought her to her beach house, where she now felt oddly at home. As they often did, they sat on the terrace and sought to make sense of their world and what they knew of it. This time, though, the profusion of details she and Emily traded overwhelmed her. "It's almost as though we have *too* much information," she said.

"And we don't know what is true and what isn't," Emily said. "How do I know what to think of this story of Elizabeth Weatherall's going renegade, especially when she sends me half a dozen boxes to keep for her? And why pick me? Supposedly because I wouldn't be suspected of helping her...yet I have to wonder, given her patent interest in you and your uncle and your relationship with me. And I also have to wonder about the coincidence of her going renegade at the exact time the aliens imposed a new Blanket on Washington DC."

Celia took a long swallow of water. She felt as though she would never overcome the dehydration of that desert camp. The area had been so dry that not even the usual chaparral plants grew there. And they had had to sweat so much, too. Yet their keepers hadn't increased their water ration to compensate. The frequent light-headedness, the cracking dryness of skin, the parched thickness of tongue had been something they had not talked about in the camp. Only now could Celia acknowledge how frightened being that short of water had made her. "But you say that Lisa Mott says it was Weatherall who initiated this plan for the camps?"

Emily said, "I know. That makes it even stranger. Lisa's really uptight on the subject of Elizabeth. She says they haven't gotten a countermand of the order, so they've continued to implement it. But neither have they received orders concerning either the transport of people out of the camps or the reception of monitors at the camps." Emily popped a raw sugar peapod into her mouth, crunched and chewed it, and swallowed. "We can find out more about that from the other end when we're talking to those people in Seattle."

"You're sure it's a good idea, going up there?"

Emily nodded vigorously. "It's essential, Cee. We'll talk first to the people at the Austrian Consulate and then introduce ourselves to some of the Co-op people—if our contacts at the Consulate think it wise. If we don't go, by default that group Mujeres Libres operating out of LA will be considered to speak for all of Southern California. And as we've already agreed, that's not what we want."

Celia sighed. "Certainly we don't want violent revolutionaries to hold a monopoly on the human rights issue."

"Then we're all set?"

"It has to be tomorrow?"

"The sooner the better. Don't worry, Cee, once you've gotten a solid night's sleep you'll feel much more like tackling this challenge."

"I hope the relevant electronic files are still intact," Celia said, thinking of how just a few days out of contact with the Center underscored how vulnerable they were, how quickly things could change should any of the police forces take it into their heads to act against them.

"At least you have the flimsies you've been keeping here," Emily said. "Which will be better than nothing. But that's only one part of our mission to Seattle. The main thing will be to find out what the hell has happened to Elizabeth's plan since she went renegade."

Celia crunched a peapod between her teeth and thought longingly of bed. But Elena would be joining them for dinner. Elena would not believe she was safe until she'd seen Celia with her own eyes. Celia understood that—she was the same where Elena was concerned. *One more time, survival.* How many more times would either of them survive detention? Could the process continue indefinitely? Or was there a limit to the number of times they would release arrested people?

Emily believed that these thugs were disorganized and lacked any rationality in their methods, any communication between competing branches about the individuals they were surveilling and holding. That made it almost more frightening, as though it were all random and the fate of each of them hung upon the frayed thread of chance.

Would it ever be over? Celia could see no end, could not believe there was one. Why then did she go on struggling? Why not give in and be the kind of lawyer she had once intended to be? When she was younger they had wanted to send her to Stanford, to continue her scholarly work as preparation for teaching jurisprudence to executives training as judges. She had considered the idea, had played with the notion of influencing future judges, but after her interview at Stanford had decided against it. That was a road closed to her now.

What roads—if any—remained open now that she had been named?

For the first time Celia realized that she no longer had much choice about continuing with the struggle. Once she had been named, that had been the end of their pressuring her to "straighten herself out" as that pig and Judge Barnes had put it. She had been judged hopeless. Did that mean she had now become an expendable professional?

Celia watched Emily sipping her fruit drink and wondered when they would make the same decision about her. When did an executive become expendable? "They haven't tried to put pressure on you?" Celia asked.

Emily looked startled. "What do you mean?"

"Has anyone talked to you, warned you not to get involved with simpaticos?"

Slowly Emily shook her head. "No. And I don't think they will, either. I think they'll let me do as I please until they decide I'm dangerous. And then..." She shrugged. "I may get an anonymous message, or someone like Lisa might drop a few hints, or Aldridge might drop a hint to my father. But that will be the extent of their attempts to tamper with me."

"Until they've decided you've gone too far."

"Yes," Emily said, "until they've decided I've gone too far." She smiled. "Don't look so worried, Cee. That day will never come."

She has no fear, Celia realized. She's a fool for it, but lucky. It must be wonderful to have no fear; one could do almost anything then. It would make all the difference in the world not to be afraid. Celia couldn't begin to imagine what it would be like.

[ii]

The Steering Committee meeting ground on. Only half-listening to Beth's report on the housing situation in the Puget Sound area, Martha checked her watch. Lenore had told her she was to speak on the Night Patrol issue after all the committees had finished making their reports and before the extra-Puget Sound reps made theirs. The housing committee was the last of the Puget Sound committees.

It had been years since Martha had been this nervous about public speaking. Angry people had packed the room. And as usual, the Steering Committee meeting was being streamed live via the Free Zone's net. Friends and relatives of several of the men the Night Patrol had killed had told various Seattle newspapers that they were "out for blood" and would not be satisfied until "the entire Co-op falls and a rational system of law and order has been reinstituted." Many of her auditors would be merely looking for ammunition when they listened to her speech; and, Martha feared, most of the others, though staunch supporters of the Co-op, would be equally unheeding to her words. They would want only to get past this "scandal" and get on with the "real business" of the Steering Committee meeting. Most of them envisaged the expulsion of Louise as the answer and believed that once that had been accomplished they could return to business as usual.

Since talking to Sorben, Martha had decided that it was far too important that everyone learn from her mistake to allow the Co-op an easy out from the situation. She was keenly aware of the irony that the people supporting her would probably be as deaf to her words as those out for her and Louise's blood. Would anybody hear what she said, would anybody think seriously and deeply about the insights she intended to share with them? "Just say *mea culpa, culpa maxima,*" Laura had advised her. "Offer to resign. Confess that your intimacy with Louise at that time got in the way of your thinking. Admit to being human. And then let us take the floor and beg you to stay as we expel Louise. We can thunder reproach at her and refuse her legitimacy. We know she won't last long, now that she's brought the wrath of the entire SIC not to mention the Executive down on her head." In fact, Louise was hiding out somewhere with her hostages, no one knew where. She might never be heard from again, some people suggested. Martha didn't believe that. Louise was too ambitious and thought she had an advantage holding important executives hostage. No question, she would be heard from again. They could not forget her; they could not ignore her. To do so would be to condone her behavior. Martha would not make the same mistake twice, and she would do her best to see that the Co-op did not, either. They had ignored the Night Patrol. She would not let them ignore Louise's abduction of living human beings.

"Next on the agenda," Lenore was saying, "is Martha Greenglass, to speak to the issue of the Night Patrol." Martha gulped water as the people sitting on the main area of the floor shifted to face her. Then she leaned back against the cushion she had placed between the riser and her back and shuffled the papers she had taken into her lap. Finally, she switched on the mike she had been given to wear in anticipation of her speaking.

This is it, Martha. Do what you have to do and do it right.

The podium had dropped back into the floor, and Lenore had seated herself among the others sitting in the central area. Martha was conscious of Sorben and most of Sweetwater's presence, as well as of the rest of the Inner Circle scattered around the periphery. She drew a deep breath. "When the *Examiner* came out with its exposé of Louise Simon's Night Patrol activities and my knowledge of them, I along with other members of the Co-op insisted on postponing the issue until this meeting to allow us to give it the serious attention it demands. Anything that might have been done or said at that time would have been in reaction and so would likely have been hastily defensive. One of the things the Marq'ssan have made me see is that until humans begin to scrutinize their mistakes and learn from and remember them, nothing will significantly change.

"Many of us here today would like to 'settle' this matter and lay it to rest. Which is to say we want to satisfy our consciences or desires— depending on which 'side' of the issue we are positioned—and then go on as though nothing had happened. Deep change is painful— and frightening.

"You've all probably read the *Examiner's* account of my discovery of Louise's participation in the Night Patrol. I would like to tell that same story, but through a different lens than that used by the author of the article. I would like to share with you what I understand of what happened.

"One day about eight years ago I returned to Seattle after several weeks' absence. I arrived a day earlier than I had told Louise to expect me because I finished my business earlier than I had estimated. I thought I'd surprise her. When I returned home, Louise was not there. I unpacked and began sorting my laundry. It was then that I discovered, under the bathroom sink, a garbage sack full of bloodstained clothing. While waiting for Louise to come home, I speculated about the clothing and the reason for its being in our bathroom. Not one of my speculations came near the truth. Later, when Louise told me, she remarked that I should have known, that she had given me enough hints that she thought I *had* known. She told me she had assumed I simply didn't want to talk about it, wanted nothing to do with it. I told her I thought what she had done, and was doing, was horrible, and that I was leaving her."

Martha glanced around the room and found expressions of impatience on almost every face she looked at. She drew a deep breath and continued. "I told no one. No one at all. Not even my closest friends. I said only that Louise and I had irreconcilable differences, and that was that. Perhaps I hinted to a few people that Louise had changed. But I told no one. Why not? That's one of the most important questions I have to ask. At the time, I thought I said nothing out of loyalty to Louise.

"But consider. I discover my lover is murdering people, and will go on murdering people, and I do nothing. *And I didn't even think about it.* Not once did I think about the people she murdered. I dismissed them from my mind as though they hadn't even existed. Because they were rapists? That's something to be considered. But I'll come back to that later. The important point here is that I didn't think about it because I didn't *want* to think about it. By not telling anyone, I *avoided* thinking about it. It was too horrible for me to face. So I didn't face it. I shirked my responsibility as a human being. I walked away from it. And oh how superior to Louise I felt. Here I was, keeping silent, protecting her, while I alone knew what a horrible person she was. I must have felt superior, right?" Martha shrugged. "I don't remember.

But after that I did my best to pretend Louise didn't exist. And I tried to forget all about the Night Patrol. Every time I heard about another man killed by the Night Patrol, I blotted it out. As though it were none of my business, as though it were nothing to me. Even though I knew Louise was one of the Night Patrol, one of the murderers."

Martha paused to sip water. "And what about the Co-op? The Co-op did the same thing. Not that we knew who belonged to the Night Patrol. But we did our best to ignore it. As though somebody else should take care of the matter, as though it wasn't our responsibility. And of course many people in the Free Zone whispered that the Night Patrol did the community a favor, that its violence helped to protect women. Basically, we all closed our eyes to it, I more than the others—since I knew more—but we all did." Martha could hear breaths hissing in all over the room. The rest of the Inner Circle were probably furious with her for implicating them, for giving the Co-op's critics ammunition for attacking them for moral negligence or even turpitude.

"I'd like to propose an analogy that's going to upset many people in this room," Martha said. "I'm not saying that the situations are the same. But there's a certain insight to be drawn from this comparison. Currently many of us are very much caught up in the human rights crisis in the US. It's upsetting and frightening to hear the stories of people who have been abused by Military and Security and other police forces solely to maintain the Executive's power and authority. We have dedicated ourselves to stopping these abuses and to helping the people who have been abused and are threatened with abuse. One of the questions we need to be asking is how this could have happened. Throughout history people have wondered how various large-scale atrocities could have been committed and allowed. Because this is so, it's a question central to the future of our species. Surely everyone sitting in this room must be committed to a future in which all people respect one another. But until we can come to terms with this horrible repetition plaguing our history, we will never achieve such a future.

"Therefore I pose this question now: how is it that human rights violations have been perpetrated and have been allowed to be perpetrated in the US today? And how is it that I allowed Louise to go on killing people? And how is it that the Co-op did nothing to stop the Night Patrol? The analogy is unfair, some of you will say, and I hope that's true, for I don't think the situations are comparable. But *structurally* they are identical. In the case of the Co-op and the Night Patrol, let me remind everyone that the Night Patrol is not a massive physically powerful force intimidating the entire community. I couldn't possibly claim that Louise personally intimidated me. Therefore, fear for one's personal safety is not an answer for why a society tolerates such abuses—though many people in the US will claim that as their excuse for not having opposed human rights abuses going on all around them. Perhaps we can say fear has something to do with it, but it must be obvious that that's only a part of the story, and in fact may be a rationalization, just as my notion of loyalty was a rationalization.

"If fear belongs in this story, it is that of one or two other kinds entirely. One kind of fear that might be at work is a fear that one's desire for absolute safety is being threatened. In the case of the Free Zone, that might include a fear of personal violence premised on the notion that people do not commit violent crimes only because they fear being punished should they do so. In the case of the US, such fear also includes the desire to silence dissent, since dissent and a lack of unanimity and social conformity are widely perceived as a threat to public safety.

"But there's another kind of fear. And this is the fear I suffered from: a fear of facing one's self, a fear of facing things we can't bear to look upon in people who are like or close to one's self. All I wanted was to run from what it was that I suddenly saw in Louise. Why? Because I might find that same thing in myself? It was a possibility, you know, since for two years I identified myself very closely with Louise. The question naturally occurred to me: how could I have loved someone who had *that* in her? The obvious conclusion to be drawn was that there must be something wrong with me for me to have been able to love someone so monstrous."

Martha took several long swallows of water and wondered if there was any human in the room who understood what she was saying. "When I first told Sorben my story, she asked me a question: if I had discovered someone I knew less intimately than Louise on the Night Patrol, would I have stopped that person? Which people would I have stopped, and which would I have simply recoiled from, the way I had from Louise? She pointed out that if I had discovered someone

I considered an enemy to be killing people, I would definitely have stopped them—presuming I had it in my power to do so. When I thought about Sorben's questions, I realized that it wasn't on account of personal attachment that I had failed to stop someone close to me, but because I in some way identified with that person and was thus unable to look the truth in the face. Whereas I could easily confront it in an enemy whom I would consider completely other than myself. Which is to say, I couldn't bear to see evil so close to home. Because if I looked more closely, I might see it in myself."

The room was utterly silent, utterly without movement. Martha trembled, but she made herself go on. "I asked Sorben: do you think this is all a part of the us-them mentality? Louise is one of 'us,' her victims—rapists—a part of 'them.' Do you think that once we see things in those dualistic terms it becomes impossible to see clearly? That maybe I didn't *really* consider the rapists human? When would I have stopped Louise? If her victims had been women, would I have stopped her? If her victims had been people I knew, would I have stopped her then? It's obvious that in such a case I would have inter-vened. Why not with the rapists?"

Martha took time to clear her throat, for it had so filled with phlegm that she was having a difficult time talking. "I would also like to add that it isn't a simple matter of morality. Suppose I had exposed Louise and had stopped the Night Patrol. That doesn't nec-essarily mean that I would have faced the thing I'm talking about. I could have taken the line that Louise was not like me—just as you all could be right now taking the line that Louise is not like anyone in this room—and felt morally superior. The way we feel superior to the Executive. But the answer is not that this evil is outside of ourselves and entirely other than us. The us-them mentality is the problem, not the solution. The us-them mentality makes it possible for Louise to kill rapists. And it makes it possible for the Executive to be complicit with the killing and torturing of thousands of people."

Martha inhaled deeply. "What I am urging today is that we not treat this as an us-them problem," she said passionately, her gaze held by Beatrice's streaming eyes. "If we expel Louise, it must not be so that we can absolve ourselves from any moral responsibility for the kind of evil she perpetrates. It must not be so that we can feel morally

superior to her. It must not be so that we can feel clean as we make
her the communal scapegoat. It must not be so that we can look away
from what is inside the entire human community of which we are still
a part, separate though we sometimes like to think ourselves. If we
expel Louise, it must be for the right reasons, political and moral. And
so I urge you all in our discussion of what has happened and what we
must do, to take this opportunity to thoughtfully explore one of the
most important issues that will ever face us. Don't let us resort to dualism as I did. Don't let us recoil in horror as I did. We must stop the
Night Patrol, yes. We must refuse to condone what the Night Patrol
does, yes. But we must remember that we are all a part of one another, and that our reason for expelling Louise is not to deny that but
to halt and condemn behavior that is morally abhorrent and socially
unacceptable to the human community." Martha tore the cap off a
new bottle of water and drank. When no one spoke, Martha located
Lenore's face. "That's all I have to say, Lenore. I'll answer questions
if anyone likes. And I'll resign if that's wanted, too." Martha switched
off her microphone.

Lenore stood up; the podium whined as it lifted off the floor. "The
mike is open for discussion," Lenore said. Martha, still trembling,
braced herself for an onslaught of misunderstanding and a dismissal
of what she had said as "intellectualizing." People shifted restlessly,
as though sitting still for so long had cramped them, had made them
need to fidget. Martha wished she could leave now; the hard part was
just beginning. But she took heart when Beatrice claimed the floor.
Perhaps something would come of it, Martha thought. She had expected either Toni Farren's faction or Cora and her "pragmatists" to
battle to seize the floor first.

"I think," Beatrice said when she had been given a mike, "that
what Martha said in her speech is the most important thing that has
ever been said within the circle of these walls." Martha breathed a
shuddering sigh of relief and blinked against tears. Beatrice, at least,
had understood. Beatrice and Sorben. Martha shifted her legs into another position and got out her yellow pad. She felt ready, now, for the
frustrations this discussion would bring her. She felt ready to struggle to make herself understood. And she was glad Louise was absent.
Louise would have made an abstract discussion impossible. Everyone

would have hated her so much that there wouldn't have been a chance to talk about dualism.

To the Co-op, Louise had become anathema.

[iii]

"We're going to have to go for a long walk, sweetie, or you'll be too sore to move later on. And then after the walk we'll plunge into the hot tub." Elizabeth smiled at the look of protest on Hazel's face. "You'll feel great tonight, you'll sleep like a baby."

"I'm so tired, Liz."

"I know, darling, but you need to do the walk." Elizabeth extended a hand and helped Hazel drag herself to her feet.

"I'm such a hopeless klutz I'll never learn any of this," Hazel said. "I'm sure it won't be worth your wasting your time on me."

They began to dress. "You'll do fine, darling. That wasn't a bad first lesson for someone who never gets more exercise than walking to the bus stop. And believe me, you'll begin to appreciate it once you realize you'll be able to defend yourself against the average male." Not against Company people out looking for them, of course, but against muggers and rapists. They couldn't count on Hazel's continuing to live such a sheltered life. And Elizabeth needed to know that if anything happened to her, Hazel would have a shot at taking care of herself.

"Let's see if there's a path along the river," Elizabeth said. The river was running fast and high, swollen with the first stage of the spring thaw. They went out the back; carefully Elizabeth locked first the door to the house and then the gate. "Though we can't see much of them, there are mountains all around us," Elizabeth said, her eyes straining to see through the trees. She longed to go cross-country skiing. The cabin offered a good selection of skis, there was plenty of snow, and for the first time she had seemingly unlimited free time. But she was reluctant to leave Hazel alone in case they had been tracked—or betrayed.

Elizabeth trusted Margot Ganshoff, but she was sufficiently cautious to keep her M-27D under the bed at night. She had taken to listening to the radio and browsing Internet news sites, but skeptically. (She was, after all, well acquainted with Allison's job.) It still seemed incredible to her that the Marq'ssan had struck DC and the surrounding area (including Norfolk, which rather pleased her) with an EMP. What she could not make out was whether her bombs had gone off before the EMP. It would have disabled them if they hadn't, for every last one of them had silicon chips in them. The radio reports had given six a.m. EDT as the time of the Blanket. But that was no guarantee... "How long are we going to stay out here?" Hazel asked.

At last, a question. "I don't think we're going to be able to walk along the edge of the river much farther," Elizabeth said. "The path seems to be ending. I'm not sure how long we'll be out here, darling. I thought maybe a week or two—which will give us time to think and replenish our energy." Elizabeth halted and looked down into Hazel's face. Smiling, she said, "I haven't had a vacation in eleven years. I'm trying to think of this part of it as something like a vacation. But mostly I want to think. And we'll be safe here." She said this with a confidence she did not fully feel. But there was little point in Hazel's worrying. It was all in her own hands, her fate as well as Hazel's. Which meant she must take as few chances as possible, since she must not gamble with Hazel's life. Hazel was not her pawn and never would be. She, Elizabeth, differed from Sedgewick significantly in that. Whatever he said about Zeldin, he knew nothing of love, nothing at all. Loving Hazel had taught her that if nothing else.

They bushwhacked on for several yards, until they ran up against impenetrably thick scrub that prevented them from continuing along the bank. "Let's go back, darling," Elizabeth said.

"Wonderful," Hazel said. "I'm thinking of that hot tub more and more every minute."

Again, Elizabeth smiled down into Hazel's lovely amber eyes; she touched the nape of the soft, delicious neck. She felt amazingly happy and light-hearted. They would lie in the hot tub and listen to the rush of the river and smell the cedars and firs towering around them. They'd done that the night before, laying their heads back on the rim of the tub to stare up at the thick crust of stars in the moonless sky. So much pleasure, after such fear and humiliation, made her feel as though she were recovering from a long illness, taking her life back into her own hands, strong and whole and charged anew with energy. She had never guessed that going renegade would feel so good.

[iv]

Celia had never been out of the southwest, had never been in a world so green, so fresh, so soft. The air fairly caressed her skin (still suffering from exposure to the scorching desert sun and air). "The trees," she said to Emily, "the trees are incredible!"

Emily glanced at Celia and smiled, then returned her attention to the road. "It's pleasant, isn't it. Exotic, even."

"It's like scenery out of old movies."

"There are a few other places on this continent like this," Emily said. "Though not many, it's true. They say that a lot of the country used to be this green and lush, that there used to be trees like these everywhere but in the southwest."

"And they let all that go?" Celia felt cheated.

"Yes," Emily said wryly. "They let all that go. They were blind about the cost of things. They didn't understand the concept of the long-run, and their cost-effective formulas were simplistic and naive. That shortsightedness was the main reason the executive-system was born, you know. Ah, here's our exit."

The car moved through a tunnel lined with yellow tile and emerged into a forest of towers. When they came to an intersection, Celia glimpsed the water a few blocks to the west. Remembering that she was in the midst of a city of anarchy, she felt oddly exposed. Yet they seemed to be in a business district, and she could see dozens of men and women, many of them professionals, walking about in apparent unconcern. People got used to anything, Celia reminded herself. And the buildings were intact, unlike the many sections of LA and San Diego that had been ravaged by the Civil War and Global War, and then by rioters.

"If the map is correct, this is our hotel," Emily said. Celia stared up at the tower, then into the fluorescent-lit garage they were entering.

"So many big buildings," Celia said. "And so many vehicles."

"This is a real city, unlike San Diego," Emily said, stopping the auto near the panel marked **REGISTRATION**. Emily lowered the window. "Emily Madden party of two," she said into the mike attached to the panel. "You should have had my request for reservations by email yesterday."

After a few seconds a male voice came over the speaker. "Reservation confirmed. Suite 75B. If you will insert your plastic into the intake slot and take the form that will then come out of the hopper and print it with your right thumb, your registration will be complete." Emily did as instructed; Celia stared as she had on all the other occasions she'd seen Emily's blue plastic and mused on the things she'd heard blue plastic could do. The voice came over the speaker again. "Please follow the purple signals, which will take you to the elevator. You will be met there."

Emily raised her window. Moving at a snail's pace, she followed the neon purple arrows directing them to the elevator. "Are all hotels like this?" Celia asked curiously.

"I've no idea," Emily said. "I've always been chauffeured in such situations." She grinned at Celia. "This is an adventure for me, too, Cee. Do you realize I've never piloted my plane this far from home without a co-pilot? This is the most independence I've ever enjoyed!"

Four service-techs awaited them at the elevator—one to take charge of the vehicle and three to carry their luggage and conduct them to their suite. Over-kill, Celia thought. But that, too, probably went with the blue plastic.

When they were finally alone in the suite, Emily took out her jammer and set it on the low table between their chairs. "What we have to do now is contact Margot Ganshoff and either Martha Greenglass or Maureen Polaskey," Emily said. "Margot Ganshoff is the person in the Austrian Consulate I was referred to by the PA of Austria's San Diego Consul. Martha Greenglass is the leader of the group that runs the Free Zone, and Maureen Polaskey is one of the people overseeing their human rights project."

Celia folded her hands over her knees. "I don't know why, but I'm feeling incredibly stressed, Em."

Emily nodded. "Because this is it. These are the people who can either make it work, or not. Without their help we'll just have to continue struggling along as we've been doing."

"Getting nowhere but jail," Celia said.

Emily stared hard into Celia's eyes. "If we can work with these people, everything will change, Cee. Everything."

Hope—belief, even—long dead, stirred in Celia. In spite of herself.

Emily opened her handset. "Let's do it and see," she said. "Let's do it now."

Chapter Twenty-eight

[i]

Venn set five glasses and two bottles of wine on the top step. "Someone else can fetch the water," she said as she poured the wine. "Everyone knows where it's kept."

Martha leaned forward to take the glass Maureen passed her. She said, "I must have had to drink a couple of gallons of water today just to keep my throat moist enough to talk."

"I'd say none of us did too badly today in the talk department," Beatrice said.

"Shall we congratulate ourselves?" Laura asked dryly.

"I for one was amazed," Venn said. "I didn't know we had it in us. And it was all spontaneous, too, once Martha set us going. You realize that the Toni Farren and Louise Simon contingents probably think we planned the entire thing."

Maureen said softly, "I don't think Toni Farren's group will be trying to discredit us. Louise's, yes. They had the most to lose today, and they lost big. But as for Toni Farren and her crowd, I think we made sense to them."

Laura snorted. "That's crap. They simply knew themselves outflanked. You don't seriously believe they took in what Martha was saying?"

"What *we* were saying," Venn said. "But maybe Maureen is right. Maybe I'm too cynical about our political groupings. We tend to think Toni Farren is only out for herself and her small clique, out to carve herself an empire. But maybe we've misjudged her. Most people *do* have ethical values that in certain circumstances can be prodded into play, even when they work against self-interest."

"Yes, but for how long?" Martha said.

"Does anyone besides me want a cushion or two?" Beatrice said. "My back is too old to take porch railings so blithely."

Maureen and Beatrice went inside to fetch cushions for all of them. "The next step," Martha said softly, "is to introduce the global human rights project. Maybe we should bring it up tomorrow. Even if we don't have the details worked out with the other Zones and activists groups, it might be a good idea to put the world on notice that not just the US will be under scrutiny."

"I don't think we should let them know we're going for a global project," Laura said. "Or we'll lose what little support of the governments that we have."

"I disagree," Venn said. "I think most of the governments supporting our human rights project don't think of themselves as being violators." Venn paused as Beatrice and Maureen returned with cushions that they distributed before reseating themselves. "We're talking about making an announcement tomorrow about the global human rights project," Venn said to them. "Laura was arguing that we will probably lose the support of the few governments that back us if we make such an announcement. But I believe otherwise. I think that the governments supporting our smaller project don't consider themselves violators. If they did they wouldn't be giving the project their support in the first place, since they'd feel too defensive. No, I think Martha's right about introducing it into the meeting, although maybe we ought to run it by our counterparts in the other Zones first. Or at least check with the Marq'ssan who are attending who would probably know if any of the other Zones have strong ideas about timing. What I'm thinking is that two important things might come from such an announcement: some rethinking, and possibly advance cooperation with rights activists on the part of marginal governments. But even more important would be the signal it would send to activists everywhere. It could be a great psychological boost."

"I agree," Beatrice said. "Activists struggling against repression need something to hold onto. Not to prick our balloon, though, I feel that I have to point out that we're probably going to need to achieve concrete progress in our struggle against the US Executive before anyone takes the global project seriously. So far we haven't helped anyone in the US. All that's happened is that a state of emergency has been declared in the area the Marq'ssan struck with a Blanket."

"Because the bastards are so stubborn," Laura said. "They can't indefinitely hold out against Marq'ssan pressure, you know."

"Oh no?" Martha asked. "I wouldn't be too sure. From what Elizabeth Weatherall told me, the people holding us up still don't really believe the Marq'ssan exist. She says they're all crazy."

"And considering the general level of self-destructiveness among us humans," Beatrice added sadly, "it's not beyond the realm of possibility that they would rather lose everything they own than give in."

"You think *all* executives think that way?" Laura said. "If enough executives continue to take losses because of the obstinacy of the Executive, there might be a palace revolution."

"Coup," Venn said. "Not revolution. Coup. Let's not get those terms mixed up."

"Semantics." Laura sniffed. "Typical intellectual snobbery." Martha reflected that the truce between Venn and Laura had been bound to fray sooner or later.

"What do you think Louise will do next," Beatrice asked Martha. "And what will happen with the Women's Patrol?"

Martha took a sip of wine before answering. Louise's response had been something she had refused to consider while preparing her speech. "Some of the Women's Patrol will stay with us, some will splinter with Louise. As for Louise herself, I suppose she'll set up shop on her own. Shoshana, by the way, told me this morning that Louise is trying to arrange a prisoners' trade with the Executive. I suppose if she succeeds in doing that her stock will rise even higher with the militant feminist groups we have ties with all over the US. After all, she's been helping to train them for years."

"You mean you think she'll strike out on her own," Laura said.

Martha leaned her head back against the porch railing. "Yes. You don't think she'd just give up?"

"I can see it," Maureen said. "The Co-op isn't the center of the anti-executive world by any means."

"Yes, but we have the Marq'ssan," Laura said.

Beatrice laughed shortly. "That's a little much, Laura. 'Have' them? Can the Marq'ssan be possessed?"

"You know what I mean. I think you've been hanging with Venn too long."

"Christ," Maureen said half under her breath.

"So let's talk about this global vid project," Venn said.

"The first thing we have to do is set up a network of coordinators," Martha said. "Of our counterparts in the other Zones and people like Inez Monteforte. Magyyt will help with Latin America, Tyln with Asia and the Pacific, Flahn with Europe and Morghuas with Africa. And some of my trade contacts should be useful, too."

"The Marq'ssan must think we're ready for this now," Venn said thoughtfully. "The possibility for it has always existed. But they've for some reason decided to go with it now. I wonder why?"

"You think all this is the Marq'ssan's idea?" Beatrice said. "That they put the idea in our heads? Even though we started the clinics and set up asylum arrangements?"

"Who knows to what extent they bring us around to their way of thinking?" Maureen said, frowning. "We humans are pretty slow—and gutless. Maybe it *is* their doing. But that's not necessarily bad, you know."

"I can tell you right now," Martha said categorically, "that that's just such bullshit. The Marq'ssan don't operate that way. They're deeply opposed to managing us. Yes, they teach us—indirectly, by asking us certain kinds of questions. But they leave the actual insights to us. Sorben didn't spell this problem with the Night Patrol out to me, you know. She merely asked me a couple of questions. Everything else followed from that. They provoke thought, not manage perception. There's a big difference. I've often wished they *would* covertly manage us into changing. It would be so damned much simpler." Martha held out her glass for more wine.

Venn leaned forward and poured from the second bottle. "So. Do we make the announcement tomorrow? And should we try to get in touch with our counterparts in the other Zones tonight?"

"I'll have more while you're pouring," Laura said, passing her glass to Beatrice who passed it to Venn. "You're premature, Venn. Not everybody agrees that such an announcement is appropriate."

Martha sipped her wine and sighed. More arguments, more discussion, more struggle for consensus. God she was tired of it. It was at times like this when she sympathized with Venn's dislike for "politics" (as she called such wrangling). As though no matter how far they went they'd still be pulled down by endless wrangling. But she supposed that was the price of having neither a hierarchy nor a democracy.

[ii]

Celia and Emily watched Margot Ganshoff read the letter from Charlotte Engheim that Emily had handed her as soon as they had been served drinks. "So," the foreign executive said, laying the letter down on the table beside her. She looked from Celia to Emily. "According to this, you are both active in the cause for human rights in Southern California. She doesn't mention any specific organization."

Emily spoke. "Neither of us is affiliated with an organization. As is the case for many activists in San Diego. Every time an organization forms, it's almost immediately banned. What would be the point of wasting one's efforts trying to hold such structures together? We work in loose networks."

The executive's eyes widened. "How do you get anything done? Who knows or cares about doing anything?"

Emily looked at Celia. "You start, Cee. Tell her about your work. And your mother's and your uncle's."

With the fingers of her right hand Celia picked at the paper napkin wrapping the glass of fruit juice she held in her left. "I'm an attorney. A few years ago one of my clients disappeared. Later we discovered he had been shipped out to a work camp. No charges were ever brought against him, and he had no trial. Our guess now is that most of the inmates in that camp were there simply to provide cheap labor, mostly agricultural, although I had a hard time believing that for a long time. I had been representing him in a civil suit at the time, against an insurance company. The firm I worked for handled only civil suits. When in the course of seeking justice for my client I discovered that his plight was commonplace, I decided to move to a different firm, one that was prepared to represent clients in such situations. Eventually I became a target of the Military Police and ODS myself. I've even been harangued by a judge about the ethical obligations of my profession to uphold the executive system. Apparently he believes that representing clients whose human rights are being violated is

a direct attack on it. No one recruited me, Margot. No organization
directs my work. Over the years I've built up a network of contacts
with other simpaticos, as people like Emily and me are called. As for
my mother, she is an emergency-room physician. She has seen and
treated the results of the brutalities. She took it upon herself not to
report to the authorities—as she is required by law to do—certain of
the cases she has treated. When appropriate, she protests the atrocities
she has seen. My uncle is also a physician. He was even more vocal,
more active, and did not confine his activities to the hospital—with
the result that he has been banned and is no longer legally allowed to
practice medicine. He worked—until his last arrest and current incar-
ceration—in an unofficial clinic, where I myself have been working
since my naming. We are typical 'movement people,' as simpaticos
are also called. We simply do what we see needs doing." Celia swallowed a gulp of the fruit juice. What could any of it mean to this
executive, anyway?

"And you, Emily?" Margot said. "What is it you do?"

Emily shrugged. "I provide credit and make connections between
simpaticos and potential simpaticos."

"You are dedicated to this 'movement,' then."

"Yes. It hardly seems subversive to want to restore justice, to demand civilized behavior of government forces. In my opinion, many
executives have jumped the track since the Blanket. They need to be
forced to take stock of themselves and how they are overturning their
own values."

The executive's smile suggested cynical world-weariness. "My
dear you are young. In short, you're an idealist."

Emily shook her head. "No. I'm talking about working within
the narrow bounds of what we've already had. Of what the executive
system stood for in the past."

"What it stood for in the past?" the executive said. She sighed.
"Do you know how old I am, Emily?"

"Naturally not."

"I'm eighty-five, my dear. Eighty-five years old. Which means
I was around to see the birth of the executive system. Granted there
were a few people who thought like you about what the executive
system should be, morally. But for the most part all that was a line

developed explicitly and cynically for public consumption. The executive system was born solely because our world would have otherwise deteriorated into an uncontrollable cascade of death and chaos. It was a question of the survival of the West. Of Western Civilization, if you will." Margot sketched a wry smile. "It's that simple. And so we were able to pull ourselves out of the mess somewhat and manage to get everything into reasonable shape. But I wouldn't say we were motivated by the moral values you're talking about. And I wouldn't say there weren't human rights violations back then, either. Because there were. In fact, during the first upheavals, when water and oil shortages began to become murderously acute for the first time in the privileged North, a lot of people were killed. The numbers aren't available on how many, at least not to people as low in the hierarchy as I am. That bit of history is not a pretty picture, Emily. And you're making a big mistake if you think you can appeal to that pretty picture when you talk to executives who count." Margot glanced at Celia. "I probably shouldn't be saying this in front of a non-executive." She shrugged. "But what does it matter?" She looked back at Emily. "You see why I'd call you an idealist?"

"But ending hunger?" Emily said. "And poverty?"

Margot snorted. "Because it was convenient. And neat. And orderly. And all around favorable. But look at the situation now! Poverty everywhere and plenty of hunger, too. If the *raison d'être* of the executive system was and is moral, don't you think it wouldn't have coped with those things first before plunging into war? What happened in this country after the Blanket? A Civil War, Emily. We in Europe began rebuilding. But here, a Civil War. It could have happened with us, too. Only we didn't have to cope with the same degree of factionalism as that which existed within your Executive. I'd say that was more a matter of luck for us than superior moral values."

"You're so cynical!"

"Yes. To repeat: I'm eighty-five-years old. I've been an executive for a long, long time."

"And your reasons for participating in this human rights project?" Celia asked, afraid the executives might go off on another tangent.

Margot shrugged. "My government has decided we can benefit handsomely from the aliens' technology. We've heard that there's a possibility that the ground water here in the Free Zone will be rehabilitated. If they can do that…" Margot's eyes gleamed. "And there are other things as well, sure things. We have a promise that they will help clean up our most important lakes. The US Executive has been sinking for some time. Since the war many of us smaller Western-aligned nations have been rethinking our positions. Austria sees its chance—and is prepared to take it. It's that simple."

Emily looked upset, Celia thought, and wondered why. Surely she must have been around such reasoning all her life. Her father must be just as cynical as this Austrian.

Celia said, "Obviously the most efficient thing would be for you to put us in touch with the appropriate people in the Co-op."

"That's easily done. I'll contact Martha Greenglass tomorrow. But I must warn you they're in the midst of one of their Steering Committee meetings, and it may be difficult to make the contact as long as the meeting is in session." Her smile flashed out. "I think you might be interested in meeting her, Celia. And you too, Emily. She made a remarkable speech today—which they broadcast only a couple of hours ago. I have a copy of it, if you're interested, and of course a recording of it will be available on the Co-op's website. It is marginally relevant to the human rights project. And is an extraordinarily risk-taking speech." Margot snorted. "In spite of so many years of responsibility, that woman is still as much an idealist as you are, Emily. It's simply amazing. Only time will tell whether she'll survive the gamble of her speech."

"I would like to hear it before meeting her," Celia said. Emily's silence worried her. What Margot had said about the executive system seemed to have upset her.

The door opened and a service-tech wheeled in a cart. "But now, we dine," Margot said, rising. "I hope you like salmon?"

Celia rose and bent over Emily, who had not moved. "Are you all right, Em?" she whispered.

Emily nodded her head three times, very slowly, then rose to her feet. Celia took her arm and walked her to the table. She wished they could go back to the hotel now, for obviously Emily was in no mood for dinner with this hard-talking diplomat. Could Emily really have believed all that propaganda about the executive system as the means to achieving a universal utopia? Wasn't it enough that it had for a time eliminated poverty and hunger and had at least briefly worked to curb the old corporate abuses that had run so many countries close to collapse and revolution?

How sad, Celia thought, that Emily should be so disillusioned. If she had known much of life before the Blanket she would have been more realistic about the executive system and its purposes. As she, Celia had always been—without the need to abolish it, but also without the need to worship it. And what of Emily's father? Celia dipped her spoon into the bowl of won ton soup. How did Emily fit him into her idealism? It was something Celia had never wondered about, though she saw now that it had always been an obvious question to pose. How little she knew of Emily. Not because of any reserve on Emily's part, but because she, Celia, had been too absorbed in her own problems even to notice. But now Emily needed her. She only hoped she'd be able to understand, be able to help. Disillusion of any sort was a terrible thing. But disillusion of what looked to be the major premise of one's existence?

Watching Emily listlessly lifting her spoon to her mouth, Celia swelled with sad, tender affection. She always forgot how young Emily was; she never thought of how Emily herself might be in need, so amazingly self-sufficient had she always seemed. But that had been a mistake. No one was beyond needing others—not even Emily Madden.

[iii]

"I seem to have worked up a huge appetite." Elizabeth stretched her arms over her head. "How about you, love?"

"You're always hungry," Hazel said. "Me, I'm feeling more lazy than hungry. I could even go to sleep right here on the floor."

Elizabeth turned her head and nibbled Hazel's shoulder. "You taste really scrumptious, love, but somehow where my stomach's concerned you lack a certain substantiality. How about if I put together a snack—I did have the foresight to take some goodies out of the freezer this afternoon—and bring it in here?" So nice having a fireplace in the master bedroom. If she had still had her house to design... No. That was behind her now. No point in playing what-if games.

Elizabeth went into the kitchen and assembled a good-sized supper. The whole set-up was almost too idyllic, she thought, getting out a liter-and-a-half bottle of water. She tried to imagine spending the rest of her life living in such leisure. Could this be what the maternal-line life—once the contracts had been fulfilled, that is—was like? But it would grow boring, eventually, even if one traveled constantly, even if one found all sorts of pursuits to throw oneself into.

Elizabeth wheeled the cart she had filled with food, drink, and all the accoutrements for eating into the bedroom. She parked it just inside the door and looked around for Hazel, who was no longer lying on the floor in front of the fire. "Where are you, darling?" she called out, unreasonably anxious. She was too stressed about security, too jumpy about the possibilities... She found Hazel in the dressing room, choosing something to wear. Elizabeth laughed at her. "So you don't like eating in the nude, darling?"

Hazel made a droll face. "It feels too decadent or something to eat while naked. Maybe for you it wouldn't be so bad, you don't have such big tits. But for me...bread crumbs or anything else drifting down onto them is annoying."

Elizabeth, chuckling, moved behind Hazel and cupped those "such big tits" in her palms. "We could mix food and sex," she said before sliding her tongue into Hazel's ear.

"Oh Liz." Hazel giggled. "I'm too inhibited for things like that."

"Are you sure?"

"I really have to put something on. I was thinking of wearing one of those dresses you got me."

An unthinkable idea suddenly came into Elizabeth's head. "No, darling, wait," Elizabeth said. "I have something else I'd like you to wear." Elizabeth hesitated: did she really want to see Hazel wearing it? Part of her did, part of her absolutely longed to cover Hazel with that silk. As an exorcism, perhaps? "Just a minute, darling, it's something I haven't unpacked." Elizabeth withdrew from Hazel and went to the section of the closet holding their luggage. She pulled out the suitcase she knew held the jouissance silk, opened it, and stared at the plastic-wrapped, tissue-swathed silk. A shudder rippled over her, raising gooseflesh all over her body. Elizabeth retrieved the package and shoved the suitcase back into the closet. With trembling fingers she opened the plastic and unfolded the silk from the tissue paper. She looked across the room at Hazel. "Try this, darling." Her voice was almost breathless. "I think it's your size."

Hazel approached. "But it's red, Liz. Red isn't my color."

"Forget the color," Elizabeth said. "Wait until you feel it on your skin." She urged Hazel with her eyes to take the gown and put it on. "Please, darling. Just this once?"

"It belonged to another lover, didn't it," Hazel said, her eyes wary.

"She wasn't my lover, darling. Someone I cared for, but not a lover."

Hazel bit her lip. "There's something spooky about this, Liz."

"Please, Hazel. Please. Please put it on." Once having thought of it, she *had* to have Hazel wear the gown. There was nothing she wanted more in the world than to see Hazel in it, moving, living, breathing, *alive*.

"This is important to you, isn't it," Hazel said. Elizabeth looked away. "I wish I knew why."

Elizabeth watched Hazel in the mirror. "Can't you bring yourself to wear it for just a few hours?"

After another long moment, Hazel went to Elizabeth, and Elizabeth draped the gown over Hazel's arms. Elizabeth watched Hazel's hands caress the silk and turn it over and over until finally she located the Velcro seam and the holes for the head and arms. As Hazel slipped into it, Elizabeth saw that she had been right about the size: it fit the girl perfectly, far better than it had fit Zeldin when she had worn it, for the gown had been sized to Zeldin's pre-incarceration measurements.

Hazel stared in the mirror at herself and at Elizabeth behind her. "Who is it you see when you look at me wearing this?" Hazel said softly.

"I see you, darling," Elizabeth said. "I see my Hazel, beautiful, resilient, sexy, alive." As long as Hazel wore this gown Zeldin could not haunt her. Hazel was the antithesis of Zeldin. Hazel was alive. *And you are my murderer.*

Hazel said. "What is it?"

Elizabeth flushed. "Nothing, darling, nothing at all. Let's eat, shall we? Our food will be getting cold."

But she was no longer hungry. Zeldin had ruined her appetite, damn her.

[iv]

Celia came to the end of the two-hour recording Margot had given them of Martha Greenglass's speech and the discussion it had provoked and looked at Emily, who, though lying stretched out on the bed with her eyes closed, had been listening. "I'm confused, Em. She makes it all so complicated."

Emily opened her eyes. "What in particular confuses you?"

Celia considered the question and realized that it did not imply that Emily herself had escaped confusion, only that there were many things that might be sources of confusion. "What are we to do with people who don't treat other individuals as human beings?" she said. "Are we to send them away the way this Martha Greenglass talks about expelling the woman who has been killing rapists? I see that she's saying rapists shouldn't be killed. As well as that the woman who killed rapists shouldn't be killed. But what do we do with rapists, torturers, and murderers? Simply let them alone, simply let them do what they want?" For as the discussion had progressed, Celia had been unable to shut off the images of that beast—and her longing for his death so that she could feel safe, so that she could forget that he had ever existed...even though she knew that his death alone would not make her "safe," that there were many more than him and that he had probably been following orders from a superior when he had done those things to her. And yet the fact remained, his very existence was an attack on *hers.*

"I don't know, Celia, I really don't." Emily's voice was slow with fatigue and very low. "I don't know what we can or should do with people who are unfit to live in society. What I thought she was saying is that by killing such people we only damage ourselves. That such a response is a part of the same disease that afflicts those who lack respect for others' lives. It seems to be a vicious circle, doesn't it."

"Us and them. There is an elemental difference, isn't there? We aren't *really* like those beasts, are we?" Celia's throat was tight. The more she thought about it, the more the force and scope of Martha Greenglass's argument felt like an oblique, clever attack on her.

"There is a difference, but not the kind of difference we want to believe in, Cee. I think that's what she was saying. And that seeing things always in divisions of us and them is dangerous. That that's where things go wrong. That the killers and torturers and rapists are such precisely because they see such a division. That if they saw others as a part of themselves they wouldn't be able to do those things. That's what I thought I heard her and some of the others saying."

"It is unbearable," Celia whispered, "thinking that I might be like those beasts, that I am a part of *that*."

"It's true, she was saying that," Emily said. "But I don't think she meant it as a necessarily negative thing. Not in the way you're thinking of. She thinks it's a bad idea to withdraw from looking that in the face." Emily sighed. "I suppose she's right. I know I've been fooling myself. Thinking that there was something good about being an executive, that the problem was merely one of abuse and fear. That the basic impulse behind the executive system was fairness and benevolence..." Emily sighed again, long and heavily.

Celia sniffed and reached for a tissue. What was it she was doing in this world, anyway? Why was she still alive? What was the *point*? Celia struggled with herself and in the end did not say any of these things to Emily. Emily was aching, hurting, was perhaps self-despising tonight. Emily, who had done so much for her, needed her. Celia reached for Emily's hand. "It doesn't change what you are, Em," she said softly. "It doesn't change your goals, your values, your inner being. You'll still be what you were."

Emily squeezed Celia's hand. "I appreciate the thought, Cee. But it's not true, you know. I am a part of all that, whatever I might like to think. It's my world; it's the world I exist in. No one can separate themselves from their world."

"No, but they can struggle against it. Otherwise why would we even be here in Seattle right now? Because we don't accept the way things are, because we don't accept our world." But what that woman had said, didn't that mean that they were all hopelessly contaminated? How could anything change if it were true they all had that ugliness inside each and every one of them?

Celia watched Emily roll over onto her stomach. No one at that meeting had talked about what to do with the beasts. Or what it really

meant to be a part of that. They'd all talked about honesty and intro-
spection and changing social structures, as though the beasts could
be wished away. But Celia knew they couldn't. And so did Emily,
despite her sheltered, protected, privileged life. For obviously Emily
had her own beasts, too. It was something that hadn't occurred to
Celia before now. But then she had never wondered much about
Emily before tonight.

Without thinking about it Celia slid down on the bed, rolled
onto her stomach, and laid her arm across Emily's shoulders. "I love
you, Emily Madden," she whispered. A few seconds later, listening
to Emily's breathing, she realized that Emily had fallen asleep. She
didn't know whether she was disappointed or relieved. She continued
to listen to Emily's breathing and conjured up an image of the ocean.
And then she drifted into sleep herself, as if it were the easiest thing
in the world to do.

Chapter Twenty-nine

[i]

They waited for Martha Greenglass in a wedge-shaped room. Celia fidgeted with the clasp on her belt; Emily stared out the window. And Celia wondered if she should have brought the files with her after all. She had reasoned that they would not be needed in this first meeting, that there would be no point in lugging them along. But perhaps these people would want figures, numbers Celia wouldn't be able to remember and Emily wouldn't know.

The door flew open and an oddly dressed woman broadcasting excitement and energy bounded toward them. This, Celia realized, was the woman who had made the speech. The woman held out her hand. "How do you do?" Her smile radiated warmth and confidence. "I'm Martha Greenglass. You're from San Diego?"

"Celia Espin." Celia shook hands with the woman. "And this is Emily Madden."

"So," Martha said when they'd settled themselves on the rug. "Margot Ganshoff tells me you're prepared to act as coordinators for your area. It will be a big job. And possibly a dangerous one."

Celia was not exactly comfortable sitting on the floor with a stranger while talking about serious, professional matters. She said, trying not to sound as stiff as she felt, "Danger won't be a new element in my life. I've been in and out of jail many times over the last few years."

Martha said, "The idea, of course, will be to get them to stop these practices. But the first phase may be difficult. The Executive seems to be balking pretty stubbornly."

"There's a question that's been in my mind since I listened to the speech you made yesterday," Celia said, abruptly launching the issue most on her mind.

"Yes?"

"It seems to me there are two ways of going about this, ah, project as you call it. One can either insist that the people guilty of human rights violations be held responsible for their crimes—arrested, tried, and punished, thereby stopping the crimes and making our homes safe again. Or one can try to 'rescue' the victims without doing anything about the criminals. The problem then is that the victims have to live as refugees and outcasts, while the criminals have everything their own way and get off scot-free." At the statement of each new point, Martha nodded. "I have to say, there's something about the latter approach that sticks in my gullet. I'm one of the victims you're talking about. Doing it your way, I'd have to flee, become a refugee, except that I can't do that, can I, since I've dedicated myself to stopping it. I'm a lawyer, Martha. I believe in the processes of law. I would like to see justice done. The thought of these criminals remaining free to pursue their bestialities..." Celia's throat grew tight; she knew she was close to tears. "What I'm asking, is, what, on the practical level, are you going to do with so many thousands of people who will need refuge? And on the level of justice, how can we simply help people to flee—thus continuing to break up their lives—while new abuses go on piling up as the criminals are allowed to continue unchecked? Why should the victims be forced to lose their homes and be severed from their closest ties? Do you see what I'm saying?"

Martha nodded vigorously. "Yes. I do. You're disturbed at my insisting that we break the spiral of violence. But I don't know that what I want is necessarily in contradiction with your idea that we not further victimize the victims while the torturers and murderers go on thriving. Though I have to say at the outset that I'm philosophically opposed to all jails, and to legal systems. I'm an anarchist, Celia." Martha's eyes glistened with excitement. "We don't have prisons or judges in the Free Zone. And you see, when you don't have prisons, there can't *be* the kinds of crimes we're talking about, at least not on the scale practiced by the Executive. I'm not saying that people would never be abducted or murdered. But that it would be much harder for that to happen."

For the first time, Emily spoke. "Why can't you include in your demands on the Executive one that those guilty of human rights violations be publicly prosecuted and brought to justice? In the past such trials have been important in avenging the pain and suffering of the victims and their friends and relatives, and in satisfying the moral outrage of the community. Shouldn't your project include that sort of redress? Evacuation would be unnecessary then, wouldn't it."

Martha's teeth worried at her lower lip. "Well, there are two things we need to bear in mind. First, historically such trials have been used for political purposes, masquerading as an exhibition of moral outrage—thus sending, pretty consistently, the message that abuses matter only when they're committed by the losers of military or political conflicts, since no one ever holds governments accountable for as long as they're in power. Second, a couple of weeks ago the Executive sent someone to negotiate with us. In fact, it was Elizabeth Weatherall, who's—was, I should say, since she just went renegade—somebody important in Security."

"We know who Elizabeth Weatherall is," Emily said. "So she was here, negotiating with you? Gotta say, that woman sure does get around."

"Well they did send her here, and everything seemed to be going smoothly. The plan was for Security to clean its own house—with the help of monitors. Information would be solicited from victims. And then Security would publicly punish its wrongdoers. That all fell apart, though, when Elizabeth was summoned back to DC. And since then…" Martha shrugged. "We've gotten no cooperation from them at all. In an anarchy there are different ways of dealing with people who commit crimes. Obviously we can't ask that our methods be applied in the US, where there are law courts—of a sort. But if we aren't going to get cooperation from the Executive, I don't see how we can do as you'd like. The best we can hope for is getting people out of their bad situations."

"You know what they'll do?" Celia said. "Once they bow to your pressure they'll say 'Good riddance, these people don't belong in our wonderful great country. If they don't like it here, let them get the hell out.' And the victims will be refugees, with no sense of redress, always living under the shadow of having been treated as though *they* were the ones who were criminals, when their tormenters are the real criminals."

Martha nodded. "I get what you're saying, Celia. Certainly we will want to take down testimony and compile lists of the guilty and so on. We'll have to see what we can do, taking it from there. It all depends on how the Executive responds to us." She looked from Celia to Emily and back to Celia again. "There's another angle to this you are not yet aware of. And that's that this project will be global, not simply national. We intend to bring pressure to bear all over the world. For that reason, there will probably be a lot more resistance. We're going to try to press a demand for serious change in the world." The current of Martha's excitement ran so strongly that it made Celia shiver with tension.

Emily said, "If the aliens couldn't force the governments to do their bidding immediately after the Blanket, why do you think they can do so now?"

"Several reasons," Martha replied. "First, the Free Zones have been around for a decade now and are beginning to be recognized by the governments. Second, the governments have grown increasingly weaker because of their wars. Third, this is an issue upon which people, given a certain amount of leadership, can unite. Do you think most governments will be willing to lose in a single stroke what they've been rebuilding over the last ten years? Another Blanket would wipe them out, and they know it. I wonder if every government will be willing to risk those kinds of losses. Surely they can't all be as crazy as the US's Executive."

"Perhaps," Emily said. "But I think *you* will be risking a lot, too. What if the governments threaten to kill their prisoners if the aliens strike? Have you considered that?"

Martha's excitement visibly dimmed. "The thought has crossed my mind," she said, "but I refuse to believe that would be the universal response. Maybe in the US...though would even the Executive dare to slaughter thousands of people like that?" Martha shook her head. "I don't think it would be tolerated by the rest of the population."

"Look what is tolerated now," Emily said.

Shocked, Celia stared at her. "Overnight you've become a consummate cynic," Celia said. "You don't really believe they'd do that, do you, Em?"

Emily shrugged her shoulders. "I don't know what I believe now. I'm just saying: you'd better be prepared for bloodshed. The executives you're talking about won't give up their power without a fight. And from everything I've seen and heard, they fight dirty. Most of them have no scruples at all. I should know," Emily said. "Some of them are my father's closest associates."

Martha rubbed her face. "It's been a long day. I'm feeling drained; so my brain isn't working as well as it ought to be." She sighed. "Maybe you're right, Emily. But I still think it's time for us to try again. As far as I can tell, there are at least a hundred times more activist dissenters worldwide now than there were ten years ago. And public support for the executive system has been eroding all this time."

"Because people have lost their accustomed standard of living," Emily said. "But believe me, most people blame the aliens more than they blame the Executive. It was the aliens that caused the Blanket, which is the perceived source of all economic disruption. I think you're overly optimistic, Martha."

Martha shrugged again. "Well, we'll just have to see, won't we," she said—doggedly, Celia thought, as though she'd lost all the zest and confidence she had brought with her into the room.

"We are neither radicals nor anarchists," Celia warned. "If there should be a conflict, I want you to know in advance which way we will go. We're not like the Mujeres Libres group. We're non-violent, and we're non-revolutionary. All we want is justice and fairness."

Martha smiled wearily. "Which you no doubt think will flow from a properly regulated government."

Celia nodded. "Yes. I believe in doing things legally, Martha."

"Even now, after seeing what a travesty the legal system is?" Martha asked. "You who say you've been in and out of jail many times?" When neither Celia nor Emily replied, Martha shrugged. "All right, I accept you as you are. There's no reason we can't work together on this project." She glanced at her watch. "Maureen's probably gone home already. I suggest the four of us meet sometime tomorrow, to get down to specifics."

Celia and Emily agreed to this, and Martha walked them to the elevator.

As Celia and Emily stepped out into the cool, breezy night Emily said, "She may be right, Cee. It may be that no government can provide fairness and justice."

Celia halted a moment; she searched Emily's face. "There have to be rules, order, and the keeping of promises, Em. And there can't be without some kind of government. Don't throw away the baby with the bathwater."

Emily half-smiled. "I'm just keeping an open mind, Cee."

"Let's go eat," Celia said. "I'm famished." This malaise was only temporary, she told herself. Emily would bounce back, would find a way of coming to terms with her disillusion; Celia knew she would. Emily was just too strong not to.

[ii]

Elizabeth and Margot took tea in Margot's "study," an electronically shielded room lined with cedar planks. Hazel, Elizabeth knew, would not come in unless called, which meant that she and Margot could talk freely. "I'm glad you came when you did," Elizabeth said, watching Margot pour. "I was trying to nerve myself up to chop off my braid. Your arrival put off the moment of truth." Elizabeth accepted the cup and saucer Margot handed her.

Margot took the cup she'd poured herself and set it down on the table beside her. "Oh? Why would you be cutting off your braid—so apparently unwillingly?"

"Apart from my size, it's the most easily identifiable thing about me," Elizabeth said. "It can be hidden, true, but why go to so much trouble? Besides, without my girl I won't be able to groom it properly."

Margot shook her head. "My dear, your reasoning eludes me. Are you trying to tell me you're going to live on the run?"

"What else?" Elizabeth said. "You know the Executive will have people combing the globe for me."

"That needn't matter all that much, you know." Margot's eyes narrowed. "If, say, you pursued one of your many interesting options."

Elizabeth leaned back in her chair. So. They had now arrived at the real reason for Margot's visit. "You have a proposition to make me?"

"Why don't you simply acquire some protection? Considering all the amazonian warriors running around the Free Zone, surely you could suitably surround yourself with a difficult-to-penetrate defense."

Elizabeth frowned. "Simon's women?"

Margot shrugged. "They aren't all attached to her, you know. She's helped organize a number of training camps but doesn't necessarily command the personal loyalty of everyone trained in them. As I mentioned before, there's one not far from here."

"And then what?"

Margot sipped before answering. When she had set the cup back in its saucer, she looked at Elizabeth. "And then you decide whom you are interested in working for."

Elizabeth drew a deep breath and slowly let it out. "Working *for*. I don't know that anyone would want me now that I've gone renegade," she said.

Margot snorted. "I'm quite certain the Austrian government would take you on in a heartbeat But there are others. And then, of course, there's the Co-op. If you were so inclined. Frankly, they could sorely use someone like you, whether they know it or not." Margot smiled sardonically. "Just imagine *your* conducting negotiations with the Executive. Wouldn't that be delicious."

Elizabeth could not help joining Margot's laughter, though the very thought of such brashness made her stomach queasy. "I'll have to think about this a bit," Elizabeth said. "I'm afraid I haven't given much thought yet to the future."

"Well I'd do so if I were you."

Elizabeth sipped tea. "What's the news?" she said casually.

Margot slanted one of her driest looks at Elizabeth. "The news is that DC is reeling under the effects of the Blanket. The Pentagon is in a stew about Norfolk's disabling. And there's a rumor that most of Security Central burned following a series of explosions that occurred *before* the Blanket was imposed. Apparently, given the timing of the Blanket, they were unable to fight the fire that resulted from the explosions." Margot's smile was sour. "You of course would know nothing about that kind of sabotage."

Elizabeth hastily gulped another swallow of tea. "Any other news?" she asked, hoping to cover up the sudden lift of relief singing joyously in her ears.

"Had a visit from somebody I believe you know."

Elizabeth's eyes met Margot's. "Oh?"

"You do know Emily Madden?"

"She's in Seattle?"

"Yes. For a few days. She's involved in some way with a San Diego human rights group."

"I'd like to see her," Elizabeth said slowly. "I wonder if we can arrange something."

"Surely," Margot said. "In case you haven't noticed, I've become something of a go-between here in the Free Zone. I'd be delighted to get you two together."

Elizabeth frowned. Was that sarcasm in Margot's voice? "And what else?" she said, an unspecified discomfort prompting her to shift the subject. "Has Simon's enterprise failed? Or has the Executive taken to dealing with her?"

Margot shrugged. "I've heard nothing. But the Steering Committee meeting has been most interesting." Margot lifted her attaché case onto her knees and opened it. "I've brought you a couple of recordings I thought you might find interesting." Margot removed two data keys and set them next to her tea cup. "Just in case you decide to do business with the Free Zone."

Elizabeth sighed. "Can you actually imagine my working for Martha Greenglass?"

"Working *with* her, Elizabeth. People don't work *for* her, but *with* her. She doesn't even have a secretary, you know."

"Then she's a fool."

Margot smiled. "Yet she gets things done. She and her colleagues. At any rate, take a look at these recordings. Greenglass makes a major speech on one of them. And on the other is a discussion of a massive project they're starting, one which—considering that the aliens will be backing them—is guaranteed to shake up the entire world."

Elizabeth frowned. "Just what is your interest in all this, Margot?"

An enigmatic smile drifted onto Margot's face. "I'm easily bored these days, my dear. I'm frankly fascinated to see if they can pull off what they intend. More important, Austria will probably benefit. We're in on the ground floor with the aliens. So while the basic geopolitical structures are being shaken down and possibly dismantled, Austria will be on solid footing. For quick minds and daring hearts, this is a time of opportunity such that countries like mine scarcely encounter. Austria may not have to live on long-past glories much longer." Margot shrugged. "If, that is, my government doesn't behave foolishly."

"Which is asking a lot," Elizabeth said. "My opinion of males is lower than ever. I think they're all mad. Something to do with their being fixed, or perhaps a genetic inferiority. I don't know which it is, but I wouldn't count on anything but weakness and foolishness and delusions from your government if I were you."

Margot sighed; staring down at her hands she toyed with one of the many rings on her fingers. "If I were fifty years younger, Elizabeth, I think I'd be tempted."

"Tempted?" Elizabeth said. "Tempted to what?"

Margot looked up and met Elizabeth's gaze. "To organize a takeover of control from the males. The world is going to pieces because of them, and I'm tired of watching it." She shrugged. "But I don't have that kind of energy or will now. My age makes me too cynical to attempt anything serious."

Elizabeth's breath came uncomfortably fast. "What a fantasy, Margot," she whispered. "But I don't see how it could be done. They own most of the property, which is what gives them control, as I'm sure you know."

"It could be done," Margot said. "I've thought about it for the last five years. During the war I thought about it. I'm so tired of incompetence and instability." She shrugged. "But it would take someone less jaundiced and jaded than myself." Her gaze plunged into Elizabeth's. "It would take someone like you. Someone with your experience, your energy, your connections."

Elizabeth's head reeled. "You're putting me on, Margot. You're so bored you want to see how I'll react."

Margot did not smile. "Let me tell you something. Living here in the Free Zone, watching the women running the Co-op, you begin to get ideas. Things look different. Nothing looks impossible; nothing looks necessarily permanent or inevitable."

Still too stunned to speak, Elizabeth offered the Austrian a feeble smile. "It sounds like suicidal madness," she finally said.

"Oh you'd have to believe in it yourself in order to attract converts," Margot said. "You'd have to believe in the power of your own plan, in your own will and abilities to get others to join you." She picked up her tea cup. "Think about it, Elizabeth. And we'll talk again another time."

Elizabeth sagged back into her chair. Everything had gone crazy, everyone had run mad. She must not even *fantasize* such a thing.

[iii]

When the video-file ended, Elizabeth sat motionless, staring at the gray, blank screen. In the sudden silence of the room, Kay's accusation—*Are human beings so little to you?*—echoed in Elizabeth's head. It seemed to her that she could hear Kay's voice speaking the words, could hear that voice she could no longer shut out of her mind.

With a great wrenching act of will, she tried to imagine how Booth and Sedgewick would react to Greenglass's speech. But Sedgewick, no, Sedgewick would never be listening to anything like this again. The old Sedgewick, then: she could imagine his sneer, his dismissal, his confidence that Greenglass and her people had made a capital error that could be taken advantage of, an error that would lose them the Free Zone. But such a dismissal would make no sense. So that dismissal would be meaningless. Yet Elizabeth felt certain the Executive would dismiss it.

"I'm confused, Liz."

Elizabeth looked at Hazel; she had forgotten the girl was even there. "I'm not surprised, darling. I'm confused, too. It's something of a fantasy, you know. To talk about one's enemies as being part of oneself. But in the end, that kind of thinking merely gets one killed."

"You think that's what will happen with Martha and her friends?"

"Perhaps," Elizabeth said. "It depends on how crazy the Executive is. I can easily imagine them deciding to kill the top leaders in the Free Zone as an example to anyone else daring to defy the executive system. So that even if the aliens retaliated, warning would have been given that collaborating with them can be dangerous to one's health." Elizabeth shrugged. "Or they might not even reason that far. But I'd like to see Greenglass in a room with the Executive, showing me how she intends to transcend the us-them dualism she's railing against."

Yet some of the things Greenglass had said made sense. In talking about her relationship to her ex-lover, for instance. Or in the Co-op's relation to the Night Patrol. Elizabeth and others like herself—Lisa and Allison, for example—had always felt uncomfortable about the Wedgewoods and Krebses and Harrigans Security employed and sanctioned. They tried to avoid such people and the fact of their existence as much as possible. Yet there was a sense that they had to be tolerated, not only because Sedgewick said so but also because they served a function, ugly but necessary, for the survival of the executive system. Us or them, she had insisted to Lisa when they'd come away from the El Cajon facility. Us or them. *Are human beings so little to you?* But I thought I had to do it, Kay. I believed it was necessary. Maybe I was wrong. But it wasn't a matter of my despising you. On the contrary, I deeply admired you. But there were things more important to me than you personally. Anyway, you would have been tortured and executed outright if I hadn't... No. That was wrong. She could always have stepped in and preserved Kay, she could have kept her merely locked up. But remembering what Kay was like when they'd captured her, the thought was inconceivable, even now. Dangerous, she had been dangerous; she had been the enemy if ever there was an enemy. Elizabeth had known just how dangerous Kay was. Kay was the woman who had single-handedly destroyed Sedgewick, had duped and deceived him as no one else could have. She was the woman who had negotiated the origins of the Free Zone. She was the woman who was hot on the track of their entire science and technology program. Kay had embodied "them." Only later, when she'd weakened, could there be any possibility of communication between them. And then, Elizabeth had begun loving her... But was that true? The sense of that woman's strength after those first three days in detention... She had been counting on Kay to handle Sedgewick as she had known she herself could not. It hadn't worked. But Kay had been her hope.

And all she'd succeeded in doing was destroying her.

No. *She* hadn't destroyed Kay. All those accusations had stemmed from Kay's fear, anxiety, hysteria. Her accusations had been melodrama, not truth. For Kay had been strong enough to make Sedgewick kill her. Would she herself ever have been that strong?

"Crying again, Liz?" Hazel said softly, getting up and moving to sit on the arm of Elizabeth's chair. She put her arm around Elizabeth's shoulder. "What is it? Why are you so upset? Is it the thought of everything you've left behind?"

Elizabeth smiled through her tears. "Oddly enough, darling, I can say now for the first time, I don't regret leaving. Isn't it strange, but I suddenly feel certain I've made the right decision."

If I'd stayed I would have lost everything, Elizabeth thought, I would have lost all respect for myself. For it would have meant becoming Booth's creature; it would have meant giving up all attempts to follow my own way, all attempts to get around the Executive's collective madness.

"It must be so hard for you," Hazel said. "I keep trying to imagine what it must be like, your suddenly losing all *that*."

Elizabeth raised Hazel's hand to her lips and kissed it. "I think, darling, that I lost 'all that' some time ago and never realized it. If I ever had it. No, I want to think ahead now. I'm not out of the game yet."

Hazel's eyes widened. "What game?"

Elizabeth bit her lip. How to explain to Hazel? And could Hazel understand? The game of power? No, that wasn't it exactly—or was it? That's surely how Sedgewick would put it. But why put anything in Sedgewick's terms now? That was all behind her, she could forge a new way of talking about things, a new outlook all her own. "The game of mattering, of making a difference," Elizabeth said finally. "Though *game* may not be the right word, for it's a serious pursuit. It's the pursuit of doing, of taking responsibility."

"Isn't there a name for it?" Hazel asked, frowning.

Elizabeth thought. "I don't know. I can't think of one. *Governing* won't do, *controlling* won't do, and *politics* won't do, either. Isn't it strange that it's so hard to name?"

"So you have to call it a game?"

"Maybe calling it that is the only way to keep from paralysis," Elizabeth said. "Otherwise one might do nothing at all." If she had stayed, it would have been out of paralysis. If Kay had gone on living with Sedgewick, that would have been out of paralysis, too. Elizabeth stared into Hazel's eyes and wished she could tell her about Kay. But Hazel would never understand, and she would lose the girl. And that she would not risk. "Let's go make a snack," Elizabeth said. "I'm starving."

Hazel smiled indulgently and gave her a hand to help her out of the engulfing armchair. Hand in hand they went out to the kitchen, Elizabeth's taste buds already anticipating the treats Margot had brought them from Seattle.

"You're a hedonist, Liz," Hazel said.

"So I am," Elizabeth said, goosing Hazel. But that pleasure was for later, after they'd eaten. Hazel liked to keep her pleasures separate, and Elizabeth liked—when possible—to please Hazel. She dropped Hazel's hand and opened the refrigerator. "Let's see what we have here, darling. Duck pâté, sweet butter, mustard, *explorateur*, feta, calamata olives, pickled mushrooms and artichoke hearts, pasta salad, fresh cauliflower, pumpernickel, oh look at this, strawberries, they must be from California, it's too early for them to be local, marinated baby asparagus, smoked salmon..." Elizabeth dumped all these items on the cart and grinned at Hazel. "Isn't it fun being a renegade, darling?"

Hazel smiled back. "With you, Liz, everything's fun."

"I hope, darling, you can say that a year from now," Elizabeth said, suddenly sober. "I hope you won't regret leaving."

Hazel shook her head. "Never. I had nothing to lose. Not like you."

Elizabeth sighed. Some day Hazel would realize that wasn't true. And then? But Elizabeth seized the cart and pushed it through to the bedroom. She wouldn't worry about that now, she'd face that day when it came. Tonight they would celebrate the beginning of their new life...whatever that might be.

Seattle, June–September 1985
Revised: Seattle, September 1996

Chronology of Significant Events

Feb 2076   The Marq'ssan "blanket" Earth in an EMP

                     Beginning of negotiations on *s'sbeyl*

Mid-March 2076   Marq'ssan Taskforce ends negotiations and creates six "free zones" (in he North American Pacific Northwest, Southern Mexico, Western Australia, Korea, and in parts of Brazil and Kenya)

Late-March 2076   Collapse of the US Executive and outbreak of the second US Civil War

Mid-June 2076   Return of Marq'ssan fleet to Marqeuei

Jan 2077   Henry "Mr. Clean" Lauder's SIC covert action team begins penetration operations in the Pacific Northwest Free Zone

Aug. 2077   Lauder's CAT abducts Kay Zeldin and attempts to capture Sorben I Sorben, who thwarts the CAT and frees Kay.

Sept 2077   Elizabeth Weatherall captures Kay Zeldin and announces her execution

Jan 2078   Robert Sedgewick kills Kay Zeldin at her request.
                     The US's Civil War ends
                     Russia invades Poland, Austria, and the Slovak Republics

Feb 2078   The US requires all citizens between the ages of sixteen and fifty-five to register for a possible draft into military service

April 2078   NATO is expelled from Estonia and Latvia
                     Russia signs "mutual protection pacts" with Estonia and Latvia

Aug 2078   NATO is expelled from Lithuania
                     Russia and Lithuania sign a "mutual protection pact"
                     The US institutes a "bonus procreation allowance" for all persons who perform military service
                     The US and UK take control of the Baltic Sea

Sept 2078	The US occupies Cuba and signs the Guantanamo Pact with Cuba
	NATO forces cross the German-Austrian border and seize control of Salzburg
Dec 2078	A border skirmish between Greece and Macedonia culminate in Greece declaring war against Macedonia
Jan 2079	The Albanian Unity Front attempts to overthrow the government of Macedonia
Late-Jan 2079	Albania and Kosovo join forces to invade Macedonia
Feb 2079	Greece withdraws from NATO
May 2079	NATO is expelled from Romania
	Russia and Romania sign a "mutual protection pact"
June 2079	The People's Republic of China attempts to invade and occupy the Korean Free Zone
	The Marq'ssan destructure all weapons, planes, ships, and ground vehicles used in the Chinese invasion of the Korean Free Zone
Oct 2079	Greece, Albania, and Kosovo sign an accord partitioning Macedonia that reserves Upper Macedonia for ethnic Albanians
Jan 2080	Led by the People's Republic of China, forty-nine nations sign a Declaration of Neutrality to defy the pressure being put on them to enforce demands by the Eastern Alliance as well as the NATO Alliance to enforce embargos against one another
Aug 2080	One week before the first elections to be held under US occupation, the Cuban insurgency instigates a popular uprising that shuts down Havana for twelve days and expels the US-sponsored government, and the Provisional People's Government of Cuba takes power
Sept 2080	The US begins the siege of Havana over the protest of the International Red Cross and Human Rights Watch
Dec 2080	NATO mistakenly bombs a British naval vessel, killing 351
March 2081	The Czech Republic withdraws from NATO and signs a "mutual protection pact" with Russia

July 2081	NATO is expelled from the Czech Republic
Sept 2081	A long-range conventional missile takes out NATO Headquarters in Brussels
Sept 2081	A long-range conventional missile takes out the Government of Russia Building (a.k.a. the "White House") The Eastern Alliance makes its first air-strikes against the West Coast of the US
Dec 2081	Yuri Petrov, Russia's top intelligence officer in Hungary is assassinated as he is leaving a restaurant in Vienna The Eastern Alliance makes its first air-strikes against the East Coast of the US The US shoots down a private Canadian plane in Canadian airspace The Pacific Northwest Free Zone agrees to provide safe haven to executive women and children in exchange for extending the Free Zone's territory south to the fortieth parallel
Jan 2082	Gabor János, Prime Minister of Hungary, is assassinated by a sniper
Feb 2082	The first International Assembly of Free Zones is held in Oaxaca, in the Southern Mexico Free Zone
March 2082	The Provisional People's Government of Cuba surrenders to US forces
July 2082	The Eastern Alliance begins nightly air-strikes against Hungary
Nov 2082	Thirty-eight members of Parliament and scores of officials are detained and charged with conspiring to overthrow the government in Hungary Martial law is declared in Budapest and a military junta is installed
Jan 2083	The US announces it will enforce an embargo on all imports from Eastern Alliance nations to anywhere in the Western Hemisphere
June 2083	The US Navy blows up three Chinese merchant vessels The People's Republic of China rescinds its Declaration of Neutrality and joins the Eastern Alliance

July 2083	A group of officers overthrows the military junta in Hungary and forms a new government
Feb 2084	Australia withdraws from NATO and signs the Declaration of Neutrality Thailand signs the Declaration of Neutrality
March 2084	Hungary withdraws from NATO and signs a "mutual protection pact" with Russia The Eastern Alliance begins massive aerial bombing of Berlin
July 2084	The Eastern Alliance drives US and UK forces out of the Baltic Sea
Dec 2084	Japan is invaded and occupied by the People's Republic of China NATO is driven out of Japan Ground war breaks out between the Eastern Alliance and NATO in eastern Germany
March 2085	The US and NATO begin peace talks with the Russians and the Eastern Alliance
Jan 3, 2086	The Madrid Accords are signed, bringing an end to the Global War

Afterword

I began writing *Tsunami* in the summer and fall of 1985, just days after I moved back to Seattle from New Orleans. Though I felt as though I had come home, my perceptions, sharpened by two years of living in what felt like the capital city of a third-world country, made everything about "home" look and feel different. In New Orleans, I had found the domination of everyday life by extreme racial and class divides as inescapable as the city's heat and humidity and its pervasive smell of rot. The comfortable duplex in which I lived perched precariously on the border between a white neighborhood of opulent mansions attended by dark-skinned uniformed servants on one side and a poor, mixed-race neighborhood of narrow shotgun houses, where the street just happened to lose its paving, on the other, and from my second-floor vantage, over several months' time I watched and listened to an enormous construction crew rip up a few blocks of the smooth, wide, gracious Fontainebleau Boulevard (about a hundred feet from the unpaved street), repave it, and then rip it up again. (New Orleans, of course, was as notorious for its corruption as Louisiana's "let the good times roll!" governor, Edwin Edwards.) Many stores in my neighborhood kept private guards armed with shotguns posted at their entrances, and having to walk nonchalantly past them never failed to add a special chill to my shopping experience. Once or twice a week I had to wait in a long line at the bank to cash a check, and I inevitably witnessed the tellers according very different treatment to customers depending on their apparent race and socio-economic status; the official I opened an account with had informed me that none of the banks in New Orleans had ATMs and that they probably never would because "most people around here are illiterate." The students at the best public high school in the state had to eat their lunch outside on the public sidewalk because the school could not afford to give them a cafeteria, and the city boasted almost no parks, because, as several residents told me, taxpayers did not care to spend tax dollars on amenities that would be available to everyone. And while just about all the city's residents I encountered were friendly and charming, I could never escape the continual consciousness of my classed, raced, and gendered place in that world until I returned to Seattle—which, because of that new consciousness I had acquired while away, I couldn't help but notice was not exactly a refuge from racist behavior itself.

Increasingly, I had human rights issues on my mind. The campaign resisting South Africa's horrific apartheid regime had come to the US, and my interest in El Salvador in particular and Central America in general intensified. I began to read about human rights issues, and by the time I finished writing "Blood in the Fruit" in February 1986, I was steeped in the extensive literature, which ranges from epidemiological and medical case studies to personal witness and testimony, from philosophical microanalysis (most notably Elaine Scarry's *The Body in Pain*, which examines how pain "unmakes" the world and renders the victim of torture abject) to political analysis. Still reeling with the shock of discovering that a major city in the US was in important respects more like the third-world than the first-world, I found myself speculating about aspects of the issues that were largely absent from my reading. The literature made it clear, of course, that the US had used torture outside its own borders to advance its foreign policy objectives and that the US had instructed and advised the agents of other governments or political organizations (like the Nicaraguan *contras*) in the techniques and uses of torture, assassination, and terrorism. But although the US has typically employed a variety of tactics of calumny, intimidation, and blackmail to quash domestic dissent, it has not (so far) resorted to large-scale use of torture to do so. (The ad hoc abuse of inmates prevalent in US prisons, though a related issue, is too complicated to go into here.)

Why, I asked myself, did the US not substantially employ such methods on its own political dissidents? And under what circumstances would that be likely to change? As I puzzled over this, I concluded that this restraint was not due to an inherent moral repugnance to torture in US culture and politics (which was what most people in the US in the 1980s imagined to be the distinction between themselves and white South Africans or Argentines or other Latin Americans), but rather to the perceived lack of necessity for it. As oppositional groups in the US can attest, the corporate media have always done a fine job of keeping dissent marginalized and muted. If the day ever came, I thought, that the interests of the wealthy and powerful were materially threatened by public dissent, the US would likely be no different than any other country in using torture to stifle it. As has been repeatedly demonstrated, political torture, rather than winning sympathy for its victims, renders them abject. I've no doubt this would be true in the US as well, since the media consistently portray those in opposition as losers (a perception reinforced by an electoral system in which winners take all). Consider, for instance, how the US Government's display of images of degradation of the Guantanamo Camp Delta prisoners in January 1992 evoked open cheers and gloating across the US; the fact that the majority of prisoners have been found to be bystanders with no connections to terrorist organizations, carelessly swept up, has changed nothing. Moreover, US politicians are practiced and adroit manipulators of the fear of difference (which has lately become *the* driving force in US politics), and fear compounds potently with images of abjection. I've no doubt at all that Hegemonic Power's use of torture within the US itself would simply amplify its message. The US is, after all, a society of genial and insensitive conformists.

Since I had set out in the Marq'ssan Cycle to write about significant political change, my realization that human rights abuses tend to be prevalent wherever large numbers of people are overturning or seriously threatening to overturn the status quo led to my (quite unintentionally) bringing these issues into the third and fourth books of the series: not to make a point, but simply as a necessary aspect of the series' worldbuilding. Arguably, it is a theme present in every book of the series. Given the executives' lack of respect for anyone daring to oppose them in any way and their lack of interest in anything not advancing their agenda (ever greater accumulation and control of resources), it seemed unlikely they wouldn't play "dirty" (*qua* Argentina's infamous "Dirty War").

While preparing each volume of the Marq'ssan Cycle for publication, I've been uncomfortable to note an increasingly harsh similarity between the executives of my invented world and the real-world elite in

DC today. Earlier this month, Judge Anna Taylor Diggs, ruling against the National Security Agency's warrantless surveillance program in a suit brought by the ACLU, infuriated the Bush Administration when she contended in her decision that even the President of the United States is subject to the US Constitution: "There are no hereditary Kings in America and no powers not created by the Constitution. So all 'inherent powers' must derive from that Constitution." The issue is expected to be resolved in the government's favor by the Supreme Court (which is packed with ultra-conservative Bush supporters). To this point, Bush's "inherent powers" have not found their limit. Perhaps more significant is that the Bush Administration, emulating foreign dictators like Augusto Pinochet, has drafted amendments to the War Crimes Act that would give Administration officials and CIA personnel retroactive as well as future immunity for authorizing "humiliating and degrading treatment" of detainees (which is a violation of the Geneva Conventions).

It looks bad, I know. But voices in opposition *are* much louder than they were when I wrote the Afterward to *Alanya to Alanya*. If enough of us refuse to be genial conformists, there is hope yet.

L. Timmel Duchamp
26 August, 2006

Acknowledgments

During the months in which I composed the third and fourth books of the Marq'ssan Cycle I read widely in the human rights literature. The works that stand out in my mind today are Jacobo Timerman, *Prisoner without a Name, Cell without a Number;* Elaine Scarry, *The Body in Pain;* the American Association for the Advancement of Science volume, *The Breaking of Bodies and Minds: Torture, Psychiatric Abuse, and the Health Professions* (ed. Eric Stover and Elena O. Nightingale, MD); *Mission to South Africa: The Commonwealth Report;* and *Psychological Operations in Guerrilla Warfare: The CIA's Nicaragua Manual* (published in a single volume with essays by Washington Post reporter Joanne Omang and NYU law professor and Vice Chairman of America's Watch and Helsinki Watch Aryeh Neier). Glancing through the shelves in my library, I shivered when my eye lighted on the illustrated pamphlet put out by the CIA titled *The Freedom Fighter's Manual*, which provides simple instructions for sabotage and would be invaluable for any would-be terrorist today; as I recall, this manual for sabotage simply confirmed what I had been reading about CIA tactics and ideas about civil order. As I've noted previously, although everything about Security Services, a fictional government agency of the equally fictitious Executive, is a product of my imagination, I found three books of great assistance in structuring my creation of this fictional institution: Philip Agee's *Inside the Company: CIA Diary;* Victor Marchetti's *The CIA and the Cult of Intelligence;* and John Stockwell's *In Search of Enemies: A CIA Story.*

It gives me great pleasure to thank the numerous individuals who, over the course of the two decades since I first drafted *Tsunami*, read the novel in ms and offered me usefully frank comments on it. Among these I especially appreciate the efforts and support of Tom Duchamp, Professor Ann Hibner Koblitz (to whom I owe a particular debt for proof-reading), Elizabeth Walter, Dr. Joan Haran, and Dr. Joshua B. Lukin. The critiques they offered were a labor of love; I will always be grateful to them for their engagement with my work. Kathryn Wilham, who edited *Tsunami*, was absolutely key from the beginning; her confidence in my vision for the Marq'ssan Cycle was vital to my completing and then deciding to publish it.

About the Author

L. Timmel Duchamp is the author of a collection of short fiction (*Love's Body, Dancing in Time*), a collection of essays (*The Grand Conversation*), four novels (*Alanya to Alanya, Renegade, Tsunami,* and *The Red Rose Rages (Bleeding)*), and dozens of short stories.. She has been a finalist for the Nebula and Sturgeon awards and has been shortlisted for the Tiptree Award several times. A selection of her essays and fiction can be found at

http://ltimmel.home.mindspring.com.

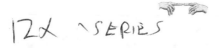

12X ^SERIES